I, THE SUN

JANET MORRIS

I, THE SUN

Perseid Press
P. O. Box 584
Centerville, MA 02632

I, the Sun

Cover art: Seal of Suppiluliumas

IIllustration Chapter 1 and subsequent odd-numbered chapters: Egyptian chariot, drawing by Mikey Brooks after a mural in the Ramesses II temple at Thebes (Ramesses II's victory over the Kheta [Hittite] people and the Siege of Daipur).

Illustration Chapter 2 and subsequent even-numbered chapters: Hittite chariot, drawing of an Egyptian relief by Mikey Brooks from drawing of an Egyptian relief, after Paul Volz: Die biblischen Altertumer (1914), p. 514 (itself copied from de Hethitischer Streitwagen.jpg in U.S. public domain).
Mikey Books illustrations (c) Perseid Press 2014
Book design: Sarah Hulcy, 2013; Mikey Brooks and Sarah Hulcy, 2014.
Map © Christopher C. Morris, 1977
Map design: Roy Mauritsen

Trade Paperback edition: ISBN 13-978-0-9914654-5-3, ISBN 10-0991465458
KindleDigital edition: ISBN 13-978-0-9914654-7-7, ISBN 10-0991465474
ePub Digital edition: ISBN 13-978-0-9914654-6-0, ISBN 10-0991465466

Library of Congress Control Number: 2014948884

Published in the United States of America

10 9 8 7 6 5 4 3 2 1

Other Works By Janet Morris

Silistra
High Couch of Silistra (1977) aka
    Returning Creation
The Golden Sword (1977)
Wind from the Abyss (1978)
The Carnelian Throne (1979)

Kerrion Empire
Dream Dancer (1980)
Cruiser Dreams (1981)
Earth Dreams (1982)

Threshold (with Chris Morris)
Threshold (1990)
Trust Territory (1992)
The Stalk (1994)

ARC Riders (with David Drake)
ARC Riders (1995)
The Fourth Rome (1996)

Novels
I, the Sun (1983)
The 40-Minute War (1984) (with
    Chris Morris)
Active Measures (1985) (with
    David Drake)
Afterwar (1985)
Medusa (1986) (with Chris
    Morris)
Warlord! (1987)
Kill Ratio (1987) (with David
    Drake)
Outpassage (1988) (with Chris
    Morris)
Target (1989) (with David Drake)

The Sacred Band of Stepsons:
    Beyond Series
Beyond Sanctuary (1985) (2011)
Beyond the Veil (1985) (2013)
Beyond Wizardwall (1986) (2013)

Sacred Band of Stepsons:
    Sacred Band Tales
Tempus (1987) (2010)
the Fish the Fighters and the Song-
    Girl (2012)

The Sacred Band of Stepsons:
    Farther Realms
City at the Edge of Time (1988)
    (with Chris Morris)
Tempus Unbound (1989) (with
    Chris Morris)
Storm Seed (1990) (with Chris
    Morris)

The Sacred Band of Stepsons:
The Sacred Band (2010)

Heroes in Hell
Heroes in Hell (1986)
The Gates of Hell (1986) (with C J
    Cherryh)
Rebels in Hell (1986) (with C J
    Cherryh)
Crusaders in Hell (1987)
Angels in Hell (1987)
Masters in Hell (1987)
Kings in Hell (1987) (with C J
    Cherryh)
The Little Helliad (1988) (with
    Chris Morris)
War in Hell (1988)
Explorers in Hell (1989) (with
    David Drake)
Prophets in Hell (1989)
Lawyers in Hell (2011) (edited
    with Chris Morris)
Rogues in Hell (2012) (edited with
    Chris Morris)
Select short story bibliography:
"Raising the Green Lion" (1980)
"Vashanka's Minion" (1980)

"A Man and His God" (1981)
"An End to Dreaming" (1982)
"Wizard Weather" (1982)
"High Moon" (1983)
"Basileus" (1984)
"Hero's Welcome" (1985)
"Graveyard Shift" (1986)
"To Reign in Hell" (1986)
"Pillar of Fire" (1984)
"Gilgamesh Redux" (1987)
"Sea of Stiffs" (1987)
"The Nature of Hell" (1987)
"The Best of the Achaeans"
    (1988)
"The Collaborator" (1988)
"[...] Is Hell" (1988)
"Moving Day" (1989)
"Sea Change" (1989)
"Boogey Man Blues" (2013)
    appeared in *What Scares the
    Boogey Man?* edited by John
    Manning

**Select non-fiction
    bibliography:**

"Nonlethality: A Global
    Strategy" (1990, 2010) (with
    Chris Morris)
"Weapons of Mass Protection"
    (1995) (with Morris and
    Baines)
The American Warrior (1992)
    (Morris and Morris, ed.)

Series contributed to:
Merovingen Nights
The Fleet
War World
Thieves' World

TABLE OF CONTENTS

PREFACE...i
CHAPTER 1 1
CHAPTER 2 29
CHAPTER 3 53
CHAPTER 4 65
CHAPTER 5 71
CHAPTER 6 85
CHAPTER 7 93
CHAPTER 8 97
CHAPTER 9 117
CHAPTER 10..131
CHAPTER 11..143
CHAPTER 12..165
CHAPTER 13..171
CHAPTER 14..195
CHAPTER 15..207
CHAPTER 16..213
CHAPTER 17..229
CHAPTER 18..243
CHAPTER 19..273
CHAPTER 20..297
CHAPTER 21..315
CHAPTER 22..323
CHAPTER 23..335
CHAPTER 24..341
CHAPTER 25..353
CHAPTER 26..369
CHAPTER 27..383
CHAPTER 28..403
CHAPTER 29..449
CHAPTER 30..471
CHAPTER 31..595
CHAPTER 32..517
CHAPTER 33..531
CHAPTER 34..547
ACKNOWLEDGEMENTS I
BIBLIOGRAPHY V

Praise for *"I, the Sun"*:

"I, the Sun is a masterpiece of historical fiction. It tells a great story while accurately creating the world of the Hittites and their best known emperor."

—Dr. Jerry Pournelle

"...[Janet Morris] is familiar with every aspect of Hittite culture."

—O. R. Gurney, Hittite scholar and author of The Hittites

PREFACE

From the annals of the ancient Hittite king, Suppiluliumas, from the Amarna letters of Egypt and the court records of a wealth of "lost" civilizations, comes this saga of kingship and greatness, love and death, politics and treachery in the second millennium, BCE

Beyond a few cursory references to the Hittites in the Bible, for thousands of years nothing has been known of this first mighty Indo-European culture. Now, based on translations of the ancient texts themselves, comes the story of Suppiluliumas, Great King, Favorite of the Storm God, King of Hatti, who by his own count fathered forty-four kings and conquered as many nations, who brought even mighty Egypt to her knees. Tutankhamun's widow sent him an urgent letter begging for a son of his to make her husband. The earliest Hebrews knew

i

him as their Protector. The entire Mediterranean world revered and feared him.

But though he conquered armies, countries, and even foreign gods, he could not conquer his love for the one woman fate denied him, Great Queen Khinti.

With the exception of a single slave girl, every prince and general, mercenary and scribe, princess and potentate in these pages actually lived, loved and died nearly fourteen hundred years before Christ. Now they live again in I the Sun.

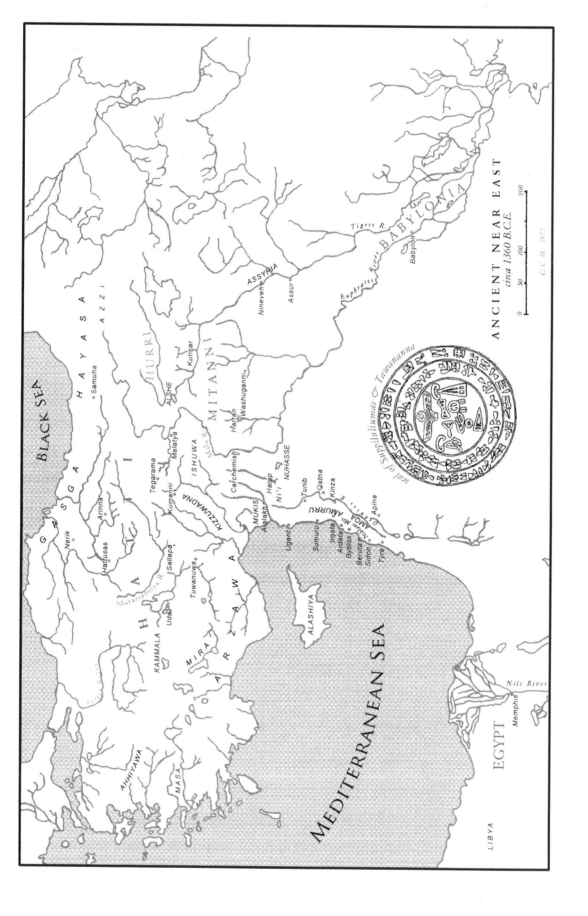

BLACK SEA

MEDITERRANEAN SEA

ANCIENT NEAR EAST
circa 1360 B.C.E.

C.C.M. 1977

0   50   100   200

Seal of Suppiluliumas & Tawananna

EGYPT

LIBYA

Memphis

Nile River

BABYLONIA

Babylon

Tigris R.

Euphrates River

ASSYRIA

Nineveh

Assur

HURRI

ALSHE

Kutmar

MITANNI

Harran

Washugannib

Carchemish

Halap

Ni'i   NUHASSE

Tunib

Qatna

Kinza

Apina

AMQA   AMURRU

Nahr   Mt. Lebanon

Ugarit

Sumuru

Irqata

Ardata

Byblos

Beruta

Sidon

Tyre

ALASHIYA

MUKIS

Alalakh

KIZZUWADNA

ISHUWA

Malatya

Tegarama

Kumanni

AZZI

HAYASA

Samuha

GASGA

Nerik

Arinna

Hattusas

Sallapa

Tuwanuwa

Udao

KAMMALA

MIRA

A R Z A W A

AHHIYAWA

MASA

H A T T I

Marassantiya R.

I, THE SUN

Thus speaks the Sun Suppiluliumas,
Great King, King of Hatti:

CHAPTER 1

There is a man who stands always on my horizon: large, cloaked and formidable. I have seen only his back. Over the years, that back has preceded me, on occasion dropping clues for me to read when I come to where he has passed. I have never been able to catch him, though I am coming closer. He has been in my dreams before every moment of crisis, for every tumble onto truth that has ever befallen me, striding away, his shoulders like a second horizon. I know that when I overtake him, I will have what it is that has eluded me over the years. Then, I will learn a thing. Then, I may truly say that I have done it. Now, I am still following. Last night I was able to see that he wore sandals, and their soles were worn. But he is getting dark.

When I first saw him, he was bright and shining. The Great King Arnuwandas, my father, had just died. I sat atop the rock sanctuary while the moon rose, looking down on the mausoleum stone-house, its grounds alight with mourners' torches, as they had been for thirteen days. I moved only to hunt or elude the *Meshedi*—the Great King's bodytroops—whom my mother periodically sent to search for me. Otherwise, I sat below the black eagle's nest, and we watched the ashes of Arnuwandas receive the adulation he had never been accorded in life. They loved him for dying. Their relief was a palpable thing, and that grieved them, so their grief was real enough.

The black eagle screeched and flapped as I snuck, hunched up, to my hideaway. I was due for my manhood ceremony this year and, at fourteen, was barely able to fit into the crevice I had found five years past.

"Tasmi*sarri!*" Gruff voices called my name with mounting fury. "Tasmisarri!" Then: "We *know* you are up there, brat." There was no mistaking my uncle Kantuzilis' commanding squeak.

My throat tightened. I was big for my age, but not ready to tangle with any of my relatives, Kantuzilis in particular. I half stood.

And that was when I first saw him, the man, and he was shining. Up the slope to my left, in a long blue cloak, he ascended. In the unabashedness of youth, I thought him the most striking figure I had ever seen. I leaned forward, Kantuzilis forgotten. The man, walking somehow in the moonlight, wore a braid swinging to his waist, as once did the old empire's Tabarnas, their Great Kings. I heard men muttering. Stones clicked and dark shapes cut across the shelf below me to intercept him. The full moon went behind a cloud; the eagle bated, then rustled round his nest in the sudden dark.

A time later, I heard Kantuzilis' steps, and others, descending to the mausoleum below. The moon had winked out all trace of the blue-cloaked man with the long braid.

I lay back and stretched out on the rock shelf, eyes closed, thinking of the blue-cloaked lord. There was something so desirable about his carriage that he seemed to me ultimately kingly, so much so that if I could just be as he was, then none would ever doubt my right to the throne or my rightness upon it. But I could not recollect any detail of him except the long, jet braid dividing his great shoulders. Such shoulders came from sweat and toil, from driving the day into dusk and wielding an axe and a sword in battle. Such shoulders cannot be had by adolescent boys, even large ones. So I dismissed the figure, and with a shake of my head tossed my unbound hair. The shining one, I decided, was a warrior, a lord come to pay homage. Since the Meshedi were gone, I set off toward the interment ceremony, curious, to seek him out. For the first time in anybody's memory Tasmi would willingly attend a state occasion.

My mother broke into ashen tears and grabbed my hands, thanking me. I was a head taller than she, even then.

I hushed her and glared around at the flying wedge of relatives who had come to pay tardy homage to the Sun Arnuwandas. There on my mother's right was my uncle Kantuzilis, commanding general of the armies, prince, misshapen in body and mind. His skin was pale like the inside of a loaf, his hair like dog-soiled snow, his eyes like bleeding wounds. He bared his yellow teeth and I gave him a stony, grim stare I had learned from a bronze mirror. He looked away. Whether it worked or he was amused, I could not tell.

Great Queen Asmunikal, my mother, laid her raven head against my chest and wrapped me round and wailed. I had thought by now she would have been wailed into a whisper. But she was, in every sense of the word, Tawananna, wife of the king, and she found strength to weep in my arms.

Asmunikal grieved mightily, although Arnuwandas' death must have been to her a blessing. For five years my father had lain helpless, dead as stone from the waist down. The blow that had maimed him thus had been struck in his own palace, by the invading Gasgaeans while the city of Hattusas flamed around us. Since then, my uncles had ruled. Now, one among them would become Tabarna, the Sun, the king of the Hatti land—what was left of it.

Next to my mother, eating a sweet cake, was a man I did not know: a young lord, a chariot man from his dress.

Counting heads absently, I searched for the azure-cloaked man. Such dye comes from the Lower Country. I saw no hint of it among the skin-cloaked crowd-within-a-crowd that was my family. What I saw, in my mind's eye, was that other night, the night I had first found the eagle's nest and the crevice in the stone with the city burning bloody below and my eyes tearing from the smoke and the rage of the helpless.

Five years later, I saw the end of helplessness approaching. I unclenched my fists, and turned to reply to the greeting of Kantuzilis, the "hero".

"Tasmi*sarri*," he said again, using that excuse to step closer. The malicious smile matched his nature. He accented the third and fourth syllables of my name. Always he called me thus—never Tasmi, like everyone else. *Sarri* means 'king' in Hurrian, and my mother's choice in my naming had taught me early how to bleed and how to fight. If Kantuzilis had his way, I would be king of a stone-house, like my father.

As he stepped to my side in a rustle of fox fur, I saw the young lord—who stood among the family and yet was unknown to me—speak over his shoulder, to a darkness that I then saw was Muwatalli, Kantuzilis' counterpart on the battlefield of palace politics.

I disengaged my mother's arms, aware of her sobbing only as it stopped. She smiled bravely, then sought one of my brothers.

Kantuzilis did not speak again, but waited with his vulture's eyes on me until I acknowledged him. Which I did not immediately do. The short hairs on my neck rose as I took a closer look at the way the crowd had shifted. Around me were four of my grown uncles; three Chiefs of 1,000; six lesser generals—all Great Ones, all related to me; all adherents of him who had ruled in deed while my father ruled his bed: the tuhkanti, my father's successor, Tuthaliyas the Second. This ring of men around me lacked, to become a war council, only that one's presence. But the new Sun of Hatti was nowhere about.

Kantuzilis swore deep in his throat and shifted his weight.

The music took up, an Old Woman's trill wheezing a new dirge. I saw my mother, her face pale, her brows knit, leaning against my brother Zida, beyond the stranger's back.

The men, all fourteen, sauntered inward, elaborately casual. It seemed as if no sound could reach us within their circle. Kantuzilis' breath whistled in his chest.

Watching the sharp-faced stranger (who himself was staring around, his hand under his cloak, casting tense shadows in the torchlight), I wondered where his interests lay.

I made a show of noticing that the lords circled round me in formation, and when I had my back to Kantuzilis, I said, "What are you waiting for, Hero?"

His hand came down hard on my shoulder, and he spun me around.

I only looked at him.

He slapped my face openhanded. "You are not too big for a strapping, nor will you be deprived one, boy!"

I bared my teeth at him and spat blood. Three men left the circle: Himuili; the stranger; another lord, Takkuri.

"When I have my majority, uncle—" The circle tightened, moving slowly toward me, pushing us away from the light.

"Silence!" snarled the hero who had burned Sallapa to the ground for the good of the Hatti land. "You were up there, Tasmi*sarri*. Admit it." He pointed toward the eagle's nest.

I shrugged. Perhaps I could talk my way out of this yet. I had taken worse from Kantuzilis than a slap. But my fists ached.

"Your mother—"

"Leave her out of this."

He was taking off his belt. It was wide, hardened leather, bronze studded, the kind chariot drivers wear to support their backs.

"You would not dare," I said through a red haze, and stopped moving back before the circle's darkward progress.

The Pale One had the belt doubled in his hand. I was a hair taller than he and not twisted of limb; but his strength was greater than mine—alone. And boys do not strike men in the Hatti land. Then why the convocation of lords? "Did you bring them to hold me for you?" I asked him.

He slapped the doubled leather strap on his palm. "That is a possibility."

If I attacked him, they could make whatever they wanted of it: no one would disbelieve the Great Ones.

I must have spun wildly; I remember their faces blurring together. I retreated as far from my uncle as I could, until a hand pushed roughly against my back. I wore no cloak—a vanity, a boy's desire to hurry the hair of manhood. I wore a light dirk at my hip, all a boy is allowed. Reaching down, I unbuckled my belt and let the dirk drop.

Kantuzilis took a measured step. Leather cracked sharply in the dimness.

It was myself I fought there. Not before the lords would he shame me! And yet, I dared not strike him.

No help would be forthcoming from behind—not from Tuttu, expressionless, huge as a hill; nor from my uncle Muwatalli the Elder, whose restraining hand was again laid against my spine.

"Tasmi*sarri*," said my uncle Kantuzilis, taking a step that brought us chest to chest, "you are going to learn respect for the Great Ones and the laws of the land, and you are going to obey them, henceforth! No one will need to chase you anymore." Muwatalli still had his hand on me. "Take off your kilt, boy, and kneel down."

I shoved back hard and tried to bolt through the opening made by the off-balance Muwatalli as he staggered leftward. They were all warriors. I got two steps.

Someone knocked my legs out from under me, and I went down. All thought of what boys do, and do not do, left me. I bit hard into an arm seeking my throat. A kick connected with my kidneys. I swung wildly with feet and fists, my face pushed into the dirt; but the men on me were princes, not street brawlers, and I became witness to the effectiveness of Meshedi training. They held me spread-eagled as one stripped me. Then, amid much jocularity and taunting jibes, Kantuzilis strapped my back and buttocks until I gnawed the ground.

When at last the restraining hands were gone and the snap of the strap ceased, I lay very still.

Muwatalli picked my head up by the hair, shook it, and when he loosened his hold I let my head fall back.

"His father's son, by that," said Kantuzilis, close to my ear. His sandaled foot turned me. A wad of spittle fell on my face. Then the men, amid conjectures as to whether the whipping would in truth improve me, drifted away.

It was Zida, my brother, who came around to see if I was dead.

By then I had wound my torn kilt about me and reclaimed the dirk from the ground. I had ceased tasting blood in my mouth, had found a way to lie on my side.

"Tasmi—"

I did not look up. "Go lie with Kantuzilis."

"Asmunikal—"

"Go lie with her."

Zida sat, remonstrating softly that I would speak so of the Great Queen. "She has her troubles. She's just trying to protect us—" He was squinting surreptitiously in the moonlight, trying to see if I was badly hurt without being obvious, gathering his report.

"She can marry Tuthaliyas, for all I care."

"If she did that—"

"Fool! He will demote her, not marry her. Once he has done it, he can take just about everything—not including the stone-house, of course. Would you like to live there, Zida, with our father's ashes?"

"Tasmi, be easy on her. She worries about you."

"I assumed that was why you were here."

"Did they say anything to you?"

"About what?" I asked, cautious.

"Asmunikal will tell you." He rose.

I grabbed his ankle and pulled it from under him.

He swore.

I slammed my fist into his ribs, rolled over on him and, when I had him pinned, did a little damage that would not show.

"Tasmi— By the Lady! Stop!"

I beat an apology out of him, for not coming to my aid.

Before I let him up, I told him what I would do to him if again he turned away from me when I battled heavy odds.

"I could not. She would not let me. Tasmi—"

"You are a man. Recognized, oath-bound. Are you not?"

I pounded his head against the ground until he said that he was. Then I made him swear by the Oath Gods to come of his own initiative to my aid, always. He was the first I ever put under my overlordship, but neither the method nor the wording has changed much over the years.

Before I released him, I related certain intimate details about his concubine that I could not have known if I had not seen her unclothed. He almost struck me then. But he was a man, and sworn to me. He snarled wordlessly, stood swaying for a time. At last, he said: "Please come, for our mother's sake."

"What do they want with me? No one was too interested when the moon was high."

"Kuwatna-ziti is here from Arinna. I do not know what they want. . . ."

"Kuwatna-ziti!" So that explained who one strange lord was. I had seen two strangers that evening: one had left the circle of relatives before it closed in on me; the other. . . "Is he wearing a blue cloak?"

Zida said, "What? No, but Kantuzilis' men saw the Storm-god leaving the stone-house with Arnuwandas' spirit, to take him up to kingship in heaven, and the Storm-god was!" His eye-whites flashed, peering around.

"By the droppings of the Great Bulls! You are beyond re-demption." I turned and started down the hillside.

Kuwatna-ziti, then, was the stranger who had left the circle just before it closed in on me. His reputation was growing. Most in the Upper Country had heard about him: they called him the Great Shepherd, a mighty leader. He and his lords had been hold-ing their own against Gasga this whole fighting season. Now, in *gimant,* the season of snow and impregnation, all the Great

Ones rested; and the armies lay snoring. Soon, with the thaw, they would form up and naught would be left in Hattusas, or any other city, but a skeleton garrison and a few Meshedi to keep the people right with the law. This spring, I, Tasmi, would not stay behind with the children.

That thought, the cheeriest I could find, steadied me through the crowd.

The shelves of the stone-house's grounds were richly planted, terraced, thick with folk. I saw Tuttu, one of the Chiefs of 1,000. He caught my eye and guffawed loudly. My neck burning, I turned away, hoping that on my dark skin the bruises and weals would not be too noticeable in the torchlight.

The pavilion before the stone-house was well dressed up: Asmunikal had had five years to prepare her husband's burial. The slaves belonging to the place were sparkling, dressed in white, passing beer to the mourners.

She sat in her carven chair, the one with the copper standards of twelve-point stags rising from its arms, and the strange lord sat beside her.

Cloak thrown aside, he squatted on a stool at her feet, listening raptly. His hair was clubbed into black locks curling down his broad back. Pressed against short sleeves, his muscles stressed his woolen tunic. His curtate shirt was cinched with a chariot belt. Below that he wore a curling sheath of tooled leather. His legs, from knees to sandals, were bare. They were legs that had braced against many a half-wild team, knotted, rolling with sinew, bulging at the calves.

As he turned his head to me, slanted eyes peered out above a close-cut black beard, measured my frame, returned to meet mine. Rising, he touched his hand to his heart casually while Asmunikal flew from her chair and hurled herself against me, blithering her distress and demanding an account of my condition.

The big man, suppressing a grin, looked at his sandals. I stared over her head at him steadily.

"Tasmi, please, please. . ."

I pushed her away. Her hands running over my back made the welts burn. "Great Queen," I said sternly, trying to find my mother behind those glittering, half-mad eyes. But on she babbled, making no sense. "Tawananna! What need have you for my presence here?"

The formal title brought her to herself. "Tasmi, this is Kuwatna-ziti."

"My lord." Kuwatna-ziti slowly inclined his head to me. In the torchlight's dance, it seemed that he fought his face.

I acknowledged him, since he had chosen to acknowledge me, and turned my attention back to her. "What is it you want, Mother?" I shook her.

"My arms," she whimpered. "Tasmi, this—thing that happened, I—"

"I know," I said gently. "When the moon turns full again, all this will be behind us." She knew what I meant. I was a boy only until then. Then I would be a man. I could challenge whom I chose; I could bear man's weapons; I could settle up some debts long owing.

"No, no, no—" She caught herself in mid moan and bit her bottom lip between her teeth. Even then, she was beautiful. Still the most beautiful woman in Hattusas. She looked up at me in horror. "Tasmi, that is not what I want. It is not what any of us wants."

"It is what I want!"

"You are hurting me! There are more important things for you to want. Look you, child of my heart, you know what must come to pass—" Her voice lowered suggestively. "You must live that long. Get your hands from me!"

I let her go. This, surely the latest of her endless schemes to put me on the seat of kingship, was not worth the trip down from the ledge. "Mother—"

"We have arranged for you to go to Arinna, to join the lords fighting there."

Despite all that seethed in me, my heart leapt. "Under whose direction? And who is 'we?'" Behind her, the lord from Arinna leaned his weight on one leg and his palm on his sword's hilt and tried to look unconcerned.

"Tasmi, they will kill you if you stay here."

"Tell me something I do not know."

"I cannot protect you—"

"Answer my question!"

"'We' is . . . everyone. Your uncles, the commanders, the Great Ones—"

"Are you saying that *everybody* held a meeting to decide what to do with me?"

Tears streamed from Asmunikal's eyes. She sniffed. "Not *every*body. There will be other changes. I am to marry. . . ."

I whirled around and strode off through the crowd. If *they* were sending me to Arinna, it would be under armed guard and the famed Kuwatna-ziti was marked for my jailer.

I wanted none of it. For the thousandth time, I considered turning my back on the whole nest of scorpions and becoming a mercenary: a Sutu. Sutu ask no questions of lineage; a good sword arm is their blood bond. And the arm, even then, I had, though the swords boys get are wooden and clumsy. I had not done it before, because I was not a man and not hard enough pressed. When Arnuwandas first died, I ran as far as the Red River; but I came back. I had waited all my life to become what the next full moon would make me: a man. But it was no use being a dead man.

When a hand came down on my shoulder, I acted instinctively: I slid my dirk from its sheath and whirled in one motion, reaching out for the assailant behind me, hugging him close—they never expect you to do that. So I paused, my dirk at the jugular of the man I embraced, to see whose throat I was about to slit: the whole maneuver took only a moment. A wary breath slid down through the long aristocratic nose of Kuwatna-ziti, who was still as stone in my grasp, his eyes almost crossed, looking down at my blade-hand.

He cleared his throat. I felt the muscles bunch in his back, and knew that in a moment I would have no advantage: he was too big, too filled with war. He said: "If you will put that knife down, and promise not to tell my men that I languished in your arms like a lover, I will buy you some wine in town and we will discuss this."

Two men had stopped; one touched the other's arm; they stared at us, conferred; one shouted; the other gestured our way.

I either had to kill this Great Shepherd, Kuwatna-ziti, and run, or let him go. I let him go.

"You are fast as the Storm-god's lightning," said the Shepherd wonderingly. "None have had me that close to a crematory urn this whole season."

I sheathed the dirk.

"Let us go into the town, and you can collect your wine." He grinned.

I found that I did not want to like him, but that I did. "No," I said, crossing my arms over my chest. The beating Kantuzilis had given me throbbed. "Tell me here."

"And then, if my words have worth to you—"

Three Meshedi came running up, pushing through the crowd.

"Trouble, Great Shepherd?" queried one of the Meshedi, blade drawn, moonlight running along its curve. His two companions made no secret of their intent, flanking me on either side.

"Trouble? Not unless you would like to start some."

The foremost of the Meshedi blinked and looked pointedly at me.

"Tasmisarri," said Kuwatna-ziti, "let us find that wine."

He took my arm, and we walked away from them. I heard the snick of their blades as they sheathed them.

"Do not call me that. Just Tasmi." I shook my arm free.

"This way, then, Tasmi," and he struck for the chariot road that winds down into the city.

"There is a quicker way, for walking." I saw, as we passed through the gate that led to the mausoleum's stables, the next king of Hatti—the moon-gleam on my father's crown drew my eyes to him. Tuthaliyas sprawled against the stable wall, an offering vessel overturned beside him, snoring softly.

"Are you not cold?" asked Kuwatna-ziti. I changed sides with him, blocking his view of the king. Kuwatna-ziti made a movement, as if to offer his cloak.

"The cold keeps me numb. I would not feel Kantuzilis' little gift."

"You are a strange one, my lord prince." He chuckled, and we turned the corner, leaving the tuhkanti Tuthaliyas to sleep in peace.

Kuwatna-ziti was then taken up with a man of his, and the harnessing of his team. They were fine, deep-bodied grays, fit for such a chariot: an open-backed fighting machine, lean and unornamented.

I sat on a low stone wall and watched the men of Kuwatna-ziti and the slaves and two somewhat anxious Meshedi watch me. The moon took refuge behind the rock sanctuary's jutting crown. I wondered why I was doing this, playing into their hands.

Then Kuwatna-ziti strolled over to me and said, "If you will drive for me, it will be just us two."

Did he think I was a baby, to be lured by a sweet-cake? I made a noncommittal noise, careful to conceal my anticipation.

The grays were as savage as the Gasgaean enemy. I ground my teeth together and braced my legs and concentrated on keeping both wheels on the narrow, elevated road. Kuwatna-ziti leaned against the chariot's side as if the racing steeds were walking in review, a hand casually upon the leather braces that line its sloping rail.

"Pull up," he said after a time, though he had only bared his teeth when I let the grays tear through the stable yard, scattering Meshedi and nobles and slaves like dust. But it was not my driving which concerned him, I found as I rubbed the back of my forearms each in turn.

We were at that flat clear place where the road swings wide and the city lies like a woman exposed. The light she threw hovered over her like a red veil. The palace, a city within a city, was nearly whole again. Down the slope from her, evidence of the burning still scarred the streets. But things were almost right with Hattusas once more. Right, and ready for our enemies to loot and pillage.

Kuwatna-ziti turned full about, inspecting the empty road. "Let them crop." I loosened my hold on the grays. "Good. Now, let us sniff out what we may, with none to overhear us."

I looked at him. "A nice team, this."

"For the right man. Will you drive for me when the weather breaks?"

My heart leapt again, then quieted. Bribe. I folded my arms over my chest.

He scowled at me in the dark. "We fight, in Arinna. We tolerate no sinecures. There is no safe place among the Shepherd's flock. We number three score, and there is not one of us unbloodied. Or is the frontier too wild. . . ?"

"My lord," I said, vaulting over the chariot's side to the ground, "drive yourself."

"My lord prince," he roared, so that the horses shied and he grabbed for their reins. He wheeled them about and drove them between me and the city. They snorted and danced. I went left. He took them off the road to follow me. It occurred to me, as he jerked them hard around, that I deserved this, for being fool enough to trust my mother. I fingered the dirk, trying to judge his heart in the dark, as the wheels creaked and the grays lunged in place and Kuwatna-ziti howled, "A curse upon every oath I ever took to your demented family! You get in this car, or by the Sun-goddess of Arinna, my lady, I will grind you to mud under my wheels!" Then he sawed on the reins so that his horses lunged toward me, wild-eyed.

At the last moment I stepped aside. As he rushed past, Kuwatna-ziti leaned down out of the chariot, grabbed me by the arm—and heaved.

For a moment I dangled, half over the car's side. Then he pulled me by the belt and I tumbled inward, cracking my head against the blunt side of a war axe fastened to the chariot's curving leather-padded innards.

The chariot lurched to a stop. I felt myself shoved out onto the ground, heard a loud squeal from the grays.

Then Kuwatna-ziti was on me: "My lord prince, I see I must talk to you in the only language you understand. Get up." His sandaled foot connected with my belly. "Go on, get up. Let us fight!"

I did not get up: I pulled him down. It did not last long.

*

I could barely see through my right eye, and my left arm was half pulled from its socket. Kuwatna-ziti, his cloak torn, his cheek sporting three long angry gouges, said: "There," and pointed to a tavern still open.

"By Serris' organ, no!"

"Why?" demanded the Shepherd, still combative.

I touched my tongue to my split lower lip. "I cannot go in there. The owner has a daughter—"

"You are popular with the people, also. That is good," said the lord for whom I would thenceforth drive. "Is there a place in Hattusas where you are welcome?"

"I have never been in there," I offered, pointing to the Blue Ram, whose prices and policies were beyond a boy's reach.

We headed for it. The proprietor looked dubious until Kuwatna-ziti palmed him some shekels. Then he led us through a sparsely-crowded room with low benches into an irregularly-shaped chamber with thick plastered walls and a stout door which might be shut. This room had a small, high window with bars; two benches around a table; and, in the corner, stacked kegs.

Kuwatna-ziti approved it, and ordered a certain wine that lit the proprietor's face with pleasure. From the larger room, I could hear low voices and a piper playing softly.

I slid between one bench and the table and leaned gingerly back in the corner. My gut still hurt when I breathed.

A girl came, sleepy, with a sealed clay vessel and two cups. She had reddened hair and wide-set eyes; her neck was strung with copper beads that dangled down between her breasts. When

she turned, her kirtled hips were sweet and my eyes went with
her to the door.

"Girl, not so fast." She turned in the doorway, hipshot. She
was one of the reasons boys could seldom gain entrance to the
Blue Ram.

"Come here." It was Kuwatna-ziti's order. Eyes downcast,
smiling, she did as he bid. He tugged on her tresses and whispered in her ear. She had a throaty laugh, a deep voice. On the
threshold, she stared at me brazenly, licking her lips slowly with
her tongue, before she took her leave.

"And close that door!" Kuwatna-ziti commanded.

The door muffled the low men's voices and tremulous pipes
beyond. Kuwatna-ziti broke the jug's seal and served us both.

The wine was elegant. I downed it as if it were not.

Loosened by the drink, I examined Kuwatna-ziti's puffy
face, his rent woolens, and felt better about my faring with him.

"That oath you took from me—what good is a boy's word?"

Kuwatna-ziti's beard wobbled. "As good as you make it.
I was not fighting a boy out there on the slope." He rubbed his
neck. "Before, I was going to ask you if you would take your
majority in Arinna. Now, I am telling you."

"Or you will beat me again?"

"If that is the only thing you understand. You might beat
me, though I doubt it: I would rather leave out the battling and
make a treaty. We have not much time. I am not your adversary."

I grunted at him, reached out and filled my cup with Murmurigan wine.

He sighed. "Tasmi, I know things have not been easy with you.
You are a prince of the realm. Times are unsettled. Kantuzilis—"

I suggested that he entertain himself with a sheep.

"Look you, princeling, you will be in the wars soon enough.
Save it. You will take your majority in Arinna, in the temple of
the Sun-goddess—"

"—Arinniti, who regulates kingship and queenship." I re-
cited the formula. "Asmunikal chose well, with you."

He ignored that. "Have you chosen a tutelary god yet?"

I sprayed wine. "Not you, too."

He smiled grimly. "War brings a man to his gods. A strong hand is not enough. To vanquish such enemies as has the Hatti land, a man needs a strong deity riding with him."

I squirmed to find a way to sit without resting on Kantuzi-lis' work. "I am not much for gods. None have called me. I grant them the same peace." Talk of the Thousand Gods of Hatti always made me uncomfortable. Though the men make much of them, and most of the decisions of kingship are made in their names, I had never had even the slightest glimpse of them, either with my eyes or my heart. Still, if only to satisfy convention, I would have to declare myself soon.

"It would benefit a lot of people, and please me—should you come to care about that—if you would consider the Storm-god of Hatti."

There are many Storm-gods. Tarhun, the Storm-god of Hat-ti, husband to Arinniti, the Sun-goddess of Arinna, stands upon the twin bulls Serris and Hurris. He is mighty, a warrior's god, a god for whom every king of Hatti performs certain functions.

"Who will my mother marry?" I said into his appraising stare.

"Are you going to start swinging if I tell you?"

"Smite the wicked before they smite you."

"Hassuilis of Ziplanda."

Hearing the name, a tightness eased in my chest. It was nec-essary, by the law, for a brother of Arnuwandas to take my mother into his house. Hassuilis was a priest of the city of Ziplanda's Storm-god, an ethereal man to whom the machinations of the court meant nothing. I had met him twice only. He seemed to me a good man, and his position in that city was one from which he could protect my mother. There is a certain autonomy dealt the holy cities: like the estates of the gods, they are exempt from tithes, existing as states within states. This condition obtained also in Arinna, which was one of the reasons my mother had ar-ranged to send me there.

Since Tuthaliyas had no intention of making her his wife, nor of allowing her to remain Great Queen, Hassuilis was the most preferable of the available alternatives. I said this.

Kuwatna-ziti narrowed his slanted eyes at me and unlatched his cloak. "Your mother is a heroic woman. She will triumph in the end."

I had no answer for that. What Asmunikal wanted, she usually got. But the cost in the past had often been too great. She had laid down ruinous policies for the land through my father, whom she ruled. Her pacifist leanings had drained the treasuries and convinced our enemies that indeed we were ripe for conquest.

I said what I thought of women mixing in government, and men who let them, and that my mother would never rule through me.

"By Tarhun's beard, you are astute, for a street brawler."

"I grew up with my ear to the floorboards. Where did you get that wound?"

"Arziya. Kantuzilis called us up. We had no choice but to aid him. When I got back, we had to reconquer all the ground we took the whole season." He shook his head, grim. "Tuthaliyas has the right idea. Burn them out. Deport the citizenry, use the namra, the deportees, for slave labor."

He refilled my cup.

"What is it like?" I asked, and he knew I meant war with the Gasgaean enemy.

"What is it like? Like the streets. Like this life you have been living. Most times war is polite. The Gasgaeans are not polite. They do not walk away at sundown, or go home for the winter. They do not nicely form ranks, or exchange a mannerly challenge, or set up a battle in an orderly fashion. They jump from trees, attack sleeping camps, hide behind bushes. They ride horses, dig pits, shoot flaming arrows. . . . They keep us on our toes."

As he leaned forward, the deep scar on the inside of his bicep slithered. "Driving for me, you will get your fill of Gasgaeans. I send no man where I have not already gone." He drained his cup; I did the same.

The warm wine lulled me, eased my wrenched muscles and battered flesh.

Kuwatna-ziti, too, seemed to feel the wine. His tone became conspiratorial: "There is a lot in this for both of us, young prince, my lord. Both on the short, and on the long."

"What mean you?"

"Tomorrow, we may pick two teams from the royal stable: one for me, for taking Your intractable Majesty in hand; and one for you, for being a good boy and going away, and not reminding anyone that if Arnuwandas had not died when he had, you would soon be tuhkanti. There is another value, too, in this, which you may not have seen."

"Since I cannot think of anything at all which I value in this, then you may be right," I slurred cautiously, adding, "but I have been thinking about all this longer than you. If there were advantage here, by now I would have sniffed it out."

"Perchance. Look: you are out of the way; Tuthaliyas is Tabarna. Unless he drastically changes, he will name no tuhkanti himself. They—the princes—might just kill each other off before it comes time for us to make our move."

I sat straight up. Kuwatna-ziti peered around him, then said, "There's no one here to overhear," in an irritated voice. "Have wine."

I took wine. Forgetful, I rubbed my sore eye and regretted it. "We should go," I said.

"Go? Go upstairs, you mean." He grinned like a wolf.

"Then let us do it," I said, rising. I would make to him no statement about my intentions. He might speak of "we" and "our move," but I was not sure that I was ready to be included in his "we."

"You know," he said, meeting me at the door, which was jammed, "it is men that a king must master. Learning man is the school of kingship. Nations rise and fall upon just that—"

"Like the proprietor of this place?" I grunted, putting my shoulder to the door. It did not budge.

"Let me try," said Kuwatna-ziti, and threw his weight against the door. Thrice he struck it, until its hinges groaned. Rubbing his shoulder, he stood back and bellowed.

I was on the table, trying the barred window, when the door burst inwards and the henna-headed girl went to her knees before us, stammering about the bolt.

Wrenching her up by the hair, Kuwatna-ziti held her against the wall.

I slid past him: the proprietor was nowhere about, the hearth banked, dawn coming in through the windows.

"Come then, girl," said the Shepherd, and to me explained that the night-boy must have shut the bolt from without by mistake, thinking no one was within. In the large room, three slumped over their tables.

"You do not believe that?" I demanded, as Kuwatna-ziti slapped the girl's rump and gestured that I should follow her up the stairs. "That wine-sot will be back with Meshedi."

Kuwatna-ziti, unperturbed, shepherded the girl up the stairs.

"You have not been long enough in Hattusas!" I shouted after. "You will wake with your throat slit."

The girl's thighs winked on the landing. "And you have been too long in Hattusas. Where go you, to your safe palace bed? Come on—" Then he stopped, his eyes widening incredulously. "Unless . . . that is . . . if you've never. . ." And he grinned widely.

I vaulted the railing after him.

He laughed. "This one is mine, then," and slapped the kirtle before him.

"You are paying," I agreed, following Kuwatna-ziti, who followed the harlot down a passage and through a door.

"What did Kantuzilis say to you?" he asked me softly, pausing in the doorway, his eyes flitting about the roughly square room before he stepped down three steps into it.

"You should have stayed, if you wanted to know that. You could have helped him." The floor was board. On it were spread covered piles of straw. From one rose the first harlot's friend and I was glad Kuwatna-ziti had chosen the former; though I was so sore in need of sleep that my body grumbled, even through the good Murmurigan wine. I strode over and flopped down on the straw and let her strip me, lying still with my hands behind my head, making a valiant effort to pretend that such things happened to me every day.

"Shepherd," I said in Babylonian, as much to impress the girl as to keep my words secret, "what business had you with Himuili and Takkuri?" Those were the two lords with whom he had left the circle. Both were regular army, not free nobles, nor Meshedi. The girl loosed her black hair and knelt between my legs.

"If I told you that," said he, "you would have something on me. I keep no lions on my roof."

I rolled onto my side, and let the harlot drink me.

I had found something else to do with her when the flimsy door burst open.

Kuwatna-ziti sat slowly up on the straw as three Meshedi poured into the room. His hand held the girl with reddened hair down on his belly.

An arrow thunked dully into the sill behind his head.

I was backed into the corner, the girl at my feet, not recollecting how I had come there. In the doorway beyond the three Meshedi were two others, both with bows nocked, although the quarters were close.

The foremost one snarled, "My lords, tuhkanti Tuthaliyas requires your presence. Up. Move!"

Kuwatna-ziti's face darkened. He removed his hand from the girl, reached back without looking to pull the arrow from the wall, snapped it in two and lay the pieces on his right. The Meshedi took a step, retraced it, and growled.

"Tasmi, what is the going price of an ear in Hattusas?"

"What? Twelve shekels of silver," I said, slowly reaching down for my kilt as one of the Meshedi gestured to me. Out of the corner of my eye I saw Kuwatna-ziti rise, then just a blur. Then the blade before my face retreated.

I straightened as Kuwatna-ziti bellowed, "Do you know who I *am?*"

On one knee was the foremost Meshedi, hand to the side of his head, blood streaming from between his fingers down over his kirtle. By his leg lay his ear, and Kuwatna-ziti's dirk. And even as I took that in, a shower of silver shekels clattered to the boards beside them.

The room was absolutely silent. The girls did not weep. The maimed Meshedi did not whimper. None among his companions moved.

Sword bared, nude, Kuwatna-ziti strode up to the bleeding man.

"Pick him up!" he snapped. The two other Meshedi did so. The two yet in the doorway followed everything with their bows.

"*Do you know* who I am?" he yelled into the bleeding man's face.

No one was paying any attention to me. I strapped on my dirk, since my faction seemed to be winning, and stepped over my girl.

The Meshedi, from a fog of pain, mumbled that he did not. Kuwatna-ziti made him add "my lord."

Then he said: "I am Great Shepherd of *Arinna,* Man of the Storm-god. With a snap of my fingers I can blot the sound of your name from the earth. Speak it!"

The terrified man did so. Kuwatna-ziti drew names from each in turn. I have seen snakes do such things with their prey. "Now," he hissed, and even my skin crawled, though he hissed not at me, "not all the clay tongues in the world, nor all the black wool, nor a thousand purifications of the twelve parts of the body will aid you. Go back to Tuthaliyas and tell him that we will be with him presently. And put yourselves under arrest."

Now, 'man' in that context is a euphemism for priest, and clay tongues and black wool are weapons used by priests and Old Women against sorcery. The twelve parts of the body must be cleansed to cure impotence. Those Meshedi fled the room as though pursued by demons.

I realized I was staring, and busied myself with sandal straps, studying the Shepherd anew. There is a high college of priests in Arinna. I was cold. The room was cold, colder than the rock sanctuary had been. The girl at my feet had wound her arms around my leg. I touched her shoulder, and her skin was risen in little bumps.

The Shepherd fussed with his bloodied knife, wiping it in the straw. When he looked at me, I stared back into the eyes of a wolf.

"I told you," he said softly, "that a man needs a strong god behind him. And that learning man is the school of kingship." He straightened, stretched.

"And out of the holy city they sent you, to give me lessons."

"Something like that." The chill had fled the air. I wondered if it had ever been there. "Let us hope I have a long temper. The rabbit should not chase the wolf, and yet it seems this audacity runs in your family. No one sends Meshedi after a lord of Arinna!"

"—and Man of the Storm-god," I tossed back as we gained the first floor landing, where I squinted through the gloom toward the hazy morning brightness of an open doorway. The clay floor had been raked; a meal boiled beyond my view. I swallowed my hunger, thinking to sate it at the palace if Tuthaliyas did not have both of us thrown into the pit.

Tuthaliyas was reasonably sober, or reasonably drunk, as the case may be. We drove the chariot through King's Gate, cut through the flowered court at the family quarters, took the covered hall that leads to what used to be the main garden court but would soon be the new throne room. Pillars lay on their sides, ready to be raised. A small mountain of purple marble waited in one corner, for the new King's Road. I myself thought we would be better off strengthening our perimeter. The old audience hall was big enough for me. But not for Tuthaliyas.

Three times had different Meshedi tried to take me in hand, until Kuwatna-ziti shouted at the third party so loudly the walls shook: "Have you nothing better to do than chase children?" which made me angry but brought the high chamberlain hustling out from the king's wing to tell us that Tuthaliyas was out at the building site.

Slaves worked there; guards lounged. A golden bull whose mouth spouted wine had been set on a table, and the tuhkanti stood by it in a full-length, long-sleeved robe of white wool trimmed with gold, my father's crown upon his head. Out from under the crown — round-domed, like a war cap, coming low over the ears — his wispy curls straggled. Around his belly was a cinch of jewels.

He smacked his lips when he saw us, filled two more golden goblets and bawled, "Well, come on! Come here, you little bastard. You too, wild man of Arinna."

I looked at Kuwatna-ziti, whose lips twitched. The chamberlain, white-haired and tiny, hobbled over, demanding in a crackling voice that we cede our arms to him. "But you must; you must," wheezed the ancient.

"What's this? What's this?" Tuthaliyas stomped around the table, his jowls quivering with every step. One of my brothers raises boars with jowls like that, bristly and always moist. His stature was such that he had to peer up to meet my eyes. Old Hittite, looked Tuthaliyas, with a nose sharp as an evergreen and meeting brows that swept around his eyes like a permanent elbow thrown out for protection. Some said his thick lips showed the invaders' blood in him, but he was hefty like a bull and wide as a doorway, and they do not grow men like that in the reedy wombs of Egypt.

He and my father were two sides of a coin. I had Arnuwandas' height, his litheness, his long aquiline nose and thin lips. In all else I was my mother's. Only in the neck, like the trunk of a tree, and in the hands, on him too large for his stature, did Tuthaliyas and I show common blood. As I thought those things, the fact that Arnuwandas was no longer in his bed in the palace, and never would be again, was brought home to me with a snap louder than Kantuzilis' belt on my back. The raked clay beneath my feet seemed to shift, and when I looked back at my uncle it was through eyes filled with uncertainty.

He nodded and took a drink from the goblet he held, then nodded again. Looking steadily at me, he said, "Kuwatna-ziti, did neither you nor anyone else think to consult me about the disposition of my nephew?"

"We had to catch him first, my lord."

I stiffened.

"And catching him necessitated slicing off one of my Meshe-di's ears?" Still the dark, tiny eyes of the tuhkanti rested on my face. Still he sipped his wine. His greasy hair curled over the trim of his woolen gown. Wine dripped onto its front.

"My lord, I am not used to being dragged out of bed by bad-mannered henchmen."

"Next time I will send a diplomat. Asmunikal tells me you want to take our young mountain lion off our hands."

"I would consider it a favor if you would let me take him."

"Why?" snarled Tuthaliyas, wheeling around. The wine slopped. He threw the goblet to the clay, strode to Kuwatna-ziti and pressed his barrel chest against the taller man's, until Ku-watna-ziti stepped back.

"My lord," said Kuwatna-ziti quietly, "I was such a youth. Someone took me in hand. He is a warrior, born. Let him make war. He will be no trouble to you when he is occupied with what he does best."

"You consider this a personal favor, you say? Mind, I am not drunk. Not drunk enough to accept that answer. You play your game. I will play mine. Do three things for me, and you take him with you."

"Do not," I said. They both turned to look at me. "Old boar, I do not want to go with him. I do not want to stay here. Most fervently, I do not want all of you deciding when I will eat and when I will be shod and when I will sleep. I am not a horse. I—"

"Tasmi, say one more word and you can hang your tongue on your belt for a remembrance." That was Kuwatna-ziti.

Tuthaliyas grinned broadly, peered pointedly at me and said, "Wonderful. When My Majesty asked you, Kuwatna-ziti, to do for him three things, what was your reply? I did not hear it in the din of these noisy slaves."

The slaves were silent. I flushed, ground my teeth harder, and did not move.

Kuwatna-ziti looked down at tomorrow's king, whose jaw jutted out as far as his belly, and said, "My lord, ask of me what you will. Did I not put thirty lords, each with thirty other lords, into your service at Arziya? Did I not labor the season past, and the one before, and the one before that, to keep the frontiers clear?" Kuwatna-ziti's eyes glittered. "There is little I and my brother lords cannot accomplish to serve the Hatti land."

His threat hung in the air like a vulture.

The Sun Tuthaliyas muttered to himself and brushed past me to the table. From behind it, fortified anew with drink, he spoke: "'I can do anything I want to you, Kuwatna-ziti. Anything. How goes the law? Ah, I have it: 'If anyone rejects the judgment of the king, his house shall be made a shambles.' Just for my Meshedi's ear, I can take your estates as security. Do not try me. You and your lords are a factor. We know that you have many friends."

"What do you want, Tuthaliyas?" said Kuwatna-ziti with unconcealed weariness.

"I want you at formal audience tomorrow, there to swear before the Oath Gods to serve me."

"That I will do. I had rather expected it today."

"I need not hurry. There has been enough stretching of form in this interment. There are two other conditions. You will take a general's commission in the regular army, and cause your flock to put itself at the disposal of My Majesty and whatever agents I shall appoint. You will—"

Kuwatna-ziti closed his eyes, then opened them.

Tuthaliyas loomed over the table, his huge hands gripping its edge. "Yes, Shepherd?"

"My lord, please continue."

"And you will promise to maintain such surveillance on my . . . nephew . . . as to be able to cede him to me on command at any time. If, under the bond of this oath, you should not then cede him to me, your life is forfeit, as well as for any of the standard reasons: if he speaks ill of me, and you hear about it; if he plots against me, and you do not deliver him to me, thinking I will not find out. *I will find out.* And it will be as if you had spoken evil. For you the punishment will be the same as for him, even if your crime is only not presenting him at my request."

I straightened my cramped fingers and looked at the imprints of my nails in my palms. It sounded like a treaty with a foreign country, this bargain they made over me.

"Do you agree?" Tuthaliyas demanded of the Shepherd.

Kuwatna-ziti stared stonily at him and pulled on his nose. "I see no other choice. But bringing my fellow lords into the regular army — that is no easy thing. It will take more than one season."

"You must do it in one season."

"Then," gritted Kuwatna-ziti, "I will manage."

"Come over here."

And the Shepherd did.

I heard Kuwatna-ziti's low exclamation and sidled near. They had been ready for him: a tablet repeating the conditions of his guardianship awaited his seal, as did his commission in the regular army.

When he had done it, first impressing his seal on the clay, then replacing the circular seal around his neck, Kuwatna-ziti asked leave to retire. Lines worked in his forehead, and his hands were nervous.

Tuthaliyas snapped a slave to him and dispatched the tablets to the scribes, as if the Shepherd had not spoken.

Then Tuthaliyas turned to me and with a contemptuous sneer said, "Your father has gone to become a god; your mother is as good as exiled; by my leave you will live to fight as a man. I have proved myself a loving uncle, in the land's eyes. Now tell me, for I have long yearned to know: who was your real father?"

I have never been able to recall how Kuwatna-ziti got me out of there.

CHAPTER 2

Arinna lies on a mound rising above the tableland, like a miniature Hattusas, her plastered walls gleaming. North of her, where the land humps mountainous, Kuwatna-ziti's family had its estates, themselves like tiny replicas of fortified towns, enclosed within walls of bricks laved with plaster. From the southernmost of his holdings Arinna could be seen, baking in the harvest heat.

I rubbed the scar that runs from my wrist up the middle of my forearm to my elbow, just beginning then to fill with flesh. I had gotten it, not in battle (though I had acquired others in that fashion during the season), but while taking my majority under the auspices of the Sun-goddess of Arinna. The Upper Country ritual differed from practices in Hattusas only in its incorporation of a night-long vigil during which the candidate sits on the hilltop above the Lady's temple until an omen of favor comes from one of the gods.

I had had no trouble with any aspect of the ritual: my reading was fluent; my behavior within the Sun-goddess' temple

29

impeccable; I enjoyed the eight prostitutes and sent them away weaving tales of me which would dispose the lords of Arinna to my favor and bring me many women in the months that followed.

But that evening as I climbed the hill, oiled, dressed in a long woolen robe and shawl and a conical cap, to wait the night for some god's hand to touch me, I had little hope for it. What if the omen did not come?

I had contrived a tale to tell them, if all else failed: so small a thing as being deaf to the gods' words would not keep me from my manhood. I stripped off my robe when halfway up the hillside: it fouled my steps. A torch was burning at the summit, where waited only the empty night and the will of the gods—if indeed there were any about.

All day the sky had been gray. No moon, no stars shone through the clouds. I sat upon the stone bench, my robe folded under me. After a time, I began to feel foolish, waiting for nothing, and my thoughts turned to Kuwatna-ziti, and all the trouble I had brought him. When the lords first learned of Tuthaliyas' decree, there were clenched fists and angry words; ultimately a crowd gathered outside the walled estate slinging mud and insults, howling that he had sold the lords to Tuthaliyas and suborned Arinna, writing curses on the wall in sheep's blood. Few among even his staunchest supporters were ready to join the regular army, commissions or no. There were long passionate meetings after Kuwatna-ziti suppressed the crowds by force and I learned, in them, sitting silent while Kuwatna-ziti worked his wiles, the worth of words and the wielding of honor as a weapon. In those meetings he spoke unequivocally for the unification of the troops and the benefits the Hatti land would reap thereby.

In private, he chewed his nails and paced and muttered, and went frequently into the barracks among the troops and into the town's taverns to gather the mood of the folk. He surely worried over the possibility of Tuthaliyas doing harm to me once I was enlisted: he searched procedural records for a way to keep me in his sight. This, I thought privately, he did to keep his own neck in place. If something should happen to me he would forfeit his

life for it: Tuthaliyas had him neatly trapped. The military dispatches we had been receiving from Tuttu, in whose 1,000 fell
Kuwatna-ziti and his men, stole away his sleep. I sleep little,
usually less than a third of an evening, and often I would meet
him, those first weeks in Arinna, walking his walls in the dead
of night.

Then he would talk to me, as if I were already a man, of what
the lords would do this season: of Samuha; of the Gasgaeans
who held the lands from Samuha to the sea beyond the northern
mountains. Also he would speak of the Storm-god of Hatti.

I dozed on the bench and dreamed a vivid dream in which the
blue-cloaked lord with the long black braid wielded a dripping
battle-axe from a racing chariot, and woke to the roar of thunder.

A downpour commenced. I rose up, thinking to seek shelter as the world shook with thunder, then exploded in a blazing
whiteness that stabbed me behind the eyes. When I next knew
anything, I knew a blinding headache and a roaring in my ears;
and knew that I was falling, rolling. I struck a rock, clutched it,
gasping. Pain washed over me with the downpour. I cradled my
left arm with my right and yelled my agony into the rain. Above,
on the hilltop, the torch was doused, but I did not need to see. I
could feel my torn flesh, blood dripping off my arm.

I sat there in the mud a long time; grating bitter curses into
the wind. All that immediately occurred to me was that my arm
would not be fit to bear a shield for a long while. Before that
thought I fled the hillside, no longer caring enough about my
manhood to wait for the touch of the gods. I did not climb back
to the summit to search out the cap and the long gown of wool,
but ran on downward in the dark, my arm held stiff and close to
my body.

In a daze, I misjudged the slope and careened down the in-
cline. Thus it was that I stumbled into the girl, who was crossing
between the outer and inner temple at the hill's foot, and took
her with me into the mud.

She yelped in surprise, sputtered, cursed, and scrambled
away from me.

I called her a clumsy slut. She drew a quick breath. Then I heard her sandals slap away on the rain-slick flags.

Next I was blinded with torchlight and surrounded with officials of the temple. Someone tried to help me up by taking hold of my left arm. I snarled and shook off the hand, getting my feet under me. Faces swam in the torch-flickered rain. A scribe came soft-voiced up to me, offering assistance in the pedantic manner of his class.

"Look at his arm!" crowed a rusty female voice. "Get clean cloth, Daduhepa, and bandage, in the rectory. Run, girl!"

A disturbance came from the temple; torches wavered. Then Kuwatna-ziti's anxious eyes peered into mine, sleep still riding their corners. Slowly he eased my left arm around his neck. Supported thus by him and the short scribe I was half carried through the Sun-goddess' immaculate halls, my muddy feet hardly touching the flags.

I tried to shake them off, but Kuwatna-ziti dragged me grimly on. A crowd of robed women flowed with us, its members always changing, full of giggles and pious exclamations. Every so often one would dash inward and peer at my arm.

Myself, I tried not to look at it. I saw my feet, and the stones beneath.

We came into a small, dark wood chamber rich with bronze appointments. Under some shelves at its rear, three covered benches had been hastily flung back from a low table on which were a copper laving bowl and a number of clay vessels.

Kuwatna-ziti eased me onto a bench. "Gently, my lord prince," he advised, though I was not to be called that in this place. "Let me see that arm."

"Great Shepherd, my lord, may I?" It was a wise woman, an "Old Woman," a shawl drawn about her, who hunched over me. "Move that table. Good. Now, young man, just lay your arm there. Daduhepa, I said *hot* water."

A girl in a muddy blue dress fled the room. I squinted at the priestesses in their long embroidered skirts, at the walls; at the

clay tablets banked on shelves against the farthest wall, never
once glancing at my arm.

"What happened up there?" demanded Kuwatna-ziti.

As I told him, trying to ignore my rolling stomach, the girl
came back with a steaming basin, thumped it down upon the table and turned to go.

"Stay," snapped the Old Woman through pleated lips. Tossing her wet black locks, the girl took up a position behind the
table, staring at me archly. Her nose was smudged with dirt; mud
slashed her cheek. "You, Pikku, stay also." The stubby scribe
bowed his head and squatted on a low stool by the Old Woman's
feet. "All the rest of you—begone." Muttering their disapproval,
the priestesses filed out.

"Kuwatna-ziti, shut the door!"

"Yes, Tunnawi," said the Shepherd meekly.

"Young man, this may hurt. There."

It hurt. Wiping the mud and blood from my arm, she cleaned
the wound with hot water. A chasm of raw, open flesh seeped determinedly. I swallowed sour bile, at last daring to watch. When
a pile of reddened cloths lay upon the table, she had the girl mix
honey and butter and oil from the vessels, and applied it herself
to the channel that ran up my forearm.

"Girl, get him some wine," ordered Kuwatna-ziti, and
when she had gone he said to the Old Woman: "What think you,
Tunnawi?"

"About the wound? Nothing. It will heal. A decoration for
him, is all."

"That is not what I mean." The Shepherd looked sharply at
the scribe.

I flexed my fingers; they moved. I tried to stop the jagged
sound of my breathing; my ears were ringing.

The Old Woman sat back from her work, her mole-strewn
cheeks humping into furrows of amusement. "Kuwatna-ziti, you
are like a mare with a foal. Young man, do you think you can
keep that clean?"

"He cannot," said Kuwatna-ziti positively. "Bind it."

"Pikku, more cloths. Only for the night." Her gnarled finger pointed at me. "Can you hear me? Or did the Storm-god of Hatti sear your tongue from your mouth? Kuwatna-ziti, can he speak?"

Kuwatna-ziti laughed mightily, startling the girl just returning with a tray.

"Pikku!" snapped the Old Woman imperiously, and the little scribe hustled over, took the tray from the girl, poured and served. His skin and eyes were pale, like a southern slave.

I decided I had nothing to say.

"Young man," said the Old Woman Tunnawi, "I asked if you could speak."

"Tunnawi, may I be excused?" huffed the girl, picking at the mud drying on her gown. Unlike the priestesses, whose breasts were bare, she was covered from neck to toe.

"You may not."

The girl, her chin lifted high and her mouth squeezed into a pouting red line, sniffed, swished to the benches and sat with an exaggerated flourish. "Pikku, serve me wine!"

The scribe scurried to obey her.

"Young man," Tunnawi warned, "if you would not remain a boy forever, you had best answer me."

"Old Woman, I have nothing to say. My arm hurts and I am wet and in need of sleep. Kuwatna-ziti, let us get out of this place."

His hand came down hard upon my good arm and dug in. While squeezing, he said, "Tasmisarri, follow my lead," so low the others could not hear. Then louder: "You must hear the words of the Old Woman, you must perform a sacrifice under her direction to the Storm-god, you must—"

"Kuwatna-ziti," wheezed the Old Woman impatiently, "he *is* the sacrifice. He *has* performed it. Look," and she reached forward and raised up my arm while I stared at her. "What do you see? Is the worship of the Storm-god alive, or is it dead? When the god Tarhun himself performs a ceremony, should we try to supersede him? You caution this boy of me, and follow after form to humor me? *He* is the form. The Storm-god of Hatti has proclaimed his patronage on this child's very flesh! Shall I now pour some oil on a sweet loaf and break it in two?"

"What, then, do you want with me?" I said.

"The wound is to be tended in the temple. You will stay here and be served by her whom the Storm-god and the Sun-goddess, in their wisdom, have chosen for you, until it is healed."

I said something one does not say in a temple.

"What?" exploded the blue-gowned girl and came straight up on her feet. "Old Woman! Tunnawi!"

"Sit down, Daduhepa, my lady," said Kuwatna-ziti, and turned my way, his eyes slitted with laughter, his teeth bared, his fingers in his beard. He was dressed as a man of the Storm-god, robed to his toes, a red shawl draped over one shoulder and bound about him by a belt bearing the long, curl-tailed ceremonial sheath. On his feet were cultic slippers with upturned toes. "I cannot leave him here, Tunnawi, you yourself must see that."

"Then stay yourself, Shepherd. We see you little enough at your god's service. Stay and spend some time at your devotions. I—"

"Old Woman, the situation—"

"—is political, and has no meaning within these walls. When the machinations of men determine the due of gods, the towns will crumble to dust. I care nothing, for politics. This man"—she patted my hand—"is Tarhun's, and the Lady's. No lesser can determine his time."

I drew my hand from hers and stood, whereupon a wave of dizziness assailed me, so that I leaned with my good arm upon the table.

"Old Woman," I said, "no one determines my time. I am not anyone's; I am my own."

"So you may think," she responded, snaggle teeth gleaming. "So you may think."

I took a step toward her; she did not retreat. We glared at each other.

Kuwatna-ziti pulled me away from her. His speech was a distant buzz when compared to the throbbing of my forearm which reached upward to echo in my ears. "I will stay here with you. You will get some sleep; we will sniff things out. Go on, sit there. Let me talk to her. Girl, attend him!" That last was very loud, and as I put my head in my hands to ease the pounding in my temples, I heard Kuwatna-ziti talking to the Old Woman, and the door scraping against its frame.

"My head hurts," I said, as much to the air as to the girl and her scribe, and slumped forward.

The headache was gone with my waking, but returned when I struggled upright to survey the little room. Kuwatna-ziti's cloak was cast over the other bed, but it was the high-chinned girl, Daduhepa, who sat on it, wringing cloths in a basin.

"You!" I said. "Go fetch me something to eat." I eyed the pot near the bed.

"I will get you a meal," she agreed, equable, but only went as far as the door where she instructed some other as to what food to fetch.

"Get out of here." My mouth was dry and fuzzy. Swinging my legs to the floor, I made it to my feet, then had to hug the wall.

I pushed her away when she tried to help me, sending her sprawling across the bed. I had not meant to push her so hard. I looked at my white-wrapped arm, then at her. Her high-browed face was flushed.

"What is the matter with me?" I muttered as the room twirled slowly.

"The Storm-god touched you."

"Get out of here. I have to—"

She laughed. I looked down at myself, hard with morning, naked.

"Who do you think cleaned you up, dressed that precious skin of yours, put you to bed, princeling?"

"Are you a lady?"

"What do you think?" Her delicately hooked nose sought the air. She had mane enough, but under the blue dress she seemed a dead stick.

"I think you should act like one and go out and let me use the pot."

"I will turn my back."

"No. If you propose to stay in here, you must help me."

To my surprise and chagrin, she did that, with her face turned away and a disdainful look on her. I judged her a few years older than I.

"You're Hurrian?" I asked. "Your name, I mean—'Daduhepa?'" I rolled the 'h' in my throat. She shot up like a startled bird, her cheeks burning, that anyone might mistake her for a Hurrian. "Surely that name is Hurrian." I had just done to her what the boys in Hattusas used to do to me. I wondered why I had done it, yet did not apologize.

Her eyes sparked. "And you? You *are* Tasmisarri, are you not?" she purred as I cautiously sought the bed, too tired to argue the insult she implied.

"I am. Can you give me one good reason why you will not take my order and get out of here?"

She gave me an interminable recitation of who she was, back almost to the legendary Anittas. I was unimpressed, but enlightened. A spoiled lord's brat, serving a short spell in the Sun-goddess' temple to make her holy, before she was traded off for peace on someone's boundary and bred by the man who bought her.

"You must be the only person in Hatti to whom I am not related," I said flatly, letting the inference that she lacked even a drop of royal blood among all her progenitors do its work for me. A flush rode her long neck downward, disappearing beneath her dress.

"I should spank you, little boy! I would, if you were not so weak."

"Keep a lady's silence, or I will pay your father his bride-price and have you scrubbing floors in Hattusas."

She paled and hurried wordless out the door, not knowing that I could not buy a cart ox and did not have a floor to call my own.

A day later, I had had only one more headache and was allowed, after a long and difficult session with the Old Woman, to walk outside on the condition that I took the girl, Daduhepa, along.

The blight of her presence was almost bearable in the crisp air. I felt the first stirrings of life as if the season's change champed upon its bit. Kuwatna-ziti had been avoiding me, for his own reasons, and I was rank with being pent up so long. I refused to wear a woolen dress, saying I wanted no fouling of my stride, but what I wanted was the feel of the weather on me. The pale sun was high. We climbed in silence, she scrabbling behind me. I pushed the pace viciously, to show her that I was no longer weak, and when we reached the summit she cast herself on the ground, lying face up, her hand between her breasts, panting. Sweat glistened on her forehead.

I stalked off to see if the lightning had left any marks on the hillside.

I was not disappointed: I found a seared patch of ground.

"Tasmisarri, please wait!"

I broke a budding branch off in my hand and drew in the dirt. The third time she called I went back to her. She still lay on the ground in her blue, high-necked gown, but her right leg was drawn up and her left arm bent back under her head, pushing her breasts against the wool. She had traced along her eyelids with kohl, as do the Egyptian women; until now I had not noticed it.

"I have heard, from some, that Kuwatna-ziti sold the lords to Tuthaliyas for you," she said sweetly.

An anger that would not let me walk away rose and filled my throat, bitter.

"Women should not mix in politics," I growled, and hunkered down on the balls of my feet, playing with buds on the branch; flicking them off, one by one, onto her dress.

"So speaks the son of Asmunikal?" she smiled viciously, and added: "Or are you?"

Her long, curving eyebrows raised, she pushed up on her arms. Her tongue wet her lips. "Do you think things will be any better for the lands with Tuthaliyas as Tabarna? Or must we wait for you, my lord?" Her white teeth flashed.

"I think you have waited long enough," I said, reaching out to take her by the throat. At the last moment, I took her by the gown instead and ripped it to her waist. She got out only one startled yelp before my palm closed over her mouth and my weight bore her to the ground. Her eyes huge and rolling above my hand, she bit and screamed into my palm as I pulled up her dress and thrust my knee between her thighs.

"Say please," I suggested when my fingers touched her moisture, but she only tossed her head about and moaned low in her throat. Under the wool her breasts stood, anxious, straining toward my tongue.

I was aware of her virginity only when I took it; by then it did not matter. When she began to shudder under me I took my palm from her mouth and replaced it with my lips. Her teeth were clenched; her hips thrust up begging under me.

I muffled the sound of my triumph against her pulsing throat, and when she cried like a kitten she cried my name.

Thereafter I lay with the blood of her violation on my fingers, staring from them into her eyes. "Why did you do this to me?" I asked her. "What are you going to do now?" I made her lick the blood. The trap, once closed on my foot, became clear.

But she did not admit to it, even then. She lay with a softened mouth under me and said woodenly, "I do not know, my lord, what it is that you mean. You have violated me and, be you prince or no, you will pay."

"I can imagine."

She made sharp angry gestures against my chest.

Still lying on her, I stretched out my good arm and, leaning on my fist, said, "Now you 'my lord' me. Have you tired of your taunting? Just what is it you expect me to pay, your bride-price?"

Her eyes filled with tears. Little fists beating against me, she squirmed so fiercely that I slid off her. She pulled her dress together over her breasts and curled her exposed legs under her.

"I expect nothing from you, Tasmisarri." She gulped, her upper lip trembling, and burst into tears.

I went down the hill and left her there.

*

"You *what?*" roared Kuwatna-ziti when I told him.

We stood in the temple stable. He pushed the gray's searching nose irritatedly away from him. I explained once more, although I was sure he had heard me the first time. "She deserved it. She asked for it. She has been at me since she first saw me. . . ." I trailed off. There was something odd about his face, and in the fact that he was not lecturing me or pounding his fist against the wall.

"That may be," he said levelly, "but it is a weak man who uses his strength on a woman. That is no start for a marriage."

"Marriage? She nearly raped me."

"That is no harlot up there, no namra bitch to use and throw back in the slave pens. I, that is . . . we . . . Tasmisarri, I can arrange this so that there will be no repercussions. You might even profit from it—"

"Rein in. I am not marrying the sharp-tongued hunting dog."

"A girl of that rank cannot be just a concubine."

"Kuwatna-ziti, you are not listening." I slid down onto a pile of straw and picked my teeth with one.

"Tuthaliyas might stand the bride-price, what with his urge to consolidate the lords." His back was to me; his fingers, clasped behind him, twined each other. "There will be reciprocal gifts from her family, because of who you are. We might just heal all our troubles here in Arinna with this one—"

"Kuwatna-ziti, look at me." The Shepherd turned. His face was impassive. "You planned this! You and the rest of them!"

"Tasmisarri, you are now a man. So I will to talk to you like one." He sat down beside me. "You have split my ranks from behind me, you have caused dissension between brothers in their own houses. Your presence here has made it difficult for me to finance certain expeditions, and more than difficult for me to retain the confidence of the lords here. Now with one concession you can quiet all the uproar you have started. Does it matter so much to you whose legs you split, or does all that I have done for you matter so little?"

"You did plan it then! Am I now to have copper nails driven through my wings? Will you divine the future from my entrails?" His hand lay on my thigh. I drew up my leg.

"It is true," Kuwatna-ziti sighed, "that we thought perhaps you and the young lady might make a match. However, I didn't expect you to storm her battlements. I must wonder, now, if she will even accept you. Have you dropped a civil war into my lap?" His slanted eyes adamantine, his lips drew thin as he spoke. "Tasmisarri—"

"I told you not to call me that."

"It is your name. If you do not like it, pick another. You are too old for 'Tasmi'."

We had no proper wedding: announcements of our elopement were sent to the parties concerned, and so in keeping was this with my image that no one questioned it. Asmunikal saved Kuwatna-ziti from financial ruin by standing Daduhepa's bride-price: my mother's wealthy new husband was pleased that the ill-reputed Tasmisarri was showing signs of settling down. Daduhepa's family, heavily landed and conservative, was very powerful in the Upper Country. The bride-price started a river of wealth flowing from my mother in Ziplanda through Tuthaliyas in Hattusas to my in-laws in Arinna. But although my house was much enriched, I had no more than I had before.

My wife and I communicated by means of the young, light-colored scribe, Pikku, who ran with messages back and forth between my wife's estates and Kuwatna-ziti's, where I continued to abide.

We had a very polite relationship that conformed to all proprieties but one: we did not sleep together. Tuthaliyas himself attended the family gathering that celebrated the affair. He had been doing the New Year festivals, and was on a swing that would take the kingly presence through all the inner towns before the campaigns began—or so he said. My wife bowed to the Great King; my in-laws beamed; Tuthaliyas found time to take from me my word before the Oath Gods, a thing he had not been able to do at his accession, since I was then not yet a man. One would have thought it was he who had taken a new wife, so jovial was he.

Daduhepa stood beside me and greeted endless people whom she knew and I did not. "May the Sun-goddess grace your house," she would simper, kissing some old hag on the cheek, then whisper to me: "I hope the Gasgaeans geld you," smirk, and greet the next.

When I finally retorted, beneath an aching smile, that she might start keeping snakes, for she would never have me again, she pounced on that, and held me to it as a promise. Cursing her so roundly that one of the bejeweled crones who waited to greet me stumbled over her cane, I stalked away to begin getting drunk, taking a gilded jar of very imported wine—Amurrite; I was holding a soldier's weekly wage of it in my hand—out into the fresh air.

Sitting down against the courtyard wall, I began drinking the wine. When I had made my way half through the jug, a crash sounded on my right and then a form slid heavily down the wall by my side. I steadied the jar. "Greetings, guest."

"Greetings, nephew," eructed Tuthaliyas. "Nice looking girl. Is she good?"

"Terrible."

He burped again. "That's the way with the ladies. Take concubines, my boy—and slaves. And leave that kind to their child-bearing and their genealogies."

I was silent, wondering if I had already said something I shouldn't.

"Kuwatna-ziti's trying to find out without offending anybody whether I—You know . . . you can call yourself anything you want. I care not about it. Just you mind your oath, and you'll come out of this a general." His hand slapped down on my arm. "I'd even give your mother that winter villa she likes so much,

if you'll turn some of that revolutionary fervor against the Gasgaean enemy. . . ."

I leaned my head back against the stone and tilted it his
way. "I take my oaths seriously, O Great King, even if you are
an old snake."

He scowled at that.

Three days later the weather broke, and I took a billet with
the Great Shepherd's men. Meanwhile Kuwatna-ziti had put me
on the role as an auxiliary (thereby avoiding having to decide
whether or not we dared call me "prince"); assigned me back to
himself as a driver while requisitioning another chariot for my
personal use; allotted me a marshal's pay scale while having me
draw special funds from the auxiliaries pool; found two men to
teach me what I was already supposed to know and put *them* on
double wages. When furrow-browed scribes came bearing arm-
fuls of contradictory tablets he would listen patiently, nodding,
smiling, and when they were done reiterate that he had meant
exactly this, and send them away. I thought it might not be so
bad, being a general.

I dropped into bed each night with every muscle in my body
screaming, rose before dawn and ate more than I once ate in a
full day, and worked the sun into bed. My arms and shoulders
and legs put on muscle. I took to wearing a driver's belt and
did exercises to strengthen my back. I learned how to stay alive
against a battle-axe and how much heavier a bronze war sword
is than a boy's wooden one. I grew like a weed. We were in the
field before I knew it.

The Shepherd's men understood Gasgaeans: we burned them
out; trapped them; strung a few on pikes. Some of us younger
men used to go down to the booty-train and bring out live namra,
offering them freedom if they could win it wrestling. Snapping
a neck takes practice, and practice on them we did. This lasted
well into the spring, until one of the lords had his neck snapped,
and the rest of us were assigned to fortifications as a disciplin-
ary measure.

It was Samuha we were fortifying, seemingly house by house. In former times the enemy from Hayasa had come and sacked all the Upper Country and made Samuha its frontier. Tuthaliyas had reclaimed it. All the Shepherd's men had to do was keep it. The location was not altogether peaceful: the enemy from Hayasa and the Gasgaean enemy both abutted the land, which had been sacked so many times that trees were scarce and the wind blew ash and the sky was always yellow.

I did not mind the construction work, though I took pains to conceal that from my fellow penitents, who were much demeaned by it. I liked the feeling I got when a sketch in the dirt became a wall, and I went thrice to Kuwatna-ziti with ideas to improve the strength of our defenses. When our punishment was over and we returned to the main business of making war, I found I had made a friend of the commander of fortifications, one Hattu-ziti; and when I took a deep gash in my side and was camp-bound, he and I spent long nights drawing Hattusas in the dirt and fortifying her.

Some say the driver's craft takes the strongest nerve of all; I disagree, but it is no easy thing to go into war without a weapon in hand. Two fists on the reins and a quick eye for flying missiles and tight corridors among steeds and wheels are what is needed. I became good at flicking a man from his feet with my whip, and better at ducking. We say of war that it is a season, but it is actually two seasons: after New Year, in the warming spring called hameshant, the campaigns begin, lasting through the harvest, until zenant, when the weather comes down low on the Upper Country and the rivers rise. There had been no snow in the winter of my passing into Kuwatna-ziti's care, and the lands were dry all year.

This threat of famine was what had brought the Shepherd's flock to Samuha, whence we were expected to hold the Upper Country while Tuthaliyas split the armies and sent Hittite forces raiding rich towns along all our borders, to bring back sheep and cattle and grain for the winter.

Tuttu—in whose 1,000 we fell—commanded the Upper Country, and did a bad job of it, even managing to die awkwardly: his death caused Kuwatna-ziti to be made commanding general; thus I found myself with his place to fill—at the head of the flock.

I filled it well enough: the men with whom I had built walls and towers were in my personal thirty, and we became as one hand.

So when, reluctantly, I came home from Samuha to Arinna with Kuwatna-ziti, I left the commander of fortifications, Hattu-ziti, as field commander in my stead. It seemed to the Shepherd and me that if the troops were to winter in Samuha, we should be there too, but we had no choice: Great King Tuthaliyas commanded us to meet with him in Arinna.

I scratched the scar that marked me "favorite of the Storm-god," and picked a weed and chewed it.

"Just say nothing about it," Kuwatna-ziti was advising me while trampling a circle in the high grass of the hill.

"You will make us both dizzy," I complained. "Tabarna Tuthaliyas, the hero, surely must know that I have my own command. He *said* to—"

"You told me what he said to you, but he was drunk. And the raids are not going well." He sat down cross-legged and rested his chin on his fist. His club he wore braided now, as men once did in the Old Empire. Putting the end of the braid in his mouth, he sucked it absently.

"It is his own fault for spreading the troops so thin. They'll be burning down Hattusas while he's out looting villages. You watch."

"Tasmisarri, try not to criticize the policies of the Sun, Great King, your, uncle. What would you do, were you Tabarna?" He had that casual smile which meant he was intensely interested.

"You know very well what needs done," I said, rolling onto my belly, staring down at Arinna glittering coldly amid the yellow hills. "And you know it will not be I who does it. I am content doing what I am doing."

"Except when someone gives you a direct order. Tasmis-arri, men like you are fit only to give orders; a soldier's craft is

to take them. The kingship, alas, is the only work to which you
are suited."

I said that I would make a sacrifice to Istar of the Battlefield, to ensure that the Lady of the Armies withdrew her support from him.

"Have you seen your wife?"

"No, nor do I intend to." We had been in Arinna three days.

"You had better."

"Are you drunk?"

"Let me make that an order, from your commander."

"Must I let you determine my personal life, too?"

"Until you can determine mine, my lord prince."

"You cannot order me to lie with her."

"I would not even think of it. Just talk to her."

"Do you want me to move up there? To Daduhepa's? Your
wife has lost her love for me." It was not just me. It was me and
a fine-boned namra girl I had with me. Kuwatna-ziti's wife had
wrinkled up her nose in disapproval, stamping around, putting
dirt in the girl's food, lecturing me on the meaning of the word
'Hittite.'

Kuwatna-ziti barked a laugh. "You worry about your women,
I will see to mine." Eyes narrowed, he pulled me by the club until my face was close to his. "I want you to promise me that you
will try to reach an accommodation with Daduhepa. You're here
for three days more, then back to Samuha—*if* all goes well. In
times like these, any move is precipitate. We do not know what
Tuthaliyas wants. It is imperative that I be able to trust my back
to the Arinnians. Talk to her. Be civilized. *Leave that namra bitch
with me.* If I hear that you took her up there, or even *mentioned*
her to Daduhepa, I will beat you so that you cannot sit down until New Year. I still can do it."

I had been intending exactly that: to take the namra. I dared
not leave her to Kuwatna-ziti's wife, had been hesitant to even
come up to the hilltop. Although the Shepherd had lectured me
repeatedly about the little namra; saying that I was smitten with
her, I did not believe it. Yet, she was a problem. In the end I took

her over to one of my men and left her happily engaged in what she did best. Then I drove alone up to Daduhepa's.

I found the servants slow to obey a master they had never seen, and by the time I had been ushered into a cedar bower to await my wife, I was furious.

She came with a train of attendants, whom I tried to no avail to dismiss.

"Tasmisarri," said my bejeweled wife, palms on her belly, "this is *my* house and these are *my* women and you will not order them about." Her complexion was clear and flushed, her eyes sparkled. She minced to a bench and sat herself down with a beatific smile.

By that time I was standing over her, my hands grappling the air. "Why did you not tell me?" I bellowed like the Shepherd, so that one of the women who floated about her squeaked. "Get these servants out of here!"

With a slight pursing of her lips, she signaled to her woman and they were gone.

I sat down on the far side of the bench from her and stared at the crust of dirt on my sandals. "Why did you not tell me?"

No answer.

"Are you well? Does it hurt? Some get sick—"

"I am fine, thank you. To what do I owe this unexpected visit, my lord?"

"We will name him Arnuwandas," I said.

"*We* will not name him anything. *I* will name him—*or her,* as the case may be. What do you want, Tasmisarri? I have heard that your time is well taken up."

I squirmed on the bench, not looking at her. "I want to make some kind of truce with you, for my son's sake."

"Go away."

"You cannot withhold him from me. 'If a woman sends a man away, she must give him his children.' It is you who care how things look. How will this look? You cannot so shame us both."

"*I* shame *you?* Impossible. Go back to your Gasgaean harlot."

"She's not Gasgaean."

"Do you think I care what she is? Get out, go on. "

She rained blows on me with her diminutive fists, until I held them away from me, then started to cry.

I sent word to Kuwatna-ziti to write me when he wanted me, and to one of my men to keep my little namra in his charge, and spent two days with my wife.

On the third day, Kuwatna-ziti sent for me. By the time I arrived at his estate I felt that I had returned, unscathed, from a war. But my feeling of well-being lasted only a moment. "Guess what lurks within," suggested the Shepherd.

"Sixteen harlots, a pig roasting, a—"

"Muwatalli the Elder."

"I thought Tuthaliyas was coming himself."

"Well, he did not. How went it with the princess?"

"Did you know she was pregnant?"

"I? Never considered it."

"You mean you never considered telling me. Does my mother know?"

"I believe she might," said Kuwatna-ziti absently as we entered the main house, which had escaped pillage for a hundred years: a cool, dark place of old woodwork mixed with modern terracing, its rooms growing progressively larger and more irregular as each level gave way to the next, until we turned down a pillared hall to the court around which the estate curled.

Muwatalli the Elder sprawled there by a tiny pond, the sun glinting off his bald pate. My pretty namra was just coming with a pitcher from the kitchens.

"I forgot to tell you, I had her sent back up here. If you are angry, I will make a settling with you over her," said Kuwatna-ziti in a low voice.

"For yourself? I thought you did not like her."

"For my wife, to teach her a lesson. Are you displeased?"

"No, take her as your own, whenever you like." I touched his arm. "The hatred Muwatalli has for me is rivaled only by Kantuzilis'."

"I know. Be at ease, keep your temper, do not say anything he might twist to your disadvantage."

Then my little namra saw us, hurrying with a soft, delighted cry to me, and there was no more time for caution or plot.

I disengaged her, bidding her await me in my rooms. By then Kuwatna-ziti was already drinking to the foremost among the Great Ones of Hattusas, my uncle, the elder Muwatalli, the prince.

His pig's eyes followed my lithe namra into the house, then fastened on me as I squatted by Kuwatna-ziti's side and took up a drink.

"Ah, Tasmisarri," my uncle said. "We have heard such glowing reports of you that scarcely any at court can believe them. Tell me how Kuwatna-ziti worked such magic." Even his fingers were swathed in rolls of fat.

"You had best ask him that."

"That's an odd scar — is that the famous mark of the Storm-god?"

"So some say. I fell down a hill in the dark, nothing more."

"Glad to hear it."

Kuwatna-ziti said, "I hope Great King Tuthaliyas is well. We had heard he would come himself."

"The Tabarna is *not* well, and you know it. Do not play with me, Shepherd."

I had not known it, but did not want to evince interest.

"I am just trying to find out what you want, Muwatalli. We leave for Samuha tomorrow —"

I stared covertly at Kuwatna-ziti, wondering why he would speak so.

"By my leave, you go, or not at all," said the elder Muwatalli.

"Of course, Muwatalli, my lord; of course. But are we not all of one mind? Samuha needs supervision if we are to hold her over the winter."

"Civilized people do not make war in winter. Will your men not balk at staying in the field?"

"Those who are there now will stay, if we set an example and stay ourselves."

"I have orders to bring the prince back to Hattusas," he said flatly.

I measured the jump to the nearest roof.

"Can you tell me why, my lord? He has a good start with the men; pulling him out for the winter will make him less effective in the spring."

"Ah, yes," said Muwatalli slowly, pinching his lower lip. "We have heard about your young protégé's success. But that is not my concern. Here—this is why I have come up here, and it might explain. I just follow orders." Only he laughed.

The tablet, once extracted from its envelope of baked clay, would doubtless tell us what Muwatalli was pretending he did not know.

He and Kuwatna-ziti sparred awhile, making swords of innuendos, until at last the Great One rose and stretched, saying that if someone would send the pretty little namra to his rooms he would be much pleased, and waddled into the house, leaving us to open the message from the Tabarna in private.

"He is not getting my woman."

"It is her virtue or yours, Tasmisarri."

"What does that say?"

"It says that the Old Boar requires your presence, what do you think?"

"I think I am about to be adjudged in contempt of a royal order—I am not going."

"Yes, you are."

"*Why?*"

"Because the king is sick, and has asked me to deliver you to him. But consider: the Hayasaean enemy and the Gasgaean tribes sleep in each other's camps. Tuthaliyas has his back up. There is nothing better than outward threat to heal inner discord. Now if you do not want to give that namra to Muwatalli, then, for your own good, I will buy her from you or fight you for her, and *I* will give her to him."

"You do not know him!"

"One namra does not matter, Tasmi!"

He was wrong. She did matter, and the loss of her haunted my sleep a long time: her screams rang in my dreams.

Kuwatna-ziti apologized to me, pale and drawn from what he had seen in Muwatalli's rooms.

I did not go in there, only gathered my things together to take to Hattusas. Never again did I trust Kuwatna-ziti's judgment above my own.

CHAPTER 3

Once I arrived in Hattusas, the joyous days spent with the army receded like a daydream, for I was Tasmi*sarri* once more. Taller, seasoned, sprouting hair on my chest, with a plumed helmet marking me as the Shepherd's, a high-born wife, and a child on the way, I could not understand why no one saw the change in me.

By the evening of our first day in the city, I had acquired a number of abrasions and needed a change of clothes, this last coming about over the taunt that my parents were brother and sister after I had withstood all lesser insults.

Kuwatna-ziti gritted his teeth, saying that he did not blame me: if they would see nothing but the past, there was nothing else to give them.

But insight had visited me while I scrapped in the streets: Kuwatna-ziti had made a fool of me. I was wroth. I thought of my command, of those men who had so energetically accepted me among them. What Kuwatna-ziti's troops had seen in me was what they hoped I might become—what he had enlisted their aid to help make me. And I, who had never known comradeship, had not wondered why a green youth who was not yet blooded could demand obedience and respect from those veterans and get it. He had 'princed' me with his men, and I had flown so eagerly into the trap my pinfeathers fluttered.

Hattusas recalled me to myself. She is the most unforgiving of cities, the coldest of mistresses. Full of soldiers back from the wars and farmers trading their harvests, her streets ran with sheep and cattle and the markets overflowed into the town. The Festival of Haste was a week away; the air snapped with laughter and the coming of the cold.

Journeying here had not been pleasant. The Shepherd, for all his astute words, was uneasy, and Muwatalli loomed always in my sight. He had offered to pay for the namra, so Kuwatna-ziti told me, but the Shepherd had refused, making a gift of her to him in my name.

"She cost you nothing," he had said to my stare.

"Nothing at all," I had agreed, and laid the whip to the grays.

We had hoped to rid ourselves of Muwatalli by going directly to the palace and announcing ourselves. There I saw that the gigantic, pillared hall would be finished by first frost.

We were in that open, colonnaded corridor flanked with Meshedi on one side and pages on the other, called the bodyguard's court. At the end of this way of bodies was the old *halentuwa-house*. Within its cypress walls were the throne, an offering table, a burning fire on the hearth, and Great King Tuthaliyas.

Kuwatna-ziti left me waiting there, then returned, asking, "Has he come out yet?"

"No."

"He's probably still in the seraglio."

That was possible, I thought as the Shepherd and I stood listening to the crowd, but not very likely. The halentuwa-house, from which the king traditionally emerges to perform official functions, is attached to the residential palace; but the Great King loathed women.

"All the Great Ones are in the city, so I've heard," said Kuwatna-ziti very low. We made our way toward the doorway through which the king would emerge, and as we did so, the curtains in the windows were drawn up. It was early morning. We had not slept or even changed, and Kuwatna-ziti's army woolens were dun-colored with dust.

"Half of them are here now," I muttered back, deciding that I was better off walking on the Shepherd's left, toward the pages, than his right where, as we moved up the line, Meshedi touched their weapons, straightening perceptibly when they recognized me.

Muwatalli had been hurried off by a tight-lipped commander of ten when we passed through the gatehouse.

As a murmur ran through the crowd and the Great King emerged from the darkness—flanked by priests and men of the Golden Lance, preceded by a scribe—my mother swept down upon us, the congealing crowd parting for her.

"Tasmi! Little one!" She threw herself into my arms. I held her, resting my chin on the top of her head, as my sister stared, straight-browed and appraising, at Kuwatna-ziti.

"Asmunikal, how can you carry all those clothes around?" I stepped back. Under a stiff cape worked with silver thread, she was wrapped thrice in fine colored woolens; her piled hair was pinned with copper.

Soon the priest's droning gave way to Tuthaliyas' reedy voice, lauding the noble warriors just returned to the city. He did not look badly indisposed, save that his skin seemed yellowish, but I put that down to the early hour and his sobriety.

My mother had my hand and would not release it. She was introducing my sister—who looked like I did at her age, all hands and feet—to Kuwatna-ziti. He was his most ingratiating self with her, treating her as if she had breasts.

While Asmunikal whispered to me of her pride in me and my wife, and of her plans for our child, the Great King began to hear grievances. A lord had found some other lord with his main wife, and demanded the death penalty for both. Tuthaliyas scratched his ear, careful not to dislodge the blunt-tipped conical

cap he wore when dispensing judgment, and made the merciful
decision: death to both. The cuckolded noble smiled grimly and
bowed himself back through the crowd.

My mother had hold of Kuwatna-ziti's hand, too, and pulled
him close.

"Great Shepherd, my lord," she whispered in that voice which
always waxed sensual when about her machinations, "have you
seen the commander Himuili?"

"My lady, I have just this morning arrived, and hardly shaken
Muwatalli's companionable surveillance."

"Stay away from that snake Muwatalli!" hissed my mother
so loud the man in front turned around. "Stay away. And keep
Tasmi clear of him."

"As you say, my lady," said Kuwatna-ziti, pained, and put
his lips to her ear.

"You have grown," I said to my sister.

"And you. You're getting hairy. But you are not any cleaner.
I heard you have been killing the enemy. And doing other things
to them."

"Your teeth are crooked," I observed.

She stuck out her tongue. She was dressed the double of her
mother, and her bare arm stuck out gawky from the stiff finery. "I
was hoping Kuwatna-ziti would have taught you to wear clothes."

The army has a choice of dress: I was there in a regulation
uniform, one which included a cloak but did not include a tunic,
only a belted kilt wrapped round the loins, whose oblique edge,
folded in front of the body, bore the Tabarna's device and rank
stripes. I made a lewd comment with my hand, gave her a look
she knew well. She flushed and pulled on our mother's arm.

I continued to stand there while Asmunikal shushed my sister and ignored us both, deeply involved with Kuwatna-ziti. The
empty scabbard, the slot on my belt where my Hattian war axe
usually rested, discomfited me, in this crowd of my fellow lords.
Even the puny weight of a dirk would have been welcome, but in
Hattusas I was, as I have said, Tasmi*sarri,* and I had been relieved
of my weapons. They had not stripped Kuwatna-ziti of his arms.

We waited through the whole day without being granted audience with the Sun of Hatti, though he certainly saw us. Near sundown Kantuzilis, the Pale One, made a show of seeing me, complete with long, slow malicious grin. Muwatalli, beside him, broke out laughing.

But the laugh died on his lips when the young commander Himuili, in a military maneuver of wondrous inventiveness, separated Kuwatna-ziti from Asmunikal and my sister and, one arm over my shoulder, extracted us with consummate skill from the audience chamber by a series of introductions and reunions that ended only when we stood between the inner and outer palace gates and I had my weapons returned to me.

Our shadows were long, their edges fuzzy, climbing the new wall of plastered mud brick that ringed the residential palace. These new, winged, doubled gates were too narrow for chariots; I wondered what Tuthaliyas had had in mind when he built them.

"Shepherd, let us go find a tavern," suggested Himuili in an odd voice.

"My lord, what is going on?" asked Kuwatna-ziti.

Himuili looked pointedly at me. I recalled that time he and Kuwatna-ziti had walked away from the circle of relatives in which I was trapped. I looked steadily back at him. The man had never laid a hand on me, but had never aided me either.

"You'll not see the king for a day or two, Tasmisarri. I have the roster. Why not go on down to my house in the lower city? I have business with the Shepherd."

So did I go off on my own, starting at the Blue Ram where I had first been with Kuwatna-ziti, ending in the streets. When I pounded on the gate of Himuili's modest town lodgings, the sky was getting light.

The man who opened it did so with blade in hand, and he was fully awake. He stared uncertainly at my disheveled appearance and sent someone to find out from Kuwatna-ziti whether or not I should be admitted.

Leaning on the doorpost, I glared at him wordlessly, half-drunk, truculent, my hackles yet up from brawling. The only thing in my mind was to let Kuwatna-ziti know that I knew how he had princed me before his men. The marshal who had called me "the Shepherd's pup" had found out the pup had teeth: I had made him eat garbage; but it was I who came away with a bad taste in my mouth.

When I was ushered into Kuwatna-ziti's presence, in a hall before a closed room, I lunged at him, going for his throat.

"Tasmi— *What? Get out!*" That last was to the servant who tried to aid him. He needed no aid. His fingers closed on my wrists and he pinned me up against the wall. "Stop it. *Stop!* That's better. Now, what's wrong? What happened to you?"

With all my strength, I tried to twist my wrists from his grasp. Putting his knee in my belly, he held me against the wall. "You demon's bastard, stop it! *Tell* me what's wrong, or I'll grind your—"

"You know well enough what is wrong. 'Shepherd's pup,' they are calling me."

"Where were you? What happened?"

I told him, and he let me go. I rubbed my wrists, wondering how long it would be until I had such tricks of defensive skill as his.

"When will you stop caring?" The Shepherd was grim. "I have had a bellyful of their feelings for you, myself. Look, you: I cannot leave here right now. And because of the way things are, I cannot invite you to join us. Come on." And he led me away from the closed doors to the room Himuili had given him, extracting from me a promise to stay there until he came from his mysterious business with our host.

"When are we leaving?" I sank down on the bed, tremors of unspent fury abating as I stretched out. A groan escaped me.

"I will send somebody to dress those cuts. I wish I knew when we were leaving, but . . . I just wish I knew."

"Send someone pretty," I called, but he was gone.

*

The days wore on my nerves, stretched into weeks. Kuwatna-ziti spent all the time he could with Himuili, which meant that I

only saw him while we loitered from dawn to dusk at the palace
and Tuthaliyas studiously ignored us. Each time a new docket
was drawn up our names were appended to the end of it; we had
no recourse but to await him.

My mother went to Arinna, so that she might be there when
Daduhepa's time came upon her. Before she left, I asked her to
convince my wife to accept my choice in the child's naming. Eyes
filled with tears, my mother said she would do what she could.

Kantuzilis took it into his head to keep the Shepherd awake
nights by evincing inordinate interest in Samuha and the faring
of the Upper Country. He spent a whole day querying me of my
exploits while Kuwatna-ziti fended off what he surely thought
were leading questions, although where they were leading I had
not the slightest idea. The veins showed through my uncle's pale
skin, and in the daylight he wore a cowled cloak; his eyes, red as
his gums, were glittering with some private humor.

"I cannot take another day of this," muttered Kuwatna-ziti
as we were checked out through the gate by a guard who waved
friendlily — he knew us well enough. That night Kuwatna-ziti
did not leave me for Himuili's company, but took both me and
the young commander on a tour of the better inns, spending silver like copper.

Himuili was covered with hair. It fringed his fingers, his
cheeks, peeked out from beneath his uniform's short slit sleeves,
curled about the leather braces on his wrists and up his neck to
meet his black mane, cut square to give no handhold in close
quarters. His eyes were startlingly large, with flecks of green in
them, and doubtless accounted for his success with the women.
We talked horses and chariots, and the placement of foot soldiers in the field.

One of Tuthaliyas' policies rankled him, and in that he had
my concurrence. This policy, that of taking few namra, amounted
in his eyes to massacre. With such sentiments I was wholeheart-
edly in agreement, but when I said so, Kuwatna-ziti found that
a piece of lamb had lodged in his throat.

We were halfway through the meal when winded Meshedi burst through the curtain into the alcove we had taken and their marshal announced that a message had come for me from Arinna and I might collect it at the palace. "What else?" demanded Himuili, for the Meshedi lingered and Kuwatna-ziti, not raising his eyes, stabbed with his dirk at a chunk of meat on his plate.

"Himuili, my lord commander, the boy is supposed to come with us. Now."

"Now?" echoed Himuili pensively while Kuwatna-ziti ate, then, squinting at the Meshedi, added: "He will be along."

"Let him go," rumbled Kuwatna-ziti. "There is nothing else to do." He was chewing determinedly, staring at his plate.

Something died of frostbite inside me. Behind the marshal I counted six other Meshedi. "May the Oath Gods take you!" I cursed Kuwatna-ziti's bowed head. My vision swam. I was tired of fighting them all.

Himuili's cautioning hand came down on my leg beneath the table. "What names have you, Meshedi?" he snapped. The men, straightening up, gave their names. "Hear me, my lord marshal," the light-eyed Himuili continued, "if you — personally — do not return the prince unharmed to my estate by the time the midwatch call is heard, I will strangle you with your own entrails."

I slid out from under his hand, saying, "Take me, then," to the Meshedi, knowing as well as anyone else there that Himuili's threats were empty.

When the seven Meshedi had closed around me, I looked back through the crowd. Himuili's head was bent to Kuwatna-ziti's.

I was in my own world on that march through the streets and into the residential palace. The Meshedi watched me warily and kept their hands to themselves.

They handed me over to the inner-sanctum Meshedi, most of whom were family, sons of concubines, cousins. But none of those spoke to me, nor I to them.

Tuthaliyas was in the king's wing, in a newly refurbished room sweet with cedar. A priestess of the Sun-goddess of Arinna and a scribe were also there.

The Meshedi marched me up before him where he sprawled in a chair carven grand like a throne, then stepped back.

He drank long from a silver rhyton, disdaining the cup bearer who hovered behind him, and said, "Your wife is ill, a suitably winded messenger assures us. Convenient, do you not think?"

"My lord king? She is heavy with child."

He ran his ringed hand across his lips. Even at that late hour, Tuthaliyas wore the round-domed crown my father had favored. I wondered if he slept with it on, and said nothing more.

"Why are you not petitioning me for leave to go to your wife?"

"It would be a waste of breath."

He grumbled, half rose, then fastened his hands on his wool-robed knees and sat back. "Just as well you know it. But I did bring you here for a reason. Will you have wine?"

"No, my lord king." I looked at the priestess, waiting patiently. The Sun-goddess of Arinna regulates kingship and queenship. I felt some concern for Daduhepa, about how she would fare on her own. I glanced at the Meshedi out of the corner of my eye. Behind my back, the stout doors were closed. This room, one of the few so constructed, had no windows. Tuthaliyas well knew me.

He shrugged and swigged again, then smacked his lips. "Well, this is not how I had intended to do this, but let's get on with it."

I stiffened, waiting for the blow to fall.

The Meshedi closed in, the scribe knelt by Tuthaliyas' throne, and the priestess came forward. She was halfway through the ritual when I realized it was my adoption, not my death, she commended to the numerous gods and goddesses whom she must invoke before the reason for their attendance could be revealed. I started visibly, raising my eyes to the king's. He put his jeweled finger to his thick lips, but his gilded belly shook with suppressed laughter.

When it was done he ordered them all out, even the Meshedi, and waved about him. "I wish I could offer you a chair, son." There were none but his throne.

Wondering if this were some further torture, some trick, I yearned for Kuwatna-ziti, then recollected his eyes, which could not meet mine.

Then the great king began to cackle. He chortled until tears came, until he wobbled on the seat of his kingship. "If only you could see your face," he gasped. And, a time later: "I do you no favor, you know."

By then I had a cup in my hand. I sipped from it. "I know."

"The princes will be all over you now, but they're off each other's necks. And I have shut your thrice-cursed mother up. I expect you to provide me with peace in the Upper Country. I do not want to hear a single grumble from the Arinnian lords—" He thrust his chin toward me, round eyes swimming with drink. "Well, you little bastard, say something."

"What am I to call you, my lord?"

"Don't call me, and I will be as happy. I suppose you had better call me 'father', to get people used to it. Bah! I hate dissembling! You understand what you have gained, and what you have not?"

"I am not sure that I do."

"You are now my son: I have need of an heir, if only to keep my brothers from murdering one another—and eager daggers from my own back. If I die and have named no tuhkanti, you can squabble with the others over my bones. For now, call yourself prince and strut your rank all you please in the Upper Country; I'm assigning you as permanent commander there. But hear this: when the Shepherd is a wolf, all the flock grows thin with fear; if this continues, evil comes to all." He sprayed my face with his winy breath. "Take for me the Upper Country, and I will make you tuhkanti—" He cocked his head at something I did not hear, then staggered away from me. "You are growing chest-hair, and my pubic hair is falling out. That must mean something. What, do you think? Ah, here's your adoption gift. Never let it be said that I am not a good father."

The doors opened inward. In marched Kantuzilis, my pale uncle, and Himuili, whom I had left with his lips to Kuwatna-ziti's ear. Kantuzilis' clothes were as bloody as his eyes. The commander Himuili's usually impeccable attire was in disarray. Between them they bore a grisly burden which no longer lived, but which once had been part of a living body.

Hard-eyed, Kantuzilis presented the head of his brother, Muwatalli the Elder, to the king for identification. Meanwhile, Himuili stood at ease, his hand on one cocked hip, his bearded visage impassive.

"There you go, son, and welcome," said Tuthaliyas to me.

Kantuzilis' pale face drained paler as the king, with obvious relish, told them of my adoption. Then he commended them on their successful evening's work, and dismissed us, all three.

No one spoke until we stood outside the palace gate. Then Kantuzilis, his calm slipping momentarily, snarled at me that I would spend the short season of life remaining to me in Samuha, and stalked off.

"I would say, Tasmisarri, that you have gained a father who cannot protect you from the new enemies you have made tonight." Himuili squinted after the Pale One's retreating form. "But I expected next to see you as dead as Muwatalli. Let us go shake Kuwatna-ziti from his mourning. Tuthaliyas is a serpent among serpents. This will set the lords back on their haunches. What did he say to you?"

"Daduhepa!" I broke into a run. Himuili did not catch me until I burst in on Kuwatna-ziti, panting, demanding that he leave with me that instant for Arinna, where my wife languished close to death.

The Shepherd was sitting by the low-burning hearth, his head in his hands, when I flung open the door.

He snapped to his feet, pale as Kantuzilis. "Tasmi!" Grabbing me, he swung me full about as Himuili skidded through the doorway. Behind him, more footsteps thudded: we had wakened the entire household.

"But we must leave *now!* I tell you, Daduhepa is—"

"Perfectly all right. Hold still." He held me in an embrace like a bear's. "Look you, I had your mother send that message when she reached Arinna, in case we needed a reason to leave. I thought," he said as I scowled and shook him off, remembering his behavior when the Meshedi came for me, "that it had worked too well, when they took you away."

"He gave me Muwatalli's head."

"That's nothing, he was intending to collect it anyway — it was planned before you two arrived here," put in Himuili. "Merely a warning for the lords, and a way to clip Kantuzilis' claws, it was. But tell Kuwatna-ziti, Tasmisarri, my lord, what else came to pass there."

I put my hand on the embrasure's sill, leaning back against it. "Kuwatna-ziti, Tuthaliyas adopted me. A priestess of the Sun-goddess did it. He said it was no favor he did me."

"You know truth when you hear it. He wants you to stay in Samuha, I imagine. Hand him the Arinnian lords, too? Are you free to leave? Good. We'll go by in the morning, I'll pay my respects, and we'll be out of here."

"But, Daduhepa. . . We should leave."

"I told you, I made that up. If I had not, what would you do, hold her hand?"

"I . . . I should be there. Anyway."

"Tomorrow, my lord prince. Tonight, we celebrate having survived today."

CHAPTER 4

"Who performed the Festival of Haste, if Tuthaliyas stayed in Hattusas?" asked my mother, perturbed, as I paced the bed-sitting room of our house in Arinna. "Who accompanied the god to his stations? Who performed the sacrifices to the dead queens?"

I struck a foppish pose for a moment, bent-wristed, and lisped one of my uncle's names. She did not laugh: Tuthaliyas' preferences were, to her, no laughing matter. Usually, a queen sacrifices to her predecessors. Hatti had no queen under Tuthaliyas. My mother had been sore distressed that, considering the circumstances, she had not been asked to make the tour with the god as he traveled to his stations in the different towns. But Tuthaliyas was smarter than that.

"Tasmi, that is not nice," she reproved me.

"Do you think I care what is nice? The dead queens will survive going hungry this once. Now, by Istar of the Battlefield, if you do not make her see me, I am going to break down the door!"

Daduhepa had given birth while I was in Hattusas. I had not seen

65

it or her, nor would anyone tell me the child's sex: Daduhepa had so decreed it.

Kuwatna-ziti had driven as far as his own estates with me, departing with a promise to meet me in Samuha. His audience with my new father Tuthaliyas had not pleased him: he had not been released from his oath concerning me, nor had any of the boons he had sought from the Great King been granted. Worse, Himuili had received the permanent appointment Kuwatna-ziti had held temporarily, and so by Tuthaliyas' inscrutable will, the Shepherd and I were now equals — in the sight of the armies, at least.

Using Daduhepa's petulance as an excuse, my mother followed me everywhere. In my wife's behalf, she even watched me with a critical eye as I stripped and bathed, meanwhile extracting from me all that had happened in Hattusas. Upon hearing that Tuthaliyas had adopted me, she sank down upon the imported Egyptian settee that dominated Daduhepa's sitting room, far from pleased, silent as if the Storm-god had struck her dumb.

"Go see if she is awake yet; tell her she must admit me," I pleaded, touching the polished sun disk of the goddess. It was a princely house, in all but truth: the servants ignored me as if I were made of smoke; I could not even get a meal out of them without Asmunikal's word behind me. And my mother seemed to think of the place as one of her own villas. I had been in her rooms; she was packed in for a long stay, had even brought my brother Zida along.

"Tasmi, when she is ready to see you, she will let us know."

"How is she? At least you could tell me that. The message you sent —"

"She will be glad to hear of your concern." Asmunikal set a copper pin more firmly in her hair. "Did you know Zida will enter the Meshedi at New Year?"

"It is past time he crawled out from between your legs. It's three years late, if you ask me."

"How dare you! Your brother —"

"There. Did you hear that? She is awake in there!" I strode over to my mother and took her by the elbow, propelling her to the door. "She'll see me whether she wills it or no." I said. "Now!"

"Ruffian!" Asmunikal spat, jerked her arm free and pushed me away, her furrowed brow smoothing. "Go sit and wait." She pointed firmly to the settee, and when I sat she disappeared into Daduhepa's rooms.

I stared a long time at the bulls carved above the doorway.

Within, a baby cried and I tried to determine whether it was a girl or boy that howled its displeasure to the world.

When the screaming ceased, my mother emerged, holding one door open for me. Once inside, I pulled it from her grasp and locked her out.

Daduhepa, her high-chinned face drawn and unsmiling, held a small, red baby with a bush of black hair to her breast. It suckled noisily, pumping her teat with tiny hands.

I strode to the bedside, where the both of them lay swaddled, to see if I could tell whether or not it was a boy. I could not tell.

"Do not touch me."

"I want to see —"

"Do not touch him either. What do you want?"

"Daduhepa, please. I came as soon as I could."

"Do you think I care?" The baby gurgled.

I stood stupidly with my hand outstretched, wiped it against my hip and wished I had not come.

The little red thing kicked her belly, trying to climb her. "No one said you could sit down." Daduhepa's eyes were very bright.

I seized her free hand and held it against her struggles. "How are you?"

It was the wrong thing to say. She screamed at me and exploded in a flurry of covers.

"This is how I am! *Look at me! You* did this to me! I'm torn asunder inside from your hairy brat!" She reared up on her knees amid the covers, naked, the child pressed to her swollen udder.

She was not easy on my eyes, her belly yet hanging in folds from the child. I took her and the little squirming thing to my breast; after a time her struggles ceased, and she and the baby both wailed in my arms.

When she quieted him, she called him Arnuwandas, and my heart warmed. So I kissed her eyes and her throat and told her that things would mend with us. Then I proved it. When I had done with her, she plucked my son up from his bed and asked me if I did not think he was beautiful, and if I did not think he looked like me, then put him into my arms. She had been wide as a cow inside, and as flaccid: stretched from him. I scowled down at infant Arnuwandas.

I have held dying men. I have embraced men seeking my death. I have never been so weak-limbed as when I first held my eldest and he sought to conquer my chin with his flailing, white-nailed fingers.

"Not like that, like this," she smiled, and adjusted my hold on him.

"He will be tuhkanti, someday," I promised her — and myself. "I will take him to Kuwatna-ziti's and we will acknowledge him before the lords." I would not have his status be questionable, as mine had been. Kuwatna-ziti was a man of the Storm-god; by acknowledging the boy in his presence I acknowledged him my son before the god. "Daduhepa, you do not know!"

"Know what?" she said, snuggling into my arm, watching me hold the baby.

"We have to send word to his grandfather — to my *new* father. That is . . . Tuthaliyas adopted me."

"What? Oh Tasmi, how *wonder*ful! We must have seals made! I will get a place in Hat*tus*as! Here, give him to me."

"Hold, princess. I'm commander of Samuha. From the sound of it, for the rest of my life. He only keeps me out of the way. I am not tuhkanti, yet — just his son."

Arnuwandas yawned widely, content in her arms.

"You are his *heir,* " she sniffed, rubbing her nose. Then her eyes widened. *"Samuha!* That's not even in Hatti."

I chucked her under the chin. "Now you see it. It surely is not, and it's no place to raise a child. There's been war in those lands so long the dirt is red, not brown. I am not putting you, or Arnuwandas the Second, in the way of the Hayasaean enemy, the wild Gasga tribes —" I was counting them off on my fingers.

"Stop! I am supposed to stay here while you live in the . . . the . . . Oh, Tasmi," and she began to wind up to weep again. "I do not care about the enemies. I will write the Great King — My parents will not let —"

"No. Stop this, I command you, wife! You be a good girl and stay here and help me keep the lords quiet. Sonship has its price. Do you hear?"

But she was not listening. Her face was stony, puffed with tears. She did not pull away, but went stiff as a dead thing.

"You hate me," she said, very low. "You've hated me since Arinna. Go on, go to Samuha and your war and your harlots. Just do not expect me to aid you." She reached blindly behind her, caught up her robe and pulled it about her, all the while holding the baby, who squirmed and began to scream. "Now see what you've done. You've scared him. Get out, go on. And stay out. *Leave us alone!*"

I went first to Asmunikal, on whom I laid my displeasure, holding her and her influence responsible for my troubles with my wife. I was deaf to her injured explanation that often women fresh from childbirth act thus, though experience has taught me that she was right, over the years. Then, I blamed her, and slammed from the estate, black of temper.

I almost killed the horses driving to meet Kuwatna-ziti, but to no avail. I missed him, and Himuili, who was with him. So I swapped teams there and left the grays, driving my own blacks down to Samuha, no longer caring whether or not I acknowledged my firstborn before the god.

CHAPTER 5

The garrison at Samuha billeted anywhere from thirty men to three hundred. Hattu-ziti, the commander of fortifications, was like an extra hand to me, taking the administrative details of the fortified town onto his shoulders, leaving me free to war. And war I did, all that fall and into the winter, against the Gasgaean enemy.

The problem with the Gasgaean enemy was that they had no real organization, no one king with which to treat. The wild tribes fought in a loose brotherhood, and when one tribe was vanquished two others would come to take its place. Just before the winter froze everything with heavy snows, I got a message from Daduhepa that she was pregnant once more, the result of our brief assignation in celebration of Arnuwandas' birth.

I took some ribbing from the men over it, and sent her an invitation to come to Samuha and bring Arnuwandas, boasting that I had made it safe.

There were rumblings in the air of meetings between Hayasa and the Gasgaean enemy: Gasga and Hayasa as one power would

be difficult indeed to fight. Kuwatna-ziti came in with the first
break in the weather and was stranded with us when the storms
recommenced. With him he brought news of foreign lands: of
Hurri and Amurru and Babylon and Egypt; and of the lords and
the game of kingship.

The Shepherd tutored me, that winter, in the ways of the
Storm-god. I struggled with him futilely about it but at length
gave in, assisting him in performing ceremonies long neglected
by the troops. He provided me with the formulas for discerning
truth by incubation (a sort of meditation), and expected me to
remember my dreams. When I had managed to master that, he
was much pleased but insisted that I must then learn to divine the
meaning of them. At that I threw up my hands and stalked off to
see if any of the namra still remembered my name.

Which was where I lay when my wife's light-skinned scribe,
Pikku, arrived from Arinna. In a spiteful mood, Kuwatna-ziti
merely told him where I was. Though I tried, during those days
Pikku was at Samuha, to suborn him and, failing that, to brow-
beat him with threats of violence upon his person, I had no doubt
that when he rode out toward the setting sun that he would tell
Daduhepa everything he had seen and heard in camp. None of it
would be to my benefit.

Her message to me had been polite, but firm: she was closing the house in Arinna and moving into Hattusas. She did not
say where in Hattusas or who had provided the wherewithal for
the move.

Kuwatna-ziti and I speculated as to whom among the con-
tenders had precipitated these events, but came to no conclusions.

"So much for her coming here," I said glumly to Kuwatna-ziti.

"You didn't really want her. You'd have to sleep at night.
What would the namra do? We'd have a revolt in the pens."

"What should I say?"

"I think you're doing badly enough with your wife without
my help. Let us write this treaty." He tapped the clay before him.
I was learning statecraft, so he said — spelling and punctuation

in Babylonian, the diplomatic language in use from Assyria to the Upper Country—and I did not like it.

"Look you, this Pikku could add to my troubles. Let us put this aside and concentrate on writing something to my wife which will work a spell on her and turn her into a woman. I will take this up again when Pikku leaves."

"Your wife, lord prince, needs your arms about her, nothing more."

"I embraced her when I saw my son, and now she is pregnant again and hates me even more, from the sound of this." We were in the officers' hut, huddled under blankets on our haunches around the hearth. Despite the fire, I could see my breath.

"She will when she hears Pikku's tale, that is sure. Why not see to it he never reaches her?"

"She would know I did it."

"Let us think, then."

We thought. Eventually we composed as beautiful a love missive as any woman ever received, slowly, drinking our way to inspiration.

"Do you think 'your thighs smeared with honey' is too much?" I asked him, rubbing my eyes.

"No, no." He emptied the jug. "Fine. Fine. Look here, this should be 'pouting lips'."

I had a headache all the next day, and gave it no more thought. Kuwatna-ziti had the message sealed and gave it to Pikku, who had reins in his hands and orders to be back by New Year.

At dusk Kuwatna-ziti brought me a meal and an eager prescription for my headache, and we made a treaty over her in Babylonian: he got the east and I got the west.

We had by midsummer seemingly come to the end of the Gasgaean tribes.

My new father Tuthaliyas sent word that he was making a rare excursion into the field, and that we should meet him on Mount Nanni.

I had written previously to him three times to allow me to raid outside my territory, and he refused each time. I had asked

twice to leave Hattu-ziti with the command and come down to
Hattusas to see my wife. That, too, he had denied me. When the
invitation to meet him on Nanni came, I was in the car, as some
call the body of the chariot, before the horses were hitched.

I took thirty chariots up Nanni's slope, holding two men
each. It was a habit of mine to take these particular men, and
one that may have saved my life, for I had not expected fighting
there. Tuthaliyas' march was quasi-religious: he was visiting
stations for the gods.

The population of the town had revolted and gone over to the
wild tribes, which explained why we had not been catching any
Gasgaeans in Samuha, and Tuthaliyas' overburdened, slow-moving processional was encircled and besieged before the drunken
Great King's eyes. Soft they may have been, but Tuthaliyas' men
were still Hattian soldiers. When we rode into the smoke-filled
town we found them in possession of it. Their archers almost
put out my driver's eye before identifications were made. Then
I set my men at what they did best, and we slew Gasgaeans until
they slunk away in the dusk.

Tuthaliyas was full of senseless talk about reestablishing
the people of this town in their place, and of what he had heard
here and there about various men and towns plotting against
him. But he thanked me, and even said that he believed I might
have saved his life.

"Then send me against the Hayasaean enemy," I said back
to him, as we sat with our cars pulled close and the light of the
flaming town flickering through the dark.

Tuthaliyas took another drink and coughed mightily, holding his side. "I need you to watch the Gasgaeans."

"I can do both."

"I will give you no more men."

"My thanks, my lord father." It was a tacit acceptance. My
heart leapt. And sunk at his next words.

"Take me to Samuha. My back hurts, and the wine is running low. You love the Hayasaeans, they are yours. But you stay
based in Samuha. Whenever you set foot out of there I will know

it, and approve it, beforehand. And if it is not so, then Kuwatna-ziti will suffer for it, just as you will. I'm not that drunk, and I'm not that sick."

"Yes, my lord," I said. I could not get accustomed to calling him father.

I went, soon after, out to meet the Hayasaean enemy, full of expectations. I did not meet them. I could find none along the borders. So I went after them, into Hayasa, but still I did not meet them. I met the Gasgaean enemy instead.

And it discomfited me that this should be so. I wrote to Kuwatna-ziti, saying that the Gasgaean enemy, in great force, had met with me and that I had defeated them. The mention of where I had defeated them was casual, but I knew he would mark it, in its position just before the god-list.

Indeed, it was as I wrote him: the male and female gods stood by me: the Sun-goddess of Arinna, the Storm-god of Hatti, the Storm-god of the Army, and Istar of the Battlefield, so that the enemy died in a multitude.

I took many namra and brought them back to Samuha.

When we had enlarged the pen, I went back out again, for I had not yet met the enemy from Hayasa and that was what was in my heart. The season was getting late and the grass turning brown. I scratched the line of hair that had come to be on my belly and surveyed the trap I had laid for the enemy. My archers were secreted, my foot in plain sight. Kuwatna-ziti held one ridge-top, I held another. In between, on the flat, stood the Hittites who would serve as bait. We had borrowed troops from Himuili, and the three of us would be in dire straits if the battle turned out not to our advantage.

Himuili's troops, waiting below, had driven the tribal troops from his station—farther east—to ours. But of all the massed tribes whooping like demons as they swarmed across the table-land, none were Hayasaeans.

I took some small consolation in the ending of that season: we smote the massed Gasgaeans; whomsoever we met there, we slew. As we were setting our trap for the Gasgaean enemy, all the shepherds from the country which had been laid waste by the enemy came down from the hills with their dogs and their flocks to help us, and their bowmen mixed with ours. The Gasgaean enemy had brought hired Sutu and auxiliary troops down on us from the rear, but still we triumphed. Into the dark did we fight, by torch and burning chariot, and the Gasgaeans with their auxiliaries died in a multitude. Of the Hittite troops, all but a very few survived.

And the captives that we took were countless. We divided them up and apportioned the booty before Himuili's men departed westward with the dawn.

I had chosen a pair of Gasgaean horses and wanted to see if they would drive. So in the morning, as the army made lazy preparations for a triumphant march home, I hitched up the Gasgaean horses and took them out on the tableland.

Hittites do not ride horses; we are not barbarians. But it seemed to me that a horse who has a bit in his mouth feels it whether the rein is long or short, and even for a horse it is not too difficult a thing to understand a center pole and a pair of traces. They were wild at first, not knowing how to run together nor caring to learn; but I turned them loose to dull their edge running themselves out across the plain before I tried to teach them any fine points.

Soon the army was out of sight and all that existed in the world were the horses and the terrain and the yellow sky where it met the mountains draped in morning mist. The road, old and grassy, led through a gutted village—hardly more than steaming timbers and a few of those round-topped, mud-brick hovels that the barbarians make.

As we came into the village, I touched my whip to the horses' flanks, for they were both tired of running and leery of the steaming ruins. They snorted and struck out with their feet, just as something ran into the road from between two of the hovels. I sawed on their reins, but even as I drew them up I knew it was too late. When I came around to their heads and backed them off, I saw that the corpse they trampled was a young boy's.

Perhaps it was that I was newly a father; perhaps it was the uselessness of the death: I found my stomach was queasy.

I was calming the horses, who knew what they had done, when I heard a noise like a sob or a muffled scream. I put my palm on the near horse's muzzle and listened. The noise came again. Tying the horses to a heavy, overturned wagon, I went seeking among the huts for its source.

The hut from which the sounds came was battened closed from the outside. Prying the boards loose, I slid back a heavy bar painted with warding signs against sorcery, and ducked within. The sounds had stopped.

Those huts are shaped like eagles' eggs cut in half, and have no windows. The barbarians curve the mud bricks inward, so that the circular wall becomes a dome at whose apex is a small opening. It was dark, steamy, and stinking within. When my eyes adjusted I saw why: its occupant was bound to a post dug into the ground—had been for several days, judging from the filth about the post's foot.

Huge eyes in a pinched, sweating face watched me silently as I cut away the ropes, holding my breath against the stench. She was unable to stand on her own. I carried her out into the light and lay her in the dust of the street. She could not have been more than fourteen.

"Can you speak, little sorceress?" She blinked eyes the like of which I had never seen—colored like the sky when drizzle comes from it—and touched my hand, then seemed to go to sleep. I stripped her, cleaned the filth from her at the village well, wrapped her in my cloak, and took her back with me.

She lay unmoving on the chariot's floor, except that she put her head against my sandal. It is not easy to drive that way, but somehow I did not push her away.

"What's that you've got, Tasmi?" teased Kuwatna-ziti, leaning from his car to peer into mine.

"A souvenir." She had drunk a little wine for me, but still huddled against the high curve of the chariot's side, my cloak pulled around her, her legs drawn up under it. Her hair had dried; clean, it was the color of ripe wheat.

"What is she?" he said, squinting.

The girl hugged the leather padding by my leg.

"A woman. What does she look like, Shepherd, a goose?"

"You know what I mean. Where's she from?"

"She hasn't said. Not Gasga, that's certain." She hadn't said anything. I was beginning to wonder if she could speak. "I found her in the sacked village to the west."

"Well?" said Kuwatna-ziti.

"Well what?"

"Aren't you going to put her with the namra?"

"No, I am not."

"So it's like that, is it?"

"I don't know what you mean. I simply do not want to misplace her." That was a real possibility, considering the number of captives we had to herd back to Samuha. Some always escape. "Besides, she's too weak, she'd never survive it."

"That," said Kuwatna-ziti, taking up his reins, "is what I thought."

I found her some old clothes of mine, and set about the business of shepherding my men and their spoils back to Samuha.

The omens are cast at the end of the season: A seer goes through the motions and speaks a ritual which proclaims that it is too late for more fighting this year. And thus the season is ended, so far as the gods of Hatti, our lords, are concerned. Whether the enemies abide by our rules or not is never certain.

At Samuha two tablets awaited me: my wife had sent word that I had a second son, named Piyassilis; Great King Tuthaliyas had written me to say that some enemy had penetrated into the Hatti land itself, and was razing the houses of the gods with fire; also he instructed me to send down the booty from the season to a certain town, where the Tabarna's troops would receive it.

I wrote Tuthaliyas back immediately, saying that it was not too late in the year for my men: If he would send me after the enemy into Hatti then the gods would not be wroth the winter long.

Should he send me on the campaign I proposed, then, I promised, what was in my heart, the gods would fulfill. I had seen this in a dream, I assured him.

Meanwhile, I prepared the Gasgaean namra to go down into Hatti, and all the cattle and sheep and the deportees I readied to become gifts to the palace. I took my time with this, for I was sure the Great King, in dire straits, would not refuse my plea.

He did not. We drove down into the Hatti land, and where the temples had been desecrated, we cast away what was burnt, and built the gods' places anew. We brought along our trained namra, and as we went through the country we left some here, some there, fortifying the border towns. But we did not meet the enemy who had been scourging the land with fire. We were always a town behind them.

I sent to my stepfather Tuthaliyas saying that the enemy would need to be chased into our arms, but the Great King was not in Hattusas. The sky grew low and the farmers took in their harvests and still we were in the Upper Country, patrolling the borders.

When Tuthaliyas returned to Hatti he sent word to me that the enemy who had been burning towns had attacked the king on his campaign, and that the Sun of Hatti had barely escaped with his life. Further, he gave me leave to do what I chose about the Gasgaeans, of whom nine tribes still stood in the land of Hatti.

I sent the fastest team I had to Himuili while Kuwatna-ziti and I contrived a trap for the Gasgaeans. By the time we arrived in the Upper Country where the tribal troops had gathered, they had chased all the Hittites from the land. But when they saw our forces blacken the plain, they became afraid, and all nine tribes of Gasgaeans lay down their weapons before me.

So we took them captive; and Himuili led them into Hattusas, to bring joy to Tuthaliyas' heart by parading them through the streets at the Festival of Haste.

Before we went back to Samuha, since we had built fortifications behind the towns emptied by the enemy, we scoured the countryside and brought the Hittite people back, so that they could occupy the land anew. I have never seen such joy in folk's eyes as when they walked dazed among houses they had never expected to see again. Because they no longer faced the winter as refugees, they fêted us, and we went home to Samuha heroes after the Festival of Haste was done.

There I received word that Tuthaliyas was ill, and this was why he had not met us in the country. I tried to send back condolences, but the snows closed down early, so that the messenger could not get out to take the message down to Hattusas, but had to stay the whole of that blustering winter with us in the northeast.

My little concubine flowered under my eyes. I never thought of her as namra, not even at the outset. Although a slave in Hatti can do anything but hold office or make magic, she was never that to me. She refused, in her lilting, strangely-accented voice, to tell me her name, so I called her "Titai." We played the winter through, and though Kuwatna-ziti scowled about her at first, she even won the Shepherd with her sweet mouth and eager ways, and it was good with us.

It was good with us all, in Samuha that winter. We had come home heroes from Hatti, arms laden with booty and namra and wine. Samuha grew new streets; some of the men built houses when the ground thawed; children were born and children conceived. Even Kuwatna-ziti's fortunes were increased by a daughter, although we only heard of that when the passes cleared and word came up from Arinna in the person of Pikku, who appeared like a bad omen with an armful of clay tablets.

Kuwatna-ziti and I were invited by Tuthaliyas to come for the New Year to Hattusas. The Shepherd looked at me and I returned his stare and we both said nothing for a long time. "We have to go," he offered at last.

"You go," I said, tickling Titai's straight nose.

"You would have killed for this invitation, last season."

"This is not last season."

"Do you not want to see your new son?"

"Not that badly."

But in the end I went with him, after staying awake all night long, wondering what to do with Titai. By taking her with me, I was satisfying two desires: first, to keep her safe; second, to confront my wife with her. A concubine is different from a harlot or a slave. Too, I wished to chastise Daduhepa for moving into Hattusas and ignoring the fact that Samuha was, by my efforts, a safer place to live than half of Hatti.

In Hattusas, Titai craned her neck, owl-eyed at its glory, and snuggled closer under my arm. I bought her all manner of baubles and fine garments, which she strewed about the house Kuwatna-ziti rented on a side street in the upper city. Ours was not a big house, only three angular rooms cut into the hillside, but Titai had never had better than the one tiny chamber I shared with the Shepherd in Samuha, and she played mistress so intensely that even Kuwatna-ziti brought her presents, to see her winged brows wriggle with delight.

My wife might have been already a great queen, by the style in which she lived. Tuthaliyas, I found out, was the person who had subsidized her emergence into Hattusas society, and I was greatly displeased by the debt she had incurred for me. But there was nothing I could do about it, except to thank my stepfather and swallow the bitter beer of indenture.

Arnuwandas was beginning to walk; my second son, Piyassilis, cried the whole time I was in my wife's house. Daduhepa did not invite me to lie with her, so I did not have to refuse her. This may have been on account of Titai—of whom she was already well-informed and with whom, at first, she refused to meet. I thought that very uncivilized of her, and said so:

"Look, you," I stormed, "with every gift you take from Tuthaliyas you add a link to the chain binding me to him. Now you refuse to let me bring my lawful concubine into my own house!"

She smiled demurely, saying only, "Lawful, is she?" I marked it odd that she was not ranting, or screeching, or threatening to have me thrown out her door. "Did you know that we are in the king-lists?" she asked smoothly. "And that our seals have been duly recorded? Wait. Here. . . ." She made as if to rise.

I pushed her back into her chair. "Do not change the subject. I have brought my concubine up from our house in the city. You will meet her, and be polite to her, or I will—"

"You will what, Tasmisarri?"

"Or I will never acknowledge either of your screaming brats. I will divorce you and take her to wife!"

She slumped down in her seat, hand over her heart. But even then she did not scream and rave, only sighed. "Bring that slut to visit. Show her your sons, your home, your wife, if you must. In my relief at being spared her presence as a houseguest, I am magnanimous."

Although I was primed to confront her, and had planned what I would say, she gave me no opportunity to start the final quarrel for which I yearned. So I went and got Titai and showed her my sons while Daduhepa presided over all with the cold dignity of a goddess. Even Piyassilis' constant screaming did not shake my wife's calm, albeit the wet-nurse was foul-tempered from his howling.

Daduhepa offered us a meal, but Titai tugged upon my fingers, pleading *no* silently, and I took her out of there, unsure that I had triumphed over my wife, though it seemed so on the face of it.

During our walk across the upper city, Titai was silent, unsmiling. Her eyes were darkly shadowed, even when I took her through the palace gardens on the excuse that it was the quickest way back to the house, although she loved sightseeing, gardens best of all. When we came to the less desirable streets among which we lodged, I stopped at a stall that sold jewelry. Not even this rekindled her eyes. "What is it with you? Surely you are not jealous of *her?*" Previously, Titai had shown no sign of jealousy, no matter what I did. I had often praised her for this trait to Kuwatna-ziti, who agreed with me that such was a rare quality in a woman.

"She gave me this for you." Titai extended her hand.

I took the circular stamp seal, set in silver, she held out, turning it in my fingers, watching her. I spied no anger in her face, only despair and uncertainty: Her shoulders were drawn up and in, as if I had just now found her in the sacked town.

"Here, wear it." I slipped the seal's chain about her neck, pulling her hair from under its links. "You can buy what you want now, on my credit. Do not ruin me while you're about it."

Fingering the seal, which hung low between her up-tipped breasts, she smiled uncertainly. "My lord, yours are beautiful sons."

I touched her where she was ticklish. She twisted, giggling, but sobered too quickly.

"Come and I will show you the Great Bulls, Serris and Hurris. And perhaps my black eagle, if he is still up there and recollects me." I saw her interest flicker, then pass away.

Pulling her by the hand, I hurried her into an alley, backing her more roughly than I had meant against a wall. Two went by and made lewd comments, seeing a big warrior leaning threateningly over a slip of a girl in festival clothes, but I was too busy holding my temper to call them out.

Under my scrutiny, she fidgeted like a skittish filly. "We are not going anywhere until you say what's in your mind."

Her fingers battled one another, an open revolt of the hands. She struggled with them, her eyes downcast: "My lord, your wife is a princess. Your children . . . I—" With a miserable wail she flung herself against me, her smooth arms locked around my waist, sobbing of how much she loved me. So I forsook squiring her to see the festival bulls, and took her home to show her who meant what to me. It was then that I realized the truth: I was in love with her.

Once admitted, it is not such a hard thing to accept, and we were still celebrating the occasion when Kuwatna-ziti came in.

"The Bulls be with you. By Tarhun's thunder, what's this? What happened? Are you both unhurt? Tasmi, answer me."

"Kuwatna-ziti, I am fine. We are fine. I have decided that I am in love."

Kuwatna-ziti groaned and kicked our mantles from the hearth and sat there. "Realized it, you mean. How did it go with Daduhepa?"

"She was more restrained than I had expected, but you cannot make a pet of a snake. I threatened to disown those screaming brats of hers, and she came into line."

"You *what?* You continually amaze me with your obtuseness. Get dressed. We're late for Tuthaliyas' meeting."

"I heard nothing about any meeting."

"You're hearing it now. Move. Titai!"

"Yes, Kuwatna-ziti, my lord?"

"Lock the door after us. Admit no one, for any reason. When we return, we will ask if the grays are still lame—*before* we knock. If we should not ask that, even though you think it to be us at the door, do not open it."

"Yes, my lord," said Titai, dressing and listening and biting her lip over the complexity of it all.

"Ready, my lord prince?"

"Tell me what this is about, Shepherd."

"On the way, Tasmi, on the way."

CHAPTER 6

"Well, son, if Kuwatna-ziti's taught you nothing else, he's convinced you to wear clothes."

"Yes, my lord Tabarna," I said, taking my seat among my relatives, the Great Ones, the palace officials, and the generals and commanders of the armies.

The man is a fool who says he has never known fear; he is worse than a fool: a liar and a pauper both. Whence but out of fear comes that surge to superhuman deeds that makes of a man a hero? I would not say I felt no fear that night, ensconced among those who had made of my childhood a misery. While in Samuha, I had forgotten the machinations of the lords. There the killing was clean and the enemy well-defined. Here. . .

Kantuzilis sat on Great King Tuthaliyas' right hand, running pale fingers through his white hair, with all my boyhood tormentors ranged about him. Himuili, on my left, leaned close to me and asked without moving his lips if Kuwatna-ziti had bespoken me. I nodded, sitting back, crossing my arms over my woolens, to see what might be seen.

What I saw was that Tuthaliyas was both very sick and very drunk. Slumping in disarray over the head of the table, his crown askew, he looked as if he had not bathed in weeks. He was yellow as the sky over a sacked town, and tremulous of voice: "As you all by now should know, we are gathered here to discuss the greatest threat that has come upon the land in generations." He peered around the table. "I had wanted to talk of Kammala, of Masa, and of Lanni, king of Hayasa, when next I called you together. But things have shifted themselves about. You!"

He was pointing at us—at Kuwatna-ziti, Himuili, or myself. We looked at one another, and I said, "My lord?"

"Do you heroes of the Upper Country have a good grasp of the situation?"

I looked to my right and left. The warlord Himuili made an upward motion with his huge green-flecked eyes, shaking his head imperceptibly. Great Shepherd Kuwatna-ziti chewed his nails. "I think so, Tabarna," I said at last.

"Good, my son. Then you explain it to the rest of us."

Having fallen into his trap, I cursed myself.

"What was that?" gurgled the Great King, his mouth full of beer—such was the gravity of the situation that there was no wine served this night in the palace.

"Well-known is the treachery of the Hurrians," I began. "And well-known also that princes slay princes when they can. What *I* have heard is that one Tushratta of Mitanni has slain the rightful heir to the throne and acceded in his place, that—"

"*You would* think that. That is *not* right!" snarled Tuthaliyas. "The old king was to be succeeded by a son whom he had chosen, Artashuwara. This prince was murdered by a treacherous official, one Utkhi. Tushratta took revenge on the official and his helpers. *Then* he usurped the throne." Spittle shone in the stubble on his chin. "Well, go on, Tasmi, what else do you know?"

"That Tushratta's brother, Artatama, does not recognize Tushratta's overlordship and has seceded from the Mitannian empire,
taking the title 'King of Hurri,' splitting the Hurri land in twain."

"Very good, Tasmi. What else?"

"That the people are calling their contentions a lawsuit before the gods, whose settlement will be determined in the usual
fashion." When a man breaks the Oath Gods' laws by slaying
one to whom he is sworn, then the family of the guilty party falls
upon one another: the Oath Gods cause them to slay their own
kin until none of that blood which did evil is left in the land.

"And what else?"

"I can think of nothing else, my lord."

"Well, there is *else*. There is the fact that both brothers
claim to be true kings. Both have written to me to uphold them,
the one against the other. Both seek to hold me to agreements
we had with the land of Hurri when it and the political dynasty
of Mitanni were one." Tuthaliyas rubbed his chin.

"My lord Tabarna," said Himuili softly, "may I ask a
question?"

"Ask."

"Whom does Egypt support in this? I would not like to tangle
with the 'Panthers Southern,' no matter how weak it is rumored
they have become."

"Egypt will support Tushratta," growled Kantuzilis, as if he
had Pharaoh's ear, without first asking if he might speak.

"It is not a question of whom Egypt supports, but of whom
we will support," glowered Tuthaliyas. "Yes, Kuwatna-ziti?"

"Armed neutrality to both parties might serve, coupled with
our insistence that since Mitanni is no longer able to exercise
dominion over the Hurri lands, then she cannot fulfill her previous obligations as set down in the alliance, and we must write
a new treaty with them. As for Artatama, king of Hurri, offer
him the same. If Hurrian fights Hurrian over names and empty
speeches, it is to our benefit. Treat with both, and we will surely
have treated with the lawful. Let them exterminate each other,
if they can. Long has Mitannian thought ruled in Hurri; those

years have been costly to us. If we find it expedient to offer aid, I would offer it to Hurri's new king." He looked around at us. "Who among you has not had a wrong done him by Hurrians under Mitannian direction? How many with Hurrian blood in their veins cannot forget how it got there? Even our language is filled with reminders of Hurrian overlordship. In my grandfather's days we paid tribute to Mitanni, yearly, when she waggled Egypt's swords under our noses. Let us put our sandals to *their* throats, now." Kuwatna-ziti was on his feet, impassioned. Many others had risen.

I yet sat. So did the Great King. But the debating of feasible schemes went on until the middle night-watch was heard to cry, "And the fire will be guarded," whereupon we got on to the problem of Lanni, king of Hayasa. That done, the Great King dismissed all into the dawn but me. "Wait for me," I whispered to Himuili and Kuwatna-ziti, "by the gatepost where the demons guard."

Tuthaliyas was succinct: "Hero, I am not sending you back to Samuha."

"My lord, have I not well served you? I have—"

"You have done so well that I no longer need you there. Your reputation grows, Tasmisarri. I want you in Hattusas, where I can use you."

"But—"

"What is the problem? Your wife is happy here. You have a lovely estate."

"Yes, my lord, and I thank you once again for all you have done. It is just that I am settled where I am—content enough. There is much yet to be accomplished in the northeast. The Hayasaean enemy. . ."

"My boy, we will smite the Hayasaean enemy together, this next season. Now go on with you, and tell Kuwatna-ziti he does not have to share the Upper Country any longer."

By the gatepost where the demons guard lounged Himuili and the Shepherd, talking politics and watching the sun rise. They did not at first mark me.

"It is not so confusing as you may think," Kuwatna-ziti was saying, exasperated, trying to answer some question I had not heard Himuili ask. "The river Mala divides the land of Hurri. Just so, the kingdom has split, and becomes two. What you must realize is that 'Mitanni' is only a state of mind: it has no language other than Hurrian; its people are Hurrians." I saw Himuili rub his face, muttering. "Just fight them, if you're told to. You need not understand it." Kuwatna-ziti turned, sensing my gaze. "Tasmi! What's wrong?"

I pushed away from the gatepost wall. "I'm thirsty. I will buy you each a draught." I wondered if my fear showed, if the Shepherd would scent its sourness issuing forth from my mouth.

But then Himuili frowned, saying that he knew a place, his green-flecked eyes darting about in the ruddy light as he reviewed suspicious shadows.

We heard the night-watch change to day as we entered a just-opening establishment and gave the crusty-eyed proprietor something to do.

Kuwatna-ziti was worrying his braid, always a sign of agitation. "So, my lord prince, what could possibly keep you quiet this long?"

Lacing my hands behind my head, I leaned back against the plastered wall. Above me, light poured in an open window; I knew they could not see me well. "Himuili, what is the slowest way you know to kill someone?"

"The slowest? Or the most painful? Whom do you intend to kill, and how slowly?"

"About a quarter-watch would be enough. My wife, that's who."

Kuwatna-ziti silenced me by decreeing that since I had invited them, I must pay the proprietor, then setting food and drink before us. Himuili was detailing suitable methods of torture, displaying that little-boy's smile he takes up with his sword. I sipped my drink and studied Kuwatna-ziti while he squinted at me. Finally, he put his hand on Himuili's arm and said, "What's this about, Tasmisarri? If I did not know better, I'd think something happened to upset you."

"Daduhepa knew about this all along. She was polite, restrained, prattling on about being listed with the royal family. I should have known, when she offered me no fight about Titai. She knew then! I'm going to kill her before she gets me killed. I—"

"Stop! *What* are you talking about?" Kuwatna-ziti demanded.

Himuili picked a hair out of his cup, held it up to the light, and swore that he would have the place closed down.

"Tuthaliyas has reassigned me to Hattusas," I said as Kuwatna-ziti stroked his long nose and Himuili twirled the offending hair between his fingers, both men seemingly unperturbed. "I cannot stay *here*. The lords will make short work of me!"

"Are you frightened, hero of Samuha, favorite of the Storm-god? Or do my ears deceive me?"

"Yes, Shepherd, I am frightened. If you listen you'll hear my teeth chatter. There are too many of them and they are too smart for me."

The lord Himuili chuckled, but Kuwatna-ziti silenced him with a fierce glare. I looked between them.

"Did you *know* of this? If you knew and did not tell me—Shepherd, the days are gone when you could pin me against the wall."

"Tasmi, eat your food and let me think. You'll need more than a little height and a couple of years in the field to make good that threat. I'll forget I heard it."

Himuili's face mirrored my own consternation in the ensuing silence during which I emptied my plate without noticing what I ate. Then Kuwatna-ziti said, "Who has Samuha?"

"You do," I replied.

He grunted, entwining his fingers before him on the table. "Tasmisarri, Tushratta of Mitanni is not yet seventeen. A mere youth. Your age. Do you see the parallel? Tuthaliyas thinks to avoid any similar ideas the Hattian lords might have . . . he's sick, but he's not feeble."

"I can*not* stay here. I don't want to."

"You can. You will. And you'll get used to it. But no more talk of laying hand on Daduhepa, or you'll answer to me."

I got up abruptly, causing the whole table to teeter. "I smell my mother's spoor! If ever I thought you were in league with Asmunikal," I warned him, "if ever I even suspect it, or if you plot to aid me without my knowing it, and I hear about it, there is nowhere in the Hatti land you will be safe from me, Kuwatna-ziti."

The Shepherd's eyes narrowed into crescents. Himuili muttered about his bladder and disappeared.

"It's that tawny bed-warmer of yours, that's what's troubling you," called Kuwatna-ziti as I stamped out the door.

When I pounded at my own threshold, demanding admittance, there was a scurrying within, then nothing. The curtains across the alleyway slammed down, after the neighbor I had awakened cursed me roundly.

Then I remembered to ask if the grays were yet lame. Still the bar did not slid back, within. I was about to forsake door for window when I heard the wood grate.

The main room of the house was dim and its air blue with acrid smoke. The curtains were rolled down, and something ill-smelling boiled on the hearth. Beside it, the new winter cloak I had bought her was thrown. Titai's hands were behind her, and she backed from me toward the hearth.

"What's this? What are you doing? What's that awful smell?"

Her upper lip trembled. Above it, her eyes were wide. "I was afraid for you, my lord."

Pushing the door shut with my foot, an awful foreboding crawled up my spine. Sniffing the air repeatedly, I bore down on her.

She sank to her knees beside the cloak at the hearth, whispering something unintelligible.

I remember such hesitancy as has never come over me in battle, a rage of conflicting emotions so that I shook like a woman.

"Pick that up," I ordered her. "I would see what is underneath."

Head bowed, Titai wadded up the cloak and held it against her. Beneath was what I did not want to see, but what the smell told me must be there: tiny jars and bits of feathers and small molded clay figures. I crouched down and, one by one, crushed the clay figures in my hands.

"*Sorcery,*" I growled at her, my voice thick to my own ears. "Titai, what are you trying to do to me?" She began to weep. "For striking a snake and speaking a man's name, a slave must die. How much more for this? Titai, even your name would not be spoken for fear of contamination. Girl, mark me: The death of a witch is very long and painful." As I spoke I was methodically emptying, then crushing, jars and casting their shards into the fire. I could not look at her, so dark was my heart.

The door was thrust open; I had not slid the bar. I sprang up.

Kuwatna-ziti and Himuili poised there, and the Shepherd's nostrils quivered. Himuili made a warding sign and backed with a curse from our threshold.

"Kuwatna-ziti, she's not Hittite, she—"

"*Do not say anything, Tasmi.* It is not what you think. You are mistaken. So is Himuili. As for me, I see nothing but a barbarian cooking her meal. *Nothing!* Get rid of this stuff, and air out the house. I will be at Himuili's a few days." His face bore no expression as he pulled the door shut behind him.

I found myself braced against the window, my fingers digging splinters from the sill: Not daring to look at her, I stared blindly through my rage at my hands. I heard her, behind me, rustling around—little hiccoughs and sobs marking her progress as she did Kuwatna-ziti's bidding.

"If ever again you make magic in my house," I grated at last, "I will take you back where I got you, and bind you again to that post, and write the warding signs on the boards myself."

CHAPTER 7

"Abuya! *Abuya!"* screamed Arnuwandas in delight when he saw the black eagle bating in his nest. There is something about it when your firstborn calls you father, successfully, at last. . . .

"No," I said, "not 'father.' *Eagle.* And there." I pointed to the town, below. "Hattusas."

Dutifully, black eyes narrowed to the task, Arnuwandas repeated the words after me.

I had been hesitant to bring him up here: a climb I had made a hundred times in pitch dark seemed suddenly hazardous, with the child's arms locked around my neck. Below, by the opening to the rock sanctuary on whose crest we perched, my blacks cropped the sparse grass, then raised their heads, ears pricked. I followed their gaze and saw a chariot driving slowly toward us.

It was not Kuwatna-ziti, but Himuili who put his car next to mine and assayed the climb. "What are you, Tasmisarri, a goat? No wonder we could never find you when we needed to."

I had had to hail him twice.

He was there because I had sent a message to his house, inviting him or Kuwatna-ziti to meet with me. I had not seen either since we had found my little sorceress at work: there were things that needed to be said. A lot of those things were said by Kuwatna-ziti's absence — although I had realized he might send Himuili in his place, I was hurt.

"Fine big boy," said Himuili of Arnuwandas, who was exploring my old hiding place in the rocks.

"Where is Kuwatna-ziti?"

"In Arinna, by now. He has gone to cleanse himself before the god. He asked me to request that you, too, perform a sacrifice."

There was no doubt in my mind as to why the man of the Storm-god felt in need of cleansing. He had dwelt in the house of a sorceress, had congress on occasion with one. "Gladly. I will sacrifice a sheep for him, also. Tell him that."

"He will be pleased. Tasmisarri, I have not much time."

"Nor I. I have to go with Tuthaliyas on his tour of the god's stations. My lord, you and the Shepherd have my life in your hands. Are you going to hold it, or drop it?" He was, as I had hoped, somewhat taken aback.

"My lord prince" — he toyed with his sandal's strap — "I could kill you in a fair fight by the time this rock" — he threw one over the ledge's edge — "strikes the ground. Therefore, I have long been able to take your life, if I wanted it. I keep out of the lords' games."

I remembered when he had walked away while Kantuzilis and my uncles took a strap to a boy's behind — and the time he and the Pale One had liberated Muwatalli the Elder's head from his body. I said nothing.

So Himuili continued, "And I am no carrier of tales. If you end with a death sentence because of your sorceress, it will not be on my account."

In Hatti, if the crime is severe enough, not only the guilty but that one's wives and children, his servants and *their* children, may also be sentenced to accompany the wrongdoer to his fate.

And Titai's crime — mine by implication — was severe enough. Still I made no reply.

"But you must consider your sons, and your wife."

"I have considered them."

"And you will continue to keep the namra?"

"I will."

"Then may the Storm-god protect you," he said, gathering his legs under him. "Such an unnecessary danger she brings you, I find that hard to accept. But Kuwatna-ziti said you would feel thus, and —"

"I want you to take this to him. It is a list of what is mine in Samuha. Say that I ask this of him only because I have no other to whom I can turn. If he will aid me in settling these affairs, in respect for what we once shared, I will be grateful. Say also that I will ask nothing further, henceforth, and that I am . . . sorry . . . about all this. . . ." I waved my hand aimlessly, and wished I had not come upon such humiliation.

Himuili stuffed the list in his pouch and straightened up, his hands to the small of his back. "Tasmisarri, a lot of folk think you might make a king. Get rid of that barbarian bitch, or she will be as a wall up to heaven between you and the kingship."

I found it necessary to go fetch up my son, and when I had done that, Himuili was already climbing down toward the chariots.

CHAPTER 8

I sold all that I had gathered in Samuha—the booty, the building namra, the girls—and with those funds procured a modest house in the better quarter of the upper city. There I installed Titai, in spite of the uproar caused by Daduhepa (who preferred lodging both me and my concubine to enduring the impropriety of it all). But I dared not, because of the sorcery. If Daduhepa ever even suspected the truth, I would wear her leash forevermore.

I managed to have the thirty men who had been the nucleus of my strength in the Upper Country transferred to me in Hattusas, and to bring the architect and commander of fortifications, Hattu-ziti, into my house to live.

I made him my aide and second-in-command, advising him to think seriously about fortifying Hattusas. When I went out on campaign with the Great King, I left Hattu-ziti in charge of my house and what resided therein, as well as of my correspondence and my finances—as perilous as ever.

I have not spoken much of war and the waging of it. To some extent, I have done this because my life as I look back upon it was one long campaign, and in my mind all the battles of my youth have flowed together: the Samuha campaigns were for the most part small guerrilla actions, only noteworthy when strung together.

But war with the Great King's chariots was different. My heart grew heavy that first season, watching the ever-besotted Tabarna misuse his men, and my thoughts turned toward the kingship, and how it might better be administered.

Once I found Tuthaliyas so soaked with wine that he slumped spread-legged against a six-spoked wheel, snoring while all around us the enemy of the country of Kammala howled and died. Once he sent us west when everyone knew the enemy was in the east; we had no choice but to go where he commanded. Let me tell you about man and drink: as a man ages, the drink that would only have warmed him in his youth takes him prisoner and vanquishes his mind. So it was with Tuthaliyas, and the army grumbled, growing dull-eyed and sour.

Often he split the force so small that I had only my thirty, as if we fought handfuls of Gasgaeans in the Upper Country and not the civilized, canny warriors of the steppes. Sometimes, when Tuthaliyas' imagination overcame him, we would be sent like Sutu to kill this man or that or to subdue a fantasized rebellion of a loyal, quiet town.

It was not good with the armies, that season. While we were down in Kammala, the Gasgaeans awoke, entering into the land of Hatti, and burned down the empty towns behind which my men had built fortifications, despite all Kuwatna-ziti's efforts to hold them at bay.

So when Tuthaliyas and I came back from Masa, although the summer was done, we had to go into the lands of Kathariya and Gazzapa, who—backed by Gasga—kept destroying our towns and carrying away their goods: all the silver and gold, bronze utensils, and articles of the gods. But the gods helped the army of Hatti (which we all sourly observed could not help itself), and we destroyed Kathariya and Gazzapa and burned them down. And all the Gasgaean troops who had come down to help Kathariya we smote, so that the Gasgaeans died in multitudes.

Though the season was late for it when I and my stepfather Tuthaliyas came back from there, he immediately prepared to go to the country of Hayasa and fight with King Lanni, who had sent him a taunting invitation.

I would have stayed in Hattusas, but no one asked me. We had two nights and a day in the city, long enough to refurbish our gear and hitch fresh horses; then we were gone on campaign once more.

My men were tired beyond forbearing; there were fights in the camp. I went to Tuthaliyas and asked him to reconsider. This was the wrong thing to do. He was seeing enemies all around him that night, and became wroth with me. And I spoke harsh words back to him, and pushed him from me into the mud. But in the morning he did not remember. So, in a way, his drinking saved my life.

Lanni, the king of Hayasa, was late arriving for battle at the agreed spot below the town of Kummaha, which gave my men time to rest and Tuthaliyas time to get falling-down drunk.

Thus, when the enemy king's chariots appeared below the town, it was I who led the men out to face him. I learned that day just how much Samuha and Kuwatna-ziti had taught me: the advantage of unpredictability is incalculable in war. My thirty mountain fighters led the charge, and Lanni's Hayasaeans fell under us like wheat under a scythe. They were polite, impeccably mannered, perfectly disciplined; they died polite, impeccable, disciplined deaths.

I found myself in the classic position: chariot to chariot with the enemy king. I had a bowman with me, and a driver who knew my blacks. My sword slipped through Lanni's neck like butter; and when Tuthaliyas woke he saw the Hayasaean king's head piked up before him in his tent.

No one had been able to wake our Tabarna to receive the royal permission to follow when the Hayasaeans broke into retreat, so

we failed to destroy the enemy multitude. When we received the
Sun's order that day to depart for Hattusas to spend the winter,
we left Hayasa taking only some loot and horses.

"This is idiotic!" fumed Mammali, a man of my thirty. "Did
Tuthaliyas not *expect* to overcome them? Just go home? Why
not leave enough men to occupy the country? We'll only have to
fight them again next season."

But there was nothing I could do about it: the battle was
won, decisively; the war was not. There came some talk from
Tuthaliyas of a treaty with Lanni's sons. To this I listened glumly, as disheartened as my men: none of us were accustomed to
going home for the winter and expecting the war to simply go
away until spring.

He may have been right, old Tuthaliyas, about Hayasa; then
he seemed very wrong. Thus his mismanagement of the kingship
was common jest among the troops, despite the dangers of sedi-
tion. Almost as common were stories of me and my thirty that
waxed out of proportion to our actual value.

In Hattusas, men whom I did not know began to seek my
company, high-born women sent me invitations to functions both
public and private, and I was the subject of many joyous offerings during the Festival of Haste.

My men and I grew closer while the city made much of us:
they were as uncomfortable as I with Hattusas society, with our
decorations and our honors and the endless parade-ground cer-
emonials at which we received them.

My mother came down to Hattusas and with furrowed brow
tried to cajole me into moving in with my wife. The scandal, she
said, was such that she could not raise her head in the streets.
Remarking that she had been bearing up well enough at the numerous fêtes she'd been attending, I saw a smile flicker across
her lips.

Titai had flowered over the season; her litheness was now
swathed in woman's curves. Her joy at my homecoming was
overwhelming, and though at first I had little time for her, not
even one sigh of dissatisfaction marred her pliant beauty.

On the other hand, Daduhepa was ever more aggrieved, and seemingly felt her sons were weapons she could wield against me with impunity. She wasted much of my time with her society dinners—attended by all the proper, boring people—until I simply let a few of these insipid non-occasions go by without my presence.

Then she granted me my first private audience since my return from the field. Frost paled the ground that day, and I had brought a pair of very old, very small horses for Arnuwandas.

"Do you not think you are rushing things a bit? With the horses, I mean?"

"He is almost three years old."

"Indeed. Am I supposed to get him a driver?" She had regained her figure; her eyes were traced with green paint. Her chin lifted so that I had thoughts of taming her anew.

Remembering little Titai, whose hips were not made for begetting, I replied, "Daduhepa, this game is wearing on me. If you would remain my wife in name, then you will be one in truth. I shall put another child in you."

Her hands went to her throat, fingering the Sun-goddess' amulet she wore. But I had planned it well: the danger of her with nothing to occupy her time deeply concerned me.

Nevertheless I did not expect her to come willingly into my arms, to moan and clutch me, or that afterwards her face would be alight with love. When she begged me once more to bring Titai with me and move in, I could only answer her that I would not do so.

Had I struck her, she would not have flinched more. She rolled onto her back, her throat grasped with her hands, croaking. "Ah, I had forgotten how you hate me."

I was clothing myself, anticipating her rage, expecting to be thrown from the house. But Daduhepa fought tears, not wrath. So I said, "Ask me why."

"Why, Tasmisarri?" she whispered thickly.

"Because it is not safe, that is why. Because three of my men have come home bloody from fights in the street with those who hope to become a hero by killing one, and because neither the Meshedi nor my relatives have forgotten me."

"Hattusas loves you. Your men are renowned, covered in glory."

"Hattusas is a harlot; with all the blood we spilled for her, we bought only a moment of her time. Things brew in the palace, ferment in the streets. Tuthaliyas does not think like a man, but like wine. If anything happens to me, I prefer it not to happen before my children's eyes."

Springing up from the bed, she embraced me, telling me that things would not always be thus. "Soon you will be king, and—"

"Do not *ever* say that. Do not even *think* it. I value my life, even if you care nothing for yours."

Now, I have said that men whom I did not know sought my company, that we were fêted in Hattusas. And we were. But the harvest of high repute is sweet only at first, and can become deadly. Hattusas was still the same city as had bred Tasmi*sarri*—and if some folk loved me awhile, more were spiteful behind my back.

The wedge of men whom I brought down from Samuha were waiting when I arrived home from Daduhepa's, all crowded into the front room while a sleepy Titai in one of my robes padded among them, serving beer and a pungent hot wine.

Hattu-ziti, my second-in-command, had been sitting by the stable in the cold to catch me alone, so I did not walk into it unwarned, but met him first: "Are you counting snowflakes?"

"Tasmisarri, my lord, we have trouble."

"Who was it this time?" As I have said, my men were heroes to some. The reaction of a woman of the nobility to a hero is fleeting but passionate: women had been the cause of most of those altercations which sent my men home bloody and battered—a cuckolded lord unsure of his chances in court; a desperate suitor confronting his competition. I expected nothing more.

What Hattu-ziti told me made my exaggerations to Daduhepa seem the mildest of devaluations: "The Meshedi jumped Mammali and four others in a side street, something about being rowdy. Mammali is the only one who came back."

I turned away from him and went in, not even asking whom we had lost. A head count told me. My men crowded round, all twenty-five talking at once.

"Are they dead, Mammali?" I demanded, shouldering my way through to him. He was somewhat battered, but he would survive. I crouched down beside him, thinking of a time I had taken an arrow in my arm hoisting him up into my car when his had overturned. He had lost an eye in that engagement. If he lost his other, which it seemed to me he might, he would be a bowl-carrying mendicant. His condition and the deaths of those four men were my responsibility as surely as if I had hired Sutu to perform the deeds myself. Hattusas treated my men as she had always treated their commander: they got my due, in the streets.

He mumbled, "My lord, I did not run. . . . I foxed them. All the rest—dead . . . sure."

I said, "Titai, make my bed ready. Lupakki, Hattu-ziti, carry him in there."

When that was done, I bade them be seated and when they were quiet looked them over slowly. "Welcome to Hattusas. I grew up here. I've told you before: those who cultivate you have a reason; all others seek your blood. Now, who knows the identities of the foul Meshedi responsible for this?"

"I do," said Lupakki, reentering the room. He was a big hulking youth, the only man there younger than I—a cold and deadly plotter, but a berserker in the field. "And I claim the honor of offering their heads, one per night for ten nights, to Istar as sacrifice."

"Sit down, and listen well. All of you, harken! We'll draw straws for the honor of smiting them. I only retain the right to tell you when," I said firmly into the mutters swelling around me. None would take exclusion from the avengers lightly. "From this day forward, do as I bid: not less than four men together, whenever you're in the streets; billet with each other—no man sleeps alone, henceforth. I'll see if I can find somewhere that will hold us all. Who among you has looked past your immediate reaction and seen what has happened here?"

"The Meshedi jumped Mammali and—"

"I expect better from you than that, Hattu-ziti."

He shook his head.

"This is nothing unexpected," growled Lupakki. "I have had men call me out for being yours. My lord prince, the people . . . they don't like us, some of them."

I laughed. "You're right but you're too polite. The Great Ones don't like me, and they're taking it out on you. Certain of my family drink blood with dinner. But this is a bold move, using Meshedi against us. . . . I'd feel better about it if they went to the trouble of pretending that some hero-hunters got the best of us."

Suppositions were voiced as to why they had not. I let them work it out. When Lupakki summed up the consensus that we'd be fools to go after the culprits now, when we were expected, I applauded him.

Then we drew straws for the ten Meshedi, and when the long-straws were decided, they accepted their tasks before the Oath Gods. I did not get one. But I cared not.

I spent the time until dawn working out various Meshedi traps, and impressing on my men the need to stay together. I divided them into units and assigned watches—both for my own house, and at either end of the quarter into which I compressed them: two men had houses on the same street, and two more on alleys adjoining. They were good men, receptive enough to moving in together, and to all my suggestions, for they had realized this night that the city waged war on them.

From then on, Hattusas was a campaign.

The next day I sought out Tuthaliyas when he was sober and secured a loan. I went to see my brother Zida, who was in the Meshedi. Then I dispatched three messengers from the palace: one to my mother; one to Himuili; one to my uncle, Kantuzi-lis, requesting an audience. My letter to my mother in Ziplanda would take time to deliver, due to the inclement weather. But my uncle had come north to commune with the Great King and make assessments upon his illness, and by first night-watch call I had an invitation from him in my hands. From Himuili I expected no answer, and he did not disappoint me.

When middle night-watch rang out I was at a lower-city inn, unobtrusively settled in a corner, listening. Disobeying my own orders, I had come alone, grimy-robed over a full panoply of weapons. In my pouch I carried ten minas of silver, more money than I had ever had on me at one time in my life—enough to buy a herd of horses. But horses were not what I was buying, and the money was part of what Tuthaliyas had advanced me against my share of spoils in the coming season.

The establishment I had chosen was notorious even among those infamous holes making up the foreigner's slums which cluttered Hattusas' skirts. I was watching with interest as one man split another's skull over a harlot. The fight was over in moments; the dancing girls did not even slow their whirling.

Summoning a serving wench to me, I allowed I would buy the victor a jar. There were perhaps ninety men in the sunken L-shaped tavern, and she went off to seek him.

The man who showed at my table, hesitating, undecided, had a head shaved all over but for one long braided lock growing above his right ear, which was notched. He weighed perhaps a fifth again as much as I.

"Sit, Sutu," I suggested and just then the girl came with the jars.

Still standing, he put his hands around one jar and drained it, smacking his lips.

I signaled the girl for another.

"What would you with me, young Hittite?" he rasped in a voice whose timbre was in no small way related to the white, narrow scar encircling his throat—and sat, folding his arms on the table.

As I casually pushed the oil lamp from between us, I let my robe fall open.

His eyes rested on the bronze axe glinting at my belt, then met mine frankly. "I said, what would you with me? Was that asp some kinsman of yours?"

I chuckled. "I am seeking Sutu, a number of them. I offer steady employment through the winter and a place with the armies come the season." One reason such men wintered in Hattusas was hope of mercenary work when the weather eased; the other was that we had no extradition policies with the southern lands. This Sutu was from far south, perhaps Libya.

"At what wage, my lord Hittite?"

"Twelve shekels hire, plus whatever the army will pay. And if, in due course, any man should accidentally kill someone for whom a person is required in payment, I will provide the person." It was a more than generous stipend.

"What are you planning, a revolution?"

I sat back. "You really don't expect me to answer that, do you, Sutu?"

First he rubbed his scar, then grunted as if just seeing the second jar, then downed it. "I am Hatib." He bowed his head ever so slightly.

"And are you interested, Hatib?"

"It is winter." He shrugged. "There are not many good men in the city, and those subsist in deplorable poverty, undernourished, sleeping in doorways."

"For what I propose, I must control where the men billet. And it will not be the lower city."

He twisted in his chair, surveying the room, then turned back to me: "How many men, and what shall I call you, my lord employer?"

"I am Tasmisarri."

He swore by Kubaba, and his face opened up in a gap-toothed grin. "I fought you when I was in Gasgaean employ. I was lucky to come away with my life." His smile fell away. "I see why the hire is so generous. I can tell my men that they will fight under you in spring? It will help."

"Tell them that, then. This, too, will help." I unhooked my pouch and lobbed it between us, onto the table. I was taking a chance, giving a Sutu that much money.

When Hatib opened it, his breath whistled. He stirred the silver with his fingers. "How many men?"

"Twenty-five at the least, thirty at the most. Keep the difference yourself, as contractor. But they must be very good men, and capable of taking direction."

He pushed the pouch toward me, just a little.

"I'm not sure. When would you want them?"

"The most I can give you is two days." In my turn, I nudged the pouch his way, telling him the time and place I would expect him, then called for my bill.

"You'll leave me this money, all of it?"

"I said so. Do not ask me things twice. I can find you, if I need to. And if I need to, this time you will not escape with your life." With that I left him, sucking his thumbnail, deep in thought.

Soon thereafter, I woke Daduhepa and used her, a precaution in case she had not yet caught, and told her to get ready to take the children to Arinna. She only argued until I explained I was moving fifty-odd men into the estate, half of them Sutu. When I went out again, she was yet debating what she would need to put the long-closed Arinna house in order, humming to herself and making a great show of not being afraid.

Upon reaching my own house I sent Hattu-ziti to Daduhepa's with four men and more of Tuthaliyas' money, to examine the defensibility of the place, determine what was needed to turn the stables into billets, lay in such supplies as he saw fit. I told him to make no secret in the market of what he was about.

In the midday I slept fitfully and awoke to find Titai softly weeping against my shoulder. For a time I tried to pry from her the reason for her tears, to no avail. Annoyed, I told her I had enough troubles at the moment, and her eyes were like a doe's when the shaft pierces true to its heart. And I was sorry, and wondered again about her history, and how she had come to be in Gasga.

But then my men started drifting in, and I was busy with arranging the moving of them to Daduhepa's, and eyeing the sky and the streets and wondering about a certain sharp-faced Hatib.

He came sauntering down an alley at sunset, having somehow eluded my watchmen. But they stopped him there and brought him to me at sword's point.

"Ah, my lord employer," he sighed, "your men have captured me, more's the pity. And you stand by watching, not telling them I am your most devoted servant. Lord employer, do you not trust me?"

"Let him go, Lupakki. You men, sheath your swords. Sutu, you'd better show them how you got in here. Noble lords, this is Hatib. If you are nice to him, perhaps he will give you Sutu lessons."

Lupakki voiced some excuse.

"Never mind it, there will be more Sutu coming. Now that you're warned, perhaps you can catch sight of them before they get this far. But be gentle, they're ours." I sent them back to their posts before bringing the Sutu into the house, where we discussed what success he had had, and I informed him that his first task in my employ would be to deliver my wife and sons safely to Arinna despite the season. As we made clear the details of that, other Sutu appeared by twos and threes, until fifteen of them stood about the big room. I was busy enough committing names and faces to memory, and assessing what Tuthaliyas' silver had bought me, and answering my own men's questions on the relocation, that I did not think to wonder why Titai had not extended the hospitality of our house to my motley, multi-racial crew of brigands—until Hattu-ziti came in, calling out explosively for drink. When she made no answer, I went to look for her.

I found her in our room, where Mammali snored in my bed. She was under it, trembling like a newborn foal, curled up, staring blankly through eyes puffed nearly shut with weeping. Since I could get no response from her, I dragged her out by the ankle. When I let her go, she curled up again.

"Titai, I have twenty men out there. *What* is it? Are you sick?" I touched her. She only whimpered. So I picked her up and carried her into the better-lit main room, both to examine her and to avoid waking Mammali, who needed what sleep he could get.

As I carried her across the threshold, she began struggling wildly in my arms, making a noise like a throttled scream. Every other sound in the room ceased while the men cleared a space in the middle of the floor. She struggled violently, even biting me as I lay her down. "Hattu-ziti, hold her arms. Lupakki, watch that foot."

We held her, but she only struggled harder.

"Let me see the little lamb. Let me see." Up came Hatib. When he squatted by her she went stiff, her eyes rolled up in her head, and she passed out.

"Now what demon's work is this?" muttered Hattu-ziti.

"Demon's work, or man's?" I snapped. Then, to Hatib: "Do you know this girl?"

"Oh no, my most respected employer, I know her not."

"Any of you?" The Sutu, to a man, answered that they did not. "I must see to her now. If you have questions Hatib cannot answer, ask Hattu-ziti. And know that I am pleased to have you. At sunrise, be at work on your new lodgings."

With mumbled leave-takings in dialects spoken from the Niblani Mountains to wretched Kush they drifted from the room.

"Here." Hattu-ziti handed me a jar of wine.

"Water would be better, and some cloths." I pulled open her eyelids, let them close. Then I picked her up and carried her into Hattu-ziti's little alcove and lay her on his narrow pallet and sat by her. Neither wine nor water aided, and somewhere in that endless night I fell asleep, still sitting there.

The next evening when I arrived at the palace enclosure for my audience with the prince, my uncle, Kantuzilis, I had five chariots supporting me, three men to a car. The watch had been told to expect me, and waved us through into the labyrinthine palace enclosure. We clattered by many buildings, into the area in which Kantuzilis had his apartments, across a paved courtyard from the house of the Gal Meshedi, chief of the royal bodyguard.

"Now remember what I have said, Lupakki: if the Meshedi should challenge you further, have them send for my brother Zida.

And if he should come and disclaim you, or in any way even hint at treachery, make sure he is the first to die."

"And if you do not come out by midwatch call, we are to come in and get you."

"If you can."

"We can," he said, grinning widely.

I clapped him on the shoulder and slid out of the car, wishing I felt as confident as he, that my mouth was not dry, that my limbs did not feel as if I had borrowed them from a stranger.

As the demon-gate guards passed me in, I smelled goat cooking, and heard the far off droning of an Old Woman. Then two high officials chasing a mouse tore by me in the corridor, and I knew that the purification ritual engaging the help of protective demons was being performed in the palace: Tuthaliyas was ill indeed.

Once they were gone, I was alone with the slap of my footfalls and the sick taste of my fear. When my father Arnuwandas yet lived, my pale uncle had taken my pet falcon—a wise, trained bird—and impaled her upon his organ while he wrung her neck unto death and I was forced to watch. That was not the worst he had done to me, when I was too small to do anything about it. And I felt small, then, as I passed through his personal guard and into his suite.

"Ah, Tasmi*sarri,* my dear boy. Or should I say, 'favorite of the Storm-god'?" He had been talking with his face averted, peering out the window. Letting the curtain fall, he turned slowly toward me. More gnarled than ever, he was; his back more bowed, his joints more swollen. Those pale eyes went slowly over me from head to toe. "My, we have become a comely young man, have we not?" The doors closed at my back. "What is this, outside? An invasion?"

"That is up to you, pederast."

"Tsk, tsk. Sit down," and, hobbling, he obeyed his own command.

I leaned against a pillar, refusing the chair he offered. "Call your Meshedi off my men, now."

"*My* Meshedi? You always were dull-witted."

"*Your* Meshedi, now that there is no Gal Meshedi commanding and Tuthaliyas lies abed." The Great King had had the last chief of the royal bodyguard executed, and appointed no successor.

"How is your mother? I have not seen her since —"

"Kantuzilis, four of my men are dead; another may lose his sight. I'm paying in advance for the ten of your men my avengers will dispatch." I threw a pouch into his lap. He winced. Behind me, the curtains rustled — and behind him, in the corner of the hall, I caught a similar disturbance.

"Those men are going to do you little good, swathed in wool. Call them out."

Smiling humorlessly, he snapped two commands, and then we really were alone.

"By the dragon who spawned you," he hissed, spurning pretense and casting the pouch to the floor, "I should have dispatched you years ago."

"But you did not, and now I am too big for you to strap. And I am telling you, if one more of my men dies by violence, I will take you out and put your neck to the plow and drive you like the ox you are through the city streets until your heart bursts."

"Try it now, fool. I invite you." Kantuzilis' eyes gleamed. "Let me assure you of one thing," he added, when I only stared at him, "you will never sit on the seat of kingship. And of another: you and your blood will be wiped from the land; none will survive. None will recollect you, even your name, when I am done. But first, you will bow at my feet. Now! Do it! Or in the king's name I will separate your head from your body this very night! I *am* Great King of Hatti while my brother is ill." His face was as red as blood.

Making as if to obey him, I wondered if I could do what I had come here to do. As I knelt there, he chortled, "Good, good," and leaned forward to run his fingers through my hair

By that hand I jerked him from his seat, my other hand stopping his mouth. Then, my heart pounding like the ground under an approaching army, I pulled up his long woolen dress and knotted it over his head, wrapping the thick shawl around him, imprisoning his arms and muffling his voice. My knees on his back, I took the broad chariot belt from my own waist and with it gave him back what he had given me while his legs kicked and his buttocks welted red and began to bleed.

Hardest was to walk out of there through his guards, closing the doors behind me dejectedly, seeming to endure their whispered taunts with bowed head.

When I had almost reached the courtyard, I saw a flicker from the corners of my eyes (which were trying to crawl around to the back of my head) and in that flicker was a lord—blue-cloaked, with a long, black braid.

At the stairs, my back muscles ticcing, I broke into a jog, and my men into a low cheer. Zida had been true to his oath, if belatedly.

"Lupakki, get us out of here!"

The clatter of the horses through the gatepost guard was to me a most welcome music.

When we had gained my wife's estate, I forsook joining the men in their celebration. Instead, I went out into the gardens and retched. When I had sat out my fear, I made a heartfelt offering to the Storm-god, my lord. Then only did I remember my little concubine, and headed for the house.

Within it, the men waxed triumphant. I was fatigued beyond relief: I had been near sleepless for four days, trying to outrun my qualms. Passing through them, I congratulated my heroes, and when I entered my wife's room (which I had appropriated), I dismissed the guard.

Titai stripped me without a word and spent a time fastidiously putting my gear away. I lay stretched out, my whole body one vociferous complaint. When she came to me, solemn-eyed, I fended off her attempts to distract me, holding her wrists in one hand and her body against mine with the other. "Will you tell me about the Sutu, or must I beat it out of you?" I said, though I never would have hurt her.

She shivered and whispered into my armpit, "My lord, please do not give me to them."

"What? Where did you get that idea?"

Then came her long discourse: how she had failed me; how she knew when a man had tired of her. Finally, in a choked voice she pleaded that I must not sell her back to the Sutu—for this boon, she would love me always in her heart.

When I gathered my wits, I assured her I entertained no such designs, and demanded to know how many times she had been sold before (thinking to myself that she had been no virgin when I found her, although her breasts were only budding then).

So I heard from her what I might have guessed if only I had thought about it: how she fell into bandits' hands when her parents' entourage was waylaid; how she'd been sold and traded ever eastward, away from that land where she was born. She retained few words in her native tongue—none of which were familiar to me—and recollected, of her family, only her father's appearance. As she recounted to me her various masters and her sojourn on an island which must have been Alashiya and her eventual disposition to the northeast where I had found her, I was sorry I had asked, and vowed to myself that not again would she be traded off like a dray-horse. But I only said to her that she would have to get used to my Sutu, and soothed her to sleep.

The next day, no Meshedi put us under siege. But not until the moon waxed full did I begin to breathe easier, and to believe what I had told myself: Kantuzilis would not spread word of his ignominy at my hands.

When the moon had turned around twice more again, the weather broke, and since Tuthaliyas was still ill he called the generals, the commanders, and the Chiefs of 1,000 together to offer up postings for spring.

He had had news from the frontier west of Gasga: a certain Piyapili, a martial governor of ours, was accused of letting the Gasgaeans into the country, and even into the houses of the gods. When the Tabarna asked "Who will go?" I said that I would, and there he agreed to send me.

Himuili was at that meeting, and Kuwatna-ziti also, and despite myself, I sought out the Shepherd.

"Tasmi," Kuwatna-ziti smiled and embraced me. He had shaved off his beard. We were on the purple marble path leading from the residence to the audience hall. "Himuili told me of your decision, and I think it realistic."

Himuili, with a wry shake of his head, made a show of searching for spies behind bushes.

"Let us go to my house, my lord Shepherd," I suggested.

His eyes clouded. "To your fortress, you mean. I would, if not for reasons you well know—I am assuming you still have her?"

"I do."

"Then I cannot."

"Thank you for setting men to watch over my wife."

"Thank the Arinnian lords. They have not forgotten you."

"This is no *place* for this," Himuili hissed, offering his own house as an alternative. We went there, and talked long into the night about whose support could be counted upon, and whose not.

"Tasmi, your mother occupies a very difficult position in this. I . . . do not know how to say this without offending you. . . ."

"Say it and take the risk, then."

"Her loyalty is not sure." The Shepherd received a bitumen cup from Himuili's deaf-mute slave.

"I know that. *She* knows she can control Zida, and that she cannot control me. When last I wrote to her, she recommended that I supplicate my god, so that he would purify my heart and bring peace to it." Zida, from his titulary in the Meshedi, could accede to the kingship as easily as I; even then, he resided in the house of the Gal Meshedi, taking Kantuzilis' orders and attentions and doing scribe's work.

That long night's conference ended only when we ran headfirst into the wall Titai had built between us: divesting myself of her was the price of their aid; I could not pay it.

With a bitter heart I left them, going to inform my men that we went out on the morrow at the head of the Great King's force, taking half our own Sutu with us, to see what might be seen in the matter of Piyapili and his town on the Gasgaean frontier.

It was a job for a magistrate, not a general, and when Piyapili stood exonerated and his defamers were separated from their tongues, Tuthaliyas still lay abed in Hattusas. So he sent me further orders, and I proceeded with the army into the Lower Country, where the Gasgaean enemy had been burning towns. And the Gasgaeans who were inside the Hattian border had treated the land very badly. So we met them, all twelve tribes who were in the country; we slew the tribal troops wherever we caught them. With the gods' aid, we took from the Gasgaean warlord all that he held and gave it back to the Hittites.

By that time Tuthaliyas was well enough to come down from the Upper Country, and met the army in the town of Zithara, where we were campaigning. From there we went on a tour of the Lower Country towns, reclaiming some who had gone over in fear to the Gasgaean enemy, and some who had joined the Arzawaean enemy. Great King Tuthaliyas drank his way from one town to another, and the men slept uneasily.

At length — after three months of indecisive battles and needless coercion of loyal towns; and after such mismanagement of a major engagement with the Arzawaeans that my Sutu began looking longingly south, toward the distant Niblani Mountains — my patience grew frayed. But just when I was about to confront him, Tuthaliyas once again became sick and prepared to return to the Upper Country.

So I went to my stepfather and pleaded the men's case: "We are much demeaned, filled with wrath. O, my lord, send me against the Arzawaean enemy, and we will return triumphant to Hattusas, bearing Anna's head." Now, this Anna stood an ally of the Arzawaeans, who in my father Arnuwandas' time had come up from the Lower Country and taken Hittite towns, making Tuwanuwa and Uda their frontier. Uda, especially, was a loss to the land, and my palms itched to reclaim it.

The Great King was very drunk that day, calling me demon's bastard and cursing me for my youth and my strength. But he sent me against the enemy, and if he sent me short-manned, I did not mind.

As soon as Tuthaliyas and half the army had departed northward, I took what remained to me—ten units of thirty, a hundred chariots and the difference in foot—and set out against the Arzawaeans. When I had marched for the first day, I came upon the enemy barricaded in a town. And the gods helped my army: the Sun-goddess of Arinna, the Storm-god of Hatti, the Storm-god of the Army, and Istar of the Battlefield, so that as we were slaying the Arzawaean enemy, their lords came out to treat with me personally, and thus I triumphed over them.

But I had not met Anna; I did not have his head. I did not turn around. I went onward, and met three more tribes and slew them. Since my men were still willing, we strode through the country occupied by the Arzawaean enemy, striking fear into them, so that they massed their forces and came against us near Uda in a multitude. And we slew that multitude in a battle so fierce blood coursed in the dirt and entrails clogged the streets.

Then two princes of the Arzawaeans sent word: since a whole tribe was slain, they would withdraw from certain towns. Thus I wrote my first real treaties, though only with princes. But seven times those princes bowed down before me; seven times they praised my men; and the gifts that they brought us were rich indeed, so that when we turned around in the browning grass to return to Hattusas, we were loaded with booty, although we still did not have Anna's head.

It seemed to all of us that Tuthaliyas would rather possess living towns than dead princes. We had done valiantly in Hatti's behalf; we felt ourselves heroes and entered the city accordingly.

CHAPTER 9

A man has certain moments in his experience, days that he
will recollect unhazed by time throughout his life—and beyond,
if there is truly kingship in heaven:

We drove triumphant through the lower city while the people
threw flowers at us and stones at our captives; young girls danced
in the streets and boys ran with our procession. I snatched up a
curly-haired girl and perched her for a moment on my car, kissed
her, then let her down. The crowd roared. To my right drove Lupakki, whose grim smile showed the shadows of strain. I caught
his eye and made a sign with my hand that put real humor there.
His helmet gleamed, its plume swaying. All of us gleamed: I had
made sure of it.

Also I had made sure that my wife was protected in Arinna,
and that Titai was hidden safely where none would think to look
for her. Both of these I accomplished by Sutu messengers before
we even saw the citadel rising up from the plain. Too, I had sent
word to Himuili and Kuwatna-ziti of what I was about; they were

117

due that courtesy. Although the price of their aid was too high, I owed them each time to think of their own futures.

At the end of such a parade, the procession stops at the pedestrian gate leading into the palace citadel. There heroes and their honor guard mount the stair in full war regalia: bronze axes, bows, spears as well as swords. My honor guard that day numbered fifty, and the heroes I had put upon my list fifty more. Among my guard, below a helm here and there, a Sutu's pigtail jutted, a toothed necklace gleamed.

I had a braid myself by then, drawn tight under my helmet and dangling down my back. Customs in Hatti are diverse; none questioned my inclusion of Sutu in my honor guard, although several marked it.

The men were passed through the small citadel gatehouse atop the stairs and up the ramp to the southeast ascent, the only one suitable for the ornate ceremonial chariots waiting to meet us.

After being driven by chariot between the colonnades into the lower courtyard, we were lauded before the people. When the sun stood high and that was finished, we were admitted through the inner gate building to the middle courtyard, and eventually through the double guard of Men of the Golden Lance and pages lining the pillared way into the halentuwa-house forecourt itself, where lords and high officials and representatives of the gods of war awaited us.

I picked out my brother Zida upon the stairs by the right doorpost. He was pale as Kantuzilis, but not because he knew anything from me.

"Lupakki, something is amiss. Give the caution signal." And he did, so that silence overtook my ranks.

I saw my mother, clutched among the Great Ones, with Kantuzilis not far off. The Pale One was smiling.

With my men positioned next to the other Hattian soldiers to be honored for their good works, I took my place next to Himuili who, along with Kuwatna-ziti, had again made it to the heroes' roll. Beside them one other hero waited, and of him I knew very little.

Himuili looked straight ahead. We three and this other commander, one Takkuri, were the ranking officers in the ceremony. The Chiefs of 1,000 (robed in long woolen dresses, man-length shawls folded diagonally over their shoulders) wore only huge ceremonial swords—curled, clumsy things—at their hips. The palace officials and the Great Ones sported nothing better than fashionable, bejeweled stickers over their finery.

"Nice day for it," I told Himuili.

His lips twitched; his huge, green-flecked eyes stared straight ahead. Mine followed in time to behold Great King Tuthaliyas stumbling down the steps on Kantuzilis' arm. Weaving, pushing Kantuzilis away, Tuthaliyas looked as if his eyes would pop from his head as he glared at us, one section at a time.

The clergy, attempting to preserve normalcy, began their incantations, offering loaves and oil and honey to the gods. Only a moment had they been droning when Tuthaliyas, arms swinging, stomped over to the priestess of the Sun-goddess of Arinna, stuck his face close to hers, and screamed at the top of his lungs for silence.

Having got it, he peered around him, jaw outthrust, swaying. Then suddenly the king faltered and lurched forward until he bumped the offering table, which careened, tottered, crashed to the stone.

There came a gasp from the crowd.

Tuthaliyas again screamed for silence. In it, I heard men shifting, the clink of gear.

"You!" roared my adoptive father, the Sun of Hatti, his pointing hand wavering wildly, so that no one knew who was meant. "Heroes! I spit upon you! You are not heroes! You come thieves, come to steal away the people's love! *I will not allow it!*" Then, as he turned to me, I saw Kantuzilis slip through the crowd, his brow furrowed. "You, you filthy bastard. You have *deceived* me. *Where is Anna's head?*"

Behind my back I made a certain sign with my fingers, one I could only hope Lupakki saw—this had been no part of our plan. Stepping forward, I heard Himuili's voice, but not what he said. To Tuthaliyas, I replied, "Anna's head"—I was slowly approaching the three stairs I would have to climb to get to him—"is yet on his body, but the frontiers of the Hatti land are enlarged."

The crowd was shifting. I chanced a glance at Zida, whose hand was perpendicular to the ground in the Meshedi holding signal.

"You *liar.* I am—"

As Kantuzilis' white claws came down on Tuthaliyas' shoulder, I shouted: "You are *nothing.* You have made a mockery of this kingship before the people. Let the Oath Gods decide between us, or cede me the seat you cannot hold!" I whirled around, checking to be sure that my men awaited me, that their resolve was strong, that their courage would hold. Then I faced the Great Ones, the chiefs, and the lords, saying, "I give you each warning! Make your decisions!"

Even as I spoke, Kantuzilis screamed *"Take them,"* springing on Zida.

At that moment I loosed my men and, with bare sword and axe, waded into the battle suddenly boiling around the Great King. To get there, I hacked my way through one Meshedi neck with my axe, tore another Meshedi off my back—too late to avoid a long slash on my chest. By then I could see no king, no brother, no allies, just the enemy: the Meshedi, the hostile lords.

Never have I laid about me with more satisfaction. My uncle Tuttu went down under me, then another uncle, followed by my useless stepbrother Tuthaliyas the Younger, and a chief took my axe in his mouth. Long did we fight there, until a hoarse voice calling repeatedly for a halt to the carnage could be heard, and heeded.

When I had wiped the last blood and sweat from my eyes, I was standing calf-deep in Hittite highborn. Shaking gore from my axe, toeing away corpses, I peered around me: most of the men left standing were mine. Far from the battle ground, my mother, two Arinnian lords and a few palace officials huddled; from behind the halentuwa-house, the clergy peeped, lamenting.

The hoarse voice had been Kuwatna-ziti's; in it he now proclaimed the day ours. I turned corpses until I found the dead Tabarna. While digging down to Tuthaliyas' corpse, I first found Kantuzilis, his fat body split like a slug's; it looked as if they had died in each other's arms.

Then only did I take thought to whom I had lost, and whom I had not. My brother Zida limped toward me—a sign that he had fought for me in the fray: I had put Hatib to watch him closely, with orders that he should not survive if he raised hand against us. Hatib, unscathed, was bending over a richly-clad body, drawing a jeweled girdle from its hips. As I counted heads, I found that I had lost two of my Sutu and five Hittites. Kuwatna-ziti, too, had lost a few men. But the Meshedi and the foul officials we slew were uncountable.

Tightening a bandage on his arm with his teeth, Himuili strolled over to me, spit out the cloth's end, and gave me his little-boy grin: "Tabarna, my lord the Sun, Great King and all suitable appellations, don't you think you should do something about that slice? Even a king can bleed to death."

"I will. I had forgotten." I fingered my wound. The cut was high, almost under my collarbone; a clean slash, and stanching itself well enough: it was a sword cut, not an axe blow. So I did not see to it.

Instead I went to speak with my mother, who was being rather roughly told that she would have to wait where she was, with the other captives.

"Tasmi! Explain to these men who I *am!* They will not let me go."

"They know who you are: that is why they will not let you go," I said. Her hair was in disarray—the only time since the burning of Hattusas I had ever seen it so. "Do you understand?"

Asmunikal's beautiful eyes looked at me from a great distance. "What are you planning to do?"

"Do? Send you into exile, on the isle of Alashiya, with the rest of your playmates."

She did not plead, nor scream, nor even pale. She looked at me with unutterable contempt, and stepped forward so commandingly that my men drew back. When she stood in clear view of all, and certain of their attention (close enough that I could see the pulse beat in her throat), she reached down ostentatiously, then drew up the hem of her robe while stepping back from me.

That done, she whirled about and walked into the midst of the prisoners. I had been, before them all, disowned.

Kuwatna-ziti chose that moment to put his arm around my shoulder and drag me off to have my wound tended.

"I've got to find a place to sit down; that's all I need, just to sit."

"Tasmisarri, from now on you can sit wherever and whenever you want."

"Then I've got to make a blood sacrifice, lest I, too, enrage the Oath Gods."

"I think," said Kuwatna-ziti, squinting, "that you have already done that."

I did not ask him whether he meant that I had enraged the gods or performed the sacrifice.

The palace has a healer, if such those can be called. Under his ministrations I winced, on the halentuwa-house steps, trying to get my mind to realize what my eyes saw as the uncountable were counted, corpses laid out neatly by rank, and my loyalists came up periodically to ask what to do about this or that. It might have been the subtle difference in Kuwatna-ziti, or the extra pace my men kept back from me; or the blanched, channeled face of the palace healer as he bowed his way from my sight, that made me feel the truth at last.

"It is done. . . . I have done it! What was in my heart the gods have fulfilled!"

Hearing my words, my men took up my belated cheer so that bedlam rang in the open hall.

"Zida, weed out the rot in your Meshedi. Hatib, take ten and help the Gal Meshedi at his task. Himuili, I need you."

"My lord king?"

"You are from Hattusas. Send Lupakki and ten of your best to round up the families of those lords who have opposed me, and any not yet dead who should be, and their adherents. I want them all corpses or exiled. The details are yours to determine."

"My lord? It will be bloody."

"A little now, or a lot later. Do it. And one more thing, Himuili—you are now Chief of One Thousand. Which thousand, I leave to you: chariot or foot, on the left, the right, whichever pleases you. Make me a list of what these dead lords had in their estates. I shall reward my men."

"What does the king of Hatti wish me to—?

"I am standing before you, so speak forthrightly, not as if I am gone. And you know my name."

"Tasmisarri. About Takkuri—and the many lords like him, those who would follow him—He fought *with* us. . . ."

"I'll talk to him. Go on, Himuili, go!" I turned away before he had gone: "Kuwatna-ziti—"

I saw the Great Shepherd stroke his chin as if lamenting his shaven beard; his kirtle was in shreds, his left eye socket turning purple. He made no reply.

So I gave him instructions: "Have the palace personnel assemble, and make final judgment in their cases; those who shall live to serve us, set them about it. I want a feast for our men, set out in the largest audience hall. Tell them to take what women they want from Tuthaliyas' seraglio. I will start anew there. . . . What is it, Shepherd?"

"My lord, I'm not—" Eyes slitted, Kuwatna-ziti sat down on the steps beside me. "Tasmi, I'm not condoning all this killing. Not in Hattusas. I'm not your man."

"You were not saying that when lord fought lord."

"I had to. . . Look you, I couldn't let them hack you to pieces. But I have not changed my position. I want no spoils from this slaughter. I'm going home to Arinna, back to the god's service."

I leaned against the steps. "You'll go where I tell you, and when."

"*Yes,* my lord king," he said, voice like a knife.

"It's still Titai, isn't it? And the fact that I foxed you, forced your hand. Well, do not worry, I was not going to offer you any reward. You saved your own neck this day. It is no gift from me to you. But *do you* as I have commanded, and this: have the army's lords, the palace officials, the Great Ones, and all the rest here tomorrow to swear to me before the Oath Gods. Now you perform these tasks allotted you!"

In my planning, I had sought this early culmination of events so that I might take the lords' oaths before court let out for winter and they scattered to their estates. But I had not expected Kuwatna-ziti to balk.

Watching the Shepherd thread his way through the living and the dead, I thought that things would be different when he was under oath to me. I called after him: "And one more thing: you're not going to Arinna; you'll deliver the exiles to Alashiya."

I summoned Mammali (who had not after all lost his sight) and had him bring before me the strange commander Takkuri, whose curly hair was matted with blood and manner uncertain. I said to Takkuri, once Mammali withdrew, "You fought with us, Takkuri. Himuili says you will be content to continue to fight with us." I motioned him to sit.

His squat form matched his Luwian dialect: pure southern Hittite, judging by his dark craggy face and substantial bones. He searched obviously for composure, then for a suitable form of address.

"Why are you so nervous, Takkuri? If I wanted to kill you, you would already be dead."

"There are relatives of mine lying there, more on your list."

"Keep your family's estates; show mercy to women and children who mean something to you. More than that I cannot do. Find Himuili and tell him I have said it."

His eyes met mine for the first time. Slowly he nodded, pausing long to fluff his oily, full beard. Then: "My lord king, I can promise you joyous acceptance in the Lower Country, and what you need of my men to fill up your Meshedi—they would gladly serve you."

"But?"

"But, my lord, a sister of mine was to be chosen for the palace women, and even now she is up there—"

"Go bring her to me."

With a bound, he was gone. I decided that if she were comely, I would keep her, and a good hold on Takkuri therewith.

She was, and I did.

When I got a count of Meshedi, I found that nearly half remained alive. I saw Zida's softness in that, but said nothing, only reassigned my Sutu and part of my foot there to temporarily fill out the guard while I sought suitable replacements.

I moved into the Great House, a fortress within a fortress within a fortress, and brought Titai out from hiding and my wife and sons down from Arinna. I invited my sister and all her handmaidens into the palace, and fattened up the lords' ranks with my partisans, creating a new aristocracy of fighters.

By the time the clouds came down into the streets, Hattusas was functioning normally. But I stayed in the Great House, not moving to a southern estate for the winter, as Tuthaliyas so often did. I made sacrifices to the Storm-god, my lord, and refurbished both his great temple and the smaller shrine in the king's quarters. I had Tunnawi the Old Woman brought down from Arinna, and installed her in the palace to oversee its purification (so I told her). I spent ten days in the temple of the Sun-goddess of Arinna, reading tablets of bronze, wood, and clay, delineating treaties and other matters concerning kingship and queenship, over all of which she reigned.

My wife Daduhepa fell to queenship with a will: she was born for it; the halls sparkled and smelled of sweet cedar and evergreen, and harpist's strains sounded soft in the night.

On Hattu-ziti I laid all the details of managing the palace, and news that in the spring we would begin the refortifying of Hattusas as we had always dreamed her. "For that, my lord, we will need greater wealth," Hattu-ziti cautioned; "levies of men, materials—"

"I will get it," I promised him. "You will have building namra and slaves beyond counting, and the finest of wood and stone, and money shall be no object."

"And how are we going to do that?"

"You worry your tasks, and I'll handle mine. Just make me lists of what you need." He did. I levied men and contributions from the fat nobility such as had not been pried out of them since the old empire, but they were yet mourning near half their number, and none refused me.

I overheard two Meshedi talking of how my heart was of good iron and how the people feared my wrath. "Any man who could exile his own mother, kill uncles and cousins like goats to be offered up to the god . . . watch yourself, is all, or you'll end with nails in your wrists."

I marked their names, but I was pleased. I had strung up a pair of Meshedi, nailed them like omen-birds on the palace gates. They were dead beforehand, but it made a lasting impression.

Hatti's Great Queen, the Tawananna, my wife, was pregnant once more. She languished happily in her wing with her dawn sickness and my sons, and bothered me not about filling the seraglio, nor about the commander Takkuri's sister, nor about Titai.

But I was bothered about Titai, and when the Old Woman Tunnawi had seen to the king's purity and the inviolability of the palace to evil demons, I had her brought before me to begin the task for which I had truly called her down from Arinna.

"Ah, favorite of the Storm-god. How is the Sun, my lord, today?" she wheezed in that feeble display I had learned was only a disarming ploy.

"I am fine. But my concubine, Titai, is not."

"I saw her only yesterday, and she seemed well enough," said the Old Woman, easing herself down by me. We were at the offering pool—a room sided with pillars and open to the sky, which lies between the king's residence and the gods' temples, in the midst of a five-room complex containing the royal library and implements of the gods. I had been through that whole library without finding a way to raise a foreign, untitled, barren girl any higher than chief concubine.

Left to me was only one alternative: "I have had her nearly five years, and she has not conceived," I said.

"My lord, if a woman does not conceive, then that is the man's fault."

"You jest."

"Does the Sun, my lord, want his concubine to conceive, or not?"

"Old Woman—"

"Does the Sun, my lord, harbor any uncleanliness in his parts?"

"I do not." I growled, leaning back on my elbow and rubbing the sword cut, healed but still itching, on my breastbone. "And I have certainly proved that I can produce children, so it is not that."

"That is what it must be, my lord, if you are cohabiting with her in the normal way and she is not bearing."

I argued with her about it, to no avail. And it was incumbent upon me to take her advice, since I had asked it. Thus I underwent a long and demeaning ceremony involving being bathed by a virgin and a eunuch, and various goings-in and comings-out through gates made singularly magical with wool and libations.

When all that was done, there was no doubt in anyone's mind that I was capable of sustaining an erection, or of spending three days meekly carrying mirrors and distaffs around in the countryside. I was feeling like a horse in training by the second day.

I balked when Tunnawi gave me the bow and arrows, saying to me in the antiquated, formulaic Hittite which the ritual demands: "See! I have taken womanliness away from thee and given thee manliness. Thou has cast off the ways of a woman, now show the ways of a man."

But after showing the wrath of a man I continued, getting through the last day of it, and we went down again into the city.

Despite the ritual, Titai was not improved, although Takkuri's sister missed her moon-flow, so I called the Old Woman again. "I am like Serris the Great Bull with her, and still she will not bear. I have spent more time with her than with all the others combined. What say you now, Tunnawi?" We were in my own apartments. Two Sutu sat in a corner, whetting their blades.

"I say," she replied, "that I must perform upon her the ceremony for uncleanliness in *her* parts."

When she had done that, the Old Woman came back to me, her brow like a field at planting time. "That girl," hissed Tunnawi, "is a sorceress. She is cursed by all the gods."

My surprise that she had divined this was not feigned. "What has given you that idea?"

"When she proved clean, I cast omens, my lord, both for you and for your house. I am telling you, there is a demon in her which eats your seed as it enters her body. And I will tell you something else, my lord, if you allow it."

"Speak." My two Sutu lounged at the window, enjoying a king's spectacular view of the countryside.

"Try not your strength against Egypt, or the land will perish thereby."

"*Egypt?* Are you not a little premature? I cannot even get down off the plateau!" I shouted instantly, faking rage to hide my relief. Still loud-voiced, I had the Sutu take the Old Woman out and dispatch her, though I could not meet her eyes. Nor could I fail to shiver at the curses she laid upon me as they dragged her away.

I had no choice: It was the Old Woman, or Titai. But I slept badly, encountering in my dreams the Old Woman Tunnawi's rheumy eyes.

*

When Daduhepa bore me a third son, we called him Telipinus, after the god of that name. She was late with him, and labored as badly as she had carried. When we saw the size of him we knew why.

Poor Titai looked upon the baby with longing eyes, her cheek pressed against my arm. But Daduhepa was jealous of her children and vengeful toward my tawny concubine: she would not even let her hold him.

I made it known among my men that I would take a suitable orphan baby if any heard of one, and kept trying to settle a child on my barren girl.

On Arnuwandas' fifth birthday, I made him tuhkanti and set Hatib the task of teaching him how to draw a bow and sneak around like a Sutu. Piyassilis, a season younger, waxed wrathful, so that I had to discipline him myself. It seemed like the only time I ever saw my second son was to welt his behind, until Titai softly observed that he, of the three, was the most like his father. She begged me to lighten my hand on him, or at least to give him some good memories to mix with the bad. So I took to carrying Piyassilis with me when Titai and I went out, and the starved look in her winter-sky eyes slowly faded. But when the weather began to break and war loomed once more, Daduhepa was less busy with infant Telipinus, and took Piyassilis back under her skirts, and my concubine cried herself to sleep at night.

I was impatient to get out and fight, since rumblings from Mitanni and Hurri (countries which had long lain quiescent despite Tuthaliyas' prognostications) were finally heard in the land.

So before I went out on campaign, I wrote to Artatama of Hurri, and to Tushratta of Mitanni, and to all the foreign lands with which we had relations, announcing that I, the Sun Suppiluliumas, Great King, the valiant, favorite of the Storm-god, ruled in Hatti.

For that was whom I had become. My mother had disowned me, and so I disowned the label she had put on me, throwing off the Hurrian stigma with which my name had tagged me.

Suppiluliumas: 'pure spring'. It was a fitting name for a king to enter in the king-lists: "the Sun," a reference to kingship in heaven—to the winged disk that is the Tabarna's—was how the old empire kings styled themselves. Since I was intending

to restore Hatti to the greatness of the old empire, I felt entitled
to so call myself.

In Egypt, in Amurru, in Ugarit, in Babylon and Byblos my
new name was being sounded out by scribes, then secretaries,
then kings. In Hatti, I myself had trouble adjusting to it: I had
been Tasmisarri too long. But it was as "the Sun, Suppiluliumas"
all would come to know me, and from the isle of Alashiya to Assyria men would soon be whispering it over their wine, and over
their dead, and over their fear.

CHAPTER 10

So it was that I began to concern myself with the matter of
fortifying Hattusas, and in that context I made my efforts the
subject of an oracle, for my exercises in kingship had brought
to my mind the curse laid upon the land by Anittas, the king to
whom all kings of Hatti owe Hattusas. Said Anittas of his sack
of Hattusas: ". . .and during the night I took it by assault. But in
its place I sowed weeds. Him who will be king after me and plant
Hattusas again, the Storm-god of Hatti shall smite!"

And the oracle was favorable, but the bird omens were not.
Furthermore, since the curse was an echo of the one laid upon my
head by the Old Woman, I made it the subject of an incubation—I
slept in the palace with the matter written on a tablet beneath
my head. All that came to me therein was the blue-cloaked lord,
him with the long braid. He was walking the crenellated walls
of Hattusas, and they were whole, unbreachable.

Satisfied, I caused new clothes of gold and silver to be made
for the Storm-god Tarhun and for his wife, the Sun Goddess Arin-

niti, and turned my attention elsewhere, leaving Hattu-ziti a free hand to make us walls as I had seen in my dream.

There were, in truth, more places to turn my attention than I might have wished. Kingship is heaviest in the cold months; nor is it greatly lightened in the warming of New Year, for then the king and queen must perform many duties for the gods, going with them upon tours and officiating at festivals. These things, which Daduhepa found wondrous and fulfilling, were odious for me from the first. I, who had led point into battle while still in my teens, grew dry-mouthed and dimwitted when concerned with leading people in their worship of the gods. The memorization of form and formula was as swamp tundra, so that however cautiously I tried to get across, I would sink in the mire. I was forever losing my place and my poise with it, and seeking hard for some scheme by which I might place the religious burden of kingship on some other's shoulders. That, however, I was not able to do, and fell exhausted into my bed, all those gray days long, from my efforts to get close enough to the Storm-god's chariot to at least offer myself in service. However I tried, my heart stayed empty and my performance of rituals likewise; and while thus engaged, I would find myself sniffing out the hearts of my lords and communing with my agents in the different towns, so that my heart ached for an end to all mummery and a pair of reins in my hands.

Nor were my duties only religious: I had the youngest court in the history of Hatti, and men like Himuili and Kuwatna-ziti were not so pliant as the aging aristocracy would have been under a king such as I. Unease and dissent were subvocalized among the remaining elders, and as a block they sought to weigh us down, to slow us, to act as a buffer state between us and the rashness they saw in our coming campaigns.

But there is a thing about buffer states: on one side of them is the frontier; beyond that, the enemy, so that no matter how one tries to stay the process, the buffer state is consumed by the expanding empire within it, until there is no buffer state anymore; just the enemy eye-to-eye with the empire. Notwithstanding how far one treks, regardless of how many countries a man brings under his control, one fact remains ineluctable: wherever there is a frontier, there is an enemy just beyond it.

So as I mentally expanded the frontiers of Hattusas, absorbing those neutral and those undecided and enlisting them to my cause, always and to the exact extent that I strengthened my position did my detractors bring up reinforcements for their own.

My throat became sore from talking and my patience thin from stretching, and often I considered glumly the disadvantages of clearing away the brambles of my court with sword and axe. But I did not, lest by that law which I have just described, I finish only to find more grown up in their place.

I ordered the palace smith to make for me a full arsenal of good iron weapons — even to fit my chariot with iron rather than bronze. This ostentation had a purpose beyond irritating the conservative: the ice-colored metal, long reserved for gods and kings, strengthened my image: they claimed that my heart was made of iron; I gave them proof of it. If the people saw an omen in the bleeding metal, it was no less true than a thousand other omens concocted in the past by kings and priests to serve their intentions. Half of becoming invincible is becoming renowned. I was much concerned with making Hatti fear me, so that the fear might spread to my enemies and numb their souls. Good iron is mystical stuff to most: kings do not have it in Babylon, nor in Egypt, nor in Mitanni; they try to wheedle it out of us by sending costly treasures, so that we must dispatch precious gifts in return; even now, only infrequently do I send it.

I spent many days working with the smith's products, accustoming myself to the differences in balance and weight of my new weapons. I could come to no terms with the first axe, and the smith and I drew in the dirt together once again. At length he brought me another, this one thinner, with a marked flare to its head and longer claws on the tearing side. The sword, however, was good on the first try: we only weighted the hilt, to get a feel like my old one. I gave the first axe to the Storm-god, but still he did not break his silence and speak in my heart.

The room in which I slept overlooked the joining of the palace and city walls and a day's drive of countryside, forest and plain. One morning, when the trees were first budding, I came in from an interminable wrangle with the Lower Country lords—just up from the winter's recess which they so piously observed—and found there a great oval mirror of bronze, hinged on a standing frame gilded with electrum, placed near the tall window opposite my bed.

"What is this?" I asked Titai, though I knew perfectly well what it was; and even whom that looming warlord behind his curtain of bronze, haughty and challenging, might be. He and I turned our backs upon one another, each taking a moment of privacy, for kings must not show such emotion as I then felt. In that first glance, before recognizing myself, I had seen him whom I had become. Had it happened in a night, this transformation of Tasmisarri into Suppiluliumas? Had the form come with the name? Or had it simply occurred so slowly that, glimpsing myself in pool and stream and shield, I had not seen? I wore a turquoise cloak, an accession gift from Amenhotep III whom we call Nimmuria, Great King of Egypt; I wore the conical crown of Hatti; and I wore the aspect of a lord glimpsed in moonlight by a boy on a hill. For an instant, my counterpart image misted and softened by the haze of bronze between us, I had thought it even him: the blue-cloaked one, come again to whisk round a corner and rub his hands together at the edges of my vision. But while I, the Sun of Hatti, wore my black hair braided, lately my visions of the lord in blue had shown him with his hair cropped square at his neck. All this I experienced in a blink's time, then saw myself, and found need to turn away, to growl at Titai. . . .

She answered: "It is a gift from your wife." Softly, disapprovingly, she added, "Do you see in it what she wishes you to see?"

"Must I have weighted words from you, too? If your tongue curls like Daduhepa's, you may find yourself sharing her bed instead of mine. Can I not have peace even between the women of my house? How can I unite the land if I cannot unite the palace? Mirrors from Hatti are not fine enough for my wife, who must import better." Thinking ill of all things Egyptian, I ripped the gift-cloak from me and cast it to shroud the mirror. "And my concubine is not content with being a foreign sorceress so inept as to be unable to protect herself from discovery by Old Women and sniveling seers—is not content even *now,* when a convocation of priestesses has lodged a formal complaint against her; but *is* content indeed to flaunt her ignorance of and disinterest of all things Hittite; is content not to—"

I had my hand in her hair by then, and her back against the window sill. Windows, in Hatti, extend almost from floor to ceiling. Though they may be curtained, these were open to the day, and high above the ground—high enough that my view of the countryside was unobstructed by the palace walls.

Totally yielding, tears streaming from wide eyes, Titai conquered me without a word, in an instant. Her terror and her abject pliancy dousing my rage, I pulled her against me and said unkingly things for a time. For I was disquieted: Titai had in no way earned my wrath; I had long ago sworn to myself never to vent my temper on her; I had made gentleness my custom. "Titai, I am . . . pressed. Patience—Bah! I resolve to acquire it, but I have little. I am the Sun, Great King: words only! The lords ring me round with words. One thing is said, another done."

She sighed. I let her go. She sought the bed and sank, trembling, onto it.

I faced her. "A man can be called king in their mouths, and not be king in their hearts. I did that which I must; many hold it against me. They say that I sacked Hattusas. If I did, it is because she would not yield. And if they fear me, since they will not love me, then that is the next best thing. Later, they will love me: my deeds will speak for me. Even as at first you served me in fear, and now serve in love."

"I loved you from the beginning," she demurred. Titai seldom wasted thought on things that did not directly concern Titai. What did concern her was the Old Women and their feud with me over her, grown open since the death of one of their number. "What will you do, Suppi-luli-umas?" she asked, dutifully sounding out my new name in her musical, foreign accent. "About the priestesses, I mean?"

"I want you to choose a Hittite god, and I have arranged with the Old Women and a seer from the palace to oversee your instruction. . . ."

She was shaking her head slowly back and forth, neck bent, so that her tawny hair brushed her knees, whispering "No," repeatedly.

But I insisted. "It is the only thing that will quiet them! Once they take you in hand, the hierophants are responsible to me. Otherwise they will never overlook your foreignness, nor the loss, on your account, of Tunnawi, one of their mighty. In a sense, I owe them a person, though the king cannot truly be held accountable. But there is our advantage: they demand a person; the person is you. If I cede them your education—which is long overdue—I do not have to be concerned for your life. What is familiar is less threatening than what is strange. They will come to know you, to see you are no evil witch. Thus my troubles with the clergy and, hence, the great preponderance of unfavorable omens now attending my every plan and proposition will drop off like a snake shedding an old skin. Now, Titai, I have not asked you for anything, ever. Now I am asking this. I will not force you, nor even order you, only say that if you behave with love in your heart toward me, you will come to my aid. . . ."

In the end she did as I asked her, although she was right and I was wrong—as wrong as I was to feel humiliation because Hattusas did not love me. Everything said of my first year of kingship is true: I sacked Hattusas, entire, and all her entrenched bureaucracy with her. I have treated conquered cities more kindly. Twenty years later I would treat the capital city of my most hated enemy more gently than in those days I treated Hattusas. I occupied my capital as a foreign town. I took nothing on faith, not one allegiance on trust, and those who opposed me I ground into dust. But it is from the easing of that siege, by my very passage from warlord-in-possession to overlord, that I derived the vision that I have made law as far south as the Niblani Mountains. And if now I can look Egypt in the eye and spit upon her pythoned brow, it is because then I was tireless and implacable in the face of exhaustion and despair.

It is a lonely thing to be a king unloved by his land. It is anguish deep beyond measuring, to be a general separated from his armies. Power's curse comes in an ache behind the eyes from reading and folds around the belly a snakelike girdle of fat from sitting. Therefrom had Tuthaliyas turned to drink and Arnuwandas before him to endless rituals aimed at placating the gods. I aimed my rituals at my nobility, that each be an arrow in my quiver. I would make them what they had to be: true vassals, as tight under my command as had been my thirty in Samuha. To that end, I abstained from drink, lest I stumble from it as my stepfather had done.

But the fear of losing my armies to other men while I must stay in Hattusas, in those days, I could not allay. To leave Hattusas would be to lose her: Himuili had resigned his titulary as a Chief of 1,000 in favor of a field command—had done it before the ranks of the armies, so that I had no choice but to accept. He was possibly the only man who could have done it and survived, but the fact that he had done it left me with no alternative but to face the result: I must remain in Hattusas while my armies went out to war. I consoled myself with my newfound wisdom, saying that the real war was in Hattusas this season, but though it was true I did not believe it, and conjectured endlessly as to how I might hurry my consolidation attempts and where I might meet up with the armies in mid season, should I have a working court by then.

I cursed Kuwatna-ziti endlessly. The Shepherd had gone deep into the temple, shaved back his forehead and cut off his nails and taken up the work of the Storm-god with ardor. Now, when I most desperately needed him, he mixed the god's dinner and worked his diplomatic skills on cattle and sheep due for sacrifice. I sent a series of more and more querulous messages, inviting the "Man of the Storm-god" down from Arinna, but always he could not come. Finally, white-knuckled with rage, I summoned the highest official of the Storm-god's temple to my palace yard, where I was working with Hatib at wrestling behind the residence.

"Am I not High Priest of the Storm-god?" I demanded, pacing before the hierophant who knelt, nose in the dirt, and would do so until I saw fit to bid him rise.

He sneezed, and agreed that I was.

"Get up. I want Kuwatna-ziti here, and he will not come. I am the Sun, am I not?"

The priest, arisen, agreed that I was.

His nose was pale with dust, but I did not look away long enough for him to wipe his face; rather, I transfixed him with a hostility which was not feigned. This cleric, whom the gods favored with their counsel, had lost no time informing me of that fact. In truth, he routinely informed me of intelligence gleaned from gods' mouths which countermanded my orders and made naught of my most meticulous plans. "Then, as the Sun, as your Tabarna, as the favorite of the Storm-god, I order you to present Kuwatna-ziti here by the full of the moon." This I was saying very slowly, as if the priest might have trouble understanding.

"But—Does the Sun, my lord, realize that I am but a poor priest? I cannot order—"

"Have the Storm-god order it! Begone!"

Hatib, who had been engaging a Man of the Golden Lance in deliberate conversation, sauntered casually away from the steps leading diagonally up the inner wall to the gatehouse. I have not spoken much of Hattusas and her fortifications. Later she came to wear all the gilded armor the labor of my years has provided. In those early days, she was aglitter in my mind only: where I saw great crenelated bastions only rubble awaited the building crews; the postern gate was but a clay tablet crudely sketched, shelved until time and funds allowed its undertaking.

"Hatib, show me that hold again." The wrestling of Egypt is equally of mind and body; perhaps because they are slight, they have developed it, but in any case I found lessons more far-reaching than brawling practices in Hatib's southern wiles. If overbalancing a man upon his left allows you to throw him to his right, how much more in the land of scheme and counter-scheme could such a ploy be worth? What we learn from a man's eyes is dependent upon only what we have learned about men; Hatib had taught me a great deal more than canny holds in those months he had been wrestling me into the dirt. He had taught me so much that when he crouched down beside me (when the king squats, no man may stand erect) I felt sure of my capacity to throw him. And I did throw him, because as he squatted down I came up out of my crouch and pulled him forward while levering myself onto his back; in a moment I bestrode him in the dust, holding his one arm pinned with my knee and twisting the other up behind him, whereupon he yielded with that thick, hissing laugh of his, and I rolled away, so that we both lay on the ground. Out of the corner of my eye I could see the Golden Lancers hunched down uncertainly, not daring to either lie down or stand up, their gaudy uniforms gathered about them:

"Hatib," I grunted, sitting erect, "when are you leaving?"

He stared, raised an eyebrow, and sat up also. "Is the Sun, my lord, getting messages from the mountains?"

"From your manner: it speaks plainer than the mountain gods. Don't 'Sun' me, either. Can I not convince you otherwise?"

"My friend, my lord employer, young king, we both know that you can order. . ."

"And make you run? And an outlaw?"

The big Sutu caught the braided lock growing above his right ear and tugged on it. "There is that. I was going to ask you to release me. Most of mine would be content to stay." He paused, perhaps waiting for me to speak, tracing with a finger the thin, white scar that collars his throat. When I said nothing, he added, "How did you know?"

"Great Queen Daduhepa took exception to the parting gift you gave Arnuwandas." My wife had taken exception to more than the amulet Hatib had given our eldest son: the boy had picked up such oaths from Hatib, in pidgin Babylonian, in Egyptian, in Hurrian, that had he been a man, he would likely have been brought to trial for blasphemy.

"The Bastet? She is a potent goddess, fit for a kinglet, who must be fierce as She upon the field. She and Istar of the Battlefield, they are one and the same."

I did not say to him that the cat-headed, full-breasted woman's body carved in lapis that young Arnuwandas now wore around his neck bore little resemblance to our own battle-goddess, although I was aware of the convention that equated them. "They are Oath Gods, both. But I think it the womanly form to which my wife objected, as women will."

We both laughed, as I had intended. When he sobered, I asked, "Hatib, how is it that you, a Sutu, can teach my son Egyptian curses? How is it that a man with the style and stature of a Libyan can invoke Kubaba"—I had not forgotten that moment, in his consternation, when he had called on the Hurri god while bending over Titai's unconscious form— "*write* Babylonian, and give gifts like Pharaoh's?"

"When a man becomes *Sutu,* " said Hatib stiffly, "he forgets the answers to those questions, Great King, my lord."

"Hatib, let us walk awhile."

We did that until we came to the stairs, and climbed them, coming out atop the wall. Leaning between two of its plastered teeth, I bespoke my proposition to him: "Hatib, if you are willing, you shall wander wheresoever you choose while serving me as if you were yet in Hattusas."

"How may that be, my lord?" asked Hatib, trying not to smirk.

"Continue to advise me in matters of foreign affairs." Hatib, whose sources of information seemed limitless, had at my order been gathering intelligence: of Mitanni's King Tushratta; on the machinations of the Syrian princes; about Alashiya, where my mother and most of my relatives now resided. "Your holdings here in Hatti I shall protect and increase, even as you roam."

"And all Hatib must do is whisper in the king's ear from afar?"

"By caravan, by messengers bought with silver. You already know what I would hear. Soon enough and thanks partly to you, my boundary with Mitanni will be farther from Hattusas. . . ."

"Kizzuwadna?" He guessed rightly.

"Once I have reclaimed that country, Tushratta and I will be neighbors."

"And then?"

"Who can say? Perhaps we will live in peace, the king of Mitanni and I."

Hatib chuckled. "My lord, I bow down before you. I only wonder how I may fulfill your expectations from my destination: I go from here to the Two Lands." He meant Egypt. "Still, it could be done. All true knowledge comes to reside in Pharaoh's hands—or in his scribes'."

I was staring, in spite of myself. A man who robes himself a Libyan, shaves his head to a mere lock, and commands Sutu should not dare to speak so casually of Pharaoh's court. But Hatib, I was beginning to learn, fits no man's mold, even when that man be king.

"My lord king, the Two Lands are troubled. Her children flock to her. The Good God—Pharaoh—seeks to separate himself from the priesthood. A prince has died at the hands of the hierophants. I have family there, and a woman to whose safety I must see."

Somewhat more Egyptian rolled off Hatib's tongue than I could follow: I caught the pharaoh's name; then a city's; then a god's: Aten. *Aten:* None of us could know, then, what that name would come to mean, how much of the world would be transformed by its speaking. Sometimes I have been tempted to offer to that god, regent of the solar disk, for he has brought me better fortune then he did to any of his own Egyptian children. Then, it was just a name heard dimly through ignorance. No one—least of all (if I may presume) Nimmuria, Amenhotep III, who first elevated him—knew who the Aten was.

What we did know, Hatib and I, was one another. We talked the sun down, and as it blew out the day's crimson breath across the sky, we devised a method of service and payment flexible enough to grow with my empire, if indeed I managed to remake it.

So when I released Hatib he knew more about what was in my heart than any Hittite. And if indeed the gods fulfill what is in the heart of a Hittite king, from my early days to late, Hatib has been one of their finest instruments. That day, I was concerned only with retaining what I might of Hatib's multinational intelligence. When we parted there I had not only done that, but laid the foundations on which the new Hittite empire would mount to heaven. Filled with visions of a thousand scribes singing our glories to the ages, I descended the staircase alone.

When I had reached its foot a shrill hawk's challenge sounded stridently from above me: Hatib, leaning out between two of the wall's teeth, waved me a final farewell.

Until the first "dusty men" mounted to Hattusas and sought out service behind the armies, I wondered whether Hatib's laconic solution to my need for mercenaries would work. I have never established how the plainsmen get their news, but the years have taught me one thing: be they Sutu, Hapiru, or any other homeless wanderers, they know kings' business before the kings themselves.

Innumerable times since I threw open my borders to the landless nomads (who in Hittite service grew dusty indeed behind the chariots, behind the pikemen, behind the Hittite foot) have I been repaid for allowing their women to glean and their children to sing and their men to fight for me. From these men I have received more loyalty than from my own, though what I offered them was merely a chance to die for the Hatti land—no more than I have done for all the repossessed towns and recovered citizenry who yet hate me for it.

About men's hearts, I was just learning, there is no fruitful conjecture.

CHAPTER 11

"What is it, Abuya, to become a wolf?" My eldest son's eyes, as he asked his question from the relative safety of his ancient horses' far side, were as big as the royal seal of Hatti.

A man hates to think that his children are avoiding him; Arnuwandas' behavior, during the months since Hatib's departure, had forced me to that conclusion. In my presence he stood stiff and pale, silent, grim as a foot soldier on the battle line.

I had noticed his odd demeanor before I joined the campaigns in midsummer, but graver troubles were oppressing me. On this side and on that—within Hatti and without—I had been beset by my enemies. Aided by Anna (whose head could not be got last season), the Arzawaean enemy had become so presumptuous that their rampaging magically solved the most stubborn problems dogging me at court, freeing me to get about what I do best. My blacks were joyous, swift as the wind—as if they knew that the good-iron bedecked chariot they now pulled belonged to a king.

As a king, I performed my first ceremonies at the borders of enemy lands. When we crossed back over this ground, it would mark borders no longer, but be part of Hatti again. We fought in the town of Anisa and below; we met six tribes in one town and seven in another. Fiercely we slew them, so that the Arzawaean enemy died in a multitude. Farther south into the country we pushed, to meet Anna and the Arzawaeans he was helping, who had attacked the towns around the Salt Lake and taken all of Mount Ammuna, along with its inhabitants, sheep and cattle.

When I had finished smiting the enemy in the towns above the lake and gone back to Tiwanzana to spend the night, a messenger brought me word while I rested in the king's estate there, that Anna himself was fighting below the lake in the town of Tuwanuwa.

Now in my formal annals I have listed my conquests, and what is said therein is truth. But a man nowhere says, in such reportage, that he was tired, or cranky, or that he might have erred in his judgment. In the matter of that first campaign it is nowhere stated why, with only six chariots supporting me, I went back to Tiwanzana to sleep while my tattered troops rested as they could in the homes of newly liberated Hittite citizens of Sapparanda and its neighboring towns.

I did this because of a woman I had seen bathing in the moonlight in the Salt Lake while her belled attendants held torch and towel and sang softly to her from the bank. Pulling up my blacks, I had watched from a distance, amazed, while the ritual languorously lilted through the night as if the land were not torn asunder by war so that the ground was a red mudflat to the horizon. Truly, I could not conceive of anyone so foolish as to linger at lakeside in deepest night, although I myself circled the shore unaccompanied and this girl had a score of attendants, male and female.

When she came up out of the salt-pale water, I forgot everything else: She was the moon goddess arisen from the mountain. When her gilded wagons filled with laughing women and went rumbling off toward the town, I followed. When they turned into a courtyard, I pulled up my blacks and tarried, one leg thrown over the car's side, until no more lyres could be heard.

The next day's fighting saw me preoccupied; if not for the gods, my lords, I doubtless would have lost the battle to Anna's troops. Possibly because Anna's head was not my utmost concern, I did not acquire it.

When, after an indecisive engagement, I led my six chariots back to my commandeered lakeside estate, I went directly to the official I had charged with fulfilling what was in my heart:

He told me the girl's name was Khinti. Her breeding was such that, considering my precarious situation in Hattusas, I could not simply order her delivered up to me. So I proposed to make her a wife and install her by the lake in a summer palace I was willing to build, which—considering her age and Daduhepa's jealousy—seemed the safest course. So long had it been since I had enjoyed trouble-free thoughts about a woman, I had forgotten the pleasure of it: the day dawned sparkling clear, and in my heart was a quiet that had eluded me since I first sat upon the seat of kingship.

I had with me twenty men; we were carrying a third fighter in each chariot. This third man might wield spear or bow, and though in former times the spearman found his place upon unmoving ground, I was weighing alternatives: my chariots' heavier loads against increased mobility of a larger segment of my force.

Driving down into the country that morning, I was lighthearted. Day dawned bright; men called to each other over the drumming of the teams; the noise of my own iron-shod wheels masked their words. Around a bend we thundered and were amid the enemy without warning. It seemed that the whole Arzawaean army surged around us there.

My third man was Lupakki that day. I remember most clearly his gleeful tallying of his dead—a shriek accompanying every successive loosing of a shaft. He had thirty arrows; twenty-eight times I heard him howl a higher number, assigning each kill to one of the gods.

Later I chided him, saying that human sacrifice is no longer performed in the Hatti land. "In former times, we did it thus, but no longer. If you must consecrate the spirits of your dead, do so in silence."

Solemnly he stared at me: "Shall we not say that the gods helped the army: the Sun-goddess of Arinna, the Storm-god of Hatti, the Storm-god of the Army, and Istar of the Battlefield, so that we smote the enemy?" Battle fever had deserted Lupakki, and the sick soul which follows after was plaguing him. Over time I have learned not to mock what he does and says in battle: he hardly remembers. Then, sensing his disquiet, I clapped him about the shoulders and slid down from the car to see if Anna's head might somehow lie on the field. But it did not.

When we had stripped all the corpses of weapons, we burned only our own dead and set out to rejoin the rest of the army. On the way I saw what pillage the enemy had wrought: the namra, the deportees, the cattle and sheep that scattered my way were countless. From this I determined that still more Arzawaeans must be abroad in the land, but had fled in fear while we battled their advance. So when I rejoined the strength of the army and heard that the enemy who had cast away the booty had retreated and taken hold of the mountain, I was not surprised.

I drove up to Tuwanuwa and bound the enemy there with what portion of the army I had. I had been there fighting one whole day before my gathered troops, and the chariots I had left behind to accompany them, arrived on the mountain. When we drove down from there, I had Anna's head.

But still I could not quiet the Arzawaeans. That entire season we fought in the south, in a score of towns, and always I would return to the Salt Lake. But although I slept there, I slept alone. Khinti's parents sorely tried my patience, but their every excuse and delay was bound up carefully with temple obligations and lordly protocol and there was little I could do about it with a war raging like flame through the country.

Hattusas grew dim and dreamlike. Great Queen Daduhepa ruled in my name. She sent word of my other commanders, and

of the Gasgaeans and of Hayasaeans, but since none of the aforementioned news was good, I paid it little heed. Himuili and Takkuri had the Upper Country; if they could not hold it, I could
not help them.

As it happened, they did not need more help than the free
hand I gave them. While I was finally preparing to return to Hattusas, word came down that Himuili's troops and chariots had
smitten the enemy with the aid of a certain Mariyas of Hayasa.
This chieftain's son had appeared out of the Upper Country, bearing aid and an enigmatic message for me from his father. Both
now awaited me in Hattusas.

I have told you of the taking of King Lanni of Hayasa's head,
which later I piked up before old Tuthaliyas. And I have intimated
that Tuthaliyas began treaty negotiations with Lanni's sons. But
intimations and negotiations were all we had: no treaty existed
between us at that time. Thus, no one was more surprised than I
to hear of the new king of Hayasa's generous support.

I wrote back right there in my own hand, inviting him and
his warlord Mariyas to Hattusas.

No longer did I dread going up to the city. For if my wife
and my court awaited me, soon also would a man whose kingly
overture to me was the first of its kind I had received from any
of my "brother" regents.

A king, to be effective, must treat with kings. If instead he
spends his days mediating underlings' disputes and defending
his kingship, it becomes as though he never sat the throne at all.
Though I knew this (it was a bitter knowledge I had swallowed
along with the god's meals which the king shares), in bringing
it about I had had little success. When I wrote to the other great
kings, it was as if I were a child. New to them, unknowable, I had
entered forcibly into their brotherhood. They would wait and see;
by my deeds, they would accept me or not. Or so I had wagered,
casually writing to each, making reference to the esteem between
our lands in former times, and of past treaties and my desire to
rework some or ratify others unchanged. All kings do it; it is
the form for friendly relations. But with each change of rulers,

countries consider anew whether it is to their betterment to *keep* relations peaceful—or to war. And if a king should determine, as I have had to do, that a treaty no longer serves the people he represents, then all the Oath Gods in the world cannot maintain those boundaries set out on bronze, or in clay, or on wood.

Good or bad, this is truth, which in my eyes has taken on a value which to all men is not apparent. Often it is said that gods make treaties, and we great kings, stewards of the gods, are merely instruments of their temper. This runs contrary to life as I have experienced it. If the gods themselves contest through men, then Tushratta—the greatest enemy of my youth—and I would have had the face-to-face confrontation which the Oath Gods denied us:

As deeply as one great king could hate another, I hated Tushratta of Mitanni. As fiercely as one god's steward could defy another, just so fiercely did we vie for the lands and people of the plains. And as thoroughly as I cursed him, I loved him; as fully as he earned my despite did he garner my respect. No king should die as he did, at the hands of his own children—alone, friendless in the cloudy streets of age. People say, wrongly, that the Oath Gods took Tushratta, and call it a lawful resolution of his affront to kin and gods; I do not believe it.

There are things that happen in life so poor in grace and empty that no god could condone them, unless he be meaner even than a man. So say I, the Sun, who have come from god-deafness to true stewardship over forty years of kingship, although in my first year I was as bereft of gods as a Hapiru wanderer chasing his Hidden One toward the Promised Land.

Upon arriving in Hattusas, I found little changed but the paintings on the palace walls. The Shepherd had still not come down from the temple at Arinna. The king of Hayasa's letter was as enigmatic as Daduhepa had adjudged it. Himuili and Takkuri were yet in the field. Titai wore that same haunted look in her huge eyes and if she had a priestess' robe around her, she was even more the foreign sorceress wrapped in it. The complaints of the Old Women had gotten no quieter. My court was a bitumen cup dropped upon the stair: fragmented but just possibly salvageable. It remained to me to fit the pieces back together. But although I had hardened myself to the loathing of my detractors and the temerity of my supporters, and accustomed myself to the people's fear of me so that I hardly noticed, when my children fled my presence on the day of my return, I was struck speechless. My face flushed hot and to cover my shame and confusion, I accused Daduhepa of turning them away from me.

In reply she spat: "I did not have to say a word, Tasmi*sarri.*" She never called by my throne name. "Your reputation speaks for itself. Should children not flee from an eater of children? Don't you wash that good iron sword in baby's blood to keep the metal shining?" Lines grooved her forehead, deep as scars; her skin was sallow, the bones under it sharp and graceless; black ringed her eyes. I had heard she never recovered from Telipinus' birth, yet refused to believe it. She seemed as aged as the scarp upon which Hattusas rests. Her hands, twisting together, shook so badly I could see their tremors.

Finally she ran dry of imprecation and I promised to speak to Arnuwandas and Piyassilis. Telipinus, barely walking, did not yet consider his father a demon, although I was strange to him: he had still been suckling Daduhepa's teat when I drove out to fight in the south.

I left the testy Great Queen then, forfending her when she tried to direct my attention to this woe and that. Although I wanted nothing less than a fight, in her presence I would soon have had one; I had had enough fighting for one season.

Standing aimlessly in the hall, leaning against the door I had closed on her, my eyelids weighed heavy. And though I wanted desperately to sleep, I could not think where in the whole of the palace I could find a bed. I could not sleep with my wife — not in that room I had just left; I had not the strength for Daduhepa, either in my body or my heart. The very thought of Titai caused me to wince as if some part of me were badly bruised. I should have gone to her; I had seen her only briefly. I did not. Her pain, a palpable shroud of barren alienation, I had not the fortitude to add to my own. Takkuri's sister was ripe with child, somewhere in the palace women's rooms among the various girls I had received as gifts (most of whom I had not even had a chance to look over).

A Meshedi in the corridor stepped back against one wall.

We scrutinized each other in silence—the guardsman and his king, neither acquainted with the other, each with a predetermined relationship of mutual service which had not yet been ratified in our hearts. He was about my age and size, noble blood stamped on him like a royal seal. We probably could have taken up one another's lives without any but our intimates noticing a swap had been made. "Meshedi, find somebody to take your duty, and come sniff out my brother Zida with me." A great king can quell a thousand rising rebels, but in the citadel if a Tabarna walks the corridors alone it is an occasion for the tearing of official hair and the gnashing of highborn teeth. To the extent that a bodyguard did not inhibit my movements, I was willing to abide by tradition. That night, if Hattu-ziti's intense young man insisted on sleeping on the floor beside my bed, I would not have argued.

In the end, he did almost exactly that, after we found Zida where I expected, in the house of the Gal Meshedi, fretting his commanders about increased security now that I was returned. Chasing out everyone but the bodyguard (who was some distant cousin of my wife) and my brother himself, we drank what wine remained from the meeting. Then Zida and I shared the small officer's room and the Meshedi curled himself up before the door.

The whole of the next day I spent in contemplation of the matter of my sons, utilizing the Shepherd's favorite ploy: I went into the sanctuary of the Storm-god of Hatti, and there I stayed until the Seven Stars twinkled in the sky. Entering the citadel directly from the eastern bridge, avoiding the city, I had preceded the bulk of the army by three days into Hattusas. When I went out early tomorrow to rejoin my army and its train of namra-borne booty for a triumphant entrance into the city, I would take my two eldest boys with me.

Having given orders to that effect, I slunk like a jackal through the night to my concubine and my bed. When I entered my apartments, although the hour was late, scented smokes thickened the air and cymbals tinkled. Titai fell to kiss my feet with heaving breasts and lips swelled as if by passion. She had been studying her lessons, she assured me, and I did not pursue it further, content to let her strip me and serve me as she would. In truth, I was more concerned with what I might say to my two sons to undo what the Great Queen had done, thinking hard about it long into the night while Titai murmured and tossed and sought me in her restless sleep.

But when I arrived at the stables in the morning it was only one son who awaited me: Arnuwandas, his young shoulders squared as if he faced his death rather than his sire.

Two shamefaced Meshedi were waiting with him; the other two had gone in search of Piyassilis, who had, they said, "escaped." I dismissed them with orders to call off their brothers who chased my second son. Too many times had I fled such men, twice my size, running me to ground on orders from king or prince.

My firstborn stood still for a moment, watching the Meshedi depart, his fingers stroking the amulet Hatib had given him. Then, looking up at me, in a small voice he said that one of his horses was lame and therefore he could not accompany me, all the while backing slowly into the shadowed stable.

Not following, I leaned against the stable wall and suggested he let me look at the ailing horse. The time it took for him to produce the animal was time I dearly needed. As I gave certain orders to the stablemen who appeared from the shadows once my boy had disappeared into them, I wondered whether Arnuwandas would return, or find that his fear was stronger than his pride and follow Piyassilis into hiding.

When at last Arnuwandas led his gray-muzzled old horse before me, I found I had been clenching my fists. A cursory examination proved the ancient horse a victim of age's infirmity: those swollen joints would get no better. But as I worked my way leg by leg around the horse, Arnuwandas moved also, always keeping the beast between us.

Then, having given the old horse ten times the scrutiny he deserved, I straightened up and, leaning my elbows on the swayed back, said, "When a horse, even a prince's horse, cannot serve, he deserves service. This old man has many sons, who carry on for him. If he were mine, I could put him in the south pasture of the Storm-god to live out his days; I would choose from among his children a fit successor."

The boy gave me his mother's cold stare.

"But," I continued, "I see you have problems similar to my own, and cannot risk a loyal servant's loss with no replacement in sight. So, if I may advise you, you might accept aid from me, an adherent who seeks your good will." By then the stablemen had brought up my blacks, not in the traces of my war chariot, but hitched to Arnuwandas' own. The near horse snorted, striking out with a forefoot, and his sire wrinkled up his white-whiskered muzzle and let out a trumpet that made me reconsider all I had said.

Only Arnuwandas remained unmoved: there was—and is—a great deal of Daduhepa in my eldest son.

Fleetingly, I thought he had not understood. When I was his age, had anyone given me a seasoned war team in its prime I would have been halfway to Arinna by the time the giver had finished speaking.

But as I have said, there is a great deal of Daduhepa in Arnuwandas.

So did he come to ask me: "What is it, Abuya, to become a wolf?"

I found a tangle in the old horse's mane and began unknotting it. "In the laws it says: 'if a man takes a woman and makes her run (elopes with her), and if avengers go after them, if two or three men die there will be no compensation, for he has become a wolf.' He has, like a wolf, taken what he needs to live; he will die, if need be, to protect it; he expresses his nature and cannot do otherwise. In the matter of wolves and the matter of kings, whoever stakes a territory, or claims that which his nature demands, cannot be held accountable for the force he applies to take and retain it—his success or failure are accounting enough. In Hatti, we do not bring a man following his nature to task for it: it is not right."

Still the boy looked at me unblinking.

Very slowly I removed my hands from the horse's mane and started walking around it toward him: "If you do not understand, then this is my fault. When I was your age I had seen the head wolf at bay, seen desperation upheld by strength and free from qualm. You have heard me call the Shepherd a wolf: he is a wolf for Arinna. Sometimes I think he is also a wolf for the Storm-god."

When I had reached his side of the horse and he yet held his ground, I squatted down. "What did you think it meant? And who is the wolf?"

Very gravely, through sticky lips, he replied, *"You* are the wolf," and I thought, *'Now* he will run.' So I stayed very still, like a man hoping to snare an eagle, saying only, "Who told this to you?"

"Mother. Hattu-ziti. Zida. *Everyone.* They say you are a wolf for the Hatti lands; that you run in your wolf-form at night and cover the moon with blood; that—"

"That is enough!" I dared not laugh: I made my voice deep and grave. "Do you believe it? That I run, I mean? If I were a wolf, would I not howl in the palace? The wolf of which they speak is a spirit-wolf, no fleshly beast. It resides in my heart. And if they say I am a wolf for Hatti, then they are not wrong, just speaking a subtle sort of truth. Men do not become animals, no matter what Hatib has taught you, any more than gods have the heads of beasts."

Arnuwandas was fingering his little cat-headed lapis amulet, and I thought that my wife had been right: I never should have let him keep such intimate company with Sutu. After a thoughtful silence, he cocked his head, and his eyes flickered toward the black team, their coats shining blue in the morning light. "If you are not really a wolf," he said, wanting to believe, but not quite daring, "then why does mother say that you are?"

I thought of a number of answers, and discarded each, settling on: "If your brother Piyassilis called you a snake because
you two were fighting, would you *be* a snake? Would you slither
through the palace halls?"

"No."

"And if you beat Piyassilis every time you fought him—I
am assuming that you probably do—"

"I do!"

"Then, if he said that the reason you beat him was because of
your snake-magic; that it was your fangful, venomous bite which
weakened him rather than your superior warrior's skill which
bested him—thus making nothing of a victory fairly won—would
it be true? Or would it only *seem* true, although he said it so many
times that others began to say it, and eventually to believe it?
And if people began avoiding you because they had heard you
were a sorcerer who could turn himself into a snake—people,
remember, who had only heard about you from others and did
not know you themselves—would it not then be as if you were
indeed a snake? Would you not be just as fearsome and powerful
as if you could really do snake-magic, simply because people
believed that you could?"

The answer might have been written in the packed earth
between his feet, so intently did he stare at it. "Yes. I think. . ."
He raised up his face, eyes tearing, and threw himself into my
arms, sobbing that he never did believe it; it was only Piyassilis
who believed.

Lifting him up, I carried him to the chariot and set him down
inside it and joined him in the car, whereupon I asked if he did
not think he might be able to sniff out his brother and handed
him the black team's reins.

While we were hunting Piyassilis, I mentioned that since
Arnuwandas had accepted the team from me, in the way of kingship he owed me a service: thus Piyassilis was soon convinced
by Arnuwandas that his father was no hairy-muzzled howler-
at-the-moon. Then with my eldest's permission I took back the
team's reins—only because I knew the way, of course—and set

a pace that had my two brave little kinglets clutching the braces for their lives, but made up for the time I had lost while proving my humanity.

We caught the army just entering the southwest gate and the procession took on the tone I had intended. Driving into Hattusas before the armies at harvest would raise the hearts of the dying. Ours was a triumphant return—and a rich one.

Also as I had intended, my sons were not unmoved. I made two wolves for Hatti there that day, for all the people to see. Arnuwandas drove the lathered blacks and Piyassilis bore my shield. The light of kingship shone from their eyes and the roar of it dried their mouths and made them breathless. Flushed with honor and glory, they cried out wordlessly to the crowd who ran up with outstretched hands to touch them. For Hatti, and for two boys destined someday to rule her, it was a good beginning.

But for Daduhepa and myself, the morning's revelations boded ill; indeed I had prepared much to say to her, but when the procession ascended to the inner citadel and the heroes formed up to get their due before the halentuwa-house court, my wife was not awaiting me.

The ceremony, however, was. It was my first of these as king: when last I had observed this rite I had been lurking among the lauded, ready to take down the king when he emerged into the day.

As they wrapped me in the Tabarna's robe and replaced my helmet with the conical crown, the pages within the halentuwa-house informed me hurriedly that my wife's condition had greatly worsened; that healers attended her and my presence was required urgently by Hattu-ziti as soon as I was finished with the ceremony. When I demanded to know if my chamberlain was with my wife, I was informed only that he was unavailable.

I sent a page to find Hattu-ziti and one to my wife's bedside and a third to my apartments to fetch Titai to the courtyard. By then the halentuwa-house was filling with dignitaries and the clergy necessary to the ceremony, each followed by a Man of the Golden Lance, a Meshedi, and a page.

I missed two responses before I could set my mind to it, but before my sons, the heroes and the ranks of the armies, my adherents and my detractors, I soon fell into the rhythms of call-and-answer I had learned by rote. Himuili was there, in the forefront of the triumphant, hairy as ever, with darkly handsome Takkuri close beside. Mammali, whose one eye was better than most men's two, stood squat and immovable with a cloth-of-gold patch over his empty socket. Lupakki had earned his honors with me in the Salt Lake campaign, so I decorated him first.

While I read aloud of deeds done in the Upper Country and congratulated my commanders, Kuwatna-ziti's absence struck me ill—the Shepherd did me yet another disservice. I had not officially commanded him to come down to the capital previously, fearing that he might ignore my summons, leaving me no choice but to punish him: no man may disobey an order from his king.

As Himuili received his honors from me and stepped back, I motioned to my brother Zida (who stood ever on my right in those days, as conscious as I of how easily we had usurped the kingship here a year before), then whispered a terse command while Pikku, the pale scribe who knelt close by, wrote it down. If Kuwatna-ziti stayed much longer in Arinna, it would be because he lay in his mausoleum there.

That done, I decreed a feast for the valiant, made the libations to the gods, backed into the shadows of the halentuwa-house to the singing of an appropriate hymn. Then foreboding struck me squarely: still no Titai nor Hattu-ziti had appeared; not even one of the pages I dispatched had returned. Hidden from public view, I threw off my robe, thrusting the crown into a page's chest, and walked as fast as is kingly down the covered hall that connects the palace and the halentuwa hut. When I was within the residence, I ran.

Encountering the page I had sent to find Hattu-ziti and hearing he had met with no success, I put him into the hands of a convenient Meshedi with orders to help him find another trade, and left it at that. Pages and Golden Lancers are exactly the useless decorations that they seem, but what else we would do with the soft-palmed sons of palace officials and numerous scions of gods who come out of the bellies of temple priestesses, I do not know. If a Golden Lance bearer errs, his sandals are unlaced and he serves his duty thus, mortified, and of this shame such men stand in mortal fear. So I was not any more surprised that the page had been unsuccessful in turning up Hattu-ziti than I had been at receiving his summons to an unspecified meeting place.

Hattu-ziti was, as I suspected, in his own apartments, which bore no resemblance to living quarters, but looked like an archive just after an enemy sack.

"We missed you at the Halentuwa-house. And my wife, also. Are the two events connected?"

He was sitting on the floor, amid piles of tablets forming a half-circle around him. I knelt down beside him. At one end of the crescent of piles, the uppermost document had its origin in the far south. Opposite I recognized a letter from Samuha. "North to south? What's this? Well? Can I get a civil answer? Why are secretaries summoning kings, great queens absent from their duties, and clay tablets purloined from the Sun-goddess' temple decorating your floor?"

"Does the Sun, my lord, have doubts about me? Because if you do, then what I have to say may cost us both more than this whole thing is worth."

"*What is it?*"

"Daduhepa is seriously ill. You yourself must have seen it. But you have not seen what the Old Women are making of it. Whatever possessed you to enter that namra into the temple?"

It had been so long since I thought of Titai as "namra" that for an instant I did not know whom he meant. "It is not within your scope to question my motives." I picked up a tablet, threw it down; it cracked in two.

"Is the king, my lord, aware that our Great Queen might well be dying? Every omen taken has said this, and the Old Women have been busy ascertaining that the cause of your wife's illness is sorcery: *Even now* they gather to divine whom the sorcerous killer may be!" Hattu-ziti had been with me a long time, since

Samuha, long enough to know I would hear him out, whatever the matter. Yet he hesitated, pulling at his ear.

I waited unspeaking until he continued:

"Surely the Sun recalls how often Your Majesty has left Titai in my care. . . . Those foreign ways of hers, she did not hide from me." He fingered a small bag strung on a thong at his neck. I have seen these bags in increasing numbers over the last few years; men today will wear anything around their necks: human teeth, feathers, all manner of cultic devices fashioned from clay; but in those days, charms were uncommon, heretical. "Nor am I the only one to whom Titai has given an amulet or potion. . . . When we lived in the upper city and you fought for Tuthaliyas, all the men came to her to heal them." Hattu-ziti looked up, as if expecting me to berate him.

Instead, I rose, saying, "Is that why my concubine was absent from the halentuwa-house? Does Titai attend my wife in her sickbed? Or shall I find them both in the temple of the Sun-goddess?" I hardly heard my own words over the pounding of my heart. I could not say to Hattu-ziti that I had not known about Titai's sorcery, or that I had known and forbidden it, any more than he could say to me that my concubine was about to be indicted for performing sorcery upon the person of the great queen, my wife.

"In the Sun-goddess' temple," said he, very low, "the Old Women and their acolytes and your Titai divine. Your wife lies abed in the residence."

I got slowly to my feet, hefting the weight of defeat up with me. If things had gone so far that Titai was divining her own doom in the temple, then the outcome rested in the gods' hands.

With muted thanks, I left him. At least they would not surprise me with it. I proceeded to my wife's side as if I were yet unknowing, and when the most nearly divine of the hierophants, and the two oldest among the Old Women, and a robe-swathed Titai whose eyes were so big they seemed entirely black, requested an audience, I had them admitted.

Their addition made eleven people in the Great Queen's bedroom, the rest being healers, handmaidens, and my sister who sat quietly in a corner biting her nails. When healers work there is always fire: this and that burned around the room; white and gray and black smoke mingled so that, though I had rolled up the curtains, the chamber was filled with an odorous pall. A middle-aged Old Woman droned tirelessly from her table by my wife's head.

When the doors were closed behind the newcomers, I silenced the Old Woman. Then all that could be heard were the fires crackling, the cauldrons' contents bubbling, and the labored breathing of my wife, who saw and heard nothing but bespoke us unintelligibly from her own private world. To the first of these intermittent speeches I made reply, but not thereafter. The limp hand pale at her throat was cool, dry, and unknowing when I took it.

Daduhepa had spent freely of her waning strength to appear before me haughty and contentious two nights ago; on my way here, I had decided that she must have contrived some illness to blame upon Titai. I had been determined to drag the truth from her, by force if need be. There was no forcing my wife even to recognize me; everything I had thought to say fled my mind at the sight of her, from whom all life seemed to hasten while I watched.

I heard a flurry of disturbance from without, and as one of the Meshedi slipped through half-opened doors I saw why, and instructed him to allow the crown prince and Piyassilis to enter. Fate comes upon us when it will; wisdom is no respecter of age. They had ridden as princes before an army whose triumph and glory were profit from a deadly harvest; now they would become acquainted with that commodity in which all kings trade.

Before the adults, my sons were dry-eyed, sitting where I placed them, one on either side of their mother, even keeping silent as I decreed they must.

There is a gift the gods have given me of which I have not heretofore spoken: in those moments when a man eyes the unknowable, the world gets back from me; I am like a man encased in armor from head to foot so that only his eyes feel the wind.

My heart becomes quiet. No pain nor fear nor doubt assails me, though later I suffer all which, when I am imperiled, the gods allay.

In the wilds of her affliction, Daduhepa moaned, and Piyassilis grabbed her hand and buried his face in it.

"Now that we are all at last assembled, Great Ones, perhaps you can tell me by whose order my concubine was absent from my side this day, and at whose behest minor priests attended me while those present tended more pressing concerns?"

A priest of the Sun-goddess, who regulates kingship and queenship, stepped forward and began to explain what had been done in the way of sacrificing and omen-taking in the matter of my wife's condition, the surmise of each investigation undertaken, and to what and whom the divined answers portended.

From his initial chronicling of unfavorable bird omens through a display of a clay liver, I kept silent. At last, when Titai's name had been thrice mentioned as having been the subject of an oracle considering her complicity in these affairs, I stopped him. "And will you tell me how you came to *ask* questions like these?"

"My lord Sun?"

"The Great Queen lies abed and the priesthood convenes a court in her chambers! Hattusas has become a shambles while I have been gone! How did you come to take these omens considering my concubine? Who gives you the right to adjudge sorcery? Is that not the king's prerogative? Or have you appointed yourself in my place, and just forgotten to inform me?"

The priest's shaven forehead furrowed, but he stood his ground. Titai, just behind him, stared steadily at me, half supported by the Old Women around her.

"My lord Sun, I took my orders from the Great Queen herself. This woman Titai's name was entered into the temple; she is a servant thereof. She offered her services in the matter of our queen's illness, and from her ministrations our Great Queen has suffered. It was by your wife's—"

"Titai! Is this true?"

The priest melted back, and Titai was borne forward by two stolid Old Women.

I forsook my wife's side and went to meet her. Her tawny hair was tangled and damp against her cheeks; her hands jerked convulsively at her sides, as if she would throw herself against me at any instant.

"I said, is this true? Did you do this?" We were so close I could have kissed her, but I did not. My eyes spoke to hers, counseling silently.

"Yes, my lord."

Arnuwandas tells me that I stepped back from her. I do not recall it. I remember my own moment of blankness—all she would have had to do was deny it. I had been afraid she would refuse to speak, as she sometimes did, and put herself in danger thereby. It had never occurred to me that she would admit to it, although it had occurred to me that indeed the priest might speak the truth.

"Do you know what you are saying?" I wondered into the utter silence.

"Yes, my lord."

The two Old Women took firm hold on her then, as all about us a buzzing like bees began. The high priest of the Sun-goddess of Arinna put away his tablets, fussing long to hide his satisfaction. I heard more than one sigh of relief.

I said, "There will be *no further* oracles on the subject. No trial at the river, no additional interrogation, no sessions in the cellars—nor another with me.

"Titai, take this moment to recant, or be '*Ti—*', bereft of name, banished from Hatti, my wife's ills taken upon your head—" Quickly, I pronounced my judgment, the lightest possible, as the priests and priestesses voiced their disapproval and my little concubine began visibly to tremble.

"Get back from her, you hags! Titai! *Once more: did you do this? Are you responsible for my wife's condition?*" At that moment Piyassilis' control deserted him, and he began to sob. Titai, swaying, reached out a hand, pulled it back, and once more affirmed her guilt.

"Why?" I spoke harshly, forgetting our audience, but she only whispered that she had done it for me.

"Take her," I ordered, incredulous that she would speak so and planning to seek her later and find out why.

As a man will, when the ground rumbles and his life tumbles stone from off of stone to lie about him in ruins, I searched among the wreckage of my heart, hoping to salvage what I might. I had done as well by Titai as any man could do. I would send her to one of the islands with which I had relations, I thought, and visit her whenever I could.

But when I went down into the cellars to say everything that I, High Priest of the Storm-god, could not say under those circumstances in which she was indicted, I found that she had had no faith in me. Who gave her the dirk I never determined. When I had arranged her on her prisoner's pallet and said what I had to say to ears which could no longer hear me, and when I had smoothed her hair back and kissed her cool lips and covered her bloodied chest with a blanket, I took the dirk and hacked off the braid I had been growing since first manhood and closed her little fist around it.

I went from there straightaway to the stables, putting Arnuwandas' blacks in harness myself. The day was nearly ended, and I drove into hills on which the dying sun dripped fire. Flaming tongues flashed from the mouths of purple dragons whose underbellies were of purest gold and whose venom, dribbling over the distant hills, made it seem that the mountains leaked flames of their own. Death always turns my eyes upward; perhaps I believed, even then, in kingship in heaven. But notwithstanding, on days of death I always recollect the weather, as on days when the gods have touched me outright.

I drove to a hill shrine a short distance north, past the burial grounds, past the rock sanctuary. Later I put a finer altar there, and caused other shrines to be built; my second queen and I put our seals thereon, and a town grew up where that night there existed only a slope and trail.

I tethered the blacks and walked from where the cedars break. It was deep dusk; above me I heard low chanting and saw a glow as the priests lit their torches. So I waited until the singing died away, then climbed up to the altar of the Storm-god of Hatti which crowned the hill. It was plain then, no columns adorned it, just the old worn stair and the rectangular terrace defined by the torches' line.

When I had satisfied myself that all the priests had gone down the other side to their lair, I spoke to him:

"Storm-god, my lord, hear me. See, I am praying to You. Take off this weight from my spirit. Show me the truth. A man comes to his god saying: 'I will do what is right. Show it to me!' And his god shows it to him. Show me in a dream, tell me by incubation. If evil has been done, let him who has sinned be shown to me: let punishment be meted out. Let the lightning come down and point him out to me. Let the thunder chase him across a hundred empty fields so that he gets lost and cannot find his way. If any have broken their oaths, let these persons be made known to me. If a woman has forsworn the king, may it be as if she has forsworn You, my lord. And whosoever has forsworn the king, Your steward, may it then be as if he has offended the whole company of the gods. May no seed come from his loins nor child from her belly; may the spirits of the dead come up from the ground and take them, any that You the Storm-god have decreed. And may I know it! May the Storm-god make a servant out of me; may I be a son whose deeds are welcome in Thy house. If a son comes to a father, then that father tells his son what is right; he answers his questions; he does not let him go home unsatisfied; he shows him the way. Show me what has angered the gods and let me take the cause of that anger away and make things right."

After I had done that, I poured out a libation I had brought. And while I was doing so it began to rain.

CHAPTER 12

"After I spoke the curses," I told Kuwatna-ziti over the rumble of my chariot, "I came back to the citadel and waited to see whether the Storm-god had indeed heard me. First a temple official coughed his spirit out during the night; then one of the priestesses was bitten by a brown spider, and she also died. So I thought the gods had heeded me, even though that very night my wife went up to heaven to become a goddess." This euphemism for death I could not speak in those circumstances without smiling; seeing me grin, the Shepherd frowned. Although he had come down from Arinna immediately upon receiving my official summons, by the time he arrived, Daduhepa was dead; Titai was ash upon the wind. He had brought a peace offering: the orphaned babe I had sought to ease Titai's hollow belly. This baby came too late for her, but showed me that Kuwatna-ziti had submitted to me in the matter of my concubine. So I took the infant anyway, a last service to my dead girl, giving him into my sister's care. Thus my relations with Kuwatna-ziti became once more as they had been before Titai's sorcery drove him away. And when he refused to utter her name or hear anything about her, then I would recall the orphan, Zidanza — the apology he was too proud to speak — and let it go at that. I needed Kuwatna-ziti. "So what think you? Did Tarhun hear me?"

"Tasmi, you question too closely the will of the gods."

"Still," I insisted, "it cannot be that my every curse is efficacious, any more than my every triumph in battle is to the gods' credit, but every defeat is debited to me. How is it that all good is ascribed to gods, yet all evil to man? *If* Daduhepa died of my curse, then she died because she had done evil, *not* because I pointed that evil out!"

"Tasmi, as Tabarna, you have the Thousand Gods of Hatti behind you; your curses brought a reckoning upon the guilty heads of those involved. Do not take the gods so lightly. If you are wise, you will henceforth save your curses for treaties and kings. Let us speak no more about it, but consider matters at hand."

Matters at hand were twofold: firstly, the chasing down of my son, Arnuwandas, who had bullied a gatekeeper into letting him out Chariot Gate with his blacks before first light, and had not returned when the day was half spent and my sister finally worked up her courage and informed me; secondly, the question of Hugganas, king of Hayasa, who slept away the toil of his journey in a palace bed between a pair of twins I had provided while Kuwatna-ziti and I, with six Sutu supporting us in chariots, went searching for my son in the cedar forest above the rock sanctuary, even up where the Storm-god lies in the hills.

All the while I was driving and Kuwatna-ziti was lecturing, I kept wondering whether my curses had *truly* brought low the evildoers in the matter of Titai and Daduhepa — and if so, whether it might not be a good idea to have someone remove those curses laid on me by Tunnawi the Old Woman, since it was her magic and her murder that started all the others dying.

I spoke of this to Kuwatna-ziti. He gravely agreed it would be wise to have the ceremonies performed promptly since her imprecations had related, as curses will, not only to me but to my seed.

This was good, sensible advice. Yet, when I heard it, I jerked my horses down on their haunches so the Shepherd nearly toppled and the teams behind split left and right to avoid trampling us. The Sutu oaths at my driving which rolled back to us on the wind were nothing compared to the vengeance I swore — not only upon Kuwatna-ziti and the institution of Old Womanhood, but upon the Thousand Gods themselves — should ill befall my eldest son.

Kuwatna-ziti said nothing until I had turned back to my team and shaken their reins. At my command they lunged forward, unwilling to be thought the least bit hesitant to obey. Then, very deferentially, the Shepherd remarked that he, too, was concerned about the young prince, but that the blacks were nearly ten years old, and Arnuwandas surely competent to drive a team so long under the Sun's tutelage.

I recollect looking sidelong at him to see if he mocked me, as I charged through the Sutu to the head of the wedge. He did not; he spoke in earnest. The time had come for Kuwatna-ziti to acknowledge the Tabarna he had helped make: he had just done it. It felt strange, though I had long desired it. In all ways but one did the Shepherd from then onward become as valued a vassal as any brother king later won to my cause: never, in all these years, has he stopped calling me Tasmi.

When we finally found Arnuwandas, and the wreckage of his chariot and the corpses of the blacks and, close by, a bear impaled upon a spear jammed into some rocks, no one said a word — not even the Sutu, who will mutter and make signs over a smoky fire if the wind blows wrong. This bear was about half the size retelling has made him; and all bears are slow, irritable, and hungry at that time of year. Still, it was no small feat, albeit the gods doubtless helped my son who, when we found him, was sobbing over the blacks, one of which yet struggled to rise while his blood soaked into the ground.

After I had lifted up the boy and determined that — though shaken and hysterical — he was sound, I carried him over to where my Sutu crowded around the slain bear lying face down amid the rocks with the spear's head protruding from its back.

Although I eventually convinced Arnuwandas that he bore no guilt for the loss of the team (finding it prudent to ignore how he had come to be there in the first place), I could never convince the Sutu that my firstborn son was not divine. From that day forward, none of mine enjoyed less than slavish devotion from the mercenaries.

We killed the crippled horse, then butchered the bear and took its carcass back to Hattusas, wrapping the meat in cedar bark to fool the other horses (who were not fooled but bore with us for Arnuwandas' sake). Thus when the Hayasaean chieftain sat down to feast with us, he sat on the right of my eldest — who in my mind had won a place at any man's table — and ate of his kill.

Afterward, the skin was displayed to all, exactly as if the hero who had performed the feat were old enough to be awake past the rising of the moon. My sister took that opportunity to pull me aside:

"How can you *do* this? He will be *worse!* He should be *disciplined,* not congratulated!" she hissed through angled teeth marring what had come to be an otherwise peerless beauty.

"Then he will be *worse!*" I mimicked her. "How perfectly did you behave when our father died? I seem to recall that you were much tended by everyone about."

"You recall nothing of the sort! You were not even *there,* hero, but ran for the hills and missed the whole funeral — all but the last day, and that only because the Meshedi dragged you! Shall I —" She faltered, began again, stopped, silenced by something she sensed in my demeanor.

"That is right, sister, I was not there. And if young Arnuwandas, who was like a mountain through the entire thirteen days of mourning, and who did more than anyone to console Piyassilis and the baby, feels like running off his grief, I will not move to stop him." I looked over her shoulder, draped in ebony curls, at my son, trying desperately to hide his fatigue and stretch himself a bit taller as our Hayasaean guests toasted his prowess.

"Look at him, sister: is that not a king, born, sitting there?"

She peered up at me out of almond eyes ringed with sooty stibium and red with weeping, and agreed that Arnuwandas II was a child of whom his grandfather would have been proud.

"You could make his spirit proud, yourself," I said, laying a hand on her slim waist and heading her back toward the feasting board.

"Tasmisarri — pardon me — *Suppiluliumas,* what *is* it you want? Surely my duties as nanny to your brats are not sufficient cause for this sudden show of brotherly affection." She slipped from my grasp with an irritable shake of her body, not unlike a dog shedding water. "No, my caretaking of your children is not what you have on your mind at all."

I stopped so that she must, for the Hayasaeans' eyes were on us rather than the slain bear's toothy grin. I said nothing, so she continued:

"I am right, am I not? It takes something more momentous than concern for your offspring to bring you, so solicitous, to my side." She had not forgiven me for deporting our mother; until she died, she bore that grudge.

"You are right — it is my concern for you."

Her laughter pealed. "For *me?*"

Glancing about my guest-filled hall, I thought I should have chosen a better time, prepared her aforehand. Although she was a woman, she came out of Asmunikal's belly, and if I had been born with her wits, I would have put the entire world under tribute by the time I turned twenty.

"You are getting too old to remain a maiden" — that silenced her mirth — "and too meddlesome to remain a princess. Have you considered wedding some suitable lord, perhaps some fellow king of mine, and thereby attaining the position for which, by nature, you are eminently suited but to which, while you remain a Hattian princess, you can only aspire in vain?"

"Bastard! Demon's spawn! You cannot mean this. You cannot!"

Kuwatna-ziti arose from the board and started toward us with a countenance showing equal measures of annoyance and trepidation.

"I mean it. Take your time. Be calm. I will not force you to accept a man for whom you have no tolerance. I am only telling you to start looking closely at those men you see brought to my table. Eventually you will have to choose among them."

She stared at me, then at the Hayasaean chieftain, a man ten years my senior with a lion's head on which black hair curled thickly, shot here and there with silver; then at young Mariyas, his son — the warlord who had distinguished himself at Himuili's side — who was of an age with her, but shorter than she and thrice as broad. Then, with a wail, she fled into the Shepherd's arms.

CHAPTER 13

Shall I tell you of every battle that I did between that night and the consummation of the marriage of my sister to Hugganas of Hayasa? Shall I detail each campaign by means of which I shored up the foundations of my kingship and ensured my sleep? I paid for Hayasa's chariots and foot soldiers in the same coinage as procured for me autonomy on the plateau, the necessary precursor to the restoration of Hatti's boundaries and her glories: my youth. Like the various meals set out for the gods, I gave it up in sacrifice. And like the steward-king who comes and eats of the sacramental meal, the ravenous New Empire gobbled up my years, swallowing them in great untasting gulps, I sometimes think: without notice, without pleasure, without satiation; the only import of all my sweat being the satisfaction of an empty bowl so the heavenly herald may cry, "It is finished!" as they do when the Sun consumes the Storm-god's meal and steals away back to the palace. When the bowl of my life is licked clean and all that remains is a wine-soaked pyre and the flame, someone will doubtless say that ancient formula over me. And if indeed I have gone up and become a god, then the Storm-god and I will laugh about it.

Then shall I be free from trepidation and forgetful of long evenings spent agonizing over what is right and what is not, and the compromise between the two that kingship perpetually demands.

It was hard for me to send my sister to Hugganas, "king" of Hayasa; harder than I imagined it might be, when first I was bedazzled by his offer of fellowship and beguiled by the strength of his army. A man does not become king in Hatti without laborious tutelage in foreign affairs: yet nothing I learned had prepared me to send a woman of my own blood into the arms of a barbarian who arranged marriages between his own sons and daughters and who took his brothers and sisters, even his offspring, to his bed without compunction. Hence the stringent warnings and conditions I levied on Hugganas, tribal chieftain more than king (though for diplomacy's sake in Hattusas he was referred to as my brother). And yet, I have had no vassal more steadfast. From those days down to these, relations have been friendly between our two countries, notwithstanding the trend lately to speak of the "Azzi" interchangeably with "Hayasaean"—even in those days Hayasa and Azzi were a confederacy: mere fashion decrees which name is applied to those lands over which my sister and her husband rule.

That he had come offering aid to me, appearing on his own initiative at the citadel in those most troubled times, has been construed by many, including the Great Shepherd, as a favor bestowed on me by the gods, my lords.

On manifold occasions the Hayasaean would shake his lion's head to and fro and, with a twitch of his bearded lips, turn peril to advantage, uttering judgments more sagacious than a priest's, unveiling alternatives where I had seen only entrapment, always in a manner which allowed him to remain the faithful vassal and I the magnanimous overlord. Indeed, he made it seem that I myself had suggested every canny stratagem he authored, and he was simply recapitulating. To my fulmination against my precariously unsettled court and what amounted in my eyes to near imprisonment by kingship, he added the honey of patience, and that same cup which seemed brimful of bitter dregs when I drank alone became a soothing draught when he swilled with me.

We would sit like two hunters awaiting the eagle under cover, though our cover was no brake of branches but the gap-toothed walls of Hatti, and our prey, far distant lands, was as yet only imagined at the horizon of our line of sight. The wooing of the country of Kizzuwadna, the projected capture of Ishuwa and, interspersed, analyses of our interminable indecisive battles with the enemy from Arzawa—all came under discussion that season of our first meeting, the second of my reign while my sister peeked, coy and decorated, from behind column and fenestration and took a sudden interest in the affairs of the land.

For his assistance I have well repaid him, looking with favor upon his country and with leniency upon its merchants and profiting him exceedingly thereby. Yet, I am what I have become: overlord to the very gates of Egypt; ruler of kings, and Hugganas is no more than he was in those days—more comfortable, perhaps, but a paltry hero, nonetheless.

The protracted delay in formalizing our relationship was not upon my sister's account—she warmed to him that winter and in spring urged me to consummate the affair as soon as I might, nor upon Hugganas' account—he was anxious to make firm our bond and turn my attention toward Ishuwa and Kizzuwadna (both in the east of Hatti and south of his own lands). Indeed, to facilitate movement of our joint forces down toward the Hurrian-controlled plain, he even committed his troops to aid mine in our war with the far western Arzawaean enemy, then my greatest concern. But on my own account, I held the matter pending while I wrestled in the arena of words with my court and warred the seasons through.

When I went finally to join Takkuri and Himuili who were overseeing the troops and beating back the Arzawaeans hill by hill, I took Hugganas himself with me. For us two rulers, overseeing the western campaign was more a welcome respite from priestly duties and civil judgment (and endless evenings of wheedling merchants and foreign emissaries with duplicity in their hearts and doggerel on their lips) than a duty.

Thus we became acquainted with each other as two men; as two commanders; as two charioteers—which was what I had in my heart. In war a man's lusts ride close to the skin, emprise sparkles brighter than the golden clothes of the Sun-goddess, and there is no time for posturing. Hugganas revealed himself a fearsome opponent, a general who could draw from his men the extra measure of valor that brings with it victory. In everything but his comportment during our long crackling nights of encampment, when his aches were eased with wine and his Hayasaean nature sharpened by it, did he meet with my approval.

But his handling of captives and his choices of bed partners were scandalous to a Hittite. Though I bespoke my concern to no one, green-eyed Himuili unknowingly voiced my qualms for me: "They're welcome enough until the spoils are divided and the namra and captive soldiers apportioned. I have heard they do such things to men in Assyria; I have not heard that Hittites do it. Not even an Arzawaean deserves protracted mutilation. No man of common rank knows the answers to such questions as condemn those poor bastards to death inflicted on them limb by limb. Half of one man, half of another on the same pyre; arms and legs scattered about the landscape. . . I tripped over a foot lying in the dirt on my way here. Their screaming keeps my men awake at night."

"May it keep the Arzawaeans awake also," I growled at him.

"Are you condoning this torture?" My commander's eyes flicked from fire, to tent, to me, then back to his feet. The king's tents are traditionally pitched amid the baggage train surrounded by his foot and his Sutu and what Meshedi he has brought along. I habitually forsook that security and took my rest wherever I chose among the men. It was my way of keeping them alert and, in a sense, romancing them. None knew when he might turn and find the Sun of Hatti, as dusty and trail-worn as himself and his comrades, hunkering down at a stewpot presided over by some commander of ten and settling in beside him for the night. Recalling all their names was impossible, but I began to know just what I had fighting for me, under this commander or that; and they began to know just what they had, in their king. Also, since no one knew just where I might be resting of an evening, my chances of ascending to heaven in my sleep were greatly lessened. If my officers needed me, they sent up a call.

I had determined when the sun went down to seek out Himuili — whose feelings could be divined in the dark during a thunderstorm by one who knew him — and learn just what he thought of our Hayasaean allies.

Arzawaean fires burned, presumptuously arrogant, on a rump of hills that paralleled those on which we were entrenched, visible from the revetment of timber astride which I found him, staring outward at the enemy encampment.

As soon as I scrambled up beside him he began telling me, in a low but emotional tone, all I had come here to the far edge of the camp to learn.

I assured him that I condoned no dismemberment, but quietly added that should we lose our engagement, Himuili himself would be called upon to halve a likely prisoner or two for the armies to ride between, thus assuring both our revenge upon those who had defeated us and, by the way of the spilt guts of the enemy, transferring to them any curse which might have hampered the Hittite army.

"It is not the same!" He scoffed, then took himself in hand. "Does the Sun see no difference between two or three men sacrificed in the unlikely event that we should lose this, this —" his hand spread out to encompass the Arzawaean hills — "exercise, this training for my troops, and a multitude tortured? These Arzawaeans have no god strong enough to preserve them: The fact that the Hayasaeans cut Arzawaean generals into pieces like they were spring lambs proves that!"

"I wish I were so confident as you."

Himuili, having no need to do temple service, had the option of growing whatever amount of hair he wished. His forehead was bound with a band and his black hair tumbled loose down his back, shining and damp, doubtless the result of a trip to the latticework of springs that dotted the gently rolling chain of hills we had bought with Hittite lives. He scratched a season's worth of beard, staring out at the enemy fires, not answering. I waited. At last he said, "Suppiluliumas, my lord Sun, are you *sure* about this? Do we *really* need them?"

"Are you sure we could triumph without them?"

"Yes! I am." Defiant, he locked his stare on me. Great power has that look on women—I have seen it.

The king and commanding general of the Hittite armies, however, was no woman: "And could we hold the whole plateau, and the plain below, and the coast down to Tushratta's navel, in such a fashion?"

His eyes widened when he realized what I meant. "No, we could not do that," he admitted, quite low, obviously taken aback by the audacity of my implication. In the firelight, his lips twitched beneath his beard, then twitched again; a chuckle rose up from his belly and danced upon the air: "No easier than Mammali could wed that Arzawaean noblewoman he's got following him around camp."

My turn came to stare into the flames: I was thinking of the girl Khinti, whose beauty had nearly brought me death on the shores of the Salt Lake, and whose body I did not yet possess for reasons of political affiliation and public opinion similar to those my one-eyed field commander must be facing. Each of my original thirty from Samuha had I given field commands, according to their abilities, putting them all under Takkuri, whose second in command was Himuili. Himuili's punishment—that of not himself being field commander of the armies—I had levied on him in response to his rejection of the appointment I had offered him as a Chief of 1,000. Seemingly he had accepted his demotion without an objection. Actually, he performed Takkuri's function and the latter subordinated himself to Himuili, and everybody knew it. It was Himuili who kept track of the hearts and minds of the Samuha veterans who made up the core of my army and, in the off season, the backbone of the Great Ones. Especially now, since I had drafted into service every lord's son capable of drawing a bow, the influential Hattusas-born commander was like a living omen on the state of the troops' morale and, more even than previously, a shaper of opinions.

"Tell me of Mammali and this woman," I suggested.

He snorted, spat, and looked at me as if weighing his words. "Mammali happened upon her in an estate he commandeered; she has spent not a single night among the namra, but has her own chariot and a driver he's assigned to her. He accords her all the rights of a Hittite lady. Show me the Hattian woman who hikes up her skirts and becomes a camp follower. . . . Men snicker at him behind his back; soon, they will dare it to his face! He should have better sense . . . an *Arzawaean,* yet!"

"Himuili, you disappoint me. Once, all these lands were Hittite. The people who lived here when the enemy came from Arzawa and made Uda and Tuwanuwa their frontier were Hattian people previously. Can you tell an Arzawaean from a Hittite by looking at him? No, you cannot. The blood that they carry is Hittite, the names that they bear are as Hittite names. . . ." He was chewing on a stalk, clearly not in agreement. "Good commander, what we build is empire. Love your Arzawaean captives, for they are Hittites once again."

"As I must love the Hayasaeans?" he asked.

"Exactly the same."

"It is *not* the same, my lord Sun."

"Then how is it different?"

"It is . . . we have been fighting Arzawaeans for years."

"How much longer than we have been fighting Azzi-Hayasa?"

"Suppiluliumas, I am having no easy time loving Hayasaeans," he rasped. "These so-called 'Azzi' fighting women are enough to give any man restless nights. If you would welcome Arzawaeans-who-were-once-Hittites back into the country and make them again your subjects, you had better find a way to stop the Hayasaeans from hacking them up!"

"That is true. See to it that there is no more torture. But be gentle with our Hayasaean neighbors. Love them as your brothers. You will need the practice. Soon enough you will have to love all manner of former enemies. Perhaps someday even Hurrian subjects, or worse. And as for Mammali, I will marry him to this Arzawaean woman myself, if he wishes. We must all learn new ways in which to deal with both our former subjects, and those who shall become Hittites for the first time. To that end, accompany me on a tour of the camp of the Hayasaeans; I will introduce you to an Azzi woman or two who may change your mind about their sisterhood."

When the Hayasaean king and I came down from Hattusas, we had brought with us the remaining fifty chariots of his pledge and five hundred foot. Among them was a unit commanded by and composed of these ladies of the battlefield, daughters of the Istar who presides over war; they bind down their breasts and pull back their hair and wield bow and axe as well as any man. Contrary to popular opinion, what warrior-women I have encountered evince no repulsion toward men, nor had any such girls whom I have bedded sacrificed a breast to their goddess to improve their aim. But the stories of their prowess in war are not exaggerated from what I have seen, and I found one among them whom I gladly would have made Great Queen and Tawananna beside me, although the matter was decided for us by her goddess, who called her up to whatever fate awaits the Daughters of the Field, doubtless saving us both from a long, difficult interlude of coming to terms with the disparities in our beliefs.

Once, long ago, before the first empire and all that came with it, women ruled the cults and men bowed down to them. A vestige of that culture hides behind the ridges of Hayasa, and it is said that the Daughters still demand the begetting parts of a man in some of their rites. It was, I think, a blessing from my gods that my Azzi girl did not survive that season; for rituals I later saw performed by certain of the Daughters might have caused me great unrest had I attempted to make a queen of her, as the Hayasaean continually urged me.

True to my word, I found Himuili a fighting girl with the help of mine, and took leave of him to seek out Mammali and see how much of what Himuili told me was true. Searching for him, I skirted the edges of the camp, for I had my red-haired warrior woman by my side. Also, I was loath to meet Takkuri, whom by rights I should have sought before taking council with his second-in-command, Himuili: I did not have any intention of listening to my field commander's delicate reproaches, framed around inquiries as to the health of his sister—and of his nephew, Kantuzilis, the son she had borne me and named after the Pale One himself (presumably in ignorance of the enmity between me and my deceased uncle, the prince). As things presently stood, this woman had whelped me a son of the second degree. But if Takkuri had his way and I elevated her to great queenship, the child would then be a son of the first order and eventually eligible for any honor including kingship, should it come to pass that my eldest prove insufficient to the task or die prematurely.

A predecessor of mine, one Hattusilis, objected vehemently to the institution of the Tawananna. This barbaric custom, he said, would be the end of us all. Women, he said, should not wield the power with which the title "Tawananna" invests them. The title itself devolved from a mighty queen in ancient times whose name it was, and now a woman who is Tawananna can render judgment and perform ceremonies and act unilaterally in a great king's stead when he is at war. A Tawananna, unless demoted, retains her title and power until her death, and a Tabarna who inherits a predecessor's Tawananna may not raise his own wife to equal heights until the old Tawananna dies. Now, whether Great King Hattusilis was right about the barbarism of the institution I would not venture to say, but those duties that my Tawananna Daduhepa had formerly discharged for me were a weight heavy upon my shoulders, amounting to fetters binding me close to Hattusas, now that I had no great queen, no Tawananna to perform them. One example is the driving of the deified fleece to its stations in the different towns at New Year, which takes nearly forty days, each one filled with rite and benediction. I had not realized how much of the load the Tawananna bears until I had lost mine.

By the same token, I was hesitant, cautious in choosing another woman to wield such power, for she can be to a great king the most insidious of enemies should their wills not coincide. Daduhepa, who loved me and in her own way did me honor while she lived, had on occasion opposed my wishes. What worse might befall me, should the next Tawananna of Hatti be Takkuri's vacuous sister? Aside from the hold she afforded me on her brother, the woman's main function was decorative, and her concerns ran to the mundane. I was seriously considering sending her to one of the southern winter palaces before I returned home to Hattusas so that I would not have to listen to her simpering, and my temper was so frayed that I would have decreed it in Takkuri's presence should he question me about her. Thus I took pains to avoid him while I kept company with my Hayasaean girl, ruminating upon the advantages of that diplomatic marriage for which Hugganas of Hayasa pressed, weighing it against some future, indeterminate wiving with more far-reaching benefits.

The glorious days and nights I spent with my warrior girl convinced me to postpone the whole question, and after her blood had soaked my tunic as she died in my arms on some nameless hillside I had no more interest in such as she: it is romantic, so appealing to a man who lives a warrior's life, to take a woman who can fight upon his right during battle and warm him during the long evenings, but when that man sees her soft flesh rived from breastbone to gullet in her own chariot, all he can do is try to fight his way to her in time to hold her while life flees, lest when she cries out in fear as the dark comes over her eyes, no one is there to answer. . . . I dreamed it a score of times before I lost her to a length of Arzawaean bronze: when it occurred it was almost a relief.

I buried her there on the hillside; her sisters assured me that she would have wanted to go full-fleshed back to the soil. Although it sat uneasily with me, I allowed it, and then got so drunk I thought not of worms and grubs and slugs and those long-lashed, round eyes.

The next day I married Mammali to his Arzawaean girl and endured her confidences as to her new husband's precarious health and his enemies who resided within the very camp itself, paying her worries little mind. Mammali, my one-eyed commander—for whom I had taken an arrow in Samuha and who in turn had taken a beating for me when the original thirty of us first laid siege to Hattusas—was well known to me, his resilience near legend in the Upper Country. So I made light of her words, distracted, with my lost girl on my mind, and the tenacity of the Arzawae-ans, whom we were having to push back hill by hill. And, even had I agreed with her, it would have been an inopportune time to meddle in affairs rightly the prerogative of the field commander Takkuri and his second, Himuili.

Instead, I held council with Hugganas as to how we might put an end to this costly war. There was sorrow in the king's al-mond eyes, not just for me, but for what might have been lost to our two countries. He ran thick fingers through his hair and knuckled his brow, and tried once again to follow the shifting of border battles that had led to this state of affairs. The latest of these, which had occurred even while my girl died fighting beside our troops, caused me to write the Arzawaean as to these Hittite towns he kept reclaiming for Arzawa just as soon as I had finished subduing them. Having written, I sent the message to the Arzawaean camp, which I could see across the valley, by way of a prisoner.

And my words were strong: what had been border skirmish-ing would soon become something else. I had lost more than a hilltop fighting the Arzawaeans and, for my warrior girl, my heart needed retribution. I gave the Arzawaean warlord, whose name was Anzapahhaddu, an ultimatum: either he return my subjects, those in the towns he had recently taken and those who were in former times Hittite citizens, or be my avowed enemy and be destroyed. This I did hurriedly; for I wanted to set out straight-away for Hattusas, taking Hugganas with me, but leaving all the

Hayasaean support troops I dared. To accomplish the plan I had in my mind, it must look as though the armies were splitting, reassigned; and everyone must see the two kings heading, unconcerned, back upcountry.

So did it look.

Takkuri and fifty chariots accompanied us at a leisurely pace northeasterly while Himuili with some few Hittites and all our Hayasaeans, foot and chariots both, went deeper into the Arzawaean country. He was to advance until he came to a strategic mountain range in which the Arzawaean leader himself reportedly resided.

The rest of the troops, each under their respective field commanders or commanders of ten, went about their business, policing the frontier and taking whatever advantage came to them under each commander's initiative in the different towns.

No sooner had we bid farewell to Takkuri at King's Gate in Hattusas than a messenger came clattering in, gasping out the news:

"Himuili and the Hattians, my lords, have been defeated!" With that not-unexpected news, the man—a Hayasaean upon horseback—then slid off his mount, bowing to his liege while all around us Hittites pricked up their ears, sauntering over to the gatehouse to meditate upon the stone warrior who looms just within the inner arch: a man on horseback is to this day a remarkable sight in Hatti.

I waited until the Hayasaean messenger had recovered himself and around me more Hittites gathered. When I deemed the moment most propitious, I loudly bade the man repeat all he knew of the affair. But the Hayasaean courier only mumbled a few unintelligible words.

"You! Get this man water." A gate guard went running. "And you, find my Master of Horses and get him here." The Golden Lancer minced away. "You, fetch the Gal Meshedi Zida." The Meshedi saluted, disappeared. "And you, go after Takkuri and bring him hither!" This last, to a passing charioteer.

Hugganas of Hayasa conversed in low tones with his equestrian scout, his wide brow furrowed, no hint of satisfaction on his kingly visage. In response to his king's prompting, the scout related the details of his message before the crowd gathering about the gate: "Himuili took us into the country of Arzawa and we attacked it; we held it. But when Anzapahhaddu and his helpers heard this, they came after him out of the mountains. He was. . . My lords . . . Himuili was with the Hittite troops and we. . . Our Hayasaeans were not accompanying them . . . the Arzawaeans surprised him and defeated him on the way. . . ."

Hugganas looked steadily at me with an expression that said, 'It is as I have predicted.'

"And how many died?" I boomed into the silence.

The man blinked and sputtered that he did not know, for he was expecting me to question him as to the whereabouts of the Hayasaeans while Himuili was being so ignominiously defeated. But since I had been expecting it, I said no such thing, only ranted awhile about the Arzawaeans and gave orders to mobilize all the troops and chariots of Hatti at once, that I might take them myself down into the country of Arzawa.

Said Hugganas to me that evening on the palace ramparts: "Well played, my brother."

By that time triumph had ebbed from me and I was wondering whether Himuili himself had survived. "This is the last time," I vowed, "that I will have to resort to subterfuge to field an army." It was not the last time, but the first.

"It is the last time you will need to, with Arzawa. Any king in receipt of such an ultimatum as you sent Anzapahhaddu must respond with battle; any court, hearing of such a defeat, cannot do otherwise than support a retribution."

"A curse upon all scheming! Why is it not enough to say 'come let us fight'? Why these games and why these sacrifices? It should be sufficient that two warlords desire a settling of affairs."

"And you call me uncivilized! Try it thus, and you will spend your years chasing here and there amid the mountains for your adversaries. . . . Not every king is as anxious as yourself to test his gods and his armies on the field. Most are content enough where they reside in their fortresses; to roust them, one must bait the kind of trap we laid out for the Arzawaeans. Most men, my lord and overlord, will accept a gift; few will accept a challenge unless they have nothing to lose."

"By making them a gift of Himuili and my own men—" At that moment my sister sniffed us out and, having heard this last, had to be placated.

But though I got my way, mounting by this subterfuge the punitive expedition my court would never have sanctioned otherwise, and though Himuili survived to fight another day, never suspecting the use I had made of him, I was ill at ease until I saw with my own eyes that these things were so.

By the time I gathered the armies and joined the offensive, the enemy had a firm hold upon the mountain called Tiwatassa, and my own men had taken its sister peak and built there three fortified camps. When I drove up with my chariotry and my foot behind me blackening the distance, the howling from our beleaguered troops could be heard to the borders. So great was the army I had gleaned from every corner of Hatti that when we had marched through the country of Mira, their prince came out and threw himself down before me and I took his submission formally before the armies, his and mine. This we were all pleased to construe as an omen from the gods. I added the Mirans to my care and their troops I levied on the spot into service.

But when we saw our besieged camps and took reports from Takkuri and a pale Himuili—who would limp evermore from the work the Arzawaeans had done upon him—the warm glow of excitement fled from me and a dark, chill purpose took its place. Sometimes it is said that in the early days of my kingship I was more idealistic than conditions warranted, but this Arzawa campaign saw the end of the boy-king who loved war above all else. It is one thing to risk yourself; it is almost as easy to risk a company of chariotry, be those men mere numbers on a tablet; it is another thing to spend your friends like enemy prisoners, playing the Storm-god, deciding who will live and who will die.

I warred in Arzawa until the ground turned bare and hard and the horses snorted smoke from their nostrils — longer than I had anticipated, longer than I wished. We fought through to our own troops and I sent to Anzapahhaddu the requisite challenge: "Come let us fight." But he did not come, although a battle between us two would have saved countless lives. He wrote back to me in an insulting fashion and so began the long profitless days during which neither of us could gain a decisive advantage.

I must simply hold until the weather took its toll: when the Arzawaeans' bellies grated against their backbones, they themselves would slay their craven lord, or so the omens said. The two eagles caught and slain to determine that in the end we would be triumphant died for nothing: the Arzawaeans somehow snuck an envoy by us, and thus we in turn were besieged from the rear by fresh enemy troops. I gave Mammali chariots and men and sent him down the mountain to strike toward Mira for an additional troop levy, but the enemy overtook him on his way, capturing his troops, chariots, and even the deportees he had with him.

By then we had a permanent headquarters on the mountain, and it was there I received Mammali's defiled corpse. I sat over it a time, wroth with myself and sick from fighting.

"Every man who dies in battle cannot be your responsibility," said Himuili. "You torture yourself and the men feel it — there is unease in the camp." Himuili, his own condition yet salt in my heart's wound whenever I saw him, had insisted that Mammali was the man to lead that fateful expedition which had been his last.

I said nothing to him: he owed what life he would lead thereafter to the sickness of the spirit then upon me. Never again have I felt such loathing for war and death. Some say it is a thing of youth; personally, I think every man whose word sends others to their deaths must experience it, or become as the stone god Ullikummis, with no heart in him to speak like a mortal man's.

I pulled my men off the mountain, and many did not like it. Some liked it so little they went over to the enemy and spoke evil about the Hittite army, calling my decision cowardice before the enemy host. Because of this, the war did not end cleanly, as I had

wished, but dragged on until the Arzawaeans were convinced by
heavy losses that there was no fear in the Sun or in his armies.

By the time it ended, I had regained for Hatti all that my
stepfather and my father and my grandsire before him had lost:
although I failed to claim Mount Tiwatassa or secure a formal
treaty, I reduced Arzawa to the proportions she had formerly enjoyed, and I was content then to police those borders and maintain them. This I have managed to do, though even to this day
the Hittites who live in Arzawa cannot forget that once they had
no suzerain. I treated Arzawa in a less friendly fashion than I
have other conquered lands initially, but my heart has softened
to them: they were once Hattians and are Hattians once again;
if they are less placid than other peoples and continually testing
their bonds, then that is because they are Hittites by blood—I
expect no less of them.

The woman whom Mammali had wed I took into the palace
and she became my strongest adherent among the Old Women,
whose rituals the Arzawaean Hittites had maintained exactly as
they had been performed in former times when Arzawa was a
province of Hatti. This woman was useful to me in other ways:
she negotiated (unofficially, of course) with the parents of the
girl Khinti, whom I was now more anxious than ever to receive
into my bed—and into great queenship.

One might think that any woman would be more than pleased
to rise to such a position. I thought so. If I had not been occupied with the Arzawaean matter described above, and with my
sister's marriage to Hugganas, or if I had been longer in Hatti
that season, I should have taken offense at the protracted delays
her family proffered.

However, when I said farewell to Hugganas and winter closed
down the passes, I considered the matter anew, determining to
consummate it that season—or not at all. Gimant, the winter, is
not called the "season of impregnation" for nothing. And with
my sister (and six half-sisters and two priestesses and an honor
guard of thirty chariots) gone to spend the winter up in Hayasa,
hoping to divine whether she could find fulfillment ruling at

Hugganas' side, the burden of my motherless boys settled fully upon my shoulders.

Arnuwandas, my eldest, knew little of hunting and nothing of the tactics of war. His brothers were no better tutored, and although this state of affairs was my responsibility, I thought a mother would help set them right. Takkuri's sister was doing her best, but judging by the disarray of the residential palace and the boys' neglected schooling, she was insufficient to the task. Her own son was a deep-night wailer, lusty-lunged and as yet too young to be less than a full-time occupation, or so she protested when I brought her failings to her attention.

Biting her full lips, she apologized so sincerely that I took my first long look at her since I had given her the child she had so unwisely named Kantuzilis. Seeing fear glaze her brown eyes and stiffen her posture so that she reminded me of a namra peering through the bars of her pen, I took pains to put her at ease. But she would not—or could not—relax with me. So I dismissed her, disgusted, before the meal I had ordered us both was served.

A man in a position such as mine has little time to dwell on matters peripheral to his survival: there are always affairs pressing, situations to be sniffed out so complex that the familial and the domestic seldom come to the fore.

But that evening, as the season's first snow fell on Hattusas, I walked my ramparts—the Sun of Hatti, triumphant overlord of an empire well-started. I had Arzawa on her knees and Mira licked my sandals; my country was protected on the east and on the west. Only Ishuwa, Armatana and Kizzuwadna stood between me and the Hurrian empire of Mitanni—and in Hugganas I had found an ally as anxious to burn and pillage there as I. All these feats I had accomplished, and yet I lacked what any groom or toolmaker had; pleasures enjoyed by the lowliest soldiers posted to frontier garrisons were denied me. All over Hatti this night men were reacquainting themselves with their loved ones, huddling warm beneath bedclothes with banked fires on their hearths and flames in the bellies of their women. But in the palace there were no tears at my safe return, no heartfelt embraces. By then,

I would estimate, my concubines numbered fifty. I had chosen none of them myself: a king gets them as gifts. Often such gifts cannot be trusted; more often, they are in some way flawed. The best I could expect from those was concealed fear and loathing—a fine enough thing in the field from a namra but less than a man wants when he yearns to drive out the chill of war from his gut.

And, though I was just beginning to suspect it then, there is no flame but that in a lover's heart fierce enough to melt the ice which collects around the throne of kingship.

Of friends, I was bereft: even Kuwatna-ziti could not be trusted. I knew no man over whom I was not sovereign, who did not desire special favors or my attention to areas in which he had concerns; to some I owed my own debts, destined never to be settled—as in the case of Himuili, whose health would not again be what it was before the Arzawaean campaigns.

Spitting square into the face of despair, I sought out my brother Zida. I never made it back to the palace from his Gal Meshedi's chambers but instead, well warmed by wine, went out with him into the town in nondescript garb, as I had been wont to do when I was yet a princeling.

I found no satisfaction reveling in the streets with my brother, for I had not been able to reveal my feelings, only managing to arouse his curiosity as to what might be in my heart. To all his queries I could make no satisfactory answer: I had none to give. Something, I knew, was very wrong. What that thing was I could not have said in those days if my kingship depended upon it.

I endured this uneasiness throughout the cold months. It rode with me while I instructed my boys in stag hunting and while I did my own hunting in the archives. There I sniffed out its trail, chiefly among the shelves of precedent and treaty; sometimes between the lines written by kings of former times. This stalking in the mountains of clay tablets only caused me to become more restless, and I turned to omen-taking and awaiting answers in my dreams and sat long nights awake in the Great Temple in the lower city, hopeful of an answer through incubation.

Men say I am less than pious: that winter I had every tablet of clay and wood recopied for the Sun-goddess. Even the bronze and silver originals that had been carried away by the Gasgaean enemy in their sack of Hattusas I ordered restored from copies and placed again in Her care, although this enrichment of the goddess puffed up her priesthood as if it they, not Arinniti, were being increased. To the Storm-god I offered numerous sacrifices, pledging all manner of service if only he would speak in my heart or, failing that, take the sour taint of sleepless nights from my mouth. But neither the Storm-god nor his wife, Arinniti, spoke to me, although I listened well the winter long.

Even the blue-cloaked lord who padded silent into my future hid himself from my sight. You may think I make too much of this, but being deaf to the gods while at the same time their steward and disseminator of their will unto the people is no easy task. Others heard the gods: peasants heard them; men of my army harkened to their whispered wisdom and lived to tell of it, swearing that without divine guidance they would surely have perished. I have seen Old Women curse men thrice their size and seen those men fall senseless into the dust, never to rise again. That season, I was greatly concerned with rightness in all things and wanted above all else to see in myself some sign or talent god-given, some ratification of my kingship by those immortal beings whom I ostensibly served.

Forthcoming from the gods was only silence. I was rewarded with an all-pervasive lack of response to whatever I attempted. And yet, in that regard, I now think I got what I then truly desired: in my heart I was no gods' steward; and if they heard me at all, they heard that. In the silence, I heard my own voice and began to heed it. I had placated the clergy by my evinced interest and rich gifts to the temples; I enlisted their aid in freeing my hands insofar as the armies were concerned, saying that the Storm-god had recommended this course or that. And the god did not gainsay me, so perhaps he did prompt me, in his way.

By the time the frost had turned to mud on the tundra, I knew my own mind; and those things that had sent me into the temples I sought to remedy on my own.

I called my court in for an early session to discuss the need to put aside prejudice and accept the folk I had brought—and would continually be bringing—into Hatti as citizens. Slaves we had aplenty; and deportees, sullen and lazy doing share-work. Citizens, on the other hand, fight fiercely where their own profit or loss is concerned. I proposed as an example the treaty I had drawn between myself and the king of Hayasa, who would retain domestic sovereignty but give up the right to conduct an independent foreign policy. Once Hugganas accepted the treaty, he accepted my terms of tribute in men and chariots yearly: he would return all the occupied land, boundaries, and deportees to me. But I felt the Hattian people must accept my terms also—even the gods of the Hayasaeans they should accord respect as they did their own.

I insisted upon the right to make such decisions on my own initiative and without any counsel from the nobility, laying out the next season's campaigns for their support without any feigned interest in their cries of penury and hardship. There were grumbles, but the hierophants of the Storm-god and the Sun-goddess of Arinna, my lord and lady, aided me, and we pushed the agenda to completion without serious opposition. After all, I was giving my sister, my own flesh and blood, into the arms of a Hayasaean. Since none of them were giving up anything, but were prospering, and fully expected to be further increased by continued Hittite conquests, there was little the lords could say.

I called all the smiths together—the toolmakers and those who specialize in good iron; the smelters of tin and lead, silver, gold, copper, and bronze—putting them under my Master of Horses, Hannutti, who set them to work for the armies: the three-man chariot would soon be the rule and not the exception in Hatti. The producers of good iron I kept late at that meeting, questioning them as to the mechanics of their skill; letting them know I hoped that iron soon would become as common in Hatti as bronze; proposing incentives that sent them away scratching their heads and exchanging the secrets of their craft with one another. This was the first time, to my knowledge, any king has attempted to standardize production of that capricious metal since Hattusili commissioned an iron throne and scepter three hundred years ago.

Mammali's widow had repaid me tenfold for taking her into the palace simply by being the first Arzawaean Old Woman to practice her skills from Hattusas. So I sent her down to Tuwanuwa to bring to some conclusion the matter of the girl Khinti, either by bringing me back the young lady herself or information as to why her family was procrastinating.

I sorted out my concubines and appointed two of them to the care of my sons, for good measure adding two Meshedi whose duties forthwith would be to watch over the Hattian ladies I had chosen while overseeing the physical education of the princes Arnuwandas, Piyassilis, and Telipinus.

I received an emissary from my sister in Hayasa, assuring me that she, at least, was content with Hugganas, and had consummated the union between our houses. For my part, I had only to send a copy of the treaty I had drafted, and all would be well with our two countries, eternally.

Therefore I wrote to Hugganas, beginning with the customary phrases: "Thus speaks the Sun Suppiluliumas, the king of the Hatti land," reminding him that I had taken up a lowly chieftain and made of him a noble hero, renowned, distinguished in loyalty both in Hattusas and among the people of Hayasa, and stating for the record that I had given him my sister in marriage. In the manner of these treaties from time immemorial, I first praised him, then set out the conditions of our agreement: that he must acknowledge me alone in lordship, and then my successor when I designated him; that my other sons and my brothers must be as his own brothers. And I warned him, moreover, to acknowledge no other lord, whatever sort of man he might be, behind the back of the Sun, warning my new and noble vassal, Hugganas, that if he did not protect the Sun of Hatti henceforth,

if to him my head was not as dear as his own and the matters of
our mutual concern did not in the future take precedence with
him—indeed if he did not love as he loved his own person 'the
head of the Sun, the soul of the Sun, and the person of the Sun,'
or if he heard evil from someone about me, and secreted it, or
failed to tell me and to point out a defamer to me, then the Oath
Gods of the treaty would destroy him.

At the closure, I reiterated:

"And you, Hugganas, protect in friendly fashion only the
Sun, stand behind only the Sun, acknowledge no other. And I,
the Sun, will protect you in friendly fashion, and correspondingly protect your sons. But correspondingly, your sons will
protect my sons.

"And behold, I have placed these words under oath, and behold, for the matter we have called the 1,000 gods into assem-
bly." Here I listed the gods, those unto whom I laid the keeping
of these oaths: the gods of the barbarians; the Hapiru gods; the
gods of river and field, of earth, mountains, clouds—all the
gods of the land; even the gods of the great sea I called upon to
witness our treaty.

But upon rereading it, I thought it not strong enough, so I
added a number of cases in point illustrating what behavior the
gods of the treaty must oversee, and what these oaths demanded
from him in this case or in that. Furthermore, I detailed extradition procedures and military levies and tributes with extra care.
And still I was not content, needing to make clear my mind and
even to relate to him a special case with which I was concerned:

"Furthermore: this sister of mine whom I, the Sun, gave
you in marriage, she has many sisters of the family and of the
seed. They too may be coming to visit because you have their
sister as wife. In the land of Hatti, one custom is important: the
brother does not take sexually his sister and his female cousin:
it is not right. But he who does such a thing, in Hattusas he does
not remain alive; he dies. And because your land is barbaric, in
it they take sexually their own brother, their own sister and female cousin. But in Hattusas that is not right.

"And if ever a sister or half-sister or female cousin of your wife should come to visit you, give her to eat and to drink; eat, drink and be happy. But do not desire to take her sexually; that is not right. From that men die. And do not seize it in your mind. If someone else leads you astray to such a thing, do not listen to him, and do not do it—it too is laid to you under oath.

"And watch out about a palace woman. Whatever sort of woman it is, whether she is free or a hierodule, do not step close to her, do not say a word to her. Nor should your slave or your maidservant come close to her. Watch out carefully about her. As soon as you see a palace woman, jump well out of the way, and leave her the way far off." Then I told him the old story of the Hittite noble who had met his death from looking wantonly upon a palace woman in the courtyard where the king's father could see him defiling this hierodule with lustful glances, so that he was executed. "Even from looking from afar a man perished. And you watch out," I warned, making it clear that not even in Hayasa would this sort of behavior be acceptable to me. "Therefore, the wives of your brothers, your sisters, do not take any longer. In Hattusas you go up into the palace and here the matter is not right. No longer may you feel free to take a woman from the land of Azzi in marriage. And let that one go, whom you had formerly; let her be your rightful concubine, but do not let her continue as a wife. And take your daughter away from your son Mariyas and give her to his stepbrother."

This I followed with standard military clauses, finishing with: "And behold, these matters which I have laid upon you by oath, if you, people of Hayasa, do not keep them, then may these oaths destroy your persons, your wives, your sons, your brothers, your sisters, your families, your houses, your fields, your cities, your vineyards, your threshing places, your cattle, and all your possessions, and from the dark earth may they raise up the spirits of the dead on you."

Then I swore once more to do no evil to the people of Hayasa, providing all aforesaid oaths were kept, wrote "finished" in the wet clay and sent Pikku, my squat, light-haired scribe, to fire the original and make copies, one of which would wait here in Hatti for Hugganas' arrival.

Pikku stood poised a moment, scanning the tablets for il-legibility or mistakes in my presence before he left. The time is long gone when a king could afford illiteracy, trusting treaty composition to scribes. When he was satisfied that all was in order, he bowed as if to take his leave.

"Scribe, send immediately to my sister, congratulating her upon her marriage. But send no copy of this; it must await Hug-ganas' arrival here. Do you understand?"

The light one smirked, pursing his lips: "My lord feels his sister might not agree?"

I laughed. "It is not to her benefit to disagree, but I would not like to be her when Hugganas reads these terms. Send suit-able wedding gifts, and a notice that the treaty itself is ready for signing in Hattusas."

The scribe muttered something. I was reminded how much ill Pikku had done me when he was yet my wife Daduhepa's per-sonal servant.

"I did not hear you," I said, and motioned him toward me.

"My lord Sun, it is only that we have already sent gifts to Hayasa, and they have sent gifts here—"

"Then send more! Is it the Sun's sister who wed Hugganas, or a hierodule? Go on. Get from my sight."

The perplexed scribe hustled to obey me.

It was none of his affair, but I handled the matter thus be-cause I did not expect to be in Hattusas when Hugganas and his new queen arrived.

CHAPTER 14

The gatekeeper of my prospective father-in-law was truculent, then dubious, then uncertain. Before admitting me to the
courtyard, he personally carried my message to his lord while
I — leaning against the side of my chariot, unconcerned to all
appearances but with both hands in plain sight — counted the
number of nocked bows trained on me from the bastions and the
parapet atop the rampart, thick as three men, surrounding the
merchant's estate. From what I had learned of this lord, he had
good reason to maintain his home like a fortified camp.

Slowly and elaborately, an eye upon the two spearmen who
stood at my team's bridles, I brushed dust from my plain black
mantle. When the gatekeeper had challenged the solitary charioteer who demanded entrance, I had answered him truthfully that
I was Suppiluliumas of Hatti.

In the ensuing pause engendered by that revelation, the scuf-
fling of feet upon the bulwarks and men's voices could be heard.
When the gatekeeper returned, his narrowed eyes betrayed his

disbelief that any single warrior in worn, unornamented gear, white with dust, might be whom I claimed; but I only waited patiently until the wings of the planked gate opened inward and the spearmen at my horses' heads led them beneath a stone arch into the estate's courtyard.

There I took my ease with a score of bronze-tipped arrows trained on my back from above, as the two spearmen belittled my horses and wondered for my benefit just how many Suppiluliumases there might be in Hatti, and what unpleasantly lingering death their lord would decree for a mercenary (such as I obviously was) who would be so overweening as to lie his way into their lord's presence. From this I gleaned more substantive evidence, should I have needed it, as to the nature of the warlord whose imposing, nigh impregnable fortress stood on the shores of the Salt Lake.

His was a well-planned enclave: once inside, I understood why, in all the years these lands had been embattled, it had never been taken by our enemies or by Hattians seeking to employ it as a command post.

From within the inner courtyard arose a commotion of shouts and running feet. Then the copper-encrusted gates drew back to reveal a magnificently robed figure striding toward me, followed by the inevitable entourage of lackeys. Behind him, plantings rustled: through the foliage I glimpsed eyes peering out and caught snatches of high-pitched chatter as might come from women or adolescent boys.

This lord brushed smooth his robe's purple sleeves in a habitual gesture of irritation and leaned down to whisper in his gatekeeper's ear. My host was as tall as I, but fair, with wheat-colored hair and eyes like a panther's: not brown or yellow or green, but a mixture of all. Attendants hurried up to his right and left with beribboned standards and a sunshade appliquéd with rampant stags; others followed carrying a gilded throne, banners blazoned with the clashing-stags device of their master's house, silver flagons and rhytons, and bowls on trays. When all these had come from the inner court to the outer court, the gates to the

inner courtyard swung shut with a thud of finality. The lord's
retinue assumed a complex order around the chair beneath the
sunshade. Finally, he himself sat down on his gilded throne. All
of this with nary a misstep: the thirty-odd before me were better
drilled than many countries' crack parade troops.

As he crossed his legs I saw, peeking out beneath the gold-
beaded hem of his robe, fine shoes with upturned toes like a
king's, and wondered just what I had gotten myself into by coming alone to confront this merchant prince (who by his display
bethought himself royalty) in his citadel.

All the while the gatekeeper was hurrying toward my chariot
and the spearmen at my horses' heads warning that I had better
dismount from my car, did I know what was good for me, and the
archers holding their bows steady and their lord examining me
from above steepled fingers, I was casting about desperately for
a way to halt this train of events before I found myself having to
make war upon the man whom I had come here to make my in-
law. For not believing I was who I claimed to be, I might excuse
him; but should he insist on carrying this posturing further—if
anyone seriously expected me to supplicate the seated lord from
a rug that slaves were just now unrolling at his feet—I would
have to orphan my prospective wife before I had even met her.
In front of his servants, it would be difficult for the man to admit
an error. Belatedly, it occurred to me that Khinti's sire—whose
loyalty was at best unsure—might actually know who stared
back at him from between my horses' ears; might even have pro-
crastinated in hopes of provoking this very sort of confrontation.

Still I had not dismounted. The gatekeeper came with twisted lips right up to my car; one of the servants whispered in his
master's ear; his lord's eyes flicked upward, behind me, where
bowmen bestrode the battlements.

So I said, "Behold, father, I come to make clear my intentions, and to consummate the matter pending between us. Did
not my Old Woman inform you?" Throwing the reins contemp-
tuously to the gatekeeper, I stepped down from my chariot and
walked slowly toward him, wondering what it was about a girl

seen briefly by moonlight that had me offering up my back to a merchant prince's rabble, when I had half a hundred at home than whom this girl Khinti would likely be no better.

The sandy-haired lord tugged his beard, spoke in three servants' ears in turn and rose as those three sprung away: one back through the inner courtyard gates, one to the gatekeeper who stood now in my chariot, one to climb the stairs fretting the defensive wall.

Motioning his retinue back, he walked toward me, his lips white in their lair of beard, hands twisting the shawl draped crosswise about him.

When I judged he would halt, I stopped, crossing my arms, and said very low, "You are making this unnecessarily difficult for us both."

"I was not sure. I am not sure. You appear more a mercenary than a king. How am I to know you are the Sun of Hatti?"

"Let your archers loose their shafts, then wait to see what happens."

"What would happen? Can I be held accountable if a bandit breaches my walls and tries to make one of my girls run? For an avenger, there is no punishment."

"You are assuming someone would *ask*. We could make good use of this place as a garrison — if my zealous armies could be restrained. Rebellious towns are often burned flat and clean, especially when they host the estates of traitorous merchants who sell Alashiyan copper to Arzawa. Too much of that cargo has ended in the bodies of Hattian soldiers for the local lords to take your part, should word leak out."

He betrayed no shock, which raised my esteem for my one-eyed commander's widow, who had guessed the nature of this family's hesitancy to become royal — more than any of my staff had managed to do.

The beard fringing his lips was shot with silver. "My lord Suppiluliumas," he rejoined, smiling so that his face crinkled up as papyrus does when thrown into flames, "with all respect. . ." In lieu of obeisance, he let his gaze rove down to my feet, then back

to meet mine. ". . .I have written you that the difficulties inherent
in your proposal are insurmountable. Your presence here only
compounds them. Whatever possessed you to drive down here
alone?" Smooth as poured wine flowed his threat, made while
gesturing toward the wall at my back. Behind him, the gate to the
inner courtyard opened; a second chair on the shoulders of four
slaves appeared. Before the gates were drawn shut, I glimpsed
between them a girl's form, a pale oval face peeking through.

"I came here to make a queen, to bring a Tawananna home to
Hatti. I am not leaving here alone—and if I do not leave here at
all, you will need more than these few brigands to protect you."

The merchant followed my glance and, seeing that the slaves
had brought up the second chair, asked me to accept his meager
hospitality, his mien austere. I grunted noncommittally and, as
we proceeded in silence and at measured pace toward the chairs,
weighed my chances. It occurred to me only now that the man
might think he had too much to lose; that his actions might actually be so questionable that he could not risk further discovery.

But as I broached the subjects of his holdings in enemy
lands and his subversive activities in pursuit of the holy shekel
and mina, my host grew restless in his seat and his cheeks colored. When I explained that the bride-price I offered included
immunity from prosecution on account of any and all previous
offenses, he hastily moved the discussion indoors. There we
sat in a lavishly-furnished hall as fine as any in my residential
palace while I detailed the uses I envisioned for his widespread
and efficient smuggling operation and how Hatti could profit-
ably employ a man who had the confidence of not only the Arzawaeans, but all the western kings. For Khinti's father's interests
were multinational in scope: he was a full brother to the present
ruler of the island fief of Alashiya; he had blood ties to the pale-
haired robust sons of Ahhiyawa who controlled the far western
islands; he catered weapons and information to these and more
distant lands. I wished mostly to audit, occasionally to edit, once
in a great while to author, the communications they received. I
offered him a mandate to continue his various nefarious activi-

ties without qualm and profit exceedingly therefrom, for it must seem as if nothing had changed.

"But were I to give you my daughter, would it not appear just a bit suspicious?"

"Ah, but you will be giving your permission under duress—you have certainly proved your reluctance to call me your son. In any case, you are too important to those you serve to lose credibility on that account: a king often accepts less than he might wish in assurances from those providing services which cannot be gotten elsewhere."

"I'm not sure, my lord, that these matters are as simple as you make them, but I am intrigued." His eyes had begun to sparkle; I had noted it but gave credit to the wine. Periodically, he would chuckle and his glance would go distant, roaming his memories and his expectations. Then, when I was sure I had convinced him, his visage darkened once more and he noted that night had fallen—it was time and past time that his guest be fed.

I was not hungry. I had been walking a precipice with him and still was uncertain; I had no desire to eat at his board. Yet I could not refuse, and I chided myself: if I dared not trust him that far I was buying myself endless sleepless nights with the spawn of his loins in my bed.

Over the meal, he came around to what troubled him: "My girl, Khinti, is not what you are expecting."

"I have seen her; she will do."

"It is not her face and figure—which, to her advantage, are her mother's and not mine—but her temper and nature . . . traits she inherited from me."

"Meaning?"

"Meaning, Suppiluliumas, my lord, that she has said she will have no greasy old king if she must spend her own life to buy her freedom. Now though you are not yet greasy and by no stretch of the imagination old, I know my daughter. If she is unwilling to accept your proposal, not the whole of the Hattian army nor the will of the Thousand Gods will prevail against her."

"I have had a surfeit of unwilling women. It is a plague upon the nobility, I fear, one we spread among ourselves by so elevating our great queens. Every woman feels herself a queen at heart. When one of their number is so privileged, all crave similar power."

My prospective father-in-law put down the silver goblet from which he had been sipping. "How old are you?"

I told him I thought about twenty-five, adding: "I seek a mate who can rule in my stead, not merely warm me of an evening. I have three princes to raise, and an empire to secure so they may have something to inherit. If I cannot interest your daughter, then she is useless to me. But if I can, and she has your"—I sought a delicate phrase—"canny grasp of realities—"

His laugh boomed loudly. "That she has. And she speaks, shall we say, all the requisite languages. Nor are her blood ties to the islands unwelcome to you." He was nodding. "Well then, speak to her, my friend, and good fortune to you. But I warn you, my girl is a daughter of your Sun-goddess of Arinna. In my country, we say Hebat-Tasimis the Bloody is her Lady. So be warned: my daughter Khinti is more full of wiles than a lioness with an empty belly."

I raised an eyebrow at that, and inclined my head politely, saying only that I would see what could be seen, calling him "friend" as he had me. I did not quite believe that the man I saw before me had so little control of his daughter.

As he walked me to the doors of his study, he put a hand on my arm: "If all comes to naught with her, for the Sun of Hatti I have three younger girls who are yet malleable. I would be amenable to a similar bargain over any one of them, and more sure of a satisfactory outcome."

"My father, have no fear. It is a matter of principle with me now. Three years I have been wooing this child of yours and all my court knows it. I will take her back in the very chariot I drove down here, and she will not be unwilling. I have had some experience—"

At that moment my host pulled the doors inward and a girl, hardly more than twelve or thirteen, jumped up from her crouch and dashed down the hall. With a shout, her father leaped after her and there ensued a brief struggle, at the end of which the girl was banished to her rooms in tears, and I found my own eyes wet with mirth.

All the way to my accommodations my prospective father-in-law held forth on the tribulations of rearing girl-children, to which I could only say that I had been favored with no princesses thus far.

"I will send her to you, my friend," he promised at last, and took his leave.

My apartment had two rooms, lavish enough in a manly way, its walls covered with hunting scenes and floors strewn with trophy pelts, horned and fanged. Outside at each end of the corridor stood armed guards, to whom my host had introduced me as he commended them into my service for the evening. I paced the quarters, feeling as if I had made camp between the jaws of the dragon, Illuyankas, and thought pernicious thoughts. After a time I fed the hearth and relieved myself, then opened the shutters to roll up the curtains for the night.

Sampling his wine, I wondered once more as to the wisdom of this undertaking. When at last the double doors rattled, then creaked open, I was brooding over my drink, sprawled on a settle strewn with fox pelts and half expecting to see the pikes of the guards, for I had nearly decided I had made a mistake. It would not have been the first time a king's pride had been his undoing.

Thus I was up on my feet with dirk in hand, spilled wine dripping between my toes, when she stepped through the doors and closed them behind her.

"Truce, my lord Suppiluliumas? Surely what my father has told you of me has not made you fear for your life?" Her eyes were the colors of her father's, but thrice as wide. Her hair, black as my own, tumbled unfettered over bare shoulders, shapely and pale.

Flushed, I said that one might expect she would come announced, accompanied by handmaidens, or at least a chaperon. Hastily sheathing my blade, I stooped to retrieve my fallen goblet.

Our hands reached the cup at the same time, touched. She drew hers back; the bracelets she wore tinkled. Crouching there, I cast aside pretense, rendering her the complete and admiring scrutiny her dress—or rather the lack of it—demanded. The girl who knelt at arm's length opposite me wore a pleated length of sheer stuff wrapped once around her, bracelets on wrists and ankles—and that was all. "I had thought, from what your sire said, that you would come to me swaddled like a priestess or bearing arms like your goddess. If I stare, then I can do no different. The three years since I last saw you have only exalted your beauty."

On the lids of her downcast eyes, gilding caught the light as the banked fire flared up. "My lord Sun, you have me at a disadvantage—*I* had not ever seen *you* until you arrived this day." Raising her head, she touched her proud throat with her hand, running spread fingers down her breast to smooth the softly shining gown which concealed nothing. "And as for my attire, this garb is appropriate for greeting royalty in the palace on Alashiya, so I thought I would accord you the honor your title demands and dress as well for you. Do you not approve?"

"I approve most heartily; it is only that the memory I have carried is pale before the reality."

"Dear suitor, you are pleasing in my sight also." She sighed. "But I fear this affair can never reach a satisfactory conclusion." As she spoke she rose and, taking three long strides that belied the delicacy of the primped lady before me, sat abruptly on the couch. Her adult manners regained, she stretched out languorously and with a disarming smile gestured that I do likewise.

I pulled up a chair carved with stags and straddled it. She was fair enough to warrant all that had been risked; indeed, I no longer wondered what had driven me to seek her so ardently. Between certain women and men passion explodes like the stars that fall from heaven, bright and awe-inspiring and god-given—and brief. One woman in a thousand has had that affect on me. It is not love, but some affinity of flesh to flesh. Yet this obviously intelligent girl, who sat before me in as studied and alluring a fashion as might a temple prostitute, could not be taken merely to quench the fire she lit. And she knew it. Remembering all her father had said of her, I no longer discounted his cautions. I had a stock of well-turned phrases from my days as a young and eligible hero; I spent some of them in amenities, allowing her to serve me wine, letting her take her time coming around to it.

"Suppiluliumas, my lord Sun, Great King. . ." She spoke some of my titles with obvious relish. ". . .I have said that this marriage cannot be, and yet you have not asked me why. Are you content merely to look at me, to talk awhile and depart to your citadel and your wars? Or do you see something, now that I am in your presence, which inclines you not to press your suit?"

By then, I had been through countless negotiations with my own nobility. I said nothing at all, only drank my wine, watching her nipples harden as they felt my scrutiny. Among the armies, it is said that this is the best indication of a woman's heart: if you can raise their nipples with a glance, then they are yours already.

My silence did what I hoped: it shook her calm. She sought the open window. "My lord, my family's business will stand no close examination. It is as simple as that." She did not turn; her voice was thick, her words faint. When I came up behind her and put my hand on her bare arms, they trembled. When I turned her and saw her countenance, it was tight with restraint; in her eyes tears glistened.

"What is this? Trembling lips and sorrowful eyes before I have even kissed you?" I did that, and the body I pulled against mine was more than willing.

Released, she sank against the window frame and put the back of her hand to her mouth.

I drew that hand away. "Your father and I have no secrets, Khinti. But if we did, his burdens are too heavy for your shoulders. I came down here to make a queen. I need a wife for my bed and a mother for my brats. It is said that Lady Khinti has vowed to die rather than give herself to some greasy old king. At least I can offer you immunity from that fate."

She did not thrust herself against me, as some lesser woman might have. She took a deep breath that reminded me of how long it had been since I had lain with such as she. Pushing back an obsidian curl from her brow, she said, "Then, my lord Sun, let us discuss the details," and offered out a hand only slightly trembling.

When all her astute questions were answered and her objections overruled, I found that I had been wrong in thinking myself to be experienced, wise in the ways of love: I knew nothing about it; only lust had I mastered. Although she was strange to the touch of a man (I took blood from her that proved it), she had made, I must suppose, a study of the subject, for she was anxious as a young mare and as wondrous to watch.

She wanted, so she affirmed in short gasping breaths, a teacher; and though almost all women will ask a man that, few mean it.

I have never had a more willing or talented pupil. On her own initiative she bent her lips to the close exploration of my manhood, a thing I would not have suggested so soon to an unlearned girl I had in mind to treat with utmost gentleness; but she crouched down between my legs, saying softly: "May I? Is this right?"

So I helped her discover what it was her mouth sought there. She stiffened upon the revelation that all things have an end, but after a moment of choking surprise during which I twisted my hand in her hair and softly urged her to accept the gift she had earned, restraint left her and all things were as a man most hopes they may be. Khinti's valorous attempt to swallow her surprise endeared her to me as nothing else might have. When afterward she buried her head in my armpit and commenced sobbing, I found myself regretful and even saying so to her.

To stop her from burrowing, I sat her up, holding her at arm's length, and when I had her calmed she assured me it was not the taste of my seed that had brought her to tears.

"What then, is it?" I demanded, holding tight to my patience and reminding myself that she had just this night passed from girlish fantasy into the truth of womanhood.

"I must make a sacrifice to the goddess." She sniffed and rubbed her eyes with her fists, smearing her makeup so that she hiccoughed an unladylike oath and wiped the remains of the gilding away with the remnants of her gown.

"And is that a cause for tears?"

"No! Yes. . . . My lord Sun, it is joy that makes me weep. You cannot know the mind of a woman. You have not lived with the constant threat of being sold off to some influential lord who has a score of others and a fat belly—and something which your father wants badly enough to be willing to throw you into the bargain." Her red-rimmed eyes, peering intently at me, seemed no less beautiful than they had when the evening began.

I touched the regal line of her cheek, for a moment struck wordless. We do these things to the daughters of our seed and have done them for countless years, with little thought to how such a prospect must cloud their days and turn their dreams to nightmares.

"A barbarian girl, a peasant's child, a slave or a namra in the pens has a better chance of wedding a man she loves than a noble's daughter. They tell us it is the price we pay and call us ungrateful if we bemoan our fate. Do you blame me if I shed tears of joy, that the man whom my father has chosen for me is a man I can serve in love, rather than fear, and bear children born of passion rather than duty?"

For that I had no answer but to further embrace her, assuring her meanwhile that she would always find welcome in my arms and in my heart.

CHAPTER 15

The unprepossessing practicality of Khinti's father was a sweet loaf upon the table of my aspirations: two men of pragmatic disposition sat down to discuss bride-price and dowry. In a morning we had worked out the details of courtesy and appearance. Thus I left there with the mistress of my heart and a small swift escort of chariots and horses, but without the canopied wagons of fine wood inlaid with ivory and gold and laden with sisters of the seed and handmaidens which must inevitably follow.

As to the escort, they also were inevitable, but though the ten teams were mine to keep along with the woman who rode within the shelter of my arms, her hands upon the reins and her laughter upon the wind, I was not easy about the men who had been charged with our protection.

But Khinti's father would not hear of us taking the trail alone, and I had to agree that it would look ill to the people. Although in my heart I wondered if perhaps he had not rethought the matter and chosen to dispatch me neatly somewhere along the way, I could make no objection which would not be an admission of distrust.

So I drove upcountry with the skin on the back of my neck trying to crawl off my head and my in-law's liegemen spread out behind, and bided my time.

When from out of the forest shoring the Salt Lake fifteen chariots thundered, surrounding us from before, from either side, and from behind, I had only time enough to shout to my escort an order:

"Halt! Keep your hands away from your weapons."

There passed a long moment in which I wondered if my father-in-law's men would obey me; then their commander echoed my words, and the world drowned in dust as they pulled up their horses in compliance.

When the dust had settled, we were encircled by a perimeter of charioteers bristling with drawn bows and spears. Khinti said my name, nothing else. She squared back her shoulders and slipped from before me that my sword arm might be unencumbered—and would have freed my shield from the straps binding it to the chariot's side, had I not stopped her.

The foremost of the dark-clad warriors removed his helmet and wiped his brow and let his long, narrow eyes roam slowly over the surrounded drivers, then made a hand-signal to his men and snapped the reins on his horses' rumps. In a wood gone silent all that could be heard were the footfalls of his team and an occasional stone dislodged by the low, lean war-chariot's wheels.

When he brought his car abreast of mine he pulled his horses up short and squinted around at his troops, whose unwavering bronze gleamed in the sunlight, an unspoken promise trained on those he had entrapped.

I had not moved at all until then. Khinti, wide-eyed, only watched. I took a long slow backward glance at those warriors of my wife's retinue, then turned back to the black-haired charioteer whose braid hung near to his waist and who leaned one hip against his car's curved wall, plumed helmet under his arm.

"Lupakki, meet your new Tawananna. Khinti, this is Lu-pakki, commander of ten of the armies."

"My lady," said Lupakki, and lowered his eyes. When he raised them disappointment and reluctance mixed therein as his suspicion that all was well with me became certainty. He raised his fist and lowered it, and every Hattian soldier sheathed blade or lowered bow, and relief filled the clearing wherein men once more breathed easily.

"Gentle lords, let us all become acquainted. It is a long way to Hattusas," I suggested, and as ranks broke I introduced my personal thirty to my wife, whose laughter pealed out across the gathering and infected both her father's troops and my own.

We spent that night in Tuwanuwa, for I had it in my mind to perform the festivals which had not been undertaken by a Hit-tite king in all the years since the Arzawaeans took the lands and made Tuwanuwa and Uda their frontiers. Though the people of those lands love the Storm-god and his consort, the Sun-goddess of Arinna, and had been celebrating the holy days on their own, I was of the opinion that a resumption of royal interest therein would do more than ten garrisons to remind the citizens of those towns of their heritage.

Since there was still no sleeping in the half-refurbished es-tate which I had chosen and then forgotten three years past, we spent that night in a roadside inn just outside of the town proper.

"Why not the garrison?" Lupakki queried me.

"It is no place for a woman of noble birth." I did not say that I did not want her to see what use my garrison soldiers were doubtless making of local namra who had chosen the wrong side in the fighting. I did say: "And in the taverns, we can learn more of the mood of the folk than from a score of officials trying to guess what we want to hear. Spread word among the men that they listen well about them."

And thus it was done, and we heard what was being said about us in the Lower Country that evening before we went into the town.

The talk was surly, of the armies and the levies we had put upon the people. And as Khinti and I and Lupakki and a girl he had met sat in the tavern, I found no way to keep, even briefly, word of the coming campaigns from my new wife. Nevertheless, I tried to steer the conversation to the upcoming tour of the towns the king and his queen must undertake; and then to a side trip to the summer-palace we were building in a nearby town — a journey I'd gladly have made to keep from her even one night longer the realization that she and I had little time together before I would take up my helmet for the season.

As suspicion became certainty on her face her bright chatter slowed, turned pensive, finally stopped altogether.

Her hands, a short time later in quarters said to be the innkeeper's finest and priced like it, were cold as she ran them over me.

"And where did you get this?" she said of a long pale scar on my side.

"Samuha."

"And this?"

"My arm? Also in the Upper Country, saving a man named Mammali who died later in the mountains south of here."

"And this?"

"At my accession."

"And this?"

"Fighting my Hayasaean allies, when they were not so friendly."

"Turn over."

I grumbled, but did so. Her nail traced a long forgotten gouge. I had to think for a moment, then said: "A Gasgaean axe made that one."

Down farther she went, and her voice was almost inaudible.

"And that?"

"That?" I rolled over, thinking that if she went over me limb by limb we would still be at it in the dawn light. "That, my uncle the prince gave me when I was too young to object and too foolish to run and hide."

"And did you give him back in kind?"

"He died, later. Not by my hand. By the Oath Gods'. Khinti?"

She lay her head on my arm and her tears rolled down it. "And what of this, my lord king and husband?"

"Now that one, some say, is the mark of the Storm-god's favor, and surely not worth a single tear."

"You are going out on that Ishuwa campaign, aren't you?"

I pulled her up to me and held her close. "What other way can I keep peace?"

"From Hattusas, that's how. Suppiluliumas, stay with me. I thought—I cannot live a year wondering if you will find space for another scar or die out there. I know no one in Hattusas. How shall I survive?"

"You will not only survive, but rule. You shall have more than enough to do to occupy you. Let me tell you a truth: the season passes in an instant. No sooner will you have seen us off than we will be riding triumphant through Sphinx Gate with our sheep and cattle and deportees. I will bring you wonders from the edges of the plateau. Ssh, now, little one. . ."

All my fine words were wasted, and she wept like she was widowed already.

Now, weeping women I have seen aplenty. But a king cannot treat his queen like a soldier treats a namra; and I had been mostly with women I held of low account and was wanting to be more gentle and more understanding with her than I had been with girls in the past: my one attempt to bring a queen to heel had not been successful, and more than anything I wanted success with Khinti.

And that may have been my problem. I was dazed with her, distracted from all else at a moment when affairs great and small crowded upon my attention. The chronicling of my nicks and cuts had obtruded uncomfortably into that moment, summoning memories of all the years spent acquiring them: years in Samuha, years fighting under Tuthaliyas' impotent banner; the bloody matters of my accession, and the initial struggles of my kingship were large in my mind.

I could not find anything to say to her, only waited, thinking thoughts of my chancery and the warming of the season and what communications might await me piled on Hattu-ziti's floor from left to right in order of their origins' distance from Hatti.

So when she had consoled herself and came tear-streaked to crawl into my lap, I began to question her of her relatives on the island Alashiya as if nothing had happened.

She stiffened as if slapped, and answered: "Ask me of your own blood there, why don't you? I am back but forty days. Your mother—"

"She is not my mother."

"So I have heard, my lord Sun. And how is that?"

"Khinti, how it is, I do not know. Some say that I am not even a concubine's child, but a son of the field . . . a bastard. Is that better than being the get of two siblings?" I heard my voice grow rough and quiet, and yet could not help it, nor even leave off. "The woman who had my care used to tell me, when I would come home black as an Ethiopian from brawling, that the Storm-God sired me. Upon whom, not even she would venture to say. It is widely rumored that a great king who was in Hattusas then was asked by my father to get Asmunikal with child. I asked her that, when she was yet my mother in name and obligation, and she slapped me and had the Meshedi put me in the pit."

"Her own son? In the pit?"

"Whether or not I ever was her son by blood, she has repudiated me. As for the pit—it was one day only. It scared me but I survived it. Now answer my question."

"You are not highly held in Alashiya. Your mother and her brothers have seen to that."

CHAPTER 16

We arrived at Hattusas well before the New Year festivals were to begin. In time, in fact, to order for Khinti a marvelous festival of her own. But the gaiety of the folk and the relief of the palace officials and the peals of laughter riding up the night wind on ladders of melody were mere echoes of the rejoicing that was in my heart.

Khinti would clap her hands, her panther's eyes shining, and run to the windows to see the celebrants dance, and nothing has ever been so fine in Hatti as were those days of our first conjugal spring.

She was so much more than I had dared hope that I ceased remarking upon it lest I seem slow-witted.

All that I was lacking she seemed able to provide: she heard the gods and most especially the Sun-goddess, her lady, and was expert at divination in all its forms. She seduced the clergy and the palace women and even my relatives had no ill words to speak of her. My sons looked her over, and each in his own way accepted the mother I had chosen them: Arnuwandas hunted her a twelve-point stag; Piyassilis "found" the iron scepter with its knob of inlaid gold that had been missing since my first wife's death and gave it unto her; Telipinus. . .

Telipinus was in love. My youngest demanded sight of Khinti upon arising each morning and before retiring at night. Many were those evenings on which the king paced hot-blooded or sat among stuffed stags made of leather and Great Bulls fashioned from painted clay and listened while Khinti's soft voice related to an untiring Telipinus the story of his namesake, the Missing God.

When she would get to the part where the Storm-god sends out the Bee to search for Telipinus the Missing God, the children, even my dour and manly nine-year-old Arnuwandas, would add their voices to hers and all together they would recite the legend.

By the time the Missing God Telipinus "came home to his house and cared again for his land" that particular evening, I was short on patience.

Spoke Khinti and the children together: "The mist let go of the windows, the smoke let go of the house. The altars were set right for the gods, the hearth let go of the log. Telipinus let the sheep go forth, he let the cattle go to the pen. The mother tended her child, the ewe tended her lamb, the cow tended her calf. Also Telipinus tended the king and queen and provided them with—"

"— time enough to spend together. Khinti, finish the story tomorrow."

Up from my brood came a howl like unto the wailing that comes from a fortified town when an army puts it under siege.

But that evening I was unmoving as the warrior carved into the stone arch of King's Gate.

My eldest snarled a foul curse which earned him a gasp from Khinti and a promise from myself that when the sun rose in the morning he would pay tribute. I almost laid hand on him then but my young wife hung on my arm and pleaded his case and for her sake I left off, drawing her out into the hall and commending my demons to the night-nurse who slept with them and the

Meshedi who doubtless slept with the night-nurse when my boys
had driven off to battle in their dreams.

"I am having a meeting in the chancery."

"Pikku came and told where you were. A quick embrace,
then, and let me go back to the children."

"Khinti, perhaps I have not made myself clear: I require your
presence at council. It is time Hattu-ziti and the rest became acquainted with you, and you with the business at hand. There is
more to queenship than prancing around the temples and telling
bedtime stories. Tomorrow is the Festival of the Earth and the
whole cycle of the Missing God will be retold. Take a hand in
it—take the children—take the Sun-goddess on your shoulders
for all I care. But tonight—"

"Sire!" She made a sign before her face that I would speak
so of her goddess, but I only took her by the elbow and propelled
her down the hallway.

By the time we had reached my secretary's chambers in the
chancery I had recovered my patience and instructed my new
queen as to the duties and honors of those men with whom we
would meet: of Hattu-ziti, most private confidant, secretary,
chamberlain and my second in command; of Hannutti, florid
Master of Horses and Marshal; of Himuili, field commander; of
Takkuri, brother-in-law, Chief of 1,000; and of Kuwatna-ziti, the
Great Shepherd, Man of the Storm-god, General in Chief of all
the armies. Of Zida, my brother, chief of the royal bodyguard,
my Gal Meshedi; and of Hugganas and his warlord son Mariyas,
she had her own knowledge and needed no cautions from me.

Hattu-ziti has never gotten over those winters drawing in
the dirt when he was a commander of fortifications and I a fledgling officer with the Shepherd's flock: every council of import
over which he has ever presided has been held upon the floor.
Eventually, in exasperation, I had maps drawn in colors in the
chancery sanctum, and a benched railing built round them so
that, when the king of Hatti sat cross-legged hour after hour and
knee to knee with his Great Ones, none of us would have to feel
undignified. In those days, we sniffed out this and that without

thought to aching buttocks and stiffened knees, and none of us felt so august as to make a differentiation between the stone of the palace's second floor and the dirt of a field council.

But Khinti giggled to see kings and heroes strewn about like the cups and rhytons and pillows and piles of varicolored clay tablets among which they sat or lay, and she teased them. At which everyone struggled up to give her greeting and settled back down silent—all but Hugganas, who with a hand to the small of his back strode over and embraced her like a sister, then drew her down at his side with queries after her father's health and the quality of peace that obtained on the Arzawaean border and in the newly liberated Hittite towns.

Thus by Hugganas' example did the men soften to her, and stiff postures eased. The handsome Himuili—whom I had sent into a certain defeat in Arzawa and who had brought back therefrom a crushed knee (and, some said, a shaken valor)—limped over to her with wine, and she smiled, saying:

"Ah, Himuili, I have heard so much about you from the palace ladies I feel us well acquainted. And I see why the girls weep in the temples; and while it confounded me before, I now understand their tears."

Zida, who had spent an evening with Khinti, caught my eye and shook his head with a knowing smirk.

In less time than it takes to gird on a sword belt she had placed each and every grizzled veteran of my confidence under tribute and brought them into the empire ruled by her smile.

All, that is, but Kuwatna-ziti, whose obsidian hair was shot with gray at the temples, making him look even more the wolf; and whose approval was so obviously held in abeyance that his answers to her courtesy fell only a hair's breadth short of impudence. This too, along with Hugganas' overly warm greeting, I held apart in my mind for later investigation.

After she had spoken with each in turn she rose up from Hugganas' side and stepped carefully among the rubble of our hours to kneel before the deployed tablets. One, of yellow clay found far south on the sea's shore, she picked up and scanned, then sat back on her heels, carefully smoothing her robe down, demure, serious.

"Hattu-ziti, my husband tells me you have all been here since morning, but of the matters under discussion, he has not spoken, leaving it for you to do. . . ."

Hattu-ziti heaved up his ever more portly bulk and leaned over the pile of tablets, saying: "These letters refer to events in the Upper Country, these to the Lower Country. From here downward are communications from countries on the plains, and here at the bottom is Egypt and those lands with which you are familiar: Alashiya and Ahhiyawa." He paused, his arm outstretched, and looked inquiringly at my wife.

"My lord, I am new to Hatti. I stare openmouthed at walls thicker than four tall men laid end to end. I gawk in the Great Temple, and the Southern Citadel takes my breath away. If you would be so kind as to summarize these events and your aspirations concerning them, then perhaps I might know better where I could be of help."

Mariyas hooted, more than drunk, but his father quieted him, so I ignored it, only waiting, not taking a hand.

"My lady," sighed Hattu-ziti, scratching his thinning pate, "matters are complex." He shot a pleading look at me but I stared back, adamant. "So, then, let us proceed. . . ." He stamped over to a vacant space of floor and widened it, then collected goblets from the men. "There, give me that. You'll have it back in a moment. Here, Shepherd, yours too; and your dirk, if you please.

"Now, then, Tawananna, here is Hatti, the inner: Hattusas and her environs." He placed a ram-chased goblet in the upper center of his space. "And here"—he dipped his finger in the wine and made an oval around the goblet—"are the boundaries of Hatti as they now exist. Here is Hayasa. . . ." A second goblet, in the extreme upper right of the cleared space, marked it. "Below Hayasa, Ishuwa." He thumped that cup down so that it slopped wine. "And below and to the west of Ishuwa, the country of Kizzuwadna commands the plain at the end of the plateau. Lady, if I offend you by telling things you already know, give me a moment. Hugganas, here, has been negotiating on our behalf with the king of Kizzuwadna. This king is so much the Hurri king Tushratta's servant that Tushratta even calls him such to his face. But not so much that he would be afraid to switch his loyalty to an overlord more fraternal who would succor and protect him."

Hugganas laughed. "That is the truth: servant he is. And the king of Kizzuwadna does not much like it. If Hatti does him a favor and crushes these Ishuwans who are a problem to everyone who shares a border with them—"

"*If* we move against Ishuwa," interrupted the Shepherd, "we will do it because they have forgotten their place in relation to the Hatti land. It is the desecration of Hittite temples and the burning of Hattian fields with which we are concerned: The people of Armatana and the people of Ishuwa will rebuild in fetters all they have destroyed, and they will make those very fetters themselves, from the arms they raised against us, and even clap them on one another's ankles."

The Shepherd rose and strode into the middle of Hattu-ziti's improvised map, my secretary giving back in an ungainly scuffle of hands and knees before him.

"The enemies from Gasga, my lady,"—Kuwatna-ziti swept up a third goblet and thunked it down to the left and rear of Hayasa's—"are at peace. The king of Hayasa is enlisted to our cause. The enemies from Armatana and from Ishuwa will this season fall before our circumspection, our well-informedness, and the onslaught of our battle. The king of Kizzuwadna seeks our embrace like a new bride, unwilling on the surface but fleeing a greater evil. Then, noble Tawananna, we will be looking King Tushratta of Mitanni straight in the eye.

"Your husband's aim, if he has not already so informed you, is to set himself up as a great king of empire, as Hattian kings were in former times. To that end he has subdued the western lands, whence you come, as a mere formality, a precursor to battle on the southern plains. And where he will die, any king has the right to choose."

Kuwatna-ziti cast a challenging glance at me, whereupon I smiled a long slow smile and spread my hands wide, giving him leave to continue, and then stretched out on my side and sipped my wine.

"My dear lord Shepherd, your love for the Hatti land needs no affirmation," said my queen softly.

"You mistake me, lady from Arzawa. It is *your* love for the Hatti land which must be affirmed in *our* eyes."

The moment stretched, and stretched, and stretched unbroken into eternity.

Takkuri stroked his beard, heavy-lidded eyes half closed, unrevealed.

Hugganas, his face that ruddy brown of a man whose windburn is darkened by the flush of anger, ran his forefinger round his goblet's silver rim.

My queen rose and walked silently to stand before Kuwatna-ziti, who glowered openly down on her.

"My lord, I have heard that you were my husband's earliest mentor; your love for him is known throughout the lands. So I will excuse you all you have said for you are rightly concerned that I be fit, that I be honorable and free from deceit. But I am more than those things with which you are hesitant to credit me: I bring gifts more lasting than gold and more suitable than horses. Alashiya I can deliver back into friendly relationship with Hatti; and the fair-haired Ahhiyawans will follow my lead. My father's avenues of intelligence are streets my husband longs to call his own. So tread with care, Great Shepherd, else in your zealousness you lose the very advantages you seek to secure."

Mariyas, chortling, whistled and beat his hands together. My brother briefly joined in, so that I hand-silenced them, struggling to keep from my countenance the smile that had conquered Hugganas' better judgment and Himuili's, also.

"Great Queen, tell us of these benefits. It will be the first I have heard of them," snarled Kuwatna-ziti and strode toward the seat he had made of cushions upon the floor. As he passed me he added: "Tasmi, you have a talent for immersing yourself in distractions when you can least afford it."

Alone, in the midst of us, Khinti seemed to quail. Her eyes re-met the men one at a time where they lounged about her, and came at last to rest on me. As clear as spoken words that glance said: *"If you do not help me, I will tell them."*

So I did not help her and she told them of her father's trade in men and arms and information and where he was accustomed to sit at table and with whom; and though at first the Shepherd snorted as if she were a defendant at judgment, when she revealed that all of her sire's information-gathering organization and the whole of his singular "diplomatic" force would be turned to our use, Zida quietly mentioned just how formidable the loan of those skills to Arzawa had made the Arzawaean enemy.

"Thank you, Zida, but it is the Great Shepherd who must be convinced of my loyalty. I can hardly perform those duties the Sun expects of me without his ratification," purred Khinti. Then:

"Kuwatna-ziti, you are sprung from one of the oldest Hattian families; in the old empire all the lands you call Arzawaean were Hittite. Yet you speak to me of being 'Arzawaean' as if it were an epithet. How would it be, if we all thought thus? How will the people become united, if we hold them divided in our hearts? How—"

"Tasmi," Kuwatna-ziti interrupted, "tell her how much you loved the campaigns for Uda, how pleasant you found the battles to reclaim the cult-city Tuwanuwa. Speak to your queen of treaties ignored by Arzawaean princes. Or, more recently, of Mount Tiwatassa and all that was spent in vain there, Mammali's life not the least of it. Himuili, walk across the room for us. Tell us while you do it how you love the Lower Country." He was up on his feet. "Tasmisarri, you have not spoken of how you love your wife's people: of how cruelly you have treated those lands, we all are well informed. Are you as vengeful and spiting with this woman in your bed as you are with the cities and towns who did not bow down to you?"

"That will do, Shepherd. Sit down and keep silent until I give you leave to speak again. Khinti, perhaps you had better explain to the Shepherd that you are Arzawaean by adoption only, rather than trying to make him see the error of his Arinna-born provincialism."

She did that, with closed eyes reciting her lineage through her mother back to the Hattian lords who first became kings of Alashiya. We have controlled the free ports of Alashiya for generations. Those kings who were originally installed by the ancient conquerors yet give their children good Hittite names, and although Alashiya conducts a certain amount of her own foreign policy, she has always been a Hittite protectorate and those who claim Hittite blood make up the ruling class of that country.

I waited a long time before I spoke; waited until Khinti had come and taken a seat by my side and a gulp of wine and sat breathing short fast breaths, straight and unsmiling; until all were tense and the silence strained and no expression showed on anyone's face, and even Mariyas put aside his wine. "Anyone else? No? Hear then, what we will do:

"My Tawananna and I will do the New Year's tour of the god to all his stations.

"Kuwatna-ziti will let his nails grow and appoint some other to his stead in the temples, take the men and chariots I will furnish, plus those not needfully deployed in the Upper Country and those Hayasa will provide, and march toward Ishuwa. When the Shepherd's flock rests in Artatama, I will meet him, and we will both do the ceremony of the borders there.

"Hugganas, can you give me more than a hundred chariots?"

"Two, my lord, but then the Hittites must be responsible for the Gasgaeans respecting our shared border. And I will give you Mariyas, although myself I will stay home and make love this season, with my lord the Sun's permission."

"Done. Mariyas, I have lost you a wife and some sleep, unless I miss my guess, over the treaty your father signed. Can you battle in my cause with an easy heart? If not, it will not go ill between us — I will simply appoint another and you can do as you wish."

"Uncle, command me," said the thick-chested stepson of my sister. "Wives, I have many; but adventures, paltry few."

"Then we are of one mind. Himuili, I give you another chance at a dignity you rejected when the lure of fighting had you in its grip. Be a Chief of One Thousand, take an advisory function under the Shepherd. Whatever our sorrows and wherever the blame for them might lie, you are in no shape to lead a column and too valuable a tactician to lose."

"I bow to my king's wishes."

"Zida, I know you fain would run with the soldiers, but stay and do my work for me while I play kingly games."

I got that from him, on a chuckle, coupled with a threat to suborn my wife and make her divorce me, and marry her himself while I was in enemy lands.

"Now, I am concerned. Not one of you has seen the connection between what affairs are rising in the south and what Khinti brings us. If I spoke Hatib's name, would that jog anyone's memory?"

I saw the Shepherd, who was leaning back on his elbows with his outstretched legs crossed at the ankles, give a visible start. None of the others were that quick of wit. But Kuwatnaziti yet smarted under my reproach and my ban of silence, so I let him stew.

"Then, behold: Khinti's sources are such that she knew what the old snake who was once called my mother has done before we did: she spoke to me of how Asmunikal had filled our Alashiyan cousins with evil tales of us. I am going there, to see what may be seen." That moved them, but I held up my hand and all subsided. "I am going there, I have said. And when I am there I will ask the king of Alashiya how it is that he has come to write to the king of Egypt advising him to make no new treaty with Hatti, when he himself is a Hattian subject."

Khinti's head snapped around, her fingers to her lips, for she had not told me that: Hatib had.

"While I am there, I will meet with Hatib, whose man brought me *this*—"

I held out my hand and Hattu-ziti scrabbled about in search of the advisory in question. He found it, put in my palm, grinning though he tried not to let me see.

I held up the tablet. "Here is the news from Egypt's own chancery: all the dispatches brought in to Pharaoh's secretaries will reach our eyes as soon as his. Hatib has bought us a scribe from among the Hittites employed by the Egyptians. When I combine my roaming Sutu with the agents of Khinti's father, none will have intelligence superior to ours."

I broke up the meeting soon afterwards, turning the talk to horses and chariots in the guise of assigning duties to Hannutti, my Master of Horses.

When Hugganas and his son and Takkuri had departed, and Zida and Himuili followed, announcing that they would be lying in a drunken stupor in the Gal Meshedi's house if anyone should need to find them, I motioned Khinti to await me without. I did not have to signal Hattu-ziti, who slipped through the door behind my queen, carping about slaves to clean up the place.

"Shepherd, why must you put me in such a position? Am I an enemy, that you demean my woman and myself thereby?"

"Am I now allowed to speak?"

"Kuwatna-ziti, do you want to see how far you can push me? This season it is I who must pin you to the wall, if it comes to that between us. And don't say you'll run back into the temple. I will not allow it."

"I should have cut out your tongue when I had the chance. It will strangle you one day. You host a serpent in your mouth and another in your bed. What do you expect *me* to do?"

"Meet her at the river. Negotiate a truce. You are the diplomat, not I. For the sake of the Storm-god and the Sun-goddess of Arinna and all the years I took your orders and counsel unquestioning, please, Shepherd, do not war upon my wife."

"Which one?"

"Now you sound like Daduhepa."

"And you sound like a garrison commander. You are not yet a king in spirit Tasmi, not yet a king by far. You are a fine soldier and a passable general, and though you are less than might be hoped as a steward of the gods, at least you try. But you have not consulted the omens for this campaign. You have set no sacrifices in the temples. The Sun-goddess has not even been informed. I, for one, do not hold that our Arinniti and the foreign Hebat-Tasimis the Bloody are one and the same goddess. And if they are . . . if your new girl is so pious a priestess and has the ear of Arinniti, my lady, as she claims she does, then why is none of that reflected in her behavior? All these tablets—where were you when the weather broke and the messengers and envoys from other countries started appearing in Hattusas? Out driving around in the woods after that half-breed, that's where—and don't tell me about her royal Ahhiyawan ties: those folk may be worthy of notice in a thousand years, but now they are no better than Gasgaeans. You are so concerned with the international court of opinion—what do you think those diplomatic couriers made of arriving in Hattusas and seeing neither king nor queen, then asking and finding out that no one had any idea when Your Majesty the Sun of Hatti would be returned to his city, nor even where he had gone, nor why? The whole Hayasaean treaty almost turned to offal because you were not here to smooth Hugganas' feathers. I only thank the Storm-god, my lord, that that demented sister of yours was not with him. Let her torture the Hayasaeans. As for me, I have had just about enough."

"Stand still, Shepherd!"

I did not ask him what he wanted from me, although I thought of that. I did not tell him that if he would just wait until I had things organized all his fears would disappear. I did not even say that I would take back what I said about the temple: I would have. Instead I walked over to where he had frozen in his tracks at my order and spun him around.

He swung first and so I did not have a chance to say anything at all, only defend myself, thinking I must not hurt him, even while I sought to pin his arms. Ten years older than I was the Shepherd, and I learned that a few silver hairs do not make a man old, although in the tussle on the floor I had gained a seat astride him and was just dragging a submission from his lips when a white-faced Khinti and almost equally paled Hattu-ziti burst through the doors with Meshedi at their heels.

I shouted them out, but they had seen. I rolled off the Shepherd, who was no longer struggling, and sat with my legs drawn up, swallowing salty blood and waiting for my breathing to ease.

Kuwatna-ziti, on his knees, wiped his mouth with a torn sleeve and sank down on his haunches, staring at the floor, shaking his head. After a time he raised it up and pushed back his square-cut mane from his eyes and looked me up and down.

"Why don't you grow your hair back and give up the temples and come fight with me, as of old?" I rasped.

"Why don't you cut yours before some enemy hangs you with it, and take heed to the wisdom—" He stopped, of his own accord, and chuckled.

And I found myself laughing also, that we had come all this way and not the smallest iota had changed between us, and thus had gone nowhere at all.

When my sides ached and tears blocked my vision and the Shepherd, gasping, leaned on me for support, I made an end to it, offering peace and sealing it with shared wine.

I had forgotten about Khinti until a timid knock came upon the doors, whereupon I remembered not only my wife and queen but that these chambers were another's, and suggested we go up to my rooms.

Once, long ago, we had made a treaty over a girl in Babylonian; the Shepherd got the east of her and I got the west. Now, it was not like that, but it was almost like that as the Shepherd and I renewed acquaintance in the smooth warm sea of wine and the wine led to women less in need of honoring than my new Tawananna.

In the morning she only asked me why the Shepherd called me Tasmi, to which I answered her that though he did, she might not.

Then I bade her help me seek the iron short sword I had long favored, for I could not find it anywhere. While we looked for it I queried her of the intimacy of her relationship with Hugganas of Hayasa, and she answered me that since of old he had been a client of her father's and at length, when we could not turn up the battered scabbard anywhere in my chambers, I settled for a golden-hilted sticker whose butt was fashioned like a two-headed lion and whose blade would hardly have cut wheat, but which I had kept around because of its provenance, said to be that of ancient empire.

As I girded it on, Khinti cautioned me not to deal too harshly with my eldest.

"His troubles," I grunted, "stem from me having failed to deal with him at all. I'm just going to scare him a bit. Either he cleans up his own mouth or some other will do it for him. All I intend is to impress upon him the importance of princes remaining princes until they are kings: I would hate to be forced to act harshly later because I acted not at all today."

To that end I had sent Meshedi earlier to prepare Arnuwandas for a private audience in the huge judgment hall whose twenty-five pillars stood as my predecessor Tuthaliyas' greatest monument.

I sat upon the gilded throne of kingship with my lituus and my conical crown and my standard bearers and keepers of the cup gathered round. The walls were lined with Bearers of the Golden Lance, pages tended the doors, and the hierophants of the temples stoked their fires. All that was different from a day of public judgment was that the queen sat not in her throne upon my right, nor did supplicants and prisoners throng the vast altar hall beyond the bronze bound doors.

I heard the Meshedi's marching feet before the herald's strident call rang out. Then the doors drew back and my eldest in his finest red robe was marched between men twice his height to the foot of my throne's dais.

At my signal all but two Meshedi drew back from the white-faced child who glared up defiantly at his father. For a moment I felt regret, inundated by the thousand horrors of my youth. For an instant it was as if I became him, damned to a world in which his every thought and word were devalued by his size and age; and I recalled the pain, and the rage, and the humiliation which must bubble unvented within whenever he would hear that most terrible of advisements: *wait until you are a man.*

Then I snapped my fingers, and the scribe at my feet piped my boy's offense as if it were upon a regular docket.

"Arnuwandas the Second, son of Suppiluliumas, Great King, and of Daduhepa, Great Queen, stands accused of casting aspersions upon the person of the Sun Suppiluliumas, Great King of Hatti. How say you? Speak!"

Daduhepa's unyielding hatred seethed in my son's face.

"I say," said he clearly in his child's voice, "that if the Sun, my father, wishes ever to recover what he has lost, he will make an end to this." His small brown fists rested on outthrust hips; his chin, while it trembled, was raised high. Over his head one Meshedi elbowed the other, and the second found need to turn his face away.

Myself, I was struggling not to make a show of my surprise, twirling the lituus in my fingers, torn between doubling the punishment I had had in mind or beating the whereabouts of my sword out of him right then and there. But then as I watched the cool gold of the lituus turning in my fingers, I thought what a kingly thing it was that the boy had done.

"Perhaps," I conceded, "we could negotiate a treaty. If you wish it, that is."

"A formal treaty, wherein my rights, as well as yours, are written?" said Arnuwandas and I yet recall the low murmurs of wonder this response wrested from the corners where the braziers crackled and belched smoke.

"Even the king of Hayasa has strictures upon him whereby he must love the Sun's head as his own, the Sun's person as his own. . . . I will be no more lenient with you, though you be prince. Can you put your seal truthfully to such an indenture, knowing that the Oath Gods oversee it?"

Gravely, my son allowed, with only a momentary squeezing shut of eyes and a surreptitious exhalation of long-held breath, that he would be willing to have the aforementioned conditions laid to him under oath, so I signaled the scribe to begin taking down my words.

We had the treaty made into a bronze tablet and deposited in the temple of the Sun-goddess of Arinna; Arnuwandas demanded proof of this having been done before he would return the iron blade he held as surety.

I thought about all this on the thirty-eight day tour Khinti and I made of the god's stations in the different towns. With the long slow-moving train of wagons creeping along in our wake I had a surfeit of time to consider my sons and whatever else I chose. And I determined that Arnuwandas' behavior held in it a lesson never well enough learned between kings and princes. And so to this day I have continued the practice started then: if between fathers and sons matters of obligation and fealty can become hazy and distorted, then how much more so between kings and princes? All my sons who are kings now understand, if they did not in former times, why between each other and most especially with their sire their oaths of allegiance are preserved on bronze tablets and archived in the temple of the Sun-goddess of Arinna, who regulates kingship and queenship.

CHAPTER 17

In the matter of omens taken for the armies, either the gods had changed their verdict or the omen-takers were more disposed to my favor.

In the matter of Hatib and a sea journey to the island of Alashiya, all agreed we could not risk it that season. Khinti's own divination bespoke it as emphatically as my dreams rendered me warnings that shook me from my sleep sweating in the middle of the night. But I had promised her, and would not disappoint her if I lost all on that account, and so said nothing whatsoever about a ship swamped and smoking, her mast and sail aflame, and made preparations to debark.

But my queen came to me and laid her cheek against my throat and whispered that though she would obey me in all things and knew how much I had hoped to accomplish on our journey, the omens boded ill, and she was afraid.

So I sent an envoy in my stead upon the long sea voyage, and while he made the trip without incident, we were never sure, as is the way with omens, what might have befallen us if indeed we ourselves had attempted to cross the sea.

But in my surprise at her revelation I had mentioned the blue-cloaked lord who walked, speechless, ever before me; for it was he who had dropped a tablet on my dream-path; and what was written upon it had precipitated the dreams which made me reluctant to undertake a visit to Alashiya at that point in time.

"Perhaps it is the Storm-god who appears to you thus," she ventured.

"The vision never speaks. Nor is it confined to my dreams: I have seen him turning corners before me in the palace, walking on the walls, lurking here and there over the years. I thought I saw him at our wedding feast, although what he would have been doing there still eludes me."

"You do not think it is the Storm-god," she said, her fine brows drawn down.

"I do not know what to think. But I am glad you are not smiling."

"Smiling? Hardly. With your permission I will ask the Sun-goddess, my lady, the nature of this evanescent ally of yours."

"Ask her in confidence, then. I would not want my men knowing their commander is in the habit of seeing things."

But by the time I went out to join the Shepherd, she still had gained no enlightenment from her goddess. In the matter of the blue-cloaked lord, Arinniti was as mute as the citadel walls.

Revenge was sweet in the land of Armatana: we burned it to the ground and enslaved its inhabitants upon the spot. Some Hittite lives had been lost in the endeavor, and it was not until I myself arrived there that the fortified town surrendered, doubtless having heard that the bloody Suppiluliumas was sharpening the iron knives with which he butchered babies.

We laughed about it, the Great Shepherd and I, and the heady wine of success made me forget Khinti and our tearful leave-taking, and my three princes who had watched from the high walls with my lesser sons and their mothers, waving and shouting themselves hoarse.

But the namra were not as feisty, nor the eastern girls as nubile, nor the battle morns as crisp as I had remembered them, and the Shepherd and I held a long and fruitless debate as to whether it was that such affairs are made much better than they really were by a trick of memory; or whether indeed the spring was warmer than usual and the girls less comely and the wine a touch sour.

Now that I am sure of the answer, I will say it is a combination of true events experienced without, and reactions, no less true, experienced within.

Discrimination is a process of learning criteria by which to judge shrewdly the present in comparison to an idealized memory held of the past. A long arduous campaign such as the one that took Ishuwa is a thing a man is proud and glad to be a part of — *afterward.* Afterward, one recalls a moment of thirst, a fall or a suppurating wound differently than he experienced them: he has survived, the pain or fear or illness has passed. Heroes are fashioned from forgotten hardship gilded with retrospective pride. Once a man can say 'I have done it!' he is willing to forget, or at least try to forget, the irritable, vicious, overtired and underfed person who performed deeds from desperation for which he is later lauded and increased. In time, if he is foolish, he may come to believe the things others say of him and even that all was as bright and shining as those who stay at home and write songs about this war or that portray them.

War is a way of life, however, and though the ground may have seemed a trifle harder to my bones at first, I soon fell into the rhythm of it; and if in comforts of the flesh the field is lacking, in sustenance for the spirit it overflows. Doing what had long been denied me, I was replete. Doing what it is that I do best, I had no anxious moments, no vociferous detractors, no sleepless nights over niceties of protocol or dire diplomacy.

The months stretched before, a deepening green with the coming of summer; and we knew then that indeed it was a dry, unseasonable heat the gods granted us that year. In the early yellowing of the grass many read ill, but there was no going home with that war half won, and we took our portion of enemy soil each day, and were content.

Kuwatna-ziti and I caught our own eagles, drove with them alone into the country, and when we let them go they flew in the direction we intended. Thus we did not truly falsify the auguries, but for the first time in anyone's memory the strength of the Hattian army stayed the winter in the field, and with the blessings of the gods.

I was conducting my foreign policy from tent and chariot, dictating variously to Pikku or whatever other scribe was about, and even received a surreptitious visit from the king of Kizzuwadna while we were watching the first snow fall from a full round moon. To this willing adherent I gave wine and comfort, for he was ready to come over to Hatti and be quit of Tushratta's demeaning overlordship then and there. But I did not want that.

The Kizzuwadnan king shook his head so that the gold disks hanging from his ears danced in the firelight, but at length agreed that he would hold back his formal defection until a moment of my choosing, and supply me as many Kizzuwadnans as I had Hayasaeans if we could find Hittite guises in which to outfit them.

I explained that I would rather his men patrol Kizzuwadnan borders and trap the fleeing Ishuwan deportees and hold them in camps, as we had done with the refugees we had chased into Hayasaean territory.

With a baffled laugh he agreed to that. Thereupon he remarked as to the quantity of booty — namra, cattle, sheep, utensils of the gods and of the armies — which was scattered about our baggage train and made a mobile city of deportees on the Hittite flanks.

So I explained that in the Hatti land proper there had been a dry season, and all the goods and namra would be sent westward as soon as was feasible, but that should he have the inclination he could take whatever goods or persons he wished southeast with him.

Then came the king to what was in his heart: the wildness of my troops and the harsh treatment they had meted out to the peoples of the towns which had been in the armies' path on the drive projected to end with my Hittite forces at Kizzuwadna's frontier.

I asked him then if he had never been part of such a campaign, and quieted his fears as to his folk receiving treatment similar to what he had seen with his own eyes; and with soft words he departed to his tent and the morrow's eastward journey, saying that his house was open to me should I seek relief from what promised to be another year campaigning.

We were then in some town or other in the upper middle of what had been Ishuwa. Behind us lay blackened, charred villages and the wails of the homeless; ahead lay all who had been fleet enough to flee but foolish enough to remain within their country's borders to defend their land. Those who had fled to Hayasa had fled into a Hittite trap; but those who had gone down the river Mala into Hurrian lands I had lost, if I could not extradite them from out of Tushratta's lap.

Now, I had been hoping for just such an occurrence and did not really expect Tushratta to give me back the citizens who had fled before My Majesty. In fact it was, in my heart, as necessary that this be so as was the putative neutrality of Kizzuwadna.

It was also necessary that I write to Tushratta, king of the Hurrians who called himself Great King of Mitanni, and demand the return of these refugees so that he could refuse me.

So I sent word to the Hurrian: "Return my subjects to me."

And before we had moved much further into Ishuwa word came up from the Hurrian as follows:

"No! Those cities had previously come to the Hurri country and had settled there. It is true they later went back to the Land of Hatti as fugitives; but now finally the cattle have chosen their stable, they have definitely chosen my country."

So the Hurrian did not extradite my subjects to me. . . . And I, the Sun, sent word to the Hurrian as follows:

"If some country seceded from you and went over to the Hatti land, how would that be?"

The Hurrian sent word back to me:

"Exactly the same."

So I wrote to Sunasarra, king of Kizzuwadna, that the moment was propitious for his defection, and I sent word to all the kings of the different lands as to what I had said and what Tushratta had said and finishing:

"Now the people of Kizzuwadna are Hittite cattle and they have chosen their stable, they have deserted the Hurrian and gone over to My Majesty. . . . The land of Kizzuwadna rejoices very much over its liberation."

And, having swallowed up Ishuwa entire, my armies were fêted in Kizzuwadna before we returned across the newly reclaimed Hittite territories, home to Hattusas to spend the winter.

My men, by then having spent nearly two years fighting, were not easy on the Kizzuwadnan city. If the people of Kizzuwadna had not been so busy rejoicing over their liberation, they might with good cause have taken offense at the comportment of their liberators. But I could not blame my men: I too was touched with the madness that long campaigns bring.

I have said we were encamped in 'some town or other in the upper middle of Ishuwa' and that statement, if I may, I shall hold up as an effect of which such long arduous campaigns are always the cause.

The most commonly asked question on that tour of the increasingly Hittite east was, "What place is this?"

I myself spoke to a town who had put down its weapons at the feet of the Sun and called it by the name of another town taken scant days before.

Once I stood with Kuwatna-ziti on a hilltop and sorted hurriedly through a score of place-names to find the one applicable to the town spread out below, but none of the names in my head seemed any more familiar than the others. You may have had this experience with a girl just-met when things grow dim in passion's heat. That day, in disgust, it was I who had to say, "What is the name of this town?"

Nor is that the only infirmity such campaigns bring. A man who spends his time in company with his peers in an abode unfixed in place develops a different set of criteria than those who lead normal lives. His privacy is nonexistent, his behavior sharply circumscribed by his rank and his worth in the eyes of his fellows. It matters to him how the soldiers hold him: his survival may depend upon it. His life renders up daily reaffirmation of his ability to perform in a crisis. He cares for little but the condition of his weapons and his success on the field. He is part of a vast host of men whose loyalty he can command, and in whom he takes great pride. They grow closer than lovers, these men, and often serve even that function for one another, in the knowledge that shared peril has changed them, made them creatures only another of their kind can understand.

So it is no wonder that when a scout troop drives into a town before the hosts and the townspeople greet them with surly eyes and flat beer and moldy bread, they take offense. And when their brothers blacken the streets and the people pale and rethink their manners — then, is it any wonder that it is often too late?

A man who has not slept in his own bed nor eaten from his own board nor made love to his own woman becomes obsessed with beds free from fleas and tables free from garbage and women freed from their husbands' embraces. It is the way of it: what is denied the soldier he rips from the conquered as repayment. There is no way around it, any more than there is a salve for short tempers or a potion that will teach merchants and innkeepers that if they try to fleece the armies it is they themselves who will be decreased.

As for the Ishuwans, in my eyes they deserved it, all that they got from us. They had played the part of Hurrian subjects long ago, then had come into the Hittite fold when it suited them, and gone again to sit by the knee of Tushratta's father when Hittite fortunes had sunk to their lowest ebb. They should have kept up that manner of behavior and crawled back into the Hittite camp when I came to power. But they were subverted by their fear of their mighty Mitannian ally, and even plundered Hittite towns. So on the return drive I turned their conquerors loose upon them, and what was left of the Ishuwa land shuddered on its knees.

The land of Kizzuwadna, had they defied me and then fled my wrath into the shadow of the Mitannian throne, I would have treated no better. In the matter of Ishuwa, my heart remained hard, and later I opened the Ishuwa land to occupation by good Upper Country Hittite families, disregarding the fact that Ishuwans had been Hittites in former times.

The discrepancy between my treatment of the aforementioned country Ishuwa and that of Kizzuwadna is no discrepancy at all: the king of Kizzuwadna came to me on my brother-in-law's arm, and so I made him a "brother": yes, he was already my vassal and bound by oath to appear yearly at Hattusas with tribute in silver and chariots and men; but him I stroked gently like a young chariot horse, being always careful to allow him his pride. After all, he had delivered unto me the first success I had had against Tushratta, and by his bloodless defection had laid the foundation upon which I would build empire, and I saw approaching the opportunity to use the kingdom of Mitanni as blocks in my cellar and even to mortar them secure with Tushratta's blood.

Thus I was not displeased with the fruits of our winter-spanning journey to the east, and turned homeward with that tight, sardonic ease of a king who knows what compromises inevitably follow the acquisition of even his most coveted prize.

I had been to Hatti twice during the fighting: once to perform the harvest festivals, and once to honor the Storm-god. I had been once to Arinna, performing the rituals for the armies in the Sun-goddess' most sacred temple and then went back to the front to see how well I had done.

So when we came in sight of Hattusas — and drove in double file across the bridge that spans the gorge and up toward the southeast gate whose ramp leads directly into the citadel — I halted the column and looked awhile at my city. Nor was I the only one who took that opportunity to meditate upon all that had gone before. A man is happy to be home, but sad to be done collecting tales to tell, regretful even of an end to awful danger and worse living conditions, if it be the beginning of quiet days and simpering stay-at-homes and the dissolution of friendships grown deep with lives saved and grief shared.

Up from the rear, when I gave them their ease and men took the opportunity to walk upon familiar ground and check their horses' harness and slake their thirst, came the queries: when would we be going out again? what were the chances of this ten or that finding a post together? who was wintering on the borders? who would make the hero's roll? who would be promoted? who wanted to stay the festival month in the Southern Citadel? who knew what had been going on in this town or that?

Those who possessed confirmed commands found themselves surrounded by the hopeful; some would smile and laugh and clap a man's shoulder, and find a friend a place; others, either because they had something assured or no hope of assurances, leaned or sat in their cars and talked of what they had done as if they must catch the memory ere it deserted them.

None of them were far from tears. My blood-tempered, invincible veterans were moved to a man, and I saw expressions on the terrible and the implacable that I had never thought to see. Now I know that the hardest softens when a triumphant army is disbanded after so long. We had joined, each of us, the brotherhood of his fellows and had not known it, most of us, until then. Warriors do not much dwell upon such things; they have few moments suited. When the whole of the armies paraded up through the city the next day, no face would show a sign of what some might construe as unmanly weakness. Tomorrow there would be the cheers and the music and the fêting and the willing noble ladies after a hero for their collection.

On those thoughts, I nodded to Lupakki and he snapped the reins to the grays and shouted the signal, and we took two hundred in through the chariot gate.

That vision of Hattusas on her scarp, gleaming fanged and clawed with her white plaster throwing back shadows of purple and gold on the citadel walls, I shall always treasure: while I was warring, Hattu-ziti had much strengthened my city. Her double walls did not gape, and even the postern gate tunnel I had wanted had he dug for me. I marked it just before the gatekeeper saw us and gave the call and the double wings of the gates were drawn inward and we passed through the gate-house and into the palace yards.

I recollect only the girl flying down the corridor between the chariots with unqueenly haste. Take heart, gentle lords: if you would keep the ardor of a new bride year after year, simply make yourself scarce.

Before the host of the armies she scrambled up into my chariot to throw herself against me, barely clothed, naked of foot and head, her unbound hair damp and throwing all the colors of a crow's wing into the air. I had my nose buried in the mass of it, and her high off the ground in my embrace before I knew it, and only the hooting of my thirty brought me round so that I pushed her back and held her at arm's length.

The girl whom I had abandoned to great queenship seemed a girl no longer; the woman who had lain with her husband so infrequently the last two years was haggard around the cheeks and dark under the eyes, but those eyes were sparkling and free from accusation and as much the panther's as ever.

"Suppiluliumas, my lord," she said upon a little gulp, "you are unscathed."

"And you, also." I chuckled. "You have survived my court, and by the look of you, thrived doing it. It is more remarkable than any feat I have accomplished in the whole of the war."

Her face clouded, and I saw the pulse in her throat and the tremor across her eyelids as she squeezed them shut. "My husband, I must speak with you."

"You can speak with me all you want, Khinti: we will have a whole winter for talk . . . and other things." Her priestess' garb made any thoughts other than those of her beauty fly from me: I had not yet succeeded in planting a seed in her womb, and she was high of breast and hard of belly and carried herself with a maiden grace.

I swatted her on the rump and bade her be off and await me in the residence. She stepped back, lowered her head as if raped, and turned without a word, descending the chariot.

In former times, I would have let her go.

I leaned down, my elbows on the polished wood that railed the chariot. "Khinti," I called softly to her retreating back. I saw her fists clench, and her stride stiffen, and the black hair bouncing, and when she turned I motioned her to approach me once again. "What is it that cannot wait until the sun sets?" With my eyes I showed her Lupakki at my team's head, Hannutti the Master of Horses loitering at a circumspect distance; and when she came up to the car I leaned out of it and kissed her upon paled lips.

"My lord Sun, it is your affairs that concern me, those you have left to my care."

"Is it?"

"And your sons, for whom not even the Goddess, my lady, could serve in your stead." And then formality deserted her and I realized that she was, after all, but a girl staggering under the heavy load of responsibilities I had laid upon her.

When in a choked and broken voice she begged me never to leave her again, I could make her no answer. So then she said that if I should go again and leave her to deal with Prince Arnuwandas on her own, she would surely die. Thus she got me to promise her that until my eldest took his majority I would oversee the matter of his upbringing. I soothed her, somewhat desperately, before my men, for the heat was rising in my neck and the muscles jumping on my back, and I wished she would go into the palace and shed her tears like any other woman, where no man must look upon the sight.

I was glad when she composed herself and relieved when, with a smile like the sun breaking over the mountains she bowed back from me and turned and ran down the crowded aisle between the soldiers and chariots, and with a sigh said to myself: "You are home. It is begun," and felt foolish and a little amused, and gave no more thought to her in all the leave-taking and order-giving and counsel-rendering incumbent on a king who is a general at such times.

Not until the sun settled onto the peaks, and the shadows stretched and woke themselves up to begin the siege of the sky, did I manage to extricate myself and slip out of the citadel to seek the rock sanctuary.

On the way, I passed my "father" Tuthaliyas' mausoleum, and my father Arnuwandas' mausoleum, and almost stopped to tell them what I had done. But the day died around me, and I wanted another to hear me, so I did not stop but climbed on. I climbed past the spot where I first had seen the blue-cloaked lord strolling in the moonlight and past the spot where I had hid when no bigger than my youngest was now, and watched Hattusas burning bright and lurid in the moonless night.

It was the morning after the fire that the eagle and I had first met: the smoke from the fire must have disoriented him; he had flown into a spire of stone and damaged a wing. He was vile at first, the black eaglet, dancing around with his hurt wing outstretched and charging me with vicious beak stretched wide. Those birds around the sanctuary are said to belong to the dead: from that first time when he ate of the twitching rabbit I impaled alive in a crack on the ledge we shared, he was mine. In my heart, our fates had always been linked, and so I had brought my sons up, each one, for his approval, and always climbed to the foot of the great rock on which he nested when I had something to sniff out or some kingly deed to report.

There was hardly any daylight left when I gained the ledge, just two lines of molten gold turning pomegranate over the mountains, like chariot-ruts in the sky.

I gave my eagle-call, and heard back a soft challenge, a rustle and snap of wings. Craning my neck I thought I could just make out a beaked head, an arch of wings against the oncoming night.

"So, old bird, you have your throne yet. Is it well with you? Things are well with me, exceedingly well. I have brought you no sacrifice. Would you eat from my hand, still, after so long?"

Only a dry rustle, like twigs, answered me.

"No reply? So be it, Overlord of the Air. I have kings enough licking my palm clean, albeit none of them are better than falcons: they take to the hood and the fetter, strike at my bidding, then return to hand though the cage awaits. What think you: must a man make do with such allies?"

I heard an answer, then, and another call in reply, softer, and I began to suspect the truth, although it was not until the following day that I saw the black eagle's wife.

CHAPTER 18

When Arnuwandas' fourteenth year and his manhood trial blew in on the harvest wind, the black eagle and his brindle mate had raised a brood and thrown them from the nest, and I was feeling a like inclination myself.

That year was the year of Amenhotep III Nimmuria's First Jubilee: they sent up those faience beetles from Egypt with a commemoration of the event inscribed on its reverse in their picture language and a copy of the text in Babylonian so we could read it. It was also the year Pharaoh raised up to co-regency his son and successor, Amenhotep IV, whom we would come to address as Naphuria, or Huri. How innocent would have seemed these official communications from the Egyptians if Hatib had not been telling me what swam beneath the surface of that river of diplomatic inanities. If not for Hatib, I would never have known even the proper names for these kings with whom I exchanged cool but polite letters, and gifts of silver and gold.

For a little more silver than I spent officially, I was receiving from a man named Duttu, who was employed by the Egyptians as an official of their chancery, terse accounts in excellent Hittite of what was noteworthy in those dispatches that crossed his desk. Now, although written Babylonian as it exists in diplomatic correspondence is as corrupt as commonly spoken Hittite or Luwian when compared to ancient Hattic, it is the language of the times. Writing to me in Hittite was as good as writing to me in code: None but my own could read it, save folk like this Duttu, who had gotten his place in a kingly court because he could write the tongues of the princes of "Upper Retenu", which is what the Egyptians call everyone north of "Lower Retenu", which is all of the coastal plain below Amqa and Kinza and east of Mitanni, which the Egyptians call Naharin. I am telling you this for a reason: the barriers of language may have been breached by the polyglot called Babylonian, which contains Hittite words and Hurrian words and words for which none recall the origin, but the walls have not been tumbled. And though I am no better at the ancient Hittite tongues than the folk who mouth them by rote at cult ceremonies, I took the time to instill in my children the importance of literacy: what a king can read himself, none can misinterpret to him; what a foreign scribe will do, no man may know in advance.

I was finally to take Khinti to Alashiya, as I had promised: for three full seasons, and also as I had promised, I had kept close to Hattusas whenever I might, which was more frequently than I had expected. The matters of my concern in that period became sharply circumscribed. The comportment of my new allies needed constant scrutiny. The terms of our treaties I oversaw stringently, that they would hold over the years. I rearranged the assignment of troops levied from treaty signatories: though a treaty specified that someone's troops be posted in a certain place, I used them elsewhere, and from such simple necessities great altercations grew like weeds which must be pulled up one by one from between precious seedlings.

Increasing the flow of Alashiyan copper became my real concern, although my mother of former times had given me a final gift: she had died and rendered me an excuse to visit the island of her exile I would not have sought, but which well served me. So when I debarked from the ship with my queen and her three princes and my son of the second degree, Kantuzilis (who was the same age as my youngest, Telipinus) I did so in the most somber and suitable circumstances I could have imagined.

This was the first time I had been anywhere of strategic interest in nearly three years time, and I had been close to pawing the ground when the news of my mother's death had proffered the excuse I needed to be quit of the Hattian nobility for a while.

The Sun Suppiluliumas — who had not been ill a day in my life but for the headaches attendant on my appointment as favorite of the Storm-god — had experienced an agony near unto death at the bidding of the geniuses of the sea. Never have I been gladder to take to my bed than that first evening in Alashiya when the unctuous, dissembling solicitation of my host the Alashiyan king finally dribbled to a halt:

"In the morning, most honored Great King Suppiluliumas, my brother, I myself will lead you and your beauteous family on a tour of the island. Khinti, dearest queen, think upon what you would like the Sun, our guest, to see."

All evening he had been like that: slickly sweet, just short of insult, ever reminding Khinti that she was a part of his 'we' and I and mine were the strangers whom they together must entertain.

"Then get a commander of ten, or two commanders of ten, to put on my boys' tails if you want anything left of your island by sunset." I growled at him and pulled Khinti roughly to her feet and pushed her before me in the direction of the gilded lintel.

I heard the king of Alashiya titter uncertainly. The next day, he was not laughing. Though it was Arnuwandas whose behavior had Khinti in tears when I first got back from Kizzuwadna, and though I had taken my eldest firmly by the scruff of his neck and proved to him that might is greater than right on more than one occasion, I had apparently started on him too late. If it takes one hundred and eighty-four days to train a chariot horse, how much longer, then, a prince? I had been about a hair's breadth from throwing Piyassilis into the ocean, nor was the smug godliness of young Telipinus any easier on my nerves. Kantuzilis, whom I had begot on Takkuri's sister, was a sickly child and browbeaten by his more royal siblings, and it was Khinti's compassion that had added him to my troubles for the length of our Alashiyan journey.

Now you must realize that vandalism and theft and assault and disobedience are often part of a boy's maturing: I did. I had not forgotten. But I found myself at a loss to understand it in them, whom I had so carefully spared those agonies of childhood which had turned me into the streets. So when my sons proved as rebellious (in the case of Piyassilis. perhaps more so) as I had been without those provocations I well remembered, I was at first tempted to make light of Khinti's distress. Soon Piyassilis' looting of my brother Zida's purse convinced me of the errors of omission I had committed so far as he was concerned; and upon the heels of that, before the furor had died down among the adults, my eldest forced a concubine to his bidding in the palace halls.

My duty became clear.

I spent an afternoon knocking them down, one at a time, and when they would rise up I would knock them back to their knees; and they could not say I took unfair advantage because Arnuwandas was hard on his manhood and Piyassilis a scant year behind, and both of them and their younger brothers Telipinus and Kantuzilis I included in the bout for good measure: four against one evened the odds.

But my sleep was disturbed by my princes until, just before we left for Alashiya, I called to audience my eldest, whose head reached my shoulder and whose body had the stretched-out look of someone whose girth is but a promise to come, and reminded him of his oath and told him that if indeed he continued to behave thus, I must judge him in contempt of that agreement laid between us.

"In the case of a boy breaking an oath, it has little meaning, but in a man, this is a different matter. If you cannot mind your oath, we will get the tablets out from the temples and destroy them, and then you can proceed as you have been doing and I will not have to take your life for it."

So he had agreed to honor his obligations to the Oath Gods and I had agreed to allow the celebration of his majority to proceed as planned upon our return.

But barely a day upon Alashiyan soil, all my fears came true: Arnuwandas and Piyassilis disappeared into the city.

"How," I demanded of my host, "could they have eluded your bodyguards for so long?"

"How," snapped he in a moment of forgetful openness, "can you raise such lions? Now they are in my city jail, in our custody, but what do you expect me to say to this vendor whose premises was torn asunder, or to my shipmaster whose daughter will never be the same?"

"I will reimburse the vendor and take the girl to Hatti as a full concubine," I said flatly. "Now give me a moment to think."

Grumbling, the pectoraled monarch glared at me, then subsided.

"Leave them where they are," I told him. "A night in a cold cell will bank their ardor."

When later I held Khinti in my arms, I even managed to forget altogether my princes, who despite all the wisdom of Arnuwandas' fourteen years were doubtless shivering in each others' grasp upon prison straw. And that worked so well that I contrived with the Alashiyan king to leave them there for the duration of our stay.

I walked the pale beaches with my beloved. We ate of the sea's bounty and trod the twisted alleyways of the bazaars. We saw black Nubians on Egyptian oars, and black-sailed Ahhiyawan ships with their clean-limbed, pale-skinned crews. We saw the small folk who once ruled those far western isles, brown-skinned, yet sharp-featured like Hittites under their curled and glossy hair. Khinti called them Minoans and told me stories of their mazelike palace and its destruction that she had heard from an old man who was a functionary of Minos' court when he ruled from Knossos, before earth and sea and fire and fate rose up and swallowed his empire whole. You still see them, the disinherited children of Minos, sailing the coast dazed and silent, living artifacts from an entire culture which is no more. Some say that the gods shook the earth from under them for their wickedness, and that monstrous creatures not wholly manlike roamed their streets.

I bought my Khinti the red-striped pottery she begged to own, not caring if, as she said, it would increase in value now that the country of its origin was overrun.

She never tired of shopping; we would walk the quays and she would giggle with delight and point out a ship from Ugarit, a war galley from Amurru, or a round-bellied freighter from Tyre. And while Khinti shopped I studied the soldiers and the crews of the different ships, judging their mettle and their weapons by eye, and gathering impressions of the lands they represented.

I mentioned to Khinti that I would have some of the purple cloth dyed from the shells found on Amurrite and Ugaritic beaches, and asked her if she thought it might go well with this room or that, and she offered to arrange to have me meet her uncle the king's representatives to those countries.

I also met Hatib, for it was the night of the full moon, as we had prearranged.

I slipped away as easily as my boys from the Alashiyan watch, meeting none in the corridors of the palace overlooking the bay who dared even raise their eyes to me, and meeting my own man at quayside where the Hittite ships rocked complacent, their masts splitting the night. Hittite ships have moored in Alashiya since ancient times; we are no monarchs of the ocean, and yet a great country must have some naval forces — thus, Alashiya was conceived, to supply the clement port our mainland coast lacks. Over the years the two nations have grown unfamiliar, like dimly-recollected cousins distant in time and space, and the trading colony of Alashiya has waxed so mighty that Hittite ships no longer are the mainstay of her defenses. Still, when I had first boarded the small boat which rowed us out to the magnificent black ships adorned with gold that rocked smug off the mountainous coast, I boarded a vessel manned and commanded by Hittites and designed for the very purpose of ferrying Hattian monarchs whence they chose, and needed neither my personal troops nor a moment's thought to feel secure doing it. The sail is about the distance a racing chariot can make in a day, some say. The trip takes me a little less time than that, and I have made the journey often since then in my determination to reacquaint Alashiyan government with its responsibilities to those who created it — not in my lifetime will we lose a single arrow fit to the bow of great kingship.

That night I was pondering the difficulties of such a determination, in streets filled with folk of every color and kind known to civilization: Ugaritic people, their curled hair oiled; Egyptians with their shining shaven pates; Amurrites in blood-brown, arm in arm with slight, jut-jawed sailors from Sidon. Even Assyrians lounged in doorways stroking their squared beards and laughing. I had brought Lupakki across the sea, and my personal thirty. These men of mine were sprawled like so many trained leopards among the bales and pottery urns filled with oil and stamped with the seal of my own palace, so that I was alone and yet not alone at all. If I had put them to watch my elder boys instead of giving each and all leave to explore the city, my princes would not be spending that full moon night among thugs and murderers on beds of straw.

But a man cannot think of everything, and I had simply assumed that those Alashiyans who wore the gold and black of Alashiya's Hittite navy would be the equal of two mainland adolescents, even though they be princes of the blood.

I sighed, banished my regret and the nagging discomfort of a man out of his element and not ready to admit it, and when I had finished rubbing the salty grit from my eyes, a man sat to my left upon a bale of wool, swinging his feet and humming softly as if he had always been there: Hatib had arrived.

Seeing this, the shadow that was Lupakki lengthened, wavered as if thrown by a flickering candle and, with a rattle of bullae, sank back among the waist-high shipping jars.

The humming stopped: The man on the bale of wool said, "I bow down seven times before thy majesty — figuratively, of course, my lord, lest the sharp-eyed shipboard take notice."

"Greetings, Sutu, what happened to your princely sidelock?"

"Ah, a sacrifice for my neck's sake. It is one thing to flaunt your heritage among the ignorant, another to offend the sun folk of Pharaoh's court."

"Where you are now employed?"

"Most exactly, my astute young lord."

"And how do you find the service of the Egyptian kings?"

"Profitable; their gold is ruddy but as good as any." Hatib looked quickly around him. His snake's voice susurrused suggestively: "The very quays have ears. You are looking less kingly, like a mercenary or a pirate yourself, young lord, and such men cause less comment in a tavern than lurking about on the dock."

Neither myself nor my men had chosen to display any rank this evening. I hitched myself off the bale on which I had been sitting and scratched my bare head: once; twice in the light of the moon.

As I headed off down the pier with the tall Sutu in Egyptian dress by my side, shadows writhed and split, and if anyone was watching he saw those shadows drift one by one down the winding ally in our wake.

"My deepest consolation in the matter of the little mother, Daduhepa," breathed Hatib. "And of the pale-haired Titai, my heart is too choked to speak."

"That is old news. It reminds me how long it has been since you and I shared a cup."

"Indeed, traveler. This place, now, has a better vintage than its facade warrants." And we stepped together down three stairs, around a corner, down three again and into one of those crowded, noisomely dissolute taverns that seem to be the only attraction all cities hold in common. Although the girl dancing in the pit of sand wore less upon her sweating buttocks than would her Hittite counterpart, her bangles and beads and the thump of her belled feet mixed as well with the shouts and clapping of the men, and the air was as thick with plot and scheme and the reek of sweat and beer as in the lower city in Hattusas.

Ensconced in a corner, Hatib ordered wine and something else which I did not recognize from a girl who came and postured at our table, and who might have stayed there, her speculative leer unmistakable, had Hatib not hurried her with foul imprecations.

Myself, I was feeling more comfortable than I had since I left my plateau and its mountain stronghold.

While we were awaiting the girl's return my men drifted in one by one, wandered, settled about the long low hall in two's and three's, and prepared with unconcealed relish to await me in the style suitable to a man in such an establishment.

"There, my friend," said Hatib when the girl set down drink and a tray with a tiny brazier and a strawlike tube of metal whose end was turned up and which was balanced on an alabaster jar no bigger than my wife's unguent jars. "Try this."

Attempting to appear cosmopolitan, I did what Hatib did, and coughed, and then felt very strange as the sweet smoke did its work. That was the first time I had smoked the sap of the poppy; and I liked not at all the lethargy it imparts.

Such candor as then overtook me I credited later to the gummy black paste, but at the time I did not even notice the loosening of my tongue.

"How are you faring up on the ramparts?" Hatib asked.

"With the king, ill. While my guard was at liberty, my sons turned frisky and their escapades scandalized the palace. Moreover, when the king came to me and asked what to do about my princes, whom his guard had apprehended and incarcerated forthwith, I said: 'Leave them there.' Now according to my wife, this horrified the king, her uncle, more than anything my boys had done, and all Alashiyans are now convinced that indeed I do eat babies. Having earned the title of 'barbarian' here in three days,

I must find some way to turn it to my advantage, but I have not yet sniffed out *how.*"

My Sutu laughed his chilling gurgle and uptipped his jaw to gulp the wine, so that I saw again that pale scar encircling his throat and wondered how he had acquired it. But I could no more ask of that than of how he came to be pectoraled and kilted in linen and bearing all the gilded trappings of Amenhotep's foreign service.

"*How,* my esteemed friend? You have already done it: those posturers know only their manners and their presumption; anything unpredictable they fear. You will get more from them if they think you ready to eat their sons and daughters than if you spend a hundred double-hours in their tiresome entertainments. My lord must know that these folk faint at the sight of blood and fear most desperately whatever cannot be predicted by their astrologers and their seers. When I want some concession on the docks, I merely loom frighteningly. Sometimes I find I must snarl a little, but most times a sharp look sends them scurrying."

"You are Egypt to them."

"And you are Hatti."

"The two are not yet equally fearsome."

"Soon," Hatib promised, "soon," and with dancing eyes puffed once more on the pipe before offering it to me.

"I have heard that this paste ensnares the mind," I refused.

"And wine does not? Do I seem to you dimwitted?"

"Nevertheless, I want no more. What have you for me?"

"Many things, my lord; many things. Some for the present, most for the future. I am here with a man whom you should meet, to meet with another whose face you might wish to know, and all of us are supping with the Alashiyan king on the morrow. If the king has for you any other entertainment for the evening, demur, and you will find yourself in company and conversation which I promise will hold your interest. Only do not give the slightest sign that we are acquainted, for this man who is with me, one Lord Hani, is the emissary of the Good God of Egypt unto foreign lands — and he is sharp as a falcon. Do not underestimate him for his youth, or for his gentleness, or for his talent at making men do just that. He is a close friend to the friendless son of Pharaoh, and will someday hold the reins of Syria in his hand."

"You have written to me that the young king and the old are embattled on the very throne. What means this?"

"Impatient, my lord?"

"After a fashion. My new queen is likely to summon out the army if she finds me gone when she returns from her cousin's estate."

"Then, my lord, consider: Egypt's young king, Nefer-Kheperure Wanre Amenhotep the Fourth, is infirm and twisted of countenance and limb and has taken his father's political ploy to neuter the priesthood into his heart and made of it an obsession."

"Hatib, explain."

"My lord, when Neb-Maat-Re — Amenhotep the Third, whom you call Nimmuria — lost a son to the priesthood's 'carelessness', he raised up a minor god, the Aten, lord of the solar disk. He has continually strengthened this god, once only a part of the triune aspect Re-Horakty-Aten, and thus has put the priests of the ram-headed god Amun in the ranks of his enemies. He has taken them and made them small, and wealth they held as their god's he has given to his favorite, the Aten. His is a brilliantly conceived counterweight to the power of that rich and coddled priesthood, but it has made him great and resourceful enemies over the years. The dedication of his successor son early in life to the Aten must have seemed innocent politicking; but the boy is long of skull and jaw, and his lips thick as a horse's, and he is as mad as that mendicant there."

I looked briefly where he pointed, at a rag-covered beggar crawling among the tables on his hands and knees, spittle and gurgle frothing cracked lips.

Then I looked back at Hatib and raised an eyebrow. "You do not expect me to believe that?"

"Believe what you will, my lord. The years will tell the true tale. Amenhotep the Third will live awhile longer: the Goddess Istar of Nineveh, whom Tushratta's father sent down from Mitanni to heal the Good God of Egypt twenty years ago, did her work well. For an old man he is spry enough. Now take heed. . . ." Hatib's voice lowered as if it might fade away altogether.

I leaned forward to refill my cup.

Hatib leaned toward me, whispering: "Your correspondent Nimmuria Amenhotep the Third went to Sidon himself to quell the unrest there: he hunted and killed one hundred and eighty elephants at the headwaters of the Mala river afterwards. He is sending troops this very moment into the city of Byblos, to help Ribaddi the Egyptian governor against his neighbor, the king of Amurru. Now this king of Amurru, one Abdi-asirta, has sent his son to parlay with us, and the youth will be at tomorrow night's fête. My lord, I cannot too strongly direct your attention to the matter of these coastal principalities. Although Abdi-asirta, this Amurrite king, professes to love the head of Pharaoh, he does not love it; and although he professes to love the person of Pharaoh, he loathes the very kiss of the Two Lands. He plunders wherever he can on land and most especially on sea, and the letters that have been coming in from the governors of the Egyptian protectorates would bring tears to the eyes of a strong man, should he read them. Long those affairs have lain festering, unattended, yet no one in the palace at Thebes has time to concern their royal selves with affairs outside the family's."

"And so?"

"And so, my most honored employer, if this continues, it is doubtful that any action upon Egypt's part would be forthcoming should Mitanni suddenly fall silent. Pharaoh's lack of interest in all but barges for his pleasure lake and statues and wrestling with the priesthood could well serve the man who chooses carefully his moment."

"And the man who lends a helping hand to Amurru when none is forthcoming elsewhere might thereby acquire a valuable ally."

"My very thought. For the surreptitious sort of war you favor, the Amurrites are well suited. Myself, if besides my other sources I could add the coastal view, if I may so call it, then we would be better informed than previously I had dared hope."

"Upon that, how goes it with my new queen's father?"

"Had he but one teat, I would wed him on the spot."

"Hatib, if all ends as we now dream it, and if my queen will oblige us and bear one, I will give you a princess."

His eyes lowered, his smirk came and went, and he reminded me that he had never met my new wife.

I answered him that on the morrow he would sit to table with her, if all went well, and the talk fell to that less dangerous than what had gone before.

I went not out of there until the moon had set, but then took with me all else I had sought from Hatib: details of reportage pertaining to the next year; changes in couriers lest they have by now drawn suspicion; and his views on what my vassals had been doing behind my back. Since none of it was other than I expected and well within my tolerance, I was pleased enough: princes will be princes, and autonomy is a dream all rulers share. My way with vassals is to give them that dream in substance, and remind them only when they err that they rule with my spears to their throats.

*

"Suppiluliumas." Khinti turned from the dawn coming in the tower window, her little fists clenched behind her.

"Surely you did not fear for me in this city you love so well."

"My lord, fear is one thing, concern another."

In due time, after I had given her to drink and to eat, she lay soft and yielding in my arms like a furrow newly dug. "My husband," she whispered in my embrace, "I waited and waited, and when I saw you would not come, I had my uncle release the princes Arnuwandas and Piyassilis — upon my order, for our host could not have slept otherwise. Are you angry?"

I tickled her, wondering whether or not I had begotten my princess on her this night, and then why she was so hard to settle, and then thought of Titai who never bore me so much as a runt, and then spoke to still my thoughts: "No, I am not angry. But now they are your responsibility, released on your authority. In the matter of your uncle's sleep, I do not see how my affairs can so concern him."

"My lord Sun," she said very slowly, weighing her words, "you have left me to rule Hattusas on my own in your absence, yet when you are returned you treat me like a concubine and speak not to me of the affairs of your kingship. You say to me you would meet with the Alashiyans concerned with Amurru and Ugarit to buy *cloth*. Do you think I am so lacking in statecraft that I could not see your intention?"

I laughed, she stiffened, and I said that I was sorry I had insulted her and would try not to repeat the oversight.

"My king, why will you not take me seriously? You made me Tawananna."

I groaned, and rolled over, and fled the bed. "Khinti, I surely did not mean to devalue you. Yes, I want more than cloth from Ugarit and Amurru. I want a place at the table your uncle prepares for Egyptians and Amurrites on the morrow. Can you provide it?"

I heard her soft gasp of surprise while I was looking out the window at the harbor and the dawn-fired sea. I continued to stare down the terraced slope, awaiting her response.

"I was going to ask you if you would attend, but. . ."

"But?" Then I rounded on her: "Is there perhaps a reluctance in you to expose your barbarian husband to these privy councils of your peers?"

"My lord Sun!" Her breasts, swaying, stared accusingly at me as she crossed the floor. She stopped before me with her fists clenched on her hips. "How denigrating is my husband! I try to present a queenly dignity, and at that you carp! Dear King, I — Oh —" Fists uncurled, her fingers sought her throat. Her eyes, pupils so huge in them they were deep golden-ringed pits of black, bored into me. "Suppiluliumas, I have loved no man but you. I venerate you above all others, so much that I wonder, of late, if I am not denying the Sun-goddess, my lady, what is hers. It is hard for me to speak, yet if I do not and things go ill it will be my fault. Please, do not take offense: you are so mighty,

yet with my people you are small and uncertain, compromised
by little things. And you think no one sees it, and try to hide behind gruffness and roughness: you are a caricature of yourself
in these environs. Must you give them so completely what they
expect? If your face is any indication, you see humor here. I do
not. Talk is a deadly weapon that flies across lands and seas un-
hampered. By this first sojourn out of your homeland people will
judge you. Will you have them saying that out from behind the
reins of your chariot you are no better than a common soldier?
They will call you less formidable, not more so, if you continue
your brash show, for all know that kingdoms are not held from
any man's car, but are only looted and lost again with no lord of
astute judgment and diplomatic skill upon the throne."

"Are you entirely finished, instructress?"

She looked away, and nibbled on her lower lip, and nodded,
swallowing repeatedly.

"Then tell me what plan you have in mind to undo all the mistakes of which I am guilty, and perhaps we can set things right."

With a wordless cry she flung her arms about my neck and
it was not until much later that we found time to talk again.

I remembered to warn her that Hatib, who was with Lord
Hani, was *the* Hatib from whom she had received letters and
messengers in my stead, and not to show any curiosity; and that
I myself would let slip not the slightest sign of recognition.

Unfortunately, in the press of matters, I did not consider
warning Arnuwandas, who yet wore Hatib's gift of the lapis Bastet
around his neck. And since Khinti had no inkling that Arnuwandas had learned his rough-and-tumble ways at Hatib's knee, she
blithely arranged to seat my boys at the banquet table, thinking
it as opportune a moment as any to fill their princely ears with
those matters she considered more important than military campaigns; but not thinking to inform their father.

So when my wife and two elder sons made a glittering entrance onto the portico overlooking the terraced drop to the harbor,
it was fortunate that I was standing near to the door, and equally

as fortunate that Hatib and his master the Honorable Lord Hani were admiring the view with their backs turned away from us.

I broke off in mid sentence what I was saying to Khinti's uncle, the Alashiyan king, and pushed my wife roughly out of my path, but still only reached the boys when the frown of concentration had faded from Arnuwandas' face and he was opening his mouth:

"Ha — *aah!*" said my eldest, the first syllable of Hatib's name giving way to an exclamation of pain as I grabbed him by the hair and thrust him back against a limestone column.

"Speak that name, and you commend its owner to an untimely death," I whispered, while still the exclamation hung on his lips, one hand in his hair and the other twisted in his festive tunic so that his feet barely touched the ground.

I saw his pain fade, and surprise with it, and understanding take its place.

Nodding, I let him go and stepped back, thinking that with any luck nothing would be made of it, or no more than could be credited to my barbaric nature.

But all were staring, so I said: "You will excuse me while I clarify certain matters with my sons."

And before I turned away and motioned my two princes to precede me through the arch into the darkened interior of the palace hall, I saw Khinti's agonized face, she holding to her uncle's kingly robe as if without his support she would faint dead away; and the Lord Hani peering after me like a very Horus through keen black eyes, stroking his chin.

"We will just wait here a moment," I told my two sons, "and then we will go back in, and you both will look sufficiently chastised that none will think twice about all this."

My boys looked at me, unspeaking.

"Do you understand, princes?"

Arnuwandas fingered the cat-headed lapis amulet he wore, as if he might remove it.

Piyassilis' touch stopped his elder brother before I could.

"Piyassilis is right, Arnuwandas: the Lord Hani may already have seen it," I commended.

"And if I am asked? Where shall I say I got it?" whispered Arnuwandas.

"Never lie, it is too hard to keep track of lies. Just be circumspect in your presentation of facts. If Hani asks, tell him you got it from a Sutu."

My two sons looked sideways at each other and, as on one face, their wolfish grins flashed out and elbows jogged sides. It was then that I saw them clearly for the first time in years, and wondered on what night their boyishness had crept off, never to return. Dressed as elegantly as Khinti could manage, of a height (though Piyassilis was broader and would surely be the larger man), they lacked only the official trappings of manhood.

"Before we return to royal games, let me say something: I have been negligent as concerns you both. It happens. Now Arnuwandas, you are of an age with me when I begat you on your mother in a moment of incontinence. I paid for that moment a thousand times more than it was worth. Take care in that regard: you need nothing less than a wife. The proof of that I hold out to you in the person of the shipmaster's daughter who is now your first lawful concubine."

I left off while he sputtered, then thanked me as Piyassilis pulled at the treasured fringing of hair about his mouth. There was no mistaking the difference in them: Arnuwandas had his mother's bones; and Piyassilis the great hands and neck and thews of his sire, making him look the older though he was younger by a year. In the black Hattian tunic whose golden stags strained to encompass his shoulders, Piyassilis might have been my very self — if a man could remake his past.

Even to the sardonic worldly smile he affected was he in my image, as he said teasingly that in the morning he would sniff out some suitable female to ravish, that he too might acquire a bedwarmer.

I told him what I would do to him if he did, holding my unfamiliar pride tight to my breast. But when I followed them back onto the portico, I was glad enough to parade them before a man who had seen the pointy-skulled, inbred weaklings who were said to simper on southern thrones.

This Lord Hani was shaven and bewigged and robed in gaudy magnificence. Some Egyptians are as tall as men of Hatti or Ethiopia, and sturdy like trees. Hani was not one of those, but a small, quick fellow with nut-brown skin and eyes so elongated with paint that they seemed to extend halfway around his head. The braids of his wig must have numbered five hundred, each one bound with golden cylinders that tinkled about his shoulders. His kilt was girded with a belt of beaded mesh that echoed the lotus motif of his pectoral, which again appeared on the blue and gold cloak that brushed his sandals.

But by Khinti's wiles the king of Hatti's appearance put Hani in shadow, as rightly should a king when confronting an emissary of kings. I had almost not worn what she had laid out for me: the tunic of finest black wool from the chest hair of lambs, custom fitted to my torso so that neither my arms nor shoulders strained it, all worked with the legend of the dragon Illuyankas in silver thread about the armholes and sleeves and at the hem. On my feet I wore black boots of softest ox and goat. About my waist hung the dagger from that same festival, its silver scabbard overlaid with raised depictions of the Storm-god's attempts to defeat the dragon, all in gold but for the eyes of them, which were blood-red stones. On my head I had a plain golden circlet, the dragon with tail in mouth, and about my neck the great seal of Hatti dangled from a chain whose every link was in the likeness of a fierce beast. The short, curved sword which I wore on my hips was my iron one, though the scabbard was gold, and it and the military cut of the tunic lent the whole affair the somber air without which I would have felt foolish, for however much you may terrace and plant a mountain, its peak looms no less lofty.

I looked down at the Egyptian whom Hatib held so highly, and he was no bigger than my wife who chatted with him in her most charming fashion.

Let me say of my queen only that she had chosen to display both her figure and the riches of Hatti, and admirably succeeded. Those effects of my former mother which had belonged to the state and yet which no man dared demand from her, my Tawananna now wore about her neck and waist and on her fingers and in her ears.

"O King Suppiluliumas," said Egypt's Honorable Lord Hani upon our introduction, "I have heard your chariotry is the finest in the world. I would love to see them, and your horses."

"You will see them," I promised him.

Without twitching an eyelid, the Egyptian rejoined, "Might I construe that as an invitation to drive up to Hattusas? I have a pair of mares which you might find worthy, should you see them, and another which I would dearly love to breed to one of your famous stallions."

"Is this an official request?"

"Everything I say, my most renowned lord Suppiluliumas, is official. If ever I step out from under the sheltering arm of the Lord of Diadems, King of Upper and Lower Egypt" — there followed a number of titularies evidently necessary before the speaking of the Egyptian king's name — "or if ever I should be acting upon my own initiative, I assure you I would make such an inconceivable act well known aforehand."

"So," I said, "then you expected to see me here, when I myself only learned of your presence last evening?"

"The Sun of Hatti suspects treachery? No, my lord, there is no treachery, only good will between our two countries."

"That is good to hear. I was wondering whether the cautions of my host here, and the grousing of a certain upcountry pretender, had come between us."

"Great King, the Sun, favorite of the Storm-god, the hero, you make a jest at my expense, I think, and before I have even given you the gifts I have brought all the way from Egypt, at the behest of His Majesty —"

I crossed my arms and broke in upon his recitation of titularies. "Let us leave out all that. You call me Suppiluliumas,

and your master Pharaoh or something similarly succinct, and
we will both know who is meant. And I still want to know how
you came to bring me gifts when none knew I would be here, let
alone be meeting with you."

"My suspicious Great Prince of Upper Retenu, I had thought
to leave the tokens of my master's brotherly regard with our host
to ship northward, since the coastal shipping these days is much
disrupted, and the inland trading routes so plagued with bedawin
brigands and Hapiru bands and border skirmishes between the
Syrian princes —"

"You mean between Tushratta and the princelings he en-
deavors to swallow, do you not?" I broke in, piqued at being
called a prince.

"Most revered Hattian lord, I am trying to tell you what you
want to know."

Over Hani's shoulder, Hatib gave me a knowing look and a
cautionary headshake.

"Say, then."

With a sigh, the slight Egyptian continued: "So, this being safest for so rare and precious a cargo, we had thought to
let Alashiya, whose ships are harried by none, get the gifts up
to Hatti. Alashiyans seem to have no trouble getting other ship-
ments to you."

"And I am not going to tell you how."

"Lord Suppiluliumas, I am not a devious man." Someone
snorted, and I shifted just enough to see who it might have been:
A lean, dark warrior in the last flush of youth lounged against a
pillar near the doorway, neither announced nor marked by anyone until then.

Turning my attention again to Lord Hani, I realized that my
wife and sons had disappeared somewhere with our host.

Hatib slid off the low wall where he had been sitting and
approached the young man by the door in such a way that Lord
Hani's attention was not diverted from his speech:

"Lord Suppiluliumas, will you allow me to present these
tokens to you in honor of —"

"Yes, yes, Hani, do let me see them," I agreed, wondering where my host and wife and sons had gone, and stepping from between the diminutive Egyptian and the young warrior to see what would develop.

What developed was that Hani stopped speaking in the middle of a word and closed his mouth, and I saw in him then the danger that Hatib had warned lay under his disarming manner.

"My lords, greet Aziru, prince of Amurru," announced my Alashiyan host as he hurried back through the arch from wherever he had gone. A quick glance showed me my sons by their stepmother, pretending to pick among the delicacies laid out for our pleasure by the arch.

Aziru of Amurru stroked his short black beard, fingers smoothing its point, and thrust himself away from the pillar without his eyes ever leaving Hatib, who had positioned himself where he could protect his Egyptian master most effectively no matter what move the young Amurrite might make.

"Who's your hunting dog, Hani? Call him off," said the prince of Amurru very quietly.

Lord Hani waved, and Hatib lessened his menacing stance ever so slightly.

"Let us all have a drink and sit to table," proposed the Alashiyan king hurriedly, taking the arm of the young, somberly dressed prince.

"I came here to talk to him, not to drink" said the Amurrite, shaking free. "I don't drink with my enemies, nor with their trained apes, no matter how well they mimic their masters."

"Aziru, what use is the trouble I have gone to in this affair if you will not —" pleaded my Alashiyan in-law.

"Who is *he?*" Aziru glanced at me. "It was supposed to be just the little monkey and me. And who are they? Did you bring me that girl, there, as evidence of Pharaoh's good will? Or those warrior cubs? I have no taste for boys."

"I, my lords, will answer that," I said to Hani and Khinti's uncle who were both white as bleached bone and struck dumb with horror. Only Hatib, who well knew me, was amused, and he ran his hand over his mouth and wiped his grin away.

My boys were up straight with their hands at their hips waiting to see what I would do, ready to avenge Khinti's honor by the look of them.

The ensuing silence I let thicken until I and the young warrior in robes the color of clotted blood stood close enough to count the hairs in each others' noses, and longer: until he stepped back a pace, then stopped and met my eyes once more.

Then I said, "I am Suppiluliumas of Hatti," and offered him my open hand.

"Aziru, son of Abdi-asirta of Amurru," said he, taking it very slowly and very carefully as a flush rose in his cheeks.

"May I present Great Queen of Hatti, Tawananna Khinti." I motioned her forward, and she quit the viands table and came to my side.

"My apologies, noble Queen Khinti," spoke Aziru most sincerely. And to my sons, when I called them forth, he bespoke similar sentiments.

I adjudged him only a few years older than Arnuwandas, despite his thick black beard, and saw in my boys the same thought.

Then the Amurrite prince turned again to me and said through unmoving lips, "My lord, I have heard great things of you in strange places."

"And I have heard less of you than I might wish. Doubtless we will remedy that."

Then the Egyptian insinuated himself into the conversation as smoothly as a sharp knife slices fat, and the Alashiyan king drew us into the palace proper to the feast he had readied.

During the meal, Aziru gave me a toast and when he had made it he proposed that since I knew nothing of the affairs in which he and the Egyptian representative were embroiled, I would be a better arbiter than even the Alashiyan king, whose function it was to provide an unbiased ear — but whose ear, in Aziru's reckoning, was not unfamiliar enough with those matters under discussion.

At his words I frowned and said that while I would be glad to hear the case and render judgment, I would expect my judgment to be binding on the parties concerned, and that under the circumstances this might not prove acceptable.

This saved my host from death by terror, by the look of him, and earned me an appreciative smile from Lord Hani but frowns from my sons, who plainly had already decided the case, whatever its particulars might be shown to be, in the young warrior-prince's favor. As had I.

And so, although I could not in conscience arbitrate between them, I sat with them while affairs of the coastal principalities were discussed. When I had heard of the terrible things this Aziru had done to the fleet of the sovereign nation of Ugarit; and the even more awful persecution his father had undertaken against certain individuals who served as Pharaoh's agents in the vicinity of the city of Byblos; and the way Abdi-asirta, this king of Amurru, had been increasingly swallowing up smaller countries on his march to the sea, I became intensely interested in places which before to me had been no more than foreign-sounding names thick with the romance of palm and incense.

This curiosity about the southern coast was increased by Hani's most obvious displeasure at his faring with the young Amurrite, and I vowed that when I returned to Hatti I would make a thorough study of these tiny nations and strategic Egyptian-controlled cities. Then, I just tasted their names: Sidon, Tyre, Byblos, the kingdom of Ugarit, Aziru's own Amurru, only recently recognized by Pharaoh as a sanctioned kingdom under putative Egyptian control. So far went Lord Hani, in the heat of his anger, as to threaten in plain words to remove Aziru's father from both kingship and life itself.

Upon hearing that, since the Alashiyan did not, I felt it necessary to intervene. Should I not have, Lord Hani might go home thinking he could someday threaten to lift my butt from its seat upon the throne of Hatti in like fashion.

"Is this, too, official Egyptian diplomacy?" I asked Hani aloud. "This man is son of a king — a crown prince, unless his

bearing deceives me — duly recognized in kingship by even your
master 'Fierce-More-Than-Panthers-Southern-One-Thousand',
or whatever his name is. Surely the jackal does not take down
the wolf! Leave off, Lord Hani, or all we monarchs of Retenu,
the Upper and the Lower, might find in your unilateral manner
reason to band together."

"My bold Hittite, think what you are saying!"

"I am thinking, fey ambassador; I am thinking. Either this
man is a prince and son of a king, or he is not. If he is, then you
are not the one to be threatening to dethrone his father in such
a cursory fashion, as if all that makes a king is your master's
sanction."

Aziru of Amurru only flicked me a momentary glance but I
saw there, despite his manner, that the prince was worried, for
it was like the look of a trapped beast who has been allowed a
chance to escape, only still does not believe it.

The Egyptian, in a flutter of engaging phrases, backed down
from his position, saying he had meant this, not that; and we had
misunderstood his intention; and lastly that his master so-and-so
of this-and-that would go no farther in the affairs of the coastal
cities than would ensure the safety of Egyptian merchants.

Whereupon the talk was changed deftly by our Alashiyan
host to the Sea Peoples, whose point of origin none knoweth,
and whose piratical activities were confined almost entirely to
the barques and galleys of "Upper and Lower Egypt," while the
young Amurrite breathed an audible sigh of relief and quaffed a
full goblet of wine without lowering it from his lips.

The speculation ended with the service of a sweet tray filled
with candied figs and dates and honeyed loaves rolled in nuts
and something else that when I swallowed made me lightheaded
even before Khinti's throaty whisper in my ear warned me that
the treat was intoxicating in the extreme.

I took her hand from my arm and kissed it, and asked her if,
so far, I had met with her approval.

She allowed that I had.

I did not say to her that I had only done what I would have done normally, any more than I had told her that her advice and Hatib's had been exactly opposite. But I thought: She gives me the Alashiyan view; Hatib gives me a Sutu's view. This Aziru speaks for the desperate little kings being squeezed like grapes between the trough of Egyptian might and the trampling feet of one another. And Egypt, she sits and waits and collects tribute from each and all, and when they have destroyed one another she will still be sitting there, licking her sphinx's paws and waiting for offerings to be placed before her. And I wondered how it must feel to commission a lake built for your wife and hand a piece of gold to each of your subjects so that all would feast when feasting was decreed.

"What are you thinking, husband?"

I had been turning my goblet in my hands, trying to slosh wine round its rim as high as I might without letting it spill over. "That it is getting late."

"My friend is right," bespoke the Egyptian, who overestimated my good will. "I beg the Sun of Hatti's indulgence, for I would show the gifts I brought in celebration of the Good God's Jubilee."

Now, I had no gifts for him and did not know whether he had any for Aziru or my host and cared less, though I could see Khinti's brow knit. I bade him present what he would and, as I said it, my wife slipped from her chair and was soon lost to sight in the stream of servants who appeared at my host's call to clear away the banquet's remains.

The hall in which we sat was commodious, flagged with alabaster and slate, pillared with limestone, big enough to hold therein an audience or a troupe of dancers or whatever its king might choose.

While around me slaves bustled, and Hatib gave low orders to one of the stewards of the house, and the Egyptian strutted around arm in arm with the Alashiyan king making expansive gestures, I found a moment wherein the only ones who might have overheard anything I should choose to say to Aziru were my two sons.

Leaning over the table to grasp a rhyton whose silver sides were beaded from the wine within, I said to Aziru, "Have your father write to me. There are things for us to discuss. Or better still, come up to Hattusas when you can."

The young warrior grinned widely and raised his cup to me, then turned aside and asked my eldest if he might see the dagger that resided in so kingly a sheath.

My wife returned with a look comprised both of relief and uncertainty and slipped into place beside and hushed me when I asked her where she had been:

"Look, the bearers are coming."

"Indeed."

And they were: Egyptian pomp is not legend for nothing, though later Lord Hani apologized for such a thrown-together affair. He had not, he reminded me, expected to oversee a presentation.

The presentation commenced with him making a long speech in which he copiously praised his pharaoh. Next, bearers brought chests on poles. Behind them, more bearers brought a carrying chair which was enclosed. And all about this curtained box creamy-skinned little Egyptians cavorted, playing strange instruments and tumbling.

I remember thinking that it was a scene contrived to enthrall just the sort of person this Hani must have thought me to be.

Upon a thunder of drums, all stopped in their places and the redoubtable Hani began with a flourish to open the first small but opulent chest. From it came a silver box whose top was inlaid in the Egyptian manner, and a palette of ivory. These he gave to my wife, after showing them about for approval, and with a snap of his fingers sent the chest-bearers away.

I would rather have had the chest.

The second chest was larger and finer than the first and contained measures of precious oils in decorated pottery jars, and I then understood why the men bearing it in on their shoul-

ders had been slow and cautious as they made their way down
the hall. The chest, it seemed, was mine this time, for the whole
thing was laid to one side.

"Now, my gracious Lord Suppiluliumas, to those gifts for
Your Majesty, without further delay."

The whole entourage moved up, matching their pace to the
bearers of the tall, spacious enclosure, and they all knelt down.
From within its latticed screens a door opened, and a slave came
up to it, and another; and these let down from out of the miraculous sedan a series of steps like a ladder that unfolded until it
touched the floor.

Then went the Lord Hani over to the gauze-lined gilded cage
and down the stairs came a woman wrapped all in white linen,
whose feet upon the stairs were dusky and whose hand, when
Hani took it, was dark as night.

From around me came a rising murmur, and I slid down in
my chair and found need to pick my teeth, keeping my eyes on
Hani, who had now escorted this person to a place a bit away
from the kneeling bearers and the house of screens and returned
to the steps once more.

As for the dark female, all I could see was her upper face,
and it was like obsidian.

Again Lord Hani reached up to take a dusky hand and a second white-swathed woman whose feet were ebony dusted with
carnelian descended the stairs.

Thereupon, Piyassilis observed in a loud whisper that since
there were two of them perhaps I would give them to my princes,
so as not to split up the pair.

Khinti gasped and I heard a slap ring out, but did not even
turn to see which son had the misfortune to receive proof of their
stepmother's ire, for Hani had placed the second girl by the first
and returned to the ivory compartment once again.

At this, Aziru leaned forward, elbows on the table, and with
cocked head squinted into the doorway, remarking that "old
Shining-In-Truth" had never offered him anything but a pair of
copper bracelets, and those had had links joining them.

I chuckled politely, and then Hani announced: "Behold, the magnificence of the gift of friendship from Pharaoh (Life, prosperity, health be his!) unto his brother, Suppiluliumas, King of the Kheta, Great Prince of Upper Retenu."

And I beheld first a pointed-toed leg, then a thigh like finest diorite; then her foot found the stair. Now black skinned people are rare in the north, save for the Ethiopians in Egypt's army or an occasional Nubian slave. But what blacks I had seen had not given me even an intimation that such as the girl who descended those steps so fluidly might exist. She was dressed in only a wisp of golden cloth about her loins, the ends of it hanging down before and behind, and golden anklets between which a delicate chain ran, surely for show. Her breasts hardly jiggled on the stairs; their nipples were painted gold, their shape as perfect as the rest of her. She stood before her handmaidens proudly, her gilded eyes calm upon me and her mass of black curls swaying slightly. Then very slowly, taking evident pride in the stares upon her, she knelt down on her knees, and her attendants did the same.

Lord Hani, who had been watching her, nodded critically and asked me if the gifts suited: if so, he would dismiss the bearers.

I said that they did, and he motioned the girl and her attendants to the side of the room where they waited like so many jars of oil, and the bearers and pipe-players and drummers back whence they came, and minced over to sit beside me with a smug and satisfied air.

My wife (strangely enough considering that she had almost certainly slipped away previously to make arrangements to return some token of Hatti's esteem) apologized for our lack of suitable rejoinder and promised in a venomously polite tone to send forth things equally as "wondrous" when she returned to Hattusas.

I was thinking, chin on fist, about whether or not the black girl with the heart-shaped face and the almond eyes had truly been as tall as I myself, or only seemed so.

I was prudent enough not to attempt to find out that evening, but when at last I had a moment to myself, three days later, it developed that she was about a hand's breadth shorter than I.

One more item of interest pertains to that evening in Alashiya:

Whilst I was busy being considerate to my wife, the Amurrite forsook his chair. None could recall the moment of his leave-taking; he made no farewells.

Then, since Hani apparently had one more thing to say to this Aziru that he had forgotten, a thorough search of the premises commenced at his insistence. Inner and outer guards were queried, but none had seen the Amurrite depart.

In fact, while we were finding that out it became clear that none had passed him into the palace: they were still expecting him, both the Alashiyan palace master and the unaccountable number of Egyptians these inquiries turned up.

The next day Piyassilis and I found a grapple swinging from the portico's most secluded corner, and I thought that if I had been Aziru I would have done the same, did I suspect, as he must have, a trap. And from what I saw when they lost him, I would say he was not in error.

CHAPTER 19

In my twelfth regnal year, word came up from Egypt that the Good Gods were building a "wondrous City-of-Rejoicing-in-the-Horizon," and in so short a time as one year would move their entire court there. Now, why the Egyptian kings wished to retire from Thebes—whose magnificence was said to make the opulence of the palace at Ugarit and even Tyre's fabled spires seem tawdry—I could not imagine.

Just which of the royal personages had precipitated the move became abundantly clear: the younger Amenhotep, Naphuria, had settled into his kingship. And if not mad, this young pharaoh was indeed strange, or at least in a mystical way intriguing: building a metropolis to his god Aten on a camel-track.

But as rumors of the City-of-the-Horizon became serious consideration, and more and more of Egypt's attention focused on raising from the sand this whim of their two pharaohs, I myself was just completing my own preparations:

While the Two Lands were otherwise engaged, I would relieve them of the burden of their unconscionably abrasive neighbor: I was going after Tushratta of Mitanni.

So down from Hattusas went my determination, out to my vassals on this side and on that. I had been three years obtaining enough Alashiyan copper and Kizzuwadnan silver and Arzawaean tin to build up my armory. I had troop levies in the thousands from those countries newly Hittite, yet I added Sutu and Hapiru and bedawin fighters and paid for them with taxes from the countries they were assigned to protect.

All this I did so that I could take three hundred chariots and a thousand men down through the Kizzuwadnan pass into Mitanni, and find something left of my empire when I returned.

I had posted Kizzuwadnan levies in Arzawa and Arzawaeans upon the border of Hayasa, so that none would be tempted by the sight of their homes, and all the various novices we had schooled so that the plain beyond Hattusas looked like a battlefield two years running and the streets of the city were filled with foreign accents and costumes as varied as those I had seen on Alashiya. Almost.

I would think longingly of the days when a bad faring of one of my commanders was all I needed to slip my shackles and hitch up my cart. An empire such as fate had rendered me is buttressed by the bastions of its ruler's personality; bastions by their nature must be unmoving, else they inspire no trust. It took yearly more preparation for me to hunt a stag, let alone wage a war in person.

To all who advised me of these truths, I seemed resigned. And I was resigned—to wait until I had massed enough strength and honed my weapons, and even told them when we first returned from Alashiya that I would wait the three years' time and at the end of it I would move.

The Shepherd and my wife and my chamberlain accepted that with relief, and made no move to obstruct me as I continued to prepare. Until just before the final winter whose spring would see the forming up of troops, Hattusas seemed of one mind, man, priest, king and god. But then the omens started to go bad.

Not only the omina that could be manipulated, but things I saw with my own eyes or did with my own hand went inexplicably awry. For example, in the sacrifice to dead queens that Khinti performed, one of the lamb's livers was yellow and stinking, and the blood from its slit throat would not flow. We asked if this was because the queen was pregnant, and the omen was unfavorable. We asked if the gods were unhappy because we had omitted Asmunikal from the sacrifice to dead queens, and the omen was unfavorable. We put the deported queen in her place and performed again the entire sacrifice. *"Are the gods, our lords conciliated?"* *"No. The omen is still unfavorable."* I heard that so often I tried asking if the sun would rise on the morrow. The omen to that was unfavorable, though the sun did rise, which led some to suppose that we as the stewards and stewardesses of the gods had done something so terrible that none of us were pleasing in their sight. Now, that "we" was the whole of the temple of the Storm-god and of the Sun-goddess in Hattusas. So we sent to Arinna to have the priests there do some investigating, and what they said back to us was very vague but definitely unfavorable.

Now, life cannot stop because the omens are unfavorable.

It bothered me, that this be an ill time for divination, but not very much. Not so much as it bothered the Shepherd. I had a military campaign shaping slowly in my hands, two sons now men and with the armies, and my sharpening interest in affairs on the coast of Syria. All the jostling and bustling of the rich and justly famous little port, Tyre; of rosy-cheeked Sidon whose palace gleams with red marble; of the cowering monarchy of Ugarit, so afraid for her libraries and her esthetes' sensibilities: all can be understood in proper perspective based on a single observation: Amurru lies *between* Ugarit and Egypt, who administrates and protects "all Upper and Lower Retenu". And Amurru was a lion lying among calves, a lion who has seen the Great Bull of Egypt, their father, in his pasture, and is cautioned but not deterred thereby.

I had exchanged one letter with Abdi-asirta. The man was cautious in the extreme. But he was Aziru's father, and I had liked

well enough what I saw in the youth to deem his sire a kindred
spirit to myself, if only in my private thoughts.

I was following the Amurrite king's exploits through my
Duttu, who yet scribed for Amenhoteps III and IV, with all the
eager delight of a youth at his first flame-lit reminiscence of soldiers' feats. At that moment, the King of Ugarit was weeping all
over the clay on which he begged Egyptian support against this
Amurrite who was nibbling away at his merchants' prosperity
on land and sea, and even at his very borders. Well would I have
liked to have the depradatory Amurrite under my sovereignty. I
suggested this to him openly, which is perhaps why he wrote me
no more after that initial exchange.

Not easily offended in such matters, I waited awhile, and
thought. Probably by the time I rode down through the Gates
into Mitanni, Aziru would have waked to find moored in Amurru's harbor a slim dagger of a vessel, crafted by Alashiya's most
gifted shipwright, unmarked by any identifying device. I hoped
he enjoyed it; I had no doubt he would know whence it came.

Although Aziru was only a few years older than Arnuwandas, he was no more than a decade younger than I. I had more
hope for wooing the son, who with the squeeze of meaningful
years after twenty would soon seem my contemporary, than for
his father, who must be gray-haired and whose temper promised
that he would not live to see it change to white.

I am not a self-effacing man, yet even I had been taken
aback at the audacious nature of Aziru's father's kingly deeds.
I, were I ruling that precarious strip of land, might have been
more cautious. There has always been a country *Amurru.* But it
had no seaboard when my father's father ruled. It was said that
Abdi-asirta's swelling populace was composed partly of Hapiru,
and if those homeless found welcome with him in exchange for
military service, then we had both offered them the same. But
the drama of the upstart warrior-king and the great pharaohs
of Egypt seemed to be taking a turn for the worse, and while I
wished him well, I could not take a hand unless invited, which
I was not. So, like a man who bets on a team's racing season, I

followed with anticipation the trials of the Egyptian governors of Lower Retenu at the hands of the king of Amurru.

So enamored of my intelligence and the entertainments it provided did I become that I remarked to Hattu-ziti that it would please me if I could be kept informed of seaboard affairs even while I was on campaign.

It was when we had devised a way to do this that the omens had started behaving inexplicably, until I snarled at Khinti: "Then *make* them right! Lie, contrive, falsify, but *make* the indications favorable. *Now!*"

And she trembled for I was in my worst temper, during which no thing or person is truly safe, and fled.

When I calmed, I myself fled up to the rock sanctuary where the black eagle nested, to see what he would advise.

I shot a fat hare through the hind so it would yet be alive when I reached the ledge, and climbed up with the twitching thing tied to my belt, its warm blood trickling down my leg.

I saw him not, only the lady bird who kept his company. She dived without even a hesitation, straight for my eyes. I fended her off, taking only gashes in my forearms while I sought to protect my face, and she beat upward screaming. That had never happened to me before.

I watched her, soaring in circles, lest she drop again from the sky onto me, and slowly hitched myself up the rock, until I could peer into the nest.

My black eagle lay there, his feathers dull and fluttering, maggots crawling pale between them, flies walking on his staring eye. Great bloody gashes had he sustained in some awful battle; one wing was half torn from his breast.

I found my grip slippery, and when I lowered myself to the rock shelf, I was trembling. A short time after, I gave up the contents of my stomach. The hare still twitched weakly on my belt. I wrung its neck and tossed its carcass over the edge of the shelf, thinking that the black eagle died a valiant death, had even made it back to his roost with such dire wounds, and no hero could ask more than that. Yet I was wracked with a chill colder than the stone beneath me, and stayed there until night came and went away again and I had decided what I would do.

What I decided to do was: nothing. I told no one of the eagle's death; its discovery was inevitable, but the connection I had long assumed between the eagle's life and mine was known to no one but me. To all else he was simply an eagle sacred to dead kings, not live ones. And that mighty fighter would not have wanted his defeat to keep me, his brother, immured in Hattusas.

There is a thing about secrets: the weight of them grows daily.

Although none questioned to my face my overnight disappearance, my agitation went not unnoticed in the palace.

And as our departure into the land of my most-reviled enemy, Tushratta of Mitanni, loomed closer, I found that the weight of the black eagle's death bowed my back so that instead of seeing always the horizon, the ground upon which I trod was shown to me in ever finer detail. I walked the palace yards with my queen, and reliefs adorning the foundation stones of buildings among which I had played as a child took on a sudden poignant beauty, as if I had never seen them before.

We were sitting, she and I, with our backs to one of the man-long limestone oblongs.

"We have ten days, my husband. Ten days only, and then begins the long season's vigil. Every hurried tread in the halls will stop my heart. Every incoming dispatch will take away my appetite as surely as dreams of you will divest me of my sleep."

"Those things are not happening to you now? I go out to war to escape them, to shut forever Tushratta's mouth, whose words make little of my might before all the courts of kings. Rest easy. When I return we will build a winter palace on the Mala river, down where the Storm-god's reign is gentle, and you can eat of those warm-weather cucumbers and the hearts of lotus. And all those other things you have pined for, which misted your eyes when we were on Alashiya—all those will be there for your pleasure."

"Do you think I care for nuts and eucalyptus so passionately? Shall I trade my lover for a stand of cypress, my unborn child"—she cupped her rounding belly—"for bolts of gauze? I would rather stay in Hattusas evermore, in snow drifts so deep a horse could not walk through them, than see you off to one more assignation with the gods of the netherworld."

"Then come with me," I said, knowing full well that she could not do that.

She turned her face away and took quick breaths and said, "You tease me cruelly, my lord Sun."

Then I had to convince her that I did not mean to tease, and the conversation drifted to the naming of the child she nurtured, which irked me although I did not show it, irked me because I expected to be back in Hattusas long before the birth was due, and yet we were speaking about it as if I might not come back at all.

So it went, with the shade of the black eagle ever circling, his spirit wings throwing dark shadows about my head, and I found that my mouth went dry as we spoke of fitting names, and that my ardor for my wife was much increased.

It is not my practice, nor any man of moralities, to penetrate a woman well gone toward bearing. I had filled those evenings since Khinti's conception with my concubines, each of whom, after all, deserves at least one spawn from the man to whose pleasure her life has been dedicated without her consent, if only so that the child will fill the remainder of her empty days. Some of them I had sent away: to the winter palace in Kumanni or to the Salt Lake, or to the estates the king uses when on tours with the gods. Some, six in fact, I had passed to my eldest on his successful completion of his manhood ceremony, which gave him a total of eight, including the Alashiyan maiden whose father was a shipmaster, and one black maidservant of my tall ebony girl.

These he kept in with mine while renovations were being completed at the site of the palace of the grandfather. Since we had no grandfather to install there, I had commanded it remade to suit my princes. Therein would each of my sons, upon his assumption of the duties of manhood, be able to reign in private over the fruits thereof.

For the present, Arnuwandas, whom the troops called *Hartaga,* which means 'Bear,' was living in Samuha with the armies, as I had done. It is as good a place as any to learn the trade of war, though despite my wishes it was somewhat of a trap: he was my official successor, tuhkanti, crown prince, and though he was a good warrior I was not about to risk him and myself both in one engagement.

Piyassilis, on the other hand, I was taking out on campaign. Although his manhood rites had been undergone without the flamboyance my eldest displayed, it was Piyassilis and not Arnuwandas who had the soul of the armies in him. Stolid, silent, self-counseling Piyassilis was without doubt the best fledgling charioteer then training in Hattusas, and there was not one four-teen- or fifteen- or sixteen-year old Hattian soldier who would not have killed to win a place in a unit he commanded. All thought I would do that — give him his own command of ten, at least. I had been a commander at sixteen, however, and recollected the discomfort of station unearned and responsibility unclear until death inscribes its reality upon the heart. I put Piyassilis in a driver's slot among my thirty, which was an appointment perilous and honorific enough for a young man skilled as he, neither too light for his pride nor too heavy for his years.

He came to me soon after I gave out troop assignments and hovered unspeaking in the chancery where Hattu-ziti and I were digging our way out from under the inevitable mountain of last-moment details that humps up from the smooth plain of the most carefully conceived and methodically undertaken engagements when so many lives and borders are involved.

Finally, distracted by my son's berobed lingering in corners and his numerous journeyings unto the very verge of speech, I demanded of him what it was he wanted.

"Abuya, I did not mean to interfere." He only called me 'father' when he was troubled enough to forget his manly dignity.

"Hattu-ziti, let us have wine, and lay this aside."

My chamberlain scratched his thinning pate and stumbled up from the floor with exaggerated difficulty, grumbling about aging joints and cold weather, saying he would be glad enough when he could order the armies out from some tropical palace on the Mala's banks. To Hattu-ziti, as regards my efficacy in the waging of war, it was as if my word became fact upon speaking. I had said I would do it: to Hattu-ziti it was already done, only not yet noticed, like a beheaded corpse in a chariot that drives a length or two before realizing it is dead.

When the wine was brought, it loosened Piyassilis' tongue and eased his stiffness, and he said that if I could find the time, one of the teams he had been training had "graduated" and he would like me to see them.

Piyassilis' love for horses, and his way with them, was more than the infatuation that all boys endure and later transfer to women. His was a talent as sure as the ancient sculptor's who carved the larger-than-man sphinxes yet guarding the lower city gate.

The horses were scions of the black team I had taken from Tuthaliyas' stable when they shipped me off to Samuha, the same black team I had later given Arnuwandas and which he had lost while about acquiring the appellation 'the Bear.'

These horses were born black, surely, for their legs and manes and tails were black, but their flanks and barrels were dappled with rings of gray and on their proud necks black patches still showed.

The snorting, quivering dancers calmed as if by magic when they were backed up to the training cart, and with Piyassilis accompanying me behind a pair of white stockinged, blaze-faced chestnuts, I took them out of the citadel and down the ramp and across the bridge whose gorge ran white with the swollen water of winter's end.

The two were, I thought, as good as their ancestors, and with my son's prideful, critical eyes on them, we drove westward, until we came in sight of the encampment on the plain.

There I pulled them up on a rise, and Piyassilis wrestled down his chestnuts, and we sat on the rims of our carts and talked for a long while of the armies—only two men readying themselves for war. I had worked hard, these three years, at making my sons

believe that with their manhood they had acquired a certain sep-
arateness from the "family," so the men they were becoming and
the king they were serving could become acquainted and make
better use, the one of the other, thereby. It was harder for me to
do than for them to accept, but no other way is there for a man
who is a king before he is twenty, an overlord before he is thirty,
and at thirty-one has a tuhkanti seventeen and a charioteer of
note a year younger.

I praised him about the horses, and he said softly that he
hoped I would use them for my iron-trimmed chariot; they would
match it well. I had three teams more decorous that I was planning to drive, but I said that I would be honored to take their
virginity in the field, although they would warm to it more did
they go into their first war under the hands that trained them.

"Abuya, I know you strive to be impartial, and I respect that,
nor have I ever asked you for a favor, or played on my blood to
get my way."

"But?"

"But . . . Lupakki says I am ready to drive for a king. I believe I am. He would take the driver you had slotted for yourself.
The man whom you chose and I drink together. In the clarity of
wine, this Tarkhunta-zalma has confided that while he is honored
to have been chosen to drive for Your Majesty, he is afraid his
sonship to Kuwatna-ziti rather than his skill has precipitated it,
and that if a single thing should go amiss, he fears the wrath of
the Great Shepherd more than a thousand Mitannian charioteers.
Under those circumstances I just described, I had to warn you.
Although you may think me importunate, a man so inhibited is
not the one to drive for the Sun of Hatti."

"And you say this Tarkhunta-zalma would be at ease driving for Lupakki?"

"He has a long acquaintance with him; they could work together as easily as they spit namra. . . . And I, more than anyone
else, am free from awe as regards your person."

"Is that a polite thing to say to your father?"

"It is the truth."

"And truth is its own reward? Not always, not always." I was thinking of the black eagle, looking out upon my hosts crouched bristling on the treeless plain. Then I saw a vision of my neatly quadranted armies cast all asunder, as in the confusion of joined battle, when a man must mark closely car and helm or skewer one of his brothers instead of the enemy. But a king must have faith in his own. If Piyassilis thought himself man enough to protect and succor me in battle without thought to what his failure to do so might mean, then I must at least equal him in valor.

"You have it. But do me one service: Get your concubines with child before we leave. It never hurts to secure your line." I was watching him closely as I spoke, to sniff out any surreptitious doubt or fear as I stated the unthinkable for his benefit. A man, especially a young man relatively unbloodied, never thinks: "What if I should fail?" He thinks of others dying, but his own death whispers not in his ear. Death would be screaming at him, its icy talons deep in his neck, when at last he faced a multitude of howling strangers intent on separating his head from his body.

Piyassilis stared back at me, rubbing his finger along the manly hair which drooped around his mouth, and said nothing. So after a time I said that it is a braver man who hacks off his braid and sews it on his helmet than one so enamored of his peers as to go into battle offering out a luxurious handhold to the enemy, and turned the team toward home.

I myself did not obey that maxim, but neither did I grow hair on my chin except from laxity, and though Piyassilis' beard concerned me more than his braid, I knew than when the lice and fleas and ticks of the field started nesting in it, he would shave it off and I would get to see what my second son's face looked like now that he was a man.

When we handed the lathered teams to the grooms, Piyassilis suggested diffidently that in the matter of my youngest boy, Telipinus, I might be wise to take a hand. With that enigmatic statement he busied himself with ordering those who mix horsefeed as to a change in his beauties' rations, and from across the stable-yard a Meshedi hurried in my direction.

So it was not until two nights before we were to see the southeastward march of the troops quartered on the plain that I found time to invite my youngest son to meet with his stepmother and me.

The pace of events had quickened so by then that I had not sat for a moment the day long, nor eaten other than standing on my feet. I might as well have already been gone from Hattusas myself, so crowded were my waking moments with matters of war. Detail in those times multiplies as quickly as a beekeeper's swarm, and like such a swarm at the honey's harvest, each constituent thereof buzzed around my head with ready stinger, awaiting its chance.

But I had done it all before, and knew well how to avoid the hurry that nurtures error. I proceeded carefully, my attention on each task at hand, conscious at all times of the price of a misstep. I succumbed not to the excitement that blew in like pollen on the wind, covering everything with a soft golden pall which leant an air of unreality to that most real of undertakings.

Khinti had been watching me accelerate by reducing speed, as it were, well knowing that my tolerance for the routine and the methodical was fast being exhausted. Without even my suggestion that it be so, she arranged for us a private supper on the terraced bank of a pool amid the gardens in the shadow of the citadel wall.

This intimate feast my black concubine served us, so that even with the matter of servants I was not disturbed. Nor did Khinti show the faintest trace of the disquiet she had evinced when, the day before, she had come to me with downcast eyes and tiny voice and said that she had done it: falsified the omens and made others do likewise: all the indications were now favorable as regards our first foray into Mitanni.

And I had said to her crossly that it was nothing, that she should not fear, that soldiers, especially charioteers, are the most superstitious of folk. I recounted a tale of example, about a charioteer who would not change harness nor bit nor buckle before a battle, and Khinti tried valiantly to smile, but failed, and I had slammed out of the hall to make more constructive use of my time.

There was none of that this evening, and when young Telipinus was brought to table, all scrubbed and red of cheek and wet of head as twelve-year-olds must be before their elders, dressed princely in a fine robe of blue wool with a shawl like a man's thrown diagonally over his shoulder and girded about his waist with a dirk, there was no discord to be seen upon the table of the Sun, or about it.

I was feeling invincible and full of anticipation; after a day so stuffed with endeavor, the warm wine and the stewed lamb and the familial and elegantly measured talk made all seem distantly sure, decided, far away. I was enwrapped in a languor the like of which there is none so sweet, full-hearted, as content as a man may be at a moment of beginnings, all qualm and conjecture quieted.

"When I am a man, *I* will not drive another's chariot, but wield an axe and bow," announced Telipinus, who was struggling to conceal his jealousy, but not succeeding, as concerned Piyassilis' new posting.

"I thought you were decided upon the priesthood," interjected Khinti, for the first time showing concern. It suited me as well as her melancholy, valorous gaiety.

"I will be a warrior priest, like the Shepherd."

"Do that, and I will give you your own kingdom," I offered. "But you must be as wise as Kuwatna-ziti, and as pure of heart."

"I will be so," said Telipinus gravely. "The god has told me."

As Khinti's eyes met mine across the table, I was wondering if it was she who had instilled in Telipinus this passion for the voice of his namesake deity.

"Indeed? What did he say to you?"

"To study kingship, and meditate upon it, and make myself ready."

A shiver crawled many-legged up my spine. That shiver was my first intimation of the "specialness" of Telipinus, who talks to gods. Then, I was only glad Piyassilis had drawn my attention thence. Sound, pragmatic, Piyassilis (cast in my image and deaf as I to those whisperings which make of men fanatics and prophets) had been worried. I was only mildly concerned.

"Telipinus, there is a thing about man and god: each must remain what they are. If a man aspires to exaltation through his closeness to the gods, my lords, he may do it — but only in a manly way. Gods are the first to strike down pretenders to their company, and it is well noted that too many godly embraces drive mortals mad."

"Your father is trying to tell you that fanaticism has no place in the heart of a Hittite prince," said Khinti, and reached out to take Telipinus' hand.

He pulled it roughly away and squared back his shoulders, those black eyes of his burning priestly from out of a visage already sharpening from boy to man.

"The gods call whomsoever they will," rebuked Telipinus. "Neither I nor you, dear surrogate mother, nor my father, will have anything to say about it."

"And to what have the gods called you?" I said, forcing a grin, not allowing myself to become irritated.

"First, to repairing the archives. There are many broken tablets, and two that contradict each other, and about my mother there is almost nothing, about my grandmother, less than that. . . ."

Then I knew where the conversation was leading. So I did not wait, but broke in: "The task you attempt is laudable; you will learn much thereby. But those things you find confusing — the particulars of myself and my immediate predecessors, and events occurring between the decimation of Hattusas and when I sat down on the seat of kingship — were made that way by a number of factors. Firstly, the sack of Hattusas itself. Secondly, the prince Kantuzilis who was my uncle swore that none would recall my name nor my deeds nor anything about me, when I was a mere prince and he was sure of his power to end my life before I took the throne. So, much of what is missing is missing because of his ill will. Thirdly, your 'grandfather' Tuthaliyas was his own man in the morning, but wine's slave by midday. You will see in his writings that I was Crown Prince while I was fighting in Samuha—no one knew that, not even myself, at the time. That is a lesson for you: the histories tell us what those who write them would like to be true and, when all involved are gone to be gods, it *is* true. From former times down to these, kings have twisted new truths from out of old embarrassments. There is nothing in those archives that a man can take on faith, any more than any of my fellow kings really host in their hearts the brotherhood they expound so dutifully. Do you understand?"

In a subdued voice, Telipinus agreed that he understood, but I felt he was playing me false, and became sure of it when he asked if I would go through the records with him and set things right.

So, lest he think I was making light of him, I said that when I could I would sit down with him and explain everything, though I doubted privately that I would ever find so free a moment, and even my ability to make those matters clear. In the matter of my parentage it was certainly not possible. But I did not want him looking at me so suspiciously, although mistrust is perhaps the first sign of maturity in a boy, and when at last we parted I felt sure that I had allayed at least his most gnawing doubts.

After he was gone back to his bed, Khinti and I walked the pond's edge in the torchlight and spoke of inconsequential things until the midwatch's cry rang out.

Then, amazingly for she had said nary a word about my nightly absences since I had got her with child, Khinti stopped stock-still, pressed close and put her hand upon the buckle holding the swordbelt at my hips: "Those things that you do with your wanton black and with your namra in the field—do them to me."

I chuckled, thinking I could not very well do that, lest I injure the child she held within. But her fingers penetrated my robe, and her eyes were luminous with the intensity of her emotions, and in them I saw that it cost her dearly to say what she had, and how long she had wanted to say it. And while I was not sure quite what she thought she was missing, nor how I might fare at treating her like a piece of booty; nor even if she would find whatever it was she thought she was being denied if, like a namra, she ended the evening weeping at my feet, I did my best to honor her heartfelt desire, albeit "honor" is something decidedly lacking on the woman's part in such affairs, and I had to take care to her safety, and to the child's, which in the true situation is no consideration whatsoever.

And it seemed, when the deed was done, that she was content, that she had indeed acquired whatever she had felt herself denied in prior lovemaking — all of which left me with the uneasy conclusion that for every night of all the eight years I had had her she had been unsatisfied in my bed, feigning her passion all along.

I found myself often thinking about the irony of her pretending and my pretending, and all the agonizing care I had taken to be gentle and kind and all the agonizing care she had taken to pretend that she appreciated my gentility and my kindness, and what this revelation might portend for the future: after all, she was my queen and Tawananna, mistress of Hatti in her own right, and we both were keenly aware of the dignity, inheritable and totally separate from that of kingship, she alone could bequeath to her heirs; and after all, she could stop at any moment, by her command, any situation that she felt demeaned her. So, after all, we were not really doing it, only playing. Which meant I was no better off than I had been while trying my utmost to bring my respect for her into bed; in point of fact, I still must tote it there. . . .

Be there any answer for the above-mentioned quandary, I have not found it, unless it is this: should a man not care sufficiently to wade in the river of deceit at the outset, he will not, so to speak, get his feet wet. But I have only succeeded in doing that with women about whom I cared moderately — at least, I could not do it with Khinti; it was my feigned moderation of immoderate lust at the outset that allowed things to develop as they did. But tell me, is there such a quality as moderation in lust?

There is no moderation in war.

When I joined the armies massed in Kizzuwadna, all my vassal kings and I watched them pass in review. Hugganas of Hayasa was there, and young Mariyas who would head the Hayasaean contingent of my force, and the Little Mouse of Mira, with his fourteen chariots to lend; and from all the parts of Hatti, the Upper and the Lower, from Ishuwa to Arzawa's shrunken frontier, my warrior-governors and warrior-feoffees and warrior-priests had come with what troops they could field.

I was no fool: I made sure that every land whose care rested in my hands, no matter how restively, added their citizens to this endeavor. There was no town or village in Hatti, no matter how small, that could say, "We had no part in it."

And my Hapiru and my Sutu and what bedawins wandered my hills, they also took a part. The auxiliaries and the Hittite foot marched by, mixed one with the other, and a glow of pride suffused me: this, I thought, is how it should be.

Then Kuwatna-ziti and I did the ceremony of the border at the boundary stone dividing Kizzuwadna from Mitanni near the mountain pass, and when I waved a farewell to the Shepherd who was headed back to Hattusas to attend the war of words in my stead, I was already standing in Mitanni.

We were striking for Carchemish on the Mala river, and once down through the pass our path was almost due southeast.

I had known the heat would be a factor for the horses, if not the men, and planned accordingly. A man can fold up his robe and his tunic, bind his kilt about his loins, exchange his boots for sandals, and hardly mind the warmth. A horse cannot. Oh, they shed at great speed their remaining winter's coats, but horses in their way are most delicate, and those first few hot days were a nightmare of horse ailments: the thick sweet grass loosened their bowels; the sweaty work gave them chills and some went lame despite everything we did to prevent it; horses groaned in the night with colic and buckled to their knees in the day with founder, rivers of sweat rolling down their necks and steam spewing out from their trembling flanks. I had expected three, four days of it; we had ten.

When our horse troubles subsided like a storm blown off during the night, I called my bleary-eyed commanders in for a tally. We lost thirty horses by their dying and turned another thirty loose, and one of those was the lead-horse of Piyassilis' grays.

He seemed inconsolable, which reminded me that although he was near as tall as I he was yet a lad.

There was nothing to do but turn the surviving horses of split teams into our reserve, which was much diminished by taking fifty teams out of it. On the theory that the second bite of the snake heals the first, I set Piyassilis to patching teams up out of the single horses, even calling a camp-day to sort things out, which I had not done since we entered Mitanni, no matter how needful the cause. But we were about to enter settled country; the no man's land around the borders, the small villages in the hills, all were behind us. Imminently, if not already, Mitanni would know we had arrived.

This, while my men were sleepless from horse-doctoring and dispirited from standing helpless while their beasts lay down with bloated bellies and bellowed out their lives. And there were many sacrifices during the camp-day to this god and to that, and many mutterings, and many men just simply drinking away their fear. In a foot army, it is the plagues that men fear most. In a horse army, a man fears more to lose his lead-horse than his axe, his bow, or even the arm that wields them. A charioteer driving into battle with a mismatched team of strange horses on his center-pole is a very unhappy man.

After a talk with my grousing commanders, we took all the men and reassigned them, so that the luckless had safer spots than those whose lot had not markedly changed. Out went my commanders from my tent, each bearing an amended list which would, on the long, make up for the weakened status of more than half a hundred of my cars but, on the short, was bound to cause some confusion.

Men who had trained three seasons on each other's right were separated; tens were broken up and reassembled in different configurations. Still, in my estimation, the disruption would be transitory, the result well worthwhile.

"It is a pity," grunted Lupakki, easing himself down by my side, "that we had not made it to the flatlands over that ridge before all this occurred."

"Is it?" We were sitting outside my tent, a smallish affair of black goat's hair which I had had pitched only for the privacy it afforded in meeting with my officers: the night was much too fine to be spent in a tent. "Over that last ridge there is no cover, and Mitannian settlements on which I would like to descend like lightning from the heavens. It was no part of my plan to limp into Mitanni like a foundered horse."

"Yet this defile and its configuration reminds me too much of Arzawa."

"On Mount Tiwatassa, you mean? There I had no Sutu, who love to scramble among the rocks, nor our multitude of Hapiru, not to forget the bedawin slinkers-in-the-dark."

"Still, we are disadvantaged when not on the flat."

"Tell me something I do not know."

"What if Tushratta already knows we are here? Any one of those hill folk could have taken it into his head to run for the nearest official with a fat purse."

"I said, tell me something, not ask me something. Lupakki, I will tell you something: it is a beautiful night. We are on the plains of Mitanni, where we have long desired to be. I brought no women with me because I am tired of whining and nagging. Now, if you have no cure for our dilemma, do not detail it to me."

He got up stiffly, mouthing some salutary phrases, and strode off.

In the dawn, the Hittite chariotry resembled a basket full of snakes, writhing. I shouted myself hoarse correcting the misremembered or the misdirected, and it was nearly day when something resembling an army began to wind its way up the ridge-slope.

They hit us while we were on the slope. I can only assume that they had watched us all the night through, though Hittite scouts had reported nothing. But then, there had been no moon.

Tearing down upon us with the sun at their backs, the Mitannian chariotry punched through the ascending wagons and chariots like an awl through softest leather, until the basin between the hills was filled with milling chariots and overturned wagons and all up and down the sloping sides of the defile battle was joined.

With Piyassilis driving, I had been standing in my chariot giving last minute instructions to the commander of the baggage train, and as the din reverberated from the ridge sides and the enemy from Mitanni descended upon my force I could do nothing but watch, helplessly, and prepare to receive them as best I could. Lupakki had been with the point, high on the hillside. No order I could give could reach him in time; I had the clarion blow a signal, then another, then one directed at Sutu ears, even while the point of the Mitannian wedge pierced our defensive scythe in the gentle bowl of the valley.

They were in my lap. I thought of nothing else, not Piyassilis' death-white hands upon the reins or even that he was my own get. I snapped orders to "Driver" without even knowing that I did it, while beneath my feet the car rocked and jerked, and I fit arrow after arrow to my bow.

If we had been ready, there would have been a third man in my chariot. If we had been the aggressors, it was I who would have had the sun at my back. As abruptly as a wheel sinking into mud did the chariot beneath me stop, mired in the press. Still I let fly with bow. Someone else of the same determination glanced an arrow off my helm. Another stuck in the center-pole. A third came whistling down vertically and nailed Piyassilis' foot to the boards of the car.

But I had no attention for that. As I had been aiming round me with bow I had been looking for a worthy opponent: In the gold-gleaming chariot beyond a pool of pedestrians hacking at each other with axes I thought I had found him.

"Driver, break through and put me next to those whites. There, where that gilded helm shows!" As I spoke, I saw a man in a Hurrian helm down a Sutu, take up his spear, and turn in a momentary space that opened around him. Then the gap was closed and I only saw the spear as it whistled toward me, for a man with an axe was intent upon beheading my son from a car suddenly drawn close. Then two horses tried to climb into my chariot from behind. I was reaching around my son with sword, cursing my spent arrows, when the spear's descent, preceded by a rush of air, split my helm like a ripe melon.

There came a roaring in my ears, then vertigo, and then I knew I was lying half on my side and half on another man, and tried to struggle upright. My knees were like ice and my thighs would not hold me. I heard shouting, and the car lurched. I tried to see what was happening, but my sight was obscured by a film of red. I grabbed the rail and by it pulled myself up. When I had done that, when I was standing, legs braced wide, I tried to shake off the clouds that obscured my vision. A moment I recall very clearly: around was a deep silence; men stood frozen still in attitudes of battle, blades in mid-swing, axes buried in brains about to splatter. Then, as I tried to wipe away the blood streaming into my eyes, everything regained its motion and an axe came swinging toward me out of the grainy, blurred confusion.

All went white, and I knew I was falling, although into what I could not say.

Intermittent consciousness visited me thereafter: triumphant shouting, as in a nightmare; the word "Mitanni" spoken loud; a second when a shadow leaned over me, a voice speaking death; a kick I had not enough strength to acknowledge; a thousand years in my black isolation struggling to remember what was wrong, and where all the pain had come from; a lurching under me that took my breath and squeezed it out in long wheezing groans through my mouth. Then stillness, and dark once again where there had been a red and surging haze, and blessed surcease from all impossible remembering and forgotten urgency.

Another time, I heard all the crying that has ever come from every man wounded in the whole of all the battles fought on earth since man began, and cried along with them, unashamed. Shortly after that, I felt myself turned, and examined, and heard myself discussed in low voices, though I could not make out the words or the faces hovering over me like misted moons, sometimes closer, sometimes farther away.

When I was moved from the warm puddle of my blood into the wagon, I knew it, and when I was given to drink, I drank. But I cared not at all by then about anything but when the pain in my head would cease. This pain was every tooth that has ever needed extraction. Every searing thump of motion made me wish for death. I sought the cave of unconsciousness, thinking to defend myself from the agony therein, but each time I wriggled into it, it spat me out.

Talk rattled round me and the wagon rattled under me and within me my mind rattled on and on, urging me to open my eyes, to sit up, to look about. . . .

To find out. Soon that became an obsession more enveloping than the pain: I must be, I thought, who I think I am.

And what I recollect, it must have happened to me.

So it might be best if I just sat up and took a look at who was driving me and where.

But I could not sit up just then.

I listened to the sounds, seeking clues.

I opened my eyes, but the blaze of light wrenched a moan from between my clenched teeth, and I let the weights on my lids push them closed.

What I had seen was the sky and the wagon's sides high about me, and horses' heads, those of the team behind.

Still I did not know if I was being driven to my death; or, should it be true, if that gaudy warrior I had tried to reach was indeed Tushratta, or even if he had survived. I considered that coldly: if we were both dead, then I would not mind it so much.

And I determined to find out those things and to end my own life before I would have it taken from me, an entertainment for the gloating Hurrians.

So when next someone raised up my head, I was ready. I had accustomed my eyes to the day. I had wriggled all the muscles of my right arm and conserved my strength. When the man holding my head up brought his other hand to my lips to give me drink, I grabbed the wrist and by it pulled myself against him, embracing him like a lover.

With a shout of surprise and a splashing of wine, my bene-factor found himself lying atop me on the floor of the wagon, his own dirk pressed to his gut.

Only then did what he was shouting come clear to me: I was done from the effort, and my eyes would not focus, and I knew that for whatever desperate purpose, I could not follow through. But as the knife slipped from my numbing fingers I realized who was shouting at me, and what words he was shouting:

"Abuya! Abuya!" screamed my son Piyassilis in a choking sob. "He lives! The Sun lives!"

CHAPTER 20

"Do not try to talk, my lord Sun," Piyassilis advised, tears streaming unheeded down his face. "Here, drink this. Lupakki! Lupakki! Driver, stop the wagon."

The wagon lurched to a stop, the wine slopped down my neck, and all about me the sky filled with brilliant tiny white spots as I tried to raise my head.

"Please, please, lie still," crooned Piyassilis, although if I could I would have spoken, and if I could I would not have lain still, and within me raged a pounding fury that this might be so: never had I been so sorely wounded. And then: how hurt was I? I recollected my father Arnuwandas, who had been struck cold and dead from the waist down; and with a fear I had not felt in battle, I attempted to draw up my legs. The effort brought the sky whirling down like a dust devil, and I could not do it soundless, but one by one I raised my legs and then with a sigh let the beckoning dark take me.

And so I was not to see Lupakki until a lifetime later, when men's talk and jostling woke me, and I found that I was being borne aloft on a stretcher into my own palace in the dead of night.

Then only did I realize the enormity of the thing, as torches bobbled down the wide palace steps and a shadow flew by them.

I heard a babble of angry voices, a high imperious command cutting through them.

For a moment I thought to pretend insensibility and stave off all further anguish thereby. But I felt the heat of her cheek against my hand; heard her, low, chanting my name and calling on her Lady; and then Lupakki's soothing tones:

"Come away, my lady, until we get him in. Come now, Great Queen, and get back. He would not like to see you crying, nor so shaken before the men. Come with me. We will. . ."

Her kiss I felt, and a drawing back, and I opened my eyes and put out my hand to reassure her, but the words would not form; I saw only the men bearing the stretcher and the sky above. So I tried to turn my head to the right, and bellowed at the pain.

By then Khinti was attempting to extricate herself from Lupakki's desperate restraint, and in my ears was a mingling of his apologetic refusals and her queenly threats as to his demise upon the moment if he did not loose her. And then, as the stretcher tilted and the men ascended the staircase, they both fell behind.

It was the Shepherd who caused me to open my eyes again while his calm orders echoed incomprehensibly in my ears.

He was pacing the stretcher, a hand on it, by my side, telling a Meshedi to get a physician to my wife with something to calm her, lest she do damage to the child, and to set a guard to watch her, and to tell her for him that she would not see the king until she had got rid of her rent garments and washed herself and combed the knots from her hair.

"Now, Shepherd," I whispered, "you know he cannot tell her that."

Kuwatna-ziti whirled, hand outstretched, and caught his motion and changed it midway, so his hand came to rest on my shoulder, not on my brow.

"Tasmi, you have done it this time. . . ." He bared his teeth and patted my shoulder. "Do not talk. We heard you were dead. Then we heard you were not. Now that I see you, I see that both are partly true. Just rest now, and later we will talk about it."

I was about to be lifted ignominiously from stretcher onto bed by two men at my feet and two at my head.

I objected, and they halted, and the stretcher-bearers with them, until I said in a slow and raspy voice that they must lay the stretcher on the bed and then help me sit up.

The Shepherd opened his mouth, then closed it, bowed his head, and stepped back a pace.

This sitting up was harder than I had expected, and when I had done it I sat erect by dint of will and balance, my hands gripping the bronze bed frame with all my desperation. But my feet were on the floor and my head I held, if not upright, then upward, by my own efforts.

The Shepherd said something unintelligible and then dismissed the men.

I had not one particle of strength available for gainsaying him.

When I heard the doors close, I heard also his voice, asking me if I would not then lie down. And since everything, my knees and my thighs and the floor between my legs, was sparkling with that red-spotted tinge which precedes unconsciousness, I let him help me.

When he had made sure that my head did not snap against the soft pillows, nor bang against the cedar board, he turned to go.

"Shepherd, how many?"

"How many what, Tasmi?"

"How many did we lose?"

"Many . . . but not that many. I told you, do not worry. Get rest. Regain your strength. I will hold the borders for you. Have I not always done it?"

"Yes, you have always done it."

"I will send in food and drink. You will eat it and drink it. You must try. The fever has burned away all but the hulk of you; you will not die of the wounds, but you could die of starvation."

I closed my eyes, and sighed, and nodded: If the Shepherd watched the flock, then I could do all those things he said. Perhaps even, if I was lucky, escape the pounding behind my eyes.

My wife appeared with my meal and fed me from her hand, her eyes red and swollen but bearing a beatific smile.

It went on a long time, this business of becoming well, and the procession of that first evening would make a pattern followed for many days:

Priests came. Old Women came. Physicians came. Upon my order and fortified by whatever the potion was that steadied her nerves, Khinti turned them all away.

She was enough of a nurse and enough of a priestess and enough of a comfort. If comfort indeed there was to be had.

For she spoke to me in a mixture of child-soothings and laments, and she wept and then she smiled, and told fanciful tales of what we would do when I was well: we would go to Kumanni, the two of us, king and queen of the realm, and then sail down the Mala: we would travel round the world, go even to Ahhiyawa and down into Egypt. We needed no more honors. We would be peaceful and happy and content within our boundaries. . . .

I fell asleep to her stories as I had to gods' tales when I was a child.

And the blue-cloaked lord, who had made not one appearance for my sake since before I took Khinti to Alashiya, came to me. And three wasted years he cast down before him and the clay shattered on the rocky ground; and three times two stones he took and made of them a pyre that ascended unto heaven; and on its summit we both stood; and the lands we surveyed were bountiful with olive and fig and palm, and waving with topaz grain in the sun; and three times a thousand charioteers came over the rolling plain; but the grain in their path withered brown and smoking, and the chariot horses fell down bloat-tongued and poke-ribbed, and the men who were driving cut their chariot-poles into staves and trudged back into a dust-hazed valley which then revealed itself to my sight as a sack. Then the blue-cloaked lord bent down and scooped up the sack by its drawstrings and, throwing it over his shoulder, marched away down a path for one only.

When I woke from that I was lying in a pool of sopping bedclothes, but I sat up and red-hot flames did not course up my spine to explode at the base of my skull. I reached up tentatively and touched the bandages wrapped about my head where they crossed left to right over my forehead, and groaned as my fingers pressed on the wound there.

Khinti stirred from her sleep at my feet, and then her eyes sprang open and she sat upright with a start. Then she stood, hovering.

"Queens do not sleep on floors."

"Queens in Hatti, these days, do not sleep at all. They nap. They doze. But they do not sleep. My lord, how do you feel?"

"Weak. Hungry. Dizzy. Not ready for a woman, even one dressed as you."

She was wearing only a thin seductive robe, and it had fallen open.

She pulled at it, her eyes never leaving me, as she approached. Falling down by my side she buried her head in my lap, her arms clasping me round, and sobbed.

I stroked her hair, thinking that although Piyassilis had been right, and I lived, living as a defeated and shamed king in a world where all knew it might not be quite the same kind of life as I had previously led.

Before, I think, I had been too ill to grapple with my defeat. It had its claws deep in my neck that day my fever broke, and in my heart and in my belly. I was abruptly, unutterably relieved that I had not had to drive back into Hattusas at the head of how-ever-many men I had not led to death in Mitanni.

"Get me Lupakki. I would hear of the war. Of what happened after I went down."

"The Shepherd has an oath from me that he will be the first to speak with you when you request conversation."

"Then get him, and now. And Khinti—"

"Yes, my lord Sun?" She was already at the door. Her chiseled, piquant face was radiant in her pregnancy, and her gaze as eager and innocent as a spotted fawn's. She raised a hand and pushed her hair off her forehead without knowing she did, and the seal she wore around her neck danced between her breasts.

"Put a robe on you that is less revealing; not even the Shepherd is that privy to my intimacy. And leave me alone with him."

"Yes, my lord Sun. Husband? I love the head of the Sun, and the soul of the Sun, and the very own self of the Sun, more dearly than my own heart, my soul, mine own self. I did not know how dearly until I thought I knew too late."

"Go do my bidding, woman, or I will give you cause to love me less."

Her reassurance smacked of pity. Condescension was more intolerable to me than falsehood, more execrable than dogs in a temple, more odious than Tushratta's malefic gloatings would surely come to be.

Out scurried Khinti, closing the doors just before the bitumen pitcher I threw reached her, so that it crashed into shards. I lay back, holding my right shoulder which was not yet ready for such exertion as throwing pitchers, and cursed until my vision blurred inexplicably and my voice broke and I found need to swallow repeatedly. Inside me was a bruise that seemed to extend about the whole of my person, impalpable but unbearably exposed. Soon Kuwatna-ziti would come to tread on this aching soreness, and then Lupakki's eyes would have to be met. I wondered wildly for a moment if a man of thirty-two was too old to start a new life as a Sutu. The most awful of my nightmares had not prepared me — not for failure so dismal and so complete. A man fears such a thing so much he does not think of it. Faced with the unthinkable was I from this moment onward: I would need to learn to live with it. Three years and countless minas of silver and horses and chariots would not soon be forgotten by the Hattian people, when all went for naught.

Walking is not easy after so long abed.

But I was doing it, stumbling around the side of the room with a hand on the wall. If I kept going that way, I would come to the window, but that was not what I sought. I slumped down into the chair before its table littered with women's things and had to wait until my palms dried and the rivulets of sweat stopped running down my neck and I was no longer shaking. When that was done, I picked up my wife's hand-mirror and set about removing the gauze swathing my head.

This was slow work but not painful. My hair had been washed free of blood and bound back. Nowhere was the bandage clotted to the wounds. But the white cloth was voluminous, unwound, and my arms were soon tired, then cold, and then full of pinpricks from the effort. When all was removed, I leaned back gratefully in the fragile woman's chair of cane and cedar, and peered like Khinti at my image reflected in the silver.

I was not any longer as pretty as I once had been. Descending from out of the new, angry part in my hair above my right temple was a wide garnet scab that ended in my right eyebrow, which now was raised slightly, arched as if in sarcasm. The other end of the rough, scabbed channel was at the top of my head; the distance, from end to end, a long, straight slash.

Now, before that time I was not gentle of aspect, but arresting enough in the way that angularity and strength of feature are handsome: my cheekbones and forehead are wide and high, my jaws flare out from chin to match them. My nose drops hawkish and severe from a protruding brow under which almond brown eyes are hidden deep and secretive, narrow slashes curved a bit like a Hittite sword. My mouth has never taken to smiling, and frown lines bracket its ridges of flesh that fall off into a shadowed downslope of hollow cheeks.

The whole of my countenance was transformed by the puckering, furious scar.

I sat back from it, lay the mirror down, not really distressed. I had been curious, but the mirror sobered me. I have taken other scars, but none so fearsome as this. I stripped off the woolen robe and took further stock. About my right shoulder, extending

under my arm and up over the muscles that rise from collarbone
to neck, was more bandage. The wound underneath was, by the
look of it, an axe blow, and I remembered taking it. A notch, a
finger's joint deep, had been carved out of the upsloping flesh.
If I had been carrying less muscle there, I would not have survived to write this or to wonder, as I did then, how long it would
take for the gouge to fill in.

Nothing else worthy of mention did I discover: I had been
abed long enough for bruise to subside and laceration to disappear.

It was not until then that I realized how close I had come
to finding out once and for all if there is kingship in heaven. I
vowed three things:

I vowed never to take a son of my loins with me into war in
my own car, for I had learned that such was one too many items
about which to be concerned when battle is joined.

I vowed to squash Tushratta like a pregnant sow under my
chariot, and render down his fat that I might grease my wheels
with it.

And I vowed to acquire a winter training camp on the plains
of Syria, where my men and my horses could condition themselves ere they fought the tropical fight again.

I had just promised myself those things and was edging my
way back from chair to bed when the Shepherd was announced
and entered to find the king of Hatti naked, feeling his way along
the wall like a blind man.

"Tasmi, must you flout the gods?" This he said as his sweeping glance took in the table and chair strewn with bandage, the
rumpled bedclothes, and myself. With a whisper of sandals he
was at my side, his arm slipping beneath mine. "You gave me
your word you would rest."

"What am I doing?" I grunted, leaning against him. "Am I
hunting boar?"

"You are sweating like it. Now sit there. Good. Not on those,
they are soaked. Here. . . ." Kuwatna-ziti stripped off his mantle
and cast it about me.

"Leave off, Shepherd." I pushed his hands away. "I need no one to dress me." Still, I felt comforted. The mantle was patterned with lightning bolts, gold, blue and black, edged with an embroidered procession led by the Storm-god himself astride his cultic bulls, Serris and Hurris. I fastened the gold-chased closure at my right shoulder, over the axe-gouge, passing the embroidered edge first under my left arm, leaving it free.

"You need someone to do it, if your wife will not. She leaves you in soaking bedclothes, in a curtained room at midday in the hottest month of the year. . . . Tasmi, do not look at me like that."

I had not been listening, but thinking how little he had changed in all this time. In kirtle of matching striped cloth, with a gold arm-bracelet about his ample bicep and a fillet binding back shoulder-length hair, his aspect was no less imposing than it had been that night my mother commended me into his care before my father Arnuwandas' mausoleum. Time rode lightly on the Shepherd; his back was not bowed nor belly sagging; only at his temples, where the silver hair grew, did his person in any way acknowledge the passing of the years. He went to roll up the curtains and let the day in, then gathered all my strewn bandage and folded it neatly.

"Tasmi," he said softly when all that was done, as he stared at something I could not see beyond the embrasure's frame, "I am the bearer of some startling news. The temples are jammed with offerors; their lines extend into the streets; they are gathered in the citadel courtyard."

"I do not blame them. What do they want, my life? The Oath Gods will have to take it from me." I lay down then, my back propped against the carven cedar board, not caring if I showed weakness.

"No, no, no. . . ." The Shepherd turned from the window to drag over a claw-footed chair. Only when he sat in it, smiling slightly and looking at me like a mother at her newborn, did I ask him what course he had in mind, and then only when I realized he would sit there mute until I did.

"Tasmi, you misunderstand, but I do have an action to recommend, and I want your word that you will do what I say."

"Shepherd, I am weak, and the top of my scalp has been lifted from the bone beneath, but let me assure you, my mind is not addled. I will not do what you or anyone says without first hearing it."

"Tasmi, the people are lining up *for* you in the temples. The sacrifices they present are not from malice or fear, but from joy and relief. Never in anybody's memory has Hattusas seen the like—not for a living king. It started when they heard you were dead, yet it is still growing. You must find the strength to appear to them. . . . If you listen closely, you can hear them singing. All the steps to the public court in the citadel, and the court itself, and even the streets are filled with them—"

"Wait! What did you say?"

"I said that you need to appear to them. I have found a kingly litter in the storage magazines, and—"

"*No!* I am not going to be carried anywhere, nor displayed to harvest the sympathy of a folk who until now would gladly have nailed me like a bird to the gates. No, not like my crippled father, and in his very portable sick bed—I cannot. Do you hear?" I was up, not knowing how I had done it, and dizzy. Kuwatna-ziti reached out the flat of his hand and pushed me backward, hardly more than a shove. Yet I staggered and my calves brushed the bed frame and I sank back down and put my head in my hands, only to wince at the pain as my fingers pressed against the naked wound.

"You must, Tasmi."

I did not raise my eyes to his, but stared at my feet peeking out from under the mantle, and the floor beneath, all of which rippled disconcertingly. "No."

"Tabarna, the time has gone for mindless audacity, and for charging like an enraged bull, and for swinging an axe at the chariotry's point. The time has come for kingly words and kingly vision, for out of these alone may ever emerge a nation sufficiently united to be the sword you long to wield, with which you may someday do the ultimately kingly deeds of which you dream. If you throw away this opportunity, you will never have another. *Be a king to your people; accept their love; be man enough to take it when it is offered. Or, in truth, it is all over for the lot of us.*"

"I must be *man* enough to *what?*"

"To let them see you in your weakness, which they understand, and console you in your defeat: it has made you human in their eyes."

"I am not going anywhere in a litter."

"By the time you can walk about unaided, the moment will have passed."

"Shepherd, you do not know what you are asking." I heard the pleading tone of my words, but could not call them back.

Those sincerely adamant brown eyes pierced me through.

"Anyone else I would have skewered to a gatepost for this," I told him at last.

I agreed, finally, on the condition that I not be carried among them, but only shown from the portico overlooking the square; and that he would leave me now, but send Lupakki to me forthwith.

When he went, he forgot his mantle, and I pulled it close about me and sat a time in bitter contemplation of this price exacted from me by the gods, my lords.

"Is it not enough that I am borne home to my bed senseless, bearing heavy wounds, defeated?" I demanded of the empty air.

Evidently, it was not enough.

"Is it not a surfeit of disgrace I have suffered already, that I must be trundled out before them like old Arnuwandas? Must I be forced into the nightmare of my childhood? Is not my present humiliation sufficient to conciliate you, my gods?"

"*No. Yes. No,*" said the silence.

I determined that when I was well I would have it out with the Storm-god, my lord, once and for all.

Then Lupakki came, and I girded myself to receive him.

In army kilt and sandals, he bore his plumed helmet under his arm, and knelt down as he would never have thought of doing in the field.

When I commanded him to take his ease, he shook his head so hard his earring rattled, went to one knee, pressed my hand to his forehead and began detailing his failings as a commander.

Since I had been ready to detail mine, and as remorsefully, it struck me funny, and I began to laugh. I laughed until I choked and Lupakki had to assist me. When I was eased on my bed, I made him sit himself down thereon, and his countenance was screwed into a dark sad knot of features that constantly twisted, remaking themselves anew.

When I had my breath back, I wiped the laughter from my eyes and said to him that he must not be so grave, that I was not mad but only startled to hear from his lips all the things I had expected to be spouting bitterly to him.

He managed a grin, but it faded quickly. "Do you need anything? Drink? Clean bedclothes? When I had your care in Samuha, you would not have slept on these."

"But you are no longer my aide, and I need more from you than a neat tent and a well-whetted blade, these days."

"Command me, lord."

"Tell me about the battle—after I went down, I mean."

He looked away, and back. "I have filed a statement, my king. . . . I am guilty of—"

"Nothing but obeying orders."

"Piyassilis—"

"Was in my care, not yours. Please, I will not detail my failings to you, and you will grant me the same grace. How many did we lose?"

"Forty-four chariots, more than half of our foot. They're still straggling in. When I saw you go down, and the boy, I was halfway down the slope. A cry went up: 'The king is down.' Then the Mitannians began shouting: 'The Hittite king is dead.' I called our thirty in on the horn; they could not help their troops, the fighting was hand-to-hand. Then I rode over everything I saw, my own included. I could think of nothing but that the prince might yet live, and that they were not going to mutilate—" He broke off; started again: "There were two Mitannians in the iron car, driving it; I got them with arrows and your horses bolted. I took off after the horses, once the thirty were gathered in. But we were only in the forefront of the Hittite retreat. They chased us all the way to the Kizzuwadnan border, but the troops were scattered, so they thinned their ranks trying to pick everyone off. There must have been twice as many of their chariotry, to begin with, as we had. I wanted only to get the prince to safety. We thought you were dead . . . all that blood, and your scalp laid open, and the chunk the axe bit out of your neck. I killed my first team, hid in the bushes until I could 'commandeer' a Mitannian team, and that was when we realized you were yet breathing. Then I had about forty cars that had rallied to me, and we drove all the way to Hattusas without a stop except to change horses. Your own chariot we left in Kizzuwadna."

"Now, about Piyassilis?"

"The prince? He has a head like good iron, and a heart to match. His foot was yet skewered to the car when I took the reins, and when he woke from his little nap, it was all I could do to convince him that it was too late to regroup and counter-attack." Lupakki looked up, obviously hoping I had heard all I craved to hear.

"What of the Mitannian in the gilded chariot, who wore the burnished helm and drove the white team with the plumes—was it Tushratta? That was where I was headed when the spear caught me."

"The sharp-bearded, gaudy warrior? If it was not him, it was someone very close to him, a prince perhaps. When he heard you were down, he pulled up his team as if he were reviewing troops and called down all manner of curses upon us and lauded his gods and from his car blared the clarion's call and the order to pursue. . . ."

"Yet he did not offer to take a surrender?"

"No, my lord."

"Nor did he single himself out to fight with me, or exchange any words of challenge? Why so undecorous a battle between two kings?"

"If you will pardon me, my lord, from what he shouted at us, I think he feels we are not honorable enough: you never sent a challenge to the Gasgaeans. Well, he said that the Hattian army was no better than a pack of jackals, and its king no king, but a puffed-up tribal chief."

"Tsk. He fielded a lot of men to deal with so puny a threat. All thanks, Lupakki. You may go."

"Lord—"

"Yes?"

"I never ordered a retreat. . . . I would have stayed there, but for you and the young prince, until I died. And I would have got that bebaubled Hurrian—"

"Then I am glad you did not. He is mine, and do not forget it. Tomorrow come to the chancery, and bring with you a list of survivors; the men will not be penalized by the errors of their superiors. We will make it, as closely as we can, so that none suffers from our loss but ourselves."

And before he had shut the doors behind him, sleep came and grabbed me by the throat and pulled me down into a whirling pit wherein maimed kings passed by an audience stand on gilded litters, preceded by jesters bearing stag standards tied with mourning ribbons.

I woke to Khinti's ministrations, accompanied by a host of questions as to what I would wear and what I would want her to wear, and so gathered groggily that the Shepherd had struck: this very day, before I had chance to think it over, he would have me out before the folk.

So I told her what I would and would not do: I would not ride in a litter; I would walk; I would dress soberly in a dark cloak and mantle and expected her to do likewise; I did not want the children there; but I would need Hannutti and the Shepherd, and wanted them both at my door to accompany me down to the lower courtyard, where we might enter the administration building from the rear.

She objected on grounds of my strength, I chased her out to clear my thoughts and meditate on what I would say. But in through the doors as my wife left to prepare came my bodyservants, the black concubine among them, and I let them do what it was they did, hardly noticing, thinking hard on what Tasmis-*arri* might say to Hattusas who, now that I cared little about it, had decided to take me to her bosom.

My black girl was beyond equal at kneading muscles, and under her hands my strength seemed in part to return to me. The fine black mantle trimmed in red and gold, and the kilt and belt and shortsword with golden sheath and kingly torque and armband and curl-toed slippers were on me before I knew it, my hair brushed and shining, and only the crown remained.

This I could not suffer: not any from the most formal conical crown to the skull-shaped cap, nor even the lightest of circlets, could I tolerate.

"Enough, then," I said. "Get back from me." I took the lituus from its bearer just as the Shepherd and my Master of Horses, Hannutti came in, my wife right behind in a softly tiered gown of gold and red that left one shoulder bare.

"My lord Sun," said the Shepherd, "if we are walking, we had best get started."

And we did. But very slowly, this somewhat disguised by the formality of the procession. Palace officials and Meshedi and commanders of ten and priests went before, in their assigned places, and Golden Lancers and more Meshedi behind. Out from the residential palace and along the red marble road and through the halls between the buildings we proceeded, until we entered the archives and mounted its stairs and came at last onto the balustraded portico overlooking the lower courtyard.

There, through my bespeckled vision, I saw that the Shepherd had not lied to me: all along the walls and thick as rats on a corpse in the enclosure and on the steps and on the ramp extending as far as I could see through the open courtyard gates into the old city thronged the people of Hattusas.

"You are right, Shepherd. I did not believe it, but you are right."

"I believed it not myself when I first saw it."

Vendors passed, hawking. Musicians played. The crowd sang. Among the folk, oxen and sheep and bulls with streamered horns and garlands of flowers round their necks waited for their turn to be slaughtered in my honor.

"Now, Great King, if you are ready?"

I nodded, and the standard bearers and royal pipers and lutenists and the pluckers of harp and lyre went out under the portico and a great cheer came up from the crowd. The Sun-goddess' symbol, the winged solar disk; the twelve horned stag; the gilt eagle and all else went forth, each with the appropriate palace official. Then my wife as a priestess of the Sun-goddess gave the benediction, and Kuwatna-ziti added the miracle of my recovery to the glory of the Storm-god, my lord.

But the crowd had a single thing on its mind. I heard my name, a howl, a chant, a thunder. Occasionally, someone would shout my birth name and others take it up, so that both the old ways and the new seemed to join.

I have done it with the army, I told myself. It is just that I have not done it with these.

And before I knew it, my wife had raised up her arms and, with the sun sparking off her crown and her jeweled neck and ringed hands, she called for silence, and a moment of prayer for the king.

This was my signal. On it, I came forth.

But all the people had gone down on their knees like a forest bent flat in a winter gale.

So it was that when they rose I stood there, hands grasping the balustrade, leaning down over them, and I had never had such a moment in my life. In the clear hot sun all their faces seemed to come distinct to me, all the thousands of them. And I thought I knew then how old Nimmuria Amenhotep of Egypt must feel.

"You have reason to weep, O people of Hattusas: we have fallen to our knees before the enemy. Weep tears of rage!

"You have reason to weep, my people, for you love the Hatti land. So we will rise up again and smite the enemy. Weep tears of joy!

"Ah, you think I cannot know it. I know it. The Storm-god has put his hand on my head and made me well. You people of Hatti, you sacrificed that this be so. And it is not so because of me, but because of you. The Thousand Gods have sent me back from the very door of the netherworld to fight again. Let the Oath Gods harken unto me: for every Hittite tear shed here, a thousand women of Mitanni will weep. For every Hattian man whose fists are clenched in rage, a thousand times a thousand men of Mitanni will clench their fists in woe, never-ending!"

I waited then; I had to, for the crowd roared: upwelling, in-articulate affirmation like the roar of the earth when she shudders in her sleep.

"I will avenge us upon Mitanni, for this is what is in my heart." I leaned far over then, knowing they could not see the trembling of my hands nor hear the beating of my heart. And I spoke to them softly, oh softly, but it carried out across the courtyard and into the gatehouse and some say even down into the city streets, "I will do it, because you have come and laid your prayers upon my altar, because you have sacrificed that it must be so, even as I have done. And what is in all our hearts, *the gods will fulfill.*"

CHAPTER 21

Slowly passed the season of my recovery, when I was mostly in the palace. During these days we heard that Tushratta of Mitanni had written to the Egyptian king Nimmuria Amenhotep III, saying to him that he had slain me and destroyed my army, and was sending to Egypt samples of Hittite booty, horses and chariots.

Upon the very night we received a polite inquiry as to my health from the Egyptians, to whom we had said nothing at all, Khinti gave me twin children: one boy, one girl. The girl I named Muwattish. The boy she named Zannanza. I was almost glad I had lost the war, for otherwise I would not have been home to hold her while she thrust them out. This was the first time I had had a hand in bearing, and I was like a just-manned driver on his first campaign.

I found the twins more wondrous than all the proclaimed "miracles" coming up the Mala from Egypt.

In the spring of my thirteenth regnal year, just after my thirty-third birthday, I heard, both from my sources and from Thebes, *their* wondrous news:

315

Naphuria Amenhotep IV changed his name: henceforth he would be called Akhenaten; and to us foreigners, who craved the simple, just "Huri" would in future be sufficient.

We giggled about it in unkingly and unqueenly levity, for we were drunk on a potent spring wind and a winter filled with children and the quiet, steady perfecting of our plans.

Other news from the far south was as we had expected: all diplomatic correspondence would henceforth go to the City of the Horizon, Akhetaten, whence the court entire (or so we heard) was moving. Much was made of the city of wonders with its magnanimous welcome to northern barbarians of every stripe. It suited me. I made use of the opportunity to put some Hittite merchants in there, lest my agent Duttu, who was ascending yearly in the esteem of the Egyptian chancery, regain some sudden loyalty to those he served. So among the assorted Syrians, folk of Upper and Lower Retenu, who were resettled in Akhetaten, went a few who were well-heeled but careful not to show it. And I had Hatib there to oversee the matter of these additions, for that was just before he was posted permanently to the fractious seaboard principalities Egypt overruled.

Speaking of fractious princes, my young acquaintance Aziru of Amurru had become a sea brigand of renown, and it was said of him by Hatib that of all the princes in Canaan, from the Niblani Mountains to Byblos, he was the one to watch. I was watching him as best I could through Khinti's father's many-eyed servants; but even they found that when they blinked, the spike-bearded Amurrite disappeared; and when they would chase after him, the best they could do was tell me where he had been.

So when I came in from performing a ceremony at the rock sanctuary, having dismissed even Khinti, I was understandably surprised to see Aziru sitting in my eagle-clawed chair with his booted feet up on a footstool drinking king's wine from a golden goblet.

"Do you not recall me?" rasped the Amurrite prince, peering reproachfully over the cup's rim at the drawn sword that spoke for me. "After so fine a gift as that black ship, and such friendly letters, I am greeted with a drawn blade? And not any regnal sticker, either, but a working weapon. . . . I heard you wanted to see me. If you don't, I'll just go out the way I came, and none will know of it."

"Do you ever use doors?"

"My lot at present precludes it." Aziru was still watching the setting sun behind my back at the window, or the blade I was holding. I kept moving until I had satisfied myself that I had no other guests, and until I saw that calculating look I knew so well from my own experience go across his face: he was wondering if he could get by me and out in safety. "And since it does, I am afraid I cannot reciprocate in the matter of the ship you gave me . . . although such a timely and appropriate present I have received from no other man. Even my father could not display such largess, though he well loves me. When and how I can repay you in kind I do not know. A great king like yourself has resources. I have none. But I wanted you to know that your ship is in good shape, and myself in part because of it."

"Do not be so sure you cannot reciprocate. If you want to repay me, then we will see what you owe. After all, I am a king and always in need of circumspect confidants. And after all, I gave you the ship because I liked what I had seen, and thought I would like better what you might do with it. Now all that has become as I thought it might. So, in point of fact, by doing what you were doing for your own self, you were serving me. Do you see?"

"No." Still watching me closely, he stroked his bearded chin.

"Have you not harried the princelings unto desperation and stolen sleep from the governors of Egypt?"

He grinned. "Yes I have."

"Then you owe me nothing. That was what I had hoped you would continue to do. I merely made it more likely that you would continue."

"I am mystified. I thought . . . I mean, did you not send out those men to call me on my obligation?"

"No, just to see if you were well, or if you needed anything, or if you might like to come up to Hattusas. And I see that you are well, and presently I will hear if you need anything, and you *are*—never mind how, for the nonce—in Hattusas. I am content."

His pointed beard stabbed the air as he rubbed his neck, laughing low. "Will you let me know if you need an apprentice to your kingship? Such dissembling as this is beyond anything I have seen or heard even in the courts of Tyre, where men say perfection of the art has been attained."

So I laughed with him, to further put him at ease. "Shall I call you Aziru, or simply 'Criminal', as your neighbors do?"

"What you will, my lord. But I think I understand: if I am not obligated, then perhaps I might want to become so? Is that what you are about?"

"Perhaps. It is your father with whom I would have to treat, should ever we wish to formalize matters. Now, I am pleased that you are here and willing to aid you, to the extent that you can accept aid from me without stoking Egypt's wrath further. We will see how things progress."

"Stay! You go too fast for me, my esteemed benefactor—far too fast." He rose and set the goblet down and walked to the window. "Beautiful view, like fire on the mountains, and the city walls so white . . . fire and ice. I had no idea the palace was so large. Nor so well-defended."

"We try."

He turned. "How does my father's desire to acquire a viable seaport, which is really all he wants and all we need—Now, lord king, that is not humorous. . . . How does what Amurru does help you?"

"If I tell you that, then we are into serious matters. Before I do, think a moment on what that might come to mean: I am once-defeated. . . ."

It was his turn to make a disclaiming sound, and I went and joined him by the window.

"I heard all about that; had a Sutu friend in it for the Mitannians. But tell me what you are saying: what will it come to mean, should you and I exchange more than a politeness or two?"

"It will mean a lot more narrowing of eyes and stroking of beard on your part, I suppose. Your father's troubles with Egypt can only escalate. Mine with Mitanni will soon do the same. But I can handle my troubles, and you may not be able to dispatch yours so easily—Wait until I have finished!"

He took his hands off his hips and leaned back against the embrasure's frame, but said nothing.

"If I were to expand southerly, I would come to Amurru long before I came to Egypt. If I came to Amurru, I would like to do it in a friendly fashion. That is all."

"That is *all?* Do I understand you correctly? You are thinking of driving down as far as that? On your summer jaunt, no doubt? To Alalakh? Ugarit? What about the Egyptians? They use Ethiopians and Nubians in the northern legions, you know, not just the slight brown folk with their cosmetic palettes. . . ."

"You are jumping to conclusions. As far coastward as the country of Kinza, which is under Egyptian protection, and the country of Ugarit, the very sunshade of Pharaoh in the Canaan lands, I will not go. No, I will be coming to visit you from a different direction." I avoided mentioning the city of Alalakh, whence, as he had guessed, I would surely go.

"From the rear, so to speak?"

"More than likely. Remember, I do not share your passion for coastal expansion. But I approve it."

"Are you saying to me what I think you are saying?"

"We could have adjoining borders and friendly relations withal; nothing more am I saying."

"Let us, then, discuss how this thing might be done."

"As you wish, Aziru," and I went to refill my goblet.

"Ah . . . my lord, I am a prince, only, you know that. What my father will do I cannot say."

"Aziru, what your father will do is as clear to me as the color of your eyes. But you and I will speak together, and you will go away and think upon what I have said, and tender unto Abdi-asirta, king of Amurru, my message:

"He may enter into my vassalage on his own initiative, or not. One way or the other, very soon, under my suzerainty he and his will surely come."

"I think," said Aziru, "that it is time for me to depart."

"So? As you wish."

"But you cannot just *say* that to me—"

"I just said it."

"Everything we are doing to get out from under Egypt's sandal, and you expect me to stand here and meekly accept the fact as soon as we have done it, you will place your own foot there?"

"Why not? You are old enough to lead sea-wolves who take down the ships of Sidon, of Sumuru, and even the flagship of Byblos' Egyptian governor, so you are old enough to know the truth when you hear it."

"Bitter herbs you offer, Great King. You extended my father your formal protection, and he refused it. You offered the king of Ugarit a place in your empire. He wrote to our lord, Pharaoh, and told him what you had done. Not even a dog can have two masters. We are too poor a country to live under tribute. Do you understand? When your delicate threat arrived, we did not run to Nimmuria Amenhotep with it, because we *desire no master!* Surely you, of all people, can understand a king who wishes to be his own person, not anyone's servant!"

"I understand. I also understand that however many Hapiru people you recruit you will never find enough of them to protect you from the legions of Egypt. As for you being a poor nation: I will make you richer than your wildest dreams, and *then* I will put you under tribute. But it will be a reminder, only. And you may shake your head and speak your princely disclaimers, but consider this: I will do it. Your only choice is whether Amurru will be a *willing* adherent. By the time I am at the gates of your father's city, he had better have his mind made up."

"Or?"

"Are you sure you want to ask me that now?"

"My lord, I am sure of nothing but that I should not have come. My father will not be pleased with what I have to tell him."

"But there is something you must do for me before you leave." I reached out and clasped him by the shoulder. He stiffened, looked at my hand a time, and then up into my face. "You must accept my hospitality. In the while before mealtime, you and I are going out of the citadel the way you came in, then again we will come up here, exactly the same way. And if by then none of mine have caught sight of us and raised the alarm, I will raise such a din that the Thousands Gods will be waked from their ease by it!" I felt the tension drain from him and took away my hand as he, smiling, agreed.

"But it is not so easy," he warned, his eyes dancing.

"How old are you?"

"Twenty-three."

"When I was twenty-three, many simple things seemed difficult."

"Then, my lord," he said, throwing a leg over the window's sill, "follow me, with all haste."

Now, my men did not sight us, and I found that the rope-burns on my palms fueled the fire of my displeasure.

I called for my brother Zida, delaying our dinner. After Zida left I called in a servant to show the prince of Amurru to a chamber where he might be pleased to rest, or seek the baths, or a bodyservant's ministrations before the meal was served.

The servant who answered my call was that black girl I had gotten on Alashiya. I instructed her, when I saw his face, to be unswerving in her service of his needs, for she was the very representative of my hospitality. And I was feeling hospitable, indeed: having dug the furrow and planted the seed, it remained only for me to wait until the seedling sprouted.

CHAPTER 22

The following year, in late summer, Telipinus and his half-brother Kantuzilis took their manhood testing successfully. Privately, some of my lords and even Khinti had doubted Kantuzilis' fitness for the trial. This son of mine of the second degree, tremulous of limb and scaly of skin, suffered ever and again from one ailment or another. But he rose to the occasion, which was a great relief to Takkuri's sister, his mother.

And to my queen, as well, who seemed determined to bestow her love on not only her own children but every child of the seed whom I had sired over the years upon this woman or that, regardless of status. Khinti knew all their names and their tempers and their tribulations, while I could hardly tell one from the next and had no inclination to learn.

Zidanza, whom I had adopted for Titai and who had been in Takkuri's sister's care, Khinti took in hand and treated as a royal prince. Thereafter, he followed her like a puppy, having never had any attention at all from anyone before; and in his case I said nothing about it, for I myself felt sorry for that one. So I decided to enter him into the Meshedi the next year as if he were a full son of mine.

Zida and I discussed it and agreed that my wife would need a personal troop sooner or later, and this Zidanza seemed a likely candidate for the post and would be grown into it just about the time we were planning to go down into Syria for extended campaigning.

Like lions, we were waiting, sending out scouts and letting others do our hunting for us, and gathering in provisions for the moment when we would spring.

We heard that the old king of Ugarit—who had not liked me at all—had died. His son and successor, Niqmad II, was the subject of much discussion, both within Hatti and without.

I was in Kumanni, our holy city upon Kizzuwadna's border, celebrating a festival, when the news of this old king's death came up. Now Ugarit, I have said, lies on the coast north of Amurru. She is possessed of a magnificent harbor which hosts a cosmopolitan traffic second only to Alashiya's. Her palace, I had heard, stretched as far as the eye could see. Bristling with animal-headed gods and steles, Ugarit was more Egyptian a country than most of the "independents." Her nobility was forgetful of its heritage; pretensions more suited to Egyptian society abounded on her shores. I am sure old Nimmuria Amenhotep found this mimicry as amusing as I. Still, it served me better than it served him: when one is looked upon as a servant by those in whose image one strives to appear, condescension in the eyes of the master is as sand in the servant's bed.

So just as we were doing in other upper-plains countries from Mukis on the Egyptian-controlled coast to Ni'i and Nuhasse, both east of the river Orontes, we began seeking partisans in Ugaritic society. Now, this is slow and painstaking work, best instigated by Hittite merchants and dwellers in foreign lands but, once begun, it smoothes the path for conquest. As dissension is fomented, local supporters take a hand. The best of these I had already singled out in some places, had not yet chosen in others, but one thing was clear: those who were presently distinguishing themselves in my behalf among the southerners, I would later reward for their loyalty. Empire buildeth itself from within.

Within Ugarit, I had supporters who told me things. They told me of the new king, Niqmad; of his youth, of the delicacy of his constitution and his sensibilities, and of his preoccupation with the arts. Great plans were announced in that country for the elevation of the historian, the sculptor, the scribe.

"What do you think, Kuwatna-ziti? Can these men of Ugarit be as blind and deaf and complacent as they profess, in the face of Amurrite hostility and the increasing disinterest Egypt shows in all but the war among its gods?" We were in my private study that day; none could overhear us; beyond my window, the sun was setting, gilding Kumanni's hilltops.

"Ugarit is yet enthralled by the Two Lands, Tasmi. The people of Ugarit see the Egyptians' might all around them and think it will never fail. Egypt is not yet giving up her appearance of suzerainty, only does she seem to be ignoring what in Egyptian eyes are labeled 'princely' disputes. Or some profess it thus, at any rate. Things cannot be as bizarre as we hear they are, in the City of the Horizon. Kings do not really drive naked, with wives beside them, through the streets of their cities—do they? The young pharaoh and his consort may be playing a shrewd game that we, with foreign eyes, cannot discern. Who knows the minds of the Beautiful Woman and the Horse-face? Not even their own mothers and fathers. Indeed, the reign of those royal parents seems about to be engulfed in the flood of strangeness that surrounds their children. That the young pharaoh and his queen should behave so heretically is in our favor. Why they do, I doubt we will ever understand. Sacrifice to the Storm-god, our lord, Tasmi, and to the Sun-goddess, our lady. Give thanks and hope these royals live long, disastrous lives upon the gold-plated seats of their double thrones: and that the old pharaoh, Nimmuria Amenhotep, does not become exceedingly well, but continues to ail, so that he perishes of this new ailment. He has been king for thirty-five years. It is time for a change."

"I could not agree more heartily. What have you heard from Mitanni?"

"Not enough, my lord Sun; not enough. Only that Tushratta's sister, who was a wife of old Amenhotep, has died and that Tushratta is negotiating with Egypt in the matter of a replacement. He will send, so it is reported, his daughter Taduhepa to replace his dead sister as a royal wife. In fact, she might be there now, only we have not yet heard it. Do not look so glum, Tasmi."

"Why not? This is not good news, not at all."

"Ah, but the ailing pharaoh has also asked that the goddess Istar of Nineveh be sent down to him. She healed him before, twenty years ago. If he is so ill as to request a foreign goddess once more, then things are not that bad for us. Perhaps she will be unable to heal him; perhaps her statue will be stolen or damaged on its way to Egypt. Twenty days is a long journey. Perhaps the old pharaoh will die before the goddess arrives; or die before the Mitannian princess arrives."

"Or not die at all. Or perhaps Istar of Nineveh will heal Old Pharaoh. Even if he be now dead, how is it better? The Mitannian girl will then marry the younger Amenhotep, and their alliance will be the stronger."

"Not 'Amenhotep': Naphuria *Akhenaten*. And not if he is anything like the person of whom we have heard so much. Would you like your daughter married to something with a pointed skull, the ears of an ass, the lips of a Nubian, the belly of a sow and the hips of a woman? Some say he is man and woman both, some say he is neither; but none say he is a normal man, with normal wants—"

"Shepherd, you sound like Khinti. I care not about his sex life. Where a man wants to thrust himself is his own concern; I have known soldiers who cohabit in the field, and so have you. That is women's talk."

"So you may think, Tasmi, so you may think. It matters not to you? It will matter to Tushratta, for it is his daughter. What if it were your daughter?"

"Tushratta is a military man. I gave my sister over to Hug-ganas of Hayasa, although he wived his sisters and married a son to a daughter."

"I will not argue it. You will see."

"I hope so. Let us leave it, then. Aziru, Criminal of Amurru, is beginning to plague Ribaddi, the Egyptian governor in Byblos, in earnest. The last time the sons of Abdi-asirta nibbled at the coast, Pharaoh sent in troops. If things are going as you say—"

"As I suspect—"

"As you suspect, then; and as I hope. *If* Egypt does not send troops into Byblos to aid Ribaddi, then that will be a sign her interest foreign affairs is truly flagging. But the marriage-alliance, Shepherd: the marriage-alliance belies all. What if the sphinx, she now disguised as Tushratta, is simply waiting for us to drive between her paws?"

"Even so, my lord Sun, the road down which you are driving leads only one place."

"I am driving to Mitanni, Shepherd."

"With one eye on the coast."

"All the gods stand and hear my oath: 'I want only Tushratta.'"

"I understand that. But you must understand that whither goeth the servant, it is at his master's behest. Touch the father-in-law of Pharaoh, and touch the hand that holds the crook and flail: Strike at the head that wears the plumed helm of Mitanni, and you are striking at the shaven pate that bears the Double Crown of Upper and Lower Egypt."

"Shepherd . . . are you afraid?"

"Is the circling wolf a coward? Does the coiling of a snake betray fear? I am ready, Tasmi. It is you who are slow in sniffing things out."

"Perhaps, Shepherd; perhaps. But speaking of sniffing things out . . . when I was too weak to hold up my head in the palace, when I was spared from death, I swore I would have it out with the Storm-god. I need your help."

He had been leaning back, sprawled. No longer: the Shepherd sat straight as an arrow, his eyes attentive, his shaven jaw outthrust. "What do you mean, Tasmi? You cannot have it *out* with a god. You do not say: 'Come, let us fight!' Not to the Storm-god."

So I began to tell him about my god-deafness, and about the blue-cloaked figure who dominates the landscape of my dreams.

And when I had said all of that, he sat silent a time, running a stylus over his plump lower lip, and at last replied: "I will ask a priestess I know, one free from prejudice, to learn the truth by incubation. I will look at the matter in my dreams. Call no Old Women in on this—you have not?"

"No, I have told only Khinti."

"Khinti. It cannot be helped."

"Shepherd!"

"Your wife is a good queen, Tasmi, so good that many are blinded in her favor with regard to things she does that in others would draw criticism."

"Let us not talk about my personal affairs."

"Then what shall we talk about?"

"Finish about the god. Do you think if I went into the temple and talked to him, it would do any good?"

"You have not done that?"

"Not for a long time; and not as I would today. I have been busy. And I would not want to do it in the Hattusas temple. Here in Kumanni, the gods seem clearer." I got up; my irritation would not let me sit. "Shepherd, I am sorry I spoke of it. Let it be as if I had not said anything."

"I am only a man, although you are forgetful of that when it suits you. You said it, and I am not hard of hearing. I will let you know what I find out."

"It is beautiful country, is it not? Khinti wants to spend the winter here." The king's estate in the holy city was of finest rare woods and colored marble, and everywhere the austere grace of godliness was inscribed upon stone and modeled softly in carven wood. The laws of the field were depicted round the large L-shaped chamber in a frieze of cedar wolves who hunted and killed eternally while all their prey fled them wide-mouthed, tongues flapping, racing over the lintel toward a pastoral pool they would never reach. Kumanni had survived a long time without being sacked: the gods protect their own. The high country rolled and stretched like a dog before his master, anxious to please.

"What the queen wants," said the Shepherd, "is for you to put Telipinus in the high priest's place: king of Kumanni, he would just about be then."

"Telipinus? Priest of Kumanni? He is barely manned. And if she wants it, what of it?"

"That is for you to determine, my lord Sun."

"All right, what else have you? I do not want to pursue this."

"As the Sun wishes. Would you come here?"

I went over to the desk at which he sat; it was spread with writing materials. "So?"

"Put your seal to this, and Lupakki is a general."

"With pleasure, though I am unsure whence I will replace the thirty I am losing to 'more important' posts. Kingship is bereft of choice."

"I wish you believed that. What about this message from Tushratta's brother, Artatama?"

"Can you get me a volunteer to take an answer to him?"

"His own messenger abides, awaiting your reply."

"I would think on this. He may have a few days' wait."

"'Kingship is bereft of choice': did you not just say that?"

"Kuwatna-ziti, I like this not at all. So Artatama may be the rightful ruler of Mitanni, ousted by Tushratta the usurper. What is that to me? If I do help him, how might I explain it to the people? When the old king of Mitanni died I was but a youth, but I remember what you said in that meeting about hating Hurrians. And although I agree that, as Hurrians go, this other brother might be preferable to Tushratta, what is the difference what color a tiger is if it is tearing out your throat? The kingdom of Mitanni and the kingdom of Hurri are now two separate entities in the eyes of the two brothers who rule them. To me they look the same: Hurrian."

"Tasmi, you misremember what I said then. I argued that we must support the Hurrian Artatama, just as Egypt supports the Mitannian Tushratta."

"Shepherd: *what difference does it make?* If I put Artatama of Hurri on the Mitannian throne and he reunites those feuding lands, I have done myself a great disservice. . . ."

The Shepherd tried to hide his smirk behind clasped hands, but I saw him.

"I hate it when you watch me think!"

"But?" teased the Shepherd.

"But, old wolf, *if* I should aid Artatama of Hurri just a little, just enough to keep Tushratta looking to his rear, and *if* war broke out on his eastern borders, and *if* he weakened himself and exhausted his troops fighting; and *if* indeed neither one of them won it, but they just kept gnawing at each other, then I could see it. . . . But that is four large 'ifs' and the last of them is possessed of a deadly stinger."

"But it is something to think about."

"All I will do is offer Artatama what I would offer any vassal king; he may not like that."

"My assessment of the situation is this: if you draft an agreement that is no further below him than his feet, he will stoop to pick it up. But Tasmi, he will not dig for it in the sand."

*

The folk always turn out when the army passes, and the folk of Kumanni were no exception. They lined the meandering route by the riverbank and cheered and sang. Noblewomen throwing garlands crowded into wagons from whose standards trained birds sang in dangling copper cages. Through the throng, priests and Old Women moved on foot at measured pace beneath their slave-borne awnings. Children ran in among the cars begging rides, their hands and faces sticky with honey. It is said that the way the folk line up for the armies is the truest measure of their feelings. If so, we were better loved in Kumanni than anywhere but Hattusas.

I stood with Khinti in the elaborate state chariot, my horses plumed and gleaming, as our chariotry passed in review. They were on their way to Ishuwa, with Piyassilis among the officers under newly-promoted General Lupakki's command. In Ishuwa, as on the Arzawaean frontier, there was always trouble. But Gasga was quiet, so I had plenty of men to spare: so peaceful were the tribal folk of Gasga that my eldest son had come down from Samuha to meet us for the occasion.

As the drums beat and the auxiliaries passed before, I strove to make out my second son behind Lupakki, somewhere in the flare of the column's point.

"There." I pointed, and Khinti grasped my arm and pressed her cheek against my shoulder and spoke motherly judgments upon the princely bearing of the long-haired youth, spear-straight, who drove his grays in exact synchrony with the teams on his left and right.

We had made our private farewells the evening before, a stiff and formal affair tinged awkward by Khinti's inability to see men in her boys. I had spent the meal in delicate arbitration between queen and princes, for Arnuwandas was sporting his first few battle-scratches, of which more was made than needful by all concerned.

Piyassilis had looked at me over the heads of my wife and boastful eldest, and shook his head like an old campaigner. Of the arrow that pinned his foot to the car, and of the head wound he summarily sustained in our defeat in Mitanni, he spoke not one word. Of his horses, he could not say enough. He had shaved off his beard and revealed what I had long suspected: he was in my image. His high forehead, thick, straight hair and wide-set, narrow eyes had portended it. The arrogant, unbending sweep of his nose had promised it. But not until he shaved did I see the prominence of his chin, the flaring angularity of his jaw, the firm mouth whose lower lip curled downward. Already, at eighteen, shadows were beginning to form around it, like defensive walls whose upper boundaries were his flaring nostrils, but whose southernmost frontiers were yet in doubt.

Himuili supped with us that night; he took his place in the royal retinue on the following day.

If I were he, I would have been bitter; I myself itched for reins of plain leather. Gladly would I have traded my golden, snub-horned king's helmet with its long flowing crest and graven cone for the simple bronze one of a field commander. But Himuili wielded the staff of his infirmity like a dignity and deployed the troops of Hatti with such brilliance that none could doubt his commitment to the task.

He was to Khinti like a second head, so she said. Without him, she affirmed, she would never have been able to control the inner lands while I campaigned so long in the outer reaches.

Looking at him, amid the inescapable crowd of ladies that materialized wherever he might choose to linger, I wondered just what it was about him that attracted them so. He had green-ish eyes, which may or may not be a sign of heavenly favor but he no longer had a manly stride, nor was his stance full of vigor. And whereas before he had his yearly quota of heroic deeds to commend him to the women, now all he did was administrative work, necessary detail that few could do as well as himself, it is true, but hardly glamorous or intriguing. Still, he wore his fine mantle as proudly as ever, and he yet sported huge hairy arms and a broad back, and that may have been it.

"Khinti, what is it about Himuili? Look at him, with all the fairest flowers of Kumanni at his feet."

She did not look where I pointed. She looked at me, a long, deep staring look through those change-color eyes. Then with a toss of her head she touched my forehead, traced the scar out of my eyebrow up to the hairline, and said:

"Jealous, my lord? He bears his scars no less prettily than you; he is simply more accessible. When first I saw you, I thought you frightening, formidable. Himuili, upon first sight, is reas-suring: a woman knows he could be very fearsome, but not with her; he includes her instantly in his protection. You, my lord, present no such false security."

"Which is why Arnuwandas does better with his women than Piyassilis, I suppose?"

"Arnuwandas is next in line, that is why he is so courted. A woman got in that way bodes ill for us all."

"Khinti—I told you, as long as he takes no wives it is none of our concern."

"My lord, I do not see how the morality of princes cannot be a concern to their father, the king."

"Well, it is not. And I wish to hear no more about it." I put my hand on her waist, let it slide, felt her stiffen with outrage. But I won the argument without a word, showing her to what depths even a queen might sink while reviewing troops in Kumanni of a bright spring day, until she gasped and tried not to show what she felt, leaning against me in hopes that none would mark the raising of her robe.

Afterward, her fury knew no bounds, and, since the review had finished at about the same time as she, she insisted on being driven directly to the king's estate, whence she would be pleased to leave, upon that moment, back to Hattusas and her twins.

When I was sure she was serious, I hailed Himuili and asked if he would see to my wife's wishes, handed her down out of the chariot into his care, and thought no more about it other than re-marking the inadvisability of mixing women and armies. From there I went off to hold council with my commanders and my sons.

But she lay yet in my bed when I stumbled in shortly before dawn, and not sleeping either, but curled into a ball.

I stared down blinking a time, trying to recollect through the wine why I had been out doing what I was doing, if I had a woman ready in my bed, then managed, "You are still here, are you?"

She made no intelligible answer.

I stripped off my gear and lay back, thinking of something else to say, and fell asleep before I had found it.

In the morning I got it straight with her, and she stayed with me in Kumanni until the summer came and we sought the cool breeze of Hattusas' scarp.

CHAPTER 23

By the time I turned thirty-five, the marriage of old Amenhotep to Tushratta's daughter was an attested fact.

So, too, was the marriage of Niqmad II, young king newly
acceded in Ugarit, to an Egyptian girl. Now whether, as Hatib
said, the girl was of less-than-noble birth, or whether she was a
royal princess, she was still Egyptian, and I did not like it. In my
mind, Ugarit was already mine; and like a man courting a woman
I was disturbed at Egypt's interest even though I had half expected it, even though it showed that some few moments of sanity
were granted those 'Living in Truth' in the City of the Horizon.

And there, also, was effected the safe arrival of the goddess
Istar of Nineveh, to the sickbed of old Pharaoh. Since he was well
enough to wed the Mitannian princess, it was generally assumed
that the goddess still favored the god-kings of Egypt.

The goddess certainly seemed to have made the aged ruler
of Upper and Lower Egypt "exceedingly well" once more. The
whole of the southern lands expelled a breath of relief so heart-

felt that we heard it in Hattusas: the Two Lands had waited like citizens huddled in a besieged city to find out if their destiny was henceforth to be determined solely by the "Criminal of Akhetaten," who sought to cast out the venerable gods of Egypt from their temples and to starve the priests of Amun and Set and Thoth and all the rest, paying homage only to his beloved Aten, ruler of the solar disk.

"If young Akhenaten wants to give up being a god-king and demote himself to a steward-king like us barbarians of 'Upper Retenu', what is wrong in that?" I asked Hatib.

My favorite Sutu had a full head of hair that season, the locks over each ear gathered into Libyan side-braids, the rest hanging down between his wide-set shoulder blades.

"Nothing is wrong with it as far as we are concerned, any more than there is anything wrong with Egyptians sending me up to Hattusas on embassy business. It is wrong for them though — and if you were as close to Egypt's woes as I, you too would be filled with pity at what is becoming of the Two Lands."

"The most precipitous cliffs soften under the winds of the years."

"Exactly. But the people of Egypt are huddled under fractured cliffs of thousands of years of tradition, waiting for them to fall. They are not like Hittite people. Egyptians have not risen up against a solar king in anyone's memory. The love of their living god runs so deep in their hearts that they grieve as must Akhenaten's own mother. And yet they do nothing, say nothing, think nothing. It is the priests of Amun, the ram-headed god, who have named him 'Criminal.' And that is being said only in the temples whose lands have been taken away and given to the sun-god Aten, whom the young king loves. . . . But the people do not love the Aten . . . the people, they just weep."

"Enough, or I will be weeping too. Do you wish release from my service? Is your heart not with me any longer, but with this poor afflicted young pharaoh instead?"

The Sutu's hissing laugh gusted forth like a mountain wind.

Caution, I told myself as I came round the white gift horses I was sending down with Hatib to Egypt. Caution, for this is no panderer nor powdered priest, and as I came abreast of him I tried once more to delve beneath the paint obscuring his eyes. What scheme or temper lurked there, I must this day determine or by dint of my own suspicions Hatib would become as useless to me as a hand severed from its owner's wrist.

I reached out and fingered the braided hank dangling against his bull's neck, saying, "I need a better answer than that. I am waiting."

Now, I have said I am not small. But Hatib had not shrunken any over the years and, king or not, I had only him attending me by the pink-eyed white steeds in the stable-yard. I had wanted no prying ears. In the palace, one never knows who may pass by.

"My friend, I am still spending Hittite shekels." He looked down his nose at my fingers, and then back to me. "Therefore I am still in your employ. Therefore" — as he stepped back I let his braid slip out of my grasp — "I will take no offense. Kingship is known to make men change."

"Almost to your death are you pushing me, old warrior. Take a moment and recollect to whom you speak, and what disaffection between us must come to mean."

"My lord, I bow down before you. On my back, on my belly, I sing the praises of the Sun." He was still standing, and his big teeth gleamed between mobile lips as he spoke. "You think Hatib does not know that death drives the chariot of the Sun's displeasure? You think, perhaps, that Hatib has forgotten all that his employer has demanded in the way of treachery to those others I serve? One word from you and Hatib is no more. One whisper in the right ear, and I and mine will be blotted out from the earth, from the very memory of man. Of course, as my lord must see, a certain scribe in Akhetaten would be heartbroken unto perishing if any ill befell me."

"By the Storm-god, man, think what you are saying!"

"I am saying, dear lord who is now a king, when you were but a desperate princeling singled out for the offering block you could not afford to question my loyalty. You gave me a great sum of money on the eve of our first meeting, you did not distrust me then. And when the oft-lamented Queen Daduhepa went up to Arinna with your boy Telipinus in her womb, it was Hatib who escorted her there safely, and came back to fight beside you against your enemies."

"Hatib . . . reassure me, do not pressure me. I cannot let you go down from here until I am free of questions, at the least."

"It is said that a king does what he wills. I believe it. What you have in your heart is there already. What could I do to change it?"

"Change it."

"I cannot, my lord. I stand between the Eagle of Hatti and the Sphinx of Egypt, and both of you have eyes on Amurru, and of both I am a servant. Now how can I serve two masters whose wishes do not coincide? If Amurrite hostility to Byblos, Tyre, and the other coastal cities continues, there will be Egyptian retribution upon the rebel Abdi-asirta and his sons, whom you the Sun would protect. Now, if I am ordered by Egypt to strike down the Amurrite, I must strike him down. And if I am ordered by you, the Sun, to lift him up, then I must lift him up. . . ." He spread wide his hands and smiled broadly, so that his beard speared the air. "And I cannot do both those things. Although my person resides this moment in Hattusas, down in Thebes rest my wife and my seed. Kill me here if you wish, lord Hittite, for that will be better than having my family subjected in my stead to Egypt's wrath."

"That is the extent of your problem?"

"It is not a small thing in my eyes."

"Nor, I am afraid, in mine. But if that is all of it, I will tell you what we will do."

I thought I saw something like relief in him as he said, "It is the whole, my lord."

"Then hear this: in the matter of the land of Amurru, do what your Egyptian masters tell you. If Amurru cannot stand against its enemies, I have no need of Amurrites. Only keep me informed as you have in the past." I punched him playfully where his belly had fattened, allaying his suspicions still further. "And all else will remain as it has been, both the service you do me and what it is worth."

"My lord, your astuteness and your circumspection will surely triumph!"

I was trying to see if his relief was real, or only a sham. I could not tell.

But thereafter, I used Hatib only for certain kinds of information: things I wished others to know. And I took no action against him, none at all. Within Hatti, we do not keep hostages to insure the loyalty of our servants without. Most other nations make it common practice. Hatib, assigned to the Honorable Hani, Mouthpiece Unto Foreign Lands for Egypt, dwelled in Lower Retenu among the minions of the Egyptian commissioner; his family dwelled in Thebes, the flesh of his bond.

I cannot say I was pleased. But when I had lost the war I had learned a thing that elsewise I might never have understood: they serve themselves, all of them; only to the extent that their leader exemplifies their own thoughts and desires, and no further, will they follow. That is why god and king become close when rulers seek total power: only if faith is involved can a regent demand more. And although my own people seek the gods through me and make me their proxy and the surrogate who enjoys all the luxury of which they can only dream, through me they have it, every one. In Hatib's case, no consideration of pride or destiny applied: only a chance acquaintance and a Sutu's oath bound him to me, and at that point in time I doubted if those would be enough.

I always give a man a second chance: This strategy I employed many more times before my heart believed its worth. Much later, I would show leniency to others who more flagrantly violated my trust, and for the same reason: a man's skin is dearer to him than the Thousand Gods of Hatti; the only way he will offer that skin up willingly into your service is if you have made him sure beyond question that your displeasure is more to be feared than all the lesser enemies he has closer to hand. If you have not, whose fault is that? In the matter of Hatib and those others he served,

Lord Hani and his Egyptian masters, I had not yet proved myself incomparably fearsome. But I was almost ready.

CHAPTER 24

In the small cedar conference chamber burned a bronze brazier. The room had a smoke-hole for the torches, no window. At the foot of its central table sat Arnuwandas, flanked by Piyassilis and Telipinus on his right and left. By Piyassilis was Lupakki, then the brilliant young commander Tarkhunta-zalma, then my Master of Horses Hannutti, and myself at the table's head. On my left sat Hattu-ziti, bald pate shining, then the Shepherd, then Takkuri whose sister had borne me the boy Kantuzilis, who stood at attention by one side of the door. Zidanza, my adopted son, in Meshedi red like Kantuzilis, had the other guard post.

It was the fall of the year that old Amenhotep died, the beginning of my eighteenth regnal year, and the beginning of Naphuria Akhenaten's sole reign from Akhetaten. Protocol required that I write the new pharaoh a letter, congratulating him on his accession. So I wrote to him, saying:

"My messengers whom I sent to your father as to the desire which your father expressed for mutual relationship, let us estab-

341

lish it. I have refused nothing of what your father asked, and all that I asked, your father did not refuse me. . . . . Why have you sent no messages, now that you have ascended your father's throne? Behold, two statues of gold, one sitting, one standing, two silver statues of women, one great lapis lazuli, let my brother send. Whatever you desire, write and I will send it. Behold a present for you: one vase of silver, weight five minas, and three more vases, total weight thirteen minas, I have sent."

And indeed, I sent those things down to Egypt, to see if I might get a reaction that would help me judge this "brother" ruler. We have a fine obsidian vase in the cellar that was sent long ago when the Shepherd Kings had ruled in Egypt and debased her. The Egyptians are still trying to blot out that memory. Now, this Shepherd King's name, so it is said, was Khyan, and on the vase was incised this Khyan's cartouche. It was a copy in silver of this artifact that went innocently along with its more customary Hattian-style companions down to Egypt.

If a man wets his finger and holds it up to the wind, he does not argue with the result. I heard nothing back from the young pharaoh.

But I had heard from other "brother" kings. I heard from the newly acceded King of Babylon, Burnaburiash, whose mighty country dominates the southeast. His letter was very brotherly and as much as admitted that I was now the fourth "Great King" in the arena of international affairs, and I was pleased to receive it. Babylon means Gateway to Heaven, and thence came up an offer I had not expected: This Burnaburiash was interested in giving me a daughter in marriage. I had not yet answered him. It is permissible to have many wives, but not many queens; if I took the Babylonian princess it would have to be as a lesser wife, as indeed the Egyptians, first Amenhotep III, and upon his death Akhenaten, had done in the case of Tushratta's daughter. It would be a tremendous advantage to me to have such intimate relations with the Lion of Babylon who, after all, might still carry some Hittite blood from the Old Empire's campaigns there. My rear would be sacrosanct, if such a thing were to come to be. But there were problems, and I had it in my mind to delay an answer until spring, meanwhile spending the winter negotiating with my queen on the matter.

There are strange things said about the Babylonians, stories told of their customs that would make a strong man shiver. What went on in their temples, in the gardens on the summits of their towering buildings, was infinitely conjectured. Talk of it was not absent from our deliberations that fall evening in Kumanni, a month to the day after the Festival of Haste.

But what concerned us most was unrest in Ishuwa, grown open in its surrounding towns across the river and spreading like a plague. In spring I would turn thirty-seven, and I had been fighting the wild tribes and the dissidents since five years before my accession. I proposed, that night, to make an end to this battle of bushes once and for all.

My commanders, ranked around the map inlaid into the table, were in full agreement. At my knee, Pikku, my short light-haired scribe, ground his teeth as he struggled to take the minutes as fast as we decided matters.

I proposed, also, that Tarkhunta-zalma and thirty men of his choosing be the extent of my troops when I drove up to meet Artatama, self-proclaimed king of Hurri, in Hayasa. Although he called me brother, into the Hatti land proper he would not come. Nor was he coming into Hayasa, but would meet me where he had his border with Hugganas, on the river Mala.

To this my sons made loud objections, each feeling it was his place to be my courier. But I was adamant. Although I remembered days when I was as anxious to volunteer for dangers that bring places on the heroes' roll, I could not trust so crucial a negotiation to princes, nor would I want to risk having them with me, should something go awry.

In the silence I demanded as a simple end to the matter, my eye caught young Tarkhunta-zalma, who slouched with bowed head and the ghost of a smile on his face, toying with the tassels of his belt. He was the only brown-haired Hittite in the room, though it happens; my girl-child twin has fair hair like Khinti's father. To Tarkhunta-zalma I said:

"As Lupakki's protégé, you are expected to be taciturn, but not unduly. Great things are said of you; I will see for myself if they are true on this sortie. That is, if you are pleased to accompany me. . ."

"Great King, my lord, I am overwhelmed. I am unworthy."

"Overwhelmed by mere words, are you? How worthy you are, we will see presently. It is lucky that a man does not need to talk to fight."

He mumbled something, and I recollected that he had trained with Lupakki's half-wild scouts, and then with my now-disbanded thirty, who were no better mannered.

"Are you apprised of the matter fully? Have you requests or questions?"

He sat up, put heavy forearms on the table and craned his neck to look at me around Hannutti. "I could drive up there in my sleep, my lord Sun. I know what men I would put together: I have thought about it enough. They will be worth their strength twice over acting in concert. You will be pleased. I know it."

"And your gear is adequate?"

"What I need I can get from Hannutti, can I not? I want for nothing, but some of mine may."

I was wondering how this brash fellow could be the same youth who had been hesitant to drive for me down into Syria.

Kuwatna-Ziti and Takkuri smiled. Lupakki put his fingers to the bridge of his nose. Piyassilis, beyond him, shook his head when he caught my eye. Arnuwandas, turning and whispering in Telipinus' ear, was otherwise concerned.

"Shepherd, this is no laughing matter. You, Takkuri, wipe away your smirk! Yes, young commander, you can get what you need from Hannutti. Or from Hattu-ziti if your requirements are extensive. But if you cannot improve your manners, I will be forced to take action."

"My lord. . ." Tarkhunta-zalma half rose, sank back, then simply bowed his head.

"That is it! I know of only one remedy for such bold insolence in the presence of the king! Shepherd, do you concur?"

"Most heartily, my lord Sun."

"Then, if you will. . ."

"Pikku, come here," ordered Kuwatna-ziti.

Up with a faint groan came the scribe, and scuttled over to the Shepherd's side.

The young commander sat immobile, pale. Lupakki had a hand on his arm and was trying to spear me with urgent looks. All others, my boys and my high officials of the army, had realized what I had in mind. The low buzz of the Shepherd's instructions and the scribe sounding out his writing scratched in the silence. When it was done Kuwatna-Ziti put his seal to the clay and handed it to me. I put my seal into the clay and handed the tablet back.

"Congratulations, Tarkhunta-zalma, general of the armies of Hatti," said the Shepherd, pushing the frame of wet clay across the table to the youth, whose brown head was yet bowed. Lupakki let out a yelp and began to laugh.

Up very slowly straightened Tarkhunta-zalma, and read the matter over, and pushed the tablet back, nodding as if to himself. Then with slitted eyes he regarded me and said, "You will not regret this, my lord Sun."

"I have a feeling you are right. Now that this is done and no one can feel resentful of you, then let us see if we can do as well for Telipinus on the morrow."

Arnuwandas spoke then: "My father, you know that a troublemaker held forth in the temple yesterday, and that the guards were tardy apprehending him. This morning our mother, rendering judgment in your stead, ruled that the guards must merely haul water three days, naked, as their punishment. I would have had them slain. We cannot afford the cost of a gentle hand right now. Not with tomorrow's ceremony, and the incendiary mood of the Ishuwans. I would feel better if we cleared the temples of all the refractory peoples. We do not want any interruptions."

Crown prince, without doubt, I thought. I said to my tuhkanti: "As for the judgment Khinti made, I would have done the same. Guards in the temples must concern themselves with fine gradations in 'allowable madness' and ecstatic frenzy. And these guards are too few, and they stand always within the shadow of the gods' wrath. But I agree that no untoward occurrences must be allowed to mar Telipinus' assumption of his duties. What has the Priest himself to say? What see you with those far-gazing eyes?"

"It will be well in the temples, father. It will be well with the Hurrian king. It will be ill in Hattusas this winter. We will all lose something."

Piyassilis groaned and it looked as if he kicked at young Telipinus under the table, for Arnuwandas, between them, cuffed them both in turn. What then developed was the need for the rest of us to separate them before they did each other damage.

Lupakki and Tarkhunta-zalma, together, dragged Piyassilis out of it while Takkuri and the Shepherd and I restrained Arnuwandas. Telipinus, who had not a scratch on him, was dusting himself off with Hattu-ziti's help, and Hannutti was grumbling that it was about time Arnuwandas stopped fighting Telipinus' battles for him, after all.

The two Meshedi, whose affair it should have been to avert such matters, stood horrified, staring at their brothers.

"You, both of you: Zidanza! Kantuzilis! What good are you to me if you are afraid to lift a hand to a brawler who outranks you? Both of you are assigned to the armies, henceforth. If Zida cannot train you, maybe the Hurrians will." As I was saying that, I was shaking Arnuwandas by the hair. I pushed him away, and spat my disgust at his feet. "Go on, go to a physician and see if you can manage to appear in the morning's procession without evidence of violence upon your person. You, too, Piyassilis, *my lord* prince. And while you are at it, spend the night meditating on what it means to be sons of the Sun. Tomorrow we will discuss it, and I do not wish to be disappointed in your answers to whatever questions I may choose to ask. Go on, get out. You too, my ladies of the Meshedi. I am sure we elders of the sword can get along without your protection."

When the door had closed behind them, I loosed my aching fingers from their grip on the table's edge and said to the Shepherd: "Snakes. That is what I have raised: a basket of snakes!" and then realized that Telipinus, innocent, wide eyed and dreamy, remained.

"You! You started this. Why are you not gone with them? Get out."

"But, my lord—"

"Get out. The gods' meal is served early; be not bleary when you eat it for the first time in Kumanni." So out he went, and whatever he was going to say went with him.

Those were the early days, when I was too uncomfortable with Telipinus' gift to think to make use of it. "Great Ones, now that the children have retired, let us consider the situation in the south."

So Hattu-ziti began to detail the strides made regarding our partisan Sarrupsi of Nuhassi and the suborning of his country, and spoke of the letters of Ribaddi of Byblos that Duttu had forwarded from the City of the Horizon, which protested, in Ribaddi's own words, that he was "trapped like a bird in a net in Byblos," and requested wood wherewith to warm himself and water to drink, and soldiers of Pharaoh, his lord, to relieve the Amurrite Abdi-asirta's siege.

And I was not really listening, but thinking sourly that this quiet, broad-backed youth Tarkhunta-zalma was no older than Arnuwandas, and yet immeasurably more self-contained. But then, a crown prince secure in his position, tuhkanti since he was a babe of five, has different troubles than any other boy might have: if Arnuwandas was quick with his fists, then so had I been at his age, and younger. Next to me, all of mine were model children, but I wanted so much more from them. And now that each had come of age and differentiated themselves the one from the other, if I did not like the people they had become, then though I might not like them as much as I wanted to like them, I had had my moment for recourse: the years during which I might have molded them and remade what I did not like had passed. I had not done it. My queen Daduhepa, my lesser wife Takkuri's sister, my second queen Khinti had not done it, or had done it but not to my satisfaction.

That was the first time I admitted it: I was dissatisfied with my sons. It was not an easy thing to admit. And it was not a pleasant thing upon which to dwell, the night before the youngest of my first batch of fledglings took wing. Tomorrow, tender-cheeked but old enough by law at least, Telipinus the Priest would assume his rule in the holy city of Kumanni. I should have been proud. I was uneasy. It had been Khinti's idea. She was not compromised by the gods looking out of Telipinus' eyes; I suppose she had some of the same inside her.

While I labored developing the strategies for the spring campaign, which had to be finished and implemented before the first snow fell in Hattusas, Khinti was setting the town of Kumanni right with the gods for tomorrow's festival. She and Himuili had been at work on it for nearly a month. It had never bothered me before; now, upon the very eve of the event, I was troubled unto speech.

"What think you, my lord?" asked Takkuri.

"What? I did not hear: my mind wanders to the morrow. Can any of you think of a reason why it should bother me, asudden, that Telipinus will be installed here? Shepherd, have the omens turned? Have the gods farted in my face again?"

"Tasmi! No, I can see nothing wrong with it; the royal family spends a good deal of time here, of late. And he is astute enough; just not willing to fistfight with Piyassilis, who is four years older, and certain enough of Arnuwandas' love to know that he does not have to."

"Still, I want the Priest out in the field, at least by the middle of next season. What if harm should befall the family and he alone remained, my last surviving prince? He cannot even protect himself. I want no son who cannot be a king, and to be a king a man must know life and death. Where else can he learn but on the battlefield? How can he minister to the disparate peoples of empire if he moves not among them?"

"I will tell Himuili, my lord. We will see to it."

"Hattu-ziti, you see to it yourself. And do it before you take that spreading bottom of yours back to the citadel."

Later that same night, Arnuwandas came to me, though I had instructed him not to, and asked me:

"Abuya, I have a question about judgment."

"So?"

"If a man has a woman and cannot see to her, and if in his absence a friend whom he dearly loves secretly sees to her, and if then the husband finds out about it, what should he do?"

I had been trying one more time to extract information from between the lines of words on some Syrian intelligence tablets. "Torchlight is a poor substitute for daylight." I rubbed my eyes and set the whole clattering mass of them aside. "Sit, and . . . what did you say? Surely *you* are not having woman troubles?"

"Abuya, this is serious." He pulled a pillowed stool under him, and smiled wanly, and looked about. "Where is Khinti?"

"Out making ready for tomorrow. As you should be. I told you to have that eye looked at, and get some sleep."

"It does not matter. This other thing matters."

"Who is she?"

"I cannot tell, I am under oath. And that is part of my second question, for after you have answered the first. So answer the first and I will ask the second."

"Say it again then." I stretched in my chair and gestured that he pour us wine.

As he was pouring, he said, "If a woman sleeps with a friend of her husband, who is much away, and the man finds out about his friend and his wife, both of whom he dearly loves, what should he do?"

"You can start standing in for me in the morning judgments in Hattusas, if this sort of thing intrigues you. Any of these, he may do: he may kill them both upon the spot; he may bring them to the gate of the palace and declare 'My wife shall not be killed' and spare her life, but then he shall also spare the life of the adulterer and mark his head. Or, if he is squeamish he may call at the palace gate and demand that they both be killed. Or he may bring it for judgment to the court of the king. Then the king may order them killed; the king may spare their lives. Whatever the king's judgment, all must accept it."

"In most cases you have judged, you have not decreed that adulterers be killed."

"No, I have not. It seems a foolish waste of life to me. Banishment is better for all concerned. Women are fickle creatures at best, and easily persuaded to one thing or another. Men, when their need is on them, will stoop to whatever is necessary. Nature knoweth no rightful father but he who arriveth first. The only security in a marriage is what a man can oversee. All considered, we make too much of it, if women stray."

"But the humiliation and the pain make it hard to think. When I think of my friend, I am suffused with rage. And yet, the humiliation is greater than the pain. Here is my second question: If the man does not know, should a friend tell him or will that be worse?"

"Is this what all the long faces and secretive looks have been about recently? Because if it is, I think it is time we put a stop to it. Whoever this friend of you princes is, leave off and stay clear of his business. No one wants to be told something like that. He will find out about it, or he will not. It is not a princely concern."

"Even if we are sworn to each other's betterment?"

"Most especially then. You would acquire the taint of it forever; he would always wonder if you, too, had not been at her. No, keep far away from the whole matter of another man's woman. Do not concern yourself."

"And if he finds out and asks me what to do?"

"If he should, which I cannot weigh without knowing this person's name, then you must give a kingly answer. Always counsel a course less final than death. Death allows no room for error. Once a man is gone to the netherworld, you cannot call him back and say, 'I am sorry I was so harsh, the moment caught me.' Leave those sentiments most terrible to war, where they belong."

"Thank you. And . . . Abuya?"

"So?"

"Please tell no one, not any person at all, whoever it may be, about this."

"You have my word. But if it is Piyassilis, and it sounds most like him, then do not worry. That one is as solid as the walls of the citadel."

"I wish it were. By the Storm-god of the Armies, I wish it were."

"Go get some sleep; you are required the whole of tomorrow. And do not forget to bring your seal. You will need it."

CHAPTER 25

So it was that after Telipinus' assumed his priestly duties
in Kumanni, all the royal family and Khinti's pale-haired Ahhiyawan relatives and the officials of the palace and of the army
who had come down from Hattusas for the festival went back
there; and I, accompanied by the young general Tarkhunta-zalma and the thirty he had chosen, went up through the refractory
lands of Tegarama and Ishuwa and into Hayasa and across her to
meet Artatama, king of Hurri, at the headwaters of the Mala river.

Now I was not merely interested, I was slavering. Tushratta
of Mitanni's brother, called by many the rightful heir to all the
Hurri lands, was going to sit down with me and plead his case.
I would hear him, brother to brother. It was said that the affair
was between the two brothers, and the Gods of the Oath. When
the Oath Gods call, a man has to listen. Artatama and I had written back and forth about it, true, but there is no substitute for
physical presence in the matter of delicate treaties.

Before she left for Hattusas, Khinti had been pleased, by
the look of her, about this Hurrian treaty but too distracted by
her relatives' visit and the need to be exceedingly gracious and
exceedingly queenly before them, so that I had taken her aside
and spoken to her about her disinterest.

"You say this to me?" she had whispered, mocking me with
her disbelief. "And where go you tomorrow, husband? Are you
coming home, now that the season for war is ended? No, you are
going out even again, though all but the few soldiers you drag
with you into peril are settled down with their wives and their
children for the winter. Even at the border stations, things are
peaceful. And yet you always find a way, do you not, to avoid
the service of the gods? Do you want the twins to grow up like
your first queen's brood, only introduced to their sire when they
are fully grown and ready for use?"

"Khinti! There are folk here!" We were standing behind the
great statue of the Storm-god straddling the sacred bulls Serris
and Hurris that is in Kumanni's temple. "What is this with you?
All is well with us, better than it has ever been."

"So it may be for you, husband, who craves wars never-
ending. You go to start one, do you not?"

"Is that it? Do not fear, this time I am ready."

Then she had spun on her heels and run from me down into
the temple, her hands pressed to her head, forgetful of the queenly
dignity she prized so highly.

I thought long on the matter of her behavior, and vowed that
I would spend more time with her this winter than I had been accustomed to spending, and put it from my mind. There is a thing
that is not easy, but which must be learned: with many affairs
constantly vying for attention, those whose solution is not imminent must be subordinated to that one which may be solved.

I was concerned with resolving my differences with this Artatama, king of Hurri. If the gods, my lords, would aid me, and I
had a feeling they would, a formal declaration of my adherence
to the Hurrian's cause would be a slap in the face to Tushratta,
the sound of which would reverberate in the mud-brick streets

of the City of the Horizon, and in the tiled halls of Babylon, and throughout all the other lands.

I was ready to move southward in spring. By then, it was in my heart that Tushratta of Mitanni be enraged unto confrontation. For if this man of Hurri, Artatama, gave me even the slightest chance, I would publicly back him in his machinations to regain the throne, and declare to all the peoples of all the lands that, in my eyes, Tushratta was a usurper and even stood in violation of the strictures of the Gods of the Oath.

And that, it turned out, was almost exactly what this Great King of Hurri wanted me to do.

We were instructed to wait on the Hayasaean side of the river: we waited.

I had heard that Artatama was an older man, so for the occasion I let my beard grow. I wore near a month's growth, which itched and caught dust, but the cold of the heights made it bearable and kept away the summer parasites. I was scratching it and leaning on my chariot talking to Tarkhunta-zalma and watching the men water the horses.

We were discussing women, and I had just said that at this point in my life, "a country has become like a teat to me, a range of mountains like a spread of thighs. . . ."

Tarkhunta-zalma then looked at me askance and praised the Great Queen and my offspring and said that if he could find a woman so fine as the meanest of the Sun's concubines, then his troubles would be over and he could rest content.

I was just telling him that women like Khinti were hard to find, and that the others I had were mere obligations, when the first chariot appeared atop the eastmost hill; then a second and a third. Abruptly my camp became full of shouts and hustling men harnessing horses as down the Hurrian hills to the east bank of the river rolled a column of chariotry, fifty in all, with a gold-and ivory-bedecked car drawn by matched sorrels in the lead.

Around this kingly chariot were standard bearers and princes and also Artatama's nobles, if my eyes did not deceive me.

Even while Tarkhunta-zalma secured the last trace and vaulted into my car and took up its reins, the royal Hurrian chariot
with its gold-crowned driver broke away from the mass of his
halted troops and headed toward the water.

"Alone, then?" queried my sand-haired driver, whose general's helm clattered around his feet.

"It appears so."

Thus we proceeded through our troops to the riverbank, and
stopped with our horses' forefeet in the river.

"Hail, Great King, King of Hatti, Suppiluliumas, the Hero,
my brother!" said the purple-robed king of Hurri, and doffed his
helmet. Then I saw the grizzled mane, the bushy brows under
which black eyes darted, the broad and jutting features of Tushratta's brother, whose girth at the waist was twice my own, but
whose shoulders were curved like a Hattian bow.

"Greetings, Artatama, king of Hurri. So that we need not
shout across the river, I invite you into the Hatti land, and your
chariotry with you."

"He ought to accept that, with nearly twice as many chariots as we have," breathed Tarkhunta-zalma, his loose hair whipping his face.

"But not twice as many men; he carries but two to the car,"
I added absently, awaiting the other king's rejoinder.

When Artatama still kept silent, I wondered if I should have
been more effusive in my greeting, but then he bellowed his acceptance and urged his team into the ford.

"Meet him," I ordered. So we met him in mid-river. Axle
to axle we touched hands in greeting, and drove back across the
river into Hatti with all his personal troops following.

"Young you seem, Suppiluliumas, my brother, to have acquired so formidable a reputation."

We were sitting to a meal in the open, where all our watching men could see that neither of us instigated violence upon
the other's person, but far enough from the stiff-necked, uneasy
troops that they could not hear us. The only ones we had with us

were a pair of army scribes, who served us food and drink and awaited something worth putting to clay.

"I have heard that Tushratta is not much older."

"That scorpion!" He sprayed out his wine. "The Oath Gods will yet have him, for the murder of our father's heir."

"I am interested in being the Oath Gods' instrument in that matter. Let us get to this business at hand: tell me what is in your heart, and why you have not accepted my first offer."

"And then tell you the secrets of the city of Washuganni, Tushratta's capital, eh? Never fear, young Great King. I know them. I know my brother, better than any. I have everything you need but, for it all, the payment you have offered is insufficient."

"What do you want?"

"I want my rightful seat of kingship. I want you to help me obtain it."

"How could it serve me to do that, to exchange one opponent for another?"

"How could it serve me to become your vassal? I cannot do that. I am hereditary ruler of the Hurri lands, including Mitanni. I will sign a neutrality pact with you. I can do no better."

"Cede me those Hurrian territories west of the Mala river, all of them which I can take on my own."

"You are jesting, my lord Hittite."

I lay back from my food, regarding his thrice-chinned, greasy aspect. "I am offering to let you keep your city Washuganni, and all east of the Mala river, whereas you only have some few lands around and about the Tigris now, and a contested strip of country between you and your brother which will soon be black and free of stick or twig from fighting and useless to anyone."

"You are offering me something you do not yet have," glowered the Hurri king, brushing meat from his robe. Upon his head an ornate crown, peaked and jeweled, glittered in the sunlight.

"I will have it. I will have it before two years have passed. And when I take it, I will carry away all the gold and silver, the implements of the gods, the gold and silver doors from Assur! All that you thieves have collected will be mine. And if you and

I reach no agreement, I will tumble the whole of Washuganni to the ground; no foundation of the city will stand. In other wise, if you and I find consonance between us, I will let the city stand, and even let you into it. I will acknowledge you as brother king and friend of Hatti, and other than a mutual assistance policy upon our shared borders, will ask no service from you. No tribute must you pay me; we will be great kings together, brothers ruling with peace between them. And that is the best and the final offer I am willing to make."

"Not enough. You must proclaim to all the kings that you recognize me in rightful struggle, that I am the true lord of Mitanni and Hurri, and agree to help me unite my disaffected lands. You must say to everyone: it is Artatama who is faithful to his oaths, chosen of the gods, favorite of Teshub—"

"Aha! At least there is one thing we have in common: we are both favorites of storm-gods."

He looked at me as if I had lost my senses and glowered more. "I was still speaking."

I grinned at him. "I thought that you had finished. Surely you want to demand no more from me than that. I cannot go any farther in that direction."

"But you will go that far?"

"I will go as far in your behalf as you allow me. But not one step to my own detriment will I take. These things you have proposed, the gods look upon them with favor. I would like to be continuously friendly with you, from this day forward, and unto the days of my sons. I wish nothing but proof on your part that you can provide me with aid in the matter of casting out this Tushratta from the seat of his usurpership."

"So, proof is it? Let me see. . . . Do you know that when Tushratta got the counter-presents in the matter of his daughter's marriage to Akhenaten of Egypt, that the statues were of wood, only plated with gold? And did you know that Tushratta was so enraged by this that he called the Egyptian envoy Hani before him and complained, and even wrote to the king of Egypt and said this?" His belly was wobbling with laughter; his keen eyes watered at the precious joke. "Did you know it?"

"No, I did not know. And it is good that you tell me such things. Tell me more, and tell me of the lay of the city, and the fortifications of Tushratta's palace, and the number of guards who patrol within."

So he did that, and it was well with us. And before we left, each back to his respective capital, we had written on the spot an agreement between us, and taken each the other's copy back to our chamberlains, and determined peace between us henceforth and mutual assistance in all the matters we had discussed.

I was triumphant. I had never been happier. All things seemed assured, all the desires of my heart within my grasp.

Thus we took our time driving home, visiting first with the border commanders in the lands of Ishuwa and Tegarama, which were troublesome countries then, and when at last we arrived back in Hattusas in the dead of night we were ten days late.

I spent a time with my general Tarkhunta-zalma, instructing him to keep the thirty he had chosen in the city for the winter, for I wanted to use them early in the spring campaigns. I spent a while longer in the chancery with Hattu-ziti going over the Artatama agreement. And when at last I had visited the king's latrine in the basement and climbed the stairs to my chambers, I was feeling my weariness.

One of the Meshedi in the corridor had been leaning against the wall, talking to a palace woman. The girl flew off with a muffled squeal and the guard struck an unmoving pose. But the look on his face seemed too fearful for so small an infraction; in such matters, I am not known for hardheartedness. Or at least, I had thought I was not.

But a king cannot take council with every palace guardsman, and I strode by him into my chambers without a second glance.

I heard a noise that was not the doors, for they had closed silently behind me, and went round to the bedchamber.

And froze in my tracks. The floor shook beneath my feet. My tongue cleaved to the roof of my mouth. My whole frame trembled as if from a death-blow.

I launched myself toward the pair upon the bed, screaming curses, and even as Khinti scrambled up, naked, I had the man by his scruffy neck and was choking the breath from him. Somewhere in the moment between when I lifted the hairy adulterer from my bed and slammed him back against the wall and began pummeling him, I had a glimpse of his shocked, fearful eyes, of his mouth opening before blood gushed from his split lips.

Then Khinti jumped up on my back, locking her arms around my neck, kicking and biting and wailing.

I let go of him and pulled her off me, and cast her down to the floor. There she lay silent, unmoving, the back of her hand pressed to her mouth, her panthers' eyes pleading.

I turned back to the man, who had fallen to his knees. I lifted him up. And then I was striking him. And he struck back. So I struck until the face of Himuili, Chief of 1,000, high official of the armies, could no longer be recognized.

While Himuili's bones crunched, Khinti, sobbing, pulled desperately at my ankles: "Suppiluliumas, husband, dear lord, leave off. Oh please, please no—"

And I would strike him again, and she would plead more. Of a sudden there appeared in the room one of my Meshedi, trying to get me off Himuili. The first one could not and went for help while the queen screamed for someone to get Kuwatna-ziti.

Then two more entered, with more behind them, and a voice I knew called my name.

But I could not stop. I did not until the Shepherd pushed between us, saying: "Tasmi, Tasmi take care! If you kill him you have sentenced her to death. Is that what you want?"

And I recollected everything then, and rubbed my bleeding hands one with the other and slowly, chest heaving, retreated before Kuwatna-ziti's inexorable, wide-armed herding.

It was then that Khinti broke away from two Meshedi who did not quite dare to hold her and threw herself at my feet, her arms around my legs, sobbing my name. I looked down at the curve of her naked back, at her black curls strewn upon the floor. I felt her cheek against my ankle, her tears between my toes.

If I touch her, I am lost. If I see her face, I will be unmanned. Or I will kill her. I felt my knees weaken, and the stone floor buck beneath my weight.

"You. Take her. Hold her."

Upon my word, the Meshedi acted, dragging her up and away. She did not struggle, but hung between them as naked as a baby, clothed only in her beauty and her black curls.

I turned my back to her slowly. And I saw there Himuili, mewling in a pool of his own blood, prone. And I saw the first Meshedi, whom I had thrown bodily from my way when he had tried to interfere, on his knees with his hands to his head.

"Tasmi! My lord Sun!" The Shepherd was shaking my shoulders.

I could hear Khinti, behind my back, weeping. I love her, I thought, and she has done this to me. And with Himuili; better with some common soldier. How, how could she do this? But I said only: "Get her out of my sight. This moment, she is exiled from Hattusas; and from all of Hatti. She takes nothing with her. No child—"

"*My children!* No! You have taken everything else. You cannot take them from me—" Abruptly, she lapsed into tears.

"As I was saying: she takes nothing with her. No child. No robe. No shekel of gold. Throw her and her Ahhiyawan relatives out the gate. Tell them if they wish to avoid my wrath they will hold her in their domain, whereto I exile her evermore. And her father who is in Arzawa, and all her kin in Hatti wherever they may be, they too are ousted from the land."

"Tasmi, are you sure?" whispered the Shepherd through stiff and whitened lips, "Do you mean this? You do mean it. . . . I—"

"No one questions the judgment of the king!"

"Yes, my lord Sun. And this man?" He indicated Himuili with a prod of his foot.

At that moment Khinti recovered her voice and strained between her guards, calling my name, imploring my mercy, begging forgiveness. But I said only that I was not exiling Himuili.
He would remain in my service, but under house arrest until he
recovered, and that in my sight he had suffered enough already
from a matter most likely not his fault. Then I walked out and
left her there.

I spent a hazy interlude seeking a place where none would
find me, not any of my sons, not any palace official, not any man
of the armies. At length I went into the king's shrine and at the
foot of the Storm-god, my lord, I tasted regret. I regretted all
the times I had taken another over her. I regretted all my years
with the armies. I regretted every curse I had frothed and every
blow I had struck. Mostly, I regretted that I had not lifted her up
when she huddled at my feet and kissed the tears from her cheeks,
and pressed her against me one last time. Her eyes haunted the
sanctuary; the perfume of her was a ghost wrapped around me. I
cried for the first time since I was a child. Then, it had been over
the conflagration that had once been Hattusas, up there with my
black eagle alone in the night. But that loneliness was nothing.
Now I was truly alone; all that I had ever loved had gone up in
smoke, charred in the bonfire of my anger.

"I cannot, I cannot!" I groaned aloud to the god. But although my tears washed the hooves of the sacred bulls, I could
find no way out of what I had done. There was no going back. "I
have decreed it," a hoarse and shaking voice said in my ears. I
listened to it: it was my own voice. "I have spoken a judgment,
and all know it. Meshedi have seen her naked with the smell of
another man's seed issuing out from between her thighs. I cannot forgive her. O Storm-god, my lord, *help me!*"

And the Storm-god put acceptance into my heart. For the
first time, I heard him — or rather recognized what it was that
had been comforting me all along. For man is alone in all his
teeming millions, and no one hears anything but his own heart.
Woe to those who delude themselves otherwise: there is nothing
else. And I could not take her back. I could not, though I heard

the weakness in me screaming that I must run from the sanctuary, stop her, sweep her out from her wagon, and smooth away
all memory of this awful night from us both like some stonema-
son preparing a rock to house the god's image. No, I could not
do anything. Only could I moan her name until I became free of
it, and petition the god that he help me to forget.

In the morning, I had not forgotten, but by then she was gone.

It was necessary that I seek the twins. My little five-year-
olds were all I had left of her. The morning light was impertinent
to eyes not closed the night long, and my beard itched and all my
skin felt sweaty and dry at the same time. But I did not go and
wash. I went straight to them, although they abode in a chamber
adjoining my wife's, and I did not want to go in there.

On the way I tried not to think of what Khinti might have
said to them; or if she had wakened them, or not; or what someone else might have said to them; or what they might now be
thinking themselves.

I tried, instead, to formulate some plan that might mitigate
the disaster in the case of those who were so innocent and yet
would be most harmed.

Outside their door, I almost turned and fled. To leave off
until another time, when my own person was not aching in its
total extent, was a great temptation.

But I went in there, past two Meshedi whose countenances,
like every other I had passed, were blank and determinedly normal.

Inside was no sign that their mother was not returning: all
was in place; every comb and jar aligned.

Their nurse met me, face ashen, her robe clutched at the neck,
and bowed down low. I excused her, and closed the doors behind.

The sound of quiet sobbing, mixed with howls like some
wounded animal's, did not in any way lessen.

My sorrel-haired princess, curled in a ball where her bed
met the wall, shrank from my touch. Her eyes widened and her
sobbing took a note of terror. She threw her hand before her
face and began to scream, calling her nurse, calling her mother,
screaming that a man had come to take her.

While I was trying to do something other than squat there dumb with my hand outstretched, a small weight flew at me from behind, pummeling my back, howling. Even then I was thinking that my beard had frightened my daughter.

But young Zannanza knew exactly whom he attacked.

"Give back my mother," he wailed brokenly, as I got him in hand and held him by the wrists and he kicked at me. "You took her! You took her away! I hate you! I am going to kill you! I will!"

Then my daughter stopped her crying. She slid off the bed and came to where I yet crouched with my son's fists clasped in my left hand, my right steadying me on the bed.

I started to say something, and could not. I only held Zannanza, whose threats had become unintelligible, but who yet jerked in my grasp.

"Abuya," hiccoughed Muwattish, her round face puffed, "Abuya, I want my mother."

Like an adult she bowed, and then tottered over to Zannanza and tugged on his hair. "Brother, brother, you are supposed to be brave. Protect us! Zannanza, you said you would! Do something!"

When she stood quiet, streaming silent tears with her hands clasped together before her, like magic my son stopped his blind surging and I let him go.

He staggered back, caught himself, went to his sister and put an arm around her. His chin trembled, but he said quite clearly, "What are you going to do with us? Will we be killed?"

They both looked at me, and I had to say something. "I. . ." And I could not speak a word from my mouth, so I gathered them in against me and held them and whispered in their ears that I loved them and they were prince and princess whom I had sired, and nothing would ever change that. I promised them that things would be well with us, and when I had said that little Muwattish asked me why I sent their mother away.

"Because she no longer loved me, and no longer wanted to be my queen."

"But Abuya," Muwattish whispered back, "she told us she loves you. She told us to tell you that, and—"

It went on like that for a very long time, and all that I did over the years to erase it has come to naught. I tried every way I knew to make it up to them for what I had done. But I had lost them, and never, really, got them back. Whatever I did to elevate them brought them low, and everything that I have tried to accomplish in their behalf has turned to offal. There are occurrences in life that go ill from their inception, and no matter how ardently you pursue them the trail is ever awash with tears. A bad thing cannot be made good; a man cannot will success out of failure, any more than the Minoans could raise their island power back up again once their cities caught fire, quaked, and fell, awash in waves.

Khinti haunted me faithfully across the seasons. I suffered anguish in Hattusas, where her stamp yet hovered, so I spent much of the winter traveling in the Lower Country. I performed festivals with a fervor, for they kept me busy and on the move. Into the king's estates in the different towns I put women of this moment or that. I suppose I was working a revenge of sorts. Some men would have lost themselves forever in winey debauch. I ravished a few noble ladies and had to make wives of them, but on the whole I collected concubines and stocked my houses in the different lands and worked endless politics in a round of chariot-diplomacy that became a sort of mobile court as we readied for the spring forays.

I wrote Burnaburiash of Babylon that if among his eligible daughters he had one fit to exercise queenship that I would be pleased to take her as a wife. I listed my requirements, putting an emphasis upon intelligence and literacy and judgmental acumen, but not leaving out that I needed someone young enough to bear me children and kind-hearted enough to raise her predecessor's. And I sent rich gifts, chariots and fine stallions, and a scepter of good iron and a hand-mirror of silver and gold, and even an iron dirk, so that Burnaburiash would know that I was serious indeed.

That was the last message I got out before the snows gated the mountain passes. I sent it from Kumanni, where I had found it necessary at last to go, and where I had finally faced Telipinus the Priest, who of all my grown sons was the most incensed by what had occurred.

It was not pleasant, with the Priest, over Khinti. Telipinus had been a babe when Daduhepa died; Khinti was the only mother he had ever known. He went so far as to propose that I rescind the exile, and that he go to Ahhiyawa to persuade Khinti to return.

"I cannot do that," I said, and walked out.

The Priest and I had nothing but formal communication between us until the spring's campaigns made Telipinus' ban of silence impractical.

I was numb with it by then; I no longer cared about the matter at all. I was studding myself to sleep each night with whomsoever, and in my mind then all women were no more than mares in a pasture. It is not at all the case but, believing it, I sired a son in the city of Ziplanda and a son in the city of Ankuwa on two very wellborn women and had to recognize them. While I was thinking that way, I was hurtful to my grown sons and those who cared about me, but no one could do any good with me, not anyone who tried.

In the matter of Himuili, no one seemed to understand what I was doing, but I was not too concerned about my public image just then.

When he was healed, in the coldest month of the year, I had Himuili brought before me, and instructed him that he would be serving the armies as a field commander until he died a hero's death in battle, and that he would be well watched, but certainly free to do as he chose in day-to-day affairs and that I would in no way treat him worse than any other commander of ten whom I had.

"Why are you doing this?" he said out of that changed countenance. His nose now went markedly leftward, and the white of his left eye was blood-red for half its extent. He was not, however, more crippled of limb than he had been before, and if I had altered the way his green eyes sat in their bed of scars, then at least he had sight in them.

"Why am I doing this? I have marked your head. I know you too well to have you exiled; I might not like what you would choose to do in foreign lands. And you are sensible enough not to do anything foolish where I might find out about it. Make no mistake"—I leaned forward, grasping the eagle claws of my throne—"I *will* find out about it, should you do evil in any matter, in any matter at all. So you be very careful to be an exemplary Hattian soldier. I am giving you a great deal of rein. Do not bolt. If you arouse my anger once again, I will kill you by torturing you at great length in the Assyrian fashion. I will import someone to do it. Is that understood?"

He was kneeling down, not shackled, for he was no physical threat: his gait was halting, he could not run. He said, "It was not her fault, you know."

"Whose fault? Who remembers just what it was that went on that night? No one does, who craves to draw another breath. Zida, take him out of here and put him to bed."

CHAPTER 26

When the winds began to sweeten with spring, word came up from Tushratta of Mitanni, warning me that he was "making himself terrible" against me because I had made common cause with Artatama "the usurper." Likening his wrath unto the terribleness that had put him upon the seat of his kingship, he said to me that should I plunder across the Mala river then he would blot me out, that should my troops take one lamb then he would do likewise with thrice that many Hattian lambs.

It was a very unfriendly exchange. It was not, however, the open declaration of hostilities I had been awaiting.

But down on the Syrian plains, along the west bank of the Mala between the Egyptian coastal protectorates and Mitanni proper, awaited my partisan king Sarrupsi in the country of Nuhasse. The geographical location of this country Nuhasse was most strategic: below my Kizzuwadnan frontier were Tushratta's vassals, the rich countries Ni'i and Mukis—and Mukis' mighty city on the Orontes river, Alalakh—and a little inland, Halap.

369

All of these countries and cities I raided on the way to Nuhasse, and the cattle and sheep and implements of the gods and namra that I took were countless. I stayed well away from Carchemish, the Hurrian city on the Mala, and across the river I did not go.

But as the Hittite army plundered its way down from Kizzu-wadna toward the soon-to-be Hittite Nuhasse, my might spilled over, and here and there a Mitannian protectorate I vanquished.

Since the weather was so hot and dry that year, raiding was easy, quick work, even for my foray contingent, which was mostly foot—five thousand of them: Hapiru, Sutu, Kizzuwadnan Hittites, Miran Hittites from the Upper Country and the Lower; Hittites from Arzawa; Hittites from Hayasa, and Hittites from every conquered town upon our borders joined in battle with us. From Ishuwa and from Tegarama I levied additional troops, on the theory that if they were out fighting under me, they would not be troublesome to Telipinus who ruled in Kumanni and Ar-nuwandas who ruled from Hattusas in my stead.

I have said it was easy raiding: it is always easy when an army wants only to loot a town, not occupy it. We fired flaming arrows and the sweltering countries burst into flame like tinder, and as the armies marched southward we would send back to the plateau all the booty, so that while the southern lands were obsessed with the drought and what it portended for winter, up above, the Hittite towns were getting fat.

As I had hoped, while I was striking fear into the kings of Ni'i and Mukis, my partisans grew strong in the country of Nuhasse. Moreover, and also as I had hoped, Tushratta of Mitanni became afraid because of the ferocity of the Hattian army. Although I plundered only on the west of the Mala river, he took it as a per-sonal affront, and up into my refractory easternmost vassal states he sent arms and agitators. But since he was making himself ter-rible against his brother Artatama, he could not meet with me, and threats did not keep the Sun of Hatti from vanquishing what fortified towns stood between my army and its goal.

Let me tell you where I was headed: Amurru. I sent word to Abdi-asirta, Aziru's father, king of the Amurrites and friend of

Hapiru people, to expect me, so that he would think: "The Sun is coming. This a good time for me myself to make war."

And I was hearing, as I led my point deeper into the navel of Syria, that my message had had the desired effect.

Let it be said that I was very circumspect on this campaign: into Egyptian territory I did not so much as step. All the lands west of the Orontes I ignored as if they were covered by the ocean's waves; I did not touch a hair on the head of any Egyptian official; not the smallest of lambs nor the poorest hovel did my fires lick.

But Abdi-asirta did all that for me, as I had known he would: it was he who launched a massive campaign one midnight, and thereby Amurru gained control of all the adjacent coastal cities about whom Egypt cared little: Irqata, Ambi, and Sigata he overcame, and Amurru was suddenly possessed of a seaboard as extensive as Ugarit's. And that was not all we heard. We heard that Aziru, with a complement of Sutu helping him, had slipped into the palace at Irqata and murdered its king, one Aduna. How we first heard this was by way of refugees whom our scouts captured. And then, as I was resting with my troops in the newly Hittite land of Nuhasse, being entertained by my grateful new vassal, King Sarrupsi, I got a message from Abdi-asirta saying that he would meet with me, and asking that I not do evil upon his borders, but drive in peace through the lands of Amurru, and promising that Hittite soldiers would be treated well by his people if their comportment allowed it.

So I wrote nothing back to him, but made ready to embark southward once again.

The king of Nuhasse, whom I had not personally met until I invested the land and freed him from Tushratta's overlordship, was a fair-skinned man with a bulbous nose and feral eyes. He whined constantly that as soon as I left, the Mitannian king Tushratta, his sympathizers in the country, and the kings of Mukis and Ni'i—whom I had not treated at all well while traveling in their lands—would descend upon him and destroy him, and his land would not be Hittite anymore. So I offered to leave some troops with him, and calmed him, and told him that should such a thing occur, since the lands were Hittite lands, I would protect them as I would protect my own hearth, my own women, my own get. And although he mumbled about it, he was a vassal and there was nothing he could do.

So we went out of Nuhasse and struck toward Amurru in the yellow, wavering heat, merciless though the summer was almost done up on the plateau.

By the time we had entered into Amurru with our troops and our chariotry and seen for ourselves that the people were friendly, or at least not hostile, we heard that Abdi-asirta had procured the overthrow of the city of Tyre and slain its king, the king's wife, and all their sons, and installed a usurper, who was his man, on the throne. As it happened, this king's wife was the sister of Ribaddi, Egypt's governor in the port city of Byblos, which the Egyptians call Gubla, and who wrote to Egypt's chancery with all his woes.

"What think you, Abuya?" said Piyassilis to me as our chariot crested a high hill. "How do you estimate the likelihood of forging a sturdy peace from such low-grade ore?"

"About like the forging of good iron: chancy. But if Ribaddi is, as he says, 'trapped like a bird in a net in Pharaoh's city of Byblos,' and if still Egypt does not aid him, their own governor, then peace or war will be decided by the Amurrite, the Mitannian, and myself. This foray is like the waxing of a blade's tip before it is quenched: that which is tempered hard, but not brittle, will last forever. And if, as with good iron, at times cold pounding will improve the temper, then upon Abdi-asirta I will pound."

We were driving round the country of Amurru, just looking, awaiting its king. "If you say so, Abuya, for a man should not doubt the word of the Sun. But if Sarrupsi of Nuhasse loses his hold, then we will be cut off without a retreat from this accursed oven of a land."

"But I would then have a reason none could question for going after Tushratta of Mitanni."

"You have that, do you not, in the message he has sent?"

We were driving through the foothills of the Niblani mountains, awaiting the king of Amurru's visit. West of us lay Ugarit, into whose Egyptian lap I was not yet ready to settle. This was to be my boundary for the time being: I was not intending to enter Byblos. All that remained was to see whether Amurru would submit, or whether the friendly Hattian soldiers encamped round the town of Apina like a plague of locusts would become unfriendly, and vanquish the land of Amurru, or whether I could bring it into the Hittite lands by negotiation. I cared not too much about the method: although I liked Aziru well enough, he was no son of mine. And I was still hoping that Tushratta would come out and fight with me. Anything that kept me longer in these lands was welcome, for Tushratta had threatened me further but did not come out to meet me in battle, and my fingers itched to close about his fat throat:

"The treachery of the Mitannian is boundless. Perhaps Tushratta will rest content without avenging the loss of his western lands; perhaps the Nuhasse lands mean nothing to him, after all."

"They mean something to me," said Piyassilis, rubbing his bandaged right arm. He had taken an arrow in it in the resistance Nuhasse's anti-Hittite faction had fielded. "I could become accustomed to the heat. The land is so fertile, the sky so vast."

"I will give it to you, if you like. Would you be a king here?"

"I do not know how I would fare with Aziru as a neighbor."

"Then where would you rather reign?"

The smile on his face faded. "You are serious, Abuya?"

"Deadly serious. You cannot be a prince forever." I had lost my first queen before the age Piyassilis was then: twenty-two.

He looked at the driver we were using, one Teshub-zalma, another son of the Shepherd's who bore Kuwatna-ziti's distinctive, wolfish stamp, and ordered him to halt the chariot. Behind us, fifteen drivers did the same.

Out from the chariot we went, with silence between us, and climbed a low ridge by the road. When we made the summit, Piyassilis said:

"Carchemish, of all I have seen, interests me the most. That city, with her crenelated walls and her river view, would content me for all time."

"Well spoken, prince, but an ambitious desire. You will need to wait a year or two for that town; next to Hattusas, I have not seen a city so fortified."

"Just why I want it: it is most like home."

"Then," I promised him, "it will be yours."

I did not expect that it would take so many years to make that promise a reality.

Nor did I expect the king of Amurru to be awaiting me in my camp when my thirty rolled in to the chorus of huzzahs that always, of late, greeted the Sun wherever My Majesty drove among the troops.

Now, we were very many, I have said. I have not said that we covered the Amurrite lands as far as the eye could see, pikes burnished, fires glowing, horses and chariots littered like booty across the landscape.

Neither, evidently, had the Amurrite expected us to be so numerous, for that was the first thing he said to me after the traditional wish that all be well with me, with my lands, with my wives, with my sons, with my horses and my chariots.

The Amurrite king had come much bedecked: in his tiered kingly robe with its short cape and his circlet and his jewels he was magnificent, scintillant. His chariot gleamed, and his horses tossed their plumed heads and shook their golden manes. He stood beside it, a broad, gray-haired man, olive-skinned and flat-faced with thick lips and a regal, generous nose. I judged him fifty, or sixty if he had lightly aged.

Beside him was Aziru, looking about him in sharp, quick glances like the falcon his retainer stroked upon its perch. Fifty chariots had Abdi-asirta, king of Amurru, led into the Hittite encampment, and my son whispered when he saw the horses that we might be well-pleased at what would come out of those Hurrian-bred mares should we let a Hittite stallion climb them.

But I was concerned not at all with horses just then.

The hue and cry of the troops was just dying down when Lupakki detached himself from a knot of men before my tent and came to escort me.

"What think you, Lupakki?"

"I think I wish Hattu-ziti were here, to separate the princes from the kings."

Piyassilis was vaulting from the car and halfway to the Amurrite chariots. "Prince," I admonished, "do not commit me to anything with Aziru, not even for ten teams of horses." He grinned back and promised that he would make no treaty with Aziru on his own. It was then that I saw the cage and the dark-maned lion who waited calmly with his handler, a leash around his neck, apart from the kingly train but not far enough apart to suit my horses, who danced in Lupakki's grasp and snorted.

"How do you think I would look in one of those capes?" lisped Lupakki.

"You may wear one yet, O provincial one. That is, if you can grow so full a beard." I had kept my own beard, though I was about ready to shave it, since it had served me well in my negotiations with brother kings thus far. At that time I was concerned with looking not so formidable, but rather trustworthy and wise, and was telling myself that the beard softened my aspect.

As I strolled toward the gray-haired king of Amurru, Aziru and Piyassilis detached themselves and went in the direction of the lion and his handler.

When Abdi-asirta had finished commenting on the multitude of my troops, he still had not shown even the smallest sign of deference, but treated me exactly like a brother king of equal rank.

So I said back to him, "Come within," without any dignities appended, and went before him into the tent wherein was a small shrine to the Storm-god and little else but a brazier and some folding, footed stools.

"Now, we are alone and I think you had better submit yourself, Amurrite prince."

I sat, but did not invite him to join me. He looked out from whitened eyes filmed with the clouds of the years, then shook his head at me, and in an old man's voice said:

"Young king, you call me prince and make light of me and do not show me even the slightest courtesy. I had thought your intentions were friendly. My Aziru says the Sun of Hatti is a reasonable man." And he sighed, and sat down upon his own initiative, smoothing his long robe around his knees.

I wondered how he could tolerate being so covered in the heat, and how well he could see out of those eyes, and how long it would be before he went up to kingship in heaven.

"Bow down before me as you do to your Egyptian overlord, and you will find me very friendly. Stop sending tribute to my enemy the Mitannian king Tushratta, and do not aid him in any way, and I will increase your might. But continue to be impertinent with me, and you will not live to fight another day."

"Is this a trap then?" The old man's voice was dry, like leaves crackling underfoot.

"No, no. Submit to me, man. Do it and I will make your borders my borders, and your people, your cattle and your temples I will protect and your sons will not have to spend their lives with their noses to Egypt's sandal."

"You boast, young man. Boasts are the most insidious of poisons. I cannot defy Egypt so openly as you demand. So, if those are your conditions, cut off my head, slay my sons, roast my people, all those but the ones you want for servants—that is what you have done everywhere else. I cannot become a vassal of yours."

"Yes, you will. But under these conditions: you will continue your alliance with Egypt; you will cease to aid Tushratta; you will claim putative sovereignty over your own lands, as you have been doing. The only difference is that where you found room for Tushratta in your heart, you will put me there instead. And, of course, keep me informed of what you do."

"If I do that, young king, it will be my death."

"You will die quicker if you do not do it. And do not try dissembling with me: we both know that Naphuria Akhenaten dwells in the temples with his One God, and goes not out to deal with Egypt's woes."

"Ah, but Horemheb leads the armies; and Hani, the Honorable Lord, disseminates Pharaoh's will; Queen Tiye lives yet, and

Ay the Divine Father is not befogged by the years: underestimate Egypt, my brash young warlord, and you will be brought before her with copper shackles on your ankles."

I almost killed him myself upon the spot. Instead, I got up and stood over him, saying: "Submit to me or the whole of Amurru will shine black like obsidian in the sun."

The sound of my rage filled the tent like a lion's roar. And I heard, from without, a commotion attendant upon my bellow of exasperation that included the voices of Aziru and Piyassilis and Lupakki.

The elephant-skinned king merely looked up at me and began quietly to explain further his difficulties.

At length, by dint of implacable repetition, I extracted from him a nominal submission, and all I demanded in the matter of Tushratta he ceded me.

But there was a sadness in him that seemed to have been festering there forever, as he appealed to my mercy in the matter of his country and his son:

"As for Aziru, you must not take Amurru away from him; set no governor upon my people. He has labored too hard to be denuded of everything for which he has fought. And my Hapiru people, those I have let into the land: you must not exile them; they have no place of their own and I have promised them a place with me unto eternity."

"You know me not well enough: there are Hapiru infantrymen among my troops, and at home in the Hatti land rest their families. As far as I am concerned they are Hittite people. As far as I am concerned, your people, henceforth, will be Hittite people—"

The old king's jaw trembled, but he did not look away, only said: "All my life I have fought the hippopotamus of Egypt trying to swallow me up, and the jackal of Hurri trying to gnaw me to death. I thought, now in the end of my days, I had enough time to assure Aziru something more than servitude. I tried to solidify the lands about me; I risked everything to acquire a seaboard from which my son might hold his independence. We are a proud folk. It will not go well with him to bend his head and see always another's foot. He may die of it. Why I have struggled so long and attained so much only to lose it to you—of whom no one had even heard a scant few years ago—is a question for the gods. I will seek some comfort from them, and an answer."

And I found myself looking out from his eyes, even as if I were in his place. So I said: "Old man, I am not trying to sack the fields of your years, nor would I put any prince into slavery. By the Storm-god, keep your country! Only aid me with information and I will ask no more. Do not formally acknowledge Mitanni, and I will be content. Later, when I can protect you from those who hold the sword over your head from Akhetaten, then will I take a formal allegiance. For now, keep your self-determination if it means so much to you."

And the old king fell down upon his knees and began thanking me in a trembling voice. And I found that for some reason I, too, was saddened by the outcome of this, a triumph for which I had waited long.

So I quieted him and raised him up and we drank and ate and studied the particulars of our bond, and when we were finished with that the day was over. Then before my troops in the light of torches I received the gifts he had brought up for me: the lion, said to be tame as a kitten, and the man who handled him; four teams of horses and the ornate chariots they hauled; ten women, the same amount he had sent to Egypt at Akhenaten's request: all were paraded before us.

Of my booty from the Hurrian protectorates I gifted him back an equal number of girls, and gave him a pair of gold cuffs from the palace of Nuhasse.

After the presentations, the old king begged to retire, and since I was feeling very friendly I had Lupakki go with him to arrange for his comfort and make sure that no harm came to him that night among the Hittite host.

All the evening long, Aziru had been quiet, only listening and making casual talk with Piyassilis, trying to sniff out what had occurred. I thought he would go with his father, but instead he waited until all but Piyassilis and myself were gone from my tent, which was no more than a sunshade open to the sweltering night, its sides tied up to let in the sparse Syrian breeze.

It was only moments into the thoughtful silence that fell among us before my son excused himself, saying that since he, too, had received a gift from his brother Aziru, he would be remiss in courtesy if he did not go taste of her.

Aziru absently replied that if she did not suit, Piyassilis need only tell him, and he would provide another. Piyassilis invited him to join him in princely recreation, and departed.

Drawing up his knees and resting his elbows on them, his hands turning his cup, the Amurrite prince looked once around and then asked, "Do I wear your bracelets, king of Hatti? Is your brand on my butt and your sword on my manhood?"

"Do you not trust your father to do better for you than that?"

"Abdi-asirta is a wise man. He does what he must. You have not answered me, King Suppiluliumas. What is my status?"

"As it was before, except that your land and mine have established friendly relations. I aided you in the past without asking any recompense, what makes you think I would change my manner?"

"However-many thousand men who are out there on my father's soil make me think you are ready to collect."

"Not yet, Aziru. Not yet."

"When?"

"When I so decree. Until then, you may play your game of suzerainty with Egypt, and I will say nothing. Just do not think you can fool the Sun. When I am ready, I will bring you into my country."

"And if I do not want to come?"

"When I am ready, the time will be right for you also."

"What conditions have you levied on my father, that you will drive away with but a few women and horses after coming all the way down here?"

"Only that he cease his pretense of friendly relations with the Mitannian king Tushratta, my enemy."

His cup rolled on the grass, so violently did Aziru of Amurru throw it down as he was rising. So that he would not be guilty of standing while I sat, I rose also, thinking that this was no boy, but a man near thirty, and that for showing vile temper before the Sun, men in former times had perished.

But he only spat, "I will begin work on my father's mausoleum," wheeled around, and strode out.

I did nothing whatsoever about it, although Lupakki stuck his head in immediately upon the Amurrite prince's exit to ask if I had anything for him to do.

So I invited Lupakki inside, and we talked of the withdrawal, imminent, of my troops upcountry for the winter. And all that time I was wondering what it was about this Aziru of Amurru that caused me to give him so much rein. I am not one for men, but I felt almost that way about the close-bearded, assertive prince, and that night I dreamed of him instead of Khinti. I dreamed that he walked with the blue-cloaked lord, that one's arm about him protectively. Behind them were waves and the sea. When I woke in the morning, I woke from a sleep more restful than any I had had since I demoted my Tawananna and exiled her to Ahhiyawa, and so I sought out the prince of Amurru and took a meal with him.

His father may have calmed him, or he had come to understand my intent, for he was as pleasant as he had been acerbic the evening past, making jokes with Piyassilis, who was much taken with him, and not saying anything at all about what had passed between us.

Throughout the long leisurely campaign homeward I looked for Tushratta to come fight with me. But as we drove through town after town and met no resistance, I began to suspect that he would not come.

We went up through Nuhasse to see our vassal, whose first acts as a Hittite subject-king were to clear the rubble of the investment from his streets and exile those former Hurrians who could not adjust to becoming Hittites. Seeing that he appeared to have the matter well in hand, I advised him to continue in that fashion and the Hittite armies rolled homeward over newly-Hittite ground.

And still we experienced no resistance, although I had left much of my foot along my new borders: in truth, we marched home at half strength, but nothing came of it. And we were triumphant: we had made the Niblani mountains and Byblos our frontier.

Speaking of Byblos, when we arrived in Kizzuwadna we heard that Ribaddi, the Egyptian governor of that city, had sent to Egypt saying:

"The Hittite has overcome all the lands that belonged to the king of Mitanni" and that "Abdi-asirta has gone over to the Hittite."

Piyassilis was visibly upset.

"Do not worry, my son. Aziru has taken care of himself in the past. His father is an old man only because he was wily enough to survive to become one. They want no aid from us. I cannot send it."

"Then send to Duttu and have him make light of Ribaddi's words to Pharaoh! Something, we must do! I do not want it on my head. It is not even true! They have not come over to us . . . have they?"

"They have, and they have not. Ask, better, how the matter came to be known to an Egyptian."

All that winter, we looked for whomever it was that served Egypt from amidst our ranks. We never found him.

CHAPTER 27

Crowns wobble on the heads that exercise kingship. That which is conquered must ofttimes be reconquered.

In the spring following the campaign that made Sarrupsi of Nuhasse my vassal, Syria—Retenu the Upper and the Lower—burst apart like a ripe melon dropped from atop a citadel wall. All the coastal princes who called themselves kings (or servants or governors, depending upon to whom they were speaking) were yet playing the faithful vassals before whomsoever held them in thrall, while behind the back of myself, or of Tushratta of Mitanni, or of Naphuria Akhenaten, they postured at independence and schemed to bring reality out of dreaming.

This has always been so on the seaboard, where Egypt makes governors of hereditary kings and servants of those born to rule. It was so, inland, because my foray had shown the kings of Ni'i and Mukis and Amurru that Mitannian power was not unshakeable.

I had come, and plundered, and gone away, taking formally only the allegiance of Sarrupsi of Nuhasse. But unofficially,

I had loosened fetters from about the ankles of subject-kings whose taskmaster had long been Mitanni. Who could blame those princes of the southern plains if they cast acquisitive eyes upon one another's borders, thinking that Mitanni was afraid to come out to battle and Egypt yet slumbering in the tropical sunrays of her new god, the Aten?

I did not blame them: I cheered them on. It was the very confusion for which I had by my foray agitated.

This unrest settled nothing but enriched armorers, pyre-builders, stonemasons, purveyors of spices and urns and funerary accouterments, all across the Lower Lands.

But where was the Sun, when all this was taking place? In Hattusas, leashed, collared as securely as the dark-maned lion given me by the king of Amurru. The lion walked his enclosure, and I walked mine, and out to battle neither of us could go.

And there were battles aplenty. I kept track of them through my Egyptian informant Duttu, through Hatib's couriers, through my sons Piyassilis and Telipinus who fought in Nuhasse while I wore through the king's shoes and stalked through the king's halls and tried to hold what I had gained and waited to see what Tush-ratta would do. . . . But I shall tell it to you as it was told to me:

First came from Telipinus news of dissent and foreign agitators in my eastern provinces. The news was that these matters were escalating, fast becoming formal revolt. A favorite trick of restive provinces is to say, "We are no longer Hittite subjects: we are Hurrian subjects," whether that is the truth, or even their desire, or not. So, by sending troops into Tegarama and Ishuwa to subdue them, I had crossed the Mala river into what was now calling itself Hurrian territory.

As I was doing it, I received a message from Tushratta of Mitanni. I had just come back into Kumanni from conferring with the commander of the border guards.

Telipinus ran out to meet me, all his dour posturing over the matter of the deportation of his former stepmother forgotten:

"Listen to this, Abuya!"

And the Priest of Kumanni read to me the Mitannian's words: "'Why do you plunder on that side of the Mala? You are plundering, I will do the same. If you plunder, I will cross the Mala and do likewise; if one lamb or goat comes to harm then I will do likewise!'"

So for the second time did the Mitannian threaten me. When I had made common cause with Artatama, Tushratta had said he was "making himself terrible" against me, but he had been like a gnat: I brushed him away; I did not notice him. Something told me that this time I would notice. He must be doing something, I thought, or else his message would have been an invitation to me to take his submission.

So I quieted all battles. The Hattian army waited, expectant. Even in Ishuwa, we pressed for no advantage, only maintained the shrunken borders as they were.

Barely had I dispatched my messengers with the above-mentioned orders when I heard these things from the south:

Abdi-asirta had taken the city of Sumuru, which belonged as much to Egypt as did the city Byblos, or the city Tyre he had acquired last season in a like fashion.

All with an understanding of the grave consequences that must develop from such overt warfare among the vassals of Egypt were speaking very quietly and long into the night about Egypt's reactions. The only thing not suggested by Hattu-ziti or the Shepherd or my sons or myself was that the sphinx would not bestir herself.

I had planned to clean up the boundary problems in the east and proceed southward. I dared not.

And I was soon upheld in my caution. Tushratta launched an expedition against me, crossing the Mala. I had only just confirmed that fact, when Sarrupsi of Nuhasse's urgent request for troops was delivered to me in Kumanni by a charioteer who had killed two teams getting to Hattusas, whence I myself had just arrived.

To aid Sarrupsi I was bound by treaty. If I wanted to acquire any more vassals in Syria, I could not let this one be executed by my enemy, the king of Mitanni.

Why Tushratta did not come against me directly, I could not understand. And it occurred to me that though the Mitannian king himself was said to be leading the expedition, I could not truly know that he was. Even more, I realized that I could not take a chance on leaving my sons in Hattusas while I went out on campaign. The times were unsettled in the extreme.

So, although I swallowed the bitter bile of pent hatred and heard in my ears the phantom cry of "coward, who sends his sons to battle for him!" from a pair of fat disembodied Mittanian lips, I dispatched Piyassilis and Telipinus and Lupakki for good measure down to aid Sarrupsi.

Arnuwandas I sent eastward to Kumanni, to see if he might fare better than had the Priest in calming the lands.

I ceased to sleep. So long did sleeplessness plague me that I resorted to a priestess who made potions which forced rest upon me. As will happen with what one is not supposed to have, I craved her and took her to my bed, for due to the unsettled conditions from Hatti to Babylon and the beleaguered routes in between, Burnaburiash of Babylon was hesitant to send me his daughter just then, and I was tired of what concubines and lesser wives I had collected.

"Do you think," I demanded in exasperation of Hattu-ziti, who had been overseeing the incoming presents and the out-going counter-presents, "that Burnaburiash has changed his mind? Have I become suddenly less suitable? Is he waiting to see how I do?"

"No, no, no, the Sun must not think that."

"Then tell him for me that I will receive his daughter at Alalakh next year, when the first day of summer comes.

"My lord?"

Alalakh is in Mukis, a country which did not yet know that, by my decision, next year it would be a Hittite country. "I said, tell him that. I will have his daughter then, or not at all. Now go do it!"

And without a word, Hattu-ziti departed, to return but scant hours later with news that Tushratta of Mitanni had left a siege force in Nuhasse and marched on to war-torn Sumuru, which when last I heard had been occupied by Abdi-asirta of Amurru's soldiers.

"Tushratta is smoothing things over with Egypt. If he hands the city of Nuhasse over to the Egyptians, whose own Rabbit of Byblos, Ribaddi, could not hold it, then Pharaoh will be re-assured of Mitannian might. And if Tushratta reclaims my very first vassal in all of the Lower Country so easily, it will then be *my* might that is lessened, and *my* eyes that must look upon the ground. May the Storm-god smite him! May his head pop from his neck to be washed in the spurting fountain of his blood! May his seed fall the one upon the other, and all his kin be eaten by the demons of the underworld! May—"

"Does the Sun, my lord, wish to be alone? I have further news, but perchance I could come back—"

"Hattu-ziti!"

"Ah, yes. We have heard that Tushratta has cast his eyes upon Amurru."

"What does that mean? Has he taken it from me? I am going down there myself—"

"No, my lord Sun."

"No, what?"

"No, it does not say here that Tushratta has taken it, only that he has looked upon it."

I snatched the tablet from his hand, and indeed that was all Hatib had said about the matter. I vowed that I would choke the Libyan with his own braids when next we met, and curtly dismissed Hattu-ziti, who was now my private secretary, chief scribe, chamberlain and pillar of the portico that holds Hattusas on her scarp.

Until at last I heard again from Lupakki that all was well in Nuhasse with my sons and my vassal king, Sarrupsi, and with my new country and its people, I had not a moment's quiet in my heart. But then I was suffused with joy, for Lupakki also reported that Tushratta had been expelled by the fierceness of our battle back across the Mala into Mitanni. Of course, there was no water in Lower Retenu in the second year of the drought, and lack of water might have had something to do with Tushratta's withdrawal: thirst wreaks havoc with a horse army.

But I was delighted. I took the twins up in my arms and drove them out into the country for the day. I hunted and wrestled with the Shepherd; who joined me in celebration of the Hattian army's success, and laughter was upon the lips of the Sun once again.

I was still seeking a traitor in our midst, someone who was reporting our movements south, but not even Kuwatna-ziti had been able to nose out the slightest clue as to whom that person might be.

Two days before the armies (and Piyassilis and Telipinus and Lupakki with them) were due at Hattusas, this traitor still occupied our attention. Then my tuhkanti Arnuwandas arrived from Kumanni bearing a worrisome look.

"Evil tidings?" I surmised. Beside me in my office, Kuwat-na-ziti frowned.

"So I estimate them. What the Sun will say I have come to find out." My eldest was clean-shaven, doing the god's work in Telipinus' stead. His thick black hair hung down to curl around his shoulders. We had shared more than a woman or two in last year's campaign, and the season in the field had made a difference in the way he regarded me which I could immediately sense but could not so easily name. He had finally named it for me, saying: "I had not realized. . . . Seeing you with the armies, I looked on you from out of different eyes than those of sonship. Do I ever come to be even half of what you are, I will lay such sacrifice before the Storm-god, my lord, as he has never seen before. Do you smile, that I have come over to you as a person, and spoken it to you?"

And I had said: "You know, you think you have come over to me, and you expect me to be surprised. I smile because I have been here waiting, all along!"

After that day, I counted Arnuwandas dearer than even the Shepherd, and took heed to his opinions as if we were of an age.

"So tell these tidings to me, and we will see if they are as bad as your face says you think they are."

"Should I leave, Tasmi?"

"No, Shepherd, stay. Speak, Arnuwandas!"

"Abdi-asirta has been killed by Egyptian seaborne forces. They invested Amurru and executed him for not paying his dues to Mitanni. Aziru is fled, hiding until he sees what Egypt will do, but he has made formal claim to his father's throne."

The Shepherd whistled a prey-bird's cry, but when I asked him to comment, demurred.

"Then, Arnuwandas, what else have you?"

"Ribaddi, governor of Byblos, regained Sumuru for Egypt once Tushratta chased out the Amurrites. And one more thing: remember last year Aziru took Tyre for his father and killed its king and placed a man of his in there? Well, the usurper has been ousted by a 'legitimate' Egyptian appointee. Aziru is naked and cowering weaponless before the whole wolf-pack of them."

"Aziru is about to become a wolf, himself."

"You will do nothing?"

"I will do nothing."

"Piyassilis will be troubled."

"Over an Amurrite? Not as troubled as he would be if his own father were slain and he tossed out of Hattusas! I have to see what Egypt is about: does the sphinx wake, at last? I want no trouble with them."

"Do you fear Egypt? We have no peer upon the field of battle. We must—"

"You must recollect your place, and to whom you are speaking. I fear some things. Egypt at present is among them. Does a man not fear an enraged bull if it is charging? Do the people not fear the gods? Fear is the wine that slakes the thirst for bravery—such thirst unquenched leads to madness. Now sit down and we will discuss it."

Discuss it howsoever much I tried, I could not convince Arnuwandas that inaction was the only prudent course at present.

Something else convinced him for me: Piyassilis' very frothing vehemence. In Arnuwandas' efforts to appear more knowl-
edgeable than his newly-arrived brother, he opposed Piyassilis'
fire with water. Disagreeing with his brother, my eldest came to
agree with me.

But the factors precipitating our new appreciation of the
situation were not solely Arnuwandas' news nor Piyassilis' return from Syria: there came also a tablet from Duttu, and a letter
Aziru himself wrote to me.

As I read them aloud, Piyassilis growled like the captive
Amurrite lion, and paced the palace chancery, ranting that Aziru
was right: all was upon our heads, and that instead of pulling my
troops back from Nuhasse, I should have sent them to Aziru's aid.

Holding up the tablet containing Aziru's message, I reminded my second son quietly, "Aziru does not want us in Amurru;
he still plays his game with Egypt. Did he say 'why did you not
aid me?' No, he did not. He is not bashful about writing to me
and blaming me for his misfortunes. Nowhere does he suggest
that I go and do battle for him, nor even at his side does he invite me to fight."

"But there must be something I can do!"

"Something *you* can do? Make a wife of him, Piyassilis, if
you love him so. Duttu tells us Aziru is writing to Akhenaten
to assure his loyalty while he writes to me the same, and even
lays all his mismanagements at my feet, saying to Pharaoh, 'The
king of Hatti has brought all these ills upon me.' Look at this,
which Aziru wrote to our Duttu, who is no longer just a scribe in
Naphuria Akhenaten's court, but is now 'Chief Mouthpiece of
All the Foreign Lands'!"

And I read to him the copy Duttu had sent me via a Sutu of
a letter Aziru had written to Egypt:

"To Duttu my lord, my father. Thus speaks Aziru thy son,
thy servant: I will fall down at thy feet. . . . Whatever is the king
of Egypt's wish, I will do. The lands of Amurru are your lands,

and my house is yours. Behold, enemies have spoken words of slander before the king; O pharaoh, do not admit them. For if the king does not love me, but hates me, what shall I do?"

"Let me see that!"

So I handed the letter to Piyassilis, and he read it over, and shook his head, and said, "You know as well as I that Aziru means only to protect his neck."

"He means to have Egypt confirm his status as successor to his father, dull-witted son of mine. And he means, I expect, exactly what he says, here. . . ." And I shoved tablets around until I found the one I sought. *"This,* Aziru wrote to Pharaoh, and even sent me a copy himself: 'seven times seven times I fall down at the feet of my lord; I am thy servant forever . . . two youths I have given; they may do as Pharaoh commands. And may Pharaoh allow me to enter Amurru.'"

"He sent hostages to Egypt?"

"Egypt took them, I would wager. Aziru is exiled from his city, begging Egypt to confirm him in his rulership: although he is a king by blood, he whines at Naphuria Akhenaten's heel that he may be confirmed as an Egyptian governor. Do you still want to drive down to Amurru and rescue him, O hero?"

Arnuwandas, who apparently had been awhile standing at the door, applauded as he entered.

Piyassilis, tossing the tablet atop the pile, declared that if it were the Sun, myself, who had been slain by a greater power, and if Egypt had taken *his* beloved brother—and here he looked at Arnuwandas with a slight, appraising smile—and had made that brother a hostage, then he, Piyassilis, would probably have done and said exactly the same as Aziru had done and said.

Arnuwandas observed, crossing his mighty arms over his chest, that in such a case it would be Piyassilis who was the hostage, and *he,* the crown prince, who was the supplicant, and *he* would never have been laid as low as to find himself in so compromised a position in the first place.

I silenced Piyassilis even as that one opened his mouth to retort, saying: "Would either of you two bold princes like to go down to Egypt for this Reception of Foreign Tribute? It is supposed to be the most wondrous of events."

Now, of course, I had no intention of sending either one of them, lest I never get them back. But they did not know that.

Two princely countenances drained pale; two pairs of shoulders straightened and two chests puffed out beneath their harvest-season woolens. Two jaws jutted.

I rubbed my own shaven jaw, and waited to see which would volunteer.

Upon the opening of Piyassilis' mouth, Arnuwandas also spoke up, and if I were a fool I could have sent two fools to Egypt, both of whom knew better, but neither of whom could stand to see his sibling look the braver, even when that bravery was foolhardy unto the extreme.

So I lectured them both briefly, and those crestfallen young men who left their sire's presence would not soon forget that I cherished rash and prideful behavior not at all in my princes.

It was Hattu-ziti I was sending down to Egypt with our 'tribute': if they wanted a prince of mine, they would have to come take him from me.

While I waited alone for my chamberlain, I mused upon something that still raises my hackles when I consider it: how briefly do we touch our lives together, we who are kings, and what horrendous consequences from those brief and tenuous encounters evolve. Abdi-asirta was dead, as Aziru had said, upon my account. I would have liked to sit and talk with him at length of all he had seen and learned of Egypt over the years; I had expected to do it. But I had briefly met him, and our fates had intertwined, and he was dead from that small encounter. And now another was king and that one, Aziru, though I had met him more times than his sire, I knew hardly any better.

Tushratta and I contested, year in and year out, without ever getting a close look at one another.

To find out what the truth was in the matter of the heretic pharaoh, so-called Criminal of Akhetaten, the Horse-Face Naphuria

Akhenaten, I was sending Hattu-ziti to Egypt, into deadlier peril than might be faced on any line of skirmish or refractory frontier.

Why? Because I was a king, and the young pharaoh "living in truth" in the City-of-Rejoicing-in-the-Horizon was a king, and no matter how much we disagreed, form must be maintained between those who exercise kingship.

There were some who had advised me to send nothing down for this pharaoh's "wonder" for which a special hall had been built to accommodate gifts from foreign lands. But so long as I did not end up gifting him with the person whom I sent bearing my presents down to Egypt, I did not see any reason to waken the sphinx's ire. Especially since it seemed that affairs on the seaboard might have done just that: if Naphuria Akhenaten had been jarred from the somnambulance in which he ruled, none of the "princes" who scrabbled over Upper and Lower Retenu were safe.

Egypt, awakened, was something I did not want to face just then.

So I was sending fine and precious gifts: cedar, obsidian, Hattian silver, a blade of good iron that would make a kingly dirk, trained hunting dogs from my older brother's pack. I have not much mentioned him: he plays none of these powerful games, and never has. Sometimes I think Manninis, this brother of mine who was grown when I was born and resides in Nerik and is content to stay there, is the wisest son of my father Arnuwandas, and I am the fool.

But then, since I cannot tell if Manninis is as content as he professes, keeping bees and dogs and training hunting hawks and staying out of political affairs, I cannot be certain.

"Hattu-ziti, do not look at me that way: if you are hesitant about this matter, I will send another."

"Who?" he said, raking his fingers through the sparse gray hairs that remained atop his head and settling his bulk down with a sigh where I was piling up all the foreign correspondence according to its country of origin.

"'Who?'" I chuckled. "You have caught me: I can send no one else. But I could throw all of this"—I gestured to the tablets—"out of the window, or better yet into the offering pool, and then we would be free of the whole problem. Temporarily, at least."

"You are putting your own concern onto my countenance, Suppiluliumas. Does the Sun think I am afraid? It is long since we fought in Samuha, and I have not had as much time in the field as others you value highly. But why is that? I will tell you why it is: it is because the Sun needed me in Hattusas, and I subordinated my wishes to your own. And I have built for you the double walls of Hattusas as no other man could have done it. Let us face the mountains and the truth therein: I have no equal at such work. But since I am done with it, and the city is fortified like no other city since the beginnings of the Hatti nation has ever been fortified, and since I have trained a corps of engineers more dexterous and inventive than have ever been—even the Ahhiyawans said that!—and since I have taken care of all the Sun's correspondence with foreign lands since you, my lord, sat down upon the seat of kingship, and since I have proved that my diplomatic skills are sufficient to maintain a little man like Sarrupsi on the quaking throne of Nuhasse—since all of these things I have done for the Sun, let the Sun do something for me: *use me.* I am forty-nine years of age and fit for more than drafting polite replies to your brother monarchs. No one in Hatti knows Syrian affairs and Egyptian affairs as do I. *Send me!* Send me free of qualm and free of doubt. Let the risk be counted between us: it is nothing. I am a man whose moment has come. I am the sun's disk rising above the mountains: I am trembling with delight like a husband on his bridal night! I am full of anticipation, and free from fear. So you see, you must—"

"Cease. Cease, before I am unmanned. Go, then, and have done! I had not realized you were so unhappy."

"The chariot horse is not unhappy when he is sweating on the trail, but when the campaigning is done and he wonders whether he will be pastured the next season, then he sweats the true sweat. I did not mean that I have not taken pride in implementing the Sun's desires, only that those labors are finished. And who goes to winter in tropical splendor, fêted by the greats from every country, meeting in Akhetaten with princes of all the foreign lands, should be one who can make some use of the opportunity! I will do you service the magnitude of which will make the Egyptians' 'wondrous' celebration like a sneeze—forgotten as soon as it has come!"

"Do you know something, Hattu-ziti?"

"I know many things, my lord. What thing is it to which you refer?"

"I am not any longer concerned about sending you to Egypt. I am not concerned at all, my lord chamberlain."

"Then let us go over the bill of lading for my journey."

"Let us go over the purpose of your journey, which cannot be written out on any piece of wood, or incised in clay."

Hattu-ziti raised a stubby, white eyebrow and sat back.

"Firstly, I have two messages for Aziru of Amurru's ambassador."

"You are so sure Aziru himself will not go? All the princes from Retenu the Upper and Lower will be there."

"Not unless he wears the rope and shackle, he will not. I have said there are two messages. You will deliver only one."

"One?"

"Wait till I have done. One. You must first see whether Amurru is a country of dogs, or a country of wolves. If dogs, then tell the Amurrite that I come in spring to change their collars, and they would be best off to crawl whining to me in Alalakh and lie down at my feet."

"My lord Sun, how am I going to determine which kind of person the Amurrite ambassador may be? Dogs and wolves both howl at the moon. Shall I take Telipinus to divine me the answer?"

"As to how you will determine what kind of man you face, the greeting you receive from him will establish it. You do not need Telipinus. Harken to your own heart in the matter. I will not question its counsel."

"Then tell me the second message."

"If the Amurrite be a wolf, say unto him that the Sun desires that he herd the lambs of Ugarit into my fold. If he is yet terrible, let him strike fear into Niqmad of Ugarit. For that I will grant him the run of the coast until he seeks to establish himself as my vassal under his own initiative."

"Now I see why the Sun does not write these things. . . . Are you—?"

"I said, let me have done. Now, whichever kind of message you deliver, add to it my condolences in the matter of Aziru's father's death, and the death of his man in Tyre, and the loss of the city of Sumuru. Add quietly that I am sure he will regain it, if the man is wolfish; but say no more if he is not."

"And what does the Sun wish me to do if the Ugaritic ambassador should hear of this?"

"By then you will have told Niqmad of Ugarit's ambassador that I have expressed a desire for friendly relations with his country, and made overtures to the effect that such dialogue between us must soon commence. You may say that I have also expressed a wish to visit his country, and furthermore invite him, Niqmad the king and his Egyptian wife also, to visit me."

Hattu-ziti shook his head back and forth, gloving his smile with his hand. "I should not be bemused by you, but I always am. . . . What shall I say to the Egyptian?"

"Aha! This is best of all. It is a very delicate task I am assigning you, so pay close attention. Convey to my brother, Naphuria Akhenaten, my fondest wishes that all be well with him, with his country, with his government, with his horses and his chariots and his wives and goats and lice and what-have-you. Make sure to confer upon Honorable Lord Hani a clear understanding of the Sun's position: what is in the hearts of the Hattian people is a wish for continued peaceful relationship between us. So fervent is the respect, so unswerving the trust of the Sun toward his brother Naphuria and the people of Egypt that these depredations of the usurper Tushratta we are overlooking as far as Egypt is concerned. Say that in our hearts it has become necessary for us to separate Egypt from Mitanni, which we do not recognize anymore, since a false king came to squat on its throne. Say to Naphuria that I am not giving up one pinch of Hattian ground to this spurious Mitannian state, and that war is between myself and the Mitannian until the gods decide the victor. And tell him, Lord Hani, that you are not sure, but you think that I, the Sun, am going to go down into Retenu and restore order there, lest trade between Egypt and Hatti be continually disturbed. Cite to him Burnaburiash's reluctance to send a royal princess upon her bridal journey, and make the Sun's displeasure at Egypt's failure to keep order gently, but unmistakably, plain."

There fell a silence. Then Hattu-ziti ruminated aloud: "The Egyptians might jump right out of their holy river to take that bait. If they think you are going to settle Retenu as an act of friendly—"

"Even I do not think they are fools. I just think they know very well what I am going to do. The only way that can be to my advantage is if I am bold enough to proclaim it, and canny enough to make that proclamation a graceful garment in which they may conceal their impotence. After all, if they could do it, they would have done it by now."

"When you said they already know it: what did you mean?"

"I mean our traitor: the bird that flies from Hattusas to land on Hani's hand."

"I do not wish to contradict the Sun, but I think there is no person disloyal among us."

"Have you joined the king of Egypt in his waking dream? There is someone among us who is speaking evil to our enemies, that is sure. Who it is I have not yet determined." To this day, I have not found him.

"Who it is," said Hattu-ziti firmly, "is not in the chancery, nor among the palace scribes, nor among any one of the palace officials."

"We shall see. I and the Storm-god will consider the matter. You consider, while you are in the City of the Horizon, whether or not there is truly 'rejoicing' therein, or whether the cisterns of the city are filled with tears. Find a way to have audience with this Naphuria Akhenaten if you can. If you cannot, at least observe him closely. I would know whether he is truly a madman, or whether he plays the cripple-of-mind for some obscure purpose. And seek you the 'Sole Friend' Horemheb, and the 'Divine Father' Ay. Bring back the true word to me, whether or not they are deceiving us."

Hattu-ziti nodded as calmly as if I had asked him to go look over the chariot horses of the king and bring me back news of their faring, and brought the bill of lading again to my attention.

When I had put my seal to it and assigned him suitable honor guards, I was planning to dismiss him. But as I was naming his attendants, he begged a favor:

"Let me take Kantuzilis, your son of the second degree, with me. He is not suited to the army, but in affairs of letters and diplomacy he might someday excel."

"I am sending no son of mine, however lowly and ill-favored, into a land that practices the diplomacy of the hostage."

"Then we will not tell anyone who he is; he resembles you not at all; he is free from the habitual postures of princes. And he needs most desperately a chance to feel himself of some use."

"What is this about?" I demanded. "Take Zidanza, if you need one of my boys to make you feel secure! At least he is sound of mind and body. What use could Kantuzilis be to you?"

"He could come to feel that he is of use to *you,* and that would do his heart more good than the Sun might imagine. As for me, I still doctor broken wings and cracked hooves."

"There must be more to this."

"Not that I would divulge. Why not seek out his mother, or peruse the archives in the matter of who has recently supplicated the Sun God? Then the truth will be made known to you in that matter."

Since Hattu-ziti was like an ass with ears flattened to his head upon the subject, I dismissed him, then sent down to the archives to see if anything Kantuzilis had said to the Sun God was recorded there.

And back came Pikku my squat scribe to me with a copy of
Kantuzilis' supplication. I will not repeat it all, only this:

"Life is bound up with death, and death is bound up with
life. Man cannot live forever; the days of his life are numbered.
Were man to live forever, it would not concern him greatly even
if he had to endure grievous sickness.

"O god, ever since my mother gave birth to me, thou, my
god, hast reared me. Thou, my god, brought me together with
good men. Thou, my god, did show me what to do in time of distress. My god did call me, Kantuzilis, thy favorite servant. . . .
Much as I wearied myself pleading before my god, yet it is of
no avail. No sooner did thou scrape one evil thing off me, than
thou brought back another in its stead. . . . Through sickness my
house has become a house of misery. Through misery my soul
longs for another place. As one who has been sick on the day
of New Year, so have I become. Sickness and misery have now
become oppressive to me; that I must declare to thee, my god.
At night sweet slumber does not overtake me on my bed. While
I lie there, good tidings do not come to me. . . . How thou could
have ordained this sickness for me from my mother's womb on,
that I have never asked the seeress. Now I cry for mercy in the
presence of my god! O god, do not make me a man who is unwelcome at the king's court! Do not make my condition an offense
to mankind! Those to whom I did good, none of them wishes me
long life. Thou, my god, art father and mother to me; beside thee
there is no father or mother for me. . . ."

And I recalled how many times I had passed him over for
another more hale, or more wellborn, or more pleasing to look
upon. And that I had at times turned my gaze from him because
of the awkwardness of his gait and the scaly pallor of his skin,
or the angry pustules that made a mountain range of his face.
And I remembered how close Kantuzilis had been to Telipinus,
bobbling always behind like a shadow, being increased by Telipinus' manly beauty and brotherly love. But when I had made
Telipinus priest in Kumanni, I had not done anything about Kan-

tuzilis. And when Telipinus went east, the Priest did not ask to
have Kantuzilis, then in the Meshedi, assigned to him.

Once, in former times, I had gone to the mountain and prayed
to the Storm-god for aid in the matter of Titai and my Queen
Daduhepa. Then there was no mother or father for me but my god.

And I felt my failure laid upon me by everything this lesser
son had said, but I had simply not had the time for him. Sons of
the Sun are many; only in the cases of my royal princes had I
bestirred myself, and that less than I might, for kings may be fathers to the get of their loins only to the extent that time allows:
I have a whole land full of sons and daughters, all the Hattian
people; every head among them is my concern.

But in my grasp there was the tablet, and in my heart the
matter of my guilt on the subject of my children in general, and
I resolved to investigate the matter and put it right.

So I called Takkuri's sister to audience, and when I told her
the nature of my concern her surprise was unconcealed:

"I had thought it something about the twins, my lord. I hope
he did not importune. . . ." She cast her eyes downward, and I
felt then even worse, though I had paid the woman handsomely
for bearing me one child and maintaining friendly relations in
the matter of my Hattusas nobility. All these years I had kept
her, albeit she was no longer necessary as a throttlehold on Takkuri her brother. Not for her beauty, which had long since faded,
not for anything except mothering children of other women and
keeping the concubines in their places had I made use of her.

The emptiness of the life of Takkuri's sister was revealed
to me, and that it was I who had done it. I said:

"I called you in the matter of the child of your womb. I am
sending him to Egypt with Hattu-ziti, as Kantuzilis' first duty in
his new position as Assistant to the Chamberlain. Tell him for me
that I am confident that he can make himself great in my service,
and that whatsoever post he craves among the palace officials
will be open to him when he has finished his apprenticeship at
Hattu-ziti's knee."

And since Takkuri's sister was tearful and gushing praises which only made me feel worse, I told her that I would be taking the twins out driving in the morning and dismissed her to seek out her own son and tell him what I had said.

At last count, I have acquired twenty-eight children of various degrees of relationship which I recognize. As my empire grew, so did my family. And but for the aforementioned exceptions, I have done well by all of them continuously. Sometimes, as in the case of Kantuzilis, whom his mother should have known better than to name after the Pale One, repository of evil, I have not entirely succeeded. Sometimes, as in the case of the twins, my most strenuous efforts came to naught. But I have done my best, and there is no more a man can do about any matter than that. Things there are that attract disaster like a waterhole a thirsty horse. Lives there are that are tragic from first scream to last (as in the case of Naphuria Akhenaten's), out of which only vile despair and despite issue forth continually.

So it was that Kantuzilis came to accompany Hattu-ziti to Egypt, while all my princes I called into Hattusas and assigned each a part in the greatest undertaking of my career: the destruction of the kingdom of Mitanni.

CHAPTER 28

"I, the Sun, Suppiluliumas, Great King, King of the Hatti land, the valiant, the favorite of the Storm-god, went to war for the second time against Tushratta:

"I crossed the Mala, conquered Ishuwa a second time, brought all the surrounding lands back into the Hatti land. I left the lands free, and the people became people of the Hatti land. I brought back sheep, cattle, namra into the Hatti land.

"I reached Alshe. Kutmar, the provincial center I captured, and became its lord. To Anartali of Alshe I presented it as a gift. I proceeded to Suta and ransacked it. And I reached Washuganni for plunder. From Suta I brought its inhabitants, together with all that they owned. But Tushratta the king escaped. He did not come to meet me in battle. So I turned and recrossed the Mala. Halap and Mukis I subdued. Takuwa, king of

403

Ni'i, came against me, and behind him Akit-Teshub, his brother, caused Ni'i to revolt. Also Akiya of Arahti revolted, saying, 'We will fight.' I, Great King, became lord of Arahti. Akit-Teshub, brother of Takuwa, Akiya, king of Arahti, and their lords I took prisoner with all their goods and brought them to the Hatti land. Then to Abuzya I proceeded. I took all the lands on account of Tushratta. Then I went onward. Qatna with its goods and possessions I took. When I went to the land of Nu-hasse, I took possession of all its lands. Sarrupsi was murdered; his murdering mother, brothers, sons I took prisoner and sent off to Hatti. Takib-sarri, servant of Sarrupsi, I made king over Ukulzat. Then I went to the land of Apina. But I did not think of fighting the land of Kinza. But Shutatarra with Aitakama, his sons, and his chariotry came against me. I defeated him, and they threw themselves into the city of Abuzya. But I sealed them in the city of Abuzya. Shutatarra, with his sons, his warriors, his brothers and his goods, I captured, and sent them off to Hatti. Then I went to Apina. And I defeated its king and his nobles . . . all of them with their lands and goods I sent off to Hatti. On account of the overweening of Tushratta the king, in one year all these lands I plundered, and sent to Hatti. From the Niblani mountains, and from that side of the Mala on, I brought them into my power."

Thus have I written of that year. But it was not so simple as that, nor was that all that occurred. Nor, I am afraid, was I ful-filled by even those triumphs chronicled above.

I had not the fat of Tushratta of Mitanni with which to grease the wheels of my chariot.

And I had not gotten Piyassilis the dream of his heart: I did not acquire Carchemish; you will note that I have left it out. I besieged it, but it was a city strongly fortified, and I did not want to spend the whole year splashing about in the Mala while I tried to starve them out, although it should have been easy, since the drought yet raged in Mitanni. While we were slipping and sliding in the diminished Mala's mud, I wrote to Tushratta, saying: "Come, let us fight."

But not even when he heard that I was ravishing that queen among concubines, Carchemish, did Tushratta come out from Washuganni and join battle.

So, as I have said, I proceeded to where he lay in his lair. Deep into Mitanni to Washuganni I led the Hattian armies, and sent word to him that I was on my way, that he might come and fight with me.

But out from Washuganni Tushratta did not come; he did not answer; he pretended he knew me not. When I went into his capital after him, he was not there any longer. He had slipped through my fingers. Some captives revealed that he had retired eastward.

Since eastward lay the rival claimant for the now vacant throne of Mitanni, I let him go: seemingly he was running toward his death. I took the gilded chariots, the utensils of the gods, the doors of silver and gold, and ground my teeth together that I had ever been so foolish as to make an agreement with Artatama of Hurri that forbade me to chase into Hurri after my enemy, Tushratta.

Then I recrossed the Mala, only having sacked the city Washuganni and removed its wealth and its people and all that they owned. I did not occupy the city: that, too, was part of my agreement with the Hurri king Artatama, Tushratta's brother.

That was when I heard of the death of my ally Sarrupsi in Nuhasse, and so I struck southwest toward my embattled country under a gray and yellow sky that rained cinders upon us from all the pillaging that had been going on in the lands.

Now, Halap is a choice grape among choice grapes, and no better opportunity could have presented itself to me to pluck it, so I took it and from its northern vantage presided over the investment of Nuhasse for the second time.

It angered me greatly that this poor vassal Sarrupsi had been murdered by his own family. And even more wroth was I when I heard that the man who usurped his throne had called Egypt to his aid against me.

I had no way of knowing whether Hattu-ziti was even back from Egypt, and I worried over my chamberlain's safety, and that of my boy Kantuzilis who was with him.

But I continued my investment of the countries now making common cause against me. From within Halap, in the country of Mukis, I fought the rebel usurper in Nuhasse and his cohorts, the kings of Mukis and Ni'i.

It was near the end of spring by then, so I was not at all sure that I could make good my boast and be in Alalakh by the first day of summer to receive my Babylonian queen. But I had not given it up; in fact, I was preparing to take the city, which I could almost spit upon from my vantage in Halap.

Also while in Halap I wrote a gentle but firm letter to Niqmad, king of the great seaboard city Ugarit, inviting him to become my ally against the hostile kings of Mukis, Nuhasse, Ni'i, and whomever else we should have as common enemies. This I did knowing full well that Aziru might not be pressing Ugarit as I had wanted him to do. But the ferment to Niqmad's rear, and my very presence so close to his land, I thought, should be sufficient.

I threw all my might into the investment of Mukis, even while my scouts brought me a prisoner who carried on his person a bid from the kings of Nuhasse, Ni'i and Mukis that Niqmad of Ugarit join them in common cause against me.

Now again I wrote to Ugarit's king, Niqmad, and I told him this:

"Since the lands of Nuhasse and Mukis are at war with me, you, Niqmad, do not fear them; have confidence in yourself. Just as in former times your fathers were friends and not enemies of Hatti, now you, Niqmad, be likewise enemy of my enemy and friend of my friend. If you, Niqmad, hear these words of the Great King, your lord, and you are faithful, you will know as a king the favor with which the Great King, your lord, will favor you.

"So, Niqmad, be faithful to the treaty of friendship with Hatti, and you will see: the kings of Nuhasse and Mukis who have dropped the treaty of friendship with Hatti, how the Great King will treat them. And you, Niqmad, in the days to come, will trust the word of the Great King, your lord.

"If then these kings send soldiers to attack your country, Niqmad, do not fear them; send immediately a messenger of yours to me.

"But if you, Niqmad, by your own arms meet and attack the soldiers of Nuhasse or of Mukis, let no one take them from your hands. If it happens that cities of your borders become your enemies, and in fighting them in the days to come you conquer them, let no one take them from your hands. And if it happens in the days to come that the Great King conquers these kings, the Great King will give you a sealed tablet of agreement."

So did I write to Niqmad, bringing to his mind treaties that had existed in former times between our lands, and acting as if indeed these friendly relations were presently established. It was a generous offer, I thought.

At the time I wrote it, Takuwa, king of Ni'i, was under my very roof, clandestinely trying to establish a similar relationship with me. But while we were yet going over the terms, his brother Akit-Teshub rose up and claimed the country of Ni'i and threw in his lot with my enemies. Thus it remained for me to regain Takuwa's country for him before I could take his submission as its ruler. And as anything less, I had no need of him.

So I sent Takuwa out with Piyassilis to ride in the point chariot while we were attacking his own country, while I myself concentrated on ending the rule of the king of Mukis by installing myself in its capital, Alalakh, so that I could receive my new wife there, as promised, if indeed she arrived safely from Babylon.

Never can I remember such anxiety over any campaign, not even against Tushratta, as that I felt while the first day of summer drew nearer and still I was not sitting in Alalakh on its throne.

But I received a messenger from Niqmad of Ugarit, saying to me what I already knew: that the hostile coalition of Mukis

and Nuhasse and the usurper of Ni'i had sent a message to the
king of Ugarit. And this is what they said to him: "Why are you
not at war along with us, separating from the Sun?" And the
messenger assured me that Niqmad, his master, did not wish to
be at war with me, and instead was requesting troops. So I sent
back with his messenger chariotry and troops under Telipinus
and Tarkhunta-zalma.

And I was pleased: the hostile kings of Mukis and Ni'i and
Nuhasse now were placed between my battle on the east from
out of Halap, and Niqmad's from out of the west. When I sent
my sons and nobles and Hattian soldiers to Niqmad's aid, I had
already put Ugarit officially under the protection of the Sun:
even tribute schedules did I write out there in Halap and give to
the high official of Ugarit to take back to his master.

As for the kings embattled between us, they were like fruit
from which the juice was ready to be squeezed.

But was the Sun triumphant? Not just then, I was not: I had
interrupted one enemy messenger's journey to Egypt to beg help
for embattled Nuhasse; surely there had been others. And I was
not yet installed in Alalakh.

As I was finishing the sack of Mukis, we heard that Aziru of
Amurru had requested troops from Egypt, in case I attacked him.

This troubled me, both that he would do the deed, and that he
himself would inform me of it. I thought about the matter for two
days, and just as the Hattian army crossed the moat into Alalakh,
capital of Mukis, I decided that the Sun's armies would take no
punitive measures in the case of Aziru's proclaimed defection,
for I had sniffed out a motive in his seeming madness. Since he
himself wrote to me of his plans, I was assuming that there was
laughter between the lines.

Three days before I had promised Burnaburiash, king of
Babylon, that I would be ensconced upon the throne in Alalakh,
I was sitting there, with all my victorious soldiers turned loose
against the rebellious town. The king of Mukis had fled and given
up his country. The back of the rebel coalition was broken, so I
presumed to think. Ni'i lay in my hands. The Sun's son Telipi-

nus and my most able young general Tarkhunta-zalma, with the soldiers and chariots I had sent down to Ugarit, had driven the enemy soldiers out of Niqmad's country. All the displaced persons that my army had taken did they offer up to Niqmad.

Thereupon Niqmad the king of Ugarit did great homage to my son and the Great Ones of my armies: silver, gold and copper and other fine gifts he offered them, and even said that he was coming to Alalakh to fall at the feet of the Sun.

So it was that while the citizens of Mukis were dying and crying in the smoldering streets, I was sitting in the plunder-heaped throne room with Niqmad, king of Ugarit, his brown nose pressed to the alabaster, doing homage at my feet.

To this bewigged and most servile king I showed favor, raising him up, saying that I acknowledged his loyalty, and that whatever belonged to Ugarit, even the smallest blade of grass, I would not touch.

Now while Niqmad was agreeing to this term and to that, and affirming to me his past demonstrations of loyalty, saying, "Behold, by hostile words against the Sun, my master, Niqmad did not let himself be reduced," I the Sun was thinking that the Egyptian manners this vassal king had learned made him too comfortable on his knees. There is a difference in the way I and my brother, the Great King of Egypt, hold vassals: the Sun's strength is not built upon the fear of mutilation. We do not cut off the hands of our enemies and trundle piles of them back to Hatti; we do not say, "The Sun is a god; bow down to him." The Hattian army is not gentle—do not think that—but it is civilized. I have no wild legions of Nubians or Ethiopians. Although later I used more Hapiru, who kill slowly, then I was not using many of them. If a Hattian soldier is pillaging in a town, he may thrust the lame and halt into the flames, but children he does not rape, kings he does not flay alive, princes he does not unman for all to see. This was what brought me Ugarit out from under Egypt's sandal: that we are men, not beasts, and treat our vassals as we treat our own people. Thus, the king of Ugarit, groveling at my feet in a manner that would have caused a Hattian noble to seek death as relief from the shame of such behavior, remarked:

"Praised be the Sun, who has shown me great favor; I am the footstool under your feet; you have raised me up and treated me as a brother. I am the enemy of your enemy, friend of your friend. To the Sun, Great King, my master, I am devoted. You have delivered me from the hands of my enemies—"

After a while I tired of the novelty and silenced him, lest the very station of kingship be devalued by the king of Ugarit's Egyptian servility.

And I signaled Pikku—who was writing down the terms of the treaty to be attested by this Niqmad in my presence—to bring forth the tablet. And to Niqmad I said:

"I am your master, your majesty, your overlord; to all my terms you have agreed. When you affix your seal to this document, all the gods will know it. You are a king within my sphere of influence. When you were pressed, you agreed to tribute in specific terms. Do you still so agree?"

"Yes." His wig was jeweled in the Egyptian manner; he wore a pectoral and cuffs of gold. Yet his dress was Ugaritic: a long wrapped tunic over an undergarment with sleeves to his wrist. And his face, which was brown as an Egyptian's but regal-nosed, was pinched and drawn.

"So then let us affix our seals. Pikku!" My scribe came forward and presented the agreement, and all my generals and commanders fell silent, and before them Ugarit became a Hittite country. Her quays and ships; her ivory-latticed palace grounds; her wondrous streets with their Egyptian colossi presiding thereupon from eyes of granite: all these were ours.

There came a shouting from my lords, and a thrusting up of clenched fists, and loud praises from the one to the other when the deed was done.

The seal that I had used was the one I had had made to celebrate my wedding: within the inner ring, beneath my name and titles, were the dignities of rank I expected to bestow upon my new wife. And this alone marred my joy, for she was not yet in my hands.

So as Telipinus and Piyassilis were congratulating Niqmad, who looked near to fainting and whose smile was as weak as his slippery grip had been when I took his hand, I called close Pikku and instructed him not to fire or copy the tablet until I told him otherwise.

"What shall I tell the scribe from Ugarit?"

"That it is the will of the Sun. On the day of his master's departure, he will have it. Not before."

With expressionless face, Pikku bowed back from me.

Now, I have not much spoken of the chaos all about us, of the moaning of the Hattian wounded and the sobbing of the namra penned in the dungeons below; nor of the smoke-blackened riches and tattered glory being pounded into the mud of Mukis by my triumphant troops. But it was so: war is always war. As we walked the halls, the king of Ugarit, who had visited before in Alalakh, would sigh and his mouth would twitch, or he would squeeze shut his eyes as he looked away from this gory sight or that splintered artifact.

"Half of Ugarit, I have heard, was destroyed by fire. Would you start soon on rebuilding it?" I ordered him most politely.

"Can the Sun loan me some men to undo what they have done?"

"What did you say?"

"I said, my very own men will soon be undoing what has been done, my master."

"Good. I have heard it is pig upon the table. I have not eaten pig since the New Year."

While he was smiling and trying in his delicate fashion to make his Egyptian manners work with me and I was thinking that if I puffed his way, he would flutter like a feather, a commotion behind us caused me to touch his shoulder. He flinched, stopped, and then a messenger strode before us, breathing hard, his eyes switching back and forth between the king of Ugarit and me.

JANET MORRIS

"Pass on in, Niqmad. Piyassilis, take our guest and seat him at the victory board. Now, man, what is it?"

As my own filed past me, the messenger said: "Ni'i is ours, my lord! The usurper has been ousted, but not taken. He has gone over to the king of Arahti, taking six lords with him. But the country is secure."

"Tarkhunta-zalma, if you would keep your ears, take them elsewhere!" I spoke harshly, but I was not angry at the young general who loitered by the doorpost. "And what else, man?" I demanded of the messenger, who yet remained. Over my shoulder, the messenger's eyes followed something, doubtless the eager young general whom I had caught eavesdropping.

"My lord Tabarna," said the man very softly, his nervous fingers twirling the ends of his hair, "I have news that may not be good. I have just come from the gatepost, where waits a man of Amurru, who sends his master's greetings and word that Amurrites are escorting the Babylonian retinue that brings your wife hither, and that the Sun should wait calmly, assured that all is well."

"I see," I said. "And what else?"

"That is all."

"Go to our guest Takuwa, the would-be king of Ni'i, and tell him that the Hattian armies by my will have regained his land for him, and that he should meet with Arnuwandas when the moon rises to go over the terms of his submission. Then go to the gatepost and get this Amurrite courier and present him to me at table. Then go and inform my thirty that they must be ready to drive on a moment's notice. After that, if you will, come eat at my board and await dismissal of the Amurrite."

He departed to his duties and I to mine.

As I was seating myself at table, I brushed my lips to Arnuwandas' ear and assigned him the task of readying the king of Ni'i for formal submission. Then I informed all present that Lupakki had completed what Piyassilis and the king of Ni'i, while he was being usurped, had started.

Piyassilis looked disappointed that he had not made it back to the front in time to earn his share of glory. But aside from him, all the men began to celebrate in earnest. Even the king of Ugarit seemed cheered, seeing that peace for which he yearned was now close to becoming a reality.

When the conversations around me permitted, I sat back and sipped wine, and pondered my messenger's news. Aziru, what had he in his mind? His men were escorting my wife hither? The implied insult, that I could not myself assure her safety, could not be denied. And yet, did he truly bring her safely to me without attaching any overweening significance to the deed, then it was a plea to be treated as an equal (or at least a useful adherent), which he might not know any other way to voice.

But I had no intention of recognizing Aziru of Amurru just then, lest my new vassal king Niqmad die of terror. He had already asked me to protect him from the Amurrite. And I had had to say to him that Amurru was a state of Egypt's, and I would not mix in, other than sending troops on Niqmad's request to maintain Ugarit's borders. What troubles he had with Amurru I advised him to settle between himself and Aziru by negotiation. And Niqmad had begged my indulgence, that I at least say to the Amurrite that he must not plunder Ugarit's ships and merchants' caravans, pointing out to me that his loss was my loss, and his people my children, and were it Hatti being plundered, I would take a hand.

Just as my messenger and the Amurrite courier in his purple-brown mantle came into the chamber, I called Tarkhunta-zalma to me and bade Arnuwandas trade seats with him.

As the Amurrite crossed the floor and bowed down before me, disappearing from view beneath the heaped viands on the table, total silence fell. Even the palace women who had been playing soft music in the corner left off.

I raised him up and bade him speak, and he told me what my own messenger had told me.

"And how far is my wife-to-be's party from here?"

"They will be at your borders in the morning. I have spent most of my time explaining my mission to Hattian officers so that they would pass me through."

"And is your master with the marriage train?"

The young Amurrite tossed his massive head so that his bushy hair whipped about his shoulders, then stared me in the eye and said: "My master Aziru has been summoned to Egypt. He wishes you to know this, and that he will not go. My lord, Great King, might I speak privately with you on my master's behalf?"

I looked around me at the attentive faces: Piyassilis; Arnuwandas; Telipinus; Kuwatna-ziti's protégé Tarkhunta-zalma; my Master of Horses, Hannutti; Teshub-zalma, the young commander; Zidanza, my adopted son; and twelve other Hattian lords' who were in attendance.

Before I went with the Amurrite courier, I said, "Tarkhunta-zalma, come with me." The young general rose, coming to stand behind my chair. And:

"You others, I have a desire to acquire the country of Arahti, whose king Akiya has given asylum to our enemy, the usurper of Ni'i. Who would like the task?"

So I chose Telipinus the Priest to command the troops, and Hannutti to accompany my son. Telipinus chose Teshub-zalma and Zidanza, and all excused themselves to set the thing in motion.

To the aforementioned, the king of Ugarit had listened in silence. When at last I got up to go out with the messenger of Amurru, Niqmad leaned forward and opened his mouth to speak but Arnuwandas must have dissuaded him, for he sat back with his hands folded over his belly.

Close to the great hall in the palace was a small, intimate chamber.

Within it, I asked the Amurrite to tell me what he would not say before my lords, while Tarkhunta-zalma stood, arms folded and legs spread wide, leaning against the doors.

"Great King, my master seeks your aid."

"In what way? He writes to Egypt begging them to send troops against me! He even tells me this is so. Let him come himself, and fall down at the feet of the Sun, and I will succor him like any other vassal."

"Great King, he bade me tell you he is sorely beset. Akhenaten has commanded Lord Aziru's presence in Egypt. Worse, the Egyptian has sent Hatib the Vile to accompany my master to Egypt, and Aziru fears that he will soon have his wrists in a shackle whose rope, after being wound around his neck, is in Hatib's hands. So my master wrote to Pharaoh, saying: 'Hatib and I will come. But, my lord, the king of Hatti has come to Nuhasse! Therefore I cannot come. May the king of Hatti depart! Then Hatib and I will come!' But, Great King, my father Aziru begs you: stay in Nuhasse. Do not remove your troops from the land, else my beloved master will be as a fettered slave switched by Hatib all the way to Akhenaten's court!"

"And what does Aziru wish me to think of his brash protestations of loyalty to the Egyptian?"

"My lord, my father Aziru has placed his neck upon your plow. He bids me tell you he has gone to Tunib, and that he will reside there seven times seven days, though into your territory he dares not come. And to tell you, lest you find it out and think ill of him, that he has written further to Akhenaten, saying: 'The King of Hatti dwells in Nuhasse, and I am afraid of him lest he comes to Amurru. . . . He dwells in Nuhasse, two days journey to Tunib, and I am afraid he will oppress Tunib.' But to you, the Sun, he offers up Tunib with open hands, only wishing that you save him from Hatib, Pharaoh's fearsome servant, who is at all times overseeing him."

"I can hardly believe this candor. But I will take a chance. I will give you safe passage. Go you to Tunib and tell Aziru that though I will depart, my troops will stay in Nuhasse; that I am going to Arahti, and when I have conquered it, I am going on to Qatna. And say that if he, Aziru, comes out to aid me against Qatna, I will consider it an act of submission upon his part, and I will leave Tunib alone, so he can play out his game with Egypt to its ending. *But in that I will not aid him,* except to say that Hatib's blood is the color of gold, and some of that gold is Hittite gold, and should Hatib hear that the king of Hatti wishes to see his face in Qatna, there Hatib's person will surely be. Now, depart."

But even as I was saying that, a knock sounded upon the doors.

Tarkhunta-zalma, without moving away from the doors upon which he leaned, declared that the Sun was in conference within.

From without came an answer, while I was watching the young courier from Amurru whose jaw, though outthrust, was quivering, and who was blinking far too rapidly. "Are you a son of Aziru's by blood, or merely by the soldier's oath?" I demanded of the clean-shaven youth, while Tarkhunta-zalma pushed himself uncertainly away from the door, gesturing for my attention. "What is it, general?"

"Piyassilis desires admittance."

"Admit him, then. You, courier, speak when the Sun speaks to you!"

And the Amurrite youth said quietly that indeed Aziru was his sire. And I was thinking that I should have known that: on such a mission of treachery, less than a blood relation even I would have been hesitant to send. And, too, Aziru's axe-face looked out at me from beneath the bushy hair of the youngster, who could be no more than fifteen or sixteen.

As I presented the prince of Amurru to Piyassilis, I was adjudging my son's face, he who loved Amurru's king Aziru like a brother, and who now greeted this youth of Amurru as a peer.

It was not only myself who was scowling at that, but also Tarkhunta-zalma, who a moment ago had been smiling; and the general was once again leaning his weight against the door, gold-banded arms crossed over his chest, naked displeasure upon his face.

I had only time to note brown-haired Tarkhunta-zalma's demeanor, he who was Piyassilis' closest companion, who had recognized his voice when I did not, and then Piyassilis was speaking:

"Tell your father Aziru that my heart is with him, and that I have laid a sacrifice upon his behalf. Abuya—"

"Who sent you in here and with what message?" I snapped.

Recollecting himself at my rebuke, Piyassilis said, "My lord Sun, the king of Ugarit wished me to come and express his desire to open negotiations leading to friendly relationship with Amurru. He would—"

"The friendly relationship he will get from us is that he develops with the oar he will soon be pulling on one of my father's war galleys," spat the youth, and I saw the brown-haired Tarkhunta-zalma raise an eyebrow.

"Princes do not make decisions in such matters in Hatti. Niqmad of Ugarit is my guest and my vassal."

At this the Amurrite youth seemed to remember where he stood. His glance went from Piyassilis, pulling his lip in irritation, to myself, to the youthful general at the door, and then returned to me. He squared his shoulders: "Great King, I came here to plead your aid for my father's sake, and you have refused me. His death will likely come of it: I cannot imagine he will be too concerned about your relationship with Egypt's Ugaritic cattle."

I was not sure I had heard him correctly but Piyassilis, aghast at such bravado, put himself between the youthful courier and myself.

"Abuya," pleaded my son softly, "he is but a boy, and sorely pressed."

"Step out of the way. Boy! If you are not capable of understanding the message I have given you for your father, then at least be capable of transmitting it. Repeat to me what I have told you."

As he did, Piyassilis listened closely, and nodded, and when the boy fell silent, Piyassilis offered himself as an honor guard to accompany the son of Aziru to his father in Tunib.

"Piyassilis, I am disappointed. I have troops yet in Nuhasse; we are sending a force into Arahti in the morning; Alalakh must be held; my new wife must be safely transported here. Have you your own troops, to suggest such a thing? Are you separating from the Sun and going over to Aziru?"

While Tarkhunta-zalma battled his grin, Piyassilis stuttered that he had meant no such thing, only was he trying to be of help.

"Be of help, then: explain to this small-minded child what the message he carries means. Not here! Go. Take him to the stables, get him fresh horses, provisions, whatsoever he needs. Give him a safe-passage through the country, but send no one with him. I have done all that I am going to do in this matter. I will hear no more about it. As for Ugarit's negotiations with Amurru, I am too busy to concern myself just now. And so," I added, as Piyassilis opened his mouth to protest, "are you. Now, depart, the both, before I lose my temper."

Tarkhunta-zalma spoke soft words to Piyassilis at the door, and then just the son of the Shepherd remained with me in the conference chamber.

"So, sit down, Tarkhunta-zalma, and tell me what thoughts you have on all this."

Suddenly clumsy, awkward and shy, he took a stool and sat gingerly upon it. "My lord Sun, I was thinking that there might be trouble at the border checkpoint when the nationality of the Babylonian princess' honor-guard is detected."

"Very good. They will all likely be detained, which is why you are going from here to ready my thirty: we leave upon the moment."

Tarkhunta-zalma started to rise.

"Wait," I said. "You know Piyassilis better than any." He flushed, lowered his eyes, and muttered something. I did not have time to consider what that reaction might mean. "What is it with him and the Amurrites?"

Up slowly came Tarkhunta-zalma's head, and his eyes were frank and appraising, long slits in his face: "My lord, Great King, does the Sun not know how Piyassilis loves thee? You have shown favor to the Amurrite; Piyassilis wants above all things to be a satisfaction to you; he seeks your approval by his manner—not only in this, but in all things. . . . As you say, I am often with him. I was with him when he dredged from Lupakki every tale of your youth. I was with him when we rode into battle, in former times, behind the Sun's chariot, and in all things he endeavored to make himself like you. Twice he almost lost his life fighting, for he would be watching you and exclaiming your prowess while he should have been watching out about him. He has mastered every refinement of wrestling and horsemanship Arnuwandas learned at your knee. Every woman you have cast aside he has taken up. . . . It is perhaps not too healthy, but it is the truth. . . . There is none who love you as your second son in the whole of the armies and not any other, including Arnuwandas (though you may fault me for speaking out) who has studied your kingship so closely or who strives as indefatigably to emulate your hero's ways."

Then it was I who studied my sandals, and could not think of anything to say. At length I thanked him, and set him to forming up my chariotry for a nightlong drive toward the south.

I sat there in the blessed solitude of Alalakh's palace a long time. Although a multitude of matters crowded in upon my meditation, crying for my attention, I solved no problems. I came to no conclusions. And when I left that chamber the matter of my wife-to-be and how my sons would accept her, and indeed whether she would be acceptable, still dominated my attention.

I went straight to the courtyard where the horses and chariots awaited, thinking how fortunate it was that Telipinus would be out taking the country of Arahti while I was accustoming the Babylonian princess to her queenship: the single look he had cast at me when the Amurrite courier-son of Aziru had made mention of her, the cold disdain with which he volunteered for the campaign which would take him elsewhere, had been clear as words on a bronze tablet: Yet did Khinti's shadow stand between me and my third son, the Priest.

And yet did her soft and yielding form haunt the Sun. She was beside me in the chariot all through the dark hours, so real I could almost have taken her into the shelter of my arm; and her soft, accepting eyes distressed me without even a hint of reproach.

So preoccupied was I with the bitter wine of my recollections, of my conjectures, of my fears, that dawn began breaking before I gave the men and horses a needed rest.

I spent that time lying on a hillock watching the sunrise, Tarkhunta-zalma like a silent, protective shadow at my rear.

At length, desultorily brushing off my kilt, I bade them drive on, that we make the checkpoint before the steaming heat of midday came upon the land. All of us were grimy, stubbly and shiny-faced from lack of sleep. In dusty mantles and kilts, necks and wrists and fingers and waists bejeweled with plunder, we looked more like a Hapiru robber band than a kingly escort. But often I have driven men the night through, turning them round the following day and marching them another way to trap an enemy.

When we reached the checkpoint, the Babylonian entourage had not yet arrived. But the close scrutiny my own officers gave the chariots streaming toward them, divested of standards or gilded harness or even plumes upon the horses' heads, gave me an indication of how we might appear.

With my helmet on the chariot's deck, stripped down to kilt and weapons and sandals in the merciless sun, I had to prove my identity before an officer of the border guard, whose perplexity turned to consternation that ran out of his mouth like the water-disease from a man's anus, until I assured him that I was pleased that his circumspection was such that even a man claiming to be a king was questioned. And, in an expansive mood, my eyes roaming the horizon whence I had come and over which I now ruled, I gave the border commander the gold wrist-guards I was wearing. Moved nearly to tears, the man followed me around thereafter like a puppy, showing me this and showing me that, while his men walked our horses and refilled our water-skins and queried my thirty of affairs in Alalakh and the winning of the Syrian war.

So it was that when the dust heralded the caravan's arrival out of the south, a scruffy band of charioteers were there to escort them into Hittite territory.

Upon sighting the dust trail, Tarkhunta-zalma let out a yell that sent my men running toward their cars. When he drove up in my chariot, I mounted and we proceeded out to meet the caravan.

As we closed the distance, I could see the Amurrites' flat-topped helms and the bare heads of the Hapiru spearmen surrounding the Babylonians, spangled and plumed within their circle. The last members of this winding column had just come into view when I pulled mine to a halt and waited.

Two chariots broke away from the train: one Babylonian, with a scoop forward of its wheels, drawn by fine-boned steeds whose heads bore bunches of blue plumes; one Amurrite, crude but serviceably sleek, pulled by larger, rangy plains horses in unadorned harness.

Even as the spike-helmed Babylonian driver raised a hand and the two charioteers stopped their horses nose to nose with ours, I saw the wagons behind, their latticed enclosures gay with streamers, and the white horses with gilded hooves who drew them.

"Bow down to the king of Hatti!" intoned Tarkhunta-zalma. The Babylonian stroked his oiled, curled beard and looked me over. The man was prepared for anything: a shield rode his arm, with lions of Babylonian gold thereon: gilt spears stuck up from the chariot's innards on his right and on his left. He turned his head to the Amurrite to exchange a look, and his hooked nose bobbled as he spoke: "What think you, friend Amurrite: is this the king of Hatti? And if it is—"

The Amurrite silenced his companion with a shake of his head, removed his helmet, and performed what obeisance is possible from a chariot. His hair was held by a fillet, but over his shoulders its black mass fanned out. He too was stripped down to kilt and weapons, and his dark skin gleamed in the hot sun.

When the Amurrite raised his head, he offered his master's greetings and begged, with my permission, to depart. By then the Babylonian was hidden behind his chariot's high fore, so deeply was he bowing.

I allowed the Amurrite his wish, advising him to take all his Hapiru with him.

"My lord, Great King," said the Amurrite, "may I have your indulgence and ask a question?"

"Ask."

"Our messenger, did he reach you safely?" In the Amurrite's manner I saw an obvious attempt to hide concern.

"He is off to Tunib with a safe-passage and some fresh horses. Tell Aziru for me that as sons go, that one is above the average."

Then the Babylonian offered his apologies, and I accepted them, though if he were mine he would have lost his tongue, and we all together drove toward the train of chariots, wagons, and their Amurrite guard, who were departing on the moment at a shout from their leader, leaving the halted Babylonian train surrounded by my Hittites.

Before us waited twenty Babylonian chariots, as many footmen, and five wagons, behind each of which came a pair of gift-horses in white halters.

"What is your will, lord?" said the Babylonian nervously, for I did not order the troops to proceed toward the border checkpoint, but instead ordered Tarkhunta-zalma to dismount, take another chariot and, in it, await me.

"My will," I replied over my shoulder as I urged the horses by him, "is to see what it is I am buying before the merchant has departed. You did not think you were coming to Alalakh, did you? You and yours go no farther than the ground on which you are standing."

"Ah, I do not know—I was told to see Her Majesty safely to Hatti."

"Look over there. Do you see those men at the checkpoint? They are standing in Hatti. Borders of mine, and no one else's, are you approaching. One more word, and your men will have to get along without you. Ha!" And I slapped my horses' rumps with the reins. Snorting, they lunged down the line.

Of the first four wagons I took no inventory. In which one rode the royal princess, I had no doubt. Up to the side of it I drove while from each wagon I passed I heard high, excited whispers and saw eyes peering out through progressively more intricate lattices and around curtains of cerise and cinnabar.

When I reached the wagon, I leaned over and jerked open its door. Within I heard screams and scrabblings, but the interior was speckled with latticed light and shadow of which nothing could be made.

Still holding my horses' reins, I levered myself up and in. Three women cowered together in a corner, silent at the command of a fourth who sat alone, stiff-backed, among her cushions. Her hand was beneath one, and I had no doubt that the pillow concealed something.

"I am come for the daughter of Burnaburiash," I said in her tongue, while without I heard a noise. I looked back over my shoulder to verify that the noise came from Tarkhunta-zalma, whose chariot had drawn alongside mine. I threw him my team's reins.

The sound of movement warned me, even as I was turning back and the air whooshed near my cheek. Then a nasty little throwing dagger shivered in the doorframe.

I pulled it out and said, "A chancy throw, with so little space. Come out where I can see you, girl, or I will pick you up and carry you."

I extended my hand toward her, still crouched in the entry, not going after her at all. That brought her out of the speckled lattice-light: hers was a cat's stalk, in that low enclosure, and prefaced by a cautionary assurance to the other three girls.

"Get you out of my way, Hittite, and I will meet you outside this wagon you presume to profane. When your master hears of this, I will make a tasty dish of your scrotum and feed it to you," she said in good Hittite.

I am sure I shook my head. Hittites and Babylonians have blood in common from former times when my ancestors conquered there, but in many ways the two lands remain ignorant of one another.

As I lowered myself down into my chariot, Tarkhunta-zalma hissed at me, but I held up a hand to him and waited, to see what the woman would do.

And I did not have to wait long. Out she came, as graceful as a fawn, pausing only a moment in the entry to sweep her glance over the Hittite chariots and the wagons and the Babylonians with their hands in their kilts.

Then I reached up and lifted her by the waist into my car.

She looked me up and down, even as I scrutinized her. Around me my men were stock-still, for the Babylonian girl wore what I later learned was the latest fashion out of Egypt: a garment not only baring her left shoulder, but sweeping down to close below her left breast—which was rouged and raised, itself appraising—showing not only breast, but belly and whatever the wind dictated, for this translucence was open, slitted from navel to toes. Her hair was straight and squared above her eyes, black as mine but more massive, and it was twirled with gold pins and jangling with gold chains depending from a circlet which glittered at her brow. Her skin was very pale, pale as an Ahhiyawan's; her cheeks were pink with a rage that reddened her full lips. As a concubine, she would have been incomparable. As a queen, however, I was not sure she would suit.

I stared at her quite a while longer than she found comfortable, and all the time I was turning her gaudy sticker. I stared further while she demanded what it was I thought I was doing, and who indeed I thought I was. I kept looking her over while she told me what her new husband would do about me, until she broke off. Her gaze wavered to my men, lounging and watching in utter silence from their chariots. And her own commander she spied, standing on his feet in the dirt by Tarkhunta-zalma's horses.

Then it was that I raised my eyes from her body to her face, and saw the brown eyes widen, and the full lips almost exclaim, and pout, and submit to the bite of white teeth.

I leaned back against the chariot's side and held her eyes, waiting.

When she squeezed them shut and her fingers sought her beaded throat, I said, "Turn around. I would see the rest of you.

And when she had done that, she bowed her head and said: "I am Malnigal, favorite of Istar, daughter of Burnaburiash, Great King, King of Babylon, come to thee as was established between the Sun, my lord, and my father."

I thought then that perhaps she might be acceptable, though it was more her body that spoke to me than her words.

I raised up her chin and kissed her firmly, drawing her against me and holding her until I felt her resistance ease and a quiet trembling begin.

Then I let her go and handed her sticker to her, saying, "Queens do not throw knives in Hatti."

She inhaled deeply, so that her long nostrils flared: "As you will, my lord. I am sure if you had come to me announced and less trail-worn no such thing would have occurred. It has been a long and hazardous journey. There is no peace anywhere between here and Babylon. And when the Amurrites came to 'escort' us and would not be deprived of the privilege, we had no way of knowing whether we were not on our way to Amurru, no better than politely imprisoned."

"If I had stayed home and sent a man to fetch you, I would have had that man make sure that he was fetching a queen, not anything else which might travel in a covered wagon. But enough of this. If you have decent clothes, put them on. If you have none, borrow some. You and I are driving to Alalakh ahead of your entourage. I have a queenly duty for you to perform."

When I had spoken of her attire, she had raised her head high, tossed it, and half that curtain of hair came forward to dress her breast. A retort had been on her lips, but she swallowed it, promising that she would be but a moment, and before I could aid her pulled herself back up into her wagon.

I could feel my troops' eyes boring into my back, but I did not turn to meet them. Rather I thought that for a twenty-year-old girl facing a man twice her age, she had not done badly.

When she reappeared, in haste, she was covered at the breast and had a shawl about her, and the circlet was gone to be replaced by a golden dragon imprisoning her hair at the base of her neck. She was fair beyond speaking, scrubbed of face, her almond eyes flashing with excitement. On her arms she wore copper wrist guards, and barely had I approved her more modest tunic than she asked me if she might drive my team.

So I bade Tarkhunta-zalma ride where he was for a while, and gave orders to the Babylonians to leave the wagons and gifts at the checkpoint.

And Malnigal put her feet into the braces and wound the reins around her delicate hands and set a pace out of that traffic that I would never have sanctioned in a prince.

But I allowed it, until we reached the checkpoint, and with my finger dried the little beads of perspiration that had appeared on her upper lip, and took back my team.

Leaning against the car, her clubbed hair blowing in the breeze, she said "You are not anything like I expected. . . . They say you have grown sons, many of them, and —"

"I know what they say about me. I have not eaten a baby all season; I reformed in honor of your arrival —"

"I do not know what to *do*. . . . " she wailed while I was saying that, and then took hold of the rail and looked away, out at the country.

"It is easier than you imagine. All you must do is be yourself, and attend your instructors, and all will be well between us, between our great houses and between our children and your father's children."

"Children —"

The word came back to me on the wind just as one of the horses shied, knocking the other off balance. I had but an instant in which I must lift the faltering horse up bodily by the reins. Then I was leaning to the opposite side and pulling the girl with me, lest the horses and chariot and ourselves all overturn.

So, when it was over, I had her tight against me, and she seemed content to stay. "Children," she repeated. "Children grown. What will they think?"

"What I tell them."

"And this thing of queenship I am to do — What is it?"

"Affix your attention to some documents. I have sealed them in your name, but I want you to attest them, for they are matters of kingship: treaties I have made with vassals." I could feel her shiver. "Does the war confound you so? All kings war."

"Not as do you, Suppiluliumas." She spoke my name for the first time.

"I think you will find this a better apprenticeship into your queenship than if I had met you in Hattusas—but if you like, I will send you there and you can await me."

"How long?"

"Exactly. I know not how long I will be warring in these lands. I lost a queen once because I was always out campaigning and she succumbed to her loneliness and took a lover. In Hatti, that is not right, and from it she was exiled, losing all: her position, her inheritance, her children, even her freedom to travel beyond the borders wherein she is contained. Do you understand?"

"My lord, I am young, but I was taught at my father's knee. However, there is a custom in my country that a princess who is priestess of Istar of Nineveh—"

"I know you are not a virgin. Let us not speak about what you once did, but of what you will do in the future."

"But I would explain—"

"I explained to your father my requirements in a woman and he explained to me your qualifications, and your sisters', and between us we have chosen you."

"For which I thank my lady, the—"

"Your lady, the Sun-goddess of Arinna," I interrupted her firmly.

"My lady, the Sun-goddess of Arinna," she said faintly, eyes closed, "I understand the necessity for me to take up the state cult, my lord. But I have brought a shrine of my lady, Istar, and beg your permission to worship at it whenever I have met the needs of the Thousand Gods of Hatti."

"I am not a god-ridden man, as you will soon find out. If you fulfill your duties, you may serve your goddess. But of any like affairs which are not customary in Hatti, always inform me before you act."

So by the time we had reached Alalakh, Malnigal and I had formed the beginnings of an understanding, despite that most difficult of circumstances in which we found ourselves: at noon we were royal strangers; in the evening, she must come willingly to my bed, a royal wife.

Upon our arrival in Alalakh I took her straightaway to the room I had been using for a chancery. Then I roused Pikku. I called Takuwa, the reaffirmed king of Ni'i and Niqmad, king of Ugarit, into our presence. There all documents were formally attested by the kings, myself, and by the woman, Malnigal, Tawananna, whose dignities were already inscribed in the inner ring of the Hattian state seal.

When we had done that, I ushered Malnigal into the king's chambers, wanting most of all to avoid introducing her to my sons until I had introduced her to myself.

I called her Tawananna, and told her of the title's meaning, how it had been the name of a great queen of Hatti in former times, and suggested to her that she might choose a Hittite name.

"You do not like my name? Or. . . It is not that, is it—? As you will, my lord: I choose the name Tawananna. I will be at least as great a queen as was she."

"You do not understand, girl. The title has come to mean almost the same as 'Great Queen'; it is a dignity, not a name. Do you want people calling you 'Queen Queen'?"

"It is a name. And if I must take a Hittite name, that is the one I choose. Malnigal is my name to those who are in my confidence; others, I am content to keep at a distance. That should do it, or at least set the tone."

"Then," I allowed, "do as you please in that matter. In other matters, I will not be so lenient. Disrobe, I would see what they teach at those infamous Babylonian temples in which you are so proud of having dwelt."

This she did, and came to me with a confident smile on her lips, and I found her distinguished above all other women I had known in the matter of giving pleasure. Her narrowness proved a boon to us. Her languorous ease was like a spark to kindling. Only when she performed artful games which involved the fetching of honey did I begin to wonder if perhaps she was not too concerned with the mechanics of sensuality. Still, when she got those things for which she cajoled me into sending, from the hands of a scandalized Alalakhan palace woman, I forgot my doubts and my questions as to how she had become such a mistress of passion, for she was all of that and more.

I explored her exotic expertise until the room darkened around us, and in the semidarkness we slept. When I roused again it was to her subtle enticement: I was committed before I was truly waked.

Upon me she was like some all-devouring incarnation of her goddess. Her legs were long and thighs muscled, and inside her was a tautness which she seemed to control at will. I pulled back from her when all she had created at last overcame her, and she gasped into the pillows while I used her from behind, to see what might be seen. There are few women who can make pleasure out of that, and none who can feign it, and when her depths clenched around me, I knew I had something very special in the way of woman writhing with balled fists beneath me.

But having finished with her, lying back with my chest rising and falling and my limbs feeling like lead, I wondered if I was getting old, for I was drained as if I had been in a battle rather than a woman.

Now, that is Malnigal's way: she absorbs all opposition, and makes it small, a mere part of herself. But I could not know that, or what it was I had there licking around my loins. Exhausted, I pulled her up roughly by the hair and settled her firmly against me, my arm crooked around her neck.

And I remember her suppressed laughter, and my abstracted curiosity about her relationship with her goddess, and what her father had said to me: that she had withdrawn from the temple; and his assurances to me that this in no way denigrated her. No more than making her eligible for marriage and shipment away from Babylon at the soonest opportunity, I thought then, sourly, and queried her:

"How does a princess become so educated in these matters?"

"I have been with my goddess; my mystery forbids any further answer." She sat up, pulling out from under my arm, and stared down on me. "It was said to me by the Sun, my lord, that what was past was past, that we would not speak of it. Now, hear you this: no mortal man has ever touched me. You are the first."

And I could not help but chuckle, and my humor she found offensive. But I held her by the ankle, and soon she subsided and remarked that she was famished from her labors, and I agreed to feed her, saying to her as she dressed that I had much liked her bearing in the presence of my vassals, and letting her know that I was more impressed by gracious queenship than any number of spectacular orgasms.

And she, fastening links of gold at her waist, looked up at me in a studied fashion that brought her luminous eyes into play, and said that the Adad of Heaven, which was the same as the Storm-god, and the Adad of Hatti would witness that in matters of queenship she, Malnigal, would certainly excel.

Such poise and spirit in a woman I had not experienced since the days of my mother. One thinks of such qualities emerging out of travail surmounted: And there was over all her person a wistful sadness tempered by worldly pride which she wore like a splendid diadem up until that moment, when I saw it slip, stabilize askew, then fall from her. Then something cold and dark as the eyes of the Dragon looked out at me, calculated, and remarked:

"Niqmad of Ugarit is pale as a ghost, and not from foreign blood, either. Have we our sandal to his throat so securely?"

It was a "we" that both pleased and perplexed me. "Now we do."

"And did we put it there in the same fashion I saw in practice in the streets of Alalakh? Does it always take three Hattian soldiers to rape a girl in a gutter? Are starving children who beg food cuffed away as a matter of Hittite policy?"

"What are you trying to say?"

"Only, my lord, that I am unfamiliar with you, with your country, with your horses and chariots, with your soldiers and your children and your laws. And what I have seen is fearsome. *You* are fearsome in the sense that kings in my country who rule from their palaces, their loins girded in gold, are not. And you do not seem—"

"This is one of my palaces. Would that I could have had it cleaned up for you, but circumstances did not allow it. And furthermore, I am not much for posturing. I find satisfaction in iron and bronze: they are not so soft as gold, nor so coveted. If you have a weak stomach, my queenship is no place for you. Say now, and we will not consummate the matter before the gods. I will annul it, if you are not pregnant, and send you back to your father."

"Oh, no, my lord Sun, I meant no offense." She came and clutched my hand, and almost I was fed up with her then, but I took a deep breath and suggested she watch her tongue until she had determined what might be offensive, and warned her that my temper was at best short, and that when pressed I often took physical recourse, and I did not want her to experience my wrath.

"Tell me, then, of affairs of your kingship: of this campaign and what you desire in your heart so that you are warring; and of what I may do to facilitate your success." As she spoke thus, she was putting up a blind, that I not see how suddenly timid and awkward she was feeling. I have seen that many times in women after a first encounter: when their triumph leaves them, they are full of doubts: whether or not you again will wish their use is the kernel of it. I had not noticed any girlish fears in her before the fact, or during the act. And yet, of all the persons with whom she had presented me in that short time of our acquaintance, this coltish one most surprised me. She was striving to conceal all behind her facade of questions, and even knew she was not having success. But I liked her better in that instance than I had liked her at all until then.

"Come here," I said, and wrapped her in an easy embrace. "You do not have to be all things at all times. I am not expecting miracles. I would prefer honesty. As for your position, do not seek so desperately to convince me you are worthy of it: my mind and heart are satisfied. I will help you, and we will make a Tawananna for Hatti the like of which has not been seen since former times."

Up tipped her head and she smiled wanly, slipping her arms around me, squeezing as tightly as she could, saying: "I have been afraid. I would not fail my father, nor yourself, Great King, nor myself—For if I cannot make a life with you, then wherever will I find a place? I thought I was suited for temple life, but I was not and could not remake myself. I am like a servant on trial for his life: no other chance will there be for me. . . . So if I am anxious, forgive me. And if I am not quite myself, but more whomsoever I have determined you might want me to be, then when I know what you do wish in a wife and a queen, you will be pleased at what now is not pleasing."

And I could do nothing else than hold her at arm's length and shake my head at her, and grin in what I hoped was a reassuring fashion, and escort her to my board.

On the way I tried to explain to her that what I had in my heart was the destruction of the kingdom of Mitanni, and that in my mind I had just about done it: all that remained was to secure the half of Nuhasse that still defied me so that I could leave the land in the care of the servant of slain Sarrupsi whom I was installing as my vassal in his master's place; the punishment of the country of Arahti for harboring a fugitive from Hattian justice; and the sweeping away of a few tiny city-states whose princes still called themselves kings and who had not enough sense to come whining up to my gates and beg their way into Hittite collars.

"As did the king of Ugarit?"

"Exactly the same. But a certain sheepdog of Amurru helped drive the ewe of Ugarit into my pasture—he and the desperation of the kings around Ugarit's borders."

"All those lesser kings, have you destroyed them?"

"Not all. Not yet. And I am not so bloodthirsty as you may have heard: In the case of the murder of my vassal, Sarrupsi, I waxed wroth, but even then I did not sentence his family, traitors all, to death; only took them prisoner. I will install this other in his place, who had been his servant. In fact, very soon I will be able to say that I have done it."

"Yet you still fight in Nuhasse?"

"In half of it. But the country buckles, it is on its knees. Soon it will lie prone under our battle, and my displeasure will be felt in the land."

And I was not wrong in my predictions:

Before many days passed, Telipinus and Hannutti and Teshub-zalma and Zidanza, my adopted son, returned triumphant from Arahti, having captured the loathsome usurper of Ni'i (my vassal king Takuwa's brother and rival claimant for that much-bloodied throne) and all his nobles, and also bearing with them in fetters the king of the country Arahti, one Akiya, who had been so stupid as to give asylum to a person hostile to the Sun. Therewith, having conquered Arahti before I could even join them to support the effort, my jubilant Telipinus and the commanders of his army, and my other sons and all my greats of the army—but Lupakki who still battled in Nuhasse—convened to plan the Qatna campaign.

This was the time I chose to introduce Malnigal to my sons, so that at least formally they would recognize her, because all of my field officers would do so.

It had not been easy keeping Arnuwandas and Piyassilis from sniffing her out; I had put a special guard on her and kept her in the king's chambers, specifically to arouse my princes' curiosity and allay their hostility. They knew there was a new queen in my chambers, and I wanted them to accept the fact before they met with her. Because of her foreignness I did this, so I told myself, and not because of the easily wounded child within the woman.

By doing so, I wounded Piyassilis and Arnuwandas, my successor, most of all, by acting as if I did not trust them in her presence.

The morning of the meeting, before which I summoned them privately to take a meal, they could talk of nothing else:

"And do you know she has brought her gods with her? Tiamat, Lady of Chaos; Marduk, his Austerity; Enlil—"

"How do you know this, Arnuwandas?"

"How?" scathed my handsome son. "I went down and over-saw the reception of the betrothal gifts, that is how. Our Great King was otherwise engaged. I—"

"Tell him about the women," broke in Piyassilis. "No? Then I will tell him: Abuya, she has brought—"

"Silence, both of you." I looked from Arnuwandas, whose princely countenance was suffused with rage; to Piyassilis, less pretty, whose height had taught him early the slouch he employed even while sitting to table in the shady private garden, the only place in the Alalakhan palace not marred by our struggle to ac-quire the country. "As for those women whom my queen, your stepmother has brought—"

"So it is that sure? I had hoped she might not suit—"

"Arnuwandas, only kings interrupt other kings. You are not yet a king. Be quiet and listen, and you may live to become one. Firstly, the matter of the Babylonian women: two of those girls are for each of you, gifts from Malnigal's father." They were not: the girls were gifts to myself. But I was implementing my plan; two concubines were a small price to pay for a lessening of hostilities. Arnuwandas snorted, unremitting. Piyassilis looked slightly mollified, and peered about him for a palace servant.

"In the second matter, the matter of my new queen's faith, I am gravely disappointed in you both. You mention this to me, when all know that I have given every god of every village free-dom to be worshipped by those who love him. Is this Egypt, that I hear prejudice spoken like reason? Has Arnuwandas, the suc-cessor to the Sun, caught Naphuria Akhenaten's disease? What next? Will you raise your tutelary god over the Thousand Gods, and cast all others out from the land? Will you tread upon the people's spirit, defile their faith, as the king of Egypt has seen fit to do? War between men and men is one thing; war between men and gods is something else entirely: a man who turns against the gods and slanders them courts disaster, whatsoever sort of man he may be. Princes are not exempt from this law of nature. The Thousand Gods of Hatti and the gods of all other countries have lived in harmony from the day the world slipped from creation's womb. How else could it be? When a king goes to battle, he calls on all the gods to aid him. It has been so forever, since the beginning of eternity. As many tongues as has man, so many are the names of the gods, but the gods themselves are numbered. Men who call themselves kings perform the will of the gods; they call upon the gods to keep them straight with earth and heaven. Think upon Egypt, when you talk of debasing this god or that: even the gods make war on one another in Egypt; the priests of the land have turned upon each other; a king has set one god above all the rest. Beware the jealous gods. The destruction of Mitanni will seem like a child's game before the chaos that will come from the war between the Egyptian gods. Should this continue, should the matter not be contained within Egypt's borders, what will become of us? How can men live together in peace if the gods cannot?"

Arnuwandas regarded me, eyes hooded, and with his mother's high-chinned air answered me: "How? As men have always lived together in peace: by the efforts of a strong leader. But it is not her religion, not that at all. . . . You have had no time for the war; no time for anything, these last days, but your new entertainment. Why do you hide her? Is she like those servants she brought, immodest and bejeweled from ear to toe? Is she so much more enticing than affairs of kingship to you? We have heard strange tales of what went on—" He broke away from my glare, left off, began again: "Our brother Telipinus has prognosticated all our ruin from this taking up of a Babylonian. Her father is a slippery ally. He sleeps with Assyrians, bedawin, whomsoever can serve him. The petty nature of this woman is clear from how many trifles she has hauled up with her. No twenty-year-old temple whore will ever hear *me* call her mother. Or queen."

"He is jealous, Abuya. And he is newly a father, we have just heard, of a man-child. When word came down, you were otherwise engaged—"

Arnuwandas leapt upon Piyassilis. Both went down in a clatter of inlaid stools and bitumen tableware, and I was hard pressed to separate them.

When I had done it, we were all three sprawled on the well-tended lawn like some farm boys squabbling over a slave-girl.

"Princes, it remains for me either to talk some sense into you both, or beat it into you. I am inclined toward the latter. If you, Arnuwandas, have become a father and still have no understanding of fatherly responsibilities, I pity your get. I have two eight-year-old children in Hattusas, in need of a mother. When you lost your mother, I got you Khinti to replace her. Neither of you complained at that time, nor did you hesitate to accept her. You are both sons—*grown*, so you protest. Act like it. Malnigal will be a mother to my twins and the queen of Hatti, and you will harbor no petty jealousies against her—"

"If some evil should befall the Sun," said Arnuwandas, "then I must share my rule with this . . . person, this Malnigal. This is no concubine you are taking, but a woman who will wield power second only to the Tabarna's, and whose stamp will soon be imprinted on the land. You adjure me to take thought to my station—*I am taking it!* I should have had a hand in this deciding! I have a right to see her! Else, I tell you, I will not accept her; in no way will I look kindly upon her. I have seen what foulness she has brought up from Babylon: texts and implements of foreign magic are among them. I was not so young when my mother died that I do not remember how and why: no sorceress is going to curse my house! As your successor, you owe me consideration in these matters—that is, if you expect me to show her any respect and tolerance whatsoever."

I looked at Arnuwandas, but I saw instead Titai, lying dead by her own hand in a cellar. And I recalled the threat Asmunikal had posed to me, and what I did to eliminate that threat.

"Come, then, the both of you, and you will see this formidable, mysterious woman you have set your hearts against."

As we made our way toward the king's rooms, Piyassilis made some attempt to excuse himself from my presence, for reasons I did not then understand. And I said grimly to him that he, too, must familiarize himself with how much of a threat this

Malnigal might be, that he overcome his fears about who would be showing respect to whom in Hattusas thereafter.

Now, in Hatti, if a father and son share the same free woman, there is nothing wrong in that. In this case, I was sure it was the only method by which harmony might be restored between the Sun and my princes. And I was right, it did restore it. When they saw for themselves how easily Malnigal submitted to their majesties, they no longer feared her. When they felt for themselves what I had felt in her embrace, they were no longer suspicious as to my actions concerning her. When they saw her terror and her tears over what was not customary in her land, and her valiant attempt to rise to the occasion; when they experienced the deference of which she was capable and surmounted her each in their way and were made sure that in no fashion could this girl, younger than both, usurp them in my heart, all became well between my princes and myself once more.

But I did not realize what price the affair would exact from my new wife until it was accomplished.

When I left her to calm herself and make ready to meet my commanders, her eyes showed white like a terrified horse's, and her fingers trembled, and at the door she clutched at me and asked if the manner of her acquaintance with my generals and commanders would be the same as it had been with my sons. I suggested to her that she study Hittite morality more closely, and left her to figure out the truth for herself.

In that meeting, all was like quiet water. Piyassilis rose and escorted Malnigal to her position, and throughout the introductions his arm supported her. The only shadow upon the proceedings was her lack of understanding as to the nobility of the greats of the army. They did not notice it, for they had not seen her with my vassals. But afterward, I explained to her that the warrior caste in Hatti was elevated above all but the priestly, and that these before her, and those who served me similarly all through the Hatti land, were the bones upon which empire was growing.

In a much diminished voice she replied that she understood.

"Do you understand that I am leaving Alalakh tomorrow to raid Qatna, and that I am giving you a choice: come, or stay in Alalakh, to be sent north with the rest of the booty."

She shuddered, and pleaded to be taken along.

"There is always a chance that I might be vanquished: war is nothing if not unpredictable. If you are with me, and I fall, your lot will be difficult indeed."

"And if I am not, and you fall, I will be given over to your son Arnuwandas, is that not right?"

"Exactly so."

"Then I will go with you. And if you are taken, this shall be my salvation." And she fingered the golden sticker with which she had tried to skewer me when first we met.

So it was that she happened to be in the king's wagon among the baggage train while all the army but Telipinus' command went out plundering in Qatna under the very banner of the Sun.

I left Telipinus in Alalakh, not on account of our differences (which I believed would disappear now that I had won Arnuwandas and Piyassilis over to the protection of Malnigal), but to hold Alalakh and Halap and all the other rich trading cities we had taken, to oversee the war fast coming to a close in Nuhasse, and at all costs keep our line of retreat free from hostile troops.

He had done as I asked, and formalized Malnigal's assumption of her new name Tawananna and her Tawananna's dignities. In his capacity as priest he was most qualified for it, after myself. But the look he had given her, plus the fact that he had purposely missed both my early morning meeting with my princes and the convocation of lords I had commanded to greet her, bespoke his adamant rejection.

Telipinus, who had been yet a swaddled babe in his cradle when his mother, Daduhepa, died; who owed his title of 'Priest' to Khinti's tender guidance; who yet wrote to his stepmother, though I had forbidden it, and even made no attempt to hide his transgression from me, was in no way ready to accept a girl of his own age as queen over him.

With the Priest, I did not force the matter, only assigned him twice as many tasks as he could be expected to handle, and left him administrating in my stead while all the rest of us sacked and plundered in Qatna. Of my displeasure at his displeasure, I made no more indication than that.

And in Qatna, all went well with us. We despoiled it from one end to the other, and chased its king Akizzi hither and yon, and carried off all the gold and silver and implements of the gods. Even did we hoist up and carry away the golden statues of the Egyptian gods. The Sun God of Egypt we toted out of there, and before I left the country smoking and groaning and denuded of every thing and person that the Sun's armies—and the troops of Aziru, who had come out to fight alongside me—could carry away, I received word that King Akizzi of Qatna had written to his master in Egypt begging for gold with which to ransom the Sun God of Egypt's statue.

We were chuckling over this, myself and my sons and a certain lapsed Sutu now officially a henchman of Egypt, when a brace of chariots bearing the device of Amurru drew up before the tents of the Sun.

"Here," rasped Hatib, "I cannot stay. I have only just convinced Aziru of Amurru that those things you told his son about me are untrue. What had my royal employer in his mind, to speak so?" He was rising, but I commanded him to sit back down, and before my sons and the generals of my armies, he had no choice but to obey.

"Arnuwandas, sit you beside Hatib, and stay there." With a sigh, my son, who loved the Sutu, refolded his legs under him.

By myself, I strolled out to greet Aziru of Amurru, just then handing over his chariot to the Hittite guards.

"I am here," observed Aziru, doffing his helm and clapping the dust from his mantle. "I have survived it."

"But not with your kingly manners intact."

He shrugged, squinted at me in the bright sun, and scratched in his pointed beard. "You could have found a quicker way to kill me, if that is what you are about. What do you want me to do now that I have prostrated myself and my honor at your feet? Will you protect my sons if Akhenaten takes my life in payment for this wanton destruction?"

"If it would ease you, I will grant you that: should you lose your life as a result of what you have done here in Qatna, I will maintain your sons upon the seat of their kingship. And as for destruction, wanton or otherwise, my own sons have been looking to you, rather than myself, for inspiration in that regard."

"Better, protect me from Hatib, if you are granting boons today."

"Bow down before me, offer your submission, and then I will set things right in the matter of Hatib."

"Here? Before the Hittite host?" He grunted deep in his throat, made an assortment of incomplete motions, and with a curse bent knee and head to me.

When I had dragged a verbal submission out of him, he arose awkwardly, spat into the dust, and asked me why I felt it necessary to demean him so before his men and my own, since he had already made his submission by plundering the lands of his last master, Akhenaten, and made it so clearly that none could misconstrue it.

I thought: so you would feel it. So you would know it in your heart, by its aching; in the back of your neck, by the rising of the hackles thereon; by the heat flooding a vassal's countenance. Even then, I still had no surety in me that Aziru was coming over to the Sun. Such men do not step meekly into harness.

I said: "Enter my tent with me, and we will celebrate your submission with my princes, who shall enjoy your loyalty even as I myself."

"My son brought me your words about the color of this Hatib's blood. What have you—?"

I was watching him very carefully then, as he stooped into the tent's semidarkness beside me.

"What? Hatib and you, together! I—" Aziru exclaimed, his right arm flying to his waist.

I chopped down upon his wrist with the side of my hand. His blade fell from nerveless fingers, even while Tarkhunta-zalma and Piyassilis, as one man, vaulted the distance to aid me.

But Aziru was standing quite still, glaring around with bared teeth like the wolf at bay which he was.

In the silence punctuated by the Amurrite's roaring breath, the settling of men back upon their haunches, and Hatib's hissing chuckle, I bade Aziru take a seat.

Without a word he settled down where he was standing, just within the tent, as far from Hatib as he could get. Piyassilis' troubled face went not unnoticed by me as I signaled Tarkhunta-zalma to watch the Amurrite and dismissed all others but my sons and the man Hatib, who rocked slightly to and fro like a snake intent on paralyzing a victim with its obsidian stare.

"I was ready to announce to you all that Aziru has come over to the Sun. Perhaps I had better first explain to Aziru why our old friend the Sutu sits among us, lest he think the Sun has gone over to Naphuria Akhenaten."

Piyassilis handed Aziru his own cup, and the Amurrite drained it without concern as to what it might hold. "Yes, Great King. Explain to me, for I need to know. While I have been hiding from this man and suffering the abasement he has heaped upon my family and the advice he has heaped upon my enemies and the thefts he has made of all that was mine, has he been in your service? Am I now to believe that all this time I have been in training, and Hatib my handler? My lord of Hatti, if this man is your servant then I can only believe that you took my oath from out of a treachery that voids it. It is this person, this . . . Libyan—whose tongue is as twisted as the braids by his ears—who has imperiled my life and my kingship and even driven me into your embrace, to avoid imprisonment or worse at Egypt's hands."

Piyassilis—with whispers, with a touch—quieted Aziru before the Amurrite king bought his death there.

"I will not notice your outburst, Aziru. It is forgotten. This man, as I told your son and he should have told you, has been in my pay for near as long as you have been alive. Is it twenty years, Hatib?"

"Glorious master, I make it twenty and three."

"But—"

"Amurrite, wait until I give you leave to speak. Did you think it a coincidence that you found a way to slip your collar long enough to come and serve the Sun? It was no coincidence." And it was Hatib's face I was looking at for, if he had been suspicioned before, now he was certain that he would have nothing on Aziru any longer; or more exactly, as he held an axe above the Amurrite's head, so Aziru would hold a sword over his.

But Hatib was not Aziru: facing the inevitable, his eyes crinkled with amusement even though he was the object of the joke. He refilled his cup and toasted me silently as I continued:

"In Egypt there is a certain official named Duttu."

Aziru started, blew his breath out explosively. He had written many letters to Duttu, Mouthpiece to All Foreign Lands, both for his father and in his own behalf.

"This Duttu," I continued, "came under Hatib's aegis to be in the Sun's employ. Now, if Aziru should find himself summoned to Egypt, Hatib, would not both yourself and Duttu explore every avenue available to each, to insure that this Aziru would not be harmed in any way?"

"Yes, my lord employer, that is most exactly what Duttu, and myself, and all our underlings would do."

"And if it appeared that this Aziru needed any help while residing in Akhetaten, or even in removing himself from Pharaoh's hospitality, would not you and Duttu be concerned in aiding him? In fact, are you not both well disposed to Aziru, my vassal, and anxious to help him in whatever way you can?"

"Great King, my most astute lord, within the guise of my position, exactly that have I been doing. When I steal from Egypt, Aziru thinks I steal from him. But no matter what I have done"—and here Hatib smiled that crocodile's smile which made Tarkhunta-zalma mutter and begin combing his brown hair through his fingers—"or whatsoever I, am doing, or in future will endeavor to do, your friend the king of Amurru will not much longer be able to avoid answering Pharaoh's summons. And once in Akhetaten he will be at the mercy of the fates: against Nefer-Kheperure-Wanre-Akhenaten, there is naught that mortal man can do that is of any avail."

"But you understand that Aziru is likely to break under the strain and implicate us all," I said softly.

"I have understood that from the moment you went out to meet him, O Munificent of Justice," replied Hatib.

I turned to Aziru. "All of this could have been greatly simplified if you had given any thought to the message I sent you by way of your son."

"All of this could have been greatly simplified if you had informed me previously."

"Previously, *what?* "

"Previously, Great King, my lord."

"Better, but not perfect. A vassal king does not criticize his overlord's methods. Now, in the event that you find that indeed you do visit in the City of the Horizon, this is what I want you to do. . . ."

And when Aziru understood my wishes and Hatib, also, was informed of the Sun's desires, I called a feast in celebration of the sack of Qatna, and while waiting for it I took both my guests to introduce them to my new queen.

When we quit the king's wagons, the night had come upon the land, and namra squealed and torches crackled and pipes whined and girls ran giggling through the wagons with bellowing soldiers close behind.

"Aziru, gentle charge," said Hatib, as we were inspecting the perimeter of the campground, "I have long desired to reveal myself to you, although in such circumstances I could not, of myself, speak from my heart. It was I who called the Great King's attention to your valor while the Sun was first visiting in Alashiya. All that has come since, in a sense, was born of my recommendation."

Dryly, Aziru thanked him, saying that his life would have been dull indeed without the light from the Sun streaming always over his shoulder.

And I was amused, and feeling victorious though I was trying not to show it, and what favor and confidence I could muster I endeavored to heap upon Aziru. For despite what I had said, and Hatib had said, and even what Aziru had managed to say, we all heard what was not spoken: words of men before a trial of deadly proportions. No one of us could deny it. Aziru would likely sample Naphuria Akhenaten's hospitality, and of what that might be like, no one wanted to think. But it lay there unspoken like a cloud before the moon, darkening the space around us and draining every festive smell and sound from the air: although Akhenaten might be Living in Truth, it was very deadly truth.

Later I took Aziru aside, wresting him from Piyassilis' company with the aid of Tarkhunta-zalma, who was looking like a man whose meal has unsettled his stomach.

I had drunk a bit, and felt replete with the successes of the day, so I put an arm companionably about the king of Amurru and drew him off between two horseless chariots.

"You will do well enough, with this information to aid you. Do not keep looking at me like a sacrificial animal."

"How else? But I did not know it showed. I *will be* returned from there, not by you, or Hatib, but by myself. I am not a man who holds desultorily to life. There is no building built which I cannot climb, no dungeon from which I cannot escape. I know . . . you think you have dealt fairly with me. And I suppose you have. If I were you and you were me, it probably would have come to be just exactly the same between us. The gods, at New Year, convene; man's fate is thence decided. My gods are strong; they love me. What I do is a good thing, for the lands, for the Amurrite people, for the homeless and the unwanted whom I have made Amurrites: the Hapiru and their ilk. All of them pray for me. I will not fail. It is only . . .

"I suppose I am in a sense competing with you, more now since the vassalage into which you have forced me—more than before. Do you see? I am a man who is no stranger to plot and scheme, nor the true nature of what men call 'heroics.' I am not dull of wit. And yet you use me like an arrow you happen to have in your quiver: to serve a purpose, without thought to whether after the purpose is served, the arrow will be broken, or lost. And with no more concern in your heart. I am a man, as you. I have wives and concubines, brothers, sons and daughters, and all the countless children a man takes into his care when he becomes a king."

"In that, you are no different than this minor King Akizzi, to whose country you yourself have laid waste. I had no idea you were inclined to the maudlin."

"A man facing death often turns to philosophy. Never should I have bothered." And he turned sideways, sliding out of contact with me, and leaned up against the farther chariot. In the torchlight, he seemed younger than his thirty years, young as Telipinus, and as accusing. "Do you have any further use for me? I would depart back to Tunib with the dawn. I was longer here than I had expected. I will have more troubles when I reach Amurru, for I was supposed to be waiting there for Egypt's Honorable Lord Hani to come and lecture me about my conduct."

"No, I have nothing more for you to do, for the nonce. Just continue to keep me informed of your faring with Egypt, and remember that if in time you come to me and beg to become formally my vassal, so that all the lands notice that you have separated from Egypt, I will then issue you my full protection."

"The price of that protection, my lord Overlord, is exceedingly great. I am neither willing nor able to pay it."

"In time, that will change."

"Until it does, am I free to depart?"

"Go in peace, Aziru. And may the Storm-god aid your battle, may the Sun-goddess of Arinna put in your mouth the words that prevail in righteousness."

In the morning, I struck southward toward Apina in a move that surprised even my generals. I had not forgotten that someone among my trusted might be aiding my enemies, though I had formally put a halt to any attempt at sniffing out any such.

On the southward push, we heard from Lupakki by way of Telipinus at Alalakh that finally the country of Nuhasse in its entirety was ours, and that the kingship seat was secure under the butt of Takib-sarri, Sarrupsi's servant. Jubilant, I sent back word of my pleasure and orders to Telipinus to begin implementing the withdrawal of troops, sorting out the border guards who would remain, and seeing to their deployment.

Now, I did not want to fight with the country of Kinza. They were a dearly beloved Egyptian protectorate, and I was leaving Byblos alone, so I was willing to leave the country of Kinza untouched.

But its king Shutatarra and his grown son Aitakama and their army came out to fight with me. "Come, let us fight!" they demanded, and I could not find it in my heart to refuse them.

I defeated them on their borders, and they retreated and established themselves in one of their cities, Abuzya. With ninety chariots and nine thousand foot I had the city besieged. And I took prisoner this king and his son Aitakama, together with all the great warriors of his country, and sent them up to Telipinus to dispatch to Hattusas. On the journey, the old king died of his wounds, but I did not know of that.

I was sacking the rich trading city of Apina, and proceeded to do the same to its king: I took the king, and his sons, his nobles and whatsoever they owned and brought them all as prisoners into my camp. No farther did I desire to penetrate into the south than Apina. Because of the presumptuousness of King Tushratta, in one year I had destroyed the kingdom of Mitanni. I was greatly pleased.

In fact, but for Malnigal's constant bemoaning of the savagery of war and Telipinus' continued hostility toward myself, his sire, all was exceedingly well with me. I had both time and inclination to deal with my queen on the return march, which because of the number of namra, the great multitude of booty, and the recalling of most of the Hittite host, would have been arduously slow without something upon which to fix my attention. Not that I, the Sun, continually marched at the crawling pace of the Hittite armies northward. Once I had satisfied myself that Telipinus' unfortunate loyalty to my exiled former queen had not gotten between him and his princely duties, and once I saw for myself that all the fat cities I was keeping fortified were properly manned, and when at last I had looked with my own eyes upon the submitted but yet restive country Nuhasse, I and my personal troops, with six hundred chariots supporting, raced the autumn's end northward.

CHAPTER 29

"But the troops must get their honors from you. Should anyone else preside, they will feel cheated. Would that it were not so."

So spoke Arnuwandas to me of my army, of the heroes' roll, and of the question of which of us, my tuhkanti or myself, would perform the ceremony.

"It is so late to be performing it, and there is so much else to do, that I will risk a few bruised feelings among the Great Ones of the army. And also, it is time you, Arnuwandas, started accustoming yourself to appearing from the halentuwa-house and performing kingly festivals. Telipinus has twice your experience in that regard. Now, do not argue with your father, but do as I have commanded you."

Thus I freed myself from not only the heroes' audience, but all the processionals surrounding the end of the Festival of Haste. Nor did I intend to visit the god's stations with my new queen, who was not yet ready to perform any sacrifices. In the matter of festival rites that winter, if my sons did not perform them, they were not performed; I needed more desperately the waking hours of my day than to waste them carting the deified fleece from temple to temple throughout the land.

So why was I risking the gods' displeasure upon the closure of such a successful campaign? There was the matter of my Babylonian queen, and how the people were accepting her. There was the matter of my chamberlain Hattu-ziti, who had been in Kumanni since my arrival, and was just that day returning to my city on the scarp. There was a certain Great Shepherd whose counsel I had long been without. And there was the news: the inscrutable, wry words of Aziru; the bleatings of Ribaddi of Byblos; the death screams from the city Sumuru, turned Amurrite in the time it took me to climb back up to the plateau. There were, not least of all, many royal prisoners, now deportees in Hittite prisons, waiting for me to find time to interrogate them, a task which I happily expected to take the winter long.

Far down my mental list waited the matter of Telipinus and the matter of my twins, Khinti's children, and weaning them from their black nurse. The affairs vying for my attention were piled up around me like snowdrifts, so deep that I could not walk, but must lunge through them. And when a man feels that mired, something is always forgotten in the confusion or, worse, not seen at all.

In the matter of Great Queen Malnigal, my new Tawananna, I was by turns perplexed, annoyed, enraged, mollified by her wiles, then perplexed once again. She, whose eyes had spat a surreptitious fire the whole time I was warring, now looked discontentedly upon my palace. No Hittite oils were fine enough for her skin, which in the long months she played the part of battlefield wife had first reddened, then peeled off, then bronzed until she looked like a Hittite warrior.

As her tan flaked away, so did her awe of things Hattian, until she was disappointed in this and dissatisfied with that, and ordering all sorts of alterations in her palace quarters and costly imported cosmetics, fabrics, foodstuffs and medicines from afar. As if that were not enough, she found my palace lacking in "civilized comforts" and even said this to me.

So I had suggested she go look at the residential palaces built on the terraces of rock above the pond, there where I had rebuilt the palace of the grandfather for my grown sons, promising her that if she preferred it, I would move out of the main palace. I had done it before, when I sought privacy. But no woman had wheedled me into it.

During her nosings about in the storage magazines, she had come upon the "glorious" Egyptian antiques I had ordered removed from my sight upon Daduhepa's death. Now these pieces of furniture had plagued me with their too-low seats and too-delicate construction in the time of my first queen and before that all through my youth, and I was not at all pleased by the delight my new great queen took in having discovered them. In fact, one of the first items on my docket was to find out from Hattu-ziti why they had not been given to someone, or sold off, or even destroyed.

"I thought I told you to get rid of them!"

"My lord?" He was just entering, arms laden with letters in their envelopes of clay, his sparsely-haired head swiveling as he crossed the room and laid them with a clatter on the table, so that never did his eyes leave mine.

"Those items of Egyptian manufacture which Daduhepa collected—we were free of them, I thought. Well, Malnigal has found them, and we are not rid of them anymore."

"They are very valuable, my lord Sun."

"They are very uncomfortable, my lord chamberlain, who hates ever to discard anything, even when he is ordered. Tell me, if you can, what is the fascination women, to the last sloe-eyed one of them, as far as I can see, have with things Egyptian?"

"Aha! Now, I have become an expert on Egypt, in the Sun's behalf. In the matter of women loving Egyptian craftsmanship, it is the precious woods and the mysteriously pleasing depictions carved into them; but more than that, it is that Egypt is a land which preens as if a woman had designed it all. The colors, the magnificent excesses, the statues colossal in dimension, all are executed like the most delicate of embroideries: no woman could resist a country which holds art and grace and pomp so high. And in their government, the Great Wife is more powerful than any Tawananna: any man who would be king in Egypt must have a blood or marriage connection with a solar princess, else in no way will the people accept him and let him be their god. But if that is done, then he is their god above all other gods: no god of diorite or marble or even of lapis is as precious to them, nor as richly adorned. Ah, my lord Sun, I have seen such wonders that I know not where to begin. . . ."

"Begin by assuring me you are not ready to separate from the Sun and become a citizen of Egypt. You sound like Lord Hani, the Honorable."

"Hani is a good man: a good man who serves a demented god-king who is also, though you may not understand this, *good,* and that is bad. . . . But it is the Egyptian *people* who are truly most good. They are so good, so tractable, so accepting, so full with love for the institution of kingship that even when its seat is occupied by an unfit king who can barely keep from befouling himself—that even when such a man is their Good God, the people remain lovers of their king."

"Hittite people love me," I said uncomfortably, squinting as hard as I could at Hattu-ziti, as if I could peer between the network of lines on his skin and into his heart.

"Hittite people are not like these people. My lord, the Sun would not want the kind of love I am talking about, nor the kind of people capable of it. Next to Hittite people, the Egyptians are sleepwalkers, lost in a dream of love and not seeing anything which is not fitting—they call it '*maat,*' which means the principle of order and rightness that indicates the place in nature's scheme of each thing—"

"Enough. I can barely believe that each year at New Year the gods convene and assign us our fates. That they are peering over my shoulder every moment, I cannot accept. Rightness. . . . Harken unto this: When a king seeks the gods, he must supplicate and supplicate; when a priest seeks the gods, he goes through all manner of ritual to attract their attention. Even with the Oath Gods, one can never be sure that they, whose task it is to do so, are really overseeing the bonds of the treaties they are invoked to rule over. Tell me not of the gods of Egypt who are eternal. Tell me of their living god, he who is to die. Better, tell me in few words the tale of your journey from beginning to end, leaving out everything but what directly affects international affairs."

"I would rather tell you of all the places I have been and the phenomena I have seen: there is no one else I could tell. But perhaps when the Sun has time. . ."

"Certainly, when I have the chance, we will talk of it. But now just give me what I need to know."

"Know then, my lord, that the Honorable Lord Hani is nothing if not peace-seeking, that he is a reasonable man and that the whole time we were on the ship, and while we walked among the temples of Karnak, and even when we saw the pharaoh's mother bearing her new son—begotten on her at Istar of Nineveh's coming to Egypt by Amenhotep the Third—that whole time, not one word did Hani speak of the Sun's expedition, then in progress, against Mitanni."

"So you are saying you think they will not interfere with me in matters of expansion, and that they are raising a successor to this Akhenaten in all haste?"

"I am saying they will not be able to interfere where Akhenaten dictates no interference. And I am saying that though all seems well in the City of the Horizon, up the river lies the stronghold of the god Amun, and there reside those who are capable of interfering."

"In your opinion, then, there is need? He is truly mad, young Naphuria Akhenaten?"

"Oh, no. It is normal to appear at audiences with towering crowns but no clothing, or clothing so revealing as to be no better than nakedness. Sane kings in Egypt, they have none. But of a god on earth are they possessed, who even says this to them, and more than that: he has appointed himself sole intermediary between his deity the Aten and the people. Do not mistake me: we have powerful opponents in Egypt. In Akhetaten they were all gathered to receive the tribute of the foreign lands. Ay, the 'Divine Father,' is as tall as yourself and nearly as great in inner stature. General Horemheb also bears watching, and not only for his military prowess—"

"When has Horemheb done any good?" I laughed. "If he is responsible for Aziru's successes, he is no threat to me."

"But he is 'Sole Friend' and he is related to Ay, the chief councilor. It is they who prop up Akhenaten on his throne."

"So you are saying tread carefully?"

"That is what I am saying, my lord Sun. I had more audiences in Egypt than either you or myself expected: this Ay decreed he must see me, and the mighty General Horemheb was in attendance. Yet they spoke not a single threat nor even broached the subject of Upper and Lower Retenu. And I had been sure that they would do so, if only because the Syrian princes were using the opportunity of their gathering together to try to dispatch each other, and three attempts on the lives of this or that monarch had been foiled at great peril by that day."

"What did they talk about, then?"

"They asked me of your sons and were polite and went on at length about what I should see while I remained in their country, and queried me upon the impression I was taking back to you of their empire, and in all ways did nothing I expected and did not do anything which I, or you, or any king's subject in Hatti would have done."

"And what else?"

"Not a thing: it is quite remarkable. Everyone there pretends that all is well: that there is no war raging above their heads; that they are not losing strength and protectorates; that the royal family is untroubled and happy. Everyone strives to project the impression that he is unutterably content. I almost forgot the Sun was raiding whilst I stood there. I found it impossible to credit the actual situation with the danger I had placed on it beforehand. In the one instance when war was mentioned, they were proclaiming some triumph that either never took place or of which we in the north have heard nothing."

"Most likely more Egyptian history: once spoken, it is thus evermore. I understand that. I was ordering my deeds for inclusion in a treaty prologue while at Halap. I left out the campaign I waged against Tushratta that got me this." I touched the scar on my head, where it ran into my eyebrow. "I did not speak a word about it, though how it slips my mind now and then I cannot understand." I grinned.

Hattu-ziti did not grin, but said: "My friend, Suppiluliumas, my king . . . think upon all the years I have served you. Give a moment to the days when the great double walls about Hattusas were only our dreams in the dirt of the infirmary floor in Samuha. Then hear me: do not make light of Egypt. The sphinx is treacherous. Should she be irritated enough to arise, she will crush us with a flick of her tail. The might of thousands of years is not conceivable until your own eyes have seen it. I have seen it, and I tell you: beware."

"I had someone's life taken for saying that to me once. An Old Woman, do you recall her?"

He nodded, but he was not affrighted by me. He went on speaking as if I had said nothing at all:

"In the smaller arena of events, there is the boy Kantuzilis, who has been assisting me since our departure to foreign lands. He is a joy to the heart of a heartless old man who has begotten no children. But even allowing for that, he will shine in the Sun's behalf in days to come."

"Keep him, then. What of Duttu, our friend with the hole in his pocket?"

"Egyptian kilts do not have pockets."

"Is that, then, his problem?"

"His problem is writer's cramp: he sends twice as much correspondence out of Egypt as he receives. I instructed him to make small of Aziru's detractors, and to bother Akhenaten as infrequently as possible with the depressing affairs of foreign wars. He was at first unsure that he could afford so bold a move, but since I agreed to further subsidize him—"

"*What?* How much more does this Duttu think he is worth? I could field a column of chariotry for what I am paying him!"

"Does the Sun want to give up on the Amurrite and let Aziru lose his head? It would be half the cost to aid him openly, for it is twice as dangerous to Duttu to cause tablets to be misfiled and wrongly marked as having been under the king's attention, as to us to send six hundred chariots to his aid."

"That much?"

"Does the Sun wish me not to send it?"

"Send it. Send Duttu howsoever much gold you have agreed to send. No one helped me. It will destroy Aziru if I take things out of his hands so that he finds out about it. Aziru's troubles: you do not understand my interest, do you?"

"I am not questioning you, Suppiluliumas," he said, suddenly jowly.

"Look, then: Here I sit, and I am a great king. And off goes Aziru to Egypt, because he is not. And of all the men I have faced in battle, none have been his equal. Had Tushratta of Mitanni been as kingly as Aziru of Amurru, he and I would have met face to face ere this. When Tushratta slipped through my fingers last season, I finally became clear about why I have been so generous to the Amurrite: he is a born king. I would have Tushratta's fat rendered down to oil by now, had he half the kingship in him that Aziru has. It is a joke of the Storm-god, to cause such a man to be born into the wrong race, into the wrong station. I have no son so kingly."

"You have four sons as kingly: Arnuwandas, Piyassilis, Telipinus, and even young Zannanza. The Amurrite is but older, more desperate, more flamboyant. However, as I have said, it is not my place to tell you what to do, and I am not going to presume upon you further. Would you look at these documents I have brought?"

"No, I would not. But I must, so I will."

When we had done with them, which were all concerned with my new vassals and their various reactions to Aziru's taking of the city Sumuru, I excused him and went straightaway down into the cellars, for while I had been reading over all those honeyed, grasping protestations of my new vassals, I had remembered the prisoner whom I had promised myself I would first look over: Aitakama, the son of the king of Kinza, who had so valiantly lost to me in battle, and whose father had died on the journey of wounds sustained at my hand. The thing I wanted to do with him had not been decided in my mind until I heard all the words of his compatriots in Hittite Syria speaking from the clay: he would be ultimately useful if I could give him back his lands in a vassal king's fief and reinstall him on his hereditary throne. I would be easing tempers and soothing fears from the Niblani mountains to Byblos, should I succeed in accomplishing such a thing.

I did not have him brought out: I went myself, alone, into his cell. He was in relative comfort but he did not know it, and he spat defiantly at me, rattling his shackles and demanding to know if I would like my own sons treated thus.

Now Aitakama of Kinza had formerly shaved his head, and it was growing out since he had neither obsidian razor nor free hands to shave himself. The aspect he presented was arresting: down upon his chest lay his matted beard, and all about his skull stood out a bush of hair like a horse's bristles when they are cut so that they stand up from the neck. He had wounds that were well into scarring on both his arms, and his torso was striped here and there with them. He was not of the nut-brown, wiry variety of person, with curly hair and curly nose, which populates some of Kinza, but a burly shock-headed bear, stoutly made and inclined to a bulging belly, the kind of man for whom no feat of endurance is too arduous. He was no boy, this Aitakama, who stood somewhere in his prime between Aziru's age and my own, nor did he show any sign of contrition or fear on his sloping, boneless face.

"What do you want, king of Hatti?" he lowered, lumbering to his knees, arms held high so that the rope running between his neck and his fetters swayed as he shifted his weight from side to side.

I wondered if I had miscalculated and no real intelligence rested behind those flat, uptilted eyes.

"I want to make an ally of you, Aitakama; a vassal, should you agree. I want to win you to my cause, and restore you to kingship under my guidance. What say you?"

His mouth opened, hung there until he noticed it. Then he chuckled, threw back his head and began to roar.

I found myself also amused, but not to tears. But then, it was not my life we were talking about.

"I say," gasped Aitakama of Kinza, "let us discuss the matter in friendly fashion," and when I cut the ropes securing his shackles, he could not at once free himself from them.

He wiped his eyes on his forearm, rested a fettered wrist on his knee to steady it, and remarked that if I were making light of him, and meant none of what I had just said, then even so he thanked me, for hope had almost gone out of him.

And I was perfectly happy to put it back.

I gave him the run of the palace, in the care of Zidanza and two Meshedi, and I made sure that in all things he was treated as a prince. When my sons came to briefings, there also, I promised, Aitakama would be. And I impressed upon him the high value I placed on candor while I probed him for resentment held against me from his imprisonment and the matter of his father's death. I found none, only an appetite for life that I was more than willing to satisfy. I made plans to restore him in Kinza in the coming spring.

"Shepherd, it is the only thing that makes any sense."

"You cannot know his heart, Tasmi. Any man will jump at the chance of life when death's spittle is on his cheek. Later, when the specter is remanded to memory, abstract fear will not hold him: the horse does not respond to the memory of the bit, only the bit in his mouth will do."

"He has nowhere to go."

"He can go back to Egypt, taking his country with him."

I scoffed. "He is a prince, soon to be a king. He will remain loyal to his oath. And if he does not, I can crush him then. Then, now: it makes no difference. The only way to test the wind is to lick your finger and stick it out there. It is worth a thousand words of caution to turn him loose and see what he will do. And I am planning to keep him busy. He goes, next new moon, upon the first day of the New Year! And that is that. Let us talk of something else."

"What?"

"What? Why I, the Sun summon a certain Shepherd, Man of the Storm-god to my presence, and must languish the entire winter in Hattusas before he sees fit to arrive."

"Did I not put your affairs before my own and labor the whole year in Hattusas while you went out plundering without me? Was I not getting fat and soft and bleary in the eyes and rusty of tongue while you were romping about in the lands of eternal summer?"

"Eternal oven, you mean. Five months of blasting heat and five months of arid bleak nights and windy white days and that sky with never a cloud. . . You want the south, Kuwatna-ziti? It is yours. I give it to you. Laughing at My Majesty, are you? Keep it up, and I will do it: then you will be a poor sway-backed king trying to hold up his piece of heaven with the rest of us, and you will not be laughing anymore! Now, why did you not come to greet me?"

"Tasmi, I have a life of my own. Not much of one, has the Empire left me, but what little there is, I hold close to my heart."

"That is not right; you cannot have what is denied to me!"

"Is it not fair? You went out on the most important campaign since Mursili the Mighty raided Babylon, and you left me here to copy treaties and feed the gods their meals! Now, since you were coming back, I took a leave. I went to my daughter's wedding. I visited my house in Arinna. With my lord's permission, I reacquainted myself with my wives."

He was barking mad, was the Shepherd.

"Kuwatna-ziti, I had no idea you longed so for the field. I am sorry, truly touched. Not again will I do that to you—But this year, there was no one else who could serve in my stead."

"Will you say that to me next year? I will not hear you!"

"I have just said I would not. Shepherd, must you yet berate me like a parent?'"

"Tasmi, you have lost all sense of proportion. I am merely restoring it. I have certain delicate matters to bring to your attention."

"What, then?" I said in a deliberate, calm tone, trying to get my temper in hand, and what rode all about my anger: guilt that the Shepherd had been penned up. As he said, I had done it. But I had to do it. Still, I felt remorse.

"The matter of Telipinus. He has come to me and asked me to mediate between you."

I squeezed shut my eyes and harnessed an imaginary team of horses to an imaginary chariot, very slowly, giving attention to each detail.

"What makes him think he cannot come to me himself?"

"He wants to come to you himself, but he is not ready to meet with your Tawananna—with Malnigal. He said to tell you that his heart simply will not allow it until he speaks with you privately."

"All right, let it be done. But you are not thinking to obstruct me again, as you did in the matter of Titai, are you? Remember what sorrow came from that? This time, it will not be I who suffers. I have got this Babylonian bitch, and I care not at all about her personally, but she is and will be Great Queen of Hatti. And all will accept her, because it is expedient, because her father is a great king, my equal, and his position and his friendliness and his strategic location are important to me. I should not need to justify this marriage, which has been so long in culminating that everyone had plenty of time to accustom themselves to it."

"Tasmi, in the matters of your women, I would never again presume to interfere. In the matter of a queen, your proclamation is sufficient to command my loyalty."

"Then, Great Shepherd, help me. For in the matter of Telipinus, I cannot see how I can prevail. The very thought of confronting him turns me pale and weak, as if I were a woman myself."

"I heard of how you settled the matter in the cases of Arnuwandas and Piyassilis. Was that really necessary?"

"Think about it for a moment, and then tell me you would not have done it exactly the same. I have no room for an additional woman in my heart: Khinti's ghost yet resides there. And even if I were not haunted like a man who has failed to perform his god's sacrifice, still, I would have done it: they, my sons, must not feel that I have thrown them over. Nor must Malnigal be allowed to harbor in her heart any dreams of coming to power over them."

"Tasmi, I wonder if you are not taking out on this girl all your sorrows; and that leads me to wonder how she can possibly understand it—and you. You will make her dangerous, if she is not already, by constantly reassuring her of how little is the place for her in your life. Few concubines could accept that. How much harder will it be on a queen? And as for there being no room in your heart for another woman, she is already in your bed. Is the Sun so afraid of what he might come to feel? She is pregnant, I have heard. And when she bears, if it is a son, and if by then you have not left off punishing her for her sex and all the hurts you fancy you have endured from previous queens, then how will it go? She is not in any way aware of the ancient history that obsesses you and makes her life cold and lonely: she knows nothing of your previous queens. But she knows queenship. She was born a princess. If she bears you a son and you still treat her like a namra, she will surely fall to manipulating affairs to her son's benefit: you will have made it her only salvation. And then you will have created all the troubles you are laboring to abort aforetime."

I fled from him to the window, refused his face, and sought the view instead. To the mountains I spoke then, very softly, saying, "Then tell me what to do. For in these matters I am helpless as a child, blind as a beggar, weak as a half-starved slave."

Not until I had commended Aitakama of Kinza to the fates, sent him back to his kingship with an introduction to Aziru of Amurru in his hand and the Sun's wishes in his mind, did Telipinus deign to visit me in Hattusas.

The day was not propitious. I had just received a messenger from Amurru, whose tidings had not at all pleased me. It was midsummer and hotter than I could ever remember it having been in Hattusas at that season. When we went down into Syria and there was a drought there, and when that drought continued to plague the Mitanni lands the entire time I was attacking them, year after year, folk said that the Thousand Gods had brought drought upon the lands to aid the Hittite armies. I wondered, that morning, whose gods were getting the credit for this season's early heat: Hatti was not officially fighting anyone. Tushratta's whereabouts were unknown. Egypt's palaces seemed asleep in the summer sun: to Aitakama of Kinza's assumption of his father's throne, the Egyptians had made no reply; nor to his delicate announcement of his autonomy over his father's land; nor to his obligatory pleas for Egyptian money and troops. By my will he was continuing to suggest he was yet an Egyptian vassal.

Meanwhile, Aitakama and Aziru of Amurru were making each other's acquaintance, raiding here and there, setting small towns afire and looting in a way they must have hoped would seem to me random, but which was in reality a canny plan to extend their borders and prop up their own kingships by picking off smaller princes and absorbing the conquered kingdoms into Amurru or Kinza.

No sooner had I sent orders—by way of Piyassilis, Tarkhunta-zalma and six hundred chariots—that both Aitakama and Aziru prepare to lend their strength to Hittite forces I was just then loosing on Egypt's country of Amqa, than I received a courier from Piyassilis.

This courier brought a message, which Piyassilis had intercepted from the beleaguered princes of the Amqa area to Pharaoh, saying: "We are in the land of Amqa, in the cities of the king . . .

Aitakama of Kinza has gone to meet the troops of Hatti and he has set the cities of the king on fire."

And I was distressed, for more than one reason. I was distressed because I had not wanted it revealed that the instigators in the Amqa fighting had been Hittite: as I have said, officially we were not fighting anyone. I was distressed because Aziru's name was conspicuously missing from the document before me. In fact, where Aziru's name should have been was Hatti incriminated instead. Aziru was not following his orders, not at all. And I was distressed, finally, by the interception of the message itself: where one messenger is apprehended, five, six, or more may have slipped through.

So, having ascertained that Aziru was no longer cooperating with his brother vassal Aitakama, I had been about to call for Pikku and dictate an order to Piyassilis to arrest the Amurrite and bring him up to me, when I was interrupted by the announcement of the arrival in my palace of a messenger from Amurru.

Now, it was a good thing, the way I was feeling, that this messenger was no brother or son of Aziru. He might never have left there alive, might never have gotten to deliver his message.

But when I saw he was not, I said nothing of my wrath, only bade him leave what he had brought and wait without.

This he did, and when he was gone I cracked the clay envelope on the table's edge without any concern as to what might be broken within.

But the tablet slid whole out of its sleeve, and there was no message from Aziru to me scribed into the clay. No, there was not. But there was no need. What he had sent me was a copy of a letter he had sent to Naphuria Akhenaten, "explaining" to Pharaoh why he had not been able to rebuild the sacked city Sumuru, and why he had not been in Amurru awaiting the Egyptian Lord Hani, a prediction he had made while he was submitting himself to My Majesty after coming to meet me from Tunib, if you will recall. Truth notwithstanding, this is what the tablet said:

"As to Hani, I dwelt in Tunib, and did not know he had come. I went after him, but did not overtake him. Now may he come safely, and may you, my lord Pharaoh, ask him how I, Aziru, have taken care of him. My brothers stood before Hani, gave him oxen, birds, food and drink. I have given horses and asses for his journey. . . . When I come before Pharaoh, my lord, Hani will come to meet me like a mother and a father. You say: 'You held back from Hani.' But your gods and the solar disk know that I was dwelling in Tunib. As to the rebuilding of Sumuru, Pharaoh, my lord, has spoken. The kings of Nuhasse are hostile, and have taken my cities on the advice of the man Hatib. Consequently, I have not rebuilt it. But now I will rebuild it in haste. You know that Hatib has taken half the implements and all the gold and silver you gave me. Furthermore you say: 'Why did you take care of the messenger of Hatti, and not of my messenger?' This is the land of my lord, Pharaoh. And you have placed me under the regents. Let your messenger come. I will give provisions, ships, boxwoods and other woods."

So, smiling in spite of myself, I decided not to call Pikku to send Piyassilis an order to arrest and deport Aziru to Hatti. Rather, I called Pikku and dictated a brief condolence to Aziru in the matter of his troubles with Hatib, and a suggestion that when I next heard from him I would hear he was aiding Aitakama in troubling Amqa, the country which yet so well loved Pharaoh, and banished the matter from my thoughts, that I might prepare myself to receive my son the Priest.

It was nearly a year since I had last seen Telipinus. Since I had come back from campaigning in Syria by way of Nuhasse, he and I had not been face to face. There had been no ill words spoken between us, but there had been no words at all. A priest or a king can always lay the responsibility for his unwillingness to face this matter or that at the gods' feet: because of celebrating this festival in such-and-such a town; or performing some long-neglected ritual on a riverbank; or sniffing out the truth about whatever case by incubation, the Priest of Kumanni had always been too busy to meet with me.

And that day, Malnigal was about to go into labor. As an expectant father paces the hall awaiting the cry of his newborn, so did I pace my small, dark retreat, awaiting my intractable prince. No thought had I then for my wife's condition, only for the conditions she had brought about between myself and Telipinus. If the truth be known, I had given no thought to anything else but this long-awaited visit by Telipinus since I had heard of it eight days before. I think now that I would not have pressed Aitakama and Aziru so fiercely into line and so dangerously into service, if I had not been thus preoccupied. Then, matters flew from my attention like messenger doves once their duties had been performed. No sooner did an affair of foreign lands alight upon my hand and I make an answer, than it flew away again and left me wondering what under heaven I might say to the Priest to restore relations between us to what they once had been.

When I was sitting in my favorite chair, supported by the ever-crouching carved sphinxes of Hatti, with my son Telipinus' bony, ascetic frame opposite me and his piercing gaze reproving me, his feelings as yet unspoken, I still did not have a single glimmer of hope that things might be made well between us. So, not having any alternative, I said:

"What can I do that will heal this rift, that will bring back to the Sun the love of his son, Telipinus? What cure has the Priest for his father, who is sick with grief? What will turn my prince's face back toward me, you who have separated from me and no longer love me?"

And I could not further speak to him. Never had I spoken of love in so many words to anyone since the days of Titai. Never had I said it to Khinti, never to any of them. I found it harder to say than a submission uttered upon one knee.

Telipinus, blinking, his countenance twisting about, rose up from his chair, took a step toward me with outstretched hand, then drew back. And the hand became a fist that resounded upon the table. With a sob he put his weight on the flat of his hands, and leaned over toward me, tears like rivers inundating him, and demanded brokenly how I could speak thus. After all that I had done, how could I expect him to love me? Did the gods love me, and I ignore their worship? Did my wife Khinti, his stepmother, love me, and I banish her from the land? Did my children love me, and I take another above them?

I took him, then, in my arms like a lover. He struggled a moment, and the manly rage went out of him, and the priestly censure, and he sobbed against me, a boy once more. I stroked his hair as I had never done when he was small, and murmured things my kingship had never let me say when his ears longed to hear them. And all the while my priestly prince sobbed soft gulping sobs that choked him. Some time in that interval, when I could no longer speak, his arms went around me and pulled tight, and we stood there however long, holding each other as if by our desperation we could press so close that no person or thing could ever again insinuate itself between us.

We stayed like that until startled out of it by the importunate pounding of a messenger battering on the door to say that Malnigal had entered into her labor, and requesting my presence.

"I will come. Tell her," I called thickly, without allowing the door to open, that none see the tear-swollen faces and trembling limbs of two who ruled in Hatti.

"I will go with you," said Telipinus through puffy lips. "There is no better time than the present."

"Then," I replied; dashing water on my face and inviting him to do the same, "let us see to it."

She was lying upon a couch I had taken from the palace at Alalakh; its feet were ivory carved in the likeness of horses' hooves; its frame was boxwood into which a processional scene was inlaid with mother-of-pearl, with bitumen, with jasper and alabaster. The pitcher from which cool cloths were laid upon her brow was of solid gold. Her couch had been spread with yards of pure white linen, a fortune's worth of it; and on that snowy surface Malnigal's soundless struggles were near to consummation as we arrived.

Her legs up, taut belly shining, her head thrown back and eyes rolling, she gasped: "My . . . husband. . . . I was waiting, waiting until you had come." And with a groan deep as the earth's when it moves, she raised up her belly toward the ceiling.

I had time to reach her, through the rattling sistrums and the clouds of blue, pungent smoke; through the inevitable crowd of palace functionaries who attend the birth-throes of queens. As I stroked her brow, calmed her and offered my hand for her to bite or squeeze, Telipinus positioned himself by the birthing bed and dismissed the officiating priest. She raised her head, to which black curls clung wetly, to examine him, whose voice was unlike the other priest's.

"My son, Telipinus the Priest. Your son. . ."

"Priest," she grated, "I am ready if you are."

And even as Telipinus droned the incantation and the Old Women muttered, Malnigal screamed and arched, and beads of perspiration turned to rivulets and inundated her convulsion-wracked form. A moment, and two, and three, and Telipinus invoked his lady, the Sun-goddess of Arinna, and his hands reached for Malnigal's belly. With an abrupt shudder, my Babylonian queen lay motionless, panting. Telipinus, crooning the gods' words, reached between her legs, raised up the bloody, struggling child, laid it on her collapsed belly and cut the cord.

Then she reached out with her hands, blindly, for her eyes were closed and streaming tears, whispering, "Suppiluliumas, his name, his name. Give a name to your son."

Wiping his priestly palms, Telipinus leaned close and took the newborn prince from her, handing him into my arms.

Whereupon Malnigal stiffened, half rose, fell back, and demanded her mirror. When the silver mirror was brought, she bade me face him into the mirror and bespeak his name.

The Priest looked at me and I back at him, for it was her own Babylonian mystery she invoked upon us all then. But the girl, so beautiful, flushed with exertion and glowing in that moment of a woman's triumph, got her way.

Holding her child, who coughed but did not cry, I knelt down by the bed and spoke the child's name, calling him Mursili, acknowledging him as a full prince then and there before all.

Then Malnigal held the mirror up to his face and my own, blew on the silver to fog it and, with her finger tracing a sign upon the misted metal, said, "Mursili, king of the universe, lord over creation, son of the Sun," and a great deal more I did not understand in some ancient tongue.

As she was speaking, she took the little prince from me and laid him between her breasts. And as he wriggled sightlessly to find her teat, she said that she thought it a fine name, since if not for Mursili I, after whom I had named him, her father's dynasty would never have come to rule in Babylon. Then, smiling that knowing smile from her most beautiful countenance, she raised her gaze and extended her hand to Telipinus, who took it and was seemingly lost to her, all hostility forgotten, whilst Malnigal whispered how long she had craved the attendance of the Priest.

And I was happy enough that she had not been offended by my choice in the child's naming, for Mursili I had sacked Babylon, put her to the torch and drove away again, leaving a crippled city writhing in his wake, which then fell to the hill folk who happened along to claim her: Malnigal's progenitors, the Kassites.

So I turned to examining the child, his straight arms and legs, his wizened features, his shock of black hair and his manhood: all were faultless, of great proportion, kingly if there is that quality in a newborn. His campaign to reach Malnigal's teat was eminently successful, and he occupied the belly of his kingship as aggressively as a man might wish. I stuck my forefinger out and touched him with it. Baby fists flailed and a baby mouth opened with a cry of inarticulate rage.

She was watching me, I must suppose, for when I looked up from him her attitude was beatific, her eyes like a replete lioness, triumphant. "You are content with him," she pronounced.

"I am content with you," I said, and stroked her flaring cheek. Telipinus came to her with water in a golden cup. Then I raised her and she sipped from it, the baby clutched against her fiercely, although he screamed and kicked. She would give him up to no wet-nurse while she was living, she said, but when she drifted off into exhausted sleep we took him from her.

Then Telipinus and I went off to celebrate, and when we were deeply enmired in wine, I realized how much the sweat-glistened woman struggling to present me with an heir had aroused me. So I called out the team of dancers I had taken from Alalakh and, after they danced for us, we found other things to do with them, like stripping off their kirtles and their beads.

"What was that?" I asked him abruptly, from the valley of pleasure. "What was it she did with the mirror and the Babylonian rite?"

"You ought to leave a line of succession, if you do not want him someday to rule in Hattusas. Istar, in all her attributes, Malnigal invoked, and who is the counterpart of the Sun-goddess of Arinna in Babylon's pantheon, also." While Telipinus was speaking, he was stripping down the last dancer, whose breasts, like Malnigal's, left nothing to be desired. He mouthed brief praise of them, then knifed around to face me: "You say nothing, lord and father. The Sun-goddess of Arinna, she who regulates kingship and queenship, has been called into attendance in the matter of my new brother. He will reign over us all, one day."

"You are not displeased," I said, my attention half with the girl who kissed about my loins, half upon the conversation, reminding myself that Telipinus had second sight.

"No, it is not other than I expected. But you have stepped upon a path that will lead you back into the south. Do you wish to know why?"

"I know why. I do not need you to tell me. I will have no one son over the others in the matter of kingship. All my sons will have, each one, his realm, and he who sits in Hattusas will but coordinate the empire."

Roughly, Telipinus pushed away the three girls, rolled over, looked deep into my heart, and said: "There is death on that path."

"Better than dying in a creaking palace bed, or of the weight of years while performing a sacrifice."

"May the Storm-god, my lord, and his consort, my lady Arinniti, aid us all."

CHAPTER 30

Telipinus' invocation seemed, as the months wore on, to have been effective indeed. I stayed in Hattusas, played with my new son, acquainted myself with my queen. Her beauty was widely celebrated in the country; foreign ambassadors who came up to Hatti would compare her favorably to Naphuria Akhenaten's wife, Nefertiti, said to be the most beautiful woman in all the world.

And it pleased me, for I am as vain as any man, to think that my woman was more beautiful than the king of Egypt's woman, who purportedly rivaled the moon in her magnificence.

None were more shocked than we to hear that the king of Egypt had demoted his renowned queen, indeed had removed her name from his monuments. It was said he would marry his daughter, by those who should have known. It was said he would marry his brother, by those who liked him not. It was said by those who read portents in Hattusas that he would put the whole of Egypt in a bath of natron for seventy days and embalm it so all that would be left would be a few towering temples and sealed tombs—that is, unless the earth opened up and swallowed him whole.

It was said by Egypt that both Upper and Lower Retenu (of which she considered me and my people a part) were crumbling away into the "sea of Asiatics." It was said that as Byblos went, so would go the Egyptian protectorates above the Nile's mouth; and that Byblos, the pharaoh's city, wavered on the verge of collapsing into Aziru's waiting arms.

None of these things were said to me formally, for Egypt and I were maintaining a diplomatic silence neither wanted to break. But Duttu was sending me up from Akhenaten's chancery every letter he received in Pharaoh's name which mentioned myself, or Aziru of Amurru, or any of my protectorates: Nuhasse, Mukis, Halap, Alalakh, Kinza. So what was said to Naphuria Akhenaten was said to me also, although I must admit that by all accounts he was not listening, and I the Sun most assuredly was.

It was said by poor Ribaddi (Egypt's governor of Byblos, who had endured year after year of Amurrite hostility) that he had fled to his brother's city, and that all Pharaoh's cities were falling away to Aziru, whose hostility to him grew daily more overt. Now, I do not know what Ribaddi of Byblos expected from the Amurrite: Ribaddi had killed Aziru's man in Tyre and supplanted him with his own; Ribaddi had been instrumental in Aziru's father's death. Aziru was a man who savored revenge. But how Aziru would exact his revenge, even I was then unsure. When, at the beginning of the following year, Ribaddi's own brother expelled him from his refuge and declared himself an open supporter of Aziru's, I understood. But perhaps Naphuria Akhenaten did not understand. Or, as many said, perhaps he did not care.

I will admit some items of correspondence for your scrutiny, so you will see why I was content to school Khinti's son Zannanza in princely ways and wait like an eagle on the rock sanctuary's pinnacle, to see what might develop.

Firstly, a letter of which I made good use by subsequently demanding of Aziru that I also be privy to the intelligence of which it spoke:

Wrote Abimilki of Tyre to Akhenaten: "But behold, I am guarding Tyre the great city, for the king, my lord, until the mighty power of the king come unto me, to give water for me to drink, and wood wherewith to warm myself. Further: Zimreda, the king of Sidon, has written every day to the criminal Aziru, son of Abdi-asirta, concerning everything that he heard from Egypt. Behold, I have written to my lord: it is good that you should know."

When I informed Aziru that I too knew, I began receiving this Zimreda's correspondence, and thus had a check on whether or not what Duttu was telling me was true.

And Aziru was even gracious in this matter, for he knew as well as I that once Ribaddi was expelled by his brother, it would be only a matter of time until Aziru would be smelling his blood.

Once more did Duttu forward to me the pathetic bleatings of Egypt's loyal governor, and I had to agree with Ribaddi's own words: "Behold our city Byblos! There is much wealth of the king in it, the property of our forefathers. If the king does not intervene for the city, all the cities of Canaan will no longer be his. Let the king not ignore this deed."

But ignore Aziru's persecution of Ribaddi and his increasingly fierce besieging of Byblos, Pharaoh did. He did not lift a finger to aid his servant, not even when Ribaddi was expelled from his final refuge with Ammunira of Beruta, and fell into Aziru's trap. Death at the hands of the Amurrite's allies, the rulers of Sidon, was Ribaddi's reward for a lifetime of loyal service to his king, the pharaoh.

This affair nearly had me harnessing my team, for had Akhenaten's professed oblivion to all things not concerned with the worship of his god the Aten continued, I surely would have been rolling down into Syria again that spring of my twenty-third regnal year.

But just as I was thinking about it—convening my greats to discuss a hasty campaign to take advantage of what was by then Akhenaten's well-demonstrated disinterest, when I was finally finding time to listen to Hattu-ziti's glorious tales of Pharaoh's

naked self driving a white and golden chariot whose white horses had gold trimmed harness, and even hooves gilded so they
shone — we heard two things so unbelievable and yet so very
intriguing that I put away all thoughts of war.

First, we heard that Naphuria Akhenaten had indeed married
his daughter, one Meritaten, whom Malnigal's father referred to
as "Mayati" when he wrote to my wife about Egyptian matters
and urged Malnigal to write to her sister, whom my father-in-law
had given to Akhenaten as a wife.

Although I refused to allow Malnigal to begin any direct
correspondence with persons living in Egypt, even if the person
was her full sister, I was amused that Akhenaten and I were thus
brothers-in-law, and pleased to have such an un-Hattian affair
confirmed by a source other than Duttu. It was Malnigal, whilst
she fed Mursili his last breast-meal, who explained to me that
the marriage was Akhenaten's way of assuring his claim to the
throne, having to do with bloodlines and solar princesses and
the fact that Akhenaten had sired no male heirs.

I shrugged and said that incest, no matter what the excuse, is
still incest, and she observed that had Egypt not been practicing
the custom for hundreds of years, the cone-headed ones would
not be weak and maddened, fit for the taking.

And I smiled and kissed her forehead and observed that she
should not flaunt her ability to read the Sun's mind. She was wearing, that day, a headdress of solid gold which her father had sent,
a gift from her sister in Egypt. I had almost forbidden her to accept it. We were a rich nation then, but not rich enough for such
excess. Down to her shoulders from the top of her head extended
this mantle, like hair: a thin, linked complexity of gold rosettes
which she wore with all her black mane braided in a multitude of
tiny plaits beneath. But she loved it so, I did not deny it to her. In
fact, I was denying her less and less: all the treasures I had taken
in the southern lands were hers to choose; whatever delighted
her I gave her gladly. Khinti became like the blue-cloaked lord,
relegated to my dreams and my half-drunken dawns.

On the very day Malnigal first wore this queenly headdress, an Amurrite messenger raced into Hattusas, bearing the second astounding message of the season, a message that had me pacing my walls, barking like a froth-mouthed dog, and taking omens as if I believed in them for nearly two years afterward.

Behold this message that Pharaoh Naphuria Akhenaten sent to Aziru, containing commands that Aziru had no choice but to obey:

"To Aziru, the man of Amurru. Thus speaks Pharaoh: If you desire to do evil, or lay up evil words in your heart, you will die by Pharaoh's axe, together with your whole family. Render submission to the king, then, and you shall live.

"Did you not say, 'Pharaoh, leave me alone this year, and I will come next year.' And I left you that year. Come, and you will see the pharaoh by whom all lands live. Do not say: 'Let him leave me alone also this year.' If it is impossible for you to come, then send your son.

"You wrote: 'Send me Hani a second time, and I will send by him the opponents of Pharaoh.' Behold, I send you a tablet with the names of the opponents of Pharaoh. Send them to me, with bands of copper as fetters on their feet. Know that Pharaoh is as well as the sun in heaven; his soldiers and his many chariots from the upper land and the lower land, from rising sun to setting sun, are very well."

And with this, from Aziru, was a terse message to me, saying:

"Look you, what the Sun of Hatti has done. Remember your oath to maintain my sons, and may the Adad of Heaven make these things right."

I sent back with the messenger words of optimism, more than I felt. I offered once again my full and unstinting protection, even saying that if Aziru came instead to Hatti, then I would hold his person in my very palace, safe from all violence. But both I, as I wrote, and he, surely when he read, knew such a thing could not come to be.

In fact, so dangerous would such a move have been on my part, with Naphuria Akhenaten awakened at last, that Kuwatnaziti cautioned me to send no such offer to Aziru.

"There are some things a man does against all reason, because he must, because his heart tells him. Now, Aziru is about to be trundled off to Akhenaten as a prisoner, mostly upon my account. I must make the offer. He will not accept it, though if he were any less mad than myself, he surely would."

"Tasmi, I beg you, do not become further involved."

"You should have begged me twelve years ago, when I went out to get my head split by Mitanni, or before that, when I first crossed paths with Aziru on Alashiya. You were not saying anything then. Now it is too late."

"So Telipinus assures me. But, Great King, the Sun, Tabarna, my lord, if you will recollect, you did not consult me in the matter of raiding that season in Mitanni, or rather did not heed my consultation. And when you were on the island of Alashiya, you had not seen fit to take me with you, and never have you consulted me about your dealings with this criminal of Amurru since the beginning of your acquaintance, down to this very day. In fact, I have never set eyes on him."

"Shepherd, calm down. I am not going anywhere, and Aziru has Hatib to aid him in Egypt—"

The Shepherd snorted, suggested that I do as I pleased, since I would do only that in any case, and stalked out. But I was right.

Aziru did not call me on my offer of hospitality. He went docile as a lamb down to rejoice in the City of the Horizon. And there did he stay, as the summer spent itself and the autumn seared the land and the winter came and went. And we were chewing on our nails in Hattusas, for there was the smallest chance that Aziru would not lose his head, but only forget his loyalties. And if all the things I had been doing to obstruct Egyptian sovereignty were spoken to Naphuria Akhenaten's face, it would start a war the proportions of which had never been seen in all of former times. The Hyksos invasion of Egypt would be as bush-fight in

Gasga when compared to the carnage all my generals and officials assured me would come of Aziru's protracted stay in Egypt.

I was urged by Takkuri and some few others to have Aziru
murdered, his throat cut before out of it could issue my own
death. But though I could have done it as easily as lifting my pale-
haired princess up to ride on my shoulders, I was not so sure as
they that anything anyone said would incriminate me more than
the years had done . . . and too, this was Aziru they were talking
about assassinating. So I stolidly refused all that and waited the
year out with a calmer aspect than I felt.

I heard that Abimilki of Tyre was abandoning his city, Egypt's
city, to the brothers of Aziru and his adherents, who evidently
felt that all was lost in the matter of Aziru's life, and so warred
more determinedly, extracting what satisfaction they could by
sacking Egyptian cities, raping Egyptian women, spending Egyptian gold. Even my vassal Niqmad, king of Ugarit, they attacked,
and I could do little but support my Ugaritic interests against
Amurru, with whose present rulers, Aziru's kin, I had no surreptitious treaty. Also, while Aziru was gone, I was receiving no
dispatches from Amurru of any sort.

All my court was telling me that I had failed, that I should
have taken Aziru's country by force, or burned it down around
his ears when I had had the chance.

And I could but wait, and taste sour criticism to which I was
not ready to answer, and wait more.

My twins, those that Khinti had birthed me, were ten that
season. Malnigal's fruitless efforts to win their hearts away from
the black girl Lord Hani had given me out of Egyptian generosity
on Alashiya lessened, then ceased altogether as her son came more
and more to occupy her mind. Also, it became clear that she was
again pregnant, which was not surprising since somehow she had
come to exercise sovereignty over my nights, although I neither
expected nor desired to desire her above my others, only wanted
to allow my Tawananna her rights of queenship, nothing more.

I was not the only one she ensorcelled. No, the whole of the
palace was taken with the queenly beauty, the dignity and per-

fection of Malnigal, whose son was already labeled "precocious" by those who pay attention to such things.

We celebrated the New Year's festival together: she had been diligently memorizing Hittite ritual texts under Telipinus' tutelage; there was none better suited to make the teaching easy, for Telipinus had much studied the correspondences of foreign gods, and Malnigal was a woman greatly inclined to mysteries and priestesses' ways.

I was as content as a man can be with an unsettled empire, and since the troubles were all in foreign lands I did not have to look at them if I wished a peaceful interlude. And I took one, or Malnigal witched me into taking one, and we performed the different festivals in all the towns together, with the twins and baby Mursili at our sides.

When we had returned from that, however, the pace of foreign affairs (which comes, although it is easy to forget this, from the vagaries of men's lives and thus is increased or decreased accordingly) was greatly quickened. Some men find their seed rises like sap in spring. With men who play at power, it is their ire, their decisiveness, their battle which rises to the fore.

Nearly a year had Aziru been detained in Egypt, wherefrom we were hearing strange news upon strange news: Akhenaten had raised his lover-brother to co-regency, married this bed-partner to the same woman he had wed the year before, one Meritaten, and then himself married the next heiress in line, a girl-child of his loins called Ankhesenpaaten.

"What means this?" I wondered aloud in my chancery where Malnigal and Hattu-ziti and Kuwatna-ziti were gathered. "And why is Aziru yet in Egypt, alive and well, but silent. . . . His own sons have written Pharaoh begging for their father's release, saying that all the little kings are accusing them of selling their father Aziru to Egypt, yet Akhenaten's only answer is to send out his wedding announcement."

"Ask, better," suggested the Shepherd, "how Lupakki is faring in Amqa and Nuhasse."

"If you had not been pushing tablets the whole time I was fighting down there, you would not have to ask. Lupakki will do exactly as he chooses in Nuhasse. In Amqa we will be triumphant. I am not worrying anymore about what this hermaphroditic lover-of-boys-and-girls-to-whom-he-is-related is going to do. Any man who orders likenesses of himself loving another man in incestuous relationship to be carved in stone to last forever and ever must be mad beyond redemption."

"It is maat," put in Hattu-ziti. "Akhenaten is 'living in truth' in his city, as he has promised."

"Well, my resident Egyptian expert, it may be truth, but it is not sanity. I have got to do something about Aziru."

"What? You cannot very well send a diplomatic complaint to Egypt; we have not had any official relations with Amurru for too long," Hattu-ziti cautioned.

"You would likely precipitate Aziru's death, rather than aid him." So spoke Malnigal, who somehow was always present at policy meetings, and who somehow never aroused my anger by speaking in them.

"If I knew 'what' I would not have thrown the matter open for discussion, would I?"

But none of us could think of anything that might aid Aziru of Amurru.

So it came to pass that we did but sit upon our hands, and pick our teeth and, but for Lupakki and Zidanza and their forces raiding Amqa and maintaining Nuhasse, down into Hittite Syria I did not go.

As the months dragged by, I gave up on it and, facing the winter, only sent to the brothers and sons of Aziru a gentle message, asking if they had any word of their lord.

But when the gods came to decide our fates at the commencement of the year, I laid a sacrifice in his honor, and had my more pious sons, and Telipinus especially, do whatever it came to them to do in the matter of Aziru.

Now, the gods had not done my will in the matter of Himuili, my second queen's partner in adultery: he was still living, limping along from battle to battle though I put him ever in what should have been the position of greatest danger. The Oath Gods, to my mind, should have taken care of him for me. But if a man waits for the gods to act, he may wait forever. And yet, if I laid a hand on Himuili myself, I would be inviting the hand of retribution upon Khinti, by the law of correspondence which all Oath Gods and gods of the field obey. So I had little hope for any miraculous emergence out of Egypt by Aziru of Amurru.

On the day that marked the first full year of life of Malnigal's second child, a daughter she had borne me (with whom we had just discovered she was pregnant when Aziru went to Egypt), word came from Lupakki, who was yet harrying the country of Amqa with Aitakama of Kinza in the guise of maintaining Hittite control of ever-restless Nuhasse.

And what was this word that gathered all my greats and officials in Hattusas? It was that Aziru, having languished eighteen months in Naphuria Akhenaten's sordid court, was back in Amurru, and in violent dispute with my vassal, Niqmad of Ugarit.

At this, many mouths curled sardonically among the lords of my armies. Some even dared point out that they had predicted this sorry development to me.

Aziru, some said, had turned back to Akhenaten, his lord; had turned his face finally away from the Sun. Niqmad the timid and those who supported him, the conservatives of Hattusas, urged me to invade Amurru and despoil it in all haste.

I was close to allowing it to be done. I was close to giving up on Aziru of Amurru. I was close to making a move that went against all my instincts, to calm my court and my adherents who feared we would lose precious, bejeweled Ugarit back to Egypt because of Aziru's duplicity.

Nor was this all that was concerning me. Malnigal's sister, I have said, resided in Akhetaten as one of Pharaoh's lesser wives. Both she and Duttu of the Egyptian court, as well as my brother king Artatama of Hurri, had written to me concerning one Assur-uballit of Assyria.

"Who in the names of all the demons of the netherworld is Assur-uballit?" I demanded after a fruitless, gall-raising meeting that resembled more the old debating sessions that used to obtain in Hatti when the democratic assemblage called the "pankus" was in force: in former times, nothing could be done, because among all the folk of the pankus, nothing could be decided. I had never held with councils. That day, I was thinking about abolishing entirely my court and starting anew with younger men who did not crave curl-toed shoes and embroidered shawls above all else.

"Shepherd, I asked you—what do you know of this Assyrian?"

"No more than you, my lord Sun. Shall I speak the obvious, that Artatama of Hurri is too busy chasing his brother Tushratta through the bushes to pay attention to his own protectorates? That this Assur-uballit has managed to secure his independence and has even gained recognition from the Egyptian court? It is too late to do anything about it. And it is too far away, truly, to warrant our concern."

"With an empty throne in Mitanni, a civil war in Hurri over whether Mitanni is a vacant Hurrian fief or another state, with the most vile torturers of Assyria raising themselves up and sharpening their weapons, the Great Shepherd of Hatti, my most valued confidant, can only say, 'they are too far away'? If they start moving westward, you will not be saying that. Not when the tanned, flayed skin of their enemies starts arriving in presentation boxes, you will not. Shepherd, I want some stronger ally than Artatama—one who can protect himself, and thus ourselves. Think upon it."

"I will think. But come with me out of this crowd. I have a matter for your attention."

As I accompanied him out of the palace proper, he would not speak of whatever concerned him. While we climbed the stairs to walk the inner wall, I brought up not Aziru, of whom I had had enough talk for one day, but Akhenaten and his shocking behavior in the matter of his co-regent, Smenkhare, who was also his lover.

"Tasmi, you are getting old. You have gray hairs."

"I am wearing better than yourself."

"In body, but not in mind. It bothers you that in lands so foreign as to be considered the farthest extent of civilization, a young king much like yourself has arisen. It troubles you also, I suspect, that in the army are appearing faces wet with youth and downy of cheek. The world does not stop spitting forth beginnings because a man's thoughts turn to endings, to the stabilizing of past affairs."

"What are you saying, O obtuse one?" We were between two crenelations of the citadel wall, halfway from one guard tower to the next. He stopped me, leaning back against the plastered stone.

"I am saying, my lord Tabarna, that you are making more of Akhenaten's sexual preference than you should. It is not such a weakness as you expound."

"Is it not?"

"Was it with us?"

"Shepherd, we were never like that."

"That is true," he sighed. "We never were like the Egyptian about it. But I want you to recollect that sometimes men grow close, closer than close, and there is nothing wrong in it. . . ."

"So?"

"So, you have recollected it, have you not?"

"Kuwatna-ziti, even a king, these days, cannot afford to stroll the battlements in muzzy recollection of his youth. I remember: so what?"

"You and I have a problem."

"If you are pregnant, it is not from me, Shepherd."

"No, but close."

"What is our problem?"

"Piyassilis and Tarkhunta-zalma," said the Shepherd very quietly, looking out over the Hattian countryside.

"What about them?" I demanded, not understanding.

"Do I have to say the words? All be as the gods decide, then, I say them. Hark: your son and mine have more than a friendly relationship."

"Shepherd, you are demented."

"No, it is true."

"So it is true. They will grow out of it, as you and I did. They will find suitable mates and drift apart. They are young—"

"That is the heart of the matter, Tasmi. They are not young anymore. They are older than boys . . . my son is thirty, Piyassi-lis is twenty-eight. They have no wives; few concubines; neither has sired a son. We need to do something about it."

"Just what do you have in mind?" I said in a voice fainter than I would have liked. It was just coming over me, the sour stomach and dizzy head of a man faced with such a revelation.

"You must talk with them."

"*I* must talk with them? *You* talk with them. It bothers me less than it bothers you."

"It bothered you enough in the case of Naphuria Akhenaten; how can you be free of scandalized remarks and superior pontification in the matter of your own son?"

"Of *both* our sons. I could dispose of yours and that would end it, would it not?"

"Tasmi, I am serious."

"And I, Kuwatna-ziti, am equally serious. Do this, then: bring them both before me. I will decree that each must take a wife and beget sons upon whomsoever they choose by year's end. More than that, I cannot do."

"*Will* not, you mean."

"Shepherd, I cannot say to a prince who is, as you point out, nearing his third decade, that he cannot see his lover anymore, even if that lover be a man. I have not raised my boys that way. You think it is just about Akhenaten's choice of bed-partners that I am concerned? It is not that at all. It is the raising of one god above all others that concerns me: if such a point of view were disseminated among the nations, war would be waged until the last person among us died. How fiercely might a man who feels he is fighting for his god wield a sword? And I am not misconstruing it, either. In Naphuria's own writings are the seeds of chaos: he has said that his god, Aten, has differentiated all the

nations. He is making a holy crusade out of his god's service, and
has even said that his god has settled every man in his place."

"You mean the hymn to the Sun god, don't you, where he says:
'Their tongues are diverse in speech,
Their forms and likewise their skins,
For thou divider hast divided the peoples.'"

"That is exactly what I mean, Shepherd. He is making skin
color and nationality a matter of godly favor, of degree — of
maat, as Hattu-ziti is so fond of reminding us. He is installing
racism in the cult of his god, and in the minds of all the peoples.
Down go the gods whom the peoples have worshipped since former times; down goes their self-esteem, and their brotherhood
under the Thousand Gods of Heaven along with them. I am not
just against his methods; I am against the danger of his cult, and
what it may do to all the peoples."

Thus I bespoke my opinion, as much to change the subject
as anything else.

But the Shepherd would not be silenced: "In the matter of
making married men of our sons . . . if you, the Sun, chose the
women, it would be impossible for them to do any other than
what you command."

"Sumeris, my daughter of the second degree, is comely.
Would she suit?"

"My lord, I was not asking."

"When *you* start 'my lord-ing' me, then I know the matter is
grave. I wish I had a grown princess of full blood to offer; your
house and mine should by now have been formally joined."

So it was decided, and so was it performed.

The Shepherd left the telling of them to me, and I chose to
do it in such a way that neither man was embarrassed, so that my
son not think I disapproved of him in any way. I did not let them
know that I knew, or that I cared, only that I thought it time each
took a wife to assure his line.

Since I had not made similar demands on my other sons, Piyassilis doubtless realized what was happening. But a man must

be allowed to correct his mistakes; by rubbing his nose in them before everyone, I would only have made it harder on them both.

I sent down Piyassilis to aid Lupakki in Nuhasse and posted Tarkhunta-zalma to Kumanni, and it was then that the blue-cloaked lord appeared in my dream, gray as good iron and noticeably dimmer as he laid upon my path two tablets, first one and then another. But when I was stooping down to retrieve them, Malni-gal woke me from my dream, saying that a messenger awaited.

"Awaiting? Now? It is the depth of night. Who is it?"

I groped my way up out of sleep in a bad temper while into my hands she pressed a full cup, and by the time I had drunk it she had laid out my clothes as if she were a bodyservant.

I paused in my dressing, touched her cheek, saying: "Have I told you how beautiful you are?" for I was sorry I had been sharp with her.

She kissed my palm and asked if she should admit him, or if I would see him elsewhere.

"Admit him, for if he must wake me in the middle of the night, then he can stand the sight of rumpled bedclothes and a sleepy king."

The message was sent by way of Lupakki, but the tablet had originally come from Niqmad of Ugarit. It was a copy of a treaty, and beyond that Niqmad sent no other word to me. Thus did the treaty read:

"Dating from today, Niqmad, king of Ugarit, and Aziru, king of Amurru, have made this agreement by oath. The disputes of Aziru with Ugarit, and those of former times, from the day of this oath, they are no longer valid. Of all these disputes, as the sun is pure, so he, Aziru is pure in respect to Niqmad and the prince of Siyannu, Abdihebat, in respect to Ugarit and Siyannu. Fur-thermore, five thousand shekels of silver are paid to Aziru and he is pure as the sun. Furthermore, if there is a king who should make an act of hostility against the king of Ugarit, Aziru with his chariots and soldiers will fight him. If the soldiers of an enemy king attack my country, Aziru will fight my enemy with chariots and soldiers. If they penetrate into my land, Aziru—his chariots and soldiers—will come to my aid."

Now what this was, on Aziru's part, was extortion. On the part of Niqmad, it showed little faith in the Sun, that he would buy protection from Aziru. What it was in large, though, most concerned me. This was a vassal treaty: Ugarit, however delicately the matter was stated, was suddenly not only my vassal, but Aziru's also. If indeed the Amurrite was now a loyal Egyptian subject, I had just lost a very rich and important country.

I dismissed the messenger to await me in the Gal Meshedi's house while I tried to toss off the mists of sleep and draft some suitable reply. I had hoped Aziru would come up to Hatti upon his return from Egypt. I had been waiting for him to do so. The treaty seemed to say that he was not in any way inclined to visit me.

And yet, I was not enraged. Something in the back of my mind whispered caution, for Aziru was a master of actions whose consequences were never what they seemed.

I called for Telipinus, who was still with me in Hattusas on account of the gathering of lords, and asked him what his "sight" showed, what he would advise.

Fingering the tablet, he answered me slowly: "I am not Piyassilis, in blind love with Aziru. But Abuya, all my person screams caution: take no action. You can crush him as easily later as now. Give him a chance to explain. Summon him to Hattusas, if you must, but into Amurru send no troops. . . . Do you think I am mad?"

"Now, Telipinus, if I have asked you here to counsel me, would I be thinking that? And furthermore: my feeling is the same as your own, although no god tells me his innermost thoughts. Only stand with me tomorrow when we inform the lords of what has occurred."

He agreed, and we stood together before the doomsayers and the battle-hungry, and we won them over without my having to hand down a unilateral decree.

Barely a month later, Aziru, king of Amurru, drove up to the gates of Hattusas and turned his own country and all his territories, his alliances, his vassals over to me. Thus the entire coast, excepting Amqa and a few beleaguered Egyptian outposts, came under the overlordship of the Sun. I had Byblos, and Ugarit once again, and all between was also mine.

Now, the tribute that I laid on Aziru of Amurru was harsh, but just. Since he was collecting tribute on his own from Ugarit and all the cities he had under his sandal, I knew he could afford it. The provision that he deliver the agreed-upon tribute by his own hand yearly into mine was somewhat unusual, but in the case of such a man as the Amurrite had shown himself to be, quite necessary. Only by looking in the eyes and listening to the words of Aziru in one's own presence did a man have the slightest chance of determining in advance what the wolf of Amurru was likely to do.

I kept him in Hattusas longer than he might have wished, but there were many things I needed to learn from him about Egypt. On the day the treaty was read aloud and the copies signed by us both, I felt as if I had conquered the world entire and brought it to its knees.

I was watching his face while the words of Hattu-ziti rang out in the administration hall's chancery, for I had called all my lords and the greats of the army to witness this event, so long in coming. Intoned Hattu-ziti, as Aziru watched the eagles fly by the window beyond the Sun's back:

"These are the words of the Sun Suppiluliumas, Great King, King of Hatti, the valiant, the favorite of the Storm-god." And Aziru's face drained pale under his pointy beard as the gods were invoked to oversee our agreement.

And as Hattu-ziti continued, Aziru would sometimes nod, sometimes bite his lip, sometimes pull on his brightly colored mantle. But to the words of the Sun, spoken by my chamberlain before the lords of Hatti, Aziru made no objection, not to his yearly tribute of three hundred shekels of refined gold, first class and pure, nor to his obligation to come up to the Hatti land once a year. In fact, as Hattu-ziti spoke the customary treaty phrases of indebtedness, it might have been another whose rule was being circumscribed. But when Hattu-ziti came to the part in the historical preamble where I had written, "But Aziru, king of Amurru, away from the court of Egypt arose, and he submitted to My Majesty the king of Hatti. And My Majesty the Great King was very pleased that Aziru had submitted to the Sun, and come away from the court of Egypt. Because Aziru at the feet of His Majesty bowed down and came away from the court of Egypt and at the feet of the Sun knelt, I, His Majesty, have treated Aziru like one of my brothers."

Then, hearing those words and knowing them forever inscribed on bronze tablets and in the hearts of the Gods of the Oath, Aziru met my eyes with a cold, emotionless stare that did not waver even when Hattu-ziti was saying: "To the Sun, Great King, his lord, Aziru spoke as follows: 'Myself, together with my house I have surrendered.'"

And the whole time the military clauses were being attested and the god-list and curses invoked for breach and punishment therefore, the king of Amurru looked straight into the eyes of myself, his lord, as if to say: 'You did this to me, and made me submit myself, but I am my own man and none of this changes anything between us.'

So after the two of us put our seals to the clay copies and the celebration commenced, I took my new vassal by the arm and led him out under the administration hall's portico, where I had received the hearts of my people so long ago, after returning in ignominious defeat from my first conflict with Mitanni.

And it was there, on the portico overlooking the outer citadel concourse, that I heard firsthand about Akhenaten: about the bespangled Hall of Foreign Tribute; about the Aten's stronghold in which Akhenaten's queen Nefertiti went to dwell when her husband threw her over for his brother and the daughter of his own loins. I heard of Nefertiti's rosy-toned skin, her strong-faced beauty which was more of our northern stamp than Egyptian—although, said Aziru, next to my Malnigal, Istar incarnate, the queen of Egypt was merely plain. I heard tell of Akhenaten himself: of his woman's hips and protuberant belly, his face that was homely beyond belief, loose-lipped and long-eyed and sardonic; I heard of his electrum-plated chariot, whose horses wore mantles of silver and gold. I heard of the king's mother, Tiye, the last hope of the priests of Amun, she who had borne a late-life son to Akhenaten's father. The boy's name was Tutankhaten, and around him all the anti-Atenists had rallied in the old capital of Egypt, Thebes. Now, I was not listening very hard to Aziru's words on the subject of Egypt's royal children; I was not interested in Tutankhaten's beauty, nor in the claim that he was as "divine" as the two co-regents sharing the double throne.

I was more attentive to Aziru's tales of Akhenaten's marriage to his own daughter which occurred while Aziru was in Egypt, when the girl was at best nine years of age, but only because of the prurience of the story.

On the other hand, Aziru's impressions of Ay, Divine Father, held my attention until the night-watch blared his call and the fires were lit in Hattusas. Yes, the Master of Horses, Ay, with his red-leather gloves and his six-foot frame, which towered above the other Egyptians like some walking colossus, intensely concerned me.

What I heard of General Horemheb, right hand of this Ay, intrigued me as well. Although during all the years we had fought, Aziru and I, in Upper and Lower Retenu, this Horemheb had been impotent against our battle, Aziru's assessment of him was high and full of foreboding. Horemheb, Aziru said, had been too busy trying to keep the pyramids from falling down on top of him to pay attention to the northern lands in which his king had lost interest. Horemheb, said Aziru, was Akhenaten's "Sole Friend" and confidant, and by all reports was already practicing the Pharaonic gleam of eye and godly manner. Under a sane ruler, said Aziru, or even if the Theban opposition led by Akhenaten's mother Tiye and ex-wife Nefertiti came back to power, Horemheb would be a force with which to reckon—as great as Egypt's army of old. A general, said Aziru, is no better than the orders he receives.

"Do you think then, that the Thebans will prevail? Will all these royal folk break Akhenaten to his harness?"

"Overlord, it is very hard to say. What can be done in the matter of a king who is a god? But another god is being raised in Thebes: young Tutankhaten. Should Ankhesenpaaten bear Akhenaten no male heir, I think that pressure from his court must force Akhenaten to abdicate, or at least get rid of his lover Smenkhare and put little Tut on the co-regent's throne. Or so has the Honorable Lord Hani said to me."

I saw a shiver course over Aziru's flesh as he talked of King Akhenaten and how the pharaoh had tried to convert him, first gently, and then more and more forcibly, to his god the Aten. And I heard from Aziru's very mouth that the reason he had come up to Hattusas and thrown himself at the feet of the Sun was most specifically the revulsion that looking upon Akhenaten's twisted countenance and listening to his fanatical pontifications had engendered in my vassal, the Amurrite king. Aziru was so candid as to say that if he had stayed much longer in Akhetaten, he was sure he would have been asked to submit himself to the god-king in ways other than by oath. And that, above all things, more than political pressure or even the murder of his father at Egyptian hands, had driven Aziru to make submission to myself, the Sun. And in the matter of the oaths of allegiance Aziru had sworn to Akhenaten in order to get out of Egypt with all the members he had possessed when he was summoned there, the Amurrite had this to say:

"Surely, the Oath Gods will make an exception of me in this case. When I swore those fealty oaths, there was hatred in my heart and naked blades were all around me. Even as I was saying them aloud, to myself and to the gods in my heart I was saying: 'if I get out of this alive I am going up to Hattusas and throw myself upon the mercy of the Sun. So, Oath Gods, do not listen to these words spoken from my mouth, do not lay these obligations to me as consequence of my oath!' And I have laid sacrifices, reminding the gods of this matter, and that I never meant to be bound by what submission Akhenaten demanded from me. And furthermore: all was overseen only by this lonely god, the Aten, and the single goddess Akhenaten has allowed to flourish, their lady of truth, Maat. So if those Oath Gods who oversee Egyptian matters of kingship and queenship were not at all consulted on his part, then what degree of attention will the gods, my lords, who were ignored, bring to bear on the matter? No, I am safe from retribution by the gods. I must be. It is Akhenaten who will reap a shriveled harvest, when the gods have had their fill of his warring against them."

And Aziru, who had been to Akhetaten and seen with his own eyes the decadence residing in the City of the Horizon, was not wrong.

Barely had the Amurrite gone down to oversee our joint concerns in Syria than word was brought to me, and seconded by Malnigal's father's monthly missive: "Smenkhare, Akhenaten's co-regent and the brother who was to him the female principal of the Aten" had died of a fever, so we were told. Recalling Aziru's prognostications, I thought the fever more likely the result of a surreptitiously administered dose of mandragora, which grew in profusion around the palace gardens of Akhenaten's city.

Barely had I sent to Aziru an invitation to come up again and consult with me on Egyptian affairs, when I received a second message: Naphuria Akhenaten, Pharaoh, Mighty Bull, Lofty of Plumes, Golden Horus, King of Upper and Lower Egypt, High Priest of Harakhte-Rejoicing-in-the-Horizon in His Name: "Heat-Which-is-in-Aten": Nefer-Kheperure-Wanre, lord of heaven, ruler of eternity, was dead.

Dead. I decreed a great festival, to be held simultaneously throughout all the Hatti lands. I was as excited as a child upon New Year's day. I was generous, magnanimous far beyond my custom, both in rendering judgments for the people and in my private affairs. I even began growing a beard for Malnigal, who had long been urging me to do so; moreover, I left off my attempts to curtail her passion for things imported, which had become a constant battle between us, so concertedly did she strain to empty Hattusas' treasury.

Dead. I greeted Aziru like my own kin, and since he had been on his way up to Hatti when the announcement was circulated, even availed myself of the opportunity that fate, in league with the Storm-god, my lord, had provided: it was I who told the news to Aziru, who watched his eyes bulge, then close; who watched his face pale, then flush; who heard his icy, sharp-edged laugh peal out over Hatti. So long, and so hard did Aziru laugh that I thought they would hear it in Thebes. He laughed until he cried, until he found need to sit, until he could not laugh anymore. Then, holding his side and groaning in mock agony, he supplicated My Majesty for wine to drink.

This I had brought to him. And when he had drunk of it, he observed that whatsoever I, the Sun, chose to do in the matter of conquering towns in the Egyptian south, I might now do. And that he, Aziru, was anxious to help me, more so than he had ever been.

"What of this Ay, whom you so praised to me? And what of the general Horemheb?"

Aziru snapped his fingers: a loud, cracking sound in the tiny, windowless study I was using so that none would inter-rupt us. *"That, "* he said, referring to the sound he had made, "is what of those two, now: Nothing! They have chosen whom they must—the solar blood must be perpetuated. You and I will very soon be dealing with a son of the Aten too young to ascend his throne without a stepstool."

"How old is this . . . boy? What is his name?"

"Tutankhaten; Nibhuria to us barbarians who cannot prop-erly pronounce an Egyptian name. He is nine, or maybe ten. This high." He extended his hand at his waist.

"How can you be so sure this boy-king will live to rule? Might he not suffer this mysterious ailment that so conveniently claimed his older brothers?"

"That is a Hittite point of view, my lord, please take no of-fense. I wonder what is going on there. Did any word come of the ex-wife, Nefertiti?"

"No word. Only that they were lifting this Nibhuria onto the seat of kingship. If you are right, and I will not believe it until I hear it from Duttu, then you and I should lay a sacrifice before the gods of the armies. What danger can a lad too young to have learned to masturbate be to us?"

"Perhaps," he said, collecting himself. "And perhaps we should not thank the gods until we are sure we have been increased. The little heiress, Ankhesenpaaten, bore her father a child just recently, but I am not sure if it lived: it was sickly like all Akhenaten's get. However it came out, she was pregnant when I left the City of the Horizon. They will marry Nibhuria Tutankhaten to Ankhesenpaaten. She holds the blood to legitimize him."

"So? Aziru, you still have not made yourself clear: will this pharaoh rule, truly, and thus be no threat; or will his mother and Ay and Horemheb and the priests rule through him?"

"Great King, I wish I knew. Overshadowing all Egyptian affairs is the godhood of Pharaoh; it is possible the child will wield power because of that. Until some one of us hears from Hani, or until Hatib the Vile whispers it in your ear, or Duttu writes you of it, none of us will know. I imagine they will stop wearing those short, round Libyan wigs that they love so in Akhetaten, and go back to the long, plaited Theban ones," mused Aziru, as if to himself.

"While you are here, will you not honor my family with your presence at my son's emergence into manhood?"

Now, polite or not, I was not asking, but decreeing, and he knew it.

"Which son, though it matters not? I am, my lord Overlord, deeply honored that you ask me to attend."

"Which? My lion-rider, prince Zannanza, Khinti's child."

"And her beautiful daughter, is she a now woman in the eyes of the Sun?"

"What is that most feral look, vassal? Whether she is or isn't can matter not at all to you: that girl will marry for love, at a time of her own choosing. I have promised her."

CHAPTER 31

Not only did we hear that they stopped wearing the fashionable Libyan wigs that had obtained in the City of the Horizon, but that the whole court was leaving. The City of the Aten was to be abandoned. We in poorer nations could only shake our heads at such flagrant waste.

In the two years since Zannanza, my prince out of Khinti, had become a man, my only reliable source of information had been Malnigal's sister in Egypt and her father, Burnaburiash, king of Babylon. Burnaburiash, the only great king of my acquaintance maintaining diplomatic correspondence with Egypt, made protest after formal protest in the matter of the Egyptian court having formally recognized the upstart "king" of Assyria, Assur-uballit, in his own right and as no one's vassal. But no notice did Egypt take of Babylon's displeasure, although the Theban scribes were nothing if not polite.

My faithful Duttu had been found out and slain, or otherwise perished, and I had no eyes in Thebes among his kindred.

Hatib, also, was suffering the shifting of power whose tremors may bring a man's life down around his ears like a wooden roof.

I had my hands full keeping my Syrian dependencies quiet and peaceful. I made a few stabs at Amqa's cities, but only to let Aziru know I was still alive and well, which he seemed to have a tendency to forget, even though once a year he trundled up to Hattusas with his tribute of gold and silver and his precious gifts for my queen and the officials of the temples and of the armies to whom he, by treaty, showed deference.

Six more times did Aziru make the yearly pilgrimage to Hattusas before the Sun, myself, roused once again for battle. Another two years did I gather intelligence and sit on my buttocks with my ears pricked southward, before I was ready.

Six years and two I waited while the Egyptian priests licked their wounds and accustomed themselves and everyone else to the change in Pharaoh's name: Tutankh*aten,* Living-Image-of-Aten, was no more; Tutankh*amun,* Living-Image-of-Amun, ruled in Thebes. The God Amun and everyone else, if one could believe what the forked-tongued chose to say, were most pleased; all was once more exceedingly well with Pharaoh, the Good God, with his country, with his wives and children, with his horses and chariots. As well, I assumed, as could be a king just turned eighteen, with a wife two years older who had borne her father, the presiding pharaoh's full brother, a child: As well as a man could be, whose rule had been so hobbled that it seemed to consist only of decrees ordering the restoration of each and every monument his heretic predecessor had defaced, of endlessly placating the formerly maligned god Amun and his priests, and of restoring free worship of the gods in all their differentiated splendor from one end of Egypt to the other.

Six years I spent teaching Aziru to come to heel, and raising my twins in their puberty and Malnigal's get in their diapers, and fighting little upcountry skirmishes.

Six years: I learned to love Malnigal less during that period. Her detractors became vociferous, and I had been through that before. So instead of silencing them, for in many ways I agreed (she was a perfect woman, perchance, but a perfect Tawananna for Hatti she was far from being), I withdrew in my way from the entire affair. If she could not see what she was doing, if she could not take charge of her life and moderate her lusts and her excesses and cease trying to transform Hattusas into a province of Babylon, then I was not going to take her part.

I am not saying that there was peace in the Hatti land or anywhere else during that time. But what battles there were, were not the battles I was longing to fight. It seemed as if I was having to do everything I had done across the years a second time. There was fighting on the Gasgaean frontier, so much so that I went myself to the front to put an end to it.

Only one of those battles was especially memorable, and not because I cut off the Gasgaean chieftain's head at the end of it: I was out of patience in the matter of the Gasgaean enemy and was not only making summary execution of Gasgaean leaders my practice, but had ordered all my commanders to do the same.

In this particular battle of which I speak, in the rear of the army, a plague broke out. And although I had Hannutti, my master of horses, the field marshal, and Himuili, commander of ten, with me, and the Great Shepherd also, only Himuili died of the plague. And I was pleased about that, although I had expected he would die in his riverbank position during the battle.

So it seemed that the Oath Gods had rendered me a judgment, both in the matter of the death of Himuili and concerning the Gasgaean enemies.

Two years of that campaign I myself oversaw, and when the worst was over and the Gasgaeans were put to flight, it was Telipinus' army that made the final sweep of Gasga before driving down to start the war with which I am about to concern myself.

In that year, the eighth of the boy-king in Egypt's reign, the thirty-sixth of my own regnal calendar, I was concerning myself with accomplishing sharply circumscribed goals:

I had thought long on the matter of my son Piyassilis, and come to the decision that the only true solution to his problem was to keep my word to give him the city and the country of

Carchemish as his own kingship. There he could do whatsoever he wished in the matter of Tarkhunta-zalma and his personal life, and no one in Hatti could say a word about it.

I had thought long on the matter of my Syrian dependencies, and when I was possessed of the country and the city of Carchemish, I intended to close up all the holes in my southernmost territories through which the treacherous kings of Mukis and Ni'i and Nuhasse were wont to slip, thus stabilizing matters in Retenu so that I could turn my attention, next year, to my eastern boundaries, where King Artatama, the Hurrian with whom I had a treaty, was making such a muddle of affairs on the far bank of the Mala.

"Tribal troops came in multitude and attacked my army by night," said the Priest, eyes darting fiery pride. "Then the gods of the Sun helped me, so that I defeated the enemy and slew them. And when I had defeated the tribal troops sent by the Hurrians, the country of our enemies saw this, and they were afraid, and all the countries of Arziya and Carchemish made peace with me, and the town of Murmuriga made peace with me, too." And he handed me the tablets of submission of those countries which were suddenly Hittite countries, the lands about Carchemish-on-the-Mala, that choicest Mitannian stronghold on this side of the river.

"But what of Carchemish, the town?" I demanded, sorting through the clay tablets. We were in my estate in the town of Uda, where Telipinus had come to meet me after driving up to Hattusas and finding out I was in the Lower Country performing a festival.

"Carchemish itself, the one town, did not make peace with us. So I left six hundred men and chariots under Lupakki, in winter camp in Murmuriga, and came up to meet with you, to see what you would have me do. The town is high-walled and brash, and within it are generals and soldiers of Tushratta; and it seems to me that fighting them on the plain before the city is useless: while I am fighting them before the city, reinforcements sneak into it from behind."

So while we were in Uda, Telipinus and I devised a plan for the taking of Carchemish, which we were intent on having by harvest time so that we could present it to Piyassilis on the thirty-seventh anniversary of his birth.

This plan made use of Ugaritic boats and Amurrite siege-craft. Therefore we dispatched messengers with new orders to Niqmad of Ugarit and to Aziru of Amurru, and to Piyassilis and Tarkhunta-zalma who had replaced Lupakki in Halap as the Hittite commanders overseeing the restive Nuhasse and tickling the Egyptian toes of Amqa. I charged Piyassilis and Tarkhunta-zalma with watching my "allies" there as well.

But as we were sending these troop levies to our vassals and girding on our swords, a message came from Lupakki:

"When the Mitannians saw that the Priest was gone, the troops and chariots of Tushratta came and surrounded Murmuri-ga. And they were superior in number to the troops of Hatti who were there."

At the same time word was brought to me that the Mitannians had surrounded Lupakki's army, I heard from Piyassilis that troops and chariots of Egypt had come to the country of Kinza, which I had conquered and made my country with Aitakama, my vassal king, ruling for me. And they attacked the country of Kinza. And within the country, revolt broke out among the people, some of whom wanted to stay loyal to the Sun, and some of whom wanted to go back over to the Egyptians. And further, Piyassilis said that the government of Kinza had thrown in its lot with those who wanted to return to Egypt's overlordship. The only thing that was not clear was where the king of Kinza, Aitakama, stood in all of this. Piyassilis could not find him anywhere: he seemed not to be in his palace. So there was no way to tell whether he himself had broken his treaty with me and revolted or his councilors had arisen and wrested the country from his hands. And I was wroth so that my scars were livid. I drove up to Hattusas in the dead of night and, for the first time in all my years of driving, killed a team of horses doing so. Would that a man could get from another man that loyalty which a horse can demonstrate, which makes a horse run until his heart bursts, only because you have commanded it.

Once in Hattusas, I mobilized all available troops and marched down into the Hurrian country. When I arrived in the country of Tegarama, I made a review of my troops and chariots. From there I sent Arnuwandas and Zida, my brother the Gal Meshedi, from Tegarama ahead into the Mitanni country, though I was reluctant to expose my heir to the jeopardy a man faces leading point into enemy territory. But then, that was why I sent Zida with him, and I was not truly worried. It would have been something to worry about if Arnuwandas had not demanded to lead the column, or if I had been unable to find it in my heart to allow him his desire.

That year I was as iron-gray as the scalloped decorations on my chariot, facing my forty-first season in the field, with all my grown sons ranged about me. And it was to me a consummate justification of all struggles past, simply to see them and to hear them and to know that each was as fit as a man may be. Before leaving Hattusas, I had a terrible and lengthy argument with my Tawananna, Malnigal, which I won, but which I thought to be the formal opening of hostilities between us: I had brought her just-manned son Mursili, two months shy of fourteen, out to battle. Since all the rest of my boys were with me, and he longed to be rescued from under his mother's skirts, I could not refuse him. Mursili was ecstatic, driving for his brother Zannanza, Khinti's boy. Both I kept ever in my personal thirty. If harm came to them, it would be because I, myself, had fallen, and I was not about to fall.

Now, when Arnuwandas and Zida came down into the embattled country, the enemy came against them for battle. Ere I could even join them, the gods of the Sun helped my brother and my eldest son Arnuwandas, and they defeated the enemy besieging Lupakki. But the enemy fled in front of our forces and escaped into the mountains and into the fortified town.

So when I arrived in the vicinity of the fortified town of Carchemish, I surrounded it and prepared to besiege it. On this side and on that side, so that I surrounded it completely, I deployed men about the city. Across the Mala into deepest Mitanni I sent troops; and up the river from the west and south, from Ugarit and from Amurru the troops of my allies came by ships and boats, bringing with them disassembled siege engines and wooden mountains for scaling the walls of Carchemish.

Never in the memory of mankind had anyone seen the like of that army. It blackened the river's banks on this side and that. Its extent made the night glow as if a thousand giant fireflies had come to alight upon the plain. And all the greats of my army, and of Aziru's army, and of Ugarit's seafaring forces, were meeting in tents and making plans around bites of stew, and calling down their gods to aid them.

As soon as I arrived in the camp I called forth Lupakki and Tarkhunta-zalma, the latter being at least partly responsible for the mishandling of affairs that had allowed Kinza to defect to Egypt and Aitakama, Kinza's king, to disappear from sight like a shekel dropped into the muddy Mala's current. These two commanders, with troops and chariots, as many as they desired, I sent forth to reclaim Kinza and proceed to Amqa, an Egyptian country I had long coveted, to seek revenge: since Egypt had attacked my country of Kinza, and taken it by default, then I would do the same with their country, Amqa. So did Lupakki and Tarkhunta-zalma depart, to do my will and bring Kinza back into the Hatti land. Aziru's troops and chariots came out to help them, and they brought uncountable booty, sheep and cattle and deportees from the Egyptian country of Amqa.

By the time Lupakki's troops returned with their Egyptian spoils and namra, I had Carchemish encircled so that not a single scout could penetrate into the city.

Now, in the field, a man sleeps whenever he may, and I had just awakened from a sunset nap during which the blue-cloaked lord had ushered me into the temples of Carchemish, and I had reached out to take the golden clothes from the gods of Carchemish, and my hand had shriveled before my eyes and fallen away at the wrist like a branch falls from a blighted tree.

Rubbing the sleep and the cold sweat away, I called for food and drink. Mursili, whose voice was just cracking and becoming the voice of a man, hurriedly ran out to fetch it for me.

The tent in which I was holding court was low and not spacious, big enough for the image of the Storm-god standing on his sacred bulls, a brazier, two stools and a map board.

Into it, behind Mursili's heavy-shouldered form—Malnigal had whelped me a squat and lusty, big-boned pup—stooped Hattu-ziti, his head bald as an egg, his brow looking like a field just plowed.

The pig-tailed son of Malnigal proudly served his sire's wine, and asked in his irresolute voice if he should depart.

"Should he, Hattu-ziti? What is it that brings you here?"

"Is the Great Bull not a man?" smiled Hattu-ziti at Mursili, who had got that nickname on account of the magnificent organ with which the gods had favored him, whose proportions were in need of no exaggeration by the prostitutes who had so praised his manhood when it had become incumbent on him to prove his prowess a scant month past. "But take up your scribe's utensils, and sit yourself down inconspicuously, and you will hear, son of the Sun, what no man has heard since the gods gave us ears. That is, with the Great King's permission?"

"Stay, then, Mursili. What is this? You have piqued my curiosity, secretary."

"My lord, Great King, a messenger from the Egyptian court awaits without."

"*What?*"

"I said—"

"I heard you. I have—Did he say—No, he would not. Is it Hani?"

"No, my lord Sun. It is a man with whom I am not familiar, one of the Theban court. But he was brought here by Hatib, who—"

"Bring him here. I would see Hatib."

But it was not to be. Hatib's path was no longer that of the Sun.

"—by Hatib, my lord, Great King, who said he was sorry, but could not remain, and commended this messenger unto your mercy, suggesting that whatever Your Majesty did with him would include his safe disposition back southward."

"You do know what this man wants, do you not?"

"My lord, no amount of cajoling or browbeating could persuade this messenger to turn over to me the sealed tablet he carries. It is for your eyes only." Despite this assertion, the look on Hattu-ziti's face told me he knew what the tablet said.

I spied Mursili watching, fascinated, without letting him see me noticing his interest. "Then, Hattu-ziti, bring him in. But is Aziru arrived yet?"

"No," he said hesitantly, troubled to the extent of forgetting to politely address me. "No, he is not, though the king of Ugarit is here with his entire entourage and his upholstered couches and—"

"I can imagine. After this Egyptian messenger is relieved of his duty, I want guards at my threshold to escort him wheresoever I decide. And I will see the king of Ugarit at moon's rise. And if Aziru should arrive, even if I am sleeping, wake me."

Hattu-ziti departed, to do as I had bid. None of us were talking much about Aziru's conspicuous absence. He had sent troops, but had not accompanied them here; he was close to being in violation of his oath. But those of us who knew Aziru were wondering how close had grown his friendship with Aitakama of Kinza (who now stood in formal violation of his oaths and would, if I could catch him, lose his life for it), and if Aziru's absence had anything to do with the disappearance of the king of Kinza.

I shook those loathsome conjectures from my mind as the Egyptian messenger, dressed in a soldier's kilt, mantle and helmet, ducked through the tent-flap with Teshub-zalma and my foster-son Zidanza accompanying him, blades drawn and ready.

I took from the messenger the sealed tablet and dismissed him, whereupon he most respectfully informed me that he had been instructed to wait and take my answer back with him to Thebes.

So I suggested that he wait outside the tent, and all three filed out again, leaving only Mursili and myself. "Mursili, build up the fire," I ordered, and as he was doing that I cracked open the envelope with my dirk's hilt and pulled the message from out of it.

And it was formal, and properly attested, and I read it thrice before the words sank in, before the meaning spoke to me. And then I could only wonder at how easily, and how quickly, I had thrown fear into Egyptian hearts by attacking their protectorate Amqa, and why I had waited so long to do so.

And then, estimating the time it takes to get a message to Thebes from Amqa, high on the coast beneath the Hattian plateau, and turning the tablet absently in my hands, I wondered if fear was truly the motive for this consummately astounding document, which was, if the words incised in the clay did not lie, from the Great Wife Ankhesenamun, who had formerly been Ankhesenpaaten, wife of the Egyptian pharaoh Nibhuria Tutankhamun. Or widow thereof, if the tablet spoke truly, for this is what the message from the queen of Egypt said:

"My husband has died. A son I have not. But to you, they say, the sons are many. If you would give me one son of yours, he would become my husband. Never shall I pick out a servant of mine and make him my husband! I am very much afraid."

Mursili says I gave a great sigh like a wind-broken horse. I do not remember that, only the consternation in my heart. Was she saying she was afraid of my battle, this widow who was now queen of Egypt? Was it Ay, the Divine Father, or Horemheb, General of the Armies, of whom she was speaking when she stated she would never pick out a servant of hers and make him her husband? Was it one of them of whom she was afraid?'

I had hardly started to fight with Egypt. She had only tasted my might. On that account, had she sent to me to give her a son to be Pharaoh and rule over the richest country in all the world? Or was this some trick, some scheme. . . . My mind whirled, slowed, lay quiet.

I rose up and hit my head upon the tent pole, then growled at Mursili to go fetch Hattu-ziti, and to call together all the greats of the army: the Shepherd, my princes, the generals and commanders, with whom I would meet as soon as they could be gathered.

"Shall I get the Egyptian messenger?" cracked my son Mursili in his changing voice as he craned his neck to get a glimpse of the words inscribed on the Egyptian clay.

"Not yet. Have him wait. I will answer him in the morning. See to his billet and his safety: it is your charge. Now, run!"

Mursili ran.

And so, when all the Great Ones were gathered, I threw the matter open to discussion in the cool night air before my tent. Staring into the fire, I told them that such a thing had never happened to me before in my whole life, and solicited their advice upon the matter.

My sons' faces were guarded. Their words were cautious. Not a one said, *Send me.* But not a one said, *Do not send anyone.* Each agreed that this was an opportunity the like of which no one had ever had previously, not in the whole of former times. Piyassilis, just returned from Syria, leaned back on his elbows, mirroring my own impassive look from across the fire. Telipinus was staring into the flames as if all future events were revealed therein. Arnuwandas chewed a piece of grass, relaxed, knowing that he was not being considered, and trying to appear howsoever he thought I would want him to appear. Zannanza, Khinti's wide-eyed, arrestingly handsome son, looked at me steadily from out of his mother's wisdom and said only that whoever took the chance would earn the reward, if indeed there was to be one. Mursili tried his best to look old enough and wise enough to be sitting among heroes who had so distinguished themselves in my service.

Now among those, caution prevailed:

The Great Shepherd rubbed his white-streaked temples and said that he would be glad to go and search out the truth, but that a son I should not send them.

Hattu-ziti objected that it would take twenty days to get to Thebes by chariot at the fastest clip, and longer to return word to Hattusas — and that by the time the deceased pharaoh Tutankhamun was placed in his tomb, whoever was to succeed him must be in Egypt to perform the ceremony of the Opening of The Mouth upon the corpse.

At that moment Aziru of Amurru appeared, with a strange look and disheveled appearance I did not then understand, and pointed out that the embalming process took seventy days, so there was some need to proceed decisively, but no need to proceed without heed to the consequences should the matter be a trap. In his face I saw all the bitter months he had spent in Egypt, and the misery he had experienced therein.

And I nodded and raised myself up with a grunt that I could not suppress after so long sitting cross-legged on the ground. So, to cover this involuntary commentary on the state of my joints, I said to Hattu-ziti:

"Go and bring the true word back to me. Maybe they deceive me. Maybe, in fact, they do have a son of their lord. Bring the true word back to me!"

And with that I dismissed them, all but my chamberlain himself. I saw the Shepherd shake his head and try to catch my eye, but I pretended I did not see him and ushered Hattu-ziti into the privacy of my tent.

"You know I would not send you if I thought there was any danger we could not surmount, don't you?" I said to him.

"My lord, I am thankful beyond expression. My joy overflows all bounds. I will go and come back again so fast you will not know I have been away, and I will make smooth the way for a Hittite king to rule from the double throne, and all the gods will aid me. It is time! It is *your* time, your moment!" He was moved unto tears, overwhelmed. Thus we fell into a long, maudlin conjecture as to what to do in this circumstance or that, all tinged with Hattu-ziti's unshakeable faith that this was the beginning of a new era of peace and prosperity for the Hatti land, which, if it ruled Egypt's pharaoh, would be the master of the entire world.

When Hattu-ziti had gone to his rest and I should have been going to mine to make ready for the siege to begin on the morrow, I instead had a light meal and Aziru, king of Amurru, brought to me.

Aziru was looking no better. Still black-faced with trail dirt, he had not changed his clothes nor washed, from the smell of him.

After he made deep obeisance to My Majesty, I invited him to sit, to partake of my table, to explain what it was that had detained him when his obligation demanded he be at my side overseeing the deployment of his Amurrite and Hapiru warriors.

"My lord . . . you don't know, do you? I—"

"It is late," I warned him. "I am simply not jumping to conclusions that would be deadly to you. I am waiting for you to tell me what part you have played in the disappearance of my ex-vassal, the criminal Aitakama of Kinza, who gave his country over to Egyptian chariots so that I am warring and sacking in my own provinces."

Aziru said something inaudible; then, upon my snarl of exasperation, looked up at me like the cornered wolf and said: "I have Aitakama. I have brought him to you, as the bond of my oath demands."

"Aha! Then bring him before me, shackled and naked, and you shall see what happens to a kinglet so foolish as to defy the Sun!"

"My lord, Great King, only listen to me, and when I am finished, you can slay him if you choose. He is waiting in my tent, not chained or bound in any way, for he threw himself upon my mercy, begging me to intercede in his behalf with you, to put the matter right in the eyes of the Sun—"

"The only way Aitakama can put the matter right is to hand me back my country! And as for you, I am still not sure you have not revolted along with him, and are only now coming to your senses and trying to pretend that you were faithful all along! Why did you not send word to me that you had this rebel, who has spat upon my protection, who was treated like a prince in my palace and who betrayed me once I had set him back upon the throne of his father? Speak, you of little honor!"

I had expected anger, harsh words, even that he might come against me, for it was just us two in there.

He did none of those, but looked upon me sorrowfully, stroking his bearded jaw, and said, "I told him it was no good, I could do nothing for him. The evidence is too incriminating. But my lord, I know the truth, and it was not Aitakama who revolted against you, but his council which rose up and took the scepter from his hand and cast him out of the country. And he came to me, and begged me that since I was coming up to fight with the Sun against your enemies, I must allow him to accompany me, for those men of the Hittite army who were seeking him out would kill him without a thought, and he would never live to tell his tale."

"He may not live to spin another, that is the truth." I was feeling suddenly ill used. Within me boiled a rage that I was not sure I could hold. But there is no good in saying to a man: "You have disappointed me; you are failing yourself, and thus failing us all." My frustration at Aziru's overlordly pretensions clenched my fists, made my palms sweat. Before me danced, like a living dream, what it would be like to sink my foot into his belly, to drop him gasping to the ground, to let him know that I saw and understood every cheap and selfish trick he had ever attempted to play on me, every flaw which he himself would not admit misdirected him. But I did not—there is no use in it, if you are not ready to strike the offender down and walk away. Only resentment and a ready guard can grow in another from facing him with his inadequacies. And I still had use for Aziru. And love, or I would not have turned from inflicting violence then and there upon his person.

Instead, I said, "Bring him before me in the predawn. I will be with one of my sons in the harness area." There was a note of strain in my voice which he misconstrued.

He did not bow back immediately from my presence, but said instead in a commiserating way: "You have decided about the son Ankhesenamun requested, have you not? You had decided even before you put the matter before the council."

"I have consulted with the Storm-god," I said, gesturing to the god upon the sacred bulls in his shrine behind me. "Aziru, I have many things to do. . . ."

"My lord Overlord, I depart forthwith. But two things, and I will leave you. First, I am supposed to be overseeing the construction of the siege engines in the predawn. . . ."

"Send someone else to see to it. What is the second thing?"

"I have brought gifts for the Sun, and for Prince Mursili, gifts born of royal Egyptian stock. Where may I find the Great Bull, your son?"

I told him where he might find my youngest prince, and thanked him on my own behalf, but suggested he hold on to the girls or put them with those namra I had set aside for myself, since the last thing I needed then was a woman, and firmly dismissed him.

In the gray, misty light before sunrise it is most difficult to send a spear or arrow true to its target. I had collected Zannanza while the stars were fading, and the two of us were letting shafts fly toward a painted square on a wall the fortifications corps had thrown up to contain the captives: or rather, that the namra had built to contain themselves under the direction of the fortifications corps.

Zannanza was beginning to understand the amount of correction the tricky light demanded, or the light was getting less tricky as the sky began slowly to color, when two men became discernible, approaching out of shadow along the wall.

I was just nocking another shaft and, at Aziru's hail, turned toward them while letting fly. My first arrow tacked Aitakama's mantle neatly to the wall at waist height. My second, flying through his shout of alarm, caught his hair on the left side of his neck. My third thunked, parallel, on his right.

There came only the sound of rustling garments: my own, as I approached; my son Zannanza's, as he accompanied me;

Aziru's as he backed away from the king of Kinza, who was held against the wall as if in a collar by my arrows.

"Spread your arms," I suggested, "and stand very still. And your legs, also."

As I outlined my errant vassal's form in arrows, I suggested certain alterations in his behavior which I would in future like him to display, and he was most anxious to appear cooperative in every way. The arrow I sent into his kilt where his legs disappeared under it divested him of what remained of his composure, and he began to gibber.

Disgustedly, I commended him to my son's mercies, saying: "If you are going down to Egypt to reign as pharaoh, you should be able to do as I have done: encircle a vassal's person with arrows, and yet not draw one drop of blood. Convince me that you can do so, and you shall wear the Double Crown."

"*Abuya!* I am—This is—I cannot thank you—"

"Do not thank me, let us see what you can do. If Aitakama cannot thank you, by the time the sun is fully risen, then there will be no reason for you to thank me."

So with utmost concentration, Khinti's son sent half a score of shafts speeding into the wood about my spread-eagled vassal's trembling frame.

Zannanza's breathing, and the roaring gulps of Aitakama of Kinza, and the sounds the arrows made sinking into the wood were all that could be heard and yet, when it was done and Aitakama's outline stuck out from the wall in feathered relief, I turned away to see a number of men of the army watching.

Striding toward them with a scowl before which they scattered to their tasks, I was soon joined by Zannanza, whose fine face was full of wondering joy.

"Abuya, is it true? Did you mean it?"

"You will need to study hard between now and when Hattu-ziti returns with word. You will study with Aziru, he knows the most about Egyptian ways. I will arrange it. Nothing is sure until Hattu-ziti gives his approval," I warned. "But it is a rule of kingship to prepare to act, whether or not in the end you act at all, no matter how difficult that preparation may be."

He touched my arm, stopped me. I allowed it. With Khinti's children, I was more than lenient. With Zannanza's princely idiosyncrasies I had long practiced patience. The boy had not been able to distinguish himself in battle, though he had been in many engagements in the Upper Country. When he was not quite a man I used to take him hunting, and he would cry over his kills, although he killed to please me. In matters of language and courtly manners and metallurgy and all things abstract, however, he excelled. In Egypt, he would not need to be a field general, but rather be in a position to employ those talents which I have mentioned.

I clasped him, drawing his wiry, slight frame against me, and said as much, gruffly, and then pushed him gently off to prepare himself for the ensuing siege of Carchemish, whilst I myself did the same.

When I had besieged Carchemish for seven days lackadaisically, when I was sure that all within were tired from defending their battlements and hungry from lack of food and thirsty for want of water which I encouraged them to pour on my fiery arrows instead of down their throats, I was ready.

On the eighth day I fought a battle against them, a terrific battle during which I brought my towering siege engines and mountains into play. And over the crumbled walls and into the city my armies advanced: Hittites, Sutu, Amurrites, Hapiru and even Ugaritic soldiers howled their blood-cries and laid about them with sword.

And on the eighth day, the one day alone, I conquered the city of Carchemish.

And since I recollected my dream about the deities of Carchemish, and since I feared the gods and wanted Piyassilis to reign long and successfully in the city I now ruled, on the upper citadel I let no one into the presence of its patron goddess Kubaba and of the god Kurunta; and I did not rush close to any of the temples. Nay, I even bowed down to these gods and then laid before them sacrifices, and Piyassilis who would be king helped me.

But from the lower town, where I had laid upon the troops no such cautionary injunctions, came the screams of ravished women and perishing children and old folk roasting in the flames. And from the lower town I removed the inhabitants, the silver, gold, and bronze utensils to carry up to Hattusas. And the namra whom I brought from the town to be taken to my palace were three thousand three hundred and thirty.

This may sound like a large number, but the namra whom the Hittite armies in total brought home, these were without number, countless, so that when we added the people of Carchemish to the penned deportees they were unnoticeable, as when a man pours a bucket of water into the sea and sees that the tide shows no increase.

Then, having subdued the town totally, I called Piyassilis before me, and I installed him in Carchemish as its king. And all of the cities of the land of Carchemish, Murmuriga, Shipri, Mazuwati and Šurun—these fortified cities—I gave to my son, Piyassilis. And there was joy on the faces of all the sons of the Sun while this was being done. With the throne of Carchemish and the scepter of Carchemish and with a throne-name suitable to a ruler of Hurrian subjects such as dwelt in Carchemish did Piyassilis ascend unto rulership in the fortified city which had been the dream of his youth. "Sarrikusuh" was the kingly name Piyassilis and I chose for him, and it was as Sarrikusuh that all manner of eastern kings would learn to quake before his majesty, his circumspection, and the potency of his battle.

Then from there my armies (all but an infantry battalion and a fortifications corps which I loaned Piyassilis Sarrikusuh to shore up the tumbled walls of which he had been so enamored) descended upon the fractious western dependencies with which I had been having trouble. Countless enemies of the Sun I rounded up; some I deported, some I visited with death upon the spot.

And when I was in Halap with all the armies, I deported its king who had been plotting against me, and I had Telipinus brought before me.

There to Telipinus, who had never asked me for anything in the way of estates or countries, I gave the rich city of Halap, and the rich country of Halap, to rule over as king.

"Abuya. . ." Telipinus, wordless for the first time in his life, fled to the casement overlooking the plain which was the nexus of all overland trade going upcountry or down. "My lord, you are too generous. You do not have to do this. . . . Not because of Piyassilis. I—"

"You," I interrupted, "should have learned by now how gracefully to accept a gift. Say that you are pleased."

"I am pleased."

"Say that you will sign a treaty as did Piyassilis, obligating yourself to your brothers in peaceful relationship even after I have gone up to become a god."

"Do not say that!"

"I am getting leathery of skin; my neck is full of cords and I have enough silver hairs to fund a country, were they metal instead of old, tired strands. Are you accepting this country from me, or not?"

"Accepting! I have loved this place since I first saw it. I told you then."

"I remember," I said, trying not to be sarcastic.

"I will keep the peace as it has never been kept! I will keep all the countries loyal to you! I will oversee Aziru, and he will not stray! I will—"

"If you will do all these things, then will you take a wife? A man needs a son of the first degree. Your brood of concubines' brats will be at each other's throats trying to determine which will succeed you—or worse, none of them will be able to claim your seat."

"I will do something about it. I want no wife, not yet. I will decree a succession among those sons I do have. What is this preoccupation of yours with death, my lord Sun?"

"You tell me. It is you, and not I, who have the sight. What do the gods say?"

"The gods," said Telipinus softly, "do not seem to be decided on anything."

But it turned out that they, the gods, my lords, were quite decided on one thing. Later Telipinus told me that in matters so highly unpleasant, his second sight sometimes failed him.

It was a useless, desperate attempt at escape by persons due for deportation who had strong supporters among those mistakenly labeled "faithful." It was a commotion in the middle of the night that woke me so that I was on my feet and clutching the hilt of my sword before I was truly awake. It was the bloody, white-haired head of the Shepherd cradled in my arms while not a man's-length away Telipinus with his own hand carried out the executions of those escapees who had been captured. Heads rolled and blood spurted in the pristine corridors of Halap's great temple, where Kuwatna-ziti had been and where the escapees had made their stand.

"Shepherd," I whispered to eyes that rolled in his seamed, pale face and even as he tried to focus upon me I knew it was no good, that no physician nor priest nor priestess would avail. At the corners of his mouth were pinkish bubbles; down my arm dripped the fluids of his life.

"Tasmi, do not look so sad," the Shepherd said, and coughed a rattling sound, and raised an age-spotted, gnarly hand to touch mine. "Kantuzilis, your son of the second degree, said that life is bound up with death; and death is bound up with life. I have always remembered it. We have had good years, a harvest of them. The Storm-god will take care of me, now—I who have been his man so long. And we—we will meet again, perhaps, when you take up your seat of kingship in heaven."

"Shepherd, I need you. I cannot do it alone. I—" And I took him up and hugged him close, even as he said:

"You can do it, Tasmi. You have done it. All is finished, like a tablet waiting to be bronzed. Do not grieve, but lay one more sacrifice for me to the Storm-god, my lord. We will both—"

And that was the last the Great Shepherd ever spoke.

We gave his ashes to the gods there in Halap, for Telipinus would let no one else perform the rites, and I was sunk in an old man's despair and was not seeing anything but my memories.

The next day I went back to Hattusas for winter.

CHAPTER 32

A warrior develops a numbness to tragedy that few sorrows can pierce. But sometimes, the knife cuts deep. Sometimes, the bravest are unmanned. Sometimes, if I may suggest it, tears are not a shame but a cure.

Events, however, have no such weakness. The seasons of a man's life roll implacably onward, no matter how concertedly he sets his feet against them. Nothing stops the greening of the leaves or the brown death they carry in them as a promise even at their birth.

Zannanza had begged to stay awhile with Telipinus in Halap, and in my aggrieved distraction I allowed it. When later I realized what must have detained him so long, and what also had Telipinus absent from his new palace, it was too late. But before Zannanza raced the first snows up to Hattusas, I had had time to cool my anger, which was not the terrible anger common to the Sun but some other anger, tinged with resignation and recognition of the fleeting delicacy of all life. So I pretended that I did not know that Zannanza had gone with Telipinus to meet Khinti, Zannanza's blood- and Telipinus' heart-mother, when she put into port there specifically to see her womb's child before he became pharaoh. She had last laid eyes upon him when he was four.

I blamed Telipinus, whose instigation of this disobedience was clear; but besides, I was thinking that if Zannanza loved Malnigal, his stepmother, as much as Telipinus loved Khinti, I would not be having to pretend I did not know about this secret meeting.

So when it became spring, just before Hattu-ziti was due to arrive back from Egypt, I confronted Zannanza with the matter, for I was feeling myself once more: the melancholy that had weighed me down the winter long was melting like the snow on the mountains.

"And how was Khinti, when you saw her?" I asked him casually at table. We were speaking — Aziru, Arnuwandas, Zannanza and I — that mixed tongue known as Babylonian, so that Zannanza's ears could catch up to his eyes. If not for me, they would have been speaking Egyptian, but in that regard I was largely untutored, and thus in my presence no one practiced the Egyptian tongue.

"How *what?* " sputtered Zannanza. "How did you know?"

Arnuwandas snorted and set down his goblet with a thunk and said before I could intervene that everyone had known for years that Telipinus wrote forbidden letters to his stepmother and even went on occasion to meet with her.

"I had to, Abuya," said Zannanza, cornered but not beaten. "She is my mother. Above all else, there is that."

Aziru looked as if he wanted to leave, but I touched him and gave an imperceptible shake of my head.

"You have not answered me, Zannanza. How is your mother's health?"

"She is well."

"And is she still so beautiful?"

"To me, she is. If you mean to punish me, must you make me wait for it?"

"I think you have been punishing yourself. I am not going to do anything. But I am not going to laud you for being disobedient either, nor for succumbing to Telipinus' urgings that you keep the affair from me. All I am saying is that while you reside under my roof, you will not again disobey me."

"I will not. But when I am king in Egypt—"

"*If* you are king in Egypt," corrected Arnuwandas.

"*If* I am king in Egypt, I am going to bring her into my country and install her as King's Mother or whatever they call it. They offer great honor in that country to the mother of a king, and my mother could use some honoring; she has been dishonored most of her life."

I looked at Zannanza a long time in silence, seeing Khinti, however much I tried not to, in his compact, well-made lineaments. Then I said that should he become pharaoh, if he then did such a thing, there might be a chance that friendly relations could be reestablished between his mother and myself.

"She has never remarried, you know. . . . No other man, she said to me, could be of interest to her, having been in the arms of the Sun. She—"

"*That is enough!* I have a wife, a queen, a Tawananna! Do you not recall her? She raised you and taught you how to keep from befouling yourself. I said *friendly* relations, nothing more. Now excuse yourself, before I begin wondering if you are fit for this kingship you crave!"

When Hattu-ziti came into Hattusas the next day, he had the Honorable Lord Hani with him. And the Honorable Lord Hani had brought a new message for me from the queen of Egypt.

Now, before I sent Hattu-ziti to Egypt, I had instructed him as follows: "Maybe they have a son of their lord! Maybe they deceive me and do not want my son for the kingship. Bring the true word back to me."

Therefore the queen of Egypt wrote back to me in a letter thus: "Why did you say 'they deceive me' in that way? Had I a son, would I have written about my own and my country's shame to a foreign land? You did not believe me and have even spoken

thus to me! He who was my husband has died. A son I have not!
Never shall I take a servant of mine and make him my husband!
I have written to no other country, only to you have I written!
They say thy sons are many; so give me one son of thine! To me
he will be husband, but in Egypt he will be king!"

This woman, the Egyptian queen, was twenty-one years
old, twice widowed, forced into incestuous relationship with
her father, the product of which was a stillborn child. So, since
I was kindhearted, I complied with the word of the woman and
concerned myself with the matter of sending Zannanza to her.

I called Hani into my presence, and to his bewigged and bejeweled self I spoke as follows:

"Your queen supplicated me like a temple prostitute pin-
ing to bear a son to the god. And yet, Egyptian actions do not
match these friendly protestations. In former times, I myself
was friendly toward Egypt, but Egypt ignored me. I went far out
of my way to avoid fighting with Egyptian countries; not in any
way did I open hostilities with your country. I was friendly, but
you suddenly did me evil. Your country came and attacked the
man of Kinza, Aitakama, whom I had taken away from the king
of Hurri-land which calls itself Mitanni. I, when I heard this,
became angry, and I sent forth my own troops and chariots and
the lords. So they came and attacked your territory, the country
of Amqa. And when they attacked Amqa, which is your country,
you probably were afraid; and therefore you keep asking me for
a son of mine as if it were my duty. He will in some way become
a hostage, but king you will not make him."

Pulling on his earrings, as if by that means he could banish
the red from his cheeks and the outrage from his stiffened spine,
the Egyptian ambassador Hani spoke thus to me:

"Oh, my Lord! This is our country's shame! If we had a son
of the king at all, would we have come to a foreign country and
kept asking for a lord for ourselves? Nibhururiya, who was our
lord, died; a son he has not. Our lord's wife is solitary. We are
seeking a son of you, our Lord, for the kingship in Egypt, and for
the woman, our lady, we seek him as her husband! Furthermore,

we went to no other country, only here did we come! Now, O our Lord, give us a son of thine!"

And I was greatly mollified to hear this Hani referring to me as "my Lord" and "our Lord," since he was speaking for all the people of Egypt.

So I made a show of mulling over which son I might send, and said that since Zannanza was of the proper age, and of kingly stuff, it was him I would give in marriage to Ankhesenamun, queen of Egypt.

Then I asked for the tablet of a treaty we had found while searching the archives for precedents, and Hattu-ziti went to get it and to get also the Great Ones of Hattusas, whomsoever was there who might witness the reading.

And when the Great Ones filed in, there was no Shepherd with his wisdom shining out from among them like a beacon. So I myself read the treaty aloud before the gathered host, in which it was told how formerly the Storm-god took the people of Kurustama, sons of Hatti, and carried them to Egypt and made them Egyptians; and how the Storm-god concluded a treaty between the countries of Egypt and Hatti, and how they were continuously friendly with each other.

When I had read aloud the entire tablet before them, I then addressed the gathered greats thus: "Of old, Hattusas and Egypt were friendly with each other, and now this, too, on our behalf, has taken place between our two countries! Thus Hatti and Egypt will continuously be friendly with each other! To the end of days with each other, this agreement will endure."

And then I had Zannanza ushered in, who this long while had been waiting in the hall, and a swell of approval rose up from my greats. Then the Honorable Lord Hani looked Zannanza over in closest scrutiny, and, nodding his head so that his tasseled earrings tinkled, sat back with a huge sigh of relief.

I leveled a stare on him, wondering what kind of son he had thought to receive: one crippled in limb? one dull in mind? Whatever he had conjectured, it was obvious that Zannanza surpassed his wildest dreams. In Egypt, among those slight folk, he would even appear tall, mighty and robust.

So before all of them I told Zannanza that to the country of Egypt he would be going, to rule over it as king. And, as he had been coached, he appeared overwhelmed, surmounted by surprise, exceedingly honored in a kingly way.

Then began a spate of feasting and revelry that lasted seven days, on the last of which my sons, all of them, of every degree, and my daughters out of whomsoever, as well as Khinti's daughter and Malnigal's daughter, and King Telipinus from Halap, and King Piyassilis Sarrikusuh from Carchemish, held a private festival in Zannanza's honor.

On the following dawn, I bade farewell to Zannanza, who was dressed kingly from head to toe in the finest Hattian fashion, from the golden helm with its bulls' horns and plumed crest, to his boots made from the king's own ox-hides.

"Be you safely enthroned in Thebes. Be you under the hand of the Storm-god the whole of the journey. And the shade of the Shepherd, may that one too watch over you."

And I kissed him, and hugged him close, and promised to send down his various concubines when he was settled, and made sure he knew just what route to take and where to meet the Honorable Lord Hani, who would accompany him across the Egyptian border but had left early to see to his affairs in Amqa.

And then Zannanza, the boy that Khinti bore me, was gone, a slight, graceful figure in the lead chariot, fading into the mists of morning with Teshub-zalma, the Shepherd's youngest son, commanding his guard.

I stood there in the empty Hattian dawn until there was no more trace of them, and then went back within my double citadel walls and climbed up to the top of the chariot gate tower, and watched, and watched, and watched, as my son left on a journey whose undertaking had never been predicted in all of former times.

That evening, Malnigal and I, amid the presumptive truce in force between us since Zannanza's departure for Egypt became an imminent reality, dreamed aloud together.

When she had first heard of the matter, she had been livid that I had not chosen her son, Mursili, to go to Egypt. But alongside her obsessive desire to increase her children beyond my others rode her equally obsessive love of her firstborn. Out of her fear, her love, and her anticipation of the great benefits she would receive from her stepson's assumption of Egyptian suzerainty, I had been able to construct the truce between us.

After all, when Zannanza was settled on the throne of his kingship, she could have whatsoever she wanted of Egypt's bounty and no one would even comment, since Egypt would then be a part of Hatti and she would not be importing anything at extravagant price: all would be laid at her feet, merely hers to choose. The elegances she craved would be spread before her, vying for her pleasure.

I have said we dreamed aloud upon the greatness that would be Hatti when we numbered among our dependencies the Black Land and the Red Land: Upper and Lower Egypt. Ostrich plumes, elephant tusks, trained hunting leopards, pomegranates, and hearts of lotus danced in Malnigal's thoughts; Ethiopians, Nubians, and the fierce-more-than-panthers-southern Egyptian army occupied the mind and heart of the Sun. How it might be to lead the incomparable Ethiopian warriors eastward against the upstart Assur-uballit brought a smile to my lips as I conjectured it.

"Whose death are you planning? I know that look," teased Malnigal and, forgetful of all our differences, I leaned close and took a kiss from her.

"It has been a long time, my lord and husband," she whispered.

"We are making new beginnings, are we not?"

I made one with her, not to beget a child upon her, or to silence her, or for any other reason than the flood of success which made me generous and loving in my heart toward everyone, whatever sort of person he or she might be.

The next morning I was thinking that once Zannanza was king I would go to Egypt and see all the things Aziru had seen, and Hattu-ziti had seen, and Hatib had seen, but I the Sun had not seen, and judge for myself whether these great pyramids and sphinxes and statues of former kings were as wondrous as everyone said that they were, without having to feel that I must make little of them because they belonged to an enemy.

And while I was thinking that, Arnuwandas tried persuading me to do something about the lion, old and short-tempered and responsive only to my princess Muwattish now that Zannanza was gone. Old lions often turn man-eating, it is true. But I no more would have attempted to separate my princess from her pet than Tarkhunta-zalma from Piyassilis Sarrikusuh, king of Carchemish.

I was just saying that, when the messenger arrived summoning me to Kumanni.

Once I arrived at the front, I spoke straightaway with Lupakki about the inadvisability of going down into the Hurri land after an otherwise unidentified enemy who had been subjecting the lands to depredations when it was likely, by the strangeness he described in their dress and their manner, that they were Assyrian troops. I had come to examine the mutilated body of a slain enemy commander, to thereby attempt a definite identification of these troops who were pillaging, and whom every one of my countries disclaimed as their own.

This putrid corpse which I examined was painstakingly and completely noncommittal about its country of origin. It bore no device of any king's service, no weapon of recognizably foreign style. And yet the face, though once clean-shaven, was decidedly un-Hittite, especially when seen in profile: a man could have hoed a field with the dead officer's nose, and his chin jutted out to meet it. And more: he had, in each ear, not only one, but three tiny holes for earrings.

Shaking my head, I had the corpse removed, took a deep breath of clean air, and told Lupakki to proceed as if he were fighting bedawin or Gasgaeans or renegade Hapiru.

Mursili, who was assigned to Lupakki as a driver on that campaign but had been detained in Hattusas for the feast of Zannanza's departure, had come east with me. Mursili, now the possessor of Zannanza's second-best team, it trained by Piyassilis' own hand, could think of nothing else. Invariably, if I looked for him and asked about the camp of his whereabouts, someone would point to a dust-cloud on the horizon and grin.

I had been there twice as long as anyone would have expected, not because Lupakki needed me, but because I was relieved to have something to occupy my thoughts that was simple, physical, demanding and satisfying enough to quiet my heart.

But when Telipinus drove in, unsummoned, I was jerked back violently into the harness of my kingship, and pulled all the weight of it once more.

The Priest, so he said, had come up to join me on an instinct, a sudden whim. He followed me around as if he were waiting for me to fall so that he could pick me up. He was low-voiced and deep-eyed and every bit a man of the gods, and I have never been so beset by formless fear as when Telipinus dogged my steps for a reason not even the second sight he possessed could reveal.

The dawn light revealed it:

A messenger from Amurru and an agent of one of Aziru's vassals brought a tablet to me in the encampment. When they brought this tablet, they spoke thus:

"The people of Egypt killed Zannanza, and brought word: 'Zannanza died.' But he died at the hands of Horemheb's police, and Teshub-zalma with him. Aziru sends the true word and the false tablet to you, my lord, Great King: it is good that you should know. And know also that Horemheb's troops are attacking all along the frontier." And it was well that Telipinus had come up from Halap to hold his father when he fell . . . though I did not truly fall, but sank into the campstool as if I had shrunken.

Consequently it was not I, but Telipinus. who dismissed the messengers, for when I heard of the slaying of Zannanza, I began to lament for my son, for Khinti's son, for that one so young who had died of my desire to single him out, to distinguish him above all others. I saw his sharp, wiry frame, his handsome, guileless face as it had been when he drove out so eager to his death. And for Teshub-zalma, the Shepherd's boy, did I also grieve.

And to the Storm-god, my lord, and to the Sun-goddess, who regulates kingship and queenship, and to all the other gods I raised my fists. And in a terrible voice I spoke to them thus: "O gods, I did no evil, yet the people of Egypt did this to me, and they also attacked the frontier of my country! Give me vengeance, O ye gods, upon the heads of these who have broken their oaths to you, my lords, and to the Sun!"

And thus began my war with Egypt, which is now in its sixth campaign.

Back to Hattusas I went, and Telipinus and Mursili went with me.

We sent word to all the kings to make ready to do battle, and against the city Amqa I led troops and chariots in force.

Those who had murdered my son we captured, along with their entire regiment, and all of them we slew. First we cut off their hands in the Egyptian fashion, as had been done to my son and his guard, only we did it while they were still alive. And then we tied them to the plow, as has not been done since olden days, and split them asunder whilst still they lived; and the bulls and oxen we used were wild ones, captured just for that purpose, and their members were dragged by the wild beasts through the countryside.

All that season I fought on Egypt's borders while Lupakki handled the rebellious Gasgaeans.

We heard that Ay, the Divine Father, was sitting in Zannanza's seat of kingship in Egypt. It was he who had been taken to the widow's heart, although he was said to be in his nineties, and even related to her by blood. So to this Ay, murderer, dispatcher of murderers, I wrote in my wrath. And I reminded Ay of the destruction of Mitanni, who was barely a power at all anymore, and whose cowardly king Tushratta ran hither and yon from my battle. And I reminded him of what those of Egypt had written to me, that they had asked me twice to send my son and that in no way did I know that such a thing they had in their minds. And I said that the king of Egypt, this Ay, was lying when he wrote to me saying that he did not know about the death of my son, in no way did he decree it. But I told him that no matter how he professed his innocence, and even if he wrote me again begging, saying, "your son is dead. In no way was I responsible," that there was no escape for his country. I had sent him Zannanza, I would have given him in marriage. Instead I had given him up to be slaughtered. And I said:

"You boast of your chariotry. I have the Storm-god, my lord, the Sun- goddess of Arinna, queen of the lands. They will come, the Storm-god, my lord, and the Sun-goddess of Arinna, my lady, and they will decide the matter. Your troops you say are many. But in the sky the falcon or the fledgling is as numerous. Even if you have an army which is as numerous, what will we do to it? The falcon pursues the fledgling, but because the falcon pursues the fledgling, one fledgling does not pursue a falcon. What you wrote: 'You could come with hostile intent. I could take away your hostile intent.' Then take away my hostile intent and take away that of the Storm-god, my lord!"

And I declared everlasting war between us because of the murder of my most beloved son, Zannanza.

All the while I was fighting that first campaign, I was based in Halap; and all that while Telipinus was pleading with me to meet with Zannanza's mother, who was yet throwing dirt over her person and grieving so that none could console her. And since I refused him each time, I was taken by complete surprise when Telipinus came before me saying:

"She is here. I have brought her myself, and if you are going to punish anyone because Khinti is in the country illegally, then you must punish me." The Priest's eyes were bright and pleading, his voice trembling in an unkingly way: "And I have sent for my sister, her daughter, that they may set eyes upon each other after nearly a score of years."

I tried to say, "Young king, you importune," but not even that much of a threat could I utter. My mind was devoid of thought and inundated with mist like a swamp; and like a swamp-walker, I had to watch my feet as I sought a chair, lest I sink in the treacherous mire.

I only remember her standing in the doorway, nothing about what else I might have said or Telipinus might have said. And I remember thinking: *I cannot do anything about her. Our differences are too longstanding. Too many are the years. All is irreconcilably lost.* Even in my attempt to do perfectly, exceedingly well in the upbringing of our son had I failed, as I had failed in every other aspect of my husbandhood to her.

And then I truly saw her: smaller, older, worn as was I. And I saw the tears streaking her dirty, mourner's face and the pathetic clasp of her hands together; and that she opened her mouth but could not speak, and instead tottered back against the doorframe. I counted the silver in her black hair and the veins showing through her skin and all the years gone from our grasp, and I knew then that I loved her yet. Still, after all the things I had done to erase it, I loved her. Oh yes. And king or no, I went to her, and took her in my arms and rescinded her exile.

Then she, who in exile had never touched another, sobbed out her mother's grief against my chest, and I said to her all things the years had never let me say. After a time I brushed the tears from the cheeks of my beloved, and she lamented very softly the loss of her beauty.

And I told her that every line and pucker enflamed me; that if she could stand my leathery skin and an old man's caress, then she should not worry about how she might look to me.

So, in Halap, I lay with the queen of my heart and recollected the love that had not filled me since former times, for which no lust can substitute.

There I stayed with her until the sky began to lower, in Telipinus' palace like some adulterer, which I suppose I was. I could not take her back to Hattusas, nor would she have come with another woman ruling there. Nor was there any solution presenting itself to our dilemma, for I could not cast down the Tawananna of Hatti like a concubine out of favor.

And my love, my Khinti, quieted my growlings and pacings and said that next spring she would come down to Telipinus' court once again, and I took a tearful Muwattish back to Hattusas, sworn to secrecy as to what had occurred when she wept in her mother's arms, having promised Khinti to meet her when the first thaws came.

CHAPTER 33

But the next season I could not truly keep my promise: Khinti and I stole some evenings, to be sure, but the war against Egypt had me deeply committed while, everywhere else, my vassals took advantage of the unsettled state of affairs to enhance their status and increase their borders.

Word came to me that Tushratta had been murdered by agents of Artatama and his son Suttarna, who were plundering in Mitanni despite the fact that Assyria and her ally Alshe were taking over the Mitanni country. And soon it became clear to me that Assur-uballit of Assyria was in league with Artatama, the king of Hurri, with whom I yet had treaty, but with whom I would not long maintain friendly relations if he continued to aid and receive aid from my father-in-law's former vassal state, Assyria. Since Burnaburiash's enemies were my enemies, and Babylon was incensed to the point of incoherency, I was in a very difficult position so long as I maintained a relationship with Artatama of Hurri, and he maintained a relationship with Assur-uballit of Assyria.

My life, it seems to me, has always displayed a certain pattern: like the calm within a storm's center, my life has always had events taking place within and without at different intensities. On the outer edges matters foment and wild winds blow; on the inner, things display themselves for meticulous examination under a clear sky. When things are happening without, a man sends arrows into the dark. When the dawn shines, he may see what he has taken down. Sometimes he finds not a dead foe, but one merely enraged by his wounds. In the clarity of the center, there is no advantage to anyone. But it is a clean contest, when man faces man across the sum of each one's endeavor: the stronger triumphs and survives. I carried the hunger, yet, for that sort of contest with Tushratta of Mitanni, murdered by his own blood in the same treacherous manner that killed Zannanza. That is no way for a king, or a prince either, to die.

I was brooding upon the sad end of Tushratta when word came to me by messenger that the son of murdered Tushratta, Mattiwaza of Mitanni, begged me to come meet him at the Red River, for into Hattian territory any farther he dared not come. Those who had killed his sire were close upon his trail, awaiting his ejection from my country so they could murder him, as they had almost succeeded in doing when he had sought asylum in Babylon and was refused it by a sneering Burnaburiash, who sent him to me.

I was still sore of heart from losing Zannanza, and I thought of how this boy must feel; and so I went, with Tarkhunta-zalma supporting me, down to the Marassantiya River to give him audience.

A sorry sight was Mattiwaza of Mitanni, wild-eyed and disheveled, in a single rent garment insufficient to ward off the nip in the air, with but two Hurrians and two servants, and nothing else. No sandals, no kingly jewels, not a wagon or even an ass had the youth on the opposite bank of the river, so that I was not sure, transiently, if this even was Tushratta's son at all.

Oh, but he *was* Tushratta's son, and of an age with Zannan-za, of fine and manly form, though his bones showed sharply beneath his skin and he was faint with hunger.

At my bidding he and his crossed the ford. There he threw himself down at the feet of the Sun, calling me Great King and Hero, Beloved of the Storm-god, and father to the orphaned who are right with the gods.

And when he threw himself upon my mercy, telling me that the Oath Gods had surely decided the case in his favor by al-lowing him to escape the purge that killed his family, and beg-ging me to help him regain his kingdom, then I took him by the hand and rejoiced over him, giving him clothing to wear, wine to drink and food to eat.

On the river bank I questioned him about all things concern-ing the land of Mitanni, and as he wolfed down sustenance he explained all that I asked.

And when I had harkened to all things concerning the land of Mitanni, I spoke to him thus:

"I shall take you as my adopted son. I shall cause you to sit on your father's throne."

Then the prince of Mitanni fell at my feet weeping.

So I took him home to Hattusas, and installed him like a prince of the blood; and chariots plated with gold, horses, har-ness, splendid attire, all sorts of jewelry and everything conceiv-able did I give unto him.

Malnigal's eyes fairly shone when she looked at this boy. And, her daughter being marriageable, she asked me if I would arrange their union, and this I was willing to do for it gave me a plausible opportunity to get the boy's seal on a treaty stronger than I otherwise would have made.

When I had drawn up the treaty, my daughter came to me in tears, saying:

"How could you do this to him? How could you do this to *us?*" and I reminded myself that before me was Malnigal's daugh-ter, with all the scheming inclinations of her dam. Now this girl was a beauty, although we had expected her to be overly broad and clumsy, as had been her brother Mursili when he entered his teens. But, unlike Mursili, she had grown no more after her eleventh year, and so was not at all tall, but wraithlike, thin and supple as the king's ox-hides, with Malnigal's chiseled features and my own massive straight hair and broad shoulders that made her waist look the finer, above flaring hips so round that if we had all been Egyptians I might have been tempted to marry her myself. But then, I suppose if I chose to submerge myself in incest with any of my get, it would more likely have been Muwattish, Khinti's daughter who was still looking for a man to love although she was in her twenty-second year.

"How could you?" Malnigal's daughter demanded again, her voice breaking.

"How could I what?"

"How could you say these things to him? How *dare* you say such things? How am I to make a life with a man whom you have bound up before the Oath Gods like a kid to be slaughtered?"

"How dare I? How dare you, girl? You are queen of nothing at all right now. You will remain so, if you do not recollect your manners, and I will let this Mattiwaza kill himself trying to regain his throne without my aid."

Her eyelids fluttered, her firm jaw trembled, and she sniffed, but did not apologize. Rather, she quoted from the treaty on which I had worked long and hard, saying bitterly: "'If you, Mattiwaza, the prince, and you the sons of the Hurri country do not fulfill the words of this treaty, may the gods, the lords of the oath, blot you out, you Mattiwaza and you the Hurri men together with your country, your wives, and all that you have. May they draw you like malt from its hull. Just as one does not obtain a plant from bad seed, even so may you, Mattiwaza, with a second wife that you may take, and you, the Hurri men with your wives, your sons and your country have no seed. May these gods of the contracting parties bring misery and poverty over you. May they overturn your throne. May the oaths sworn in the presence of these gods break you like reeds, you, Mattiwaza, together with your country. May they exterminate from the earth your name and your seed born from a second wife that you may take. Much as you may seek uninterrupted peace for your country, from the midst of the Hurrians may that be banned. May the earth be coldness so that you fall down slipping. May the soil of your country be a hardened quagmire so that you break in, but never get across. May you, Mattiwaza, and you, the Hurrians, be hateful to the Thousand Gods, may they pursue you.'"

When she had finished quoting my words to me, she raised up her gaze and fire issued forth therefrom: "He cannot sign this. I will not allow him! Shall my nights in my husband's bed be blighted by the wrath and the curses of my own father?" And she began in earnest to cry.

I called for Meshedi to remove her. While awaiting them, I spoke to her as gently as I could manage, reciting to her the following clause in the treaty, saying that I was only trying to protect her in her place and all of my other sons in their places, reminding her:

"I have said this: 'If you, Mattiwaza, the prince, and you, the Hurrians, fulfill this treaty and this oath, may the gods protect you, Mattiwaza, together with your wife, the daughter of the Hatti land, her children and her children's children, and also you, the Hurrians, together with your country. May the Mitanni country return to its place which you occupied before, may it thrive and expand. May you, Mattiwaza, your sons and your sons' sons from the daughter of the Great King of the Hatti land, and you, the Hurrians, exercise kingship forever. May the throne of your father persist, may the Mitanni country persist.'

"Now, considering that I wore my youth away chasing Mattiwaza's cowardly, overweening father throughout the countryside, and considering that I have adopted this Mattiwaza and given him you, my daughter, in marriage—and considering that he has not a shirt to call his own and a mere handful of supporters and that I must also bring forth the army and fund it and field it and provide generals to direct it and even spill the blood of Hattian soldiers to install this husband of yours in any kingship whatsoever, then whatever regulations I choose to make upon him and

his country, I will make. I am a generous man, as the gods decree
a king must be, but I am not a foolish man, to make a man a king
and then call him my equal. He is married to you: so what? I am
not giving him such a critical kingship and then worrying about
how he will do ruling it so that you, his wife, can salve his pride
and save yourself a few bedroom altercations. He will be a vassal; it is better than being dead. He will be acknowledged by the
lands; he will have enough honor and glory. But that land he will
rule shall be ruled under my advisement, and that of Arnuwandas after me, or not at all. You tell him I want it sealed by him on
the morrow, or out he goes with what he brought into Hatti: one
ragged garment, two Hurrians, two slaves. Oh, and you—he can
take you with him, for if you cannot understand and implement
even this tiny portion of my will, if kingly diplomacy is so much
beyond you, then you are no daughter of mine, and your mother
has either been deceiving me, or has herself been deceived by
some wet-nurse. Now get you from my sight: I will see neither
yourself nor your spouse again until I have the attested treaty
in my hands." And I motioned to the Meshedi, who had entered
and were waiting quietly, talking among themselves and pretending not to listen, to escort my princess from the Sun's presence.

Angered the more I gave thought to the stupidity of my
daughter, I summoned Malnigal to me, of whom I had been seeing as little as possible, and who no longer shared my bed. And
upon her head I laid this matter of the prince Mattiwaza and her
daughter, and also a great number of complaints I had previously
been prudent enough not to air. Thus we had a screaming argument that rang through the halls of the palace so that no mouse
dared move anywhere in that whole extent of wood and plaster
and stone.

Snow was falling, when all things irretrievable had been
said, when I lost all remnants of control and slapped her flat-
handed so that she went sprawling. From there on the floor she
spat forth all manner of curses upon the Sun, the like of which I
had not even laid upon the prince Mattiwaza in that part of the
treaty which had so horrified her daughter.

Then I stalked out and found my brother Zida, and we sought
out Hattu-ziti together, and the three of us found Arnuwandas,
and then we four sat together and among us we divided up the
commands for spring and sketched, as well as one party to a war
may, our strategy for the season about to commence.

Upon one point, Arnuwandas was adamant: he and no one
else, whoever that person might be, would lead our forces against
General Horemheb's Egyptian troops. We had heard that Horemheb himself had been just recently in Amqa, setting fortifications to right and increasing the garrisons there; and it had been
Aziru who sent the news, so we knew it was true. Anxious was
Arnuwandas to avenge his brother Zannanza and Teshub-zalma,
the Shepherd's boy. And all that he asked of me I gave him in the
way of troops, excepting one man: Tarkhunta-zalma.

"I am going to send Piyassilis, should he be willing"—and everyone laughed; Piyassilis was the most willing of warriors—"to
install prince Mattiwaza, my son-in-law"—and I could not hold
back a grimace, for I thought of my daughter's untimely and ill-
conceived interference—"in the seat of kingship in Hurri, that
which was his father's."

"You are going to put him in Washuganni?" Zida disbelieved,
shaking his head.

"I am going to put *us* in Washuganni. We need a buffer
against the Assyrian; Mattiwaza will be it. Assur-uballit backs
Suttarna the Third for that seat: if this Suttarna, counterclaimant,
son of Artatama, resides in Washuganni, we will all be spending
the majority of our days trying to ensure Piyassilis' kingdom of
Carchemish."

Thus I envisioned it; thus did it come to pass.

Mattiwaza and Piyassilis and the armies of my second son
(whom I could hardly ever remember to call by his throne-name
Sarrikusuh), went forth into battle. And at first I, the Sun, was
not with them.

Then my son Piyassilis led the armies forth into the country
of Harran and burned it down. From Harran he went to Washuganni and razed that country, and then he went onward. But when

the Assyrian heard that the king of Carchemish had come, he marched forth with troops and chariots of Assur and went to the town of Taite in which my son and the Hurrians were fighting. And he came to the aid of Suttarna.

But when the king of Carchemish, Piyassilis Sarrikusuh, saw the extent of the troops of Assur-uballit, he went back to Washuganni and sent word to me.

And I was like a newly-manned general, as I raised up the Sun's own army, and with my personal thirty and Zida, my brother the Gal Meshedi, and all of us who pawed the stone floors of our pasture, went out to rescue the troops of Mattiwaza, my son-in-law, and Piyassilis Sarrikusuh.

When we arrived in the town where they were fighting, we were just in time to relieve the beleaguered Hattian soldiers, and the soldiers of Carchemish, and those Hurrians who had come over to Mattiwaza, else all would have died in the awful fashion that Assyrians mete out death.

Now, Mattiwaza was very grateful not to be a piece of tanned hide with his name and the date of his demise inscribed upon it, and no sooner had he finished praising me and my gods than Piyassilis pulled me aside and asked how I had done it, for when we had seen the trap in which Mattiwaza was caught like a fox, I had called upon the gods in my wrath, and raised my fist skyward.

And as I raised it, an Assyrian arrow had caught my brother Zida square in the heart, and he had died there, from the matter of trying to save Mattiwaza, who was no kin of mine.

So in the midst of the battle, I bellowed out to the Storm-god in my rage, saying: "I showed mercy in the ways the gods recommended to me. I took my enemy's son and made him a son of mine. And because of that, O my lord, my brother have the Assyrians killed! And I had done no evil to the Assyrians, but they came and started doing evil against me. Storm-god, O my lord, and all you lords of the oaths, because of that you have taken my brother from me. Now, my lords, all you gods, because of that evil the Assyrians did to me, pronounce a judgment!" I had screamed it, spread-legged, fist upraised, unconscious of the deadly shafts whizzing all around me. When anger overcame me there, and I beseeched my gods, my lords, the gods heard the words of my mouth. In the middle of the dry and arid spring, there was in the sky no cloud. But after the words issued forth from me, the sky turned dark and there was rain. First came the black clouds on a wailing wind, and the ground seemed to tremble a little, and forth from the clouds burst the Storm-god's lightning, and then it thundered vehemently.

Later we heard that in the Hatti land it never rained at all, but there in the town Taite near Washuganni in the Hurrian country it kept raining. And when the Assyrians saw my might and that the Storm-god lent me his thunder and his lightning which speared down into the midst of the enemy troops, they became sore afraid. Some howled and fell upon their knees, some turned upon their brothers and killed them and fled in chariots, others fled upon feet that slipped and twisted from under them in the mire and in the mud. And thus I defeated the enemy, so that the enemy died in a multitude. And captives the troops kept leading away from there for three days.

Then I went back to Washuganni with Mattiwaza, and with Piyassilis Sarrikusuh, and we drew up a second treaty, between kings, for now Mattiwaza was king of his father's fortress. And in that treaty I fixed boundaries and divided the captured countries, increasing Piyassilis' country eastward, and in the treaty I said:

"After I took Mattiwaza by the hand, I set him on the throne of his father that the country of Mitanni not perish. I, Great King, brought Mitanni to life for the sake of my daughter. Mattiwaza is truly king thereof, my daughter is truly queen. And you, Mattiwaza may take concubines, but no other wife. You may not allow any other woman to be as wellborn as she. None shall sit beside her. She shall exercise queenship, her spawn shall be of noble birth."

So it was in Carchemish, where she could make no objection, that I consolidated the matter of Mattiwaza and provided for Malnigal's daughter by treaty that which few fathers can ever provide: a loyal and continent husband.

When I returned to Hattusas, it was to receive word that Arnuwandas' army had defeated the Egyptian troops of Horemheb,
who were guarding Amqa's borders, and taken many prisoners.
But a plague had broken out among the captives, and soldiers of
Egypt and soldiers of Hatti were dying therefrom.

But when Arnuwandas arrived in Hattusas, he was well,
and those of the Hittite army that were with him, they were well.
And I was more concerned with whether or not I would be able
to maintain this Mattiwaza, my new son-in-law, in his kingship:
a battle is not a war. Suttarna, the counterclaimant and Assur-
uballit's excuse for making war upon the Hurri land, had not died
in the battle, but escaped.

And I fêted Arnuwandas, who was content in his revenge, but
also thought he would be awhile longer on Egyptian campaigns
until his dead brother's shade was fully placated.

Once I had done that, since Arnuwandas was in Hattusas and
the winter not yet down upon the mountains, I went to the Priest
and stayed long in his holy city of Halap, and Khinti's lap, also.

Not that I did no business of kingship; in fact, as the years
have grown smaller and more fleeting, I have been doing more
and more. Through Khinti I was negotiating with her country of
"exile", Ahhiyawa, which was growing stronger and hence less
friendly. And we set up an exchange of delegations to be mobilized in the following year: architects, princes to learn the arts of
the horse; whomsoever they chose to send, I would let them send:

"I have troubles with everyone else, in this time when I would
be bringing all my troubles and my disputes to a close so that Arnuwandas will be able to reign in peace, as I have never done."

"Ssh, ssh, my love. Does Suppiluliumas, lord of Hatti, wish
to collect less years than the king of Egypt, who has ninety and
three?" Khinti asked, disturbed though she spoke teasingly. "I
could not live through the winters without these spring trysts to
look forward to. My lord, I would not hear of death, not with life
so pleasing, after the long drought of my middle age."

"Khinti, beloved, you have just said it!" I rose abruptly,
disrupting her, and began to pace: "You are right. I will do it!"

"What? What will you do? What am I 'right' about, besides loving you?"

"I will not subject you, and myself, to these long barren seasons apart! I must find a way to rid myself of Malnigal—"

"No. Not on my account would I wish demotion on any other queen. No; it is too foul a punishment."

"And ours is not so foul?"

"But, my beloved, it is we who together made our sorrow, and she is free of that taint!"

"Women! I will never understand! Be quiet, then. No more will I hear from you on the subject. Malnigal is no jewel of a wife, and with her I will do as I choose. And when I command you to pack your things and move back into Hattusas, you will do as I say."

"No one," she said softly, "would dare disobey the command of the Sun."

It seems so long ago, that night.

I have been fighting. When have I not been fighting? I have developed the habit of working upon this, dictating it to Pikku, who as much as any of us elder chariot-horses deserves his last gallops in the field.

Those things I have long ignored, the whispered complaints of back and wrist, the crackle of loose teeth within my jaw, I can no longer ignore, for they are no longer so subtle: my back screams like a man whose eyes are poked out with a red-hot iron when I wake in the morning, although the warmth of the day eases it gradually until the cold ground under me brings it round full circle when I rise. My wrist—I did that driving with Malnigal that day up to Alalakh, when the wheel-horse went down and the car nearly overturned. It went away with time, but now it has returned. I am thankful that it is my left wrist and not my right; if I put my ear close, I can hear the snapping inside when I move my thumb.

Ay died in his fourth regnal year, and Horemheb is now in name what he has been for four years: Pharaoh, ruler of the Two Lands. I would like to dispatch him before I hand the kingship of Hatti over to Arnuwandas and take up residence in the "palace of the grandfather," which I am, twenty times over.

If I do that, I will be the first king of Hatti to survive so long and not be slaughtered, either by his enemies or his sons. But that is what I am going to do, after I have collected enough evidence to demote Malnigal and brought Khinti back into Hatti to assume the place in flesh, beside me on the throne of queenship, that she never relinquished in my heart.

When I returned from Halap this year, the Prince of Mira was waiting to throw himself on my mercy and beg my protection.

This prince was fleeing from the Lower Country revolts, which extend farther than that: because I am fighting Egypt as well as constantly supporting Piyassilis and Mattiwaza in their efforts to maintain Mattiwaza in Washuganni as king of Mitanni and Hurri, now the Gasgaeans, the Hayasaeans, the folk in the Lower Country whom I brought to their knees at the beginning of my reign—all these are revolting.

My sister died of a plague, although I have heard that it was not the same one which has been ravaging the Hatti land. Our plague turns people blue-fingered and they cough out their life. It was some other that took her, and her husband; and Mariyas the warrior also died, so that things with Hayasa are again as they were when I was sixteen and fighting them from my base in Samuha.

These matters bother me, for I am trying to order my affairs so that I can spend some time being a man, instead of all my time being a king.

But, I was telling you about the prince of Mira. . . . I am allowed, I think, this one meander, in deference to my age. Hattuziti and I and Lupakki have decided that once a moon we are entitled to get drunk unto stammering and stumbling and act just as old and foolish and crotchety as we please. But fifteen- or twenty-year-old girls no longer truly interest me, although there is a spice to them, now that I am grizzled and truly fearsome, that I did not taste when I was thirty.

So, about the prince of Mira: I offered him asylum and, over the past season while I was fighting in the Upper Country and Arnuwandas was fighting in Egypt and Piyassilis—that is, Sarrikusuh—was fighting in Carchemish and in the Hurri lands beyond, this prince of Mira (one of the Arzawaean border lands that I had taken without bloodshed when the king who was this boy's father came and laid down his weapons at my feet) fell in love with Khinti's daughter, Muwattish, and she also looked upon him with favor.

Of all my children, none had ever cleaved to my side like Muwattish. None but that princess had offered up to her father such joy. The Miran prince's name was Mashkuiluwa, and he had rejected a bid by his brothers to secede from my nation and make common cause with the rebels: all of my old Arzawaean enemies, in league—although this is hearsay—with Ahhiyawa.

When I heard of my daughter's feelings for this Miran, I wrote to Khinti about the matter, not making the situation any brighter than it was: I was full extended, fighting everywhere, and though I had promised the boy when I took him in that I would reinstate him in his kingship, I had not that year been able to accomplish it. And of the reputed Ahhiyawan influence in these rebellions, I spoke to my wife of old.

And she wrote back to me, giving her consent for the marriage, and accepting my suggestion that the ceremony be held in Halap, with Telipinus officiating as priest. But whether her cousin the Ahhiyawan king was aiding the rebellion in the Lower Country, she did not know.

So the marriage was performed, and Malnigal, who was pregnant (a king must see to his duties) and knew she was in my disfavor, if not exactly why, made no objection.

I had never minded marrying off any of my children, but I minded in the case of this daughter. Muwattish, too, though she loved the big, rugged Miran prince, cried profusely and came creeping into my room in the dark as she had been wont to do of old. And I held her, and comforted her, and told her that a grown woman should not be weeping on her wedding night, unless she could weep tears of joy.

And she sobbed that there would be no one left to take care of me, with her gone. Who would see to my meals? And the fit of my clothes? And that I would be like Zannanza's lion, all alone and, like him, without the sense to eat.

Now I do forget a meal once in a while, but I was not going to pine away to skin and bones as the old lion had done. We had turned him loose to die in dignity in the cedar forests. It was not, perhaps, the same as returning him to the plains whence he had been exiled since his youth, but had someone turned me out to roar at the moon and lurk among the trees and ravage what I might, I would have been grateful.

But no one did. My daughter, Muwattish, lived in with her husband in one of the residential palaces, and I began to prepare for the sixth campaign of my greatest war. Even while I was drafting my plans, Aziru came up from Amurru, and I noticed for the first time the silver that had come to be in the wolf's thick mane.

And the news he brought was not welcome: Nuhasse was close to open revolt. Aitakama of Kinza, caught betwixt, had said to Aziru that he could no longer hold his country, that all the folk of Kinza would by spring have gone over to Takib-sarri, my faithless vassal in Nuhasse.

"It is hard to blame them," I said. "I might do the same, if I had an overlord who seemed to be too busy to take any care about me. Do not worry, Aziru, we will burn down their towns around their ears, drop them to knees as in former times."

With lifted brow, Aziru replied: "I was not in any way worried, my lord, other than for Aitakama's sake. He has never forgotten the time you used him for a target and let your son Zannanza loose arrows around his quivering frame."

"He was rather obviously trembling, wasn't he?" I recollected, and we fell to wine and cogitation and conjecture about how to best stop this revolt before it blossomed.

At length, we sent a message down to Telipinus, to seek out Sarrupsi's grandson. You will remember Sarrupsi, that first

Syrian vassal of mine who was so foully murdered by his wives and the Hurrian supporters who did not want to stay with him in the shadow of the Sun. This Sarrupsi's grandson was well-known to Aziru, and to Telipinus also, Aziru said. So in my letter to Telipinus I asked for his opinion on the subject of the fitness of Tette, Sarrupsi's grandson, to rule, and said that if he agreed with Aziru, then, at the same time he was writing me to confirm his agreement, he should seek out Tette and make him ready to become a king.

And I sent a greeting to Khinti, and even mentioned my love, and consigned her into the care of the Storm-god, my lord, and the Sun-goddess, my lady, that she would not become ill as people had been doing with greater and greater frequency ever since Arnuwandas' army brought the Egyptian plague back into the Hatti land along with his captives.

Thus have I come here, to the battlefield once again, to my goat's-hair tent while outside ring the snorts of stamping horses and the moans of the wounded under the vast southern sky, in the forty-first season of my kingship, to subdue once more the rebellious countries of Kinza and Nuhasse.

This, too, I am doing for the Hatti land as so long ago I had sworn, to make her great, to extend her boundaries farther than they have ever been extended in former times; to make of all the little, warring nations brothers, Hittite people, that they may live better lives, free under the mandate of the Thousand Gods to worship howsoever they choose.

CHAPTER 34

It is deep, amber autumn; crackling brown grass shrivels under the graying sky. The blue-cloaked lord has come amongst the tents of the Sun, padding soundlessly on his worn sandals, hardly brighter than a shadow cast by the moon. Last night I saw his profile; this night, I know, we will sit together as brothers. I will see his face. Then, I will be able to say that I have done it. What more might any man ask?

I dreamt of him, and that I took my chariot, the war chariot with its iron scales and the black team who are the descendants of the black team I took from the royal stables so long ago when Tuthaliyas and my mother sent me off to Samuha with the Shepherd that I might live. I dreamt of him, and I dreamt that on yonder hillock I drew up my team and he, himself came to sit with me. And we sat in the rear of the car with our legs dangling down, and we spoke of many things. Still, in the dream, I could not quite see his face. Tonight, I will see it.

This morning when the Sun awoke, weakness was full upon me. My limbs trembled and my head ached and I was coughing. It is not a good sign, but somehow I have been expecting it.

I bedded a namra, a girl from the pens, taken out of Nuhasse, and that was six days past. Two days ago she died of the blue plague, and sometimes it does not take so long as that.

Telipinus and Khinti were here the day we installed Tette in his grandfather's seat of kingship.

They came down in a whirlwind of dust and with frothing horses, and Telipinus had given no explanation as to what brought him hither in such unseemly haste. I was glad enough to see the Priest, and we spoke long of the mechanics of reinstating Khinti's name among the Tawanannas of Hatti, and it will be done, so that she will be a great queen in the gods' eyes, and so that she may join me when I go up to become a god and take my seat of kingship in heaven.

She leapt like a maiden from out of Telipinus' car and thrust herself against me, panther's eyes gleaming, and with her face pressed against my breast told me that she had had an awful dream, and she thanked the gods that it was not true, that all was well with me.

And since all was well with me, I laughed softly at her, and hugged her close, and drew her into my embrace once more.

I have never been gladder of anything than that she came to me then, except perhaps that she left when she did, safe in Telipinus' care.

The Priest, before he drove back to Halap, his capital, spoke with me about what had happened when I fought the Assyrians and the lightning of the Storm-god came to my aid. And we both agreed that the Storm-god, my lord, had revealed himself at last: that he had reached down and touched the Sun, who has been all these years his servant. And at last, I have come to believe it. How, without the gods, could I have done it: all the things I have set out to do?

Ah, I am a stranger to meditation, and perhaps not the man for it.

But no higher sense, no godly insight, is needed to see what everyone's faces are saying.

Mursili, my young prince, squats in a corner, too old for his tears, but offering them up to me just the same.

"Mursili, go and fetch me Lupakki. And Arnuwandas, if he is here."

So my boy, the Great Bull, leaves to fetch them, and Pikku and I have a moment to ourselves. In it, I make provision for my faithful scribe who has served me since the days of my youth, and for my daughter Muwattish and her husband, who is not yet a king, and for my sons and their sons, and for my wives. And I have a moment to write and seal my own a message to Khinti. While I am doing it, I see the blue tinge creeping up my fingers toward my heart. Beneath my arms and in my groin there are sore swellings.

But I have this day, so the Storm-god has promised me. To-night it will rain, and his thunder will strike the hillock beyond my tent, and I will see what I have been waiting to see all these long campaigns through: the face of the blue-cloaked lord, and what is to follow.

Now I am not so calm, within. I do not know how to fight this enemy lurking inside my flesh. And yet, all my life I have gone out to meet the enemy, and I am going to do just that.

Lupakki comes, and with him the brown-haired Tarkhunta-zalma, the Shepherd's boy who so favors his sire. If the Shepherd were here it would be easier, but he is not.

And I am not moaning: I would want no death of pinches, sliding, slowing, then finally stopping enfeebled after having hung on my children's necks overlong.

"Lupakki, may the gods favor you. It is my time and I have no doubt of it. I will want my chariot, and my blacks, at dusk."

"My lord Sun, I . . ." And he went to one knee and pressed his lips against my hand, and Tarkhunta-zalma took Mursili against him while my youngest son sobbed.

"Go on, Lupakki, do this thing I have asked."

"Where am I driving you, Great King Tasmisarri . . . Suppiluliumas?"

Gods, how grateful I am that Lupakki forgot himself, bid farewell to "Tasmisarri."

"You are driving me nowhere at all, most faithful. I am driving myself this last time. I crave the reins of the team, and the wild winds blowing, and all the substance of my life this evening."

And he nodded and went away, and I called my youngest and cradled his head in my arms as if he were a child again and told him, as none had ever told me, "If aught happens to Arnu-wandas, you are tuhkanti for Hatti. It is my will."

After that I could not console him, but bade him help me upright, for the horses stamped with trembling flanks beyond the tent's entrance.

I gave up all the things I owned: the iron sword to Lupakki; the seal of Hatti into the trembling grasp of my eldest, Arnuwan-das, who stood by the chariot, leaning on it.

And with him I spent a somber moment, instructing him as to what to do in this case or in that, or if Malnigal became a greater problem with myself, the Sun, not around to control her.

"I cannot believe this," broke Arnuwandas. "Not that you will never be in Hattusas; not like this; not now." He looked about him at the drizzling, early dusk. "Please, Abuya, go you back into your tent, and rest. We will call upon the gods, and—"

"The Storm-god has called upon me, and this is what he has said: 'Go up on the hill and I will come to you, in my thunder and my lightning.' Now, is that not a befitting summons for even a king to attend?"

"Abuya—"

"Arnuwandas, my firstborn, wish me well, and be a great king over whom I can exclaim with joy should I truly sit among the gods. And take care of Pikku, who has written down what—" And the coughing hit me, so that my son supported me, and everything grew bright with blue sparks, and I knew I had to hurry, for it was getting late. "— what I have not time to say. Be a good king to your people, know that you are a joy to my heart. Over you and Piyassilis and Telipinus and Mursili I will hover like the Sun's own armies." And I kissed him, and levered myself up into the car and took hold of the reins.

And they felt cool and right to me, and the horses bobbed their heads, understanding, as horses will, and did not tax my strength.

So, it is over. I have done it. And upon the hillock I will meet him, who is both the Storm-god, and myself, and at last we will look eye to eye at one another. But it is late, and I must hurry. Already, it is raining. The Storm-god looses his lightning, and the feet of his sacred bulls, Serris and Hurris, cause the ground to tremble with their thunder.

ACKNOWLEDGEMENTS

I would like to thank Calvert Watkins, of Harvard University's Department of Linguistics, for his labors in my behalf: for translating the texts appearing herein from a multitude of languages; for gleaning therefrom every bit of historical evidence pertinent to the life of Suppiluliumas; for discussing with me the major theories held to be most probable in those 'grey' areas of my subject's life, his parentage and his accession. For my conclusions in those and all other areas, only I am responsible. There does exist a series of tablets, published first as *"Die Boghazkoi-Texte in Umschrift,"* and later correlated and translated by Hans Gustav Güterbock as *"Deeds of Suppiluliumas as Told by His Son Mursili II."* A fragment of a parallel tablet has recently come to light wherein the 'my father' of the Mursili text is replaced by the first person singular pronoun, 'I.' I have followed events as depicted in these tablets, and when possible laid actual words written more than thirty-three hundred years ago into the narrative. *"Suppiluliumas and the Amarna Pharaohs,"* by K. A. Kitchen, a

I

study in relative chronology, has been my most-consulted reference. I have followed in general the suggested chronology therein, only adjusting it to agree with *Cambridge Ancient History, Vol. II, Pt. 2,* and making small deviations from the chronology of the Amarna Letters. To these scholars, and those whose works appear in the bibliography along with the sources on which they were based, I extend my warmest thanks and admiration.

    —JEM

BIBLIOGRAPHY

A Guide to the Babylonian and Assyrian Antiquities, British Museum, 1900

A Twelfth-century B.C. Opium Pipe From Kition, Karageorghis, Antiquity, Vol. L #198, 1976

Ancient Near Eastern Texts, J. B. Pritchard, ed., Princeton, 1974

Ancient Records of Egypt, J. H. Breasted, Vols. II, III, Russell & Russell, New York, 1962

Babylon, James Wellard, Shocken, 1974

Cambridge Ancient History, Vol. II, Pt. 2, Cambridge, 1975

Deeds of Suppiluliumas As Told By His Son Mursili, H. G. Guterbock, Journal of Cuneiform Studies 10, New Haven, 1956

Die Boghazkoi-Texte in Umschrift, Leipzig, 1922

Egyptian Grammar, Gardiner, Oxford, 1974

Egypt of the Pharaohs, Gardiner, Oxford, 1964

Hattusha, The Capital of the Hittites, Bittel, Oxford, 1976

'How the Iron Age Began,' Maddin, Muhly, Wheeler, *Scientific American,* Vol. 237, #4

Hurrians and Subarians, Gelb, Studies in Ancient Oriental Civilization #22, University of Chicago, 1973

Keilschrifttexte aus Boghazkoi, Leipzig and Berlin

Keilschrifturkunden aus Boghazkoi, Berlin

Kingship and the Gods, Frankfort, Chicago, 1971

Palais Royal d'Ugarit, III, IV, Paris, 1955, 1956

Politische Documente aus Kleinasien, E. F. Weidner, Leipzig, 1939

Suppiluliumas and the Amarna Pharaohs, K. A. Kitchen, Liverpool, 1962

The Geography of the Hittite Empire, Garstang & Gurney, British Institute of Archaeology at Ankara, Occasional Publications #5, London, 1959

The Greatness That was Babylon, Saggs, Mentor, 1968

The Heretic Pharaoh, Collier, Day, 1972

The Hittite Ritual of Tunnawi, Am. Oriental Series, Vol. 14, New Haven, 1938

The Hittites, O. R. Gurney, Penguin, 1972

The Hittites, People of a Thousand Gods, Lehmann, Viking, 1977

The Tell El-Amarna Tablets, S. A. B. Mercer, Toronto, 1939

Treasures of Tutankhamun, British Museum, 1972

Tutankhamen, C. Desroches-Noblecourt, New York Graphic Society, Boston, 1976

Made in the USA
Lexington, KY
29 May 2016